CRIME AND PUNISHMENT

CRIME AND PUNISHMENT

Fyodor Dostoevsky

WORDSWORTH CLASSICS

This edition published 1994
by Wordsworth Editions Limited
Cumberland House, Crib Street, Ware,
Hertfordshire SG12 9ET

ISBN 1-57335-364-7

*Printed and bound in Great Britain
by Mackays of Chatham plc, Chatham, Kent
Typeset in the UK by Antony Gray*

INTRODUCTION

Crime and Punishment is the first of Fyodor Dostoevsky's five large
works and it reveals the author's mastery of psychological observation
and analysis and, like most of the great novels of world literature, it
has its roots in the author's own experiences of life. The story
concerns the life and evil doings of a poor student, Raskolnikoff (the
name is derived from the Russian word for schismatic). Raskolnikoff
broods long and hard over his own poverty and that of his mother and
young sister, and he resolves to murder, as a matter of principle, an
old woman pawnbroker – having elaborated a convoluted programme
of self-justification for his planned crime in which he effectively
elevates himself to the level of an amoral superman of Napoleonic
stature, quite above the law. His crime, like so many such acts, does
not go according to plan and he is forced into committing an even
worse crime than the one he had originally planned. With consum-
mate mastery of his art, Dostoevsky then proceeds to strip away the
onion peel of self-justification with which Raskolnikoff has surrounded himself. The pangs of conscience progressively ensnare the
evil-doer and he turns for sympathy to the 'pure' self-sacrificing
young prostitute, Sonia, who has been obliged to practise her ancient
profession by the indigent circumstances of her drunken father,
Marmeladoff, and her family as a whole. Already under suspicion
from the astute examining magistrate, Porphyrius Petrovitch,
Raskolnikoff is urged by Sonia to confess, which he eventually does in
a confession notably lacking in contrition. The scene is then set for
punishment, and the reader is required to decide on the nature of true
repentance and whether peace and tranquillity can ever again visit the
convicted Raskolnikoff's tortured soul. Laurence Irving wrote that
Crime and Punishment was a vast compendium of 'the piteous, the
terrible, the human and the sublime', but it is also notable for its fine
evocation of St Petersburg, with its dingy tenements and low dives,
and for its moments of outrageous humour. Dostoevsky read *The*

Pickwick Papers and *David Copperfield* while in prison in Omsk and he shared many of Dickens's prime concerns, such as the miseries of urban life, the condition of children, the causes and effects of crime, and the suffering endured by innocent humanity.

Fyodor Mikhailovich Dostoevsky was born in 1821 in the Mariinskaya Hospital for the Poor in one of the most wretched areas of Moscow. His family, on both sides, was of the impoverished Russian middle-class, his father being an army doctor. His mother died in 1837. He studied at the St Petersburg Military Engineering Academy from 1838–1843, but he turned his back on a career as an engineer for the more precarious life of a writer. His first published work was a translation of Balzac's Eugénie Grandet *(1844). His first original work to be published was the widely acclaimed story* Poor Folk *(1846). In April 1849 he was arrested with others and placed in solitary confinement in the Fortress of St Peter and St Paul for membership of the socialist Petrashevsky circle and, after a mock execution on a freezing morning which left an indelible impression on his mind and drove a fellow convict mad, his death sentence was commuted to imprisonment for four years in a Siberian penal establishment, followed by four years as a private soldier. In 1860–1861 his book* Notes from the House of the Dead, *based on his experiences in prison, appeared in the journal* Time, *which he had founded with his brother Mikhail.* Time *was suppressed in 1863. In 1862 Dostoevsky visited England, France, Germany and Italy. In England the things which most impressed themselves on him were the World Exhibition, the poverty of Whitechapel and the prostitutes plying their trade in the Haymarket.*

Some of the experiences of his 1862 trip abroad were used in his book Notes from the Underground *(1864). His wife and brother died in 1864, leaving him to support their dependants, and in the face of heavy financial commitments he wrote* Crime and Punishment, *which was published in 1866 and which became an immediate and prodigious success. In 1867 he married his young secretary, Anna Grigoryevna Snitkina, a union that was to be blessed with children and much happiness, for she nursed him in his epilepsy, loyally bore his mania for gambling, helped him to overcome his frequent depressions brought on by dark and gloomy thoughts and assisted him in his work with her flair for business – a quality her husband lacked. Other great works followed, such as* The Idiot *(1868),* The Devils *(1872),* A Raw Youth *(1875) and* The Brothers Karamazov *(1880). Despite his success as an author, Dostoevsky lived his entire life in a precarious financial state, sometimes on the brink of starvation, on occasion having to flee from his creditors, and once having to pawn his overcoat and last shirt. He died in 1881 of a lung haemorrhage associated with an attack* of epilepsy, and was followed to his grave by 40,000 mourning Russians. His reputation, founded on his acute psychological and philosophical insight into the depths of the human soul, has increased in stature during the twentieth century, and he stands today secure as one of the giants of Russian literature.

FURTHER READING

Baring, *Landmarks in Russian Literature* 1910
E. C. Mayne (ed.), *Letters* 1964
Murry, *Feodor Dostoevsky* 1916
E. J. Simmons, *Dostoevsky: A Biography* 1940
A. Yarmolinsky, *Dostoevsky: A Biography* 1971

CRIME AND PUNISHMENT

DRAMATIS PERSONÆ

ALENA IVANOVNA, *Money-lender*

ELIZABETH, *Servant and Sister of Money-lender*

PULCHERIA ALEXANDROVNA, *Mother of Murderer*

EUDOXIA (DOUNIA) ROMANOVNA, *Sister of Murderer*

NASTASIA, *Servant*

MARFA PETROVNA, *Wife of Svidrigailoff*

CATHERINE IVANOVNA

SOPHIA (SONIA) SEMENOVNA

MADAME LIPPEVECHZEL

RODION ROMANOVITCH RASKOLNIKOFF,
  Student and Murderer

DMITRI PROKOVITCH RAZOUMIKHIN, *Fellow Student*

PETER PETROVITCH LOOSHIN, *Dounia's Fiancé*

PORPHYRIUS PETROVITCH, *Lawyer*

ARCADIUS IVANOVITCH SVIDRIGAÏLOFF

MARMELADOFF

ANDREAS SEMENOVITCH LEBEZIATNIKOFF

ZOSIMOFF

ZAMETOFF

NIKOLA

ELIA PETROVITCH

PART I

Chapter 1

ONE SULTRY EVENING early in July a young man emerged from the small furnished lodging he occupied in a large five-storied house in the Pereoulok S—, and turned slowly, with an air of indecision, towards the K— bridge. He was fortunate enough not to meet his landlady on the stairs. She occupied the floor beneath him, and her kitchen, with its usually-open door, was entered from the staircase. Thus, whenever the young man went out, he found himself obliged to pass under the enemy's fire, which always produced a morbid terror, humiliating him and making him knit his brows. He owed her some money and felt afraid of encountering her.

It was not that he had been terrified or crushed by misfortune, but that for some time past he had fallen into a state of nervous depression akin to hypochondria. He had withdrawn from society and shut himself up, till he was ready to shun, not merely his landlady, but every human face. Poverty had once weighed him down, though, of late, he had lost his sensitiveness on that score. He had given up all his daily occupations. In his heart of hearts he laughed scornfully at his landlady and the extremities to which she might proceed. Still, to be waylaid on the stairs, to have to listen to all her jargon, hear her demands, threats, and complaints, and have to make excuses and subterfuges in return – no, he preferred to steal down without attracting notice. On this occasion, however, when he had gained the street, he felt surprised himself at this dread of meeting the woman to whom he was in debt.

'Why should I be alarmed by these trifles when I am contemplating such a desperate deed?' thought he, and he gave a strange smile. 'Ah, well, man holds the remedy in his own hands, and lets everything go its own way, simply through cowardice – that is an axiom. I should like to know what people fear most: whatever is contrary to their usual habits, I imagine. But I am talking too much. I talk and so I do nothing, though I might just as well say, I do nothing and so I talk. I have acquired this habit of chattering during the last month, while I have been lying for days together in a corner, feeding my mind on trifles.

Come, why am I taking this walk now? Am I capable of *that*? Can *that* really be serious? Not in the least. These are mere chimeras, idle fancies that flit across my brain!'

The heat in the streets was stifling. The crowd, the sight of lime, bricks, scaffolding, and the peculiar odour so familiar to the nostrils of the inhabitant of St Petersburg who has no means of escaping to the country for the summer, all contributed to irritate the young man's already excited nerves. The reeking fumes of the dram-shops, so numerous in this part of the city, and the tipsy men to be seen at every point, although it was no holiday, completed the repulsive character of the scene. Our hero's refined features betrayed, for a moment, an impression of bitter disgust. We may observe casually that he was not destitute of personal attractions; he was above middle height, with a slender and well-proportioned figure, and he had dark auburn hair and fine dark eyes. In a little while he sank into a deep reverie, or rather into a sort of mental torpor. He walked on without noticing, or trying to notice, his surroundings. Occasionally he muttered a few words to himself; as if, as he himself had just perceived, this had become his habit. At this moment it dawned upon him that his ideas were becoming confused and that he was very feeble; he had eaten nothing worth mentioning for the last two days.

His dress was so miserable that anyone else might have scrupled to go out in such rags during the day-time. This quarter of the city, indeed, was not particular as to dress. In the neighbourhood of the Cyennaza or Haymarket, in those streets in the heart of St Petersburg, occupied by the artisan classes, no vagaries in costume call forth the least surprise. Besides the young man's fierce disdain had reached such a pitch, that, notwithstanding his extreme sensitiveness, he felt no shame at exhibiting his tattered garments in the street. He would have felt differently had he come across anyone he knew, any of the old friends whom he usually avoided. Yet he stopped short on hearing the attention of passers-by directed to him by the thick voice of a tipsy man shouting: 'Eh, look at the German hatter!' The exclamation came from an individual who, for some unknown reason, was being jolted away in a great wagon. The young man snatched off his hat and began to examine it. It was a high-crowned hat that had been originally bought at Zimmermann's, but had become worn and rusty, was covered with dents and stains, slit and short of a brim, a frightful object in short. Yet its owner, far from feeling his vanity wounded, was suffering rather from anxiety than humiliation.

'I suspected this,' muttered he, uneasily, 'I foresaw it. That's the worst of it! Some wretched trifle like this might spoil it all. Yes, this hat is certainly too remarkable; it looks so ridiculous. I must get a cap to suit my rags; any old thing would be better than this horror. Hats like these are not worn; this one would be noticeable a verst off; it would be remembered; people would think of it again some time after, and it might furnish a clue. I must attract as little attention as possible just now. Trifles become important, everything hinges on them.'

He had not far to go; he knew the exact distance between his lodging and present destination – just seven hundred and thirty paces. He had counted them when his plan only floated through his brain like a vague dream. At that time, he himself would not have believed it capable of realisation; he merely dallied in fancy with a chimera which was both terrible and seductive. But a month had elapsed, and he had already begun to view it in a different light. Although he reproached himself throughout his soliloquies with irresolution and a want of energy, he had accustomed himself, little by little, and, indeed, in spite of himself, to consider the realisation of his dream a possibility, though he doubted his own resolution. He was but just now rehearsing his enterprise, and his agitation was increasing at every step.

His heart sank, and his limbs trembled nervously, as he came to an immense pile of building facing the canal on one side and the street on the other. This block was divided into a host of small tenements, tenanted by all sorts of trades – tailors, locksmiths, cooks, various kinds of Germans, prostitutes, petty officials, and others. People were swarming in and out through the two doors. There were three or four dvorniks belonging to the house, but the young man, to his great satisfaction, came across none of them, and, escaping notice as he entered, mounted at once the stairs on the right hand. He had already made acquaintance with this dark and narrow staircase, and its obscurity was grateful to him; it was gloomy enough to hide him from prying eyes. 'If I feel so timid now, what will it be when I come to put my plan into execution?' thought he, as he reached the fourth floor. Here he found the passage blocked; some military porters were removing the furniture from a tenement recently occupied, as the young man knew, by a German official and his family. 'Thanks to the departure of this German, for some time to come there will be no one on this landing but the old woman. It is as well to know this, at any rate,' thought he to himself, as he rang the old woman's bell. It gave a faint sound, as if it were made of tin instead of copper. In houses of this sort, the smaller lodgings generally have such bells.

He had forgotten this; the peculiar tinkling sound seemed to recall something to his memory, for he gave a shiver – his nerves were very weak. In another moment the door was opened part way, and the occupant of the rooms stood examining her visitor through the opening with evident suspicion, her small eyes glimmering through the darkness like luminous points. But when she saw the people on the landing, she seemed reassured, and flung the door open. The young man entered a gloomy ante-chamber, divided by a partition, behind which was a small kitchen. The old woman stood silently in front of him, eyeing him keenly. She was a thin little creature of sixty, with a small sharp nose, and eyes sparkling with malice. Her head was uncovered, and her grizzled locks shone like grease. A strip of flannel was wound round her long thin neck, and, in spite of the heat, she wore a shabby yellow fur-tippet on her shoulders. She coughed incessantly. The young man was probably eyeing her strangely, for the look of mistrust suddenly reappeared on her face.

'The student Raskolnikoff. I called on you a month ago,' said the visitor, hurriedly, with a slight bow. He had suddenly remembered that he must make himself more agreeable.

'I remember, *batuchka*, I remember it well,' returned the old woman, still fixing her eyes on him suspiciously.

'Well, then, look here. I have come again on a similar errand,' continued Raskolnikoff, somewhat surprised and uneasy at being received with so much distrust. 'After all, this may be her usual manner, though I did not notice it before,' thought he, unpleasantly impressed.

The old woman remained silent a while, and seemed to reflect. Then, pointing to the door of the inner room, she drew back for her visitor to pass, and said, 'Come in, *batuchka*.'

The small room into which the young man was ushered was papered with yellow; there were geraniums and muslin curtains in the windows, and the setting sun shed a flood of light on the interior. 'The sun will shine on it just the same *then*!' said Raskolnikoff all at once to himself, as he glanced rapidly round to take in the various objects and engrave them on his memory. The room, however, contained nothing remarkable. The yellow wood furniture was all very old. A couch with a shelving back, opposite which stood an oval table, a toilet-table with a pier glass attached, chairs lining the walls, and two or three poor prints representing German girls with birds in their hands, completed the inventory. A lamp was burning in one corner in front of a small image. The floor and furniture were clean and well polished. 'Elizabeth attends to that,' thought the young man. It would have been difficult to find a speck of dust on anything. 'It is only in the houses of these dreadful old widows that such order is to be seen,' continued Raskolnikoff to himself, looking with curiosity at the chintz curtain overhanging the door which led into a second small room, in which he had never set foot; it contained the old woman's bed and chest of drawers. The apartment consisted of these two rooms.

'What is it you want?' asked the mistress of the house dryly; she had followed her visitor in, and planted herself in front of him to examine him more closely.

'I have come to pawn something, that is all!' With this he drew from his pocket a flat old silver watch. A globe was engraved inside the lid, and the chain was of steel.

'But you have not repaid the sum I lent you before. It was due two days ago.'

'I will pay you the interest for another month; have a little patience.'

'I may have patience or I may sell your pledge at once, *batuchka*, just which ever I like.'

'What will you give me on this watch, Alena Ivanovna?'

'That is a wretched thing, *batuchka*, worth a mere nothing. Last time I lent you two small notes on your ring, when I could have bought a new one at the jeweller's for a rouble and a half.'

'Give me four roubles, and I will redeem it; it belonged to my father. I expect some money soon.'

'A rouble and a half! and I shall take the interest in advance.'

'A rouble and a half!' protested the young man.

'Please yourself whether you take it or not.' So saying, the old woman tendered back the watch. Her visitor took it and was about to depart in vexation, when he reflected that this money-lender was his last resource – and, besides, he had another object in coming.

'Come, fork out!' said he in a rough tone.

The old woman fumbled in her pockets for her keys, and passed on into the adjoining room. The young man, left standing there alone, pricked up his ears and began to make various inductions. He heard this female usurer open her drawer. 'It must be the top one,' was his conclusion. 'I know now that she carries her keys in her right pocket – they are all hung on a steel ring – one of them is three times as large as the rest, and has the wards toothed; that cannot be the key of her drawer – then she must have some strong box or safe. It is curious that the keys of strong boxes should be generally like that – but, after all, how ignoble!'

The old woman reappeared. 'See here, *batuchka*: if I take a ten kopeck-piece a month on each rouble, I ought to receive fifteen kopecks on a rouble and a half, the interest being payable in advance. Then, as you ask me to wait another month for the repayment of the two roubles I have already lent you, you owe me twenty kopecks more, which makes a total of five-and-thirty. What, therefore, I have to advance upon your watch is one rouble fifteen kopecks. Here it is.'

'What! Is one rouble fifteen kopecks all you mean to give me now?'

'That is all that is due to you.'

The young man took the money without further discussion. He looked at the old woman and was in no haste to depart. He seemed anxious to say or do something more, but without knowing exactly what. 'Perhaps I may be bringing you some other article soon, Alena Ivanovna, a very pretty cigar-case – a silver one – when I get it back from the friend to whom I have lent it.' These words were uttered with much embarrassment.

'Well, we can talk about it then, *batuchka*.'

'Goodbye. You are always alone – is your sister never with you?' asked he with as indifferent an air as he could assume, as he entered the ante-room.

'What have you to do with my sister, *batuchka*?'

'Nothing. I had no reason for asking. You will – well, goodbye, Alena Ivanovna.'

Raskolnikoff made his exit in a perturbed state of mind. As he went downstairs, he stopped from time to time, as if overcome by violent emotion. When he had at length emerged upon the street, he exclaimed to himself: 'How loathsome it all is! Can I, can I ever? – no, it is absurd, preposterous!' added he mentally. 'How could such a horrible idea ever enter my head? Could I ever be capable of such infamy? It is odious, ignoble, repulsive! And yet for a whole month – '

Words and exclamations, however, could not give full vent to his agitation. The loathing sense of disgust which had begun to oppress him on his way to the old woman's house had now become so intense that he longed to find some way of escape from the torture. He reeled along the pavement like a tipsy man, taking no notice of those who passed, but bumping against them. On looking round he saw a dram-shop near at hand; steps led down from the footpath to the basement, and Raskolnikoff saw two drunkards coming out at that moment, leaning heavily on each other and exchanging abusive language. The young man barely paused before he descended the steps. He had never before entered such a place, but he felt dizzy and was also suffering from intense thirst. He had a craving for some beer, partly because he attributed his weakness to an empty stomach. Seating himself in a dark and dirty corner, in front of a filthy little table, he called for some beer, and eagerly drank off a glass.

He felt instantly relieved, and his brain began to clear. 'How absurd I have been!' said he to himself, 'there was really nothing to make me uneasy! It was simply physical! A glass of beer and a mouthful of biscuit were all that was necessary to restore my strength of mind and make my thoughts clear and resolution fixed. How paltry all this is!' Yet, in spite of this disdainful conclusion, his face brightened as if he had been suddenly relieved from a terrible weight, and he cast a sociable glance round the room. At the same time he had a confused suspicion that there was something artificial in this momentary cheerfulness. There were but few people left in the place then. A company of five musicians had followed the drunken men already mentioned. When they had gone, it seemed very quiet, for only three remained. A man partly drunk, who looked like a small tradesman, was sitting with a bottle of beer before him. By his side, a tall, stout man with a white beard, enveloped in a great coat, was nodding on the bench in a state of complete intoxication. From time to time he would wake up and begin to snap his fingers, fling out his arms, and slap his chest, though without rising from the bench on which he was reclining. These movements accompanied some foolish song, the words of which he would vainly endeavour to recall:

> 'For a year I caressed my wife,
>   A whole year I ca – ressed my wife – '

Or:

> 'In the Podiatcheskaia,
>   'Twas there I found again – '

But no one chimed in. His companion even received his musical efforts in silence and with an air of dissatisfaction. The third member of the company looked like a retired official. He sat by himself, from time to time raising his glass to his lips and glancing round. He, too, seemed considerably agitated.

Chapter 2

RASKOLNIKOFF WAS unaccustomed to crowds, and, as we have said, he had been shunning all intercourse with his fellow-creatures, especially of late. At the present moment, however, he felt suddenly drawn to them. A kind of revolution seemed to come over him, and the social instinct reasserted its rights. Our hero, after abandoning himself for a whole month to the unhealthy fancies engendered by solitude, was completely wearied of his isolation, and longed to enjoy human society, if but for a moment. Thus, though this dram-shop was so filthy, he had a certain pleasure in ensconcing himself there. The master of the establishment sat in another room, but appeared from time to time in the public one. When his handsome top-boots lined with red appeared on the threshold, they attracted instant attention. He wore a *paddiovka*, a black satin waistcoat horribly grease-marked, and no neckcloth. His face seemed to shine with oil. A lad of fourteen was seated at the counter, and one still younger was serving the customers. The eatables displayed in the window were slices of cucumber, black biscuits, and small morsels of fish. A musty odour overhung the whole. The heat was stifling, and the atmosphere so heavy with alcoholic vapours, that five minutes of it seemed enough to intoxicate anyone.

Occasionally we come across strangers who interest us at first sight, even before we have exchanged a word. This was precisely the effect produced on Raskolnikoff by the individual who looked like a retired official. When the young man subsequently recalled this first impression, he set it down to a presentiment. He never took his eyes off the official, doubtless because the latter returned his gaze and seemed anxious to open a conversation. He looked indifferently, and even somewhat haughtily, upon the other guests and on the proprietor of the establishment; evidently they were too far beneath him in education and the social scale for him to condescend to address them. This man, who was over fifty, was of medium height and had a pale complexion. His head was very bald, displaying only a few grey hairs. His swollen cheeks, of a yellow or rather a greenish hue, betrayed his intemperate habits, and under the drooping eyelids sparkled a pair of small eyes, somewhat red, but full of animation. The most striking thing about his face was its expression of intelligence and enthusiasm, which alternated with a look of insanity. He wore a tattered old dress-coat; and yet, by an instinct of neatness, the only button that remained on it was correctly buttoned. Inside his nankeen waistcoat might be seen a smeared and tattered shirt-front. The absence of a beard proclaimed him an official, but it must have been a long time since he had shaved, for his cheeks were blue with a somewhat thick growth of bristles. A touch of official gravity was also evident in his manner, though at the present moment he seemed suffering from emotion. He passed his hands through his hair and sometimes buried his face in them on the table, reckless of soiling his ragged cuffs. At length he turned to Raskolnikoff and addressed him in a loud decided tone:

'Shall I be taking a liberty, sir, if I presume to enter into conversation with you? My experienced eye enables me, in spite of the simplicity of your dress, to discern in you an educated man, and not a pillar of the dram-shop. I, myself, have always attached great importance to education, when united to substantial qualities. I belong to the *tchin*. Allow me to introduce myself as Marmeladoff, a titular councillor. May I ask whether you are in the service?'

'No, I am studying,' replied the young man, slightly surprised by this courteous language, and yet annoyed at finding himself thus abruptly addressed by a stranger. Though he had felt in a sociable vein for the last quarter of an hour, the vexation which he usually felt when a stranger attempted to accost him instantly revived.

'Then you are or have been a student?' returned the official promptly. 'I thought as much! My instincts are unfailing, sir, and founded on long experience!' He touched his forehead with his finger, to indicate his own estimate of his capacity, and continued: 'You have studied! But allow me – '

And rising, glass in hand, he changed his seat to one near the young man. Though intoxicated, he spoke distinctly and with tolerable coherence. To see him thus fasten on Raskolnikoff as a prey, it might have been supposed that he, too, had not opened his lips for a month.

'Sir,' declared he with a certain solemnity, 'it is true that poverty is no vice. I am aware that neither is intemperance a virtue – more's the pity! But indigence is a vice, sir. You may be poor, and yet retain your natural pride; but, when you are indigent, you retain nothing. An indigent man is not driven out of society with a stick, but with a broom, which is far more humiliating. Yet society is justified, for the indigent man is the first to degrade himself. Here you see the origin of these dram-shops! One month ago, sir, my wife was beaten by Mr Lebeziatnikoff. Now, cannot you understand how the fact of my wife being struck wounded me in my most sensitive point? Allow me, out of pure curiosity, to ask you another question. Have you ever passed a night on the Neva, in a hay-barge?'

'No, I never have,' returned Raskolnikoff. 'Why?'

'Well, that is where I have been sleeping the last five nights.'

He filled his glass, drank it off, and began to muse. Bits of hay were to be seen clinging here and there to his clothes, and even to his hair, and he looked as if he had neither undressed nor washed for the last five days. His large red hands, with their grimy nails, looked especially dirty. The whole room was listening, though somewhat carelessly. The lads behind the counter laughed. The master had come down to the basement, on purpose, no doubt, to hear this 'whimsical fellow.' He had taken a seat at some distance, and was yawning with a consequential air. Evidently, Marmeladoff was a familiar presence there. He probably frequented it for the purpose of talking to those he met. This habit becomes a necessity to some drunkards, especially those who find themselves harshly treated by severe wives at home; they try to make up for the consideration they miss on their own hearth by seeking it from their boon-companions.

'A whimsical fellow!' said the owner of the dram-shop in a loud voice. 'But if you are an official, how comes it you do not work or serve?'

'Why do I not serve?' returned Marmeladoff, addressing himself exclusively to Raskolnikoff, as if the question had come from him, – 'why do I not serve? Is not my uselessness a source of annoyance to myself? When Mr Lebeziatnikoff beat my wife with his own hands a month ago, and I witnessed the scene, dead-drunk, did I not suffer then? Allow me to ask, young man, whether you ever – ever asked for a loan without the faintest hope?'

'Yes – that is to say, what do you mean by the term "without hope"?'

'I mean, knowing perfectly beforehand that you will get nothing. For instance, you feel certain that this man, this useful and well-meaning citizen, will lend you no money – for, pray, why should he? He knows it will never be repaid. Will pity lead him to do it? Mr Lebeziatnikoff, who is up to all the ideas of our day, explained lately that pity is now actually prohibited by science, an opinion current in England, the headquarters of political economy. Why should this man lend you money, I repeat? You are sure he will not, and yet you set out – '

'Why go, then, under such circumstances?' broke in Raskolnikoff.

'Because you feel that you must go somewhere – you are at your wits' end. The time comes when a man makes up his mind, willingly or unwillingly, to any step. When my only daughter went to have her name entered on the police register I was obliged to go too (for she has a yellow ticket),' added he, parenthetically, looking rather anxiously at the young man.

'I don't trouble myself about that, sir, not at all,' he hastened to declare with apparent composure, while the two lads behind the counter could scarcely refrain their laughter, and the master himself smiled. 'What does it signify? Little do I care for their tossing their heads, for everyone knows it, and there is no keeping things secret; I do not regard the matter with contempt, but with resignation. Well, well! *Ecce homo!* Allow me, young man: can you or *dare* you fix your eyes on me now and deny that I am a sot?'

The young man made no reply.

The orator waited with an air of dignity till the laughter provoked by his last words had subsided, and then resumed. 'Well, I may be a sot, but she is a lady! I bear the mark of the beast, but my wife, Catherine Ivanovna, is a cultivated person, and the daughter of an officer of high standing. I may be a queer sort of fellow, I allow, but my wife is an educated woman, with a fine mind and a large heart. And yet – if she would but have pity on me! Oh, sir, every man seeks for compassion somewhere. Catherine Ivanovna, with all her elevation of soul, is unjust – and though I know well that, when she plucks me by the hair, it is all owing to the interest she takes in me – for she does pluck me by the hair, young man,' insisted he, with increased dignity on hearing a renewed outburst of laughter – 'still, if she would but – But, no, no, it is useless to talk of it! I have never once obtained my wish; not once has she shown me any compassion, but – it is all my character, I am a real brute!'

'I believe you!' observed the owner of the house with a yawn.

Marmeladoff struck the table with his fist. 'Such is my character. Would you believe, sir, that I have actually drunk her stockings. I say nothing about her shoes, for that is credible enough – but even her stockings! I drank her little angora shawl too, a present that had been made her, hers before she ever married me, and thus her own property, not mine! We live in a cold room, and she has caught a chill this winter, and begun to cough and spit blood. We have three young children, and Catherine Ivanovna works from morning till night, washing clothes and keeping the little ones tidy, for she has always been accustomed to see everything clean. Unfortunately, she has a delicate chest and is consumptive, and it grieves me. Don't I feel it! The more I drink, the more I feel it. I give myself up to drink on purpose to feel and suffer the more. I drink in order to redouble my sufferings!' And he laid his head on the table with an expression of despair.

'Young man,' resumed he when he again raised it, 'I think I can read trouble in your countenance. As soon as you entered I received that impression, and that was why I addressed you. If I tell you the story of my life, it is not in order to incur the ridicule of these idlers, who have heard it all before, but because I seek the sympathy of an educated man. Let me tell you that my wife was brought up at an aristocratic boarding-school in the provinces, and that when she left she danced about in her shawl before the governor and other officials, so great was her delight at obtaining the gold medal and a diploma. As to the medal, we sold it a long time since; but my wife still keeps the diploma in a box, and she showed it only the other day to our landlady. Though she is always at daggers drawn with the woman she was pleased to be able to show her tokens of former good fortune to someone. I cannot wonder at it, for it is all over now, and her sole pleasure is to recall bygone days! Yes, she has a grand, proud, indomitable soul. She will scrub her own floor and eat black bread, but she insists on being treated with proper respect. She would not stand Mr Lebeziatnikoff's rudeness, and so, when he beat her, in order to avenge himself for the set down she gave him, she was forced to take to her bed, feeling the insult to her dignity far more than the blows she had received.

'When I married her she was a widow with three tiny children. Her first husband was an infantry officer, with whom she had made a runaway match. She was greatly attached to him, but he took to gambling, came into collision with the authorities, and died. He took to beating her at last. I have heard from a reliable source that they were not always on the best of terms, but that does not prevent her from still bedewing his memory with tears, and constantly instituting comparisons between him and myself, which *I* find by no means flattering. I am quite pleased, all the same, that she should imagine her former life to have been a happy one. After her husband's death she found herself alone with three young children in a wild and remote part of the country. It was there that I met her. Such was her destitution that even I, who have seen so much, cannot attempt to describe it. None of her relations would have anything to do with her, nor would her pride have allowed her to appeal to their compassion. Then I, sir, I, who had also been left a widower with a daughter of fourteen, offered my hand to this poor creature out of compassion for her sufferings.

'Though she had come of such a good family, and been so well educated, she consented to marry me, and by that you may gauge her misery. She received my offer with tears and sobs, and wrung her hands, but she accepted it, for she had nowhere to go to. Can you understand, sir, what it means to have nowhere to go to? You don't? Don't realise that yet? Well, I treated her properly for a whole year, never touching this' (here he pointed to the half-bottle before him), 'for my feelings were honourable. But I earned nothing. I had lost my situation meanwhile, without any fault of my own; changes in the administration led to my office being abolished, and then I took to drink!

'It was after about eighteen months of disappointments and peregrinations that we settled down in this magnificent capital, so rich in monuments. Here I succeeded in finding fresh occupation, but again lost my place. It was my own fault this time, and brought about by my love of the bottle. We occupy a room now belonging to Amalia Fedorovna Lippevechzel; but how we live, or how we pay, is more than I can tell. There are many lodgers besides ourselves. The house is a perfect bear-garden. Meanwhile, my daughter by my first marriage was growing up. I prefer to pass over what she had to suffer at her stepmother's hands. Catherine Ivanovna, though full of magnanimous sentiments, is an irascible lady, unable to control her anger. Well, it is no good talking of that! Sonia, as you may suppose, has not been highly educated. Four years ago I endeavoured to instruct her in geography and universal history, but as I never knew much about them myself and had no good manual at my disposal, her studies did not go very far. We stopped at Cyrus, King of Persia. Later on, when she was grown up, she read a few novels. Mr Lebeziatnikoff lent her Ludwig's *Physiology*, not long ago – are you acquainted with the work? She found it very interesting, and even read us a few passages aloud. This is all the intellectual culture she has had.

'And now, sir, let me ask you frankly, how is a poor respectable girl to make a living? Unless she has any special talent, she can but earn fifteen kopecks a day, and to do this she must not waste a single minute. What am I talking of? Sonia made half a dozen linen shirts for a member of the Council – Ivan Ivanovitch Klosstock – whom you may know by name; well, she has not only never been paid for them, but was actually expelled from the house, with abusive language, under the pretext that she had made a wrong measurement of the neck. Meanwhile the children were starving, and Catherine Ivanovna walked up and down the room wringing her hands, with hectic spots on her cheeks, as usual in those suffering from her complaint. "You idle thing!" exclaimed she, "are you not ashamed to live here and do nothing? All you do is to eat, eat and drink, and keep yourself warm!" You may well ask what the poor girl could have had to eat and drink, when the children even had not had a crust of bread. I was lying down – I may as well say – drunk. I heard my Sonia's sweet voice say gently (she is fair, and always looks pale and delicate) "But, Catherine Ivanovna, how could I do that?"

'I must tell you that Daria Frantzovna, a bad woman, well known to the police, had already made overtures to her thrice, through our landlady. "What," returned Catherine Ivanovna ironically, "you must have a fine treasure indeed to preserve it so jealously!" Do not accuse her, sir, do not; she did not know what she was saying; she was ill and harassed, and saw her children crying with hunger, and her words were meant rather to vex Sonia than to drive her to evil ways. Catherine Ivanovna is always like that; as soon as she hears her children cry, she begins to beat them, even when they are crying with hunger. It was then past five o'clock; I saw Sonetchka rise, put on her burnous, and leave the house. At eight o'clock she returned, and, going straight up to Catherine Ivanovna, laid thirty roubles in silver upon the table before her without saying a word. Then she took our large green woollen handkerchief, which serves for all the family, wrapped it round her head and lay down on her bed with her face to the wall, but her shoulders and whole frame kept quivering. I was still in the same condition. At that moment, young man, I saw Catherine Ivanovna move and kneel down in silence by Sonetchka's little bed; there she knelt the whole night long, kissing my daughter's feet and refusing to stir. At last the two fell asleep in each other's arms; yes, the two of them, and there I still lay, stupefied.'

Marmeladoff paused as if his voice would serve him no longer; then he suddenly filled his glass again, emptied it, and after a while resumed: 'Since then, sir, owing to an unfortunate occurrence and a denunciation emanating from malicious persons, in which Daria Frantzovna was principally concerned, attempting to avenge herself for some pretended want of respect, my daughter, Sophia Semenovna, has been entered on the register, which obliged us to shift our quarters. Our landlady, Amalia Fedorovna, showed herself inflexible on this point, forgetting that she herself had first favoured the intrigues of Daria Frantzovna. Mr Lebeziatnikoff joined her – well, ahem! – it was with reference to Sonia that Catherine Ivanovna and he had the quarrel to which I have just referred. He paid Sonetchka great attentions at first, but his self-esteem soon took alarm. "How can an enlightened man like myself live in the same house with a creature of that sort?" said he. Catherine Ivanovna promptly took up the cudgels in Sonia's behalf, and the matter ended in actual blows. My daughter generally comes to see us at nightfall now, and does all she can to assist Catherine Ivanovna. She lodges with Rapernasumoff, a lame, stuttering tailor.

'He has a large family, and they all stutter like himself. His wife, too, has an impediment in her speech. They all live in one room, only Sonia has her own corner separated off by a partition. Well, ahem! they are very poor, and all afflicted with this stutter. Well then, one morning I got up and donned my tattered garments; I raised my hands to heaven, and went to his Excellency Ivan Afanasievitch. Do you know his Excellency Ivan Afanasievitch? No? Well, then, you miss the acquaintance of a good man. He is worthy to stand in the presence of the Lord. He deigned to listen to my story from beginning to end, and tears came into his eyes. "Well, Marmeladoff," said he, "you have disappointed me once – I will give you another trial and take you on my own responsibility," – that was his very expression – "try to profit by this warning. You may go now!" I kissed the very dust on his feet – mentally, of course, for he would not have allowed me to do it in reality; he is a man far too advanced in modern ideas to receive any homage of that kind. But, good heavens! what a reception they gave me at home when I announced that I was reinstated in the Service and about to receive a salary!'

Here Marmeladoff became again overpowered by emotion. The vault was at that moment invaded by a troop of half-tipsy men. A hurdy-gurdy was heard at the door, and the shrill voice of a child of seven singing 'The little Farm.' The scene became noisy; the master and his assistants turned to attend to the fresh arrivals. Marmeladoff paid no heed, but went on with his story, becoming more and more communicative the deeper he drank. A beam of joy overspread his countenance as he dwelt on his recent reinstatement. Raskolnikoff was listening attentively.

'That was five weeks ago, sir. Yes – and when Catherine Ivanovna and Sonetchka heard the news, why, bless me, I felt in the seventh heaven. Once, it used to be nothing but abuse: "Go and lie down, you brute!" But now they walked on tiptoe and kept the children quiet: "Hush, Simon Zakharitch has returned from his office tired, he must have his rest!" They gave me a cup of coffee with cream in it before I left the house. Real cream, just think of that! And how in the world they scraped together eleven roubles fifty kopecks to replenish my wardrobe, I can't think. They fitted me out from top to toe, finding me boots, a uniform, and shirt-fronts made of good calico; everything was in splendid condition, and it cost them eleven roubles and a half. Six days ago, I brought the whole of my first earnings to my wife, twenty-three roubles and forty kopecks, and my wife pinched my cheek and called me a dear. "What a dear you are!" said she (when we were by ourselves, you understand). But was not that pretty of her?'

Marmeladoff stopped and tried to smile, but his chin quivered. He succeeded, however, in suppressing his emotion. Raskolnikoff did not know what to make of this drunkard, who had left home for five days and had been sleeping in the hay-barges, and yet cherished a morbid attachment to his family. The young man was listening with all his ears, but it made him feel uncomfortable, and he was vexed with himself for having entered this place.

'Oh, sir, sir!' implored Marmeladoff, 'maybe, like the rest, you think all this ludicrous; maybe I only weary you by relating all these foolish and wretched details of my domestic existence, but they are not amusing in my eyes, they stab me to the heart. During the whole of that happy day, I was building castles in the air; I was dreaming how I might reorganise our life, find clothes for the children, enable my wife to get a little rest, and raise my only daughter out of the mire. How many plans I made! Well, sir' (here Marmeladoff shuddered, raised his head and looked his audience in the face), 'the very next morning, just five days ago, – after cherishing all these dreams, I stole, actually *stole* Catherine Ivanovna's keys, and took from her box all the money that remained from what I had given her. How much was there left? I cannot remember. I left home five days ago, and they don't know what has become of me; I have lost my situation, I left my uniform in a dram-shop near the Egipetsky bridge, and received this cast-off suit in exchange – it is all up with me now!'

Here Marmeladoff struck his forehead, set his teeth, and, closing his eyes, leaned on the table. In another minute, however, his expression suddenly changed, and looking at Raskolnikoff with assumed cynicism, he said with a laugh: 'I went to Sonia today and asked her to give me something to drink! Ha, ha, ha!'

'And did she give it you?' cried one of the party that had just entered, with a hoarse laugh.

'It was her money that paid for this half-bottle,' replied Marmeladoff, addressing himself exclusively to Raskolnikoff. 'She looked out thirty kopecks and gave them me with her own hands; it was all she had, I saw. She said nothing, but only gave me a look, a heavenly look, such as angels have when they weep over the faults of us men, but condemn us not! It is worse than being scolded! Thirty kopecks! And she must be wanting them herself. What do you say, dear sir? She is obliged to attend to her appearance. That trimness which is indispensable to her calling, cannot be kept up for nothing. You understand me? She must buy pomade, and starched petticoats, and pretty little boots to set off her feet when she has to stride across a puddle. Do you understand the importance of this neatness, sir? Well, and here I, her father by natural rights, have taken these thirty kopecks from her on purpose to spend them in drink! I am drinking them now! They are all gone! Ah, who could take pity on such a man! Can you sympathise with me still, sir? Speak! – do you pity me or do you not? Ha, ha, ha!' He was about to pour himself out another glass, when he perceived that his half-bottle was already empty.

'And why should anyone have pity on you?' cried the tavern-keeper.

There was an outburst of laughter, mingled with opprobrium. Those who had not heard the ex-official's words were ready to join in the chorus at the mere sight of him. Marmeladoff seemed only to have awaited the tavern-keeper's exclamation to give the reins to his eloquence. He rose abruptly, and extended his arms.

'Why should anyone have pity on me?' rejoined he, in an excited tone. 'Why? say you. You are right, there is no reason why they should. The proper thing is to crucify me, nail me to the cross, and show no pity! Crucify me, judge, but pity me as you do it! I will go to meet my punishment, for I thirst not for pleasure, but for sufferings and tears. Do you think, publican, that your half-bottle has given me any pleasure? It was sadness, sadness and tears, that I sought and tasted at the bottom of this flagon; but He who has had pity on all men and sees all hearts, will have pity on us; He alone is Judge. At the last day He will come and ask, "Where is the girl who had compassion on her earthly father, and did not turn away in disgust from the habitual drunkard? Where is the girl who sacrificed herself to an unkind consumptive stepmother, and children who were not her own flesh and blood?" And He will say: "Come, I have forgiven thee once, once already, and now all thy sins are remitted, because thou hast loved much." He will forgive my Sonia, He will forgive her, I know. I felt convinced of it when I was with her just now. We shall all be judged by Him, and He will forgive us all: the evil and the good, the wise and the gentle. And when He has finished with the rest, our turn will come too: "Draw nigh," He will say to us, "draw nigh, ye drunkards, ye cowards, ye dissolute men." And we shall draw nigh without trembling. And then He will say unto us: "Ye are sots! Ye bear the mark of the beast on your foreheads, yet come unto Me." And the wise and intelligent will say: "Lord, wherefore dost thou receive these?" And He will answer: "I receive them, O ye wise and intelligent men, because not one of them thought himself worthy this favour." And then He will hold out His arms, and we shall throw ourselves into them; and we shall burst into tears; and then we shall understand everything. All the world will understand, and Catherine Ivanovna also. Thy kingdom come, O Lord!'

He fell back on the bench exhausted without looking at anyone, as if he had lost all consciousness of his surroundings; and became lost in a deep reverie. His words had produced a certain impression. The noise ceased for a moment, but the laughter and invective soon began again.

'Powerfully argued!'

'The old dotard!'

'The bureaucrat!' and so on.

'Let us be going, sir,' said Marmeladoff, abruptly, raising his head and addressing Raskolnikoff. 'Take me home to Kozel's, in the court. It is time I went back to Catherine Ivanovna.'

The young man had been wishing to move for some time, and had already thought of making himself useful to Marmeladoff. The legs of the latter were far more unsteady than his voice, and he leaned heavily on his companion. They had three or four hundred paces to go. As the drunkard approached his domicile, he seemed to grow more and more uneasy.

'It is not Catherine Ivanovna that I am afraid of now,' stammered he, in his emotion. 'I know she will begin by plucking my hair; but what is my hair? It does not matter, nay, it is even better for me that she should do it; I don't mind that, but I feel so afraid of – of – her eyes, and the red patches on her cheeks. I am afraid, too, of hearing her breathing. Have you ever noticed how people with her complaint breathe when they are greatly agitated? I am afraid of hearing the children cry, too; for, unless Sonia has found them something to eat, I don't know how they can have had any food, I really don't! But as to blows, I care nothing for *them*. I may tell you, sir, that, in fact, far from hurting me, I actually enjoy those blows; could not do without them; they do me good. Let her beat me and ease her mind. But here we are at Kozel's. He is a wealthy German locksmith, and owns this house. Come with me!'

They crossed the courtyard, and began to ascend to the fourth floor. It was close on eleven, and though at that season there was, strictly speaking, no night at St Petersburg, yet the higher they ascended the darker the staircase became, till it ended in complete obscurity. The smoky little door which opened on to the landing stood open. A lighted candle-end revealed a miserable room, about ten feet long. This was completely commanded by the corridor, and looked in the greatest disorder, children's clothes lying about everywhere. A ragged piece of stuff was hung so as to curtain off one of the corners farthest from the door, and behind it probably stood the bed. The room contained nothing but two chairs and a wretched sofa covered with oilcloth, which stood in front of an old deal table, bare and unvarnished. On the table was placed an iron candlestick, in which the candle had nearly burned down. Marmeladoff had his own lair, not in a corner, but in the passage. The door leading to the rooms occupied by Amalia Lippevechzel's other lodgers stood partly open. Some of these were noisy; they were probably playing cards and drinking tea. Cries were heard, peals of laughter, and sometimes bad language.

Raskolnikoff recognised Catherine Ivanovna at once She was of a fair height, and had a slight and tolerably good figure, but looked very ill in the face. Her chestnut hair was still beautiful, but, as Marmeladoff had said, there were red patches on her cheek-bones. She was pacing up and down her tiny room with parched lips, pressing her hands to her chest. Her breathing was short and very uneven. Her eyes sparkled with a feverish brilliancy, but their gaze was hard and fixed. A painful impression was produced by this hectic, agitated countenance as seen by the expiring light of the candle. Raskolnikoff judged Catherine Ivanovna to be not more than thirty; she was, indeed, much younger than her husband. She did not notice the arrival of the two men; she seemed to have lost all faculty for sight or sound. A stifling closeness pervaded the room, and pestilential fumes were wafted up the staircase; yet she had not thought of opening the window or closing the outer door; the inner door stood ajar, admitting a dense cloud of tobacco-smoke which caused her to cough, but which she made no effort to exclude.

The youngest girl, a child of four, was sitting on the floor asleep, with her head resting against the couch; the little boy, one year her senior, was trembling and crying in a corner, having apparently just been beaten. The eldest child, a tall thin girl of six, wore a tattered chemise; over her bare shoulders was thrown an old woollen burnous bought for her seemingly two years ago, for it barely reached to her knees now.

Standing in the corner by her little brother's side, she had passed her long thin arm round his neck, and was whispering to him, no doubt trying to quiet him. At the same time she kept a timid gaze fixed on her mother. The large dark eyes, dilated by fear, looked even larger on her thin little face. Marmeladoff knelt down by the door instead of entering the room, but signalled to Raskolnikoff to advance. At the sight of a stranger the woman paused absently in front of him, and attempted for a minute to explain the apparition. 'What is this man doing here?' said she to herself. But presently she imagined him to be on his way to some other lodger, there being a passage through the Marmeladoffs' room. So she was about to open the door of communication without paying any further attention to the stranger, when a sudden shriek escaped her; she had just caught sight of her husband kneeling outside.

'So you have come back!' cried she, in a voice tremulous with anger. 'Villain! Monster! But where is the money? Let me see, what have you in your pocket? These are not your own clothes! What have you done with them? What has become of the money? Speak!' She proceeded to search his pockets. Marmeladoff, far from resisting, at once stretched out his arms to facilitate her operations. He had not a single kopeck on him. 'But where can the money be gone?' cried she. 'Good heavens, is it possible that he can have drunk it all! There were twelve roubles left in the box!'

She seized her husband by the hair in a sudden fury, and dragged him into the room. Marmeladoff's patience did not forsake him; he followed his wife with docility, crawling after her on his knees. 'I like it! It does not pain me, I enjoy it, sir!' cried he, as Catherine Ivanovna shook his head violently; he actually knocked it himself against the floor once. The child who had fallen asleep there, woke and began to whimper. The little boy who was standing in the corner could not bear the sight. He began to shudder and scream, and darted to his sister. His terror was so great that he seemed almost in convulsions. The eldest girl was trembling like an aspen.

'It is all gone in drink, every kopeck!' vociferated Catherine Ivanovna in despair, 'and he has even parted with his clothes! They are hungry, starving!' said she, as she wrung her hands and pointed to the children. 'And you, sir,' said she, turning suddenly upon Raskolnikoff, 'are you not ashamed to come here straight from the dram-shop? You have been drinking with him, have you not? Then begone!'

The young man did not wait for a second command, but retired without uttering a word. The inner door flew wide open, and in the doorway appeared the brazen, scoffing, curious faces of several of the lodgers. They wore round caps, and smoked either pipes or cigarettes. Some of them were clad in dressing-gowns, others in airy costumes verging on indecency; some held their cards in their hand. What amused and delighted them most was to hear Marmeladoff scream when he was dragged by the hair. The lodgers were already beginning to crowd into the room, when an irritated voice was suddenly raised; it proceeded from Amalia Lippevechzel herself, who forced her way through, to restore order after her own fashion. She told the poor woman for the hundredth time that she would have to clear out next morning. This notice was naturally given in the most insulting terms. Raskolnikoff had in his pocket the change out of the rouble he had put down in the dram-shop. Before leaving, he took out a handful of coppers, and laid them on the window-sill without attracting notice. As soon as he was on the staircase, he repented his generosity, and felt half inclined to turn back.

'How absurd of me,' thought he, 'when they have Sonia and I have no one.' But he told himself that he could not take back the money, and would not if he could. This reflection decided him to go forward. 'Sonia requires pomade,' continued he to himself as he walked along the street: 'her charms cannot be maintained without money. H'm! She does not seem to have had much luck today. Hunting man is like hunting game – you must run your chance of coming home empty-handed. They would be in great straits tomorrow without that money of mine! Ah, well, Sonia, they have found you a good milch-cow, and they know how to turn you to profit. It does not trouble them now, they are used to it. They shed a few crocodile tears at the first, and then made up their minds to it. Man is a coward, and can get accustomed to anything!'

Here Raskolnikoff began to muse. 'Well! If I am wrong,' exclaimed he presently, 'if man is not necessarily a coward, he should trample on every fear and prejudice that stand in his way!'

Chapter 3

THE NEXT MORNING Raskolnikoff awoke late, after disturbed and unrefreshing slumbers. He felt very cross and glanced angrily round his room. It was a tiny place, not more than six feet in length, and its dirty buff paper hung in shreds, giving it a most miserable aspect; besides which, the ceiling was so low that a tall man would have felt in danger of bumping his head. The furniture was quite in harmony with the room, consisting of three rickety old chairs, a painted table in one corner, on which lay books and papers thick with dust (showing how long it was since they had been touched), and, finally, a large and very ugly sofa with ragged covers. This sofa, which filled nearly half the room, served Raskolnikoff as a bed. He often lay down on it in his clothes, without any sheets, covering himself with his old student's coat, and using instead of a pillow a little cushion, which he raised by keeping under it all his clean or dirty linen. Before the sofa stood a small table.

Raskolnikoff's misanthropy did not take offence at the dirty state of his den. Human faces had grown so distasteful to him, that the very sight of the servant whose business it was to clean the rooms produced a feeling of exasperation. To such a condition may monomaniacs come by continually brooding over one idea. For the last fortnight, the landlady had ceased to supply her lodger with provisions, and he had not yet thought of demanding an explanation. Nastasia, who had to cook and clean for the whole house, was not sorry to see the lodger in this state of mind, as it diminished her labours: she had quite given up tidying and dusting his room; the utmost she did was to come up and sweep it once a week. She it was who was arousing him at this moment.

'Come, get up, why are you sleeping so late?' she exclaimed. 'It is nine o'clock. I have brought up some tea, will you take a cup? How pale you look!'

Raskolnikoff opened his eyes, shook himself, and recognised Nastasia. 'Has the landlady sent me this tea?' asked he, making a painful effort to sit up.

'Not much chance of that!' And the servant placed before him her own teapot, in which there was still some tea left, and laid two small lumps of brownish sugar on the table.

'Here, Nastasia, take this, please,' said Raskolnikoff, fumbling in his pocket, and drawing out a handful of small change (for he had again lain down in his clothes), 'and fetch me a white roll. Go to the pork-shop as well, and buy me a bit of cheap sausage.'

'I will bring you the roll in a minute, but had you not better take some *chtchi** instead of the sausage? We make it here and it is capital. I kept some for you last night, but it was so late before you came in! You will find it very good.' She went to fetch the *chtchi*, and, when Raskolnikoff had begun to eat, she seated herself on the sofa beside him and commenced to chatter, like the true country-girl she was. 'Prascovia Paulovna means to report you to the police,' said she.

The young man's brow clouded. 'To the police? Why?'

'Because you don't pay and won't go. That's why.'

'The deuce!' growled he between his teeth, 'that is the finishing stroke; it comes at a most unfortunate juncture. She is a fool,' added he aloud. 'I shall go and talk to her tomorrow.'

'She is, of course, just as much of a fool as I am; but why do you, who are so intelligent, lie here doing nothing? How is it you never seem to have money for anything now? You used to give lessons, I hear; how is it you do nothing now?'

'I am engaged on something,' returned Raskolnikoff dryly and half-reluctantly.

'On what?'

'Some work –'

'What sort of work?'

'Thinking,' replied he gravely, after a short silence.

Nastasia was convulsed. She was of a merry disposition, but her laughter was always noiseless, an internal convulsion which made her actually writhe with pain. 'And does your thinking bring you any money?' asked she, as soon as she could manage to speak.

'Well! I can't give lessons when I have no boots to go out in! Besides, I despise them.'

'Take care lest you suffer for it.'

'There is so little to be made by giving lessons! What can one do with a few kopecks?' said he in an irritable tone, rather to himself than the servant.

'So you wish to make your fortune at one stroke?'

He looked at her rather strangely, and was silent for a moment. 'Yes, my fortune,' rejoined he impressively.

'Hush! you frighten me, you look terrible. Shall I go and fetch you a roll?'

'Just as you like.'

* Cabbage soup.

'Wait a minute. I was forgetting to tell you that a letter came while you were out.'

'A letter for me? From whom?'

'How should I know? I gave three kopecks out of my own pocket to the postman. I suppose I did right?'

'Bring it, for the love of Heaven, bring it at once!' cried Raskolnikoff, in the greatest agitation. 'Good Lord!' In another minute the letter was put into his hands. It was as he thought; it came from his mother, and bore the R— postmark. As he took it he turned pale. He had received no tidings from home for a long while; but it was something else that smote him so suddenly. 'And now, Nastasia, pray begone! Take your three kopecks, and for the love of Heaven begone!'

The letter was trembling in his fingers; he did not choose to open it in Nastasia's presence, but was waiting for her to go that he might read it. As soon as he found himself alone, he put the envelope to his lips and kissed it. Then he began to examine the address; he recognised the familiar handwriting; the fine and somewhat sloping characters were those of his mother, who had once taught him to read and write. He hesitated, and seemed almost to shrink from opening it. At length he broke the seal and found a long letter, two large sheets completely filled.

'My dear Rodia,' began the mother, 'I have not written to you now for more than two months, and have been so distressed about it that it has often kept me awake at nights. Still I feel sure you will forgive my involuntary silence. You know how I love you. Dounia and I feel that you are all-in-all to us; our hope and future happiness are bound up in yours. What did I not suffer on learning that you had been obliged to leave the University some months ago for lack of means, and that you were without any teaching or resources of any kind! How was it possible for me to assist you when I had nothing but my yearly pension of one hundred and twenty roubles? The fifteen roubles which I sent you four months ago were advanced me, as you know, by one of the tradesmen here, Athanasius Ivanovitch Vakrouchin, a good man, who was a friend of your father's; but, as I had signed a paper authorising him to claim my pension, it was impossible for me to send you anything till this was repaid, and I have only just been able to do it.

'Now, thank God, I find myself in circumstances to send you a little more. I must hasten to make you acquainted with the happy change in our fortunes, and must first tell you what you are not yet aware of, that your sister has been living with me for the last six weeks and intends to remain with me. Her tortures, Heaven be praised, have come to an end; but to begin from the beginning, for I should like you to know everything that we have been concealing from you hitherto. You wrote me word two months ago that you had heard of Dounia's uncomfortable situation with the Svidrigaïloffs, and you asked for further particulars. What reply could I make at the time? If I had told you all, you would have thrown up everything and come to us, even if you had to do it on foot, for I know that with your disposition and feelings you could not have endured the thought of your sister being insulted. I myself was in despair, but what could I do? Nor did I at that time know the whole state of the case. Unhappily, Dounetchka, on accepting a situation as governess in this family last year, had received a hundred roubles in advance, to be deducted monthly from the salary due to her; consequently she was obliged to remain until this debt was discharged.

'She had asked for this advance (as I may tell you now, dearest Rodia) mainly in order to send you the sixty roubles of which at that time you stood in such urgent need, and which you received from us last year. We deceived you then by writing that Dounetchka's little savings had furnished the sum. It was a falsehood; but now I may tell you the truth, that you may know what God has done for us, and how loving and true-hearted Dounia is. Mr Svidrigaïloff began by behaving very rudely to her, constantly making sarcastic and insulting remarks at table. But why should I dilate on painful details which can only vex you uselessly, since it is all over now? Dounetchka was kindly treated by Marfa Petrovna, Svidrigaïloff's wife, and by the rest of the family, but she had a great deal to bear, especially when Mr Svidrigaïloff, who had acquired the habit of drinking in the army, was under the influence of Bacchus. Had that but been all! But under his apparent rudeness and contempt the wretch concealed a passion for Dounia!

'At length he threw off the mask by making dishonourable proposals, trying, by various promises, to seduce her, and declaring himself prepared to leave his house and family and take her to live in some other village or even country. You may imagine Dounia's distress. It was not merely the pecuniary part of the business, to which I have already referred, which prevented her from resigning her situation on the spot; she feared lest she should arouse Marfa Petrovna's suspicions, and thus introduce an element of discord into the household. The *dénouement*, however, came unawares. Marfa Petrovna happened to surprise her husband in the garden entreating Dounia to fly with him, and, misconstruing all, accused her of being the cause of everything. There was a dreadful scene. Marfa Petrovna even struck Dounia and refused to hear a word, reproaching her for a full hour. Finally, she ordered Dounia to be immediately sent back to me in a common peasant's cart, in which were flung all her things, not packed, but all of a heap. Then there came on a pouring rain, and Dounia, thus insulted and shamed, had to ride with a peasant the whole seventeen versts in an uncovered cart.

'Think now, what could I have written to you in reply to your letter received two months ago? I was quite in despair. I dared not tell you the facts, because you would have felt all this so much and what could you have done? It would only have brought misfortune to you and have hurt Dounia. Nor could I fill my letters with trifles when my heart was full of grief. For a whole month the matter was the talk of the town, and it reached such a pitch that it was impossible for Dounia and myself to go to church without finding ourselves the object of contemptuous glances and whisperings; remarks were even made aloud in our presence. All our friends abandoned us, not even acknowledging us in the street, and it came to my ears that some merchants and Civil Service clerks were intending to affront us by smearing the gate of our house with tar, and our landlord demanded our removal. The cause of all this was Marfa Petrovna, who accused and bemired Dounia in every house, so that in time the tale was known not only in the town, but throughout the whole district. I felt very ill, but Dounia was stronger than myself. You should have seen how she bore up and consoled and inspirited me. She is an angel!

'But, through God's mercy, our affliction came to an end. Mr Svidrigaïloff came to his senses and repented, and, probably pitying Dounia, laid before Marfa Petrovna positive and documentary proofs of her innocence, in a letter which Dounia, before the surprise in the garden, had found herself obliged to write and give to Mr Svidrigaïloff, in which she declined personal explanations and assignations. For this letter, which on her departure remained in his hands, reproached him most indignantly with the baseness of his behaviour towards Marfa Petrovna, setting forth that he was the father of a family, and how abominable it was on his part to insult an unhappy, defenceless girl.

'One word, dear Rodia. This letter was so nobly and affectingly written that I sobbed on reading it, but now I can read it without tears. Besides this, in Dounia's justification appeared at last the testimony of the servants, who had seen and heard much more than Mr Svidrigaïloff supposed, as, indeed, is always the case. Marfa Petrovna was perfectly astounded and horror-stricken, as she herself avowed to me, but was entirely convinced of Dounia's innocence. Next day was a Sunday. She came to the church, and on her knees, with tears, prayed to the Holy Virgin to give her strength to endure her trial and fulfil her duty. Then she came straight on to us and related all, and, with bitter tears and in humble penitence, embraced Dounia and implored her forgiveness.

'That very same evening, without the least delay, she set out for all the houses in the town and bore testimony to Dounia's innocency, speaking in most flattering terms of the nobleness of her feelings and behaviour; and, more than that, she showed and read aloud Dounia's own letter to Mr Svidrigaïloff, and even distributed copies (a perfectly unnecessary proceeding, to my mind). Thus for some days she made a tour of the town. Some people began to be offended because others had been made her confidants; therefore she had to take them in turns, until it got to be known that on such a day Marfa Petrovna would be at such and such a place, and there people again assembled who had already read the letter at home or at other acquaintances'. In my opinion, much of this was quite needless, but Marfa Petrovna is such a character! At any rate it restored Dounia's reputation; but the shame and infamy of the husband was so mercilessly exposed that I felt pity for him, and thought he had been dealt with too harshly.

'Dounia then began to receive offers of engagements for teaching from many families, but declined them all. All this brought about what I am going to relate, and changed, as I may say, our destiny.

'Learn, then, dearest Rodia, that she has received and accepted an offer of marriage. Of this I hasten to inform you. I know it has all taken place without our consulting you, but I am sure you will not be angry with us, as it was impossible to write and wait for the receipt of your answer. Besides, as you were absent, you would not have been able to judge of the matter. It came about in this way. He is a councillor, Peter Petrovitch Looshin, and a remote relation of Marfa Petrovna's, who has assisted him very much. It commenced by his intimating, through her, a desire for our acquaintance. He was, accordingly, received by us, took coffee here, and the next day very politely made his proposal, and asked for an early and decisive reply. He is now on his way to St Petersburg, and being a thorough business man, every minute is of importance to him. You can understand how much we were taken aback by so sudden and unexpected an occurrence! Mr Looshin is a man of means and of solid character, and practises in two places. It is true, he is forty-five years of age; still, he is tolerably good-looking, and can make himself agreeable to women. He seems, on the whole, most respectable and decorous, though, perhaps, a little stern, and even haughty. This, however, may be only my first impression.

'I wish to warn you, dear Rodia, when you meet him in St Petersburg, which will come about very shortly, not to judge him in haste or heat, as you are in the habit of doing people, if on making his acquaintance you do not altogether fancy him. I say this, although I am sure he will make a favourable impression upon you. Besides, to know a man thoroughly, one must deal with him gradually and with circumspection, so as not to be influenced by prejudice, which it may be very difficult afterwards to correct or efface. Peter Petrovitch is, to all appearance, a man of great honour. On his first visit, he told us he was very conservative, but shared in many things, as he himself put it, the convictions of the rising generation; and at the same time he was an enemy to all prejudices. Much more he said, so that some might have called him vain, and fond of hearing himself talk; but this is hardly a vice.

'Indeed, I understood but very little of what he said, but Dounia explained to me that he was a man of little cultivation, but intelligent, and, it seemed, kind-hearted. You know our little Dounia – so full of character, so prudent, patient, and magnanimous, although high-spirited, as I well know from experience. Of course, neither on his side nor on hers is there any particular affection; but Dounia, besides being a sensible girl, is a noble being, almost an angel. She would feel it her duty to make her husband happy, if he cared for her welfare. We have no reason to question his intentions, although all has been done quickly; besides, he, too, is very sensible, and can see that his own happiness will be best secured by that of his wife. As for some dissimilarity in character, habits, and thoughts (which occur in the happiest unions), Dounia said there was no need to be disquieted on that score, as she relied on herself, and could endure much, provided he were only honourable and just. At first we thought him rather disagreeable, but this may have arisen from his being an outspoken man, and that he is indeed. When he visited us the second time, on receiving our consent, he admitted that it had always been his intention to marry some honest girl without dowry, one who had been tried in the fire, because, as he explained, a husband should in no way be indebted to his wife – it is much better for her to regard him as her benefactor.

'I must add that he expressed himself in terms somewhat more delicate than those I use. I have forgotten the exact words, and recollect only the sense; besides, he did not say this intentionally, it evidently only came out in the course of conversation; he endeavoured to correct himself and soften his speech; still, I thought him rather rude. I told Dounia so afterwards, and she said angrily, "Words are not deeds," and that is quite true. Dounia did not sleep at all the night before deciding; and, fancying I was asleep, she got up and paced up and down the room all night. At last she threw herself on her knees and prayed long and fervently before the Holy Image. In the morning she told me she had decided.

'I have told you that Peter Petrovitch is now on his way to St Petersburg. His journey is of great importance, as he intends to establish himself there as a lawyer. He has been for a long time occupied with lawsuits, and only a few days since gained a very important case, and it is indispensable that he should appear before the Senate at St Petersburg. He may be very useful to you there, and Dounia and I are confident you can now commence definitely your future career under his protection. Oh that this were realised! Such a result could only be attributed to the goodness of God. Dounia dreams about it. We ventured on saying a few words on your behalf to Peter Petrovitch. He answered cautiously, and said he certainly could not do without a secretary, and of course it would be better to pay a relation than an outsider, if only the former should prove himself equal to his duties (as if you were not sure to!); but he expressed the doubt that your University course would interfere with your attention to his office. The subject then dropped, but Dounia thinks of nothing else, and she has been in a state of great excitement about it, building up the project that ultimately you may become his colleague and even his partner; the more so because you are studying for the law. I agree with her, Rodia, and fully share her hopes and plans, and see in them much probability, notwithstanding Peter Petrovitch's obvious evasiveness (which is because he does not know you).

'Dounia is quite confident she will attain all by her influence over her future husband. At present we cannot talk with Peter Petrovitch about these ideas of ours, especially about your becoming a partner. He is a practical man, and would, maybe, take it amiss and treat us as dreamers. Neither have I nor Dounia said so much as a word to him of our strong hopes that he might assist us to send you money whilst at the University. In the first instance, this will come in due time (could he refuse Dounia such a trifle?), the more so as you yourself might be his right hand in business and receive assistance, not as a favour, but in the worthy light of a well-earned salary. Dounia intends to arrange this. Secondly, we did not speak, because I wish you to be on an equal footing when you meet him. When Dounia spoke of you with ecstasy, he replied, "It is necessary to examine every man personally to judge of him." He reserved his opinion of you until he had seen you.

'Do you know, dear Rodia – this has nothing to do with Peter Petrovitch, but my own individual, and, it may be, old-womanish caprice – but it appears to me that I should do better if I lived alone after their marriage, as now, and not with them. I am fully convinced he will be kind enough to offer for me to remain with my daughter, though he has not done so as yet; but I shall refuse. I notice in life that mothers-in-law are not appreciated by the husbands. I do not wish to be the slightest inconvenience to anyone. I want to maintain the fullest liberty for myself, as long as I have my pension and such children as you and Dounia. If possible, I will settle near you both, Rodia. I reserve for the close of my letter the pleasant news that we shall very shortly be all together and embrace one another again, after nearly three years' separation. It is quite certain that Dounia and I are going to St Petersburg; when, I don't exactly know, but, to all appearances, shortly, and very shortly. All depends upon Peter Petrovitch, who, when he has looked round a little, will send us word. He wished to hasten the wedding for several reasons, and even, if possible, to have it before Lent; but, if that is impossible, then soon after the feast of the Assumption. Oh, with what rapture shall I press you to my heart!

'Dounia is wild with joy at meeting you, and said once, in joke, that for that alone she would marry Peter Petrovitch. She is indeed an angel. She adds nothing in writing now, but bids me tell you she has much to say to you, but cannot take up pen to write you a few lines without upsetting herself. She sends you her best love and a thousand kisses. And now, although we shall soon be seeing each other in a few days, I will send you, all the same, some money, as much as I can. As everybody has got to know that Dounia is to marry Peter Petrovitch, my credit has increased. I am sure Athanasius Ivanovitch will advance me as much as seventy-five roubles on the security of my pension, so that I shall be able to send you twenty-five or even thirty roubles. I would send more, but I have to consider our travelling expenses, and, although Peter Petrovitch was kind enough to undertake on his own account the transport of our luggage, it is, nevertheless, necessary to reserve enough to pay our fare to St Petersburg, where it would be impossible to arrive without something in our purse. Dounia and I have calculated it all out nicely. I don't think it will come very expensive. From here to the railway station is exactly ninety versts, and we have arranged about a coach with a peasant whom we know, and then we will travel on third-class. In fact, I shall manage to send you not twenty-five but thirty roubles.

'But I must close, my two sheets are filled, I have no more room. This is our story; in truth, there has been much to tell you; and now, my dearest Rodia, I embrace you and look forward to our meeting soon. I send you a mother's blessing. Love your sister Dounia, dear Rodia, love her as she loves you, and believe that she loves you infinitely more than her own life. She is an angel, and you, Rodia, are everything to us, our hope and our trust. Be only happy yourself, and we shall be happy too. Do you pray to God, Rodia, as you used to do, and believe in the mercy of the Creator and our Redeemer? I almost fear in my heart that the new epidemic of unbelief has attacked you; if so, I pray for you, Rodia. Recollect, dear, how, in your infancy and during the life of your father, you lisped your prayers on your knees to me. How happy we all were then! Goodbye, or better still, *au revoir*! I embrace you a thousand times and with kisses without end – I am, yours, while life lasts,

PULCHERIA RASKOLNIKOFF.

During all the time he was reading the letter, even from the commencement, Raskolnikoff's face was wet with tears; when he had finished, it looked pallid and distorted, and a bitter smile played about his lips. He laid his head on his grimy pillow and became lost in thought. His heart beat wildly and his thoughts were agitated. He was stifled and cramped in this little yellow room, which felt like a cupboard. Neither his eyes nor thoughts were in harmony with his surroundings, and he seized his hat and went out, giving no thought this time as to whom he might meet on the stairs. He took the direction towards Vassilevsky Island, across the V— Prospect, walking as if on most urgent business, and, true to his habits, hurried along, muttering to himself, and then speaking aloud, so that many took him for a man in liquor.

Chapter 4

HIS MOTHER'S LETTER pained him. Of the principal point of the letter there was no doubt in his mind, even whilst reading it. What to do he had decided at once. 'This marriage shall never take place whilst I live. Mr Looshin may go to the devil.'

'It is plain enough,' he muttered, smiling, and maliciously celebrating in advance the success of his decision. 'No, mother, no, Dounia, you cannot deceive me: and still they excuse themselves for not asking my advice and coming to a decision without me. What capital excuses, and what a man of business this Peter Petrovitch is, who woos at post-horse, nay almost at railway, speed! No, Dounia, I see and know all you are preparing to say to me, many things. Yes, and I know, too, what were your thoughts as you paced that room all night, and why you prayed before the holy image of our Lady of Kazan, in my mother's room. This was your Golgotha! Well, so it stands decided, does it, that Eudoxia Romanovna is pleased to take this business-like and rational man, together with his fortune, this substantial well-to-do individual who practises in two places and "shares the latest convictions of the rising generation" (so she writes), and *appears* kind, as Dounia herself said. Oh, the force of appearances! – on the strength of them Dounia is going to marry this fellow! Marvellous! marvellous!

'Again, how curious my mother should write to me about "the rising generation." Is it simply to give me an idea of his character, or with the remote object of predisposing me in Mr Looshin's favour? Oh, the crafty one! It would be well to clear up one point. How far were they candid with each other on that day and that night, and how has it been since? Were all their discussions mere recitations, did they keep back their real thoughts and never divulge them? Very likely it was partly so. Apparently, from the letter, he showed himself rude to my mother, and she went straight to Dounia with her remarks, provoking her to retort angrily. Who would not feel maddened to see the whole thing so unquestioned? And why should mother write: "Love Dounia, Rodia, for she loves you more than her life'? Has she no tricks of conscience to torture her for consenting to sacrifice her daughter for her son? "You are our hope, our all!" Oh! mother, mother!'

His anger boiled more and more, and had he come across Mr Looshin at that moment he would have killed him.

'This is the fact,' he continued, following the whirlwind of thought in his head, ' "One must approach a man gradually and cautiously to know him," but it is not difficult to make Mr Looshin out. "He is a man of business and *appears* kind." What great things, too! The luggage he attends to, pays for the larger boxes. Is not that kind? And they, the mother and bride, engage a peasant's tilted cart. I used to go that way. Nothing, only ninety versts, "and afterwards we will travel third-class a thousand versts," and prudently too. You must cut your coat according to your cloth. And you, Mr Looshin, what of you? She is your bride, and must you not know that my mother has to borrow money on her pension for her journey? Of course, this is an ordinary business transaction, an affair of mutual profit and equal shares; consequently the expenses must be shared equally. Bread and salt together, but each his own tobacco, according to the proverb. But the man of business has deceived them just a little. The luggage costs less than their fare, and perhaps passes free.

'Do they not see all this, or do they mean to be hoodwinked? Still, they are content, and think this is only the flower, and the real fruit is to come. What I fear for the future is not so much his stinginess as the tone he takes. I can foresee his tone after marriage . . . But what can my mother be thinking of? What will she do in St Petersburg? With three silver roubles or two notes, as that – hem! – old woman *said*! What does she mean to live on? It is plain she already guesses it will be impossible to live with Dounia after she is married. The dear man evidently let that slip out from the very first, although my mother averts that fact with both hands, and with that "but I shall refuse." On what does she rely – on her pension of a hundred and twenty roubles, with deductions for the debt to Athanasius Ivanovitch? All through the winter she knits comforters and embroiders cuffs, ruining her poor eyes, and that only adds twenty roubles a year to the hundred and twenty. Nevertheless, she relies on the noble feelings of Mr Looshin: "He himself will offer, he will entreat." No doubt! And so it is with these idealists – it is always the case. Up to the last they adorn the man with peacock-feathers, to the last they hold to the good, and, although they have a foreboding of the reverse of the medal, they put away their thoughts, and will shut out the reality with both hands, until in the end the idealised man mocks and laughs at them and shows himself as he really is. I should like to know whether he is decorated. Yes, I'll bet he has the Anna in his buttonhole, and wears it at commercial dinners. Perhaps he may wear it at the wedding. The devil take him!

'As to my mother, God be with her! But Dounia, Dounia darling, I know you. You were nineteen years of age when last I saw you. I knew your character *then*. My mother writes, "Dounia can endure much". I knew that two and a half years ago, and, if she could stand Mr Svidrigaïloff and all the results, no doubt she can endure much indeed, and now they imagine she can endure even Mr Looshin and his theory of the superiority of wives raised from poverty and made happy subjects of benefaction, which he divulged at the first interview. He made a blunder certainly, although so precise; but it may scarcely have been a blunder, and that he aimed to make it clear as soon as possible. But Dounia must see what he is. And to live with such a man! She would eat black bread and drink water, and never flinch, sooner than sell herself for comfort incompatible with her moral liberty. Not for all Schleswig-Holstein, and not for Mr Looshin! No, Dounia never was that sort of girl, and surely she cannot have changed. True, it may be said, it is hard to live with the Svidrigaïloffs. It is hard to go from place to place as governess all one's life for two hundred roubles; but, all the same, I know my sister would sooner go as a planter's slave or to a Livonian German than injure her soul and her moral feeling by a connection with a man with whom she had nothing in common, and whom she could not esteem. Never, never, for her individual advantage! Were Mr Looshin made of pure gold or diamonds, she would never consent to become his legal concubine. Then why does she consent?

'What trickery is there? Where is the clue? The thing is clear. For herself, for her comfort, even to save her life she would never sell herself but for another. Yes, for a beloved and adored one she would. This is the whole secret. For a brother, for a mother, she would sacrifice all. Oh, then we yield up moral feeling, liberty, peace of mind, and bring everything into the market; we can even give up life – if it only makes these beloved beings happy! But that is not all – we must even invent our own casuistry and borrow it from the Jesuits if necessary, and for a time persuade ourselves that it is necessary, really and absolutely needful, in a good cause! So it is, and as clear as day! Clear as day that Rodia Romanovitch Raskolnikoff is the hidden spring and prime object in all this. And why should I object to all that is arranged for me – to keep me at the University, then to become Looshin's partner, and ultimately secure his business, and become at last a rich man, honoured, esteemed, and even die a celebrated man? As to my mother: "There is Rodia, precious Rodia, Rodia my first-born! Who would not sacrifice a daughter for such a first-born?"'

'Oh, dear and unjust hearts, who in such a plight would shun even the fate of a Sonia! Have you thoroughly measured the sacrifice? Truly? Have you strength for it? Do you know, Dounia, that Sonia's fate is no more degrading than yours with Mr Looshin? "Of course there can be no particular love," my mother writes. On the contrary, there is already aversion, contempt, and loathing. What of that? One must keep clean. But do you understand what this cleanness means? Do you understand that a Looshin's purity is on a par with a Sonia's virtue, and it may be even worse and meaner, because you, Dounia, can count on superfluities and comforts, and in her case there is no alternative but starvation and death? Such purity is costly, very costly, Dounia, but if it goes beyond her strength and she repents? What sorrow, grief, and tears will be concealed from all! You are not a Marfa Petrovna, and what will become of my mother? I see her already uneasy, and what when she sees all? And myself? What are they thinking of me? I will not accept your sacrifice, Dounia. No, mother, it shall never be whilst I live. I will not have it.'

He suddenly bethought himself and paused.

'Not have it! What can I do? You prohibit it? By what right? And what, in your turn, can you offer? To consecrate my future to them *when* I leave the University and get a place? Bosh! *Now*, what about *now*? Something must be done at once; don't you realise this? What are you going to do? All they can do is to get an advance on their hundred-rouble pension, or from the Svidrigaïloffs. How can I protect them from these Svidrigaïloffs, from Athanasius Ivanovitch Vakrouchin?

Before I can do this, my mother will have had time to grow blind from knitting, and perhaps starve, and my sister – imagine what may become of her! Do you realise all this?'

So he excited and tormented himself, though with a certain sense of enjoyment. These questions were not new or improvised, but old and sore ones, and they had long worried him. All this present anguish had been engendered in him long ago, and it was ripened and concentrated in the form of a terrible question which held his heart and reason, and cried irresistibly for solution, and now his mother's letter came upon him like a thunder-clap. It was plain, now was not the time to grieve, to be passive and reason on unanswerable questions, but by all means to *do* something, and at once and quickly. A decision must be come to at all hazards, and something done, or –

'Or renounce life altogether!' he cried suddenly with ecstasy, 'and obediently submit to fate as it is, stifle everything, and dismiss the right to act, live, and love!'

'Do you know, sir, what it is to have nowhere to go to? One must of necessity go somewhere.' And he suddenly called to mind Marmeladoff's question the night before.

Then he shuddered. Another thought from the previous evening had returned. But he did not tremble, he knew he had a presentiment that it would come, but the thought was not altogether that of the day before, and the difference was this. A month ago, and even up to the present time, it had been a dream, but now it did not seem a dream, but a definite and terrible form, and altogether new. He became suddenly conscious of the change, and his head throbbed, and his eyes grew dim. He hastily looked round, and sought where to rest himself. He was now on the K— boulevard. A bench stood about a hundred steps off, and he hurriedly made for it; but, on the way, a little incident took place which attracted all his attention.

Looking towards the bench, he observed before him, a dozen steps off, a woman; but, as usual, he did not notice her at first. Still there was something so strange about her, even at first sight, that, having her within his ken, he gradually became interested in her – at first against his will, and with anger against himself; his curiosity, however, grew stronger and stronger, until he confessed he would like to know what was so peculiar about her. She seemed to be a very young woman, and was out, in the intense heat, bareheaded, without sunshade or gloves, and walked strangely, flourishing her hand about. She wore a silk dress, very oddly put on, scarcely fastened, and torn behind. A small neckerchief was ill-arranged on her shoulders. Finally, the girl walked unsteadily, even reeling about. Raskolnikoff's interest in her was now thoroughly aroused. He came up to her at the bench, but, on reaching the seat, she fell down heavily on it, throwing her head on it and closing her eyes, apparently from excessive fatigue. He presently guessed that she was drunk. Strange – sad it was to look upon such a sight, and he thought he was deceiving himself. Before him was a small and extremely young face of no more than sixteen, possibly only fifteen; it was overhung by light hair, and looked handsome, but heated and swollen. She seemed unconscious that she was in the streets.

Raskolnikoff did not sit down, but stood before her. This boulevard was very little frequented at any time, but now, at two o'clock, in such heat, hardly anyone was to be seen: still, a little way off, on the edge of the walk, a man was standing who appeared as if he also would like to approach the girl for some purpose. He had, no doubt, also observed and followed her, and Raskolnikoff's presence hindered him from going up to her. He flung a spiteful glance at Raskolnikoff, but at the same time appeared anxious that the latter should not observe him. Standing a little apart, he impatiently awaited the departure of the inopportune ragged stranger. The whole thing was very clear. He was about thirty years of age, stout, healthy-looking, with full lips, wore a moustache, and was fashionably dressed. As soon as Raskolnikoff saw him, his anger rose, and it immediately came into his head to insult this fat coxcomb. In a moment he left the girl and went up to the man.

'Eh, you Svidrigaïloff, what are you after?' he cried through lips foaming with rage, and clenching his fist.

'What does this mean?' gruffly replied the man, knitting his brows and looking at Raskolnikoff from head to foot.

'Get off; that's what I want you to do.'

'How dare you, you ruffian?' He flourished a cane.

Raskolnikoff rushed at him with both fists, not staying to calculate that the stout man was worth two of him. But at that moment somebody firmly seized him from behind, and between them stood a policeman.

'Stop, gentlemen do not fight in the public thoroughfare. What is this? Who are you?' gruffly, turning to Raskolnikoff, and noticing his rags. His was a bold, soldierly face, with a grey beard and whiskers, and an intelligent expression. 'Here, I want you,' he said, seizing Raskolnikoff by the arm.

'I am a student; Raskolnikoff is my name; you can easily ascertain that,' and turning to the gentleman, 'and you too, sir, if you like. Come here, I will show you.' And, catching the officer by the hand, he dragged him to the bench.

'See, there, quite drunk! Just come on the boulevard. Who knows what she is? Yet she hardly can be what she appears. It is more likely she has been made drunk, or drugged, and then turned out into the street. Look at her. It is plain; and now look here. This coxcomb, whom I would have struck down, is unknown to me, and it is the first time I have seen him, but he noticed her, followed her, the poor helpless one! He saw her condition, and would have seized her for his own purposes. This is certain, believe me. I make no mistake. I watched him pursue her. I have hindered him, and now he is only waiting for me to be gone. See, there he stands a little way off, twisting a cigarette. Is this to be allowed? How can we lead her home, think you?'

The officer considered. The stout man was clearly intelligible; but the girl? The officer bent down to examine her with compassion in his countenance. 'Ah, what a pity!' said he, shaking his head. 'A mere child, too! Listen, my child,' said he, addressing her, 'where do you live?' The girl opened her eyes, gazed stupidly at her interrogator, and brandished her arms.

'Listen,' said Raskolnikoff (here fumbling in his pocket and taking out twenty kopecks), 'go for a conveyance and see her taken home. But how to find her address?'

'Lady,' again commenced the officer, having taken the money, 'I am going to take you home. Where do you live? What is your address?'

'Oh, they are seizing me!' murmured the girl, once more waving her hands.

'Ah, how sad! It is a shame! A child!' He began again to shake his head in pity and indignation. 'What is to be done?' he said suddenly to Raskolnikoff, eyeing him from head to foot, and thinking it strange that one in such rags should have money to throw about. 'You came upon them a long way off?' he asked.

'I tell you she was in front of me, reeling about the boulevard, and when she got to the seat she rolled down.'

'Shame to see such in full day! She is drunk, and has been betrayed. See her torn dress,' and the officer again bent over her.

'In the first place,' said Raskolnikoff, 'we must prevent that villain taking her. He means no good, one can see that. The wretch! Why does he not go?'

Raskolnikoff spoke loudly, and pointed at him. The man indicated heard him, and was about to break forth, but restrained himself, and was content with giving a contemptuous glance, and at the same time moving off a little and remaining standing.

'That we can prevent,' replied the officer, 'if we only knew where she came from. Lady! Lady!'

All at once she opened her eyes, looked fixedly, as if recollecting something, then rose up and went off in the direction whence she came. 'The villains are seizing me!' she cried, still waving her hands about. She moved quickly, but reeled as before. The coxcomb went after her, down another avenue, but keeping her in sight.

'Do not alarm yourself. He shall not have her,' said the officer, resolutely, as he went after them. 'What vice we see around us!' he added, with a sigh.

Something seemed to sting Raskolnikoff, and in a trice he turned and shouted to the officer: 'Eh! One moment.'

The latter looked back.

'Stop! What do you want? Let him amuse himself' (pointing to the man). 'What can it matter to you?'

The officer did not understand, and looked him in the face. Raskolnikoff began to laugh.

'Eh?' said the officer, with a movement of the hand as he continued to follow the man and girl. He evidently took Raskolnikoff for a lunatic or something worse.

'He walks off with my twenty kopecks,' said Raskolnikoff, spitefully, when alone, 'and the other will fee him to let that girl be. Why did I interfere? What right had I to meddle? Hang them both! What is it to me? And how could I give away those twenty kopecks? Were they mine?'

Notwithstanding his strange words, his heart was heavy, and he sat down on the forsaken seat. His thoughts were disturbed and he found it difficult at that moment to think at all. He could have wished to forget everything and sleep all off, and commence afresh.

'Poor thing!' said he, looking at the place so recently occupied by the young girl. 'As soon as she comes to herself, she will begin to cry, and then her mother will learn all and box her ears, following it up with a whipping to increase her humiliation, and, perhaps, turn her out of doors – or even, if not, some Daria Frantzovna or another will get scent of the quarry, and start her on the road to ruin till she is forced to enter a hospital (as generally happens to these sort of girls when they have respectable mothers). When she comes out, it will be the same thing again and again, with ever-recurring visits to the hospital; then she will take to drink, and in two or three years, at the age of eighteen or nineteen, it will be all over. How many have I seen end thus, whose life began like hers? What then? They call it a necessary evil, a percentage we are forced to pay (to the devil, I suppose) to ensure the tranquillity of society. A percentage! There is a scientific basis for it all, which soothes the mind. If the thing went by its right name it might attract more attention. Who knows whether Dounetchka herself might not be included in the percentage for next year, if not for this?

'But where am I going?' he thought suddenly. 'Strange! Apparently I was going somewhere after I had read the letter. Ah! now I remember: – to Vassilevsky Ostroff, to Razoumikhin. But why? It is strange! What could make me think of going to him?'

He wondered at himself. Razoumikhin was one of his most intimate friends at the University, although, it must be observed, Raskolnikoff had very few. He shunned everybody, went about with no one, and studiously kept aloof from all, and soon he became equally avoided. He occupied himself seriously and without sparing himself; for this he was respected. None loved him, as, besides being very poor, he was extremely proud and reserved. He seemed to make a mystery of himself. Some students used to declare that he looked down upon them all as children, with the idea that he had outstripped them in knowledge, ideas, and convictions, and that their opinions and interests were inferior to his own. But he did associate with Razoumikhin – that is, he was more communicative with him than with anyone else. It was impossible for anyone to be otherwise with Razoumikhin. He was uncommonly jovial, a frank fellow, and kind and soft-hearted. But under all was concealed a depth of worth and merit. The best of his comrades knew this, and all loved him. His appearance arrested attention: he was ill-shaven and black-haired.

Sometimes he was very turbulent and was reputed a perfect Hercules. He could drink to excess, but he could also abstain. It was noticed that no failure affected him, nor did circumstances alter his joviality. He could have lodged on a roof or endured protracted cold and hunger without losing his spirits. He was very poor and earned his own living, obtaining the necessary means by some sort of work; and he had a number of resources. Once during a whole winter he kept his room unheated, and was fond of declaring that he preferred it, as the cold made him sleep better. At this present time he found himself obliged to discontinue his studies at the University for lack of means, though he hoped it would not be for long, and he was making every effort to improve his situation. Raskolnikoff had not been near him for four months, and Razoumikhin did not even know his friend's whereabouts. Some time ago, about a couple of months since, they had met, but Raskolnikoff crossed the street to avoid him; so Razoumikhin also took no notice of him, as he saw his friend did not wish it.

Chapter 5

'Ah! I thought of going to Razoumikhin some time ago to ask him to get me work of some sort,' said he to himself, 'and he may be of assistance to me now; he may be able to get me employment, and let me have a little more money – if he has any – to buy boots and repair my clothes and make me fit to give lessons again. But what then? What can I do with a few kopecks, if I get them? Really, it is very absurd of me to go to him.'

The question why he thought of seeing Razoumikhin troubled him more than he admitted to himself, and he uneasily sought to discover some ominous meaning in this apparently natural call on his friend.

'What! Is it possible that I am resting all my hopes on a Razoumikhin?' he asked himself in astonishment. He thought and rubbed his forehead; then, after a time, a strange idea came into his head. 'Yes,' he said, suddenly and firmly, and in a tone of final resolution, 'I will go to him – that is certain – but not now. I will go to Razoumikhin the day after *that*, when *that* has become certain, and all commences anew.' He roused himself. 'After *that*,' he muttered, quitting the bench. 'Ah! *If* it happens. Will it really ever?'

He left the place and thought of turning back, but the idea of going home was exceedingly repugnant to him – there, in that den of his, where *that* had had its birth more than a month ago! He went heedlessly on. A shiver ran through him, and he turned cold from these evil thoughts. He made a desperate effort to interest himself in the surrounding objects and find distraction in the passers-by, but he soon fell back upon himself, and when, again shuddering, he raised his head and looked around, he neither knew what he had been thinking of nor where he was. In such a state he had gone all over Vassilevsky Ostroff, crossed the Little Neva, and was now on the island. The verdure and the freshness at first pleased his weary eyes, habituated to town dust, lime, and massive houses. Here were no offensive exhalations or drinking-shops. But these new and agreeable feelings soon passed away and gave place to a morbid irritability. Now and then he would stop before something attractive in the green villas, and look over the fences upon the balconies and terraces, and the gaily-dressed ladies and children running about the gardens. The flowers particularly interested him, and he looked at them long. Splendid carriages were also passing, and ladies and gentlemen on horseback. He glanced at these with curious eyes and forgot them before they were out of sight.

Once he stopped, and began to count his money, which he found amounted to about thirty kopecks: 'Twenty to the officer, three to Nastasia; then I must have left forty-seven or fifty at Marmeladoff's,' thought he, as he reckoned it up, but quickly forgot even for what purpose he had pulled out his money, and, a cook-shop at that moment catching his eye, he recollected that he was hungry. Entering the place, a kind of eating-house, he drank a glass of brandy and took a cake, which latter he finished eating in the streets. As he had not tasted brandy for a very long time, it soon began to have an effect upon him, although he had only taken one glass. His limbs grew heavy, and he commenced to feel very drowsy. He made for home, but, on reaching Petrovsky Island, he had to stop from sheer feebleness. He left the road, turned aside where there were some bushes, sank upon the grass, and was soon sound asleep.

Dreams appear much more prominent and clear when the dreamer is in an unhealthy state – they have an extraordinary semblance of reality. Most monstrous pictures are put together, but all the circumstances are so subtly interwoven, the details so artistically harmonious in every minute respect, as to defy human imitation, be the artist a Pooshkin or a Tourgeneff. Such morbid dreams are always recollected for very long, and produce strong impressions on the disordered and already excited organs of the dreamer.

Raskolnikoff had a strange dream. His childhood came back to him; he was once more in his native town. He was seven years of age, was walking with his father in the suburbs. The day was hot and stifling. The town stood revealed before him on a plain, whilst beyond, far away against the horizon, appeared a dark wood. At some paces from the nearest gardens of the town there was a *caback*, or tavern, a large place which always produced a disagreeable impression, and even dread, on him as he used to go by with his father. A crowd of people seemed always gathered there; they used to bawl, curse, and sing, and at times fight amongst themselves; whilst, in the vicinity, drunken and suspicious characters abounded. On meeting any of these, he would run up to his father, seize his hand, and begin to tremble violently. Near the *caback*, a path, covered with black dust, crossed the field; and farther on, about three hundred paces to the right of the town, was the cemetery. In the middle of the latter stood the little stone church, with its green dome, which he visited twice a year with his father and mother in memory of the dead grandmother whom he had never seen, and they brought with them a rice-cake ornamented with a cross of raisins. He loved his church and its old images, for the greater part

undecked, and its old priest with his trembling hand. Near his
grandmother's grave was that of his younger brother, who died when
six months old, whom he had also never known and could not recollect,
but they told him that it was his little brother's, and each time he
visited the cemetery he reverently crossed himself before the tiny
grave, and saluted and kissed it.

He dreamed that he was going with his father along the road which
led to the cemetery, and was passing the *caback*. He held his father by
the hand and gazed upon the house in terror. A particular circumstance attracted his attention. At this moment the place was surrounded by a crowd of gaily-dressed townspeople, their wives, and a
regular rabble. All were intoxicated, and singing and shouting. Near
the door stood a wagon, but a strange one. It was one of those very
large ones used for transporting barrels and other heavy goods, drawn
by large dray-horses. He loved to look upon these huge cart-horses,
with long manes and thick legs, moving tranquilly along, with
measured pace, under their heavy loads, which seemed as nothing to
them. But, oddly enough, to this large cart was harnessed a small and
feeble roan mare, one of those which he often saw straining under
some tall load of hay or wood, and plodding painfully along as the
peasant's whip mercilessly fell across its nose and over its eyes. To him
this was so pitiful that when he saw such a sight he could never refrain
from tears, and his mother would be obliged to lead him from the
window. All at once a number of peasants came noisily out of the
house, the greater part clad in red and blue shirts and sleeveless
smock-frocks, tipsy, of course, and some singing, with valalaikas
(Russian guitars) in their hands. 'Get in, get in, all of you,' cried out a
young stout-shouldered peasant with a thick neck and face red as a
carrot. 'Jump up, I am going to take the lot of you.'

'What, with such a jade as that? You are out of your senses, Nikola,'
and they began to laugh.

'Come on. Get in!' cried Nikola, jumping into the wagon with the
reins, and standing straight up in front, 'she only eats her head off, and
I am sick of her. Get in, I say, and see me make her gallop.' He took up
his whip, and gleefully prepared to flog the mare.

'What, gallop that thing?' laughed the crowd.

'Such a gallop as she has not had for ten years.'

'Come on, no pity, brothers; get your whips.'

They began to clamber into the wagon, amidst laughter and jests. Six
got in, and there was room for more. Amongst them was a stout red-
faced woman, whom they placed in a corner. She was clad in red
fustian, with a braided headdress, and sat cracking nuts and laughing.

All the crowd laughed with relish at the idea of seeing the old mare trot under such a burden. Two fellows with whips stood ready to assist Nikola. The mare drew with all her might, but, far from a trot, she barely succeeded in moving her load one inch, and simply sprawled her feet about. She snorted and winced under the blows from three whips, falling rapidly upon her. The laughter in the wagon and from the crowd redoubled, and served to arouse Nikola's anger, and his whip rained blow upon blow on the back of the unfortunate beast.

'Keep quiet, still, still!' cried he, 'I'll make her go,' and his fury increased with his blows until he lost all control over himself.

'Father! Father!' the boy cried to his father, 'why are they doing that? They will kill the poor horse.'

'Never mind, let us go, they are drunk, it is only their mad pranks. Come,' and he led him away. But he slipped from his parent's hand, and, with no thought of himself, ran to the mare. She was breathing heavily, and, making another effort, had stopped, and stood ready to drop.

'Beat her to death,' yelled Nikola, 'if she won't – '

'You are no Christian,' cried an old man out of the crowd.

'How can you expect her to take such a load?' said another.

'You will kill her!' shouted a third.

'All right, she is mine; I can do what I like, can't I? Come on, let us try again. I say she shall gallop!'

Suddenly laughter resounded everywhere – drowned everything else. The mare was resenting the augmented blows, and was kicking freely. Even the old man could not resist smiling. Two men out of the crowd came forward with whips, and, standing at her flanks, laid on to her ribs.

'Give it her across the eyes and the nose.'

'Let us sing, brothers!' cried one in the wagon, and all took up the cry, and they commenced a lewd song; the tambourines beat, whilst some whistled in accompaniment; the red-faced woman cracked her nuts and grinned.

The boy looked on and saw how they struck the animal on the eyes, and very eyeballs, and his heart heaved and tears rose. One of the strikers smacked him in the face; he felt it not, and ran up to the old man – the old man who condemned them all. An old woman saw him, and carried him in her arms out of the crowd, but he escaped and again ran back to the animal. She was evidently nearly spent, but had again begun to kick.

'I'll make you food for wolves!' shouted Nikola. He threw down his whip, stooped, pulled out a long, narrow board from the bottom of the wagon, held it up on end, and swung it over his head.

'You will kill her!'

'All right,' shouted Nikola, and he brought the board down upon the roan with all his might.

'Flog her, flog her, what matters!' cried voices out of the wagon.

He raised it again, and another blow, in all its heaviness, fell upon the back of the unfortunate mare. Her hind legs gave way, but she jumped up and pulled with all her last strength, and endeavoured to extricate herself. From all sides the whips came thickly, and the board rose once more, descended a third time, then a fourth, with full force. Nikola was mad that he could not kill her with a blow.

'See, she is going to fall, it is all over,' shouted one of the crowd.

'Get a hatchet and finish her,' cried another.

'Mind!' cried Nikola, throwing down the board and seizing a crowbar. 'Take care!' he shouted, and he hit the mare a heavy blow with it, and at the same time lost his balance and stumbled. The mare reeled, and the bar was raised anew and fell heavily upon her spine, and she sank to the ground, all four legs giving way at once.

'All over!' shouted Nikola, and he leaped from the wagon in great excitement. Some drunken fellows seized what they could lay their hands upon, sticks, boards, or anything, and began belabouring the expiring mare, whilst Nikola spent his fury in hitting at her at random with the iron. The mare stretched out her head, groaned heavily, and expired.

'She is dead,' murmured some.

'But she never galloped!' cried others.

Nikola stood there with bloodshot eyes, and seemingly sorry he had nothing else to beat.

'Well, really, you are no Christian,' a number of voices shouted indignantly.

The poor boy thought not of himself, and made his way through the crowd to the dead mare; he embraced her bloodstained head and kissed it, then he leaped up and rushed frantically at Nikola with closed fists. At this moment, his father, who had been long seeking him, ran up and drew him out of the crowd.

'Come, come away!' said his father.

'Father, why did they kill the poor horse?' The boy sobbed, the words coming with difficulty from his heaving breast.

'They are drunk; it is not our affair. Let us go.' He took his father's hand, but his throat began to choke, and he struggled for breath. He shouted out and awoke.

He was covered with perspiration, and even his head was wet, and he arose breathless and in great terror. 'Thank God! It was only a dream,' he said, and he sat down again under a tree to recover himself. 'But what is all this? I am in a fever. What an ugly dream!' His limbs felt disjointed, and his mind was in darkness and confusion. He placed his elbows on his knees and held his head with his hands.

'God! Am I to stand beating in her skull with a hatchet or something, wade in warm blood, break open the lock and rob and tremble, blood flowing all around, and hide myself, with the hatchet? O God! Is this indeed possible, and must it be?' He trembled like a leaf as he said this.

'What am I thinking of?' he cried in some astonishment. 'I know well I could not endure that with which I have been torturing myself. I saw that clearly yesterday when I tried to rehearse it. Perfectly plain. Then what am I questioning? Did I not say yesterday as I went up the stairs how disgusting and mean and low it all was, and did not I run away in terror?'

He stood up and looked all round, wondering how he got there, and moved off towards the T— bridge. He was pale, and his eyes were hot, and feebleness was in all his members, but he seemed to breathe easier. He felt that he had thrown off the old time which had been so oppressive; and in its place had come peace and light. 'Lord!' he prayed, 'show me my way, that I may renounce these horrid thoughts of mine!'

Going across the bridge, he quietly gazed on the Neva, and the clear red sunset. He did not feel himself tired now, notwithstanding his weakness, and the load which had lain upon his heart seemed to be gone. Liberty! Liberty! He was free from those enchantments and all their vile instigations. In later times when he recalled this period of his existence, and all that happened to him in those days, minute by minute and point by point, he recollected how each circumstance, although in the main not very unusual, constantly appeared to his mind as an evidence of the predetermination of his fate, so superstitious was he. Especially he could never understand why he, weary and harassed as he was, could not have returned home by the shortest route, instead of across the Haymarket, which was quite out of the way. Certainly, a dozen times before, he had reached his lodgings by most circuitous routes, and never known through which streets he had come. But why (he always asked) should such a really fateful meeting have taken place in the market (through which there was no need to go), and happen, too, at exactly such a time and at a moment of his life when his mind was in the state it was, and the event, in these circumstances, could only produce the most definite and decided effect upon his fate? Surely he was the instrument of some purpose!

It was about nine o'clock as he stood in the Haymarket. All the dealers had closed their establishments or cleared away their goods and gone home. About this place, with its tattered population, its dirty and nauseous courtyards and numerous alleys, Raskolnikoff dearly loved to roam in his aimless wanderings. He attracted no notice there. At the corner of K— Lane were a dealer and his wife, who were engaged in packing up their wares, consisting of tapes, handkerchiefs, cotton, etc., preparatory to going home. They were lingering over their work, and conversing with an acquaintance. This was Elizabeth Ivanovna, or simple Elizabeth, as all called her, the younger sister of the old woman, Alena Ivanovna, to whose rooms Raskolnikoff went the day before for the purpose of pawning his watch to make his *rehearsal*. He knew all about this Elizabeth, as she knew also a little about him. She was a tall, awkward woman, about thirty-five years of age, timid and quiet, indeed almost an idiot, and was a regular slave to her sister, working for her day and night, trembling before her and enduring even blows. She was evidently hesitating about something, as she stood there with a bundle under her arm, and her friends were pressing some subject rather warmly. When Raskolnikoff recognised her he seemed struck with the greatest astonishment, although there was nothing strange about such a meeting.

'You ought to decide yourself, Elizabeth Ivanovna,' said the man. 'Come tomorrow at seven o'clock.'

'Tomorrow?' said Elizabeth slowly, as if undecided.

'She is frightened of Alena Ivanovna,' cried the wife, a brisk little woman. 'You are like a little child, Elizabeth Ivanovna, and she's not your own sister, but a stepsister. She has too much her own way.'

'You say nothing to Alena Ivanovna,' interrupted the man, 'and come without asking, that's the way to do it, and your sister can manage herself.'

'When shall I come?'

'At seven o'clock, tomorrow.'

'Very well, I will come,' said Elizabeth slowly and reluctantly. She then quitted them.

Raskolnikoff also went away, and stayed to hear no more. His original amazement had changed gradually into a feeling of actual terror; a chill ran down his back. He had learned unexpectedly and positively that, at seven o'clock the next evening, Elizabeth, the old woman's sister, the only person living with her, would not be at home, and that, therefore, the old woman, at seven o'clock tomorrow, *would be there alone*. It needed but a few steps to reach his room. He went along like one sentenced to death, with his reason clogged and numbed. He felt that now all liberty of action and free-will were gone, and everything was irrevocably decided. A more convenient occasion than was thus unexpectedly offered to him now, would never arise, and he might never learn again beforehand that, at a certain time on a certain day, she, on whom he was to make the attempt, would be entirely alone.

Chapter 6

RASKALNIKOFF LEARNED subsequently what induced the man and his wife to invite Elizabeth to call on them. It was a very simple matter. A foreign family, finding themselves in straitened circumstances, were desirous of parting with various things, consisting for the most part of articles of female attire. They were anxious, therefore, to meet with a dealer in cast-off clothes, and this was one of Elizabeth's callings. She had a large connection, because she was very honest and always stuck to her price: there was no haggling to be done with her. She was a woman of few words and very shy and reserved. But Raskolnikoff was very superstitious, and traces of this remained in him long after. In all the wants of this period of his life he was ever ready to detect something mysterious, and attribute every circumstance to the presence of some particular influence upon his destiny.

The previous winter, a fellow-student, Pokoreff by name, on leaving for Charkoff, had happened to communicate to him in conversation the address of Alena Ivanovna, in case he should ever require to pawn anything. For a long time he did not use it, as he was giving lessons, and managed somehow to get along, but six weeks before this time he had recollected the address. He had two things fit to pawn – an old silver watch, formerly his father's; and a small gold ring with three red stones, a souvenir from his sister on leaving home. He decided on getting rid of the latter, and went to the old woman's. At the first glance, and knowing nothing whatever of her personally, she inspired him with an unaccountable loathing. He took her two notes, and on leaving went into a poor *traktir*, or restaurant, and ordered some tea. He sat down musing, and strange thoughts flitted across his mind and became hatched in his brain. Close by, at another table, were seated a student, whom he did not know, and a young officer. They had been playing billiards, and were now drinking tea. Suddenly Raskolnikoff heard the student give the officer the address of Alena Ivanovna, the widow of a professor, as one who lent money on pledges. This alone struck Raskolnikoff as very peculiar. They were talking of the same person he had just been to see. No doubt it was pure chance, but, at the moment he was struggling against an impression he could not overcome, this stranger's words came and gave extra force to it. The student went on talking, and began to give his companion some account of Alena Ivanovna.

'She is well known,' he said, 'and always good for money. She is as rich as a Jew, and can advance five thousand roubles at a moment's notice; yet she will take in pledge objects worth as little as a rouble. She is quite a providence to many of our fellows – but such an old hag!' And, he went on explaining that she was grasping, evil, and capricious, held articles as forfeited if one day behind the time; she advanced no more than a quarter of the value on anything, and charged five and even six per cent interest per month, and so on. She had a sister, Elizabeth, who lived with her, and Alena Ivanovna ill-treated her and kept her in perfect subjugation like a child, although the latter was almost a giantess and the former considerably undersized.

'It's quite phenomenal!' he exclaimed, and burst out laughing.

The conversation then turned upon Elizabeth. The student spoke of her with evident pleasure and still laughing. The officer listened to his friend with considerable interest, and begged him to send him Elizabeth to mend his clothes; and Raskolnikoff did not miss a word, and thus learned all. She was younger than Alena Ivanovna, and only her half-sister, and was about thirty-five years of age. She worked day and night for the old woman – cooked, washed, and slaved for her, besides doing sewing for sale and going out charing; and she gave up all her earnings to her sister. She durst not accept any work or take any order without Alena Ivanovna's permission. The latter, it was known, had made a will, according to which Elizabeth got nothing beyond the sticks of furniture: her money was all left to a monastery in the Province of N— for perpetual prayers for her soul. Elizabeth was extraordinarily tall and ill-proportioned, with long ill-shod feet. She, however, kept herself very clean. What most surprised the student and made him laugh was that Elizabeth was continually getting in the family-way.

'But you pretend she's a perfect monster?' observed the officer.

'She is certainly very dark-skinned; she is just like a soldier dressed up as a woman, but it does not follow that she's exactly a monster. She has such a good-natured countenance, and there is so much sympathy in the expression of her eyes that she pleases many people. She is very quiet, too, very gentle, very patient, and so easy-going. And she has such a sweet smile.'

'Ah, she seems to please you,' said the officer, smiling.

'Her oddness interests me. But I tell you what I would do. I would kill that damnable old hag, and take all she is possessed of, without any qualm of conscience,' exclaimed the student excitedly. The officer laughed, but Raskolnikoff shuddered. The words just uttered so strongly echoed his own thoughts. 'Let me put a serious question to you,' resumed the student, more and more excited. 'I have hitherto been joking, but now listen to this. On the one side here is a silly, flint-hearted, evil-minded, sulky old woman, necessary to no one – on the contrary, pernicious to all – and who does not know herself why she lives.'

'Well?' said the officer.

'Hear me further. On the other hand, fresh young strength droops and is lost for want of sustenance; this is the case with thousands everywhere! A hundred, a thousand good deeds and enterprises could be carried out and upheld with the money this old woman has bequeathed to a monastery. A dozen families might be saved from hunger, want, ruin, crime, and misery, and all with her money! Kill her, I say, take it from her, and dedicate it to the service of humanity and the general good! What is your opinion? Shall not one little crime be effaced and atoned for by a thousand good deeds? For one useless life a thousand lives saved from decay and death. One death, and a hundred beings restored to existence! There's a calculation for you. What in proportion is the life of this miserable old woman? No more than the life of a flea, a beetle, nay, not even that, for she is pernicious. She preys on other lives. She lately bit Elizabeth's finger, in a fit of passion, and nearly bit it off!'

'Certainly she does not deserve to live,' observed the officer, 'but nature – '

'Ah, my friend, nature has to be governed and guided, or we should be drowned in prejudices. Without it there would never be one great man. They say "duty is conscience." Now I have nothing to say against duty and conscience, but let us see, how do we understand them? Let me put another question to you. Listen.'

'Stop a minute, I will give you one.'

'Well?'

'After all you have said and declaimed, tell me – are you going to kill the old woman *yourself*, or not?'

'Of course not. I only pointed out the inequality of things. As for the deed – '

'Well, if you won't, it's my opinion that it would not be just to do so! Come, let's have another game!'

Raskolnikoff was in the greatest agitation. Still, there was nothing extraordinary in this conversation; it was not the first time he had heard, only in other forms and on other topics, such ideas from the lips of the young and hot-headed. But why should he, of all men, happen to overhear such a conversation and such ideas, when the very same thoughts were being engendered in himself? – and why precisely *then*, immediately on his becoming possessed of them and on leaving the old woman? Strange, indeed, did this coincidence appear to him. This idle conversation was destined to have a fearful influence on his destiny, extending to the most trifling incident and causing him to feel sure he was the instrument of a fixed purpose.

On his return from the market, he flung himself upon his couch and sat motionless for a whole hour. It became dark, he had no light, but sat on. He could never afterwards recollect his thoughts at the time. At last he felt cold, and a shiver ran through him. He recognised with delight that he was sitting on his couch and could lie down, and soon he fell into a deep, heavy sleep. He slept much longer than usual, and his slumbers were undisturbed by dreams. Nastasia, who came to his room the next morning at ten o'clock, had great difficulty in awakening him. The servant brought him some bread and, the same as the day before, what was left of her tea.

'Not up yet!' exclaimed she indignantly. 'How can you sleep so long?'

Raskolnikoff raised himself with an effort; his head ached; he got upon his feet, took a few steps, and then dropped down again upon the couch.

'What, again!' cried Nastasia, 'but you must be ill then?' He did not answer. 'Would you like some tea?'

'By and by,' he muttered painfully, after which he closed his eyes and turned his face to the wall. Nastasia, standing over him, remained watching him for a while.

'After all, he's perhaps ill,' said she, before withdrawing.

At two o'clock she returned with some soup. Raskolnikoff was still lying on the couch. He had not touched the tea. The servant became angry and shook the lodger violently. 'What ever makes you sleep thus?' scolded she, eyeing him contemptuously.

He sat up, but answered not a word, and remained with his eyes fixed on the floor.

'Are you ill, or are you not?' asked Nastasia. This second question met with no more answer than the first. 'You should go out,' continued she, after a pause, 'the fresh air would do you good. You'll eat something, will you not?'

'By and by,' answered he feebly. 'Go away!' and he motioned her off. She remained a moment longer, watching him with an air of pity, and then left the room.

After a few minutes he raised his eyes, gave a long look at the tea and soup, and then began to eat. He swallowed three or four spoonfuls without the least appetite – almost mechanically. His head felt better. When he had finished his light repast, he again lay down on the couch, but he could not sleep and remained motionless, flat on his stomach, his face buried in the pillow. His reverie kept conjuring up strange scenes. At one time he was in Africa, in Egypt, on some oasis, where palms were dotted about. The caravans were at rest, the camels lay quietly, and the travellers were eating their evening meal. They drank water direct from the stream which ran murmuring close by. How refreshing was the marvellously blue water, and how beautifully clear it looked as it ran over many-coloured stones and mingled with the golden spangles of the sandy bottom! All at once he clearly heard the hour chiming. He shuddered, raised his head, looked at the window to calculate the time. He came to himself immediately, and jumped up, and, going on tiptoe, silently opened the door and stood listening on the landing. His heart beat violently. But not a sound came from the staircase. It seemed as though the house was wrapped in sleep. He could not understand how he had been able to sleep away the time as he had done, whilst nothing was prepared for the enterprise. And yet it was, perhaps, six o'clock that had just struck.

Then, he became excited as he felt what there was to be done, and he endeavoured with all his might to keep his thoughts from wandering and concentrate his mind on his task. All the time his heart thumped and beat until he could hardly draw breath. In the first place it was necessary to make a loop and fasten to his coat. He went to his pillow and took from amongst the linen he kept there an old and dirty shirt and tore part of it into strips. He then fastened a couple of these together, and, taking off his coat – a stout cotton summer one – began to sew the loop inside, under the left arm. His hands shook violently, but he accomplished his task satisfactorily, and when he again put on his coat nothing was visible. Needle and thread had been procured long ago, and lay on the table in a piece of paper. The loop was provided for a hatchet. It would never have done to have appeared in the streets carrying a hatchet, and if he placed it under the coat, it would have been necessary to hold it with his hands; but with the loop all he had to do was to put the iron in it and it would hang of itself under the coat, and with his hands in his pockets he could keep it from shaking, and no one could suspect that he was carrying anything. He had thought over all this about a fortnight before.

Having finished his task, Raskolnikoff inserted his finger in a small crevice in the floor under his couch, and brought out the *pledge* with which he had been careful to provide himself. This pledge was, however, only a sham – a thin smooth piece of wood about the size and thickness of a silver cigarette case, which he had found in a yard adjoining a carpenter's shop, and a thin piece of iron of about the same size, which he had picked up in the street. He fastened the two together firmly with thread, then proceeded to wrap them up neatly in a piece of clean white paper, and tie the parcel in such a manner that it would be difficult to undo it again. This was all done in order to occupy the attention of the old woman and to seize a favourable opportunity when she would be busy with the knot. The piece of iron was simply added for weight, in order that she might not immediately detect the fraud. He had just finished, and had put the packet in his pocket, when in the court below resounded the cry:

'Six o'clock struck long ago!'

'Long ago! Good heavens!'

He ran to the door, listened, seized his hat, and went down the stairs cautiously and stealthily as a cat. He still had the most important thing to do – to steal the hatchet out of the kitchen. That a hatchet was the best instrument, he had long since decided. He had an old garden-knife, but on a knife – especially on his own strength – he could not rely; he finally fixed on the hatchet. A peculiarity was to be noticed in all these resolutions of his; the more definitely they were settled, the more absurd and horrible they immediately appeared to his eyes and never, for a moment, did he feel sure of the execution of his project. But even if every question had been settled, every doubt cleared away, every difficulty overcome, he would probably have renounced his design on the instant, as something absurd, monstrous, and impossible. But there were still a host of matters to arrange, of problems to solve. As to procuring the hatchet, this trifle did not trouble Raskolnikoff in the least, for nothing was easier. As a matter of fact Nastasia was scarcely ever at home, especially of an evening. She was constantly out gossiping with friends or tradespeople, and that was the reason of her mistress's constant complaints. When the time came, all he would have to do would be to quietly enter the kitchen and take the hatchet, and then to replace it an hour afterwards when all was over. But perhaps this would not be as easy as he fancied. 'Suppose,' said the young man to himself, 'that when, in an hour's time, I come to replace the hatchet, Nastasia should have come in. Now, in that case I could naturally not enter the kitchen until she had gone out again. But supposing during this time she notices the absence of the hatchet, she will grumble, perhaps kick up a shindy, and that will serve to denounce me, or at least might do so!'

But these were mere details, which he did not care to think about; besides, he had no time to do so. He had to come to a decision about the thing itself; when he had done so it would be quite time enough to consider the accessory part of it. This last condition, the most essential of all, seemed to him impossible to realise. For instance, he could not imagine that, at a given moment, he would cease to think, would rise up and go straight-way there. Even in his recent *rehearsal* (that is to say the visit he had paid to the old woman's in order to definitely feel his ground), he had been far from rehearsing seriously. An actor without conviction, he had been unable to sustain his part, and had hastened away indignant with himself. Yet, from the moral point of view, Raskolnikoff had reason to consider the question solved. His keen casuistry had disposed of all objections, but when he no longer found them within, he sought for them without. Impelled, apparently, by some blind, irresistible, supernatural force, he groped for something to which he might cling. The unexpected incidents of the preceding evening were working upon him half mechanically, just as a man who has allowed a flap of his coat to catch on the cog of a wheel soon finds himself hopelessly entangled in the machinery. The first question on which he dwelt was one that had often passed his mind before: How is it that almost all crimes are so easily discovered, and what puts us on the track of the criminal?

By degrees, he arrived at several singular conclusions. He argued that this was owing rather to the criminal's own demeanour than to the material impossibility of concealing his crime; that, at the fatal moment, his resolution and mental power gave way, and that hence he behaved with childish simplicity and abnormal thoughtlessness, just when prudence and circumspection were all-important. Raskolnikoff compared this aberration of judgement and want of purpose to a morbid malady, developing gradually and attaining its maximum degree just before the perpetration of the crime, and continuing to exist under the same form at the fatal moment and for some time after (to a greater or less degree, according to the individual), to vanish finally, like every other malady. One point that required clearing up was, whether the crime is the result of disease, or whether the crime, by virtue of its nature, is not always accompanied by some morbid phenomena; but this the young man did not feel himself able, as yet, to solve.

While reasoning thus, he persuaded himself that he, personally, was secure against any such mental weakness, and that he was capable of retaining his resolution and intelligence throughout his enterprise for the simple reason that the latter *was not a crime*. We have no intention of rehearsing the arguments which had led him to *this* conclusion. We shall merely observe that throughout his musings, the practical side of his enterprise, the purely material difficulties in the way of its accomplishment, were all passed over. 'Let me but preserve my presence of mind and resolution, and when the moment for action comes I shall triumph over every obstacle.' Still he did not set to work. He believed less than ever in the ultimate persistence of his resolution, and when the clock struck seven he started as if awaking from a dream.

Before he had got to the bottom of the staircase, a trifling circumstance came and upset all his plans. On reaching his landlady's landing, he found the kitchen-door wide open, as usual, and he peeped in, in order to make sure that, in the absence of Nastasia, her mistress was not there, and that the doors of the other rooms were closed. But great was his annoyance to find Nastasia there herself, engaged in hanging clothes on a line. Perceiving the young man, she stopped and turned to him inquiringly. He averted his eyes and went away without remark. But the affair was done for. There was no hatchet, he was frustrated entirely. He felt crushed, nay, humiliated, but a feeling of brutal vindictiveness at his disappointment soon ensued, and he continued down the stairs, smiling maliciously to himself. He stood hesitating at the gate. To walk about the streets or to go back were equally repugnant. 'To think that I have missed such a splendid opportunity!' he murmured as he stood aimlessly at the entrance, leaning near the open door of the porter's lodge. Suddenly he started – something in the dark room attracted his eye. He looked quietly around. No one was near. He descended the two steps on tiptoe, and called for the porter. There was no reply, and he rushed headlong to the hatchet (it was a hatchet), secured it where it lay among some wood, and hurriedly fastened it to the loop as he made his way out into the street. No one saw him! 'There's more of the devil in this than my design,' he said smiling to himself. The occurrence gave him fresh courage.

He went away quietly in order not to excite any suspicion, and walked along the street with his eyes studiously fixed on the ground, avoiding the faces of the passers-by. Suddenly he recollected his hat. 'Good heavens! The day before yesterday I had money, and not to have thought of that! I could so easily have bought a cap!' and he began cursing himself. Glancing casually in a shop, he saw it was ten minutes past seven. He had yet a long way to go, as he was making a circuit, not wishing to walk direct to the house. He kept off, as much as he was able, all thought of his mission, and on the way reflected upon possible improvements of the public grounds, upon the desirability of fountains, and why people lived where there were neither parks nor fountains, but only mud, lime, and bricks, emitting horrible exhalations and every conceivable foulness. This reminded him of his own walks about the Cyennaza, and he came to himself.

'How true it is that persons being led to execution interest themselves in anything that strikes them on the way!' was the thought that came into his head, but it passed away like lightning to be succeeded by some other. 'Here we are – there is the gate.' It struck half-past seven as he stood near the house.

To his delight, he passed in without observation. As if on purpose, at the very same moment a load of hay was going in, and it completely screened him. On the other side of the load, a dispute or brawl was evidently taking place, and he gained the old woman's staircase in a second. Recovering his breath and pressing his hand to his beating heart, he commenced the ascent, though first feeling for the hatchet and arranging it. Every minute he stopped to listen. The stairs were quite deserted, and every door was closed. No one met him. On the second floor, indeed, the door of an empty lodging was wide open; some painters were working there, but they did not look up. He stopped a moment to think, and then continued the ascent: 'No doubt it would be better if they were not there, but fortunately there are two more floors above them.' At last he reached the fourth floor, and Alena Ivanovna's door; the lodging facing it was unoccupied. The lodging on the third floor, just beneath the old woman's, was also apparently empty. The card that used to be on the door had gone; the lodgers had, no doubt, moved. Raskolnikoff was stifling. He stood hesitating a moment: 'Had I not better go away?' But without answering the question, he waited and listened. Not a sound issued from the old woman's apartments. The staircase was filled with the same silence. After listening for a long time, the young man cast a last glance around, and again felt his hatchet. 'Do I not look too pale?' thought he. 'Do I not appear too agitated? She is mistrustful. I should do well to wait a little, to give my emotion time to calm down.'

But instead of becoming quieter, his heart throbbed more violently. He could stand it no longer, and, raising his hand towards the bell-rope, he pulled it towards him. After waiting half a minute, he rang again – this time a little louder. No answer. To ring like a deaf man would have been useless, stupid even. The old woman was certainly at home; but, suspicious by nature, she was likely to be so all the more then, as she happened to be alone. Raskolnikoff knew something of

Alena Ivanovna's habits. He therefore placed his ear to the door. Had the circumstances amid which he was placed strangely developed his power of hearing, which, in general, is difficult to admit, or was the sound really easily perceptible? Anyhow, he suddenly became aware that a hand was being cautiously placed on the lock, and that a dress rustled against the door. Someone inside was going through exactly the same movements as he on the landing. Someone, standing up against the lock, was listening whilst trying to hide her presence, and had probably her ear also against the door.

In order to avoid all idea of mystery, the young man purposely moved about rather noisily, and muttered something half-aloud; then he rang a third time, but gently and coolly, without allowing the bell to betray the least sign of impatience. Raskolnikoff never forgot this moment of his life. When, in after-days, he thought over it, he could never understand how he had been able to display such cunning, especially at a time when emotion was now and again depriving him of the free use of his intellectual and physical faculties. After a short while he heard the bolt withdrawn.

Chapter 7

THE DOOR, AS BEFORE, was opened a little, and again the two eyes, with mistrustful glance, peeped out of the dark. Then Raskolnikoff lost his presence of mind and made a serious mistake. Fearing that the old woman would take alarm at finding they were alone, and knowing that his appearance would not reassure her, he took hold of the door and pulled it towards him in order to prevent her shutting it again if she should be thus minded. Seeing this, she held on to the lock, so that he almost drew her together with the door on to the staircase. She recovered herself, and stood to prevent his entrance, speechless with fright.

'Good-evening, Alena Ivanovna,' he commenced, trying to speak with unconcern, but his voice did not obey him, and he faltered and trembled. 'Good-evening, I have brought you something, but we had better go into the light.' He pushed past her and entered the room uninvited. The old woman followed and found her tongue.

'What is it you want? Who are you?' she commenced.

'Pardon me, Alena Ivanovna, your old acquaintance Raskolnikoff. I have brought a pledge, as I promised the other day,' and he held out the packet to her.

The old woman was about to examine it, when she raised her eyes and looked straight into those of the visitor who had entered so unceremoniously. She examined him attentively, distrustfully, for a minute. Raskolnikoff fancied there was a gleam of mockery in her look as if she guessed all. He felt he was changing colour, and that if she kept her glance upon him much longer without saying a word he would be obliged to run away.

'Why are you looking at me thus?' he said at last in anger. 'Will you take it or not? Or shall I take it elsewhere? I have no time to waste.' He did not intend to say this, but the words came out. The tone seemed to quiet her suspicions.

'Why were you so impatient, *batuchka*? What is it?' she asked, glancing at the pledge.

'The silver cigarette-case of which I spoke the other day.'

She held out her hand. 'But why are you so pale, why do your hands shake? What is the matter with you, *batuchka*?'

'Fever,' replied he abruptly. 'You would be pale too if you had nothing to eat.' He could hardly speak the words and felt his strength failing. But there was some plausibility in his reply; and the old woman took the pledge.

'What is it?' she asked once more, weighing it in her hand and looking straight at her visitor.

'Cigarette-case, silver, look at it.'

'It doesn't feel as though it were in silver. Oh! what a dreadful knot!'

She began to untie the packet and turned to the light (all the windows were closed in spite of the heat). Her back was turned towards Raskolnikoff, and for a few seconds she paid no further attention to him. He opened his coat, freed the hatchet from the loop, but did not yet take it from its hiding-place; he held it with his right hand beneath the garment. His limbs were weak, each moment they grew more numbed and stiff. He feared his fingers would relax their hold of the hatchet. Then his head turned giddy.

'What is this you bring me?' cried Alena Ivanovna, turning to him in a rage.

There was not a moment to lose now. He pulled out the hatchet, raised it with both hands, and let it descend without force, almost mechanically, on the old woman's head. But directly he had struck the blow his strength returned. According to her usual habit, Alena Ivanovna was bareheaded. Her scanty grey locks, greasy with oil, were gathered in one thin plait, which was fixed to the back of her neck by means of a piece of horn comb. The hatchet struck her just on the sinciput, and this was partly owing to her small stature. She scarcely uttered a faint cry and collapsed at once all in a heap on the floor; yet she still had strength to raise her arms to her head while one of her hands continued to clutch the pledge. Then Raskolnikoff, whose arm had regained all its vigour, struck two fresh blows with the hatchet on the crown of the old woman's head. The blood spurted out in streams and the body rolled heavily over. At that moment the young man drew back; so soon as he beheld his victim stretched on the floor he bent over her face; she was dead. The wide-open eyes seemed about to jump from their sockets, the convulsions of death had given a grimacing expression to the countenance.

The murderer laid his hatchet down and at once began to search the corpse, taking the greatest precaution not to get stained with the blood; he remembered seeing Alena Ivanovna, on the occasion of his last visit, take her keys from the right-hand pocket of her dress. He was in full possession of his intellect; he felt neither giddy nor dazed, but his hands continued to shake. Later on, he recollected that he had been very prudent, very attentive, that he had taken every care not to soil himself. It did not take him long to find the keys; the same as the other day, they were all together on a steel ring. Having secured them, Raskolnikoff at once passed into the bedroom. It was a very small apartment; on one side was a large glass case full of holy images, on the other a great bed looking very clean with its quilted-silk patchwork coverlet. The third wall was occupied by a chest of drawers. Strange to say, the young man had no sooner attempted to open them, he had no sooner commenced to try the keys, than a kind of shudder ran through his frame. Again the idea came to him to give up his task and go away, but this velleity only lasted a second: it was now too late to draw back.

He was even smiling at having for a moment entertained such a thought, when he was suddenly seized with a terrible anxiety: suppose the old woman were still alive, suppose she recovered consciousness. Leaving at once the keys and the drawers, he hastened to the corpse, seized the hatchet, and prepared to strike another blow at his victim, but he found there was no necessity to do so. Alena Ivanovna was dead beyond all doubt. Leaning over her again to examine her closer, Raskolnikoff saw that the skull was shattered. He was about to touch her with his fingers, but drew back, as it was quite unnecessary. There was a pool of blood upon the floor. Suddenly noticing a bit of cord round the old woman's neck, the young man gave it a tug, but the gory stuff was strong, and did not break. The murderer then tried to remove it by drawing it down the body. But this second attempt was no more successful than the first, the cord encountered some obstacle and became fixed. Burning with impatience, Raskolnikoff brandished the hatchet, ready to strike the corpse and sever the confounded string at the same blow. However, he could not make up his mind to proceed with such brutality. At last, after trying for two minutes, and staining his hands with blood, he succeeded in severing the cord with the blade of the hatchet without further disfiguring the dead body. As he had imagined, there was a purse suspended to the old woman's neck. Besides this there were also a small enamelled medal and two crosses, one of cypress-wood, the other of brass. The greasy purse, a little chamois-leather bag, was as full as it could hold. Raskolnikoff thrust it in his pocket without examining the contents. He then threw the crosses on his victim's breast, and hastily returned to the bedroom, taking the hatchet with him.

His impatience was now intense; he seized the keys, and again set to work. But all his attempts to open the drawers were unavailing, and this was not so much owing to the shaking of his hands as to his continual misconceptions. He could see, for instance, that a certain key would not fit the lock, and yet he continued to try and insert it. All on a sudden he recalled a conjecture he had formed on the occasion of his preceding visit: the big key with the toothed wards, which was attached to the ring with the smaller ones, probably belonged, not to the drawers, but to some box in which the old woman, no doubt, hoarded up her valuables. Without further troubling about the drawers, he at once looked under the bed, aware that old women are in the habit of hiding their treasures in such places. And there indeed was a trunk with rounded lid, covered with red morocco and studded with steel nails. Raskolnikoff was able to insert the key in the lock without the least difficulty. When he opened the box he perceived a hare-skin cloak trimmed with red lying on a white sheet; beneath the fur was a silk dress, and then a shawl; the rest of the contents appeared to be nothing but rags. The young man commenced by wiping his blood-stained hands on the red trimming. 'It will not show so much on red.' Then he suddenly seemed to change his mind. 'Heavens! am I going mad?' thought he with fright.

But scarcely had he touched these clothes than a gold watch rolled from under the fur. He then overhauled everything in the box. Among the rags were various gold trinkets, which had all probably been pledged with the old woman: bracelets, chains, ear-rings, scarf-pins, etc. Some were in their cases, while the others were tied up with tape in pieces of newspaper folded in two. Raskolnikoff did not hesitate; he laid hands on these jewels, and stowed them away in the pockets of his coat and trousers, without opening the cases or untying the packets; but he was soon interrupted in his work –

Footsteps resounded in the other room. He stopped short, frozen with terror. But the noise having ceased, he was already imagining he had been mistaken, when suddenly he distantly heard a faint cry, or rather a kind of feeble interrupted moan. At the end of a minute or two, everything was again as silent as death. Raskolnikoff had seated himself on the floor beside the trunk and was waiting, scarcely daring to breathe; suddenly he bounded up, caught up the hatchet, and rushed from the bedroom. In the centre of the apartment, Elizabeth, a huge bundle in her hands, stood gazing in a terror-stricken way at her dead sister; white as a sheet, she did not seem to have the strength to call out. On the sudden appearance of the murderer, she began to quake in every limb, and nervous twitches passed over her face: she tried to raise her arm, to open her mouth, but she was unable to utter the least cry, and, slowly retreating, her gaze still riveted on Raskolnikoff, she sought refuge in a corner. The poor woman drew back in perfect silence, as though she had no breath left in her body. The young man rushed upon her, brandishing the hatchet; the wretched creature's lips assumed the doleful expression peculiar to quite young children when, beginning to feel frightened of something, they gaze fixedly at the object which has raised their alarm, and are on the point of crying out. Terror had so completely stupefied the unfortunate Elizabeth, that, though threatened by the hatchet, she did not even think of protecting her face by holding her hands before her head, with that mechanical gesture which the instinct of self-preservation prompts on such occasions. She scarcely raised her left arm, and extended it slowly in the direction of the murderer, as though to keep him off. The hatchet penetrated her skull, laying it open from the upper part of the forehead to the crown. Elizabeth fell down dead. No longer aware of what he did, Raskolnikoff took the bundle from his victim's hand, then dropped it and ran to the anteroom.

He was more and more terrified, especially after this second murder, entirely unpremeditated by him. He was in a hurry to be gone; had he then been in a state to see things more clearly, had he only been able to form an idea of the difficulties besetting his position, to see how desperate, how hideous, how absurd it was, to understand how many obstacles there still remained for him to surmount, perhaps even crimes to commit, to escape from this house and return home, he would most likely have withdrawn from the struggle, and have gone at once and given himself up to justice; it was not cowardice which would have prompted him to do so, but the horror of what he had done. This last impression became more and more powerful every minute. Nothing in the world could now have made him return to the trunk, nor even re-enter the room in which it lay. Little by little his mind became diverted by other thoughts, and he lapsed into a kind of reverie; at times the murderer seemed to forget his position, or rather the most important part of it, and to concentrate his attention on trifles. After a while, happening to glance in the kitchen, he observed a pail half full of water, standing on a bench, and that gave him the idea of washing his hands and the hatchet. The blood had made his hands sticky. After plunging the blade of the hatchet in the water, he took a small piece of soap which lay on the window-sill, and commenced his ablutions. When he had washed his hands, he set to cleaning the iron part of his weapon; then he devoted three minutes to soaping the wooden handle, which was also stained with blood.

After this he wiped it with a cloth which had been hung up to dry on a line stretched across the kitchen. This done, he drew near the window and carefully examined the hatchet for some minutes. The accusing stains had disappeared, but the handle was still damp. Raskolnikoff carefully hid the weapon under his coat by replacing it in the loop; after which, he minutely inspected his clothes, that is to say so far as the dim light of the kitchen allowed him to do so. He saw nothing suspicious about the coat and trousers, but there were blood-stains on the boots. He removed them with the aid of a damp rag. But these precautions only half reassured him, for he knew that he could not see properly and that certain stains had very likely escaped him. He stood irresolute in the middle of the room, a prey to a sombre, agonising thought, the thought that he was going mad, that at that moment he was not in a fit state to come to a determination and to watch over his security, that his way of going to work was probably not the one the circumstances demanded. 'Good heavens! I ought to go, to go away at once!' murmured he, and he rushed to the ante-room, where the greatest terror he had yet experienced awaited him.

He stood stock-still, not daring to believe his eyes: the door of the lodging, the outer door which opened on to the landing, the same one at which he had rung a little while before and by which he had entered, was open; up till then it had remained ajar, the old woman had no doubt omitted to close it by way of precaution; it had been neither locked nor bolted! But he had seen Elizabeth after that. How was it that it had not occurred to him that she had come in by way of the door? She could not have entered the lodging through the wall. He shut the door and bolted it. 'But no, that is not what I should do! I must go away, go away.' He drew back the bolt and, after opening the door again, stood listening on the landing.

He stood thus a long while. Down below, probably at the street-door, two noisy voices were vociferating insults. 'Who can those people be?' He waited patiently. At last the noise ceased, the brawlers had taken their departure. The young man was about to do the same, when a door on the floor immediately below was noisily opened and someone went downstairs, humming a tune. 'What ever are they all up to?' wondered Raskolnikoff, and closing the door again he waited a while. At length all became silent as before; but just as he was preparing to go down, he suddenly became aware of a fresh sound, footsteps as yet far off, at the bottom of the staircase; and he no sooner heard them than he guessed the truth: – someone was coming *there*, to the old woman's on the fourth floor. Whence came this presentiment? What was there so particularly significant in the sound of these footsteps? They were heavy, regular, and rather slow than hurried. *He* has now reached the first floor, he still continues to ascend. The sound is becoming plainer and plainer. He pants as though with asthma at each step he takes. He has commenced the third flight. He will soon be on the fourth! And Raskolnikoff felt suddenly seized as with a general paralysis, the same as happens when a person has the nightmare and fancies himself pursued by enemies; they are on the point of catching him, they will kill him, and yet he remains spell-bound, unable to move a limb.

The stranger was now ascending the fourth flight. Raskolnikoff, who until then had been riveted to the landing with fright, was at length able to shake off his torpor, and hastily re-entered the apartment, closing the door behind him. Then he bolted it, being careful to make as little noise as possible. Instinct rather than reason prompted him to do this. When he had finished, he remained close to the door, listening, scarcely daring to breathe. The visitor was now on the landing. Only the thickness of the door separated the two men. The unknown was in the same position towards Raskolnikoff as the latter had been a little while before towards the old woman. The visitor stood panting for some little time. 'He must be stout and big,' thought the young man as he clasped the hatchet firmly in his hand. It was all like a dream to him. The visitor gave a violent pull at the bell. He immediately fancied he heard something move inside. He listened attentively during a few seconds, then he gave another ring and again waited; suddenly losing patience, he began to shake the door-handle with all his might. Raskolnikoff watched with terror the bolt trembling in the socket, expecting to see it shoot back at any moment, so violent were the jerks given to the door. It occurred to him to hold the bolt in its place with his hand, but the *man* might have found it out. His head was turning quite dizzy again. 'I shall betray myself!' thought he; but he suddenly recovered his presence of mind as the unknown broke the silence.

'Are they both asleep, or has someone strangled them? The thrice-confounded creatures!' growled the visitor in a guttural voice. 'Hi! Alena Ivanovna, you old sorceress! Elizabeth Ivanovna, you indescribable beauty! – open! Oh! the witches! Can they be asleep?'

In his exasperation he rang ten times running, and as loud as he possibly could. This man was evidently not a stranger there, and was in the habit of being obeyed. At the same moment some light and rapid footsteps resounded on the staircase. It was another person coming to the fourth floor. Raskolnikoff was not at first aware of the new-comer's arrival.

'Is it possible that there's no one at home?' said the latter in a loud and hearty tone of voice, addressing the first visitor, who was still tugging at the bell-pull. 'Good-day, Koch!'

'Judging by his voice, he must be quite a young man,' immediately thought Raskolnikoff.

'The devil only knows! I've almost smashed the lock,' replied Koch. 'But how is it you know me?'

'What a question! The day before yesterday I played you at billiards, at Gambrinus's, and won three games right off.'

'Ah!'

'So they're not at home? That's strange. I might almost say it's ridiculous. Where can the old woman have gone? I want to speak with her.'

'And I too, *batuchka*, I want to speak with her.'

'Well, what's to be done? I suppose we must go back to whence we came. I wanted to borrow some money of her!' exclaimed the young man.

'Of course we must go back again; but why then did she make an appointment? She herself, the old witch, told me to come at this hour. And it's a long way to where I live. Where the deuce can she be? I don't understand it. She never stirs from one year's end to the other, the old witch; she quite rots in the place, her legs have always got something the matter with them, and now all on a sudden she goes gallivanting about!'

'Suppose we question the porter?'

'What for?'

'To find out where she's gone and when she will be back.'

'H'm! – the deuce! – question – but she never goes anywhere.' And he again tugged at the door-handle. 'The devil take her! There's nothing to be done but to go.'

'Wait!' suddenly exclaimed the young man, 'look! – do you notice how the door resists when we pull it?'

'Well, what then?'

'Why, that shows that it's not locked, but bolted! Hark how it clinks!'

'Well?'

'Don't you understand? That shows that one of them must be at home. If both were out, they would have locked the door after them, and not have bolted it inside. Listen, don't you hear the noise it makes? Well, to bolt one's door, one must be at home, you understand. Therefore it follows that they are at home, only for some reason or other they don't open the door!'

'Why, yes, you're right!' exclaimed the astonished Koch. 'So they're there, are they?' And he again shook the door violently.

'Stay!' resumed the young man; 'don't pull like that. There's something peculiar about this. You've rung, you've pulled at the door with all your might, and they haven't answered you; therefore, they've either both fainted away, or – '

'What?'

'This is what we had better do: have the porter up, so that he may find out what's the matter.'

'That's not a bad idea!'

They both started downstairs.

'Stop! you stay here! I'll fetch the porter.'

'Why stay here?'

'Well, one never knows what might happen – '

'All right.'

'You see, I might also pass for an examining magistrate! There's something very peculiar about all this, that's evident, e-vi-dent!' said the young man excitedly, and he hastily made his way down the stairs.

Left alone, Koch rang again, but gently this time; then, with a thoughtful air, he began to play with the door handle, turning it first one way, then the other, so as to make sure the door was only bolted. After this, with a great deal of puffing and blowing, he stooped down to look through the keyhole, but the key was in the lock, and turned in such a way that one could not see through. Standing up on the other side of the door, Raskolnikoff still held the hatchet in his hands. He was almost in a state of delirium and was preparing to attack the two men the moment they forced an entrance. More than once, on hearing them knocking and planning together, he had felt inclined to put an end to the matter there and then by calling out to them. At times, he experienced a desire to abuse and defy them, whilst awaiting their interruption. 'The sooner it's over the better!' he kept thinking.

'The devil take them!' The time passed; still no one came. Koch was beginning to lose patience. 'The devil take them!' he muttered again, and, tired of waiting, he relinquished his watch to go and find the young man. By degrees the sound of his heavy boots echoing on the stairs ceased to be heard.

'Heavens! What shall I do?'

Raskolnikoff drew back the bolt and opened the door a few inches. Reassured by the silence which reigned in the house, and, moreover, scarcely in a fit state at the time to reflect on what he did, he went out on to the landing, shut the door behind him as securely as he could and turned to go downstairs. He had already descended several steps when suddenly a great uproar arose from one of the floors below. Where could he hide? Concealment was impossible, so he hastened upstairs again.

'Hi there! Hang it! Stop!'

He who uttered these cries had just burst out of one of the lodgings, and was rushing down the stairs as fast as his legs would carry him, yelling the while: 'Dmitri! Dmitri! Dmitri! May the devil take the fool!'

The rest died away in the distance; the man who was uttering these cries had already left the house far behind. All was once more silent; but scarcely was this alarm over than a fresh one succeeded it: several individuals talking together in a loud tone of voice were noisily coming up the stairs. There were three or four of them. Raskolnikoff recognised the young man's sonorous accents. 'It is them!' No longer hoping to escape them, he advanced boldly to meet them: 'Let happen what will!' said he to himself: 'if they stop me, all is over; if they let me pass, all is over just the same: they will remember passing me on the stairs.' They were about to encounter him, only one flight separated them – when suddenly he felt himself saved! A few steps from him, to the right, there was an empty lodging with the door wide open, it was that same one on the second floor where he had seen the painters working, but, by a happy chance, they had just left it. It was they, no doubt, who a few minutes before had gone off, uttering those shouts. The paint on the floors was quite fresh, the workmen had left their things in the middle of the room: a small tub, some paint in an earthenware crock, and a big brush. In the twinkling of an eye, Raskolnikoff glided into the deserted apartment and hid himself as best he could up against the wall. It was none too soon: his persecutors were already on the landing; they did not stop there, however, but went on up to the fourth floor, talking loudly amongst themselves. After waiting till they had got some distance off, he left the room on tiptoe and hurried down as fast as his legs would carry him. No one on the stairs! No one either at the street-door! He stepped briskly outside, and, once in the street, turned to the left.

He knew very well, he knew without a doubt, that they who were seeking him were at that moment in the old woman's lodging, and were amazed to find that the door, which a little while before had been shut so securely, was now open. 'They're examining the corpses,' thought he; 'it won't take them a minute to come to the conclusion that the murderer managed to hide himself from them as they went up the stairs; perhaps they may even have a suspicion that he stowed himself away in the empty lodging on the second floor while they were hurrying to the upper part of the house.' But, in spite of these reflections, he did not dare to increase his pace, though he still had a hundred steps or so to go before reaching the first turning. 'Suppose I slipped into some doorway, in some out-of-the-way street, and waited there a few minutes? No, that would never do! I might throw my hatchet away somewhere? Or take a cab? No good! No good!' At last he reached a narrow lane; he entered it more dead than alive. There, he was almost in safety, and he knew it; in such a place, suspicion could hardly be fixed upon him; while, on the other hand, it was easier for him to avoid notice by mingling with the crowd. But all these agonising events had so enfeebled him that he could scarcely keep on his legs. Great drops of perspiration streamed down his face; his neck was quite wet. 'I think you've had your fill!' shouted someone who took him for a drunken man as he reached the canal bank.

He no longer knew what he was doing; the farther he went the more obscure became his ideas. However, when he found himself on the quay, he became frightened at seeing so few people there, and, fearing that he might be noticed on so deserted a spot, he returned to the lane. Though he had hardly the strength to put one leg before the other, he nevertheless took the longest way to reach his home. He had scarcely recovered his presence of mind even when he crossed the threshold; at least the thought of the hatchet never came to him until he was on the stairs. Yet the question he had to solve was a most serious one: it consisted in returning the hatchet to the place he had taken it from, and in doing so without attracting the least attention. Had he been more capable of considering his position, he would certainly have understood that, instead of replacing the hatchet, it would be far safer to get rid of it by throwing it into the yard of some other house.

Nevertheless he met with no mishap. The door of the porter's lodge was closed, though not locked; to all appearance, therefore, the porter was at home. But Raskolnikoff had so thoroughly lost all faculty of preparing any kind of plan, that he walked straight to the door and opened it. If the porter had asked him: 'What do you want?' perhaps he would simply have handed him the hatchet. But, the same as on the previous occasion, the porter was absent, and this gave the young man every facility to replace the hatchet under the bench, exactly where he had found it. Then he went upstairs and reached his room without meeting a soul; the door of his landlady's apartments was shut. Once home again, he threw himself on his couch just as he was. He did not sleep, but lay in a sort of semi-consciousness. If anybody had then appeared before him, he would have sprung up and cried out. His head was swimming with a host of vague thoughts: do what he could, he was unable to follow the thread of one of them.

PART II

Chapter 1

RASKOLNIKOFF LAY ON the couch a very long while. At times he seemed to rouse from this half-sleep, and then he noticed that the night was very far advanced, but still it never entered his head to rise. Soon it began to brighten into day, and the dawn found him in a state of stupefaction, lying motionless on his back. A desperate clamour, and sounds of brawls from the streets below, rose to his ears. These awakened him thoroughly, although he heard them every morning early at the same hour. 'Ah! two o'clock, drinking is over,' and he started up as though someone had pulled him off the couch. 'What! two o'clock already?' He sat on the edge of the couch and then recollected everything, in an instant it all came back! At first he thought he was going out of his mind, a strange chill pervaded his frame, but the cold arose from the fever which had seized upon him during his sleep. He shivered until his teeth chattered, and all his limbs fairly shook. He went to the door, opened it, and listened; all was silent in the house. With astonishment he turned and looked round the room. How could he have come home the night before, not bolted the door, and thrown himself on the couch just as he was, not only not undressed, but with his hat on? There it lay in the middle of the floor where it had rolled. 'If anyone came in, what would he think? That I am drunk of course.'

He went to the window – it was pretty light – and looked himself all over from head to foot, to see if there were any stains on his clothes. But he could not rely upon that sort of inspection; so, still shivering, he undressed and examined his clothes again, looking everywhere with the greatest care. To make quite sure, he went over them three times. He discovered nothing but a few drops of clotted blood on the ends of his trousers which were very much frayed. He took a big clasp-knife and cut off the frayed edges. Suddenly he remembered that the purse and the things he had abstracted from the old woman's chest, were still in his pockets! He had never thought of taking them out and hiding them! Indeed, it had never crossed his mind that they were in his pockets whilst examining his clothes! Was it possible? In a second he emptied all out on to the table in a heap. Then, turning his pockets inside out to make sure there was nothing left in them, he carried the things to a corner of the room. Just there, the paper was hanging loose from the wall; he bent down and commenced to stuff all the things into a hole behind the paper. 'There, it's all out of sight!' thought he gleefully, as he stood gazing stupidly at the spot where the paper bulged out more than ever. Suddenly he began to shudder with terror. 'Good heavens!' murmured he in despair, 'what is the matter with me? Is that hidden? Is that the way to hide anything?'

Indeed, he had not reckoned on such spoil, he had only thought of taking the old woman's money; so he was not prepared with a hiding-place for the jewels. 'I have no cause to rejoice now,' thought he; 'is that the way to hide anything? I must really be losing my senses!' He sunk on the couch again, exhausted; another fit of intolerable shivering seized him and he mechanically pulled his old student's cloak over him for warmth, as he fell into a delirious sleep. He lost all consciousness of himself. Not more than five minutes had elapsed before he woke up in intense excitement, and bent over his clothes in the deepest anguish. 'How could I go to sleep again when nothing is done! For I have done nothing, the loop is still where I sewed it. I forgot all about that! What a convincing proof it would have been!' He ripped it off and tore it into shreds which he placed among his underlinen under the pillow. 'These rags cannot awaken any suspicions, I fancy. At least, so it seems to me,' repeated he, standing up in the middle of the room, and, with an attempt rendered all the more painful by the effort it cost him, he looked all round, trying to make sure he had forgotten nothing. He suffered cruelly from this conviction, that everything, even memory, even the most elementary prudence, was abandoning him.

'Can this be the punishment already beginning? Indeed, indeed, it is!'

And indeed the frayed edges he had cut from the bottom of his trousers were lying on the floor, in the middle of the room, exposed to the view of the first-comer. 'But what can I be thinking of?' exclaimed he in utter bewilderment. Then a strange idea came into his head; he thought that perhaps all his clothes were saturated in blood, and that he could not see this because his senses were gone and his perception of things lost. Then he recollected that there would be traces on the purse, and his pockets would be wet with blood. It was so. 'I am bereft of my reason, I know not what I am doing. Bah! Not at all! – it is only weakness, delirium. I shall soon be better.' He tore at the lining. At this moment the rays of the morning streamed in and shone on his left boot. There were plain traces, and all the point was covered. 'I must have stepped in that pool. What shall I do now? Boot, lining, rags, where shall they go?' He rolled them up and stood thinking in the middle of the room. 'Ah, the stove! Yes, burn them. No I cannot, I have no match. Better throw them away. Yes, yes, that is the thing,' said he, again sitting on the couch. 'At once and without delay too, quick!' But, instead, his head fell back upon the pillow, and chilly shiverings again came over him. He covered himself with his cloak and slept again. It appeared hours to him, and many a time in his sleep he tried to rise to hasten to throw away his bundle, but he could not, he seemed chained to the bed. At last he awoke, as he heard a loud knock at his door.

'Eh, open, will you?' cried Nastasia. 'Don't lie there like a dog. It's eleven o'clock.'

'Perhaps he is not in,' said a man's voice.

'The porter's voice. What does he want?' Raskolnikoff rose, and sat on the couch listening. His heart throbbed violently.

'Who has bolted the door, then?' exclaimed the servant. 'Open, will you?'

'All must be discovered!' He rose a little and undid the bolt, and fell back again on his bed. There stood the porter and Nastasia. The servant looked strangely at Raskolnikoff, while he fixed a despairing glance upon the porter.

'Here is a notice for you from the office,' said the latter.

'What office?'

'The police-office.'

'What for?'

'I don't know. You are summoned there, go.' The porter looked anxiously at the lodger, and turned to leave. Raskolnikoff made no observation, and held the paper unopened in his hand.

'There, stay where you are,' said Nastasia, seeing him fall back on the couch. 'If you are ill, do not go. What is that in your hand?'

He looked down; in his right hand were clutched the pieces of frayed cloth, his boot, and the lining of his pocket. He had evidently fallen asleep with them as they were; indeed he recollected how, thinking deeply about them, he had dozed away.

'The idea of taking a lot of rags to bed and hugging them to you like a treasure!' laughed the servant in her sickly manner.

In a second he hid all under his coat and looked at her attentively. Although little was capable of passing in his mind, he felt she would not talk thus to a man under arrest for a crime. But then, the police?

'Is there anything you want? You stay here, I will bring it.'

'No, I will go. I am going at once,' murmured he, rising to his feet.

'Very well.'

She went out after the porter. As soon as she had disappeared, he rushed to the light to look at his boot. Yes, there were spots, but not very plain, all covered with mud. But who would distinguish them? Nastasia could know nothing, thank heavens! Then with trembling hand he tore open the notice, and began to read. At last he understood; it was simply the usual notice to report himself at the office of the district that day at half-past nine o'clock.

'But why today?' cried he. 'Lord, let it be over soon.' He was about to fall down on his knees to pray, when a fit of laughter seized him. 'I must trust to myself, not to prayers.' He quickly dressed himself. 'Shall I put the boot on?' he thought, 'better throw it away, and hide all traces of it.' Nevertheless he put it on, only, however, to throw it off again with an expression of horror. As, however, he recollected he had no other, a smile came to his face, and he drew it on once more. Again his face changed into deep despair, his limbs shook more and more. 'This is not from exertion,' thought he, 'it is fear.' His head spun round and round and his temples throbbed visibly.

On the stairs he recollected that all the things were in the hole in the wall, and then where was his certificate of birth? He stopped to think. But such despair, and, if it may be so called, cynicism, took hold of him, that he simply shook his head and went out. The sooner over, the better. Once again in the open air, he encountered the same insufferable heat, the dust, and the people in drink rolling about the streets. The sun caught him full in the eyes and almost blinded him, whilst his head spun round and round, as is usual in fever. On reaching the turning into the street he had taken the day before, he glanced in great agitation in the direction of the house, but immediately averted his eyes again. 'If they ask me, I should confess, perhaps,' said he to himself, as he turned away and made for the office. This was not far distant, in a new house, on the fourth floor. As he entered the court, he saw to the right of him a staircase, ascending which was a man carrying some books. 'It was evidently there.' He did not think of asking.

'I will go and fall on my knees and confess all,' he murmured, and began to ascend the narrow and very steep stairs. On every floor the doors of the kitchens of the several apartments stood open to the staircase, and emitted a suffocating, sickening odour. The entrance to the office he was in search of was also wide open, and he walked in. A number of persons were waiting in the ante-room. The stench was simply intolerable, and was intensified by the smell of fresh paint. Pausing a little, he decided to advance farther into the small low room. He became impatient when he found no one took any notice of him. In an inner room were seated a number of clerks engaged in writing. He went up to one of these.

'What do you want?' Raskolnikoff showed him the notice.

'You are a student?' asked the clerk, glancing at the notice.

'Yes, – that is, I used to be.'

The clerk glanced at him – without, however, any particular curiosity. He was a man with unkempt hair and an expressionless face.

'There is nothing to be learned from him, evidently,' thought Raskolnikoff.

'Step in there to the head clerk,' said the man, pointing to a farther room, which was quite full of people, amongst whom were two ladies. One of the latter, in mourning, and poorly clad, sat near the desk of the chief man, writing something from dictation. The other was a stout and good-looking woman, richly dressed, who wore a brooch almost as large as a dish; she stood in a corner, evidently waiting for somebody. Raskolnikoff placed his notice before the clerk. 'Wait a moment,' said the latter, after having cursorily examined the document, and continuing to busy himself with the lady in mourning.

Raskolnikoff breathed more freely. 'He knows nothing.' Little by little his self-possession came back to him, and he grew calmer. 'How stupid of me to be so craven! I might have let all out. Pity they do not let the air in here, it is stifling.' His head and senses were in a complete whirl, and a strange feeling came creeping over him; he felt he was losing all government over himself, and tried to fix his mind on something perfectly new, but found it impossible. He kept looking at the chief clerk and sought to read his face. The latter was a young man of about twenty-two, with swarthy face, mobile features, and appeared older than his years. He was fashionably dressed, with a number of rings on his fingers and a large gold chain on his waistcoat. With one of those present, he now and then exchanged a word or two in very good French.

'Luisa Ivanovna, you can be seated,' said he languidly to the stylish dame who was standing there, evidently not daring to sit down, although a chair was very near.

'I thank you,' said she, in German; and with much rustling of silk she sat down.

The woman in mourning was at last finished with, and, just as she turned to go, an officer, with a very good figure, entered the room noisily; he moved his shoulders in a peculiar fashion with each step he took. The lady last addressed jumped up at once from her seat, and made a very low curtsy, but the officer took not the slightest notice of her as he passed, and sat himself down in an easy-chair at the table.

This was the assistant district-officer, a man adorned with red whiskers standing out on either side of his face, and with extremely small features, which, however, betrayed no particular character except perhaps annoyance. He looked up impatiently at Raskolnikoff, whose filthy attire was by no means prepossessing. The latter returned his glance calmly and straight in the face, and in such a manner as to give the officer offence.

'What do you want here?' he cried, apparently surprised that such a ragged beggar was not knocked down by his thunder-bearing glance.

'I am here because I was summoned,' stammered Raskolnikoff.

'It is for the recovery of money lent,' said the head clerk. 'Here!' and he threw the paper to Raskolnikoff, 'read!'

'Money? What money? It cannot be that,' thought the young man, and he trembled with joy. Everything became clear, and the load fell off his shoulders.

'At what hour did you receive this, sir?' cried the lieutenant; 'you were told to come at nine o'clock, and now it is nearly twelve!'

'I received it a quarter of an hour ago,' loudly replied Raskolnikoff, over his shoulder, suddenly angered, 'and it is sufficient to say that I am ill with fever.'

'Please not to bawl!'

'I did not bawl, but spoke plainly; it is you that bawl. I am a student, and am not going to have you speak to me in that fashion.'

The officer became enraged, and fumed so that only some splutters flew out of his mouth. He jumped up from his place. 'Please keep silence. You are in court. Don't be insolent.'

'And so are you in court; and, besides bawling, you are smoking, so you are wanting in politeness to the whole company.' As he said this, Raskolnikoff felt an inexpressible delight at his maliciousness. The clerk looked up with a smile. The choleric officer was clearly nonplussed.

'That is not your business, sir,' he cried at last, unnaturally loud. 'Make the necessary declaration. Show him, Alexander Gregorivitch. Complaints have been made about you! You don't pay your debts! You know how to fly the kite evidently!'

Raskolnikoff did not listen, but greedily seized the paper for the solution. He read it through more than once, and could make nothing of it. 'What is this?' he asked of the clerk.

'It is a writ for recovery on a note of hand of yours. You are called upon either to pay at once, together with all expenses, etc., or to give a written answer when you will be able to pay, and sign an agreement not to remove until payment is made, and not to sell or conceal any property you may be possessed of. The creditor is free at any time to sell your goods and proceed against you according to law.'

'But I owe nothing!'

'That is not our affair. You are pursued upon a protested note of hand, in favour of the widow of the college assessor, Zarnitzan, and for the sum of one hundred and twenty roubles.'

'But she is my landlady!'

'Well! what if she is?'

The chief clerk gazed with a pitying, but at the same time triumphant smile at this novice, who was about to become acquainted, at considerable expense, with the proceedings usually taken against debtors. But what did Raskolnikoff care for the note of hand now? What mattered to him his landlady's complaints? Was it worth his while to trouble himself about it, or even to give it the least attention? He stood there reading, listening, answering, questioning at times, but he did all this mechanically. The delight at feeling himself safe, the satisfaction of having escaped an imminent danger – that was what, at that moment, filled his whole being. For the time being, all care for the future, all worry, was miles away from him. It was a moment of unalloyed joy, immediate and purely instinctive. But just then quite a tempest broke out in the police office. The lieutenant had not as yet recovered from the affront he had received, and his wounded pride was evidently seeking for revenge. So he suddenly began roughly to address the stylish lady, who, ever since his entrance, had been looking at him and stupidly smiling.

'And you, hussy!' yelled he as loud as he could (the lady in mourning was now gone), 'what happened at your house last night? Eh? You're again becoming a scandal to the whole street! Constant free fights and drunken brawls! Do you want to be sent to a penitentiary? Come, I told you, I warned you at least a dozen times, that at the next I should lose patience! But you're incorrigible!'

Raskolnikoff dropped the paper he held in his hand, and looked in amazement at the stylish lady who was treated with such scant ceremony. He was not long, however, before understanding what was the matter, and the affair rather amused him. He listened with pleasure, and experienced a great desire to laugh. His nervous system was quite disorganised.

'Elia Petrovitch!' observed the chief clerk, but he at once saw that his interference at that moment would be useless: he knew by experience that, when once the impetuous officer was started, it was impossible to stop him. As for the stylish lady, the storm let loose on her head at first caused her to tremble; but, strange to say, the more she heard herself abused, the more amiable became the expression of her countenance, and the more seductive the smiles she bestowed upon the terrible lieutenant. She kept curtsying whilst impatiently awaiting an opportunity to get in a word.

'There was neither uproar nor free fight at my house, Mr Captain,' she hastened to say, the moment she had the chance to speak (she expressed herself in Russian without any hesitation, though with a very strong German accent), 'there was no scandal whatever. The man came there intoxicated, and he called for three bottles; then he began to play the piano with his foot, which is rather out of place in a respectable house, and he broke several of the strings. I observed to him that that was not the way to behave; thereupon, he picked up a bottle and began to lay about him. I at once called Carl, the porter; he hit Carl in the eye; he did the same to Henrietta, and gave me five slaps on the cheek. It is disgraceful to behave thus in a respectable house, Mr Captain. I called for assistance; he opened the window which overlooks the canal, and squeaked like a little pig. Was it not shameful? The idea of going to the window to squeak like a little pig! It is true that Carl, pulling him behind to make him leave the window, tore off one of the tails of his coat. Then he demanded fifteen roubles for the damage, and I paid him five roubles out of my own pocket, Mr Captain. It was that ill-behaved visitor, Mr Captain, who caused all the scandal!'

'Come, come, enough! I have already told you, I have already repeated – '

'Elia Petrovitch!' again observed the chief clerk significantly. The lieutenant gave him a hurried glance, and saw him slightly shake his head.

'Well, so far as you are concerned, respectable Luisa Ivanovna, this is my last warning,' continued the lieutenant. 'If in the future, there occurs the least scandal in your worthy abode I'll have you caged, as is said in polite society. Do you hear? Now you can go, but I shall keep my eye on you, so beware!'

Luisa Ivanovna at once began to bow pleasantly all round; but, as she withdrew backwards towards the door, curtsying the while, she came in collision with a handsome officer, with a fresh and open countenance and superb fair bushy whiskers. This was Nicodemus Thomich, the ward officer, in person. Luisa Ivanovna hastened to bow to the ground, and then gaily skipped out of the office.

'What a noise there is here!' said he to Elia Petrovitch, but in a friendly tone, 'we can hear all downstairs.'

'Here's a gentleman, a student, no – that is, an ex-student,' said he, carrying some books to another table, moving his shoulders at each step in his peculiar manner, 'he does not pay his debts, gives bills, and refuses to yield up his room; there are constant complaints about him, and yet he takes offence because I happen to light a cigarette in his presence. Just look at him, he's a nice one to take offence!'

'Poverty is no crime,' said Nicodemus Thomich, turning affably to Raskolnikoff, who immediately began, in an easy tone:

'Your pardon, sir,' he turned to the officer, 'I wish to excuse myself if I have failed in anything. I am a poor student in bad health, and oppressed by poverty. At least, I was a student, but now I cannot afford to be one. I shall have money soon. I have a mother and sister in the Government of —. They are going to remit to me, and I will pay. My landlady is a worthy woman, only she is angry because I have lost my lessons and have been unable to pay her for four months – and she does not even send me up my meals now. I do not recollect what the bill was for. Still, can I pay it now? You can judge for yourselves.'

'That is not our affair,' again observed the chief clerk.

'True, true, but let me explain,' resumed Raskolnikoff, still addressing Nicodemus Thomich, but desirous also of fixing the attention of Elia Petrovitch, who pretended to be busy amongst the books on the table, 'I have lived with her for three years, ever since my arrival here from home, and not long afterwards I gave her a promise to marry her daughter – a verbal promise, strictly verbal, I assure you. She was a young girl, I liked her, although I was not in love with her; in one word, I was young. I must also tell you my landlady gave me a deal of credit, and I led a fast life and was rather volatile.'

'Do not trouble us with such confidences, we have no time to listen to them,' interrupted Elia Petrovitch abruptly.

'Pardon me, let me tell you,' cried Raskolnikoff, much put out by the interruption, 'let me tell you how the thing was, although I know it is useless. I quite agree with you. About a year after the girl died of typhus. I remained there as I was, and the mother told me and some friends of mine as well, that she had the most perfect confidence in me; and when I gave her the bill for what I owed, she said she would give me as much credit again; and never, never, would she enforce the promissory note. But now that I am without pupils and have nothing to eat, she claims a settlement. What do you think of that?'

'All these distressing details, sir, do not concern us,' sarcastically rejoined Elia Petrovitch. 'You have to make a declaration and give a promise. As regards your having been pleased to fall in love, and all these tragic incidents, we have nothing to do with them.'

'Do not be so harsh,' said Nicodemus Thomich, as he sat down and commenced writing.

'Please write,' said the clerk to Raskolnikoff.

'Write what?' asked he rudely.

'As I dictate.'

The clerk stood near and dictated to him the usual form of declaration: that he was unable to pay, that he would not quit the capital, dispose of his goods in any way, etc., etc.

'You cannot write, your pen is falling from your fingers,' said the clerk, and he looked him in the face. 'Are you ill?'

'Yes, my head swims. Go on.'

'That is all. Now sign it.'

Raskolnikoff let fall the pen, and seemed as if about to rise and go, but, instead of doing so, he laid both elbows on the table and supported his head with his hands. A new idea formed in his mind: to rise immediately, go straight to Nicodemus Thomich and tell him all that had occurred; then to accompany him to his room, and show him all the things hidden away in the wall behind the paper. His desire to do all this was of such strength that he got up from the table to carry his design into execution. 'Reflect, reflect a moment!' ran in his head. 'No, better not think, get it off my shoulders.' Suddenly he stood still as if shot. Nicodemus Thomich was at this moment hotly discussing something with Elia Petrovitch, and the words caught Raskolnikoff's anxious attention. He listened.

'It cannot be, they will both be released. In the first place, all is contradictory. Consider. Why did they call the porter if it were their work? To denounce themselves? Or out of cunning? Not at all, that would be too much! Besides, did not the porter see the student Pestriakoff at the very gate just as he came in, and he stood there some time with three friends who had accompanied him. And Koch: was he not below in the silversmith's for half an hour before he went up to the old woman's? Now, consider.'

'But see what contradictions arise! They say they knocked and found the door closed; yet three minutes after, when they went back with the porter, it was open.'

'That's true. The murderer was inside, and had bolted the door, and certainly he would have been captured had not Koch foolishly run off to the porter. In the interval *he*, no doubt, had time to escape downstairs. Koch explains that, if he had remained, the man would have leaped out and killed him. He wanted to have a *Te Deum* sung. Ha, ha!'

'Did nobody see the murderer?'

'How could they? The house is a perfect Noah's ark,' put in the clerk, who had been listening.

'The thing is clear, very clear,' said Nicodemus Thomich decisively. 'Not at all! Not at all!' cried Elia Petrovitch, in reply.

Raskolnikoff took up his hat and made for the door, but he never reached it. When he came to himself he found he was sitting on a chair, supported on the right by some unknown man, while to his left stood another, holding some yellow water in a yellow glass. Nicodemus Thomich, standing before him, was looking at him fixedly. Raskolnikoff arose.

'What is it? Are you ill?' asked the officer sharply.

'He could hardly hold the pen to sign his name,' the clerk explained, at the same time going back to his books.

'Have you been ill very long?' cried Elia Petrovitch from his table; he had run to see the swoon and returned.

'Since yesterday,' murmured Raskolnikoff in reply.

'You went out yesterday?'

'I did.'

'Ill?'

'Ill!'

'At what time?'

'Eight o'clock in the evening.'

'Where did you go, allow me to ask?'

'In the streets.'

'Concise and clear.'

Raskolnikoff had replied sharply, in a broken voice, his face as pale as a handkerchief, and with his black swollen eyes averted from Elia Petrovitch's scrutinising glance.

'He can hardly stand on his legs. Do you want to ask anything more?' said Nicodemus Thomich.

'Nothing,' replied Elia Petrovitch.

Nicodemus Thomich evidently wished to say more, but, turning to the clerk, who in turn glanced expressively at him, he became silent. All suddenly stopped speaking. It was strange.

Raskolnikoff went out. As he descended the stairs he could hear an animated discussion had broken out, and above all, the interrogative voice of Nicodemus Thomich. In the street he came to himself.

'Search, search! they are going to search!' he cried. 'The scoundrels, they suspect me!' The old dread seized him again, from head to foot.

Chapter 2

HERE WAS THE ROOM. All was quiet, and no one had, apparently, disturbed it – not even Nastasia. But, heavens! how could he have left all those things where they were? He rushed to the corner, pushed his hands behind the paper, took out the things, and thrust them in his pockets. There were eight articles in all, and two little boxes with earrings or something of that description, then four little morocco cases; a chain wrapped up in paper, and something else done up in a common piece of newspaper – possibly a decoration. Raskolnikoff distributed these, together with the purse, about his person, in order to make them less noticeable, and quitted the room again. All the time he had left the door wide open. He went away hurriedly, fearing pursuit. Perhaps in a few minutes orders would be issued to hunt him down, so he must hide all traces of his theft at once; and he would do so whilst he had strength and reason left him. But where should he go?

This had been long decided. Throw the lot into the canal and the matter would be at an end! So he had resolved in that night of delirium, when he cried out, 'Quick, quick! Throw all away!' But this was not so easy. He wandered to the quays of the Catherine Canal, and lingered there for half an hour. Here a washing raft lay where he had thought of sinking his spoil, or there boats were moored, and everywhere people swarmed. Then, again, would the cases sink? Would they not rather float? No, this would not do. He would go to the Neva; there would be fewer people there and more room, and it would be more convenient. He recognised that he had been wandering about for fully half an hour, and in dangerous places. He must make haste. He made his way to the river, but soon came to another standstill. Why in the Neva? Why in the water at all? Better some solitary place in a wood, or under some bushes. Dig a hole and bury them! He felt he was not in a condition to deliberate clearly and soundly, but this idea appeared the best.

This idea also, however, was not destined to be realised, and another took its place. As he passed the V— Prospect, he suddenly noticed on the left an entrance into a court, which was surrounded entirely by high walls. On the right, a long way up the court, rose the side of a huge four-storied building. To the left, parallel with the walls of the house, and commencing immediately at the gate, a wooden hoarding ran for about twenty paces down the court. Then came a space where a lot of rubbish was deposited; whilst farther down, at the bottom of the court, was a shed, apparently part of some workshop, possibly that of a carpenter or coachbuilder. Everything appeared as black as coal-dust. Here was the very place, he thought; and, after looking round, went up the court. Behind the door he espied a large unworked stone, weighing about fifty pounds, which lay close up against the hoarding. No one could see him where he stood; he was entirely free from observation. He bent down to the stone, managed to turn it over after considerable effort, and found underneath a small cavity. He threw in the cases, and then the purse on the top of all. The stone was not perceptibly higher when he had replaced it, and little traces of its having been moved could be noticed. So he pressed some earth against the edges with his foot, and made off.

He laughed for joy when again in the street. All traces were gone, and who would think of looking there? And if they were found who would suspect him? All proofs were gone, and he laughed again. Yes, he recollected afterwards how he laughed – a long, nervous, lingering laugh, lasting all the time he was in that street. As he came to the Boulevard K—, where he had had the adventure with the drunken girl, his joviality left him, and other thoughts crowded into his brain relative to that incident. 'The devil take him!' he muttered. He went on, looking round maliciously. His thoughts hinged upon one certain point, and he felt that even now at the very outset he was straying from his one object, an important question which he had shunned facing for the last two months. 'To the devil with all! – the girl, the new life, and everything!' he cried all at once in a fit of anger. 'How ridiculous I am! How I lied, to try to win the good graces of that detestable Elia Petrovitch! How I set them all at defiance, and played with them all! Did I, though?' He stopped to ask himself a new, perfectly unlooked-for, but urgent question. 'Have I done this deed with discernment and with a definite aim in view, or in simple foolishness? Did I even look in the purse, and see what I had got? Was that the outcome of my cowardly work? Did I not want to cast them all into the river, and without giving hardly a glance at them? What was all this? I am very ill, that is why I have these thoughts. I am jaded and worn out, and do not know what I am doing. Yesterday and the day before, it was the same. I shall get better soon. Suppose I do not, though! How tired I am!'

He kept on walking, however, trying to divert his mind, but knew not what to do or undertake. His old repugnance came upon him stronger than ever – an obstinate, malicious hatred of everybody, his surroundings and everything; and he resolved simply to ignore anyone who spoke to him. He stopped when he came to the banks of the Little Neva, near the Vassilevsky Ostroff. 'Why, he lives here, in that house!

How strange! I said the other day that I would go to Razoumikhin *afterwards*, on the following day, and here am I going!' He ascended to the fifth floor. Razoumikhin was at home, in his small room, busily engaged in writing, and he rose and opened the door. It was four months since they had last seen each other. Razoumikhin appeared in a tattered dressing-gown, with his bare feet pushed into a pair of old slippers, his hair dishevelled, his face unshaven and unwashed. He seemed astonished.

'What! Is it you?' he cried, as he looked his old comrade over from head to foot – then he gave a prolonged whistle.

'Impossible!' he said at last, scanning Raskolnikoff's rags. 'Why brother, my more than brother, come in, sit down,' and he led Raskolnikoff to an old rickety couch, covered with American cloth, and worse than the latter's own. Razoumikhin saw at once that his visitor was unwell.

'You are seriously ill, man, are you not aware of that?' He tried to feel his pulse, but Raskolnikoff drew back his hand.

'You need not,' he said, 'I am here, that's all. I want to get some pupils – I wanted to ask, but I don't want pupils at all, either – '

'You are delirious,' replied the student, carefully watching him.

'No, I am not!' Raskolnikoff rose from the sofa. He felt he would permit no one in the whole world to argue with him, be it his very best friend, and he suddenly became livid with rage. He almost choked from excess of feeling. 'Good-day!' he cried suddenly, making for the door.

'Stay, my good fellow!'

'I am going,' said Raskolnikoff, with his hands to his sides.

'What are you come here for, then? – have you lost your senses, or what? This is almost insulting. I will not let you go away like this.'

'Well, listen: I came here because I knew no one else who could assist me, because you are the kindest, the wisest of all, and can understand. But now I see that there is nothing I am in want of, absolutely nothing. I can help myself best! It is sufficient, leave me in peace.'

'Stop a minute, Mr Chimney-sweep! You are positively out of your mind! I am giving no lessons myself either. I am at present doing translations for a publisher. I had counted on you as being useful to me. My orthography is rather bad, and I am very weak in German – indeed, I only undertook the work with the hope of its leading to something better. Look here, he will pay three roubles for translating these German pages, and you may do them if you like. Here!'

Raskolnikoff took the paper and the three roubles in silence, and went out. Razoumikhin gazed after him with surprise, which was redoubled when he saw his visitor return, lay the money and paper once again on the table, and, still maintaining silence, again prepare to quit the room.

'You must be in a raging fever!' Razoumikhin at last roared out. 'What comedy is this you are playing? You are enough to vex a saint! What the devil did you want here?'

'I don't want any translations,' murmured Raskolnikoff from the stairs, making his way down.

'Eh! Where do you live?'

No answer.

'Confound you then! Be off!'

Raskolnikoff was already in the street. On the Nicolaeff Bridge he was brought to his senses in a very extraordinary manner. He felt the lashes of a whip across his back, and heard cries from the driver of a carriage, who had called out to him three or four times before proceeding to more vigorous measures. The blows exasperated him to such an extent that he leaped to the hand-rail (how he came to be in the middle of the street he knew not). The carriage drove on, and he stood, amidst the smiles of the lookers-on, gazing malignantly after it and rubbing his back. Suddenly he felt some money thrust into his hand. A trader's wife, with headdress and goatskin shoes, was just passing, accompanied by a child carrying a yellow parasol, and evidently the woman's daughter. 'Take this, for Christ's sake!' said the former as she went on. From his clothes and appearance, he might very well be taken for a beggar, engaged in his occupation, and no doubt the blow from the whip brought him the twenty kopecks. He kept the money and went away, turning his face to the Neva, in the direction of the Palace. The heavens were without a cloud, whilst the water appeared almost blue, a rare occurrence with the Neva. The dome of the Cathedral never stood out so plainly on the horizon, and through the clear air could be distinctly seen the tracery of its architecture.

The pain from the whip abated, and Raskolnikoff forgot the blow – one disturbing and indistinct idea engrossed him entirely instead. He stood and looked afar off, long and fixedly. This spot was particularly well known to him, and in his old University days it happened, hundreds of times, that he would linger here, at this very place, and admire the beautiful panorama displayed to his eyes. An inexplicably soothing air appeared to blow upon him in this place, and the scene appealed to him mutely. He used to be astonished at the sombre and enigmatical questions which came to the surface of his mind; but, mistrusting himself, the solutions were invariably deferred to the future. He thought of standing there again and thinking as he used to do, but he knew that that would be ridiculous, and that buried below him, far under foot, were all the past problems and questions – the panorama, even, and all besides. It appeared to him as if he had escaped upwards and lost sight of everything. At last he made a movement with his arm and felt the coins in his hand, gazed a moment at them, then flung them into the water, and went homewards. He felt as if he had severed himself from everything and everybody at that moment.

He reached home towards evening, perhaps at about eight o'clock – how and by what particular way, he never recollected – but, speedily undressing, he lay down on the couch, trembling like a beaten horse, and, drawing his overcoat over him, he fell immediately into a deep sleep. He was awakened at early morn by a terrible noise. Heavens! What was that shriek? Such an unnatural sound, such howlings, gnashings of teeth, blows, cursing, he had never heard before! He could not imagine such ferocity and confusion. In horror he arose and sat up in bed. The clamour and swearing grew louder and stronger, and then, to his astonishment, he heard the voice of his landlady. She was howling and giving vent to words impossible to analyse, at the same time imploring someone to cease beating her. Her assailant, evidently in the greatest rage, joined in with loud shouts and exclamations. Raskolnikoff began to tremble like a leaf. He recognised the voice; it was that of Elia Petrovitch. 'He here, beating the landlady, kicking her? Why, what for? Impossible! It must be a dream. What are the lights?' From all quarters the occupants began to gather, and voices, sounds, knocking and banging of doors joined in the general noise. It was reality. 'Good heavens! Can it be? he is coming here?' He raised his hand towards the bolt, but let it fall again. Dread benumbed him like ice. He fell back. At last, after about ten minutes, the noise began to subside; the landlady groaned and sighed; Elia Petrovitch threatened and abused, and then came silence. The lookers-on returned to their rooms.

Haunted by Elia Petrovitch's voice, Raskolnikoff fell back on his couch in a kind of stupor; he could not close his eyes, but lay there in such a state of agitation, and with such an unendurable sensation of fright, as he had never felt before. Suddenly the door opened, and Nastasia entered, bearing in her hands a light and a plate of soup, with bread, salt, etc. She gave a glance at him, and, finding he was not asleep, placed the light on the table and began to arrange the meal.

'He has eaten nothing since yesterday, and has been running all over the town with a fever on him.'

'Nastasia, who beat the landlady?'

She looked at him steadily, and repeated his question.

'Yes, about half an hour ago, Elia Petrovitch was on the stairs. Why did he beat her? How did it happen?' Nastasia did not answer, but continued to look at him; her strange glances annoyed him. 'Nastasia, why are you silent?' he cried in a weak voice.

'It is the blood,' she said at last, quietly, and as if speaking to herself.

'Blood! What blood?' he murmured, with a pallid face, turning to the wall.

Nastasia still gazed on him. 'Nobody beat her,' she said at last.

He turned to her breathless. 'I heard them, I say, I heard all. I was not asleep, I sat up and listened all the time. It was Elia Petrovitch, and all the house came and listened, too.'

'Nothing has happened. It is only your blood; it's got clotted, and brings on dreams. Take something to eat!'

He made no reply, and Nastasia stood near him, surveying him as before. 'Give me something to drink, Nastasia.' She went below, and returned with some water in a white earthenware jug. He recollected nothing further except sipping a few drops and spilling some down his neck, then came a blank.

Chapter 3

RASKOLNIKOFF'S MIND, however, was not quite a blank during all the progress of his illness. He recollected a good deal about it. It seemed to him that he was surrounded by a number of persons who wished to bear him off, and who disputed and quarrelled a good deal over him. Then again, sometimes there would be no one in the room, all had run away, frightened of him, and only occasionally peeped in at the door to look at him. Then they threatened him, mocked him, and sometimes laughed at him. He frequently recollected seeing Nastasia by his bedside; also a man whom he seemed to know very well, and whose name he could not bring to mind, and he used to grieve about this and even cried. At times he felt he had lain there a month, at other times it seemed but a day. One thing he entirely forgot, the *one thing* that above all he should have remembered – he knew he did this and made violent efforts to recollect. Then he would struggle to rise and rush away, but someone always restrained him by force. Then he sank back, feeling weak and about to faint. At last he came to himself.

This happened one morning about ten o'clock, a time when, in clear weather, the sun always cast long rays on the couch where he lay. At the bedside stood Nastasia and a man who was certainly unknown to him. This was a man with a beard and wearing a *caftan*. He had the appearance of a workman. Through the half-open door the landlady was looking on. Raskolnikoff raised himself a little.

'Who is that, Nastasia?' he asked, pointing to the man.

'Hallo! He is awake,' said she.

'He is awake!' echoed the man. Concluding that Raskolnikoff had recovered consciousness, the landlady immediately closed the door and made off. She was always of a timid nature, and dreaded conversations or explanations. She was about forty years of age, short and stout, good-looking, and good-natured, which seemed to be the result of her stoutness and inherent laziness; altogether she was a rather pleasant woman.

'Who are you?' asked Raskolnikoff, turning to the workman. At this moment the door opened, and Razoumikhin's tall form entered, stooping.

'What a cabin this is! I always bump my forehead. Call these apartments indeed! Ah! brother, are you awake? I heard so from Pashenka.'

'He has just awoke,' said Nastasia.

'He has just awoke,' repeated the workman, with a smile.

'And who may you be?' Razoumikhin asked, turning to the last speaker.

'I have come from the merchant Shepolaeff on business, sir.'

'Please be seated, my friend. You have done well to wake,' he continued, turning to Raskolnikoff. 'For four days you have hardly touched anything. True, they gave you some tea with a spoon. I have brought Zosimoff to you twice. You remember Zosimoff? He examined you carefully, and said you had a lot of nonsense in your head, the result of bad diet and beer. You will soon get over it. We need not detain you,' he added to the workman, 'please explain what your business is. There has been someone here before, Rodia, from their office, besides this man.'

'Yes, sir, that was Alexis Semenovitch, from our office, who came the day before yesterday. By order of Athanasius Ivanovitch Vakrouchin I have to give you from Simon Simonovitch the sum of thirty roubles, remitted from your mother as before. I presume you have heard of this?'

'Yes, I recollect, Vakrouchin,' said Raskolnikoff pensively.

'What! You know Vakrouchin?' cried Razoumikhin. 'What have you there?'

'The book, sir!'

'Give it me. Now, Rodia, raise yourself and sign, take the pen. Money is the honey of humanity.'

'I don't want it,' said Raskolnikoff, pushing away the pen.

'Not want it? Now, come, friend, I will witness it. It is very simple. See, I will guide your hand. That is it. Here is your receipt.'

'Thanks, sir.'

'Bravo! And now, my friend, you want something to eat. What shall it be? Some soup?'

'I have some over from yesterday,' said Nastasia, who had been standing near all the time.

'With potatoes and rice, eh?'

'Yes, I will bring some.'

Raskolnikoff looked at them with deep astonishment and a dull feeling of dread. He decided to maintain silence and await events. 'I am no longer delirious, this is reality.'

In a few moments Nastasia returned with the soup, and announced that some tea would soon follow. She further brought with her a couple of spoons and plates, and all the proper service – salt, pepper, etc., all in such order as never had been before. The cloth was spotless.

'It would not be amiss, Nastasia, if Prascovia Paulovna got us in a couple of bottles of beer. We can manage them!'

Raskolnikoff continued to look on stupidly, and with some effort. Razoumikhin now sat down near him as awkwardly as a bear, and, supporting his friend's head with his left arm, began to feed him. Raskolnikoff took one spoonful, then another, than a third, when his friend said he must wait till Zosimoff came.

'I have dined here, Rodia, for the last two or three days, and Pashenka, your landlady, has supplied my meals. I did not object. Here comes Nastasia with the tea.'

Razoumikhin poured out a cup of tea, then another, and sat down again on the couch. He took hold with his left hand of the sick man's head, and, blowing at the tea to cool it, fed the patient with a spoon. Raskolnikoff accepted all these attentions in silence, and made no resistance, notwithstanding that he felt quite capable of sitting up and helping himself without any assistance. A low kind of cunning had come over him, and it had come into his head to conceal his strength, to sham, to lie and listen and observe. After sipping about a dozen spoonfuls, he pushed away the spoon and fell back upon his pillow. His head did rest upon a pillow now, a real feather one, in a proper case, a fact Raskolnikoff had already noticed and taken into consideration.

'Now, Rodia, I must tell you how I found you out. When you escaped from my place in such a funny manner without leaving me your address, I felt so angry with you that I resolved to seek you out to punish you. I set about it at once and asked and asked. This, your present address, I had forgotten – indeed, I could not recollect it, as I never knew it. I tried to find out your old quarters and it made me still more angry to be unsuccessful; so I went to the Address Bureau, and in a few minutes they found you out. You were inscribed in it.'

'I?'

'Yes, they would not find *me* there, though. No sooner did I arrive here than I was told all your affairs. I know all, *all*, my friend, and have made acquaintance with Nicodemus Thomich, Elia Petrovitch, the partner, and Mr Zametoff, the chief clerk in the police-office; and, lastly, I got to know your affair with Pashenka. I do not wish to tire you, and will not say anything superfluous. My last conquest was Pashenka herself; ask Nastasia – '

'You got round her,' murmured the servant, smiling shyly.

Raskolnikoff did not reply, although at the moment he could not tear his eyes away from his comrade's glance. Razoumikhin was evidently a little disconcerted at his silence, but continued: 'It was a great pity, my dear fellow, you did not be more careful with her. How ever did you come to sign the bill? I know everything – but pardon me, I see I am touching a very delicate string! I am an ass! But, apropos, it's quite true she is not quite so stupid as she looks. Is she?'

'No,' replied Raskolnikoff, turning away, not understanding that it was better to sustain the conversation.

'Is it not true?' Razoumikhin added, delighted that his hearer was evincing some interest. 'Quite an unexpected character! I can't quite make her out. She must be forty; indeed, she owns to thirty-six. I am sure she has a full right to do so. However, I must avow that I judge her more intellectually, metaphysically, or whatever you call it. All this quarrel has arisen in this way. She saw that you were no longer a student, had no pupils, and were deprived of means of livelihood, and, furthermore, that she had no hold on you through her daughter's death – this made her take fright. She saw you were allowing yourself to sink effortless, and resolved to make you give up your room. For a long time she meditated upon this, and then there was the bill, which, however, you had told her that your mother would meet – '

'It was very mean of me to say so. She herself is almost dependent on charity, and I lied in order to remain here,' declared Raskolnikoff vehemently.

'You were prudent in that. It was very unfortunate that that Mr Tchebaroff should have turned up. Without him Pashenka would not have thought of doing anything. She is too timid; not so the business man. His first question, I'll be bound, was, "Can the bill be realised?" What was the reply? "Yes, his mother has only a pension of one hundred and twenty-five roubles – nevertheless, she helps him; besides, his sister Dounia is such as would go into bondage for him." This was what they relied on. Do not be alarmed. I have learned your secret thoughts. You were right to confide in Pashenka when she looked upon you as a future son-in-law; but, you see, while the honest man tells his secrets, the business man hoards them up and turns them to account. In short, he made your bill over to Tchebaroff, and he commenced these proceedings. Fortunately, I am on good terms with Pashenka, and partly through her influence I have managed to stop the affair, at the same time assuring them you would pay. You will do so, I am sure. Do you hear? I offered Tchebaroff ten roubles down for his expenses, and here I have the honour to return you the bill! So that now they have only your promise to rely upon.'

Razoumikhin placed the bill on the table. Raskolnikoff looked at him, and, without opening his mouth, again turned to the wall.

'I see, my friend, that you are still acting the fool,' added Razoumikhin, after a pause. 'I thought only to amuse and distract you with my talk, but, instead, it seems I have simply succeeded in making you angry.'

'Did I fail to recognise you when I was delirious?' Raskolnikoff muttered at last.

'Yes, my presence seemed to excite you sometimes, especially when Zametoff once accompanied me.'

'Zametoff? The clerk? Why did you bring him here?' Raskolnikoff quickly turned and fixed his eyes on Razoumikhin.

'Why? What alarms you? He wished to become acquainted with you, as I had spoken so much about you. From whom could I have learned these particulars if not from him? He is an excellent fellow, very extraordinary in his way as well. We are friends now and see each other almost every day. I have removed to this neighbourhood. You know Luisa, do you not – Luisa Ivanovna?'

'Did I rave much?'

'Yes, but do not agitate yourself.'

'What did I say?'

'Oh, what people always say. Now, my friend, let us not waste any time; but talk of business.' He stood up, and seized his cap.

'What did I rave about?'

'It is of no use repeating. Do you fear having disclosed your secrets? Do not be alarmed. You never mentioned the Countess, but you talked a great deal about a bulldog, earrings, watch-chains, Krestoffsky Island. You spoke, also, of some porters, of Nicodemus Thomich and Elia Petrovitch, and said a deal about them. Another funny thing was, your boot seemed to be an object of great interest to you; you kept asking for it. Zametoff sought for it in every corner, and gave you this plaything, stained and washed out by your own hands as it was. Then, and then only, did you grow calm again, and the whole day you held it in your hands, so tightly that it was impossible to take it from you. It must be about now, somewhere among the clothes. But now to business. Here are your thirty-five roubles, out of which I am going to take ten, and render you an account later on; at the same time I shall let Zosimoff know, although he should have been here by now – it is twelve o'clock. I shall also give Pashenka orders. Adieu, for the present.'

'He calls her Pashenka. Oh, the sly fellow!' said Nastasia to Raskolnikoff, as she left the room; then on the stairs she stood listening, but, catching no words, she slipped down farther. She seemed very eager to learn what Razoumikhin was saying to the landlady; it was apparent that she herself was completely bewitched by him.

No sooner was the door closed, than the sick man threw off the clothes and leaped like a madman out of his bed, and stood waiting with a burning impatience until they were quite gone away. Now, at once to work. 'But what? Do what?' he asked himself. He had forgotten why he had jumped out of bed. 'My God, my God, tell me but this: Do they know all or nothing? Knowing all, do they but feign, and mock me as I lie here, and then go and tell what is already known to everybody; or do they simply – ? What can I do? I forget as soon as I think!'

He stood in the middle of the room, and looked around in a vacant manner, ran to the door, opened it, and listened. No one was about. He ran back again, and knelt down near the hole under the paper, thrust in his hand, and found nothing; then to the stove to rummage among the cinders – the bits of torn pockets lay where he had thrown them, evidently no one had seen them. Then he recollected the boot spoken of by Razoumikhin, and speedily discovered it under the clothes. It was so muddy that he felt sure Zametoff could have noticed nothing.

'Ah, Zametoff – the office! Why am I called there? Where is the summons? Pshaw! I am getting confused. It was the other day! – the same day I examined the boot; since then I've been ill. But why does Zametoff come here? And why does Razoumikhin bring him?' he murmured, sinking down on the couch exhausted. 'What is this? The fever is still on me or I would fly. Yes, I must fly quick, quick, at once! at once! Ah! but where to? Where are my clothes? My boots? They are gone. Ah! Hidden away, I have no doubt. There is my coat, the money, thank God! I will take it and go away to other apartments where they will not find me. Yes, but the Address Bureau, they will discover me; Razoumikhin will. Better fly farther, to America, and defy them. I will take the bill, too, that may be of use. What else shall I take? They think

I am ill, and do not imagine I can get away. Ah! ah! ah! I guessed from their eyes they knew all. If I can only get down the stairs. Perhaps they have placed a watch here, the police! What is this? Tea? A bottle of beer, too, that will refresh me!'

He seized the bottle, in which was about a glassful, and drank the contents off as if he had a fire in his throat. Many moments had not elapsed before the liquor got into his head, and a light, but agreeable, shiver ran through his frame. He returned to his bed and drew the clothes over him, and, his thoughts becoming soothed under the influence of the beer, he sank into a light and pleasing slumber, which was aided by the comfort of the new pillow on which his head rested. He awoke, later on, with a feeling on him that some person was in the room, and opening his eyes, they fell upon Razoumikhin, who was standing at the door, seeming undecided whether to enter or not.

'Ah, you are awake! Bring up the bundle, Nastasia.'

'What time is it?' Raskolnikoff asked, looking wearily around.

'Six o'clock. You have slept for six hours.'

'Heavens! How could I have slept so long?'

'What is the matter? There is no hurry. We have plenty of time before us. I have been here several times, but you were fast asleep; also twice to Zosimoff – he is not at home. I have been moving my things today – uncle and all. I have an uncle with me now. Never mind, though! Give me the bundle, Nastasia. Now, my friend, tell me how you feel.'

'I'm quite well. I'm not ill. Have you been here long?'

'I told you I was here a little while ago.'

'Yes, but before then.'

'How before?'

'When did you first come?'

'Why, I told you all about that. Have you forgotten?' Raskolnikoff tried to think, but all was muddled, and he gave an appealing glance at Razoumikhin. 'Oh, you are confused, but the sleep has done you good, and you look better – indeed you do.' He looked at the bundle brought in by Nastasia, and continued: 'I have been very busy in the matter too. You know, we must make a man of you. Do you see this?' diving into the bag, and holding up a fairly good, but at the same time cheap and ordinary, cap. 'Let us try this on.'

'Not now,' said Raskolnikoff, pushing it away.

'Do, please, it is getting late, and I shall not be able to sleep if I do not see how they fit, for I bought them on chance. There, that is the latest thing in caps. What do you think I gave for it?' Raskolnikoff making no reply, Razoumikhin turned to Nastasia. 'What do you say?'

'Twenty kopecks, I should think.'

'Twenty kopecks! Fool!' cried he, offended. 'Why, one could not buy it today for eighty. Now then, we approach the United States, as we call them at college,' and Razoumikhin spread out before Raskolnikoff a pair of light summer trousers in pretty good condition, without stains, and then a waistcoat, apparently much too large for its purpose. 'Rather loose, I think, but that will not matter, all the more comfortable. You see, Rodia, to be in fashion one must observe the seasons, and if asparagus is not customary in January one need not have it, and it saves money: so it is with respect to my purchase. For it is summer, and I have bought accordingly. When the time comes for darker autumn suits you can abandon this if it does not abandon you. Now, as to the price. What is your idea? Two and a quarter roubles and the old agreement; if it wears out this year, they give you another pair gratis next year. Now we arrive at the boots. One can easily see they have been worn, but they will last a month or two, for they are of foreign manufacture. The Secretary of the English Embassy was in want of money, and sold them. He had only had them a week. Price, a rouble and a half. Lucky, wasn't I?'

'But perhaps they don't fit,' muttered Nastasia.

'Not fit?' replied Rasoumikhin, pulling out of his pocket one of his friend's patched muddy boots. 'I take good care of that. I got the exact size. As for the linen, that was not so easy; but, however, here are three shirts with fashionable fronts. Now let us reckon up: eighty kopecks the cap, two roubles and a quarter the clothes, boots a rouble and a half, shirts five roubles – in all, nine roubles and fifty-five kopecks. Here are forty-five kopecks change; please to take them. Now you are completely rigged out, and in quite a fashionable style. As for socks and other little things, you can buy those yourself. There remains twenty-five roubles; and you need not mind the rent, I have arranged with Pashenka about that. Please now to change your linen.'

'No, I will not,' cried Raskolnikoff, who had listened moodily to the playful recital of the purchase of the clothes. 'Where did the money come from for these?' he asked.

'Money? Why, out of your own! Didn't your mother send it you through Vakrouchin – don't you recollect?'

'I remember now,' Raskolnikoff answered, after a long surly silence.

At this moment the door opened and a tall stout man entered familiarly, as if accustomed to the sight of the sick man. 'Zosimoff at last!' cried Razoumikhin in delight.

Chapter 4

ZOSIMOFF WAS A TALL and stout man, about twenty-seven years of age, with a round, colourless, clean-shaven face, and his fair hair stood erect on his head. He wore spectacles, and had a large gold ring embedded in the fat flesh of one of his fingers. He was dressed in a light summer coat and trousers, very fashionable in cut, and everything he had on seemed spick and span; his linen was irreproachable, whilst his general appearance was still further set off by a massive watch-chain. His manner was pompous, but at the same time studiously easy, though the effort, in spite of his endeavours to conceal it, was continually apparent. His acquaintances thought him insufferable anywhere but in a sickroom, where he was invaluable.

'I have been twice to your place, my friend,' cried Razoumikhin. 'You see he is awake.'

'I see, I see. How do we feel now, eh?' turning to the patient and sitting near him on the sofa, after having disposed of his legs as best he could.

'He is out of sorts, and when we wanted to change his linen he almost cried,' said Razoumikhin.

'You could have changed that later on if he did not wish it. The pulse is weak. Your head still aches, does it not?'

'I am quite well, very well,' Raskolnikoff replied in irritation, raising himself a little on the sofa and glancing at the interrogator with sparkling eyes. The effort seemed, however, too much for him – he fell back again in his old position, with his face towards the wall.

'Very good, he is going on all right. Has he eaten?' He was told, and asked what should be given the invalid.

'Oh, anything – soup, tea. You need not give him mushrooms nor cucumbers, though, nor beef either. The mixture as before, and I will have a look at him tomorrow. That will do for today, and – '

'Tomorrow evening I shall take him for a walk,' said Razoumikhin, 'in the Yosupoff Garden, and then we intend to go to the Crystal Palace.'

'I do not think he will be able to be moved. However, we shall see.'

'What a pity! I am just going to give a house-warming in my new rooms, not two steps away, and we could take him there. He could lie on the sofa between us. You will come?'

'Thanks, if possible. What's the entertainment?'

'Oh, nothing. Tea, brandy, herrings, cake.'

'Anyone particular?'

'Some young fellows, and my uncle, who has just arrived in St Petersburg on some trifling business. I have not seen him for five years.'

'Who is he?'

'He has passed all his life as a district postmaster, has a pension now, and is about sixty-five years of age. He is nothing to speak of, but I am very fond of him myself. Porphyrius Petrovitch, examining magistrate for the district, is to come. Then some students, teachers, a tchinovnik, a musician, and an officer – Zametoff.'

'Tell me, pray, what can there be in common between either of you, and such as Zametoff?' asked Zosimoff.

'Oh, those grumblers! They all take principles as motives and dare not follow their desires. He is a decent fellow, and I like him. That's my principle, and I want no other reason. Zametoff is an extraordinary man, and we have a matter of interest in common – '

'I should like to know what – '

'It is all about a house-painter – that is, a stainer. We have been working to release him. It is all arranged now. The thing seems perfectly plain.'

'What painter is that?'

'Did I not tell you? Oh, you only heard the beginning – about the murder of the old woman. A painter is implicated.'

'Yes, I heard about the murder; it interests me, partly for a reason – I read about it in the papers.'

'Yes, they killed Elizabeth, too,' put in Nastasia, addressing Raskolnikoff. She had remained near the door listening.

'Elizabeth?' he murmured almost inaudibly.

'Elizabeth – you knew her? She has repaired your shirts at times.'

Raskolnikoff turned, as usual, to the wall, where, on the dirty yellow paper, were depicted some tiny white flowers, which he mechanically proceeded to examine, and count the petals and leaves. His feet and arms felt benumbed, almost as if these limbs were amputated, but he obstinately continued his occupation, and did not try to stir.

'Well, and what about the painter?' said Zosimoff, with some gesture of displeasure at Nastasia's chatter.

Nastasia sighed, and became silent.

'He is charged with the murder,' replied Razoumikhin.

'What proofs are there?'

'Proofs! There are none; what they take to be proofs are not proofs. They were on a false scent, just as they were with Koch and

Pestryakoff. All is done stupidly and irrationally. By the way, Rodia, you have heard something about this? It happened just before your illness; when you were at the office and swooned, they were talking about it.'

Zosimoff looked curiously at Raskolnikoff, who did not move. 'I must keep an eye on you, Razoumikhin. You are taking too much trouble about a matter which does not concern you,' Zosimoff observed.

'Never mind that. We mean to rescue this unlucky man from the grip of the law,' cried Razoumikhin, bringing down his fist upon the table. 'What can be more scandalous? They talk and talk, fancying that that leads to truth; and they worship their loquacity. Now, for example, see the confusion in the official mind. The door is found closed; the porters come; it is open. Koch and Pestryakoff must, then, have done the deed! That's their kind of logic!'

'Do not put yourself out about it. They are simply detained – it was necessary to do that. I remember meeting this Koch once. He was in the habit of buying up expired pledges, was he not?'

'Yes, the scamp! and notes of hand also. A regular business. But have done with him. It is about this I am excited – about their crazy, trivial routine! "We have," they say, "facts before us!" But facts are not everything; it is important to know how to interpret them.'

'And do you understand how to go about that?'

'Perhaps. It is impossible to keep silence when one feels one could give assistance in the matter, if – you know the details?'

'I am still waiting for the painter's history.'

'Yes, of course. Well, listen to the story: – On the third morning after the murder, whilst they were still engaged in playing with Koch and the other – in spite of the clearest evidence of their every movement – there suddenly came to light a very unlooked-for fact. A peasant, Dooshkin by name, who keeps a beerhouse exactly opposite the house, appeared at the office, bringing with him a jewel-case, which contained a pair of gold ear-rings. This was his story: – "There came to me, the day before yesterday, a little after eight o'clock at night, a painter, whom I know well, Nikola by name, and he asked me for an advance of two roubles upon these things, and in reply to my question – how did you come by them? – he replied that he had found them in the street. I did not ask him anything further and I advanced him a one-rouble note on the thing, thinking that if I did not do so somebody else would. Besides, I know this Nikola, he is of the same Government as myself. Although he is not a drunkard, still he drinks, and we knew that he was working on the same job together with Dmitri.

' "He at once changed the note, and drank off two glasses, took up his change and went away. Dmitri we did not see at all. The next day, having heard of the murder, it struck me at once that the ear-rings belonged to the old woman, and that she had advanced money upon them. I immediately set about making inquiries, and went to their house, and, after preparing the way carefully, asked, 'Where is Nikola?' Dmitri replied, 'He is out on the spree somewhere. He came home at daybreak, drunk, and went out again after about ten minutes; but I did not see him at all, and went to work alone.' I then returned home," said Dooshkin, "having learned all that could be learned. Next morning, at about eight o'clock, Nikola appeared in my place, very unsteady, though not very much in drink, and capable of conversation. He sat down in silence on a bench. At this time we had few people in – a stranger, another man asleep, and my two boys. I asked, 'Have you seen Dmitri?' 'No,' said he. 'Where have you passed the night?' 'On a barge.' 'And where,' said I, 'did you find the ear-rings?' 'In the street.' He said this in a very fidgety manner. 'Do you not know what has happened in that house?' 'No, but I have heard something,' he replied, turning the colour of copper. I looked straight at him, and he, taking hold of his cap, stood up to go. I wished to detain him, and said 'Stop a bit, Nikola, won't you take a glass?" I signed to the boy to shut the door, and came forward – only in time, however, to see him rush out, and when I got to the door he was out of sight. Of course, I supposed him guilty." '

'Naturally!' cried Zosimoff.

'Listen to the finish. Search is made everywhere for Nikola, and they detain Dooshkin, Dmitri also, and the barges are visited and all – when suddenly they drop upon him in a tavern near — Gate. He had come there, taken off the silver cross he wore, for which he wanted some brandy. A few minutes after, a woman, milking, caught sight of him through a chink in the cowshed, trying to hang himself with a rope. They laid hands on him, and he said: "Take me to the police-station, and I will make a full confession." This was his examination when he got there:

'Question: "How was it when you were working with Dmitri you did not see any persons on the stairs at such and such a time?" Answer: "Apparently they came, and we did not notice them!" "Did you hear no noise, or anything unusual?" "Nothing extraordinary!" "Was it not known to you the same day that at such a time a certain widow and her sister were murdered and robbed?" "I heard it first from Athanasius Paulitch two days afterwards in a beerhouse." "Where did you find the earrings?" "In the street." "Why, next day, did you not return to work with Dmitri?" "Because I took a holiday!" "Where?" "Here and there." "Why did you run away from Dooshkin?" "I was frightened!" "What of?" "The law." "How could you be frightened if you felt you had done no wrong?" Now, believe it or not, Zosimoff, but these questions were proposed in all seriousness. I know it for a fact. Fancy such a thing!'

'I suppose proofs exist.'

'I do not speak now of proofs, but of such questions, and those who put them. Well, never mind! They pressed and badgered him until at last he confessed. "Not in the street," he said, "but in the room where I was at work with Dmitri." "Under what circumstances?" "We were together all day until eight o'clock, and were preparing to go away, when Dmitri took hold of a brush and dabbed in my face some rose-coloured wash, then ran away, and I went after him downstairs into the court, and caught him near the gate. The porters were there with some gentlemen. They scolded us for creating an uproar, and so as did a gentleman who was passing with a lady. We were on the ground, and I had hold of Dmitri by the hair, and he was wrestling with me. It was not in temper, but simply in fun. At last Dmitri got away and ran off down the street. I tried to overtake him, but could not, and then returned back to the room where we had been working, in order to pack up our things and await Dmitri's return. I stood waiting in the room, when suddenly I saw the brush lying on the floor. I picked it up. It was on the floor near the door." '

'Near the door? Did he say near the door?' suddenly exclaimed Raskolnikoff, with an agitated glance at Razoumikhin as he slowly raised himself up from the sofa, and supported himself with his hands.

'Yes. What has that to do with you?' answered Razoumikhin, turning round.

'Nothing,' Raskolnikoff returned feebly, turning back again to the wall. There was silence for a few moments.

'He is half-asleep, I suppose,' at last Razoumikhin remarked interrogatively, glancing at Zosimoff, who returned a slight negative shake of the head.

'Well, go on,' said Zosimoff, 'what further?'

'What further? Only that he at once left the room, forgot all about Dmitri, and ran to Dooshkin, received the rouble, and went straight off on the spree. There's the whole story. What do you think is the net result of it all?'

'I suppose it is a clue.'

'So now they accuse the painter of the murders. They have no doubt –'

'Bah! You excite yourself too much. What about the ear-rings? I suppose you agree that they did come out of the old woman's box, and on that very day? That is of some consequence.'

'The idea! Doctor! You, above all, a man of discernment and reputation, who are acquainted with human nature, do you not see any further? Can you not understand that this is the true story, and that the ear-rings fell into his hands as he says?'

'But he owns that he lied at first.'

'Listen, listen carefully. The porter, Koch, Pestryakoff, the porter's wife, the lady and gentleman, in all eight or nine persons who were in the court, are all witnesses to the fact of Nikola's struggle with Dmitri on the ground, and which they were all watching with interest and amusement. Do you hear? If they, or only Nikola had murdered anyone, and then rifled the place, then I ask you only one question: You know the bodies when discovered were warm, so that the murders could not have been committed more than five or ten minutes before Nikola and Dmitri came running out into the streets; and I ask you, could they have come out and commenced their horseplay as they did, knowing that but a few moments would elapse before the deed would be discovered? There they were, playing like children, and ten persons were witnesses!'

'It is very strange, and it seems impossible, but – '

'There is no *but* in the case. Of course the ear-rings appearing so soon after in Nikola's hands constitute a fact against him; still it ought to be counterbalanced by those in his favour. Unfortunately, our magistrates have no idea of arguing these questions from a psychological point of view – they look at nothing but bare facts, and that exasperates me!'

'I see well enough you are annoyed. Was there any proof that the ear-rings did really belong to the old woman?'

'That was proved by Koch, who recognised the things, and said whom they belonged to; the owner has established his claim to them.'

'And did no one see Nikola at the time when Koch and Pestryakoff ascended the stairs, and can't an alibi be established?'

'No,' replied Razoumikhin rather sorrowfully, 'even Koch and Pestryakoff took no notice when they passed Nikola's room. They recollect that the door was open, but could not recollect whether any workmen were about or not.'

'Well, how do you explain all these facts? Can you account for the finding of the property – that is, if Nikola's tale is true?'

'Explain it? What is there to explain? The thing is self-evident. The ear-rings explain all. The actual murderer dropped them. The murderer was upstairs when Koch and his companion knocked, and he held the door. When Koch foolishly went away, the man slipped down after him, because he could do nothing else and there was no other outlet; on the stairs he heard the porter and Koch commencing the ascent, and he must have got into the empty room just at the moment when Nikola and Dmitri ran down into the street. Their fighting attracted the attention of everyone in the yard, and the murderer thus succeeded in getting away unperceived. The ear-rings dropped out of his pocket as he stood at the door. They clearly show he was there, and that's the whole mystery.'

'Very clever! No, my friend, you are too ingenious.'

'How so?'

'Because the plot is too well arranged and interwoven – quite theatrical in fact.'

'Bah!' cried Razoumikhin. But just at this moment the door opened, and there appeared upon the scene a face unknown to anyone in the room.

Chapter 5

THE INTRUDER WAS a man, apparently not very young, of affected manner and pompous carriage, with a close and snappish-looking countenance. He remained at the door looking around with an offensive and unconcealed expression of astonishment which seemed to ask: 'Where ever have I come to?' Mistrustfully and with an affected assumption of fear and doubt, the man took to examining Raskolnikoff's low and dark chamber until at last he fixed his eyes upon Raskolnikoff himself, who, undressed and unwashed, lay upon the miserable and dirty sofa, intently regarding the new-comer with a bold glance of inquiry. The tension of silence endured for several moments, until at last the gentleman softened his demeanour a little and, turning to Zosimoff, civilly, but stiffly, said, laying stress on each syllable:

'I wish to see Rodion Romanovitch Raskolnikoff, a student or ex-student – is he here?'

Zosimoff lazily turned, and possibly would have answered, had not Razoumikhin anticipated him. 'There he lies, on the couch. What is it you want?' This familiar 'What is it you want?' seemed to wound the visitor's dignity, and he almost looked round at the speaker, but recollected himself in time and turned pointedly to Zosimoff.

'There is Raskolnikoff,' said the latter, as he nodded his head in the direction of the bed, and began to yawn, opening his mouth to the utmost, and prolonging the liberty as long as possible. That over, he dragged his watch out of his pocket, opened it leisurely, and then in the same slow manner replaced it in his waistcoat.

Raskolnikoff himself lay all this time on his back, and stubbornly continued to eye the new-comer. His face was ghastly pale and expressed the deepest anxiety and trouble, as if he had just borne a most painful operation or had come from the rack. The new arrival at first awakened curiosity in him; then doubt, then almost fear. When Zosimoff, pointing to him, said: 'There is Raskolnikoff,' he quickly raised himself, indeed almost leaped up, and, in a broken and agitated voice, said: 'Yes, I am Raskolnikoff! What do you want?'

The visitor looked at him attentively, and replied: 'I am Peter Petrovitch Looshin. I have an idea that my name is not entirely unknown to you.'

But Raskolnikoff, who seemed to await something quite different, looked bluntly and vacantly at him, and gave him back no answer, as if he had just heard Looshin's name for the first time.

'How? Is it possible you have received no information about me?' asked Peter Petrovitch, a little put out. In reply, Raskolnikoff slowly let himself down on his pillow, placed his hands to his head, and fixed his eyes on the ceiling. Looshin's anger became very visible, and it was not decreased by his feeling that Zosimoff and Razoumikhin were attentively watching him. 'I supposed and reckoned,' he exclaimed, 'that the letter which was sent off at least ten days or a fortnight ago would – '

'One moment. Why do you stand at the door?' suddenly broke in Razoumikhin. 'If you have anything to communicate, sit down. Nastasia, stand aside. Over here! A tight fit. Here's a chair.'

The guest managed to step over Razoumikhin's legs, and, stumbling past, sat down upon a chair drawn from under the table.

'Do not be put out,' chuckled Razoumikhin. 'You see Rodia has been ill for the last five days, and for three he was delirious. He is better now, however, and is picking up a bit, and even eats with appetite. This is the doctor who attends him, and I am Rodia's friend and companion, who is now nursing him. I, too, am a student. And now, sir, will you in turn please say what is your business?'

'I thank you. Am I not perhaps disturbing your patient by my presence and conversation?' returned Peter Petrovitch to Zosimoff.

'No, no,' replied Zosimoff, 'it may possibly entertain him,' again yawning.

'Oh, he has quite recovered his reason since morning,' joined in Razoumikhin, whose familiarity Looshin apparently deeply resented.

'Your mamma,' commenced Looshin.

'Hum!' Razoumikhin ejaculated. Looshin looked at him questioningly. 'Nothing. Please go on.'

Peter Petrovitch shrugged his shoulders. 'Your mamma, whilst I was there, commenced writing an epistle to you. Since my arrival in St Petersburg I have purposely refrained from paying you a visit until the present moment, in order to allow you time to become acquainted with everything, but, to my great astonishment, I find – '

'I know, I know!' cried Raskolnikoff, in a tone of irritation. 'You are the bridegroom? Yes, I know all. That's enough!'

Peter Petrovitch grew pale with anger, but kept silence, only turning as if for an explanation. During the silence which followed this outburst, Raskolnikoff resumed his former occupation of staring his visitor in the face, this time very particularly, as if he had not had time to do so before, or had discovered some entirely new feature in the man; to obtain a better view, he even raised himself up from the couch. Really there seemed something in the appearance and manner of Peter Petrovitch to justify the appellation of 'bridegroom' which had been so unceremoniously thrown at him. There was no doubt, indeed it was very apparent, that Peter Petrovitch had spent the last few days in 'getting himself up' in expectation of his bride's arrival. His clothes were fresh from the tailor and very good, only they were too new, and therefore prominent. His little elegant round hat, also new, furthered the impression; Peter Petrovitch nursed it very affectionately, and carefully held it in his hands. The gloves, too, were a pair of grey kid of the very best make, which, however, he simply carried in his hand for appearance. The shades which Looshin affected were all light, the cut youthful. A very bright tie with pink stripes completed his attire. His face was very fair and even good-looking, and he certainly seemed younger than his age, forty-five. Dark mutton-chop whiskers very tastefully thickening towards his clean-shaven chin. His hair, scarcely flecked with grey, was curled, without giving him the comical or foolish appearance which very often happens. On the contrary, if there was really something unpleasant and repellent in his fair and grave face, it was due to other circumstances. After having gazed with scant ceremony into Looshin's face, Raskolnikoff gave a malicious smile, sank back on his pillow, and turned his eyes to the ceiling as before.

Looshin apparently decided to take no further notice of his peculiarities, and spoke thus: 'I am sorry, very sorry, that I find you in this condition, and if I had known of your illness I should have called sooner. But you can understand my worry. I have, besides, very serious and weighty business in the Senate, and I do not lose sight of other matters which you may guess. Your mother and sister I expect hourly '

Raskolnikoff turned and was about to say something. His face expressed some wish, and Peter Petrovitch stopped; no remark came, however, and he proceeded: 'Yes, hourly. I have found apartments for them.'

'Where?' asked Raskolnikoff feebly.

'Not very far from here. Bakalieff's house.'

'I know it,' Razoumikhin put in. 'It belongs to the merchant Eugène –'

'Yes.'

'Most horrible place – filthy and dirty – ah! and suspicious characters and deeds. The devil knows who does live there. I got there once under very scandalous circumstances. However, it is cheap.'

'I have not much knowledge of these places, being new to the city,' replied Peter Petrovitch touchily. 'I have found two very clean rooms, and it is but for a short time, till the house I have taken can be made ready. I am lodging, for the present, close by, at Madame Lippevechzel's, with a young friend of mine, Andreas Semenovitch Lebeziatnikoff. He told me of the place.'

'Lebeziatnikoff?' slowly repeated Raskolnikoff, as if the name recalled something to his mind.

'Yes, he is in a Government office. Do you know him?'

'Yes – no,' replied Raskolnikoff.

'Pardon my asking the question. I was at one time his guardian – a very dear young man with advanced ideas. I am always glad to meet young folks, one always learns what is new from them,' and Peter Petrovitch looked round benignantly.

'In what sense do you mean?' asked Razoumikhin.

'In the most serious sense,' replied Peter Petrovitch, evidently glad of the question. 'I, for example, have been ten years absent from St Petersburg; all these reforms, novelties and ideas penetrate, it is true, to the provinces; but to understand, know, and see everything, one must be in the capital, and, to my idea, you can never learn these things quicker than in the society of our young men. I own I am glad – I may be mistaken, but it seems to me there is found among them a clearer insight, a more critical spirit, and more acute reasoning.'

'This is all very true,' Zosimoff hastened to say.

'Is it not?' continued Peter Petrovitch, with a favourable glance at Zosimoff. 'And you agree with us' – (he was about to add 'young man') – 'that that is progress.' This to Razoumikhin.

'Very commonplace!'

'Not so, sir. If, for example, they said to me, "Love thy neighbour," and I did so, what would be the result? It would simply amount to this, that I tear my coat in halves, and give one to my neighbour; we should thus be half-naked, and, according to the Russian saying, "He who hunts several hares at the same time returns with none." But science says, "Love thyself above all, because everything in the world is founded on self-interest. Follow this, and thou maintainest thy garment intact." Economic truth adds that the more society is organised on this theory – the theory of whole coats – the more solid and permanent are its foundations, and the more established are its personal affairs. By following this principle, I find I attain everything; and, as for the naked, I see that they ultimately receive more than the half-coat, not as the outcome of charity and exceptional liberality, but of the effects of common progress.'

'Pardon me, I am very stupid,' said Razoumikhin warmly, 'and there I leave you. I had some aim in my remarks, but all this chatter of self-diversion and interminable commonplaces I blush to listen to. You have hastened to place yourself before us with all your knowledge; it is pardonable, and I will not condemn it. I only wished to find out one thing – what sort of man you are! Enough!'

'My dear sir,' commenced Mr Looshin, bending with tearful dignity, 'you do not mean so unceremoniously that I –'

'Don't I? There! That will do!' cried Razoumikhin, as he turned brusquely to Zosimoff.

Peter Petrovitch wisely decided to go, after this. 'I trust that our acquaintance, upon your recovery,' said he to Raskolnikoff, 'and in view of the special circumstances of our relations, will very much increase. Particularly let me wish you a speedy return to health.'

Raskolnikoff did not reply, and Looshin now rose from his chair.

'She must have been killed by one of her debtors,' Zosimoff was saying.

'Oh, quite certain. Porphyrius has not given me his opinion,' replied the student, 'but he is examining the pawners.'

'The pawners?' asked Raskolnikoff suddenly.

'Yes! What then?'

'Nothing!'

'How does he know them?' asked Zosimoff.

'Koch gave some names, others were written on the wrappings of pledges, and others came after their things.'

'How cunning and experienced the rascal must have been! Such boldness! Such resolution!'

'That is just what he was not,' cried Razoumikhin. 'This is what you all say! I believe, on the contrary, that it was neither a bold nor a daring deed, but decidedly a first step. If you consider, you will see how improbable is your idea. Chance alone brought him out of the scrape, and what does not chance do? He seems to have foreseen no obstacles, and how did he manage all? He obtains some ten or twenty roubles, fills his pockets with them; whilst hidden away everywhere – in old rags, drawers, trunks, and such-like – were afterwards found fifteen hundred roubles in hard cash, besides bank-notes. The man knew how to murder, but not to rob!'

'You are no doubt referring to the case of the murder of the two women,' joined in Peter Petrovitch, who was still standing there, with his hat and gloves in his hands, and desirous, before leaving, of letting off a few more words of wisdom. He apparently loved notice, and his vanity got the better of his good sense.

'Ah, you have heard of it?'

'Yes, in society – '

'Do you know the details?'

'I cannot say I do, but the case interests me from another point. I do not now speak of the great increase of crime during the last five years amongst the lower classes, nor of the unusual and incessant robberies and fires: – stranger than all to me is that there is to be found the same parallel increase in offences amongst the higher classes. Here, an ex-student pillages the post on the high road. There, men of the foremost rank are found to be forgers of notes – in Moscow, for instance, a whole company of forgers of the late lottery loan-tickets has been captured, at the head of which is a professor of world-wide celebrity; then our Foreign Secretary is mysteriously murdered – from pecuniary motives; and now this old woman is killed, not by moujiks, for they were not her customers, but by men of a superior class. How are we to explain this outbreak of the civilised portion of our community?'

'Economic changes,' said Zosimoff.

'How to explain it?' said Razoumikhin. 'Why, it's simply putting your theories into practice.'

'How, my theories?'

'Follow out your theories which you preach, to the end – and you say that people may cut throats – '

'Dear me!' cried Looshin.

'No, no! Not so!' cried Zosimoff.

Raskolnikoff lay there with quivering upper lip, breathing with difficulty and deadly pale.

'Economic ideas,' loudly cried Looshin, 'are not incentives to murder, and if it is simply proposed – '

'But is it the truth?' suddenly shouted Raskolnikoff, whose voice trembled in its malicious tone, and whose face expressed a wild sort of joy at giving offence. 'Is it true that you told your future bride, in the very house she accepted your hand, that you were all the more glad that she was a beggar, because it was wise to lift up a woman from indigence, so that you could the better have dominion over her, and did you not there and then remind her that she was beholden to you in this – eh?'

'Dear sir,' replied Looshin, irritated and blushing, 'dear sir, how words are distorted! Excuse me, but I must tell you that such reports which reach you, or better say, are told you, have not the slightest foundation, and I – I suspect who – in one word, your mamma – has told you this. She appeared to me to have, notwithstanding her superior character and nature, some very ecstatic and romantic ideas. Still, it was far from my belief that she could really entertain such distorted fancies, and give expression to them – and then – and then – '

'Do you know one thing?' cried Raskolnikoff, rising and looking at him with glistening eyes, 'do you know one thing?'

'What, sir?' Looshin stood and waited.

'This: that if ever again you dare to breathe one word against my mother, I will throw you head over heels downstairs!'

'What is the matter, Raskolnikoff?' cried Razoumikhin.

'That's it, is it?' Looshin turned pale and bit his lip. 'Hear me, sir,' he commenced after a pause, endeavouring to hide his emotion. 'I divined your unfriendliness from the very first, and therefore remained here expressly to learn more. I could have pardoned much in your sick condition, but now – you – never – '

'I am not ill,' cried Raskolnikoff.

'Then all the more – '

'Go to the devil!'

But Looshin was already gone. Razoumikhin stood up to allow him to pass, but he took no notice of anyone, and quitted the room in a manner expressive of the fearful affront he had received.

'Leave me! Leave me all!' shouted Raskolnikoff excitedly. 'Leave me! You torment me! I do not fear you! I fear no one now! Away from me! Let me be alone! Alone! Alone!'

'Let us go,' said Zosimoff.

'Very well – if we may leave him?'

'Come,' firmly replied Zosimoff, going out; and his companion followed. 'We must not irritate him.'

'What is the matter with him?' asked Razoumikhin, on the way downstairs.

'There is something on his mind, something not at all apparent, which weighs heavily on him, I fear.'

'Then what does this Peter Petrovitch mean? Evidently he is to marry his sister, and Raskolnikoff had received a letter about it before his illness.'

'Yes, worse luck! and that may have brought on the whole affair. You remarked that he was indifferent to everything discussed except one point which brought him out – I mean the murder.'

'Yes, yes,' said Razoumikhin, 'it struck me, it seemed to interest him – startle him. It had the like effect upon him in the office, when he fainted.'

'We will speak further of it this evening. It interests me deeply, and I may have something to tell you then. I will return to inquire after him in half an hour; meanwhile we will adjourn the subject.'

'All right; thanks! I am going to see Pashenka, and will get Nastasia to watch him.'

Raskolnikoff looked up with impatience at Nastasia, who had been in the room all the time, and was even now loth to go.

'Will you drink your tea now?' she asked.

'By and by. I wish to sleep. Go away!' He turned abruptly to the wall; and Nastasia left him.

Chapter 6

HARDLY HAD NASTASIA left the room when Raskolnikoff jumped up, and, after bolting the door, proceeded to clothe himself from the bundle left by Razoumikhin. How strange! He felt a delicious calm in his mind; not a trace of fever or delirium; no feelings of terror, as he had felt. It was a moment of strange and unexpected tranquillity. His ideas were precise and clear, and seemed pregnant with resolution. 'Today! Today!' he murmured to himself. He recollected, however, that he was still weak, but he trusted to his newly-found indomitable will and self-confidence to sustain him in the street. He was now fully dressed in entirely new clothes, and stood up ready to go. His eye fell upon the money upon the table – the twenty-five roubles – and this he put in his pocket, together with the change left by Razoumikhin. Quickly undoing the bolt, he passed down the stairs and gained the street unobserved, although Nastasia was in the kitchen at her work.

It was eight o'clock, and the sun had disappeared. The heat was as intolerable as before, but he inhaled the dusty, fetid, infected town-air with greediness. And now his head began to spin round, and a wild expression of energy crept into his inflamed eyes and pale, meagre, wan face. He did not know, did not even think, what he was going to do; he only knew that all was to be finished 'today,' at one blow, immediately, or he would never return home, because he had no desire to live thus. How to finish? By what means? No matter how, and he did not want to think. He drove away all thoughts which disturbed him, and only clung to the necessity of ending all, 'no matter how,' said he, with desperate self-confidence and decision. By force of habit he took his old walk, and set out in the direction of the Haymarket. Farther on he came on a young man who was grinding some sentimental ballads upon a barrel-organ. Near the man, on the footpath, was a young girl of about fifteen years of age, fashionably dressed, with crinoline, mantle, and gloves, and a straw hat trimmed with gaudy feathers, but all old and terribly worn out, who, in a loud and cracked, though not altogether unpleasing, voice, was singing before a shop in expectation of a couple of kopecks. Raskolnikoff stopped and joined one or two listeners, took out a five-kopeck-piece, and gave it to the girl. The latter at once stopped on a very high note which she had just reached, and cried to the man, 'Come along,' and both immediately moved on to another place.

'Do you like street-music?' said Raskolnikoff to a middle-aged man standing near him. The latter looked at him in surprise, but smiled. 'I love it,' continued Raskolnikoff, 'especially when they sing to the organ on a cold, dark, grey winter's evening, when all the passers-by seem to have pale, green, sickly-looking faces – when the snow is falling like sleet, straight down and with no wind, you know, and while the lamps shine on it all.'

'I don't know. Excuse me,' said the man, frightened at the question and Raskolnikoff's strange appearance, and hastily withdrawing to the other side of the street.

Raskolnikoff went on, and came to the place in the Haymarket where he had met the trader and his wife and Elizabeth. No one was there at the moment. He stopped, and turned to a young fellow in a red shirt, who stood gaping at the entrance to a flour-shop.

'A man trades here at this corner, with his wife, eh?'

'Everyone trades here,' replied the lad, scanning his questioner from head to foot.

'What is he called?'

'What he was christened.'

'But you belong to Zaraisk, don't you? To what Government?'

The boy stared at Raskolnikoff. 'We have no governor, your highness, but districts. I stay at home, and know nothing about it, but my brother does; so pardon me, your most mighty highness.'

'Is that an eating-house there?'

'That's a dram-shop; they have a billiard-table. You will find plenty of princesses.'

Raskolnikoff went across the market to another corner, where there was a crowd of people, all moujiks. He would have liked to speak to them, but they took no notice of him. So, after standing thinking a few moments, he turned to the right, in the direction of V—. Avoiding the market, he now found himself in — Lane. In former times he had often sauntered down here, thinking deeply, but now he thought of nothing. There stood the large house, a drinking and eating establishment, from which, every minute, gaily-dressed women issued bareheaded. In two or three places they crowded on the path in groups, especially near where the entrance to the lower storey was, whence came the sound of singing and twanging of guitars. Women were everywhere, chattering and shouting. Some were squatting on the pathway. Here a soldier was strolling about, smoking a cigarette, drunk, spluttering oaths, and who appeared desirous of going somewhere, but had forgotten where; while scattered about were the drunk and half-drunk, rolling across the street. Raskolnikoff stopped to look at the women. All were clothed in cotton, wore goatskin shoes, and went bareheaded. Some were about forty, others barely seventeen, but almost all had disfigured faces and blackened eyes. 'Give me something to drink,' said one, and Raskolnikoff put three five-kopeck pieces in her hand, and, passing by, stopped and began to think.

'Where was it?' said he to himself. 'Where was it that I read of a condemned man who, at the hour of death, says or thinks that if the alternative were offered him of existing somewhere, on a height of rock or some narrow elevation, where only his two feet could stand, and round about him the ocean, perpetual gloom, perpetual solitude, perpetual storm, to remain there standing on a yard of surface for a lifetime, a thousand years, eternity! – rather would he live thus than die at once? Only live, live, live! – no matter how, only live! How true is this! Oh, Lord, how true! Oh, miserable race of men! – and miserable he, too, who on this account calls himself miserable!' he added, after a pause.

He went into another street. 'Ah, the Crystal Palace! Razoumikhin spoke of the Crystal Palace. What do I want? Ah! Yes! To read! Zosimoff said he had read in the papers – '

'There are newspapers here?' asked he, as he entered a room – one of a suite – rather empty. Two or three persons sat with tea before them, whilst in a farther room a group of men were seated, drinking champagne. Raskolnikoff thought he recognised Zametoff amongst them, but he could not be sure. 'Never mind, if it is!' he muttered.

'Brandy, sir?' asked the waiter.

'No, tea; and bring me some newspapers – for about the last five days. I'll give you a drink.'

The papers and the tea appeared. Raskolnikoff sat and searched, and, at last, found what he wanted. 'Ah, here it is!' he cried, as he began to read. The words danced before his eyes, but he read greedily to the end, and turned to others for later intelligence. His hands trembled with impatience, and the sheets shook again. Suddenly someone sat down near him. He looked up, and there was Zametoff – that same Zametoff, with his rings and chain, his oiled locks and fancy waistcoat and unclean linen. He seemed pleased, and his tanned face, a little inflamed by the champagne, wore a smile.

'Ah! You here?' he commenced, in a tone as if he had known Raskolnikoff for an age. 'Why, Razoumikhin told me yesterday that you were lying unconscious. How strange! Then I was at your place –'

Raskolnikoff laid down the paper and turned to Zametoff. On his lips was a slight provoking smile. 'I know you were,' he replied, 'I heard so. You searched for my boot. To what agreeable places you resort! Who gives you champagne to drink?'

'We were drinking together. What do you mean?'

'Nothing, dear boy, nothing,' said Raskolnikoff, with a smile and slapping Zametoff on the shoulders. 'I am not in earnest, but simply in fun, as your workman said, when he wrestled with Dmitri, you know, in that murder case.'

'Do you know about that?'

'Yes, and perhaps more than you do.'

'You are very peculiar. It is a pity you came out. You are ill.'

'Do I seem strange?'

'Yes; what are you reading?'

'The paper.'

'There are a number of fires.'

'I am not reading about them.' He looked curiously at Zametoff, and a malicious smile distorted his lips. 'No, fires are not in my line,' he added, winking at Zametoff. 'Now, I should like to know, sweet youth, what it signifies to you what I read?'

'Nothing at all. I only asked. Perhaps I –'

'Listen. You are a cultivated man – a literary man, are you not?'

'I was in the sixth class at college,' Zametoff answered, with a certain amount of dignity.

'The sixth! Oh, my fine fellow! With rings and a chain – a rich man! You are a dear boy,' and Raskolnikoff gave a short, nervous laugh, right in the face of Zametoff. The latter was very much taken aback, and, if not offended, seemed a good deal surprised.

'How strange you are!' said Zametoff seriously. 'You have the fever still on you; you are raving!'

'Am I, my fine fellow – am I strange? Yes, but I am very interesting to you, am I not?'

'Interesting?'

'Yes. You ask me what I am reading, what I am looking for; then I am looking through a number of papers. Suspicious, isn't it? Well, I will explain to you, or rather confess – no, not that exactly. I will give testimony, and you shall take it down – that's it. So then, I swear that I was reading, and came here on purpose' – Raskolnikoff blinked his eyes and paused – 'to read an account of the murder of the old woman.' He finished almost in a whisper, eagerly watching Zametoff's face. The latter returned his glances without flinching. And it appeared strange to Zametoff that a full minute seemed to pass as they kept fixedly staring at each other in this manner.

'Oh, so that's what you have been reading?' Zametoff at last cried impatiently. 'What is there in that?'

'She is the same woman,' continued Raskolnikoff, still in a whisper, and taking no notice of Zametoff's remark, 'the very same woman you were talking about when I swooned in your office. You recollect – you surely recollect?'

'Recollect what?' said Zametoff, almost alarmed

The serious expression on Raskolnikoff's face altered in an instant, and he again commenced his nervous laugh, and laughed as if he were quite unable to contain himself. There had recurred to his mind, with fearful clearness, the moment when he stood at the door with the hatchet in his hand. There he was, holding the bolt, and they were tugging and thumping away at the door. Oh, how he itched to shriek at them, open the door thrust out his tongue at them, and frighten them away, and then laugh, 'Ah, ah, ah, ah!'

'You are insane, or else – ' said Zametoff, and then paused as if a new thought had suddenly struck him.

'Or what, or what? Now what? Tell me!'

'Nonsense!' said Zametoff to himself, 'it can't be.' Both became silent. After this unexpected and fitful outburst of laughter, Raskolnikoff had become lost in thought and looked very sad. He leaned on the table with his elbows, buried his head in his hands, and seemed to have quite forgotten Zametoff. The silence continued a long time. 'You do not drink your tea; it is getting cold,' said the latter, at last.

'What? Tea? Yes!' Raskolnikoff snatched at his glass, put a piece of bread in his mouth, and then, after looking at Zametoff, seemingly recollected and roused himself. His face at once resumed its previous smile, and he continued to sip his tea.

'What a number of rogues there are about,' said Zametoff. 'I read not long ago, in the Moscow papers, that they had captured a whole gang of forgers in that city. Quite a colony.'

'That's old news. I read it a month ago,' replied Raskolnikoff in a careless manner. 'And you call such as these rogues?' he added, smiling. 'Why not?'

'Rogues indeed! Why, they are only children and babies. Fifty banded together for such purposes! Is it possible? Three would be quite sufficient, and then they should be sure of one another – not babble over their cups. The babies! Then to hire unreliable people to change the notes at the money-changers', persons whose hands tremble as they receive the roubles. On such their lives depend! Far better to strangle yourself! The man goes in, receives the change, counts some over, the last portion he takes on faith, stuffs all in his pocket, rushes away and the murder is out. All is lost by one foolish man. Is it not ridiculous?'

'That his hands should shake?' replied Zametoff. 'No; that is quite likely. Yours would not, I suppose? I could not endure it, though. For a paltry reward of a hundred roubles to go on such a mission! And where? Into a banker's office with forged notes! I should certainly lose my head. Would not you?'

Raskolnikoff felt again a strong impulse to make a face at him. A shiver ran down his back. 'You would not catch me acting so foolishly,' he commenced. 'This is how I should do. I should count over the first thousand very carefully, perhaps four times, right to the end, carefully examine each note, and then only pass to the second thousand, count these as far as the middle of the bundle, take out a note, hold it to the light, turn it over, then hold it to the light again, and say, "I fear this is a bad note," and then begin to relate some story about a lost note. Then there would be a third thousand to count. "Not yet, please, there is a mistake in the second thousand. No, it is correct." And so I should proceed until I had received all. At last I should turn to go, open the door, – but no, pardon me! I should return, ask some question, receive some explanation, and there it is all done.'

'What funny things you do say!' said Zametoff with a smile. 'You are all very well theoretically, but try it and see. Look, for example, at the murder of the money-lender, a case in point. There was a desperate villain who in broad daylight stopped at nothing, and yet his hand shook, did it not? – and he could not finish, and left all the spoil behind him. The deed evidently robbed him of his presence of mind.'

This language nettled Raskolnikoff. 'You think so? Then lay your hand upon him,' said he, maliciously delighted to tease him.

'Never fear but we shall!'

'You? Go to, you know nothing about it. All you think of inquiring is whether a man is flinging money about; he is – then, *ergo*, he is guilty.'

'That is exactly what they do,' replied Zametoff, 'they murder, risk their lives, and then rush to the public-house and are caught. Their lavishness betrays them. You see they are not all so crafty as you are. You would not run there, I suppose?'

Raskolnikoff frowned and looked steadily at Zametoff. 'You seem anxious to know how I should act,' he said with some displeasure.

'I should very much like to know,' replied Zametoff in a serious tone. He seemed, indeed, very anxious.

'Very much?'

'Very much.'

'Good. This would be my plan,' Raskolnikoff said, as he again bent near to the face of his listener, and speaking in such a tragic whisper as almost to make the latter shudder. 'I should take the money and all I could find, and make off, going, however, in no particular direction, but on and on until I came to some obscure and enclosed place, where no one was about – a market-garden, or any such-like spot. I should then look about me for a stone, perhaps a pound and a half in weight, lying, it may be, in a corner against a partition, say a stone used for building purposes; this I should lift up, and under it there would be a hole. In that hole I should deposit all the things I had got, roll back the stone, stamp it down with my feet, and be off. For a year I should let them lie – for two years, three years. Now then, search for them! Where are they?'

'You are indeed mad,' said Zametoff, also in a low tone, but turning away from Raskolnikoff. The latter's eyes glistened, he became paler than ever, whilst his upper lip trembled violently. He placed his face closer, if possible, to that of Zametoff, his lips moving as if he wished to speak, but no words escaped them – several moments elapsed – Raskolnikoff knew what he was doing, but felt utterly unable to control himself, that strange impulse was upon him as when he stood at the bolted door, to come forth and let all be known.

'What if I killed the old woman and Elizabeth?' he asked suddenly, and then – came to himself.

Zametoff turned quite pale; then his face changed to a smile. 'Can it be so?' he muttered to himself.

Raskolnikoff eyed him savagely. 'Speak out. What do you think? Yes? Is it so?'

'Of course not. I believe it now less than ever,' replied Zametoff hastily.

'Caught at last! Caught, my fine fellow! What people believe less than ever, they must have believed once, eh?'

'Not at all. You frightened me into the supposition,' said Zametoff, visibly confused.

'So you do not think this? Then why those questions in the office? Why did the lieutenant question me after my swoon? Waiter,' he cried, seizing his cap, 'here, how much?'

'Thirty kopecks, sir,' replied the man.

'There you are, and twenty for yourself. Look, what a lot of money!' turning to Zametoff and thrusting forth his shaking hand filled with twenty-five roubles, red and blue notes. 'Whence comes all this? Where did I obtain these new clothes from? You know I had none. You have asked the landlady, I suppose? Well, no matter! – Enough! Adieu, most affectionately.'

He went out, shaking from some savage hysterical emotion, a mixture of delight, gloom, and weariness. His face was drawn as if he had just recovered from a fit; and, as his agitation of mind increased, so did his weakness.

Meanwhile, Zametoff remained in the restaurant where Raskolnikoff had left him, deeply buried in thought, considering the different points Raskolnikoff had placed before him. 'Elia Petrovitch is a fool!' he said at last to himself.

Just as Raskolnikoff opened the street-door, he found himself face to face with Razoumikhin, who was coming up the steps. They both took another step before they recognised each other, so that their heads almost met; Razoumikhin's face expressed the greatest astonishment, and he cried in a great passion: 'What the devil are you doing here? You should be in your bed. I have been seeking you. Rodia, what does it all mean? Explain yourself, do you hear?'

'I was tired of you all, you wearied me to death. I wish to be alone,' replied Raskolnikoff calmly.

'Alone! When you can hardly move, and your face is like a sheet, and you have hardly any breath in your body? What were you doing in the Crystal Palace? Tell me instantly!'

'Get away!' Raskolnikoff said, and tried to push past and get free. This exasperated Razoumikhin, and he seized Raskolnikoff firmly by the shoulders.

'What! you dare to say "get away" to me? I tell you what I will do with you, I'll take you round the waist, wrap you up in a bundle, and run home with you, and lock you in; that's what I'll do.'

'Hear me,' Raskolnikoff commenced in an apparently calm tone. 'Is it possible you do not see that I do not want your kindness? And what is the use of wishing to do kindnesses to those who return them by – by spitting at them? Why did you search me out at the beginning of my illness, when I perhaps was only too glad to die? I have shown you today that you torment me, weary me, and all this retards my recovery very seriously, because it irritates me. Zosimoff went away and left me for this reason, and, for God's sake, you do the same! What right have you to restrain me by force? You see I speak in sober sense, do I not? Leave me alone then, and cease your kindness. I may be ungrateful, I may be base, only let me be. For God's sake, do so! Go! Go! Go!'

He commenced collectedly and carefully, avoiding giving offence, although this was ready to burst forth, and ended in heat and with a long-drawn breath, as in his scene with Looshin. Razoumikhin stood a little while in thought, and then withdrew his hands. 'Well, then, go!' he said, and Raskolnikoff went past him. 'Stop!' he roared after him. 'Listen! Take yourself off with your babble and fancies, and sit on your troubles as a hen on her eggs. There is no sign of life within you. You are made of oil, and have not a drop of blood in your veins. I believe not in such as you. Stop, I say, and hear to the end,' he cried with redoubled rage, as he saw Raskolnikoff turn to go. 'You know I have a gathering at my new place today. They are probably arriving now. I left my uncle there, and I must run back. Look here, if you were not such a fool, such a confounded fool, an infernal fool with strangers – you see I recognise your cleverness, but you are a fool, or else if you were not, you would come and join us, instead of wearing out your boots. Will you make one of us? Zosimoff will be there. Come!'

'No.'

'Nonsense!' impatiently cried Razoumikhin. 'I tell you what it is. You can't answer for yourself, and are not accountable for your actions. I'll be bound you will forget all about this, and come. Don't forget the address, Potchinkoff's, third floor.'

'I shall not come, Razoumikhin,' said Raskolnikoff, and turned away again.

'I bet you do!' cried Razoumikhin after him. 'If not, I don't wish to know you! Is Zametoff in here?'

'Yes.'

'Seen him?'

'Yes.'

'Spoken to him?'

'Yes.'

'What about? Why don't you speak? Never mind! Remember, Potchinkoff's house – 47, Babooshkin's!'

Raskolnikoff had now turned the corner, and Razoumikhin stood for a moment thinking. At last he shook his head, and turned to enter the house, but paused half-way up the steps. 'Curse it!' he said, under his breath, 'he speaks sensibly enough as if – I am a fool! All lunatics have their lucid moments. What is he after now, I wonder? Perhaps he means to drown himself, and I am to blame.' He ran down the steps, intending to follow Raskolnikoff, but no trace was to be seen of him, and Razoumikhin returned to the Crystal Palace in order to question Zametoff.

Raskolnikoff made straight for the — Bridge, and, stopping in the middle, leaned over the side and gazed abstractedly at the scene before him. He felt almost too weak to stand there, and would have been grateful to lie down in the road or anywhere. Inclining over the water, he mechanically looked at the last rosy reflection of the setting sun. at the rows of houses which were darkening in the gathering twilight, and at a window afar off, which, catching the sun's last rays, sent a stream of flame into the dark waters of the canal. Now his head became giddy, his eyes saw blood, and everything – houses, passers-by, carriages – went round and round. Suddenly he shivered violently, thereby perhaps saving himself from another swoon. He became aware that somebody stood near him, almost by his side, and he turned to see a girl with a shawl over her head, a tall girl with a yellow drawn face and red sunken eyes. She looked straight at him, but really through him, as if her eyes distinguished nothing, and then, in a moment, mounted the railings and threw herself into the water. The dirty water rose and swallowed up its victim, but the drowning woman came directly to the surface, and the current carried her silently along, her head and feet under water, and her clothes floating on the surface.

'A boat! A boat!' a dozen voices cried, and a crowd began to collect.

'Oh, save her! It is my Afrosinka!' shrieked a woman's voice, not far off. 'Save her! Pull her out!'

'A boat! A boat!' they continued to shout.

But a boat was not necessary, for a policeman, running down some steps, succeeded in drawing her out, and, with the assistance of a comrade, placed her upon the granite steps. There she speedily came to her senses, and sat up, rubbed her eyes, sneezed, and looked very stupid. She said nothing. Raskolnikoff looked quietly on, but the sight was extremely repulsive to him. The police busied themselves with the woman, and someone mentioned the police-station.

'No! Not water!' Raskolnikoff murmured to himself. 'What about the office? Why is not Zametoff there now? He ought to be at ten o'clock.' He turned round and looked about him, and then moved off in the direction of the district office. His heart was empty and depressed, and he strove again to drive off thought. No feeling of anguish came, neither was there any trace of that fierce energy which moved him when he left the house to 'put an end to it all.'

'What will be the end of it? The result lies in my own will. What kind of end? Ah, we are all alike, and accept the bit of ground for our feet and live. Must this be the end? Shall I say the word or not? Oh, how weary I feel! Oh, to lie down or sit anywhere! How foolish it is to strive against my illness! Bah! What thoughts run through my brain!"

Thus he meditated as he went listlessly along the banks of the canal, until, turning to the right and then to the left, he reached the office building. He stopped short, however, and, turning down a lane, went on past two other streets, with no fixed purpose, simply, no doubt, to give himself a few moments longer for reflection. He went on, his eyes fixed on the ground, until all of a sudden he started, as if someone had whispered in his ear. Raising his eyes he saw that he stood before *the house*, at its very gates.

Quick as lightning, an idea rushed into his head, and he marched through the yard and made his way up the well-known staircase to the fourth storey. It was, as usual, very dark, and as he reached each landing he peered almost with caution. There was the room newly-painted, where Dmitri and Nikola had worked. He reached the fourth landing and paused before the murdered woman's room in doubt. The door was wide open and he could hear voices within; this he had not anticipated. However, after wavering a little, he went straight in. The room was being done up, and in it were some workmen. This astonished him – indeed, it would seem he had expected to find everything as he had left it, even to the dead bodies lying on the floor. But to see the place with bare walls and bereft of furniture was very strange! He walked up to the window and sat on the sill.

There were only two workmen – young fellows – who were engaged in papering the walls, hiding the former green with a white paper, covered with tiny lilac-flowers. Raskolnikoff looked upon the alteration with great displeasure, and, crossing his hands, continued leaning against the window. His presence seemingly did not attract their attention; and after a few words they began to make preparations for leaving off their work. Raskolnikoff, after a few moments, passed into the other room, where the bed and the chest of drawers had once stood. The room seemed very small, and the paper upon the wall strongly marked the place where the image used to stand. One of the workmen now saw him, and cried:

'What do you want here?'

Instead of replying, Raskolnikoff walked to the outer door and, standing outside, began to pull at the bell. Yes, that was the bell, with its harsh sound. He pulled again and again, three times, and remained there listening and thinking.

'What is it you want?' again cried the workman as he went out to Raskolnikoff.

'I wish to hire some rooms. I came to look at these.'

'People don't take lodgings in the night. Why don't you apply to the porter?'

'The floor has been washed. Are you going to paint it?' remarked Raskolnikoff. 'Where is the blood?'

'What blood?'

'The old woman's and her sister's. There was quite a pool.'

'Who are you?' cried the workman uneasily.

'I?'

'Yes.'

'Do you want to know? Come to the porter. I will let you know.'

'Very well, let us go; we have finished. Are you ready, Aleshka?'

'Come, then,' said Raskolnikoff indifferently, and he went before them downstairs. 'Porter!' he shouted as he reached the ground floor.

Some people were standing near the entrance watching the passers-by, and amongst others were the two porters.

'What is it?' one of the porters shouted.

Raskolnikoff did not reply, and stood apart lost in thought.

'He came to look at the rooms,' said the workman.

'Which rooms?'

'Where we are working. "Why," he asked us, "did you wash the blood away?" Then he said there had been a murder, and he had come to take the place. He began pulling at the bell, and told us to come with him here, and he would explain himself. He insisted.'

'Who are you?' asked the porter impatiently.

'I am Rodion Romanovitch Raskolnikoff, ex-student. I live at Schill's house, in a lane not far from here, No. 14. Ask the porter there – he knows me,' Raskolnikoff replied indifferently, without turning to his questioner, and gazing down the darkening street.

'What were you doing in those rooms?'

'Looking at them.'

'What for? Come, out you go, then, if you won't explain yourself,' suddenly shouted the other porter, a huge fellow in a smock-frock, with a large bunch of keys round his waist; and he caught Raskolnikoff by the shoulder and pitched him into the street. The latter lurched forward, but recovered himself and, giving one look at the spectators, went quietly away.

'What shall I do now?' thought Raskolnikoff. He was standing on the bridge, near a crossing, and was looking around him as if expecting someone to speak. But no one spoke, and all was dark and dull, and dead as a stone – at least to him, and him alone. Suddenly, about two hundred steps from him, at the end of a street, a sound of voices was heard, and a crowd began to gather. In the middle of the road he could discern a carriage, at a standstill, and round about gleamed a number of lights. What was the matter? Raskolnikoff went up to the crowd. He seemed to wish to take interest in the least incident, and smiled coldly as he thought that now it really was decided, he would give himself up, and that all would soon be at an end.

Chapter 7

IN THE MIDDLE of the street stood a carriage, to which were harnessed a pair of fiery grey horses; it was empty, the coachman had descended to hold the horses' heads. The police were there, and a number of people crowded round. One held a lantern, the rays of which were directed on some object lying in the road, at the very wheels of the carriage; everyone had something to say, and, over all the confusion, could be heard the coachman endeavouring to exculpate himself. Raskolnikoff pushed his way through the crowd, and managed to obtain, at last, a glance at the cause of the commotion. On the ground a man lay insensible, with blood streaming from his face on to his shabby-genteel clothes. He had been trampled under the horses' feet, his face appeared literally beaten in; evidently it was no laughing matter.

'I was driving carefully enough,' exclaimed the coachman, 'but the drunken man did not see my light. I saw him crossing the street, and, just as he neared the horses, he began to reel about. I shouted, but it was too late; he fell before the horses. I pulled up at once, but the horses are young and shy, and they trampled upon him. That's how it happened.'

One or two out of the crowd shouted: 'Quite right, we saw it all!' The coachman was not so very low-spirited or frightened, and it was evident the carriage belonged to some rich and distinguished personage, who was awaiting its arrival somewhere. The police acted accordingly, and prepared to carry the injured man to the hospital; no one knew his name.

Meanwhile, Raskolnikoff had pushed still nearer, and just then the light from the lantern shone on the face of the unfortunate man. He recognised him.

'I know him! I know him!' he cried, pushing right in front. 'It is the former Titular Councillor Marmeladoff; he lives just at hand, at Kotzel's. A doctor, quick, I will pay!' He drew forth money, and showed it to the police. Raskolnikoff betrayed great agitation, but the police seemed satisfied that they knew who the injured man was. Raskolnikoff gave further his own name and address, and urged the men to hasten with Marmeladoff to his home. 'There it is, only three houses off,' he shouted, 'Kotzel's, the rich German's. I know him well. He is a drunkard, and has a wife and children, and one daughter besides. Let him be taken home, and not to the hospital; there is a doctor in the same house, and I will pay.'

Helpers were soon found; they raised the man and bore him away. The house was hardly thirty paces off, and, going on in front and supporting the head, Raskolnikoff led the way.

'Here it is, here! Carry him up head forwards. I will pay. I thank you all,' he said.

Catherine Ivanovna, as usual, was feeling ill, and was walking to and fro, with her hands pressed to her forehead, muttering to herself, and constantly coughing. Occasionally she would stop to speak to her eldest daughter, the ten-year-old Polenka, who kept her great wise eyes fixed upon her, although engaged at the time in undressing her little brother, who had been unwell all the day, in order to put him to bed. The still younger sister stood near, waiting for her turn to be relieved of her rags. The outer door was closed, in order to keep out the tobacco smoke rising from the floor below, which aggravated the cough of the poor consumptive woman. Catherine Ivanovna, it appeared, had been in worse health this week; the red spot on her cheek burned more brightly than ever.

'You cannot think, you cannot even imagine, Polenka,' said she, as she continued her march, 'the style in which we lived at papa's, and how happy we were, until this drunkard brought me and all of you children to ruin. Papa was a Colonel and almost the Governor, there was only one step higher for him; and everybody used to say to him, "We already look upon you, Ivan Michailitch, as our Governor," when I – when I – oh! wretched life!' – she clutched at her throat to ease a fit of coughing – 'when I appeared at the ball at the Commander's. Princess Bezzemelnaya asked as I passed with your father, Polya: "Is that the noble girl who danced with a shawl at the commencement of the holidays?" – You must sew that hole up; see to it at once and darn it, as I taught you. – My cough! Oh dear! It will tear me to pieces! – And then it was that Prince Tschegolsky, who had just arrived from St Petersburg, asked me to dance a mazurka with him; the very next day he wished to make proposals for me, but I thanked him in flattering terms and told him my heart was given to another. That other was your father, child. My father was fearfully angered about it! – Is the water ready? Give me the shirt and stockings, Leda' (turning to the young child). 'I must wash your things, too, tonight. – God! What is that? Again! What is the matter?' she cried, as she saw the door open, and people pressing forward with some burden.

'What is it? What are you bringing here? O heavens!'

'Where shall we lay him?' asked a policeman, as he looked round.

'On the sofa, there, place his head so,' said Raskolnikoff.

'Run over in the street, drunk,' shouted someone from the landing.

Catherine Ivanovna stood erect, deadly pale, and breathing with difficulty. The children were frightened, and little Leda gave a scream, and ran to Polya and clutched at her dress, trembling the while. Having seen Marmeladoff properly laid down, Raskolnikoff now turned to the wife.

'For Heaven's sake, be calm, do not be alarmed!' said he quickly. 'He was crossing a street and was knocked down by a carriage. Do not distress yourself – he will come to. I ordered him to be brought here. You know me. I was here once, you recollect? He will recover, I will pay!'

'He will never recover,' she cried despairingly, as she ran to her husband.

Raskolnikoff at once recognised that this woman was not one who succumb easily to faints and swoons. In an instant she had placed under his head a pillow which no one had noticed. She then loosened his clothes, although at the same time there was going on a hard struggle within. She did not lose herself, however, and kept back from her trembling lips the cry ready to burst from her choking throat.

Raskolnikoff had persuaded someone to run for the doctor, who, it appeared, lived in the building. 'I have sent for a doctor, do not trouble, I am going to pay,' said he to Catherine Ivanovna. 'Is there no water? Give me a towel at once, or anything; he is hurt, but not killed, be assured of that. Well, we shall hear what the doctor says.'

Catherine Ivanovna ran to the window, where, on a table in a corner, stood a large pan filled with water ready for the night's washing of her children's and husband's linen. This was done at least twice a week by the wife herself, and the only time when the things were available for the tub was when the owners were asleep. Catherine Ivanovna was particularly clean, and willingly made this sacrifice of her rest rather than endure uncleanliness as well as rags. She seized the pan, but stumbled and almost fell with the burden. Raskolnikoff had found a towel, and, having dipped it in the water, he set himself to wash the blood-stains off Marmeladoff's face. Catherine Ivanovna stood near, with pain depicted on her face and her hand to her throat. She looked as if she also needed help. Raskolnikoff began to reflect that he had perhaps done no wise act in ordering the wounded man to be brought home. The policeman stood in doubt.

'Polya!' cried Catherine Ivanovna, 'run quickly to Sonia. If she is not at home, say her father is run over, and that she is to come at once.'

During all this time the rooms kept filling with people, until there was not room for an apple to fall down. The police had all left, with the exception of one man, who tried to keep the crowd back. From every floor the occupants poured, and, after hesitating at the outer door, became bolder, and pressed right into the room itself. Catherine Ivanovna noted this and fired up.

'Do you wish to kill him?' she yelled at the crowd. 'What have you come here to look at? – with cigarettes too! He, he, he! – and hats on! Have you no respect for the dying? Away! Be off!'

A violent fit of coughing stopped her further speech, but her words were of avail. Catherine Ivanovna seemed to be rather feared – at any rate, the crowd began to fall back towards the door, having gratified that secret feeling of satisfaction at witnessing distress from which no man is free, though it may be accompanied by most sincere feelings of pity and commiseration. Someone in the crowd here made a suggestion to take the wounded man to the hospital, which Catherine Ivanovna no sooner heard than she rushed to the door to lecture the crowd again. Here she encountered Madame Lippevechzel, who, hearing of the accident, was making her way into the room in order to see how matters stood. She was an extremely choleric and disorderly German woman.

'Ach! Mein Gott!' – clasping her hands. 'Your drunken husband has been trampled upon by a horse; take him off to the hospital. I am the landlady!'

'Amalia Ludvigovna, I ask you to recollect what you are saying,' began Catherine Ivanovna haughtily. (She always addressed the landlady in this style, so that she should know 'her place,' and even now could not deny herself this pleasure.) 'Amalia Ludvigovna –'

'I have told you time after time not to dare to call me Amalia

Ludvigovna, but Amalia Ivanovna.'

'You are not Amalia Ivanovna, you are Amalia Ludvigovna. I am not one of your low flatterers, like Mr Lebeziatnikoff, who is grinning there at the door.' (This gentleman was really there, and saying, with a radiant face, 'Now they grapple!') I shall always call you Amalia Ludvigovna, and really I cannot understand why this title does not please you. You see yourself what has befallen my husband. I ask you at once to close the door and let no one enter, otherwise I swear tomorrow your conduct shall be reported to the Governor-General. The Prince knew me in his youth, and recollects Simon Zacharovitch very well, and has shown him many kindnesses. Everyone knows that my husband had many powerful friends and protectors, whom he abandoned from feelings of delicacy, as he knew his own unhappy weakness; and now, even now, one helps us' (pointing to Raskolnikoff), 'this noble-minded young man who has means and connections, whom my husband knew as a child. And rest assured, Amalia Ludvigovna – '

All this was spoken very quickly, but coughing at times sadly interfered with Catherine Ivanovna's eloquence. At this moment the dying man revived and moaned, and the wife ran back to him. Marmeladoff opened his eyes, and fixed an expressionless look upon Raskolnikoff, who was standing near. His breath came with difficulty and rarely, whilst large drops of perspiration stood on his forehead, and the blood oozed from his injured lips. Catherine Ivanovna watched him with a stern look, but from her eyes ran a few tears.

'Good heavens! Look at his poor chest! Look at the blood, the blood!' she cried at last, in despair. 'We must take off his waistcoat. Turn a little, Simon Zacharovitch – that is, if you can,' she added.

Marmeladoff recognised her. 'A priest!' he said, in a hoarse voice.

Catherine Ivanovna turned to the window, and, resting her forehead on the frame, cried out in agony: 'Oh, most wretched existence!'

'A priest!' repeated the dying man, after a moment's silence.

'Hush – sh!' she said to him. He heard her voice, recognised it, and became silent. She returned to his pillow, and he timidly looked into her face. He did not long remain quiet, as his glance happened to fall upon the form of his little child, his favourite daughter, Leda, who was cowering, as if in a fit, in a corner, her little eyes fixed upon her father.

'Ah! – ' he sighed, and endeavoured to speak.

'What is it?' asked Catherine Ivanovna.

'Bare-legged!' he murmured, noticing the child's half-clad state.

'Silence!' shouted Catherine Ivanovna, threateningly. 'You ought to know why she is so.'

'Thank heavens! – the doctor at last!' cried Raskolnikoff in delight.

The doctor came, an old German gentleman, who, with the aid of the wife, undid the husband's bloody shirt, and bared his throat and chest. This part was fearfully battered, and, in addition, his right ribs were fractured; whilst on his left side, near the heart, was an ominous black and yellow spot, a cruel blow from a hoof.

'I can do nothing for him,' said the doctor to Raskolnikoff.

'What do you mean?'

'He is dying.'

'Is there no hope?'

'None. He is near the last gasp. I might stop the blood, but that would be of no avail. In five minutes he will be dead.'

Some movement here took place amongst the crowd at the door, and the people made way for an old grey-haired priest, who entered the room, bearing before him the Holy Sacrament. The doctor gave way at once, and cast a significant glance at the priest. Raskolnikoff asked the former to remain, even though it was useless; he shrugged his shoulders and consented to do so. All stepped back. The ceremony took but a little time, and it was doubtful whether the dying man understood a word; occasionally he would make a vain attempt to articulate. Catherine Ivanovna took hold of Leda and the child on the table, and placing them before her, fell upon her knees. She bit her lips to prevent her tears, and, as she prayed, sought to arrange the attire of her half-clothed children a little. At the door of the inner chamber the spectators had pressed forward again, whilst beyond them the gathering of the curious still kept augmenting. Only one dim candle lighted up the whole scene.

At this moment the crowd opened its ranks to let little Polenka pass, who had run for her sister. She was quite out of breath, and, catching her mother's eye, went up to her and said, 'She is coming, I met her in the street.' A young girl made her way quietly and timidly through the centre of the crowd, and strange indeed was her unexpected appearance in the room, in the midst of poverty, rags, distress, and death itself. She, too, was in rags, and her clothes worthless, although decked out for the street with all the glaring prominence of her kind. Sonia remained at the threshold of the inner door, and stood there looking as one in a strange place, who knew nobody. Her gaudy attire, her coloured silk dress with its absurd train, the light boots, the parasol (quite unnecessary at night), her little round hat trimmed with flaming scarlet feathers, all made a striking figure in such a scene. From under her hat appeared a poor little wan and frightened countenance, with open mouth and eyes immovable from terror. Sonia was small and slightly built, with fair hair and complexion, and possessed very attractive blue eyes. She continued to stand there, breathing heavily from having hurried, until some whispering amongst the crowd, evidently about her, reached her ears. She cast down her eyes, and advanced farther into the room, although barely beyond the threshold. The last sacraments had now been administered, and Catherine Ivanovna went up to the dying man. The priest prepared to retire, and, before leaving, turned to say one or two words of consolation to her.

'What will become of these?' she asked, pointing to her children.

'God is merciful, lady. Trust in the power of the Most High,' commenced the priest.

'He is not merciful to us.'

'You are wrong, lady, very wrong,' replied he, shaking his head.

'Am I? Look there!' said she, pointing to her husband.

'No doubt those who were the involuntary cause of the accident will indemnify you for the loss of his support, and assist you.'

'You do not understand me!' cried Catherine Ivanovna, waving her hands. 'Indemnify me for him? A drunkard who rolled under the horses' feet! And as for being a help, he never did anything but cause me misery. He drank everything away. He robbed us to get drink, and my life and my children's have been ruined in the drink-shops. Thank God, he is dying, the loss is little.'

'One should forgive in the hour of death. It is wicked, lady, a great sin, to have such thoughts.'

Catherine Ivanovna turned again to the dying man, and rubbed the perspiration and blood from his brow, gave him water to drink, and smoothed his pillow.

'Ah, sir! Yours are words only. Pardon, you say?' she exclaimed. 'Had he come home drunk, as usual, and not hurt, I should have washed his clothes, along with my children's, all night long, and then, waiting until they were dry again, as soon as light came I should have stitched and darned at the window. Such are my nights. And then to speak of forgiveness!'

Her cough stopped further words, and she was obliged again to hold her throat with one hand, whilst with the other she put a handkerchief to her mouth. She withdrew it as soon as the fit had subsided, and held it out to the priest. It was full of blood. He turned his head away, and said nothing. Marmeladoff seemed now in great pain, and his eyes were rigidly staring at his wife, who was now bending over him again. He was evidently endeavouring to say something to her; his lips moved, and an indistinct sound came from them. Catherine Ivanovna divined that he wished to ask her pardon, and at once cried harshly to him:

'Keep quiet! Hush! There is no need. I know what you want to say.'

The dying husband refrained from further efforts, but at the same moment his now wandering eyes fell upon his daughter Sonia, standing at the door. At first he did not recognise her, as she was standing in the shade. 'Who is that?' he asked, in a thick, hoarse voice, as his face assumed an aspect of terror, his eyes glaring wildly to where his daughter stood.

'Lie still! Will you?' cried Catherine Ivanovna.

But he strove with all his strength to raise himself, and kept his eyes immovably fixed upon his daughter. Evidently he did not recognise her in such a costume. Suddenly he knew her, as she stood with an expression of intense grief on her little face, awaiting her turn to say farewell to her dying father.

'Sonia, my daughter! Forgive me!' he cried, as he endeavoured to seize her hand, but his strength failed him completely, and he fell back heavily, his head hanging over the sofa and touching the floor. They raised him, and placed him upon the sofa again, but the end had come. Sonia, with a feeble cry, ran and embraced him. He died in her arms.

'He is gone!' cried Catherine Ivanovna, gazing at the corpse of her husband. 'What shall I do now? How am I to bury him? And how shall I feed them?'

Raskolnikoff came up to Catherine Ivanovna. 'Catherine Ivanovna,' he began, 'last week your dead husband imparted to me the history of his life and all his circumstances. Be assured that he spoke of you with the highest respect. That same evening when I learned how devoted he was to you all, and how he loved and esteemed you especially, Catherine Ivanovna – spite of his unhappy weakness, that moment saw us friends. Allow me now to assist to discharge a debt to my dear friend. Here are twenty roubles; if they are of use to you in your need, then – I – in a word – I will come again; tomorrow – tomorrow without fail – that is, perhaps, tomorrow, again. Adieu!'

He rapidly passed out of the room, and made his way through the crowd to the stairs, where he came face to face with Nicodemus Thomich, who having heard of the misfortune, was hastening up. They had not met since the scene in the office, but Nicodemus Thomich recognised him immediately.

'You here?' he asked.

'He is dead,' replied Raskolnikoff; 'a doctor has been and a priest. All in order. Pray do not disturb the poor widow, she is in a decline besides. Comfort her, if possible. You are a kind man, I know,' he finished, with a smile, as he looked straight into the other man's eyes.

'You are wet with blood,' said Thomich, noticing by the light of a lantern some fresh blood-stains upon Raskolnikoff's waistcoat.

'Yes, I am all over blood,' Raskolnikoff answered with a peculiar glance. He smiled and tossed his head, and passed downstairs.

He descended quietly without hurrying, A new life seemed welling up within him, a feeling akin to that of a condemned man upon suddenly receiving his pardon. Half-way down the stairs, the priest, who was also leaving the house, overtook him, and Raskolnikoff, stepping aside, silently exchanged bows with him. He had hardly reached the last step, when he heard somebody behind him. It was Polenka, the little daughter, who was calling after him: 'Sir! Sir!'

He turned round, and looked at the thin but pretty face of the little child. She slid down the handrail, which evidently pleased her, and she looked at him with a little smile: 'Sir, will you please tell me your name? And where you live, too?'

He put his two hands on her shoulders, and gazed upon her with some happiness. It was pleasant to do so – he knew not why. 'Who has sent you?'

'My sister, Sonia,' replied the child, still smiling.

'I thought your sister had sent you.'

'Mamma also told me; when sister Sonia asked me, mamma said: "Yes, run quickly, Polenka." '

'Do you love your sister Sonia?'

'I love her more than anybody,' the child answered eagerly, and her smile became more serious.

'And will you love me?'

Instead of a reply, he saw the child draw nearer to him; and her swollen lips were naively put out to kiss him. Then her thin, match-like arms closed round him, and she held him tightly as she began to cry softly, her hold becoming stronger and stronger. 'My poor papa!' she said, after a while, as she wiped her tears away with her hand.

'Did your papa love you?'

'He loved Leda more than any of us,' she replied seriously and without a smile. 'He loved her so much because she was little and delicate, and he always brought her presents, but he taught us the Bible and grammar,' she said with pride. 'Mamma said nothing, but we knew, and papa knew, she was pleased. She wished me to learn French, as a lady should.'

'And you learned to pray?'

'Oh, yes – long ago. I used to pray myself, and Kolia and Leda prayed aloud together with mamma. First they prayed to "Our Lady," and then prayed, "God, forgive and bless dear sister Sonia," and then, "Lord, pardon and bless our other papa," because our old papa was dead, and this was our new one, and we prayed for him, too.'

'Polya, my name is Rodion; when you pray, pray for me too, for Rodion – nothing else.'

'All my life I will pray for you,' the child said firmly, and she smiled again, and threw her arms round him once more.

Raskolnikoff gave her his name and address, and promised he would return tomorrow. The child left him in rapture. It was now eleven o'clock as he reached the street. In five minutes he was on the bridge again – at that same spot where he had encountered the would-be suicide.

'It is sufficient!' he muttered solemnly and decidedly. 'Away, spectres! Away, fear! Away, visions! This is life. Am I living now? Did my life not leave me together with the old woman's? Heaven be hers and – Enough! Peace to her! The reign of reason and light commences now, of will, of force. Let us examine ourselves, and measure our minds,' he said conceitedly, and, as if thinking over in his mind some dark resolve: 'Ah me! it seems I agree to accept the yard of foothold and live on. I am very weak again, but it seems all the sickness is gone. I knew it would be so as I came out. Let me see – Potchinkoff's, Razoumikhin's quarters, is not far off – a few steps. No, let him amuse himself as he may. It is nothing! Strength, strength is necessary; without strength one can attain nothing, and strength begets strength. This they do not know,' he said proudly and conceitedly to himself, as he crossed the bridge with the lightest step. He was full of self-satisfaction. What had caused this jauntiness? What had changed? He knew not himself; it had simply come into his head that he must live, that there was life still, and he had not parted with it along with the old woman.

Perhaps he jumped rashly to this conclusion, and it was simply a catching at a straw, but it did not matter, and he did not think. He was in the best of spirits as he lightly sought out Razoumikhin's rooms. He soon found the house, and the porter directed him to the new lodger's. On the staircase he could hear the noise and racket of a great gathering. The door was wide open. Razoumikhin's room was pretty large, but the company numbered about twenty-five. Raskolnikoff halted at the door. The landlady's two servants were busily engaged in handing round tea, cake, etc., and also sundry bottles. Raskolnikoff called for Razoumikhin. The latter ran to the door at once. At a glance it was evident that he had been drinking unusually freely, although he was not a man who generally showed the effect of his potations.

'I am only come to tell you that you have won your bet. I cannot, though, make one of you. I am so weak, that I shall fall down directly. That is all, and, now, goodbye! Come to me tomorrow.'

'Let me accompany you home since you are so weak.'

'Attend to your guests! Who is that fellow looking this way?'

'That? Oh, I don't know – some acquaintance of my uncle's. My uncle is a dear old fellow – pity you cannot stay to be introduced. However, never mind. Never mind the lot – I must look after you. Wait a moment, I'll call Zosimoff.'

Zosimoff came out with a certain amount of readiness, and looked with some curiosity at his patient. 'You want sleep, man,' he said, examining him. 'I must give you a powder – will you take one? I have them here ready.'

'Certainly,' replied Raskolnikoff.

'It is a good thing you are going to see him home,' Zosimoff remarked to Razoumikhin. 'What tomorrow will bring we shall see, but today he is not so bad; there is a remarkable change.'

'Do you know what Zosimoff whispered to me as we came out?' said Razoumikhin as soon as they were in the street. 'I did not tell you then, because there were fools about; Zosimoff ordered me to talk with you on the way and prevent your talking at the same time; and then he told me that he had an idea – an idea that you were mad, or pretty near it. Fancy such a thing! In the first place, you are twice as intelligent as he; secondly, you are not so stupid as to be offended at his having such a nonsensical idea; and, thirdly, he has got the idea of mental disease from your last conversation with Zametoff.'

'Has Zametoff told you all?'

'Yes, most clearly. I can now understand your every thought, and so can Zametoff. Yes, in one word, Rodia, the point is this – I am a little tipsy, I fear. That is nothing; the point is this, that this feeling – you know? – the thing that none of them dared to say aloud, that story did not last long, and, when they brought the painter, all became clear and it vanished away. Now, why are they such fools? I gave Zametoff a good blow – (this between ourselves, brother, mind, not a word that you know) – I saw he was nettled, but today it is perfectly plain, principally this Elia Petrovitch! he was present when you swooned, I know.'

Raskolnikoff listened greedily, while Razoumikhin rambled on in a tipsy way.

'The smell of the paint and the foul air made me faint,' said Raskolnikoff.

'Very likely, but it was not the paint only. The fever had been gathering in you for a month past, according to Zosimoff. You quite frightened Zametoff today in the Crystal Palace and horrified him with your nonsense; then all at once you showed him you were poking fun at him. Oh, why was I not there? Now Porphyrius wants to make your acquaintance too.'

'Indeed? And why do they put me down as mad?'

'Not exactly mad, my friend; it seems I talk too freely. You interest him very much. I am a little in drink, I know, but that seems to be about his idea.'

'Listen to me, Razoumikhin,' said Raskolnikoff, after some little silence. 'I want to tell you everything straight out. I have just been at a dead man's, a tchinovnik's, who was run over. I gave away all my money; and, moreover, there greeted me a being who, if I had killed anybody I – in one word I saw there another creature, with a flame-coloured feather – I am stupid. Hold me, I shall fall. – Here is the staircase –'

'What is the matter?' asked Razoumikhin, alarmed.

'My head swims a little, though that has nothing to do with the affair; but to me it is so sad, so very sad, poor woman! Look! What is that? Look!'

'What do you mean?'

'Do you not see a light in my room! See!' Both stopped at the last flight near the landlady's door, and sure enough a light was plainly to be seen in Raskolnikoff's room.

'Strange! Nastasia, no doubt, though,' said Razoumikhin.

'No, no. She never comes at this time; besides she is in bed long ago. Goodbye.'

'What do you mean? I will see you up. Let us go together.'

'Yes, yes; but I wish to shake hands now and say goodbye here. Now, give me your hand. Goodbye.'

'What ever has come to you, Rodia?'

'Nothing; let us go in. You shall be witness.'

They mounted the stairs, Razoumikhin thinking that Zosimoff, after all, was quite right. 'Perhaps I upset him with my talk,' thought he to himself. Suddenly, as they reached the door, they heard the sound of voices in the room.

'Who can they be?' cried Razoumikhin.

Raskolnikoff rushed forward first and threw the door wide open. His mother and sister were seated on the couch, and had been expecting him for half an hour. Why did this take him by surprise? How was it he had never thought about them after hearing that very day that they were expected? During this half-hour they had been entertained by Nastasia, who was standing before them and retailing to them all the news, together with her own secret ideas. They had both started with fright when she told them that he had rushed out, ill as he was, into the street, and had been seen no more. 'Heavens! What has become of him?' Both wept, and suffered much during this half-hour of anxiety. A joyful cry greeted Raskolnikoff's appearance. They rushed up to him, but he stood there like a stone. A sudden and insupportable thought had chilled him to the marrow, and his hand was not put out to grasp theirs; it would not move. His mother and sister rushed to him with open arms, kissed him, smiling, crying. He took one step, faltered, and fell down upon the floor in a swoon. Razoumikhin, who was standing at the door, immediately rushed towards him, and, taking the fainting man in his powerful arms, deposited him on the sofa, amidst the cries and screams of his relations.

'Nothing, nothing!' he cried out to them, 'this is only a swoon. Water! He will soon come to himself and be all right. The doctor said so.'

And Razoumikhin seized Dounia by the hand and almost dragged her forward to 'see him come to himself.' The mother and sister looked on Razoumikhin with feelings of gratitude, as one providentially sent; they had already learned from Nastasia what this 'lively young man,' as she called him, had been to Rodia in his illness, in the course of her confidential conversation with Dounia and Pulcheria Alexandrovna.

PART III

Chapter 1

RASKOLNIKOFF HALF-ROSE and sat upon the couch; then, after cutting short the flow of Razoumikhin's eloquent consolations by a slight gesture, he caught his mother and sister by the hand, and gazed for two whole minutes first at the one, then at the other, without uttering a syllable. The fixed expression in his face was one of sorrow and anxiety, and had about it something uncanny. It frightened Pulcheria Alexandrovna, and she began to cry. Eudoxia Romanovna looked pale, and her hand trembled as it lay in her brother's.

'Go home to your lodgings – with him,' said he in broken accents, pointing to Razoumikhin, 'go away till tomorrow, and then – but when did you come?'

'We have just arrived, Rodia,' replied Pulcheria Alexandrovna. 'The train was very late; but, Rodia, I could never bear to leave you now! I will stay here all night and watch – '

'Don't plague me!' returned he in a tone of irritation.

'I will stay with him,' said Razoumikhin briskly; 'I will not leave his side for a minute; my guests may look after themselves and take offence if they choose! Besides, my uncle is there to play the host.'

'How can I ever thank you enough?' began Pulcheria Alexandrovna, again pressing Raskolnikoff's hand, but her son cut her short.

'I cannot, I cannot do with it,' repeated he in an agonised voice, 'do not keep on tormenting me! Go away at once! I cannot stand it!'

'Let us go, mamma,' whispered Dounia in an anxious tone, 'let us leave the room for the present at any rate, our presence merely worries him.'

'And am I not to spend a single minute with him after being parted from him these three years?' groaned Pulcheria Alexandrovna.

'Wait a bit,' said Raskolnikoff, 'you are always interrupting me, and making me forget what I was about to say. Have you seen Looshin?'

'No, Rodia, but he has already heard of our arrival. We were told, Rodia, that Peter Petrovitch had been so kind as to call on you today,' added Pulcheria Alexandrovna rather timidly.

'Yes, he was indeed so kind. – Dounia, I told Looshin just now that I was going to kick him downstairs, and I wished the devil might take him – '

'What do you mean, Rodia? You could not surely? – it is not possible!' began the terrified mother, but a glance at Dounia prevented her from proceeding further.

Eudoxia Romanovna stood with her eyes fixed on her brother waiting for a further explanation. The two ladies felt cruelly perplexed, having already heard of the quarrel through Nastasia, who had given some account of it after her own fashion and to the best of her comprehension.

'Dounia,' proceeded Raskolnikoff, exerting himself, 'I will not have this marriage, so pray dismiss Looshin tomorrow, and let me never hear his name again.'

'Good heavens!' cried Pulcheria Alexandrovna.

'Only consider what you are saying, brother?' said Eudoxia Romanovna vehemently, but she restrained herself, and added in a gentle tone: 'Perhaps you are not quite yourself at this moment – you are feeling tired?'

'Do you think I am wandering? No. You are going to marry Looshin on my account. I will not accept the sacrifice. So you will just write to him tomorrow and break off the engagement. Bring me your letter to read in the morning, and it will be all settled.'

'I cannot do that!' cried the young girl with some resentment. 'By what right – '

'Oh, Dounetchka, you are getting angry, too. Let it be till tomorrow. Don't you see – ' stammered the terrified mother, darting to her daughter's side. 'Let us go, it is the best thing we can do!'

'He is not quite himself!' chimed in Razoumikhin, in an unsteady voice which betrayed that he had been drinking, 'else he could never – but he will come to his right senses tomorrow. It is quite true that he showed the gentleman the door, today, and irritated him a good deal. He was holding forth in this room and explaining his theories, but he slunk off with his tail between his legs – '

'Then it is all true?' exclaimed Pulcheria Alexandrovna.

'Goodbye till tomorrow, brother,' said Dounia in a compassionate tone. 'Let us go, mamma! Adieu, Rodia!'

He made a final effort to address her. 'I am not delirious, sister, as you may see; this marriage would be a disgrace. I may be infamous, but there is no reason why you should be – it is enough for me. And, however great a wretch I may be, I would repudiate you as my sister, if you were to contract any such marriage. You may choose between me and Looshin! And now go –'

'You are out of your mind! You are a perfect despot!' vociferated Razoumikhin.

Raskolnikoff made no answer; he was probably in no state to do so. Utterly exhausted, he sank back on the sofa and turned his face to the wall. Eudoxia Romanovna's sparkling eyes were fixed inquiringly on Razoumikhin, who felt startled by the glance. Pulcheria Alexandrovna was filled with consternation.

'I cannot make up my mind to leave!' murmured she, half in despair, aside to Razoumikhin. 'I must stay somewhere near him. Take Dounia home.'

'You would spoil all!' returned the young man in the same low tone, feeling at his wits' end. 'Let us clear the room, at any rate. Bring a light, Nastasia! I swear,' continued he under his breath, as soon as they were on the staircase, 'that he was all but beating the doctor and myself just now! Even the doctor – fancy that! Besides, it would be impossible for you to let Eudoxia Romanovna remain by herself in those lodgings! Remember what sort of house it is. Could not that rascal Peter Petrovitch have found something more suitable for you? Well, you are aware I have been drinking a drop too much, and so – I make use of rather strong expressions; pray excuse them –'

'Well,' resumed Pulcheria Alexandrovna, 'I am going to find Rodia's landlady, and ask her to put Dounia and myself up somewhere for the night. I really cannot abandon him in this state!'

This conversation took place on the landing just outside the landlady's door. Nastasia was standing on the last step, holding the light. Razoumikhin was in a state of great excitement. Half an hour earlier, when he had been taking Raskolnikoff home, he had been most loquacious, and was conscious of it; still his head had remained clear, in spite of the immense quantity of wine he had taken in the course of the evening. He had now fallen into an ecstatic state, heightened by the effects of the heady liquor. He had caught both ladies by the hand, and began to harangue them in the most unconstrained fashion, attempting to convince them and add emphasis to each word by squeezing their fingers, while his eyes remained fixed on Eudoxia Romanovna. The poor women, suffering from his grasp, endeavoured from time to time to disengage the fingers imprisoned in his large bony hand, but he paid no heed, and only clasped them all the tighter, never thinking of the pain he was inflicting. Had they asked him to oblige them by throwing himself down head foremost, he would have done it in an instant. Pulcheria Alexandrovna felt Razoumikhin to be very eccentric, and his grip terrible; still she thought of her Rodia, and so closed her eyes to the peculiar manner of the young man, who seemed to have been sent so providentially to her aid.

Eudoxia Romanovna, indeed, shared her mother's anxieties, but, though not naturally timid, she could not endure the fiery glances cast on her by her brother's friend without some feelings of surprise, and even uneasiness. Had it not been for the unbounded confidence in this singular man with which Nastasia's account had inspired her, she would have made her escape at once, and taken her mother with her. Still she understood that it would be difficult to do without him at this juncture. Within ten minutes, however, she felt much reassured; whatever Razoumikhin's condition might be, he soon showed himself in his true colours, and revealed his real character.

'You must not think of asking the landlady any such thing; it would be the height of absurdity,' was his prompt reply to Pulcheria Alexandrovna. 'You may be Rodia's mother, but, if you stay here, you will only exasperate him, and Heaven knows what may happen. Now, listen to what I have to suggest: Nastasia will attend to him for the present, while I see you both home, for, in St Petersburg, it will not do for two women to venture through the streets by night alone. After seeing you safe, I will run back here, and, within another quarter of an hour, I solemnly promise to bring you word how he is, and whether he has gone to sleep. Well, then, listen! Next thing, I will run to my own lodging – (I have a party there, and all my guests are drunk) – and I will fetch Zosimoff, the doctor who is attending Rodia; he is at my place now, but not drunk, for he never takes wine. I will bring him to our patient, and then on to see you, so that, within the hour, you will have two reports of your son – first mine, and then the doctor's, which will be of more value. If your son is worse, I promise to bring you back here; if he is going on well, you can just go to bed. I will spend the night here, in the corridor, so that he will know nothing about it, and I will get the landlady to give Zosimoff a bed, so as to have him at hand if wanted. At this moment, I believe the doctor's presence at Rodia's bedside to be of far more importance than yours, so do you go home. You cannot get the landlady to give you a bed; she might take *me* in, but not *you*, because – well, because she is a fool. If you must know, she has fallen in love with me; and she would be sure to feel jealous of Eudoxia Romanovna, and of yourself too, but especially of Eudoxia Romanovna. She is a most peculiar woman! I am a fool, too, I confess. Well then, come. Will you not trust me? Tell me whether you do?'

'Let us go, mamma,' said Eudoxia Romanovna, 'I feel sure he will keep his promise. Does not my brother owe his life to his care? And if the doctor really consents to spend the night here, what more could we wish?'

'Come, you understand me, you are an angel!' cried Razoumikhin enthusiastically. 'Let us be off! Nastasia, go upstairs at once with the light, and stay by him; I shall be back in a quarter of an hour.'

Pulcheria Alexandrovna, though not altogether convinced, made no more objections. Razoumikhin seized both ladies by the arm, and half-led, half-dragged them down the stairs. The mother still felt some anxiety: 'He can bestir himself certainly, and wishes to do all he can for us; but can we depend on any promises he makes in his present condition?' The young man divined her thoughts.

'Ah, I see, you think I am under the influence of drink,' said he, as he strode along the pavement, without observing the ladies' difficulty in keeping pace with him. 'That does not signify in the least – I mean – that is to say, I have drunk like a beast, but it is not the wine that has got into my head. As soon as I set eyes on you, I felt struck – never mind my words, I am talking nonsense, I feel so far, far beneath you! As soon as I have seen you to your lodgings, I shall go to the canal, which is close at hand, throw a bucketful or two of water over my head, and be all right. If you did but know how I loved you both! Don't laugh, and pray don't be angry! Be angry with anyone else you like, but not with me! I am his friend, and consequently yours. It is what I wished. I had a presentiment, for you seem suddenly to have fallen from the skies. I shall not sleep a wink tonight. Zosimoff said but just now that he was afraid he might go mad – that is why we must avoid irritating him!'

'What are you saying?' cried the mother.

'Is it possible that the doctor can have said so?' asked Eudoxia Romanovna in alarm.

'He did, but he is mistaken, completely mistaken. He had given Rodia some medicine, a powder, which I saw; and, just then, you arrived. Well, it would have been better if you had waited till tomorrow. We did well to retire. In another hour Zosimoff himself will come, and report to you on his condition. *He* is not intoxicated, and I shall be all right by then. But why did I get so terribly excited? Because the wretched fellows drew me into a discussion, and I have vowed never to argue with anyone again! They will talk such stuff! A little more, and I should have seized them by the throat! I left my uncle there to preside over the entertainment. Well, would you credit it? They are partisans of complete impersonality; supreme progress, in their eyes, is to be as little resemblance as possible to oneself. We Russians have chosen to live on other people's ideas, and we are saturated with them. Is it true? Is what I say true?' cried Razoumikhin, squeezing both ladies' hands.

'Oh, good gracious! I know nothing about it,' said poor Pulcheria Alexandrovna.

'Yes, yes – though I cannot agree with you in every point,' added Eudoxia Romanovna gravely. Scarcely had she uttered these words when a cry of pain escaped her, provoked by Razoumikhin's energetic grasp of her hand.

'Yes, yes, you say? Well then, you are a fountain of goodness and purity and reason and perfection!' exclaimed the young man, transported with joy. 'Give me your hand, give it to me, and let me have yours, too, that I may fall upon my knees and kiss them this instant!' And down he went in the centre of the pavement, which was, fortunately, deserted at the moment.

'Pray, don't! What do you mean?' cried Pulcheria Alexandrovna, greatly alarmed.

'Please get up,' said Dounia, laughing, though she could not help feeling rather uneasy also.

'Never, never, unless you give me your hands! There! Now I am up, and we will walk on. I am an unlucky idiot, quite unworthy of you, and blush to think that I am in liquor at this moment – I am not worthy to love you, but all who are not perfect brutes must kneel and bow down before you. That is why I did homage. Here are your lodgings, and Peter Petrovitch deserved to be turned out by Rodion for putting you here! How dared he lodge you in such a place? – it is scandalous! – Do you know the sort of people that live here? And are you engaged to this man? Well, I must say that your future husband is an uncommonly queer sort of fellow!'

'Listen to me, Mr Razoumikhin; you are forgetting – ' began Pulcheria Alexandrovna.

'Yes, yes, you are right, I did forget, I am ashamed of myself,' blurted out the student apologetically, 'but – but you must not take offence. I only said it because I am so outspoken, and not because – well, it would be ignoble; in a word, it is not because – I dare not finish my sentence! But as soon as the man left us, we all felt he was not one of our sort. Well, come, it is all right now. You forgive me, don't you? Well then, let us go on! I know this corridor, I have been here before; there was a scandal here, at No. 3. Which is your room? No. 8? Then you had better lock your door for the night and admit no one. In a quarter of an hour I shall return and report to you, and half an hour afterwards you will see me here again, with Zosimoff. Goodbye for the present!'

'Good heavens! Dounetchka, what is going to happen?' said Pulcheria Alexandrovna, anxiously, to her daughter.

'Don't be uneasy, mamma,' returned Dounia, taking off her bonnet and mantle. 'God has sent this gentleman to our assistance; I am sure we may depend on him, in spite of his having just emerged from such orgies. What he has already done for my brother – '

'Ah, Dounetchka! Heaven only knows if he will ever come back! How could I ever make up my mind to leave Rodia? Little did I expect to find him in this condition! How strangely he received us! You might have thought he was vexed at our coming.' Her eyes were glistening with tears.

'It was not that, mamma. You could not see him well, you were crying all the time. He has been much shaken by this severe illness, and that accounts for it all.'

'Oh, this illness! What will be the end of it? And how strangely he spoke to you, Dounia!' resumed the mother, timidly, trying to read her daughter's eyes. Still she was more than half consoled when she found that Dounia was ready to defend her brother, thus showing that she had forgiven him. 'I know that he will change his mind by tomorrow,' added she, attempting to sound her still further.

'While I am confident that he will keep to his opinion – on that subject,' rejoined Eudoxia Romanovna.

The matter was too delicate to admit of Pulcheria Alexandrovna's pursuing it further. Dounia kissed her mother, who said nothing, but clasped her in a tight embrace, and then seated herself to await, with agonised feelings, the arrival of Razoumikhin. Her eye rested timidly on the daughter, who was pacing up and down the room with folded arms, lost in thought. This was one of Eudoxia Romanovna's habits when she had much to consider, and, in such cases, her mother found it best to leave her to herself.

Razoumikhin certainly cut a ridiculous figure when, under the influence of liquor, he suddenly conceived such a violent admiration for Eudoxia Romanovna. Yet the appearance of the young girl, especially as she paced the room with folded arms, lost in pensive thoughts, might have sufficed to excuse the student, even without the apology of his intoxicated condition. It was calculated to arrest attention. She was tall and fine-looking, had a very good figure, and showed in every gesture a touch of self-reliance, which, however, failed to detract from the grace and delicacy of her movements. In features she was not unlike her brother, yet she might have been called handsome. Her auburn hair was a shade lighter than Rodion's. Her brilliant dark eyes betrayed a touch of pride, which at times melted into extreme sweetness. She was pale, but not sickly; on the contrary, her complexion looked fresh and healthy. The mouth was small, the cherry-coloured lower lip projected slightly, and so did the chin; these were the only irregularities in her profile, and gave a peculiarly firm and almost haughty cast to her beauty. The expression of her face was usually grave and pensive, which made it look all the more charming when suddenly enlivened by the gay smile of youth. Razoumikhin had never seen anything to equal it; he was ardent, sincere, honest, and frank, strong as a knight of romance, and over-heated by wine – so it was easy to explain his infatuation. Besides, as chance would have it, he saw Dounia for the first time at a moment when her features were to some extent transfigured by tender affection and the delight of seeing Rodia; her expression turned to one of indignant pride on receiving her brother's insolent commands – and the conquest was complete.

He had only spoken the truth, when he had declared in his drunken frankness that Prascovia Paulovna, Raskolnikoff's eccentric landlady, might be jealous not merely of Eudoxia Romanovna, but even of Pulcheria Alexandrovna herself. The latter had retained some traces of her former beauty, though she was now three-and-forty; and she did not look her age, as is often the case with women who preserve their lucid faculties, vivid perceptions, and pure, honest, warm hearts to the verge of old age. Her hair, indeed, had begun to turn grey and grow thin; lines had already gathered round her eyes, and sorrow and care had stamped themselves on her cheeks; still she was handsome. She might have sat for a portrait of Dounetchka some twenty years later, without the projecting under-lip which gave so much character to the face of the young girl. Pulcheria Alexandrovna was affectionate and sensitive by nature, but not weak; though timid and inclined to yield, she could make a stand when principle, honesty, or convictions were at stake.

Within twenty minutes of Razoumikhin's departure, two light taps were heard at the door. He was back again. 'I am not coming in. I have not time,' was his hasty declaration when the door opened. 'He is sleeping like a lamb, and I only hope it may last for ten hours! Nastasia is with him, and has orders to stay till I return. Now I am off in search of Zosimoff. He will bring you his report, and then you must go to bed, for I can see how tired you are.' He had scarcely uttered these words when he vanished.

'What an active, obliging young man!' exclaimed Pulcheria Alexandrovna, delighted.

'He certainly seems extremely kind!' replied Eudoxia Romanovna with some warmth, and she began to pace up and down the room again.

About an hour afterwards, steps were heard along the corridor, and another knock at the door. This time the two women were confidently awaiting the fulfilment of Razoumikhin's promise; and he returned, accompanied by Zosimoff. The latter had not hesitated a second about leaving the banquet to visit Raskolnikoff, but his friend had more difficulty in persuading him to call upon the ladies, as he placed little faith in Razoumikhin's assertions, believing him to be still in liquor. The doctor's self-esteem, however, was soon reassured and even flattered, for he found himself regarded as an oracle. During the ten minutes he remained, he succeeded in allaying Pulcheria Alexandrovna's anxiety. He showed the greatest interest in his patient, while expressing himself in grave and reserved language, as becomes a doctor of twenty-seven called in to a critical case. He never wandered from his subject or attempted to enter into general conversation. Though he had at once noticed Eudoxia Romanovna's beauty, he did not allow himself to pay her the slightest attention, but addressed all his remarks to Pulcheria Alexandrovna.

All this was gratifying to the mother. He declared Raskolnikoff to be now in a most satisfactory condition. He considered his patient's illness to be owing partly to the low material condition in which he had been living for some months past, but to have its origin likewise in mental causes: it was a complex product of various physical and psychological influences, such as preoccupation, care, anxiety, apprehension, brooding, etc. Zosimoff, having noticed, without appearing to do so, that Eudoxia Romanovna was listening with marked attention, proceeded to dilate complacently on this theme. When Pulcheria Alexandrovna asked with timid anxiety if he had not observed symptoms of insanity in her son, he replied, with a calm, frank smile, that the meaning of his words had been much exaggerated. He had certainly noticed a fixed idea, somewhat resembling monomania, in the patient, and this all the more because he (Zosimoff) was now directing his attention especially to this most interesting branch of medical study. 'But we must take into consideration,' added he, 'that up to today my patient has been constantly delirious and that the arrival of his friends cannot fail to distract his mind, assist him to regain strength, and exercise a beneficial influence – that is, if we can secure him against any fresh shock,' ended he, significantly. Then he rose and bowed both ceremoniously and cordially, taking his leave amidst thanks and blessings, and a profusion of grateful acknowledgements. Eudoxia Romanovna even held out the little hand which he had never attempted to touch. In short, the doctor retired delighted with his call, and still more with himself.

'We will talk everything over tomorrow; go to bed at once, now; it is high time for you to take some rest,' were Razoumikhin's orders, as he went out with Zosimoff. 'I shall bring you news the first thing tomorrow.'

'That Eudoxia Romanovna is certainly a charming young girl!' observed Zosimoff, quite simply, as soon as they were in the street.

'Charming? You call her charming!' yelled Razoumikhin, darting on the doctor, and seizing him by the throat. 'If you should ever dare – do you understand?' cried he, holding him by the collar and pinning him against the wall. 'You hear what I say?'

'Let me go, you drunken fool,' said Zosimoff, trying to shake him off. As soon as he found himself free, he gazed at the student standing before him with swinging arms and a scowling face, and burst out laughing.

'I have no doubt I am an ass,' said Razoumikhin gloomily, 'but – so are you.'

'Not I, my friend. My head is not full of any such nonsense.'

They walked on without another word, and it was not till they had nearly reached Raskolnikoff's lodgings that Razoumikhin, who had been absorbed in thought, broke silence.

'Listen to me,' said he to Zosimoff. 'You are a good sort of fellow, but not without your vices; I know you to be a voluptuous, ignorant sybarite. You love your ease and good living, and gratify all your fancies. Now, this I call ignoble, because it is the parent of vice. You are so effeminate, that I can't understand, for the life of me, how you manage to be such a capital doctor and so devoted to your patients. Think of a doctor sleeping on a feather-bed, when he has to get up at night to go and see a patient! Three years hence, it will be useless to ring at your bell, for there will be no getting you up. But that is not the question now; what I have to tell you is that I am going to sleep in the kitchen, and you will pass the night in the landlady's apartments, to which I have had some difficulty in procuring you admission. You will have an opportunity of making closer acquaintance with her – not in the way you suggest! Not a vestige of any such thing, my friend!'

'I am not suggesting anything.'

'She is a modest woman, my friend – quiet and timid, chaste as Diana, and withal most sensitive and affectionate! I would to Heaven you would rid me of her. She lavishes so many attentions upon me that I am wearied of them, and will hand them over to you!'

Zosimoff laughed still more heartily. 'It is easy to see that you have not been on your guard; you know more than you choose to say! But why should I make love to her?'

'I assure you, you will find no difficulty in winning her good graces; you have only to go on chattering about something, take a chair by her side, and talk away. And, then, you are a doctor, and can cure her of some little ailment. I vow you will never repent it. She has a piano. I sing a little, you know, and so I treated her to a little pathetic Russian ditty. She likes anything sentimental. That was our first beginning; but you are a perfect master of the instrument and play like a Rubinstein. I am sure you will never repent it!'

'But what is to come of all this?'

'Have I failed to make my meaning clear? Don't you see that you would just suit each other perfectly? This is not the first time I have considered your case. You are sure to come to it sooner or later, and there you would find your feather-bed, and whatever else you want. Here you would be in port, secure from all agitation, and have excellent cakes and savoury dishes, your samovar ready at night, and a warming-pan for your bed. All the repose of the grave, and yet a happy life! But now we have chattered enough; let us be off to bed. Listen. I sometimes wake in the night, and, if I do, I shall go and see how Rodion is getting on; so don't be alarmed if you hear me pass. Should you feel inclined, you might go up just once, and if you notice anything unusual about him be sure to call me – though I don't expect this will be necessary.'

Chapter 2

THE FOLLOWING MORNING, soon after seven, Razoumikhin awoke, troubled by cares which had never before crossed his mind. He recalled all the incidents of the previous evening, and felt that he had undergone a new mental experience. At the same time, he was conscious that the dream which had flitted across his brain was absurdly unattainable. Indeed, he felt it to be so ridiculous that he was ashamed of it, and passed on hastily to the more practical questions bequeathed to him by the preceding day. He felt what distressed him most was the idea of having figured as a low blackguard. Not only had he appeared drunk, but, abusing the advantage given him by his position as benefactor to a young girl obliged to have recourse to his aid, he had allowed a secret silly feeling of jealousy to lead him to speak against her lover without knowing their exact relations, or even the gentleman's true circumstances. What right had he to judge Peter Petrovitch so freely? Who had asked his opinion? Besides, was it at all likely that a creature like Eudoxia Romanovna would marry a man quite unworthy of her for the sake of worldly advantage? There must be some merit in this Peter Petrovitch. There was this matter of the lodgings, certainly – but how was he to know their character? Besides, the ladies were only staying there temporarily while other quarters were being made ready for them. Oh! How miserable it all was! And how could he justify himself by pleading drunkenness – an absurd excuse that could only aggravate his misconduct! *In vino veritas*, and here, under the influence of wine, he had revealed the whole truth – viz., the meanness of a ridiculous jealousy. How could he, Razoumikhin, have allowed himself to cherish such a dream? He, the drunken, brutal prattler of yesterday, and this beautiful girl! What could be more odious and absurd than to think of linking them together?

And then the young man suddenly remembered with shame what he had said on the stairs the night before about the landlady being in love with him, and how jealous she would be of Eudoxia Romanovna; this was the culminating stroke to his confusion. He could not bear it, and down came his fist with a great thump upon the kitchen-stove, hurting his hand and cracking a tile. 'Well,' murmured he next minute, in utter dejection, 'it is done now, and it is hopeless to think of effacing my misdeeds. I shall give up all idea of that, and simply present myself before them without saying anything – merely discharge my task, and make no excuses. I shall not say a word – it is too late now, the deed is done!'

Yet he dressed himself with extra care. He had but one suit, and even had he possessed several, he would probably have retained the one he wore the previous evening, in order to avoid the appearance of having 'got himself up.' Yet a cynical disorder would have been bad taste; he had no right to offend against decorum, especially when he was wanted and had been expressly requested to come. So he brushed his clothes carefully; and, as to his linen, that was always spotless. Having asked Nastasia for some soap, he proceeded conscientiously to his ablutions, washing his head and neck, and bestowing great attention on his hands. When the moment came for deciding whether he should shave (Prascovia Paulovna possessing some excellent razors which had belonged to her deceased husband, Mr Zarnitzin), he answered the question in the negative with a sort of irritation: 'No, I will keep as I am, lest they should fancy I shaved because – No, not for the whole world!'

His monologue was interrupted by the arrival of Zosimoff, who had gone home for a short time after passing the night at Prascovia Paulovna's, and had now returned to visit his patient. Razoumikhin informed him that Raskolnikoff was sleeping like a dormouse. Zosimoff ordered him not to be disturbed, and promised to turn up again between ten and eleven. 'Provided he is to be found here!' added he.

'With such a whimsical patient, there is no depending on anything! Do you know whether he was to go to them, or they to come here?'

'I fancy they will come,' replied Razoumikhin, grasping the drift of the question. 'Of course they will have family affairs to discuss. I shall go. You, as the doctor, have naturally more right here than I.'

'I am no confessor; besides, I have other things to do besides listening to their secrets. I shall go too.'

'There is one thing troubles me,' continued Razoumikhin, knitting his brow. 'I was tipsy yesterday, and let out things I had no business to, as I was taking Rodia home; among other absurdities, I mentioned your fear that his brain was affected –'

'You told the ladies so yesterday.'

'I know what an idiot I have been. Strike me, if you will! But tell me seriously, in confidence, what you think of the case.'

'What have I to tell? You spoke of him as a monomaniac when you first called me in. Then, yesterday, we upset him completely; I say *we*, but it was really your doing, when you would go on talking about that house-painter: a suitable subject indeed to discuss before a man whose brain may have been upset by this very affair! Had I been aware at the time of the full details of that scene at the police-office, and known that he was acquainted with the suspicions of the vulgar, I should have stopped you at once. These monomaniacs make mountains of mole-hills, and convert fantastic trifles into realities. I half-understand it all, after what Zametoff told us at your party. By the way, that Zametoff is a charming fellow, but still – ahem! – he need not have said what he did. His tongue runs away with him!'

'But whom was he talking to? You and me?'

'And Porphyrius too.'

'Well, and if he did, what can it matter?'

'By the way, you have some influence over the mother and sister, have you not? They should be careful what they say to him today –'

'I will tell them so,' returned Razoumikhin with an air of annoyance.

'Adieu then for the present; pray thank Prascovia Paulovna on my behalf for her hospitality. She shut herself up in her room, and made no answer when I wished her good-morning through the door. I know she was up by seven, for I saw the samovar being carried in from the kitchen. She would not deign to admit me into her presence –'

Razoumikhin reached the ladies' quarters exactly at nine o'clock. They had risen before seven, and were expecting him with feverish anxiety. He walked in with a clouded brow, made an awkward bow, and then regretted bitterly having entered in this fashion. He had reckoned without his host: Pulcheria Alexandrovna ran to meet him, seized both his hands, and seemed ready to kiss them. The young man glanced timidly at Eudoxia Romanovna, but, instead of the mocking expression and ill-disguised scorn which he expected to read on her haughty countenance, he found gratitude and affectionate sympathy, which overwhelmed him with confusion. He would certainly have been more at his ease had they received him with reproaches. Fortunately, he had a topic of conversation ready to hand, which he at once broached. On learning that her son was not yet awake, but going on as well as possible, Pulcheria Alexandrovna said it was all the better, as she much wished for some conversation with Razoumikhin first. Then the ladies inquired whether their visitor had already breakfasted, and, hearing he had not, invited him to join them, as they had waited for him to come, before sitting down to table.

Eudoxia Romanovna rang the bell, which was answered by a ragged servant. He was ordered to bring in the tea, which was served in such a slovenly manner that the ladies felt quite ashamed. Razoumikhin inveighed vehemently against such a 'hole,' then, remembering Looshin, he stopped short, looked out of countenance, and felt delighted to be rescued from his embarrassing situation by the questions showered upon him by Pulcheria Alexandrovna. His answers kept him talking for three-quarters of an hour, telling all that he knew of the principal occurrences in Rodion Romanovitch's life during the past year, and ending with a circumstantial account of his friend's illness. He naturally passed over all that it was undesirable to mention, such as the scene at the police-office and its consequences. The two women listened eagerly, and, when he imagined himself to have given every detail of interest, their curiosity was not yet satisfied.

'And tell me, tell me, what you think – ah, excuse me, I am still ignorant of your name,' said Pulcheria Alexandrovna eagerly.

'Dmitri Prokovitch.'

'Well then, Dmitri Prokovitch, I feel so anxious to know the view of things he takes in general – I mean, as to his likes and dislikes. Is he always irritable? What are his inclinations – his dreams, if you so call them? What is his particular vein of thought just now?'

'What shall I say? I have known Rodion for the last eighteen months; he is gloomy, morose, proud, and haughty. Of late (though the germs may have been brooding in him previously) he has become suspicious and hypochondriacal. He is kind and generous, but cannot bear to show his feelings, and would sooner appear brutal than expansive. Sometimes he does not appear hypochondriacal in the least, but simply cold and absolutely unfeeling. One might almost say that there exist in him two natures, which alternately get the upper hand. Sometimes he is extremely taciturn; everything and everybody seem against him, and he will lie in bed and do nothing! He never indulges in raillery, not because he is not of a sarcastic turn, but rather because he disdains to waste his words. He never cares to hear what anyone has to say, and takes no interest whatever in what is occupying the attention of everyone else at the time. He has a high opinion of his own ability, not altogether without justification, I will own. What more can I add? Your arrival seems likely to produce a most salutary influence.'

'Heaven grant it may!' cried Pulcheria Alexandrovna, much perturbed by these revelations about the character of her Rodia.

At length Razoumikhin ventured to look a little more closely at Eudoxia Romanovna. While he talked he had often cast a glance her way, but only by stealth. She had been sometimes sitting at the table, listening to him with attention, and then, rising, would pace up and down the room with folded arms and closed lips, occasionally stopping to ask a question. It was a habit of hers, also, not to hear people out. She was wearing a thin, dark woollen dress, and a small white fichu round her neck. Razoumikhin soon perceived, by various indications, that the two women were very poor. Had Eudoxia Romanovna been arrayed like a queen, she would probably not have intimidated him in the least; but now, perhaps just because of the the poverty of her attire, he felt greatly constrained in her presence, and exercised a circumspection over his expressions and gestures which naturally added to his embarrassment.

'You have given us many curious details as to my brother's character and – with great impartiality. It is quite right; I thought you were an admirer of his,' observed Eudoxia Romanovna, with a smile. 'I think some woman must have affected his life,' added she thoughtfully.

'I never said so; you may possibly be right, only – '

'What?'

'He loves no one, and perhaps he never will,' pursued Razoumikhin.

'You mean that he is incapable of loving?'

'Do you know, Eudoxia Romanovna, how terribly like your brother you are – in almost every respect?' were the words that escaped the young man's lips. Then, suddenly remembering the judgement he had just passed on Raskolnikoff, he became confused and turned as red as a lobster. Eudoxia Romanovna looked at him, and could not help smiling.

'You may both be mistaken in Rodia's character,' remarked Pulcheria Alexandrovna, slightly piqued. 'I am not speaking of the present, Dounetchka. What Peter Petrovitch writes in this letter, and what you and I suppose, may not be true, but you can scarcely imagine, Dmitri

Prokovitch, how capricious and whimsical he is. When he was but fifteen, his character was a constant source of surprise to me. Even now, I consider him capable of doing things that would never occur to anyone else. To go no further, he nearly broke my heart eighteen months ago by taking it into his head to marry that daughter of his landlady's, as you may have heard?'

'Do you know the whole story?' asked Eudoxia Romanovna.

'Would not you have thought,' continued the mother eagerly, 'that he would have yielded to my tears and entreaties, and been touched by our distress and my illness, and been afraid of causing my death? On the contrary, he would have carried out his intentions with the utmost composure, without yielding to any consideration. Yet it is not that he does not love us.'

'He never spoke to me on the subject,' replied Razoumikhin cautiously, 'but I have heard something about it from Madame Zarnitzin, though she is not over-communicative, and what has come to my ears sounded very strange.'

'Well, what did you learn?' asked both women at once.

'Oh, nothing really very interesting! All I know is, that this marriage, which was all arranged and about to come off when the young lady died, did not at all meet with Madame Zarnitzin's approval. Then others say that the young girl had no pretension to good looks – in fact, she was very plain; they speak of her, too, as sickly in appearance, and extremely peculiar. Still there must have been something attractive about her, or it would be difficult to understand – '

'I have no doubt she had her good points,' remarked Eudoxia Romanovna laconically.

'May Heaven forgive me for having been so glad to hear of her death! – and yet I don't know for which of the two the marriage would have been more fatal,' concluded the mother, and then timidly, after much hesitation, and many glances at Dounia, who appeared to disapprove highly of her tactics, she again began to question Razoumikhin about the scene of the preceding day between Rodia and Looshin. This was the incident which seemed most especially to distress and even terrify her. The young man gave a detailed account of the altercation which he had witnessed, but added, in conclusion, that he considered Raskolnikoff to have wantonly and deliberately insulted Peter Petrovitch, no longer excusing his conduct on the score of illness.

'He must have premeditated this before he fell ill,' he ended by saying.

'I think so too,' said Pulcheria Alexandrovna, full of consternation. But she was much surprised to find Razoumikhin now speaking of

Peter Petrovitch in polite and even half complimentary terms. This struck Eudoxia Romanovna also.

'Then this is your opinion of Peter Petrovitch?' Pulcheria could not help asking.

'It would be impossible to think otherwise of your daughter's future husband,' replied Razoumikhin in a warm tone of decision, 'and it is not mere ordinary courtesy that prompts my language; I speak thus, because – it would be impossible to think otherwise of the man whom Eudoxia Romanovna has honoured by her choice. If I allowed myself to speak disparagingly of him yesterday, it was owing to my being abominably drunk and quite beside myself: – I had lost my senses, in fact I was half mad, and today I feel thoroughly ashamed of myself!'

He coloured and remained silent. Eudoxia Romanovna's cheeks flushed, but she held her tongue. She had not uttered a word since Looshin's name had been first introduced. Pulcheria Alexandrovna, however, when deprived of her daughter's assistance, became evidently much embarrassed. At length she spoke with some hesitation, glancing each moment at Dounia, she said that she found herself in a most awkward situation at the present time.

'You see, Dmitri Prokovitch – ' she began. 'I may be perfectly open with Dmitri Prokovitch, Dounetchka?'

'Certainly, mamma,' rejoined Eudoxia Romanovna in a tone of authority.

'This is the situation,' continued the mother hastily, as if allowing her to make her grief known were removing a load from her breast. 'Early this morning we received a letter from Peter Petrovitch, in reply to one we had written informing him of our arrival. You see, he had promised to come and meet us at the station yesterday, but in his place appeared a servant, who brought us here, and said his master would call on the morrow. And now, instead of coming, Peter Petrovitch has sent this note. You had better read it yourself, it contains something which causes me great uneasiness, you will see at once what it is, – and then be so kind as to give me your frank opinion, Dmitri Prokovitch! You know Rodia's character better than anyone else, and we can have no better counsellor. I must tell you beforehand that Dounetchka decided the point in a second, but I could not tell how to act, so – I waited for you.'

Razoumikhin unfolded the letter, which bore the date of the previous evening, and read as follows: 'Madame Pulcheria Alexandrovna – I have the honour of informing you that an unexpected engagement prevented my meeting your train, but I sent a reliable person in my place. My Senate business will again prevent my waiting upon you in the morning, nor do I wish to interfere with a mother's visit to her son, nor with that of Eudoxia Romanovna to her brother. Consequently it will be precisely eight o'clock at night before I do myself the honour of calling at your lodgings. I must earnestly request to be spared the presence of Rodion Romanovitch throughout this visit, as he offered me the grossest insults during the call I paid him in his sick-room yesterday. Independently of this, I wish to come to a personal explanation with you on a point which we may perhaps regard in different lights. I have the honour to give you notice beforehand that, if, in spite of my express desire, I should find Rodion Romanovitch with you, I shall be obliged at once to retire, and the blame will rest with yourself. This I write because I have reason to believe that Rodion Romanovitch, who appeared so ill at the time of my visit, suddenly regained his strength within two hours, and might, consequently, make his way to you. Yesterday, in fact, I saw him with my own eyes, in the lodgings of a drunkard who had just been run over by a carriage; on the pretext of paying for the funeral expenses, he gave five-and-twenty roubles to the daughter of the deceased, a young person of notorious conduct. At this I was much astonished, knowing the difficulty you had in procuring this sum. Requesting you to present my ardent homage to your estimable daughter Eudoxia Romanovna, permit me to subscribe myself, with all respect and devotion, Your obedient servant, P. LOOSHIN.'

'Now, what am I to do, Dmitri Prokovitch?" asked Pulcheria Alexandrovna almost tearfully. 'How can I tell Rodia he is not to come? Yesterday, he insisted vehemently on our dismissing Peter Petrovitch, and now he himself is forbidden to appear! It would be just like him to come on purpose if he only knew about it, and – whatever would happen then?'

'Follow Eudoxia Romanovna's advice,' replied Razoumikhin calmly, without a moment's hesitation.

'Ah, but she says – Heaven knows what she says, she will not explain her reasons. According to her view, it is better, nay absolutely necessary, that Rodia should be here at eight o'clock and meet Peter Petrovitch. I should prefer not to show him the letter, and to use every means to prevent him from coming, and I reckoned on your assistance. I cannot understand, either, what he can mean by alluding to this dead drunkard and his daughter in this note; Rodia can never have given this person the last coins – which – '

'Which represent so many sacrifices on your part, mamma,' put in Eudoxia Romanovna.

'He was not himself all yesterday,' said Razoumikhin thoughtfully. 'If you only knew how he amused himself in a *traktir*, not that it was such a bad stroke either! He certainly talked about a dead man and a young girl, when I was taking him home yesterday, but I did not understand anything about it. Yesterday, certainly, I myself – '

'The best thing, mamma, will be to go to him, and then we shall soon see what we ought to do. Time is getting on – why, it is actually past ten!' exclaimed Eudoxia Romanovna, looking at a splendid gold enamelled watch, secured by a slight Venetian chain, which looked quite out of keeping with the rest of her attire.

'It must have been a present from him,' thought Razoumikhin.

'Ah, it is time to go! – high time, Dounetchka!' said Pulcheria Alexandrovna, quite alarmed. 'He might think we were resenting his reception of us last night, if we stayed away any longer. Oh, dear me!' While she spoke, she was hastily putting on her bonnet and mantle. Dounetchka, too, was preparing to go out. Her gloves were not merely shabby, but worn out, and Razoumikhin felt startled on seeing the holes; yet, in spite of all, their shabby dress seemed to make both ladies look more dignified, as is always the case with women who know how to arrange their humble attire. 'Good heavens!' exclaimed Pulcheria Alexandrovna, 'could I ever have believed myself shrinking from an interview with my son, my dear Rodia? I feel frightened, Dmitri Prokovitch!' added she, looking at the young man.

'Do not be afraid, mamma,' said Dounia, embracing her mother, 'but trust in him. I have faith in Rodia.'

'And so have I, but I have passed a restless night,' replied the poor woman. The trio then left the house together. 'Do you know, Dounetchka, I was just falling into a doze this morning, at daybreak, when I saw in a dream the late Marfa Petrovna. She was dressed all in white. Ah me! Dmitri Prokovitch, you have not yet heard of the death of Marfa Petrovna?'

'No, I have not. What Marfa Petrovna?'

'She died quite suddenly, and only think – '

'Another time, mamma,' interposed Dounia; 'he does not yet know what Marfa Petrovna you are speaking of.'

'Oh, don't you know that? I fancied I had told you all about it. Pray excuse me, Dmitri Prokovitch, I have been so completely upset for the last two days! I look upon you as our providence, and felt convinced therefore that you must know all about our affairs. I look on you as a relation – please not to be offended with me. Why, what is the matter with your hand? Have you hurt it?'

'Yes, I have hurt it,' murmured the happy Razoumikhin.

'I am too demonstrative at times, and Dounia takes me to task. Oh,

what a shocking hole this is he lives in! I hope we shall find him awake!
How can that landlady of his call it a room? You were saying just now
that he never cares to unbosom himself; I may possibly worry him with
my silly talk? Could you not give me a hint or two, Dmitri Prokovitch?
How ought I to behave towards him? You see, I don't know what to
do.'

'Do not put many questions if you see him frown; and, above all,
avoid too many inquiries about his health, for he dislikes them.'

'Ah, Dmitri Prokovitch, how painful a mother may sometimes find
her position! Here is this staircase – this dreadful staircase!'

'Mamma darling, you are pale, do compose yourself,' said Dounia,
caressing her mother. 'Why torture yourself thus when it must give
him pleasure to see you?' added she with flashing eyes.

'Stop, let me go first to see if he is awake.'

The two ladies slowly followed Razoumikhin up the stairs. On
reaching the fourth floor, they noticed that the landlady's door stood
ajar, and that a pair of piercing black eyes was watching them through
the chink. When it met theirs, the door was suddenly closed with such
a bang that Pulcheria Alexandrovna all but shrieked.

Chapter 3

'HE IS GOING ON capitally!' cried Zosimoff gaily, as he saw the two
ladies enter. The doctor had been there for ten minutes, and was sitting
on the sofa as he had done the night before. Raskolnikoff was dressed
and seated at the other end; he had even taken the trouble to wash and
comb his hair, operations which he had neglected for some time past.
Though the room seemed quite full, now that Razoumikhin and the
ladies had arrived, Nastasia managed to smuggle herself in after them,
and remained to listen to the conversation. Raskolnikoff was certainly
much better than on the previous night; still, he looked very pale and
seemed absorbed in moody thoughts. When Pulcheria Alexandrovna
and her daughter entered, Zosimoff noticed with surprise the expression assumed by the invalid. It was not joy, but a sort of stoic
resignation; the young man seemed mustering all his energy to support
for an hour or two some inevitable torture. After the conversation had
begun, the doctor observed that nearly every word seemed to touch
some secret spring of grief, though at the same time he noticed with
astonishment his patient's increased self-control; the furious monomaniac of the day before now seemed able to command himself to some

degree, and disguise his emotion.

'Yes, I can see myself that I am all but cured now,' said Raskolnikoff, embracing his mother and sister so cordially as to bring a flush of pleasure to the cheek of the former, 'and I am not going to talk as I did yesterday,' added he, addressing Razoumikhin, and pressing his hand affectionately.

'I am actually astonished to find how well he is today,' began Zosimoff. 'If this improvement continues, in three or four days he will be quite well, or at least as much so as he was a month or two ago – perhaps I should go back still farther, for the illness had been coming on for some time, eh? Own now that you may be able partly to trace it,' ended the doctor with a constrained smile, as if still afraid of irritating his patient.

'It may be possible,' returned Raskolnikoff, coldly.

'Now that I can enter into conversation with you,' continued Zosimoff, 'I am anxious to convince you that it is important to remove the primary causes which developed your illness: if you can do that, you will recover; otherwise, the disease will gain ground. I am in the dark as to these primary causes, but they must be known to yourself. You are intelligent and have doubtless observed your own condition. I believe your health to have declined ever since you left the university. You cannot continue without occupation, and the best thing for you, in my opinion, would be to set to work again, have some object in view, and pursue it steadily.'

'Yes, yes, certainly, you are quite right – I shall resume my university studies as soon as possible, and then – all will go well.'

The doctor had given this sage advice partly to impress the ladies. As he ceased, he looked at his patient, and was doubtless somewhat disconcerted by the mocking expression plainly portrayed on his face. But Zosimoff was soon consoled, for Pulcheria Alexandrovna hastened to thank him and was especially demonstrative in her expressions of gratitude for his call of the previous night.

'What, did he go to you during the night?' asked Raskolnikoff uneasily. 'And you actually took no rest after your fatiguing journey?'

'Oh, Rodia, it was only two o'clock. Dounia and I never go to bed at home earlier than that.'

'I don't know how to thank him either,' continued Raskolnikoff, suddenly knitting his brows and looking down. 'Putting aside the question of money – to which you must excuse my alluding,' said he to Zosimoff, 'I am quite at a loss to know what can have excited your interest in me. I really cannot understand it, and indeed I may say that your kindness actually troubles me, because it is so unaccountable. You see how frank I am.'

'Don't trouble yourself,' said Zosimoff, affecting to laugh. 'Suppose yourself my first patient! We doctors at first are as fond of our patients as if they were our own children; indeed, some of us grow positively attached to them. And my practice is not a large one yet.'

'I say nothing about *him*,' said Raskolnikoff, pointing to Razoumikhin. 'I have done nothing but insult and plague him.'

'What nonsense he talks! You seem quite in a sentimental vein today!' exclaimed Razoumikhin.

Had he been more observant, he might have seen that his friend was in a far different mood. Eudoxia Romanovna, however, was not deceived, and began to study her brother attentively.

'Of you, mamma, I dare hardly speak,' pursued Raskolnikoff, apparently reciting a lesson he had conned over that morning; 'it is only this morning that I am able to understand what you must have suffered while awaiting my return last night.'

So saying, he smiled, and suddenly held out his hand to his sister. No word accompanied the gesture, but the smile this time expressed genuine feeling. Dounia seized his hand with joyful gratitude, and grasped it warmly. This was the first mark of attention he had shown her since their altercation of the previous evening. Pulcheria Alexandrovna's face became radiant as she witnessed this silent and conclusive reconciliation between the sister and brother.

Razoumikhin fidgeted on his chair. 'I should love him, if only for that!' murmured he, with his usual tendency towards exaggeration. 'What a noble impulse!'

'How beautiful that was!' thought the mother to herself. 'He has such fine instincts! This simple act of holding out his hand to his sister with that look of affection was certainly the frankest and most delicate manner of coming to an understanding.'

'Oh, Rodia,' said she, hastening to reply to her son's remark, 'you cannot think how unhappy Dounetchka and I felt yesterday. But that is all over now, and we may call ourselves happy again, and now I may tell you. Only fancy, we ran here almost as soon as we had left the station to see you, and this woman – (why, there she is! Good-morning, Nastasia) – she told us first thing that you had been in bed with a fever, and had run out into the street in your delirium, and how they had gone to look for you. You cannot picture our feelings.'

'Yes, yes, it was all most annoying,' muttered Raskolnikoff, but in such an absent and even indifferent manner that Dounetchka looked up in surprise.

'Let me see, I had something else to say to you,' continued he, making an effort to rack his memory. 'Oh yes, I hope, mamma, that neither you nor Dounia will think that I should have refused to come to see you today, or was waiting for you to call on me first.'

'What ever makes you say that, Rodia?' exclaimed Pulcheria Alexandrovna, as much astonished this time as her daughter.

'It sounds like the most formal courtesy,' thought Dounetchka; 'he makes peace and apologises as if he were reciting a lesson, or satisfying the rules of etiquette.'

'I wanted to come to you the instant I woke, but I had no clothes to put on; I ought to have told Nastasia yesterday to wash out that blood. I have only just been able to dress.'

'Blood! What blood?' asked Pulcheria Alexandrovna, in alarm.

'It was nothing, do not be uneasy. While I was roaming the streets yesterday, in my delirium, I came into contact with a man – a clerk, who had just got crushed; that was how my clothes got covered with blood – '

'And you delirious all the while! Yet you recollect everything,' broke in Razoumikhin.

'Quite true,' returned Raskolnikoff uneasily. 'I remember everything, down to the smallest detail; the strange part of it is that I cannot explain why I said or did anything, or why I went to such and such a place.'

'That is a well-known phenomenon,' remarked Zosimoff. 'The act is often accomplished with singular skill and ability, but the principle from which it emanates becomes altered in the diseased brain and depends on various morbid conditions.' This phrase 'the diseased brain,' threw a chill over those assembled. Zosimoff had let the words escape him unintentionally, while absorbed in dilating on his favourite theme. Raskolnikoff, wrapped in thought, seemed to pay no heed to the doctor's words. A strange smile was playing round his blanched lips.

'Well, but what of this man who was run over? I interrupted you just now,' Razoumikhin hastened to say.

'What?' said Raskolnikoff, as if suddenly roused. 'Oh yes, I got covered with blood in helping to convey him to his house – by the by, mamma, I committed an unpardonable folly yesterday; I must have indeed have been out of my mind. All that money you sent me, I gave away to the widow, to pay for the funeral. The poor woman is greatly to be pitied – she is consumptive – and there she is, left with three young children and no means of support; there is a daughter too. Perhaps you might have acted as I did, had you seen their misery. I am aware, however, that I had no right to act as I did, more especially as I knew what it had cost you to send me the money.'

'Never mind that, Rodia,' replied the mother, 'I have no doubt you always act for the best.'

'Don't be so sure of that,' returned he, with a distorted smile. Conversation languished for a while. Everyone felt conscious of something forced in his words and silence, in the reconciliation and pardon.

'Have you heard of Marfa Petrovna's death, Rodia?' asked Pulcheria Alexandrovna, suddenly.

'Who is Marfa Petrovna?'

'Why, Marfa Petrovna Svidrigaïloff, to be sure! I told you so much about her in my last letter.'

'Oh, ye-yes, I remember now. And so she is dead; well, really!' said he, starting up as if from sleep. 'Can it be really true? What did she die of?'

'Why, fancy, she fell down dead!' replied Pulcheria Alexandrovna eagerly, encouraged by her son's apparent interest. 'She died the very day my letter to you was posted. As far as we can tell, that dreadful man was the cause of her death. They say he beat her black and blue!'

'Did such scenes really occur in their household?' asked Raskolnikoff, turning to his sister.

'On the contrary, he always showed great patience, and behaved most politely to her – indeed, he was often far too indulgent, and so matters went on for seven years – then he suddenly lost all patience.'

'Then if he had shown such patience for seven years, he could not have been so very terrible! You seem to be making excuses for him, Dounetchka?'

The young girl frowned. 'Oh, he is a terrible man! I cannot conceive anything more dreadful,' replied she, shuddering and becoming pensive.

'This scene had taken place in the morning,' continued Pulcheria Alexandrovna. 'Then she ordered the horses to be put in at once, because she was intending to drive to town immediately after dinner, as she usually did on such occasions; she made a hearty meal, they say – '

'Even when she was beaten black and blue?'

'It was her habit. Then, as soon as she rose from the table, she would take her bath, in order to be ready to start at once. You must know that she was under treatment; there is a spring in the neighbourhood, and she bathed in it regularly each day. She had hardly stepped into the water when she was seized with an apoplectic fit.'

'And no wonder!' observed Zosimoff.

'And her husband had beaten her severely.'

'What has that to do with it?' put in Eudoxia Romanovna.

'Well, mamma, I can't see why you should tell such ridiculous stories,' said Raskolnikoff, becoming suddenly irritable.

'Well, my dear, I did not know what to talk to you about,' was Pulcheria Alexandrovna's frank confession.

'You both seem to be afraid of me,' resumed he with a bitter smile.

'We are,' answered Dounia, eyeing him with severity. 'Mamma was so frightened that she actually crossed herself as we came upstairs.' The young man's face worked convulsively.

'Oh, what are you saying, Dounia? Do not be offended, pray, Rodia! How can you talk so, Dounia?' said Pulcheria Alexandrovna apologetically, quite confused. 'It is true that I thought, all the time I was in the train, of the pleasure of being with you and talking to you again. I was so overjoyed that I did not even think the journey long! And now I am happy, quite happy, to be with you again, Rodia.'

'Say no more, mamma,' murmured he in much agitation, pressing her hand, but averting his eyes, 'we shall have plenty of time to talk!' He had scarcely uttered these words when he looked pale and distressed; again he felt a chill run through his veins, and owned to himself that he had uttered an awful lie, for henceforward he was cut off from all unconstrained intercourse with his mother or anyone else. This dreadful thought came home to him so vividly at the moment that, forgetting all about his guests, he rose and made for the door.

'What are you about?' cried Razoumikhin, seizing him by the arm.

Raskolnikoff sat down again and looked round without saying a word. Everyone stared at him with a feeling of stupefaction. 'How dull you all are!' exclaimed he, suddenly. 'Say something, at any rate! Why do you sit as if you had all been struck dumb? Come, speak, what is the use of our meeting unless we have some conversation?'

'Heaven be praised! I thought he was going to have another attack,' said Pulcheria Alexandrovna, who had been crossing herself.

'What is the matter with you, Rodia?' asked Eudoxia Romanovna, anxiously.

'Well, it was only some nonsense that came into my head again,' replied he, beginning to laugh.

'If it is merely nonsense, so much the better; but I was half-afraid – ' muttered Zosimoff, rising. 'I am obliged to leave you now, but I shall try to come again in the course of the day – ' And, bowing, he left the room.

'What an excellent man!' observed Pulcheria Alexandrovna.

'Yes, he is a capital fellow, so good and clever and intelligent,' said Raskolnikoff with unusual animation. 'I cannot remember where I met him before my illness; but I believe I have come across him somewhere. There is another excellent man,' added he, nodding to Razoumikhin;

'but where are you off to?' Razoumikhin had just risen.

'I am obliged to go too. I have some business to attend to,' said he.

'You have nothing in the world to attend to; stay here. You are only going because Zosimoff has left. Don't go. But what is the time? Is it twelve o'clock? What a pretty watch you have there, Dounia! Why do you keep so silent? I have to do all the talking.'

'It was a present from Marfa Petrovna,' replied Dounia.

'And it cost a great deal,' added Pulcheria Alexandrovna.

'I thought Looshin must have given it you.'

'No, he has not given Dounetchka anything yet.'

'Ah! Do you remember, mamma, how I was once in love and wanted to marry?' said he abruptly, looking at his mother, who felt startled at his tone and the sudden turn he had given to the conversation.

'Yes, certainly, my dear boy,' replied Pulcheria Alexandrovna, exchanging glances with Dounetchka and Razoumikhin.

'H'm! – yes; what shall I say about it? I seem to have forgotten it all now. She was a sickly young girl, constantly ailing,' continued he, half to himself, with his eyes fixed on the ground. 'She was fond of showing charity to the poor and was always thinking of entering a convent; I remember her bursting into tears one day when she was talking to me about it; yes, yes, I remember that – remember it perfectly. She was not pretty – rather plain, indeed. I really cannot say why I became fond of her; perhaps I felt an interest in her because she was so delicate – if she had been lame, or deformed into the bargain, maybe I should have been still more in love with her,' and he smiled pensively. 'There was nothing much in it, merely a boyish fancy – '

'No, it was more than a boyish fancy,' remarked Dounetchka conclusively. Raskolnikoff looked at his sister attentively, but either failed to hear or understand what she said. Then, rising with a melancholy air, he kissed his mother, and returned to his seat.

'Do you love her still?' asked Pulcheria Alexandrovna, much touched.

'Her? Still? Oh! – you are talking about her! It all seems such an age since, and so very far off. I have just the same feeling, however, about all that surrounds me now – ' He looked attentively at the two women. 'See, you are here – and yet I feel as if you were a thousand versts away – I don't know why I should talk about it, though – and what is the use of questioning me?' added he, angrily; then he relapsed into his reverie, and began biting his nails.

'What dreadful lodgings you have, Rodia! – you might as well be in a sepulchre,' suddenly remarked Pulcheria Alexandrovna, to break the painful silence; 'I am sure it must have had a good deal to do with your hypochondria.'

'This room?' resumed he absently. 'Yes, it has had a good deal to do with it – that is just what I thought myself – if you only knew, mamma, what a strange idea your words conveyed,' added he suddenly, with an enigmatical smile. Raskolnikoff was scarcely able to endure the presence of the mother and sister from whom he had been separated for three years, yet with whom he found it impossible to converse. Yet there was a subject he felt obliged to mention; just now, when he had started up, he had told himself this question must be settled, one way or other – that very day. At this moment he felt glad to bring it forward as a means of escape from his embarrassment. 'Listen to what I have to say, Dounia,' he began in a harsh voice. 'I am ready to apologise for what passed between us yesterday, but I consider it my duty to remind you that I keep to my alternative; you have to choose between me and Looshin. I may be infamous, but there is no reason why you should be. One is enough. So if you marry Looshin, from that moment I shall cease to consider you my sister.'

'Rodia! Rodia! There you are, beginning to talk in the same style as yesterday!' cried Pulcheria Alexandrovna, overwhelmed with distress. 'Why do you keep talking of yourself as infamous? I cannot bear it! Those are the words you used yesterday.'

'Brother,' returned Dounia, in a tone as cold and hard as his own, 'the misunderstanding between us is based on an error into which you have fallen. I thought the matter over in the night, and saw how it was. You imagine that I am sacrificing myself to someone else. In this you are mistaken. I am marrying simply on my own account, because my situation is one of great embarrassment. Of course I shall be very glad if this enables me eventually to assist my relations, but this is not what has influenced me in my decision – '

'She is lying!' thought Raskolnikoff to himself, biting his nails as a vent for his anger. 'She is too proud to own that she longs to become my benefactress! What arrogance! The love of such despicable souls is as bad as their hate. Oh, how I detest them all!'

'In one word,' pursued Dounetchka, 'I am about to marry Peter Petrovitch because, of two evils, I choose the least. I intend to be loyal in rendering all that he expects of me, and thus he will not be deceived in his wife. What made you smile just now?' She coloured, and her eyes sparkled with indignation.

'All that he expects?' echoed he, with a bitter smile.

'Up to a certain point. From the manner in which Peter Petrovitch made his proposal, I saw at once what he was likely to require. He may think rather too highly of himself, but I hope he may be able to appreciate me too. Why are you laughing again?'

'And why are you blushing again? You are false, sister! You cannot have any esteem for Looshin; I have seen and heard him. You must, therefore, be marrying him for interested motives; your conduct is sordid, to say the least of it, and I am glad, at all events, to see you can blush for it!'

'It is quite untrue, I am not saying what is false!' cried the young girl, losing her composure. 'I shall not marry him unless I am convinced that I can esteem him thoroughly. Fortunately, the means of discovering this lies within my power today. This marriage is not sordid, as you declare! But, even supposing you were right and I was taking such a mean step, would it not be cruel of you to speak as you do? Why should you exact from me a heroism which you may possibly find yourself unable to carry into practice? It is nothing but tyranny and despotism! If I am injuring anyone, it is myself only – I am guilty of no one's death! Why do you look at me so terribly? What makes you turn pale? Rodia! dear Rodia – '

'Good heavens! he is fainting, and it is all your doing,' cried Pulcheria Alexandrovna.

'No, it is nothing – a passing weakness merely! My head was swimming, but I was not faint. Fainting-fits belong to women. Ah, yes, what was it I was about to say? Oh, how are you going to ascertain this very day whether Looshin is worthy of your esteem, and whether he – appreciates you? That was your expression, I believe, unless my ears deceived me?'

'Show my brother Peter Petrovitch's letter, mamma,' said Dounetchka.

Pulcheria Alexandrovna held out the letter with trembling fingers. Raskolnikoff read it through twice, and very carefully. Some outburst was expected by all, and the mother was especially anxious. The young man seemed considering something for a minute, and then handed back the letter.

'I cannot understand it,' began he, addressing no one in particular. 'He is a barrister, accustomed to plead; he is ornate even in his conversation, and yet he writes an uneducated letter.' These words produced a general stupefaction; they were so different from what had been expected. 'At any rate, if not quite uneducated, his style is uncultivated; he writes like a commercial man,' added Raskolnikoff.

'Peter Petrovitch never boasts of having received a good education,' said Eudoxia Romanovna, slightly nettled by her brother's manner; 'he is proud of being a self-made man.'

'Well, he has reason to be proud of it; I don't object to that. You seem vexed, sister, at my making a frivolous remark about this letter; do you imagine that I insist on such trifles simply to tease you? On the contrary, my remarks on his style bear on the present attitude of affairs. His phrase, "You will have no one but yourself to blame," is perfectly explicit. In short, he announces his intention of retiring at once if he finds me with you. By this threat he intimates that, unless you obey him, he will leave you in the lurch after bringing you to St Petersburg. What do you say to that? Can these words offend you as much, coming from Looshin's pen, as if they had been written by him' (pointing to Razoumikhin) 'or by Zosimoff or myself?'

'No,' replied Dounetchka, 'I feel that he expressed his thoughts too plainly, and that he may not have the gift of style – your remark was very judicious. I scarcely expected –'

'Looking at the letter as that of a business man, he could scarcely have expressed himself differently, and he is, perhaps, not to be brought to book for his apparent boorishness. Still, I must disenchant you on another point; one clause of his letter contains a vile calumny against myself. I gave a miserable, consumptive widow some money yesterday – not, as he says, "on the pretext of paying for the funeral expenses," but actually for that object; and the sum was given by me to the widow herself, not to the dead man's daughter – "the young person of notorious conduct" to whom he alludes, and upon whom, moreover, I had never set eyes till yesterday. In all this, I can see nothing but a desire to slander me in your eyes and separate me from you. Here, again, he writes in his legal style, making his intention abundantly evident without any attempt to couch it in civil terms. He is intelligent, but discretion requires something more. All this shows pretty well what the man is, and I don't see much trace of any feeling for you. This I say on your account, as I really wish you well.' Dounetchka did not answer; her mind was quite made up, she was looking forward to that evening.

'Well, Rodia, what do you decide?' asked Pulcheria Alexandrovna, whose anxiety had been still further increased by hearing her son's business-like discussion of the matter.

'What do you mean?'

'You see what Peter Petrovitch writes: he does not wish you to join us tonight, and even declares that he shall go, if you come. That is why I ask what you mean to do.'

'The decision does not rest with me. It is for you and Dounia to see whether you feel aggrieved by Peter Petrovitch's requirements. I shall do just as you like,' added he coldly.

'Dounetchka has already decided the question, and I quite agree with her,' hastily rejoined his mother.

'I feel your presence indispensable at this meeting, Rodia, and beg you earnestly to come,' said Dounia. 'Will you?'

'Yes.'

'I shall feel much obliged if you, too, will join us at eight o'clock,' continued she, addressing Razoumikhin. 'Mamma, I am asking Dmitri Prokovitch to come too.'

'You are quite right, Dounetchka. Arrange it all as you think best,' added Pulcheria Alexandrovna. 'To me it will be a great relief; I cannot bear anything underhand, it is always best to speak out and be open. Peter Petrovitch may take offence if he chooses!'

Chapter 4

AT THIS MOMENT the door was noiselessly opened; a girl entered the room, casting a timid look around her. Her appearance caused general surprise, and every eye was inquisitively fixed on her. Raskolnikoff did not at first remember her. It was Sophia Semenovna Marmeladoff. He had seen her for the first time the day before, but in connection with circumstances and in a dress which had left quite a different impression of her upon his mind. On this occasion she seemed a girl in modest and even poor array, with becoming and reserved manners and anxious face. She wore a very simple and short dress and an old-fashioned bonnet. Of yesterday's attire no vestige was left, excepting the parasol in her hand. On seeing this company, which she had not expected to find there, her confusion was extreme, and she even made an attempt to withdraw.

'Ah! Is that you?' said Raskolnikoff, greatly surprised, and growing all at once uneasy.

He remembered that Looshin's letter, which had been read by his mother and sister, contained an allusion to a certain young person 'of notorious conduct.' He had just now been protesting against this calumny, and declaring that he had seen the identical young person for the first time the night before, when, lo and behold, she herself called! He also remembered that he had allowed the words 'of notorious conduct' to pass by without any special protest. In a moment these thoughts passed helter-skelter through his brain. But, on observing the girl more attentively, he saw her so overwhelmed with shame that he pitied her in consequence. And at the moment when, crestfallen, she purposed leaving the room, a species of revolution was effected within him.

'I really did not expect you,' he made haste to observe, whilst inviting her by a look to remain. 'Pray be seated. You come, I presume, from

Catherine Ivanovna? Excuse me, not there; but here.'

On Sonia's visit, Razoumikhin, seated near the door on one of the only three chairs which were in the room, had partly risen in order to allow the girl to pass by. Raskolnikoff's first movement had been to motion the latter to the part of the couch where Zosimoff had just been seated, but reflecting on the familiar character of this piece of furniture, which was his own bed, he reconsidered his request and pointed to Razoumikhin's chair.

'Come and sit here,' said he to his friend, whilst causing him to take the seat the doctor had just vacated.

Sonia sat down, almost trembling with nervousness, and timidly looked at both ladies. It was self-evident that she herself could not realise how she had the audacity to sit near them. This thought caused her such pain that she suddenly rose, and, greatly distressed, addressed Raskolnikoff. 'I – I have only called for a moment. Excuse my having disturbed you,' she remarked in a hesitating voice. 'It was Catherine Ivanovna sent me; not having anyone else near, she begs most earnestly that you will be kind enough to be present tomorrow morning at the funeral service, at St Mitrophane's, and to come afterwards to our place – I should say her place – to take some refreshment. She trusts you will do her this honour.' After these words, painfully uttered, Sonia remained silent.

'I shall most certainly try. I will do my very best,' stammered, in his turn, Raskolnikoff, who had now partly risen. 'Pray be seated,' added he, somewhat brusquely, 'do! You are not in a very great hurry, are you? I am anxious to have a word with you; a moment or two will suffice.' At the same time he invited her with a gesture to resume her seat. Sonia obeyed, casting her timid glances once more on the two ladies, and suddenly averting them again.

Raskolnikoff's features tightened, his pale face turned scarlet, his eyes shot fire. 'Mother,' said he, in a quivering voice, 'this is Sophia Semenovna Marmeladoff, the daughter of poor Mr Marmeladoff, who was run over yesterday, and of whom I told you.'

Pulcheria Alexandrovna looked at Sonia and gently closed her eyes. In spite of the dread she experienced with reference to her son, she could not refuse herself this satisfaction. Dounetchka turned towards the girl and began to examine her seriously. On hearing Raskolnikoff mention her name, Sonia once more looked up, but with increasing embarrassment.

'I was going to ask you,' the young man made haste to say, 'how things went off at your place today. I hope you have not been worried, or that you have not found the police a nuisance?'

'No, nothing out of the way has occurred. The cause of death was quite clear, and we have been left undisturbed, except that the other lodgers are annoyed.'

'Why should they be?'

'They say that the body has been kept too long – it is hot now – there is a smell, so that tonight, towards dark, it will be taken to the mortuary chapel, where it will remain till tomorrow. At first Catherine Ivanovna objected, but she has at last acknowledged that it could not be otherwise.'

'Then the body will be removed this very day?'

'Catherine hopes that you will honour us tomorrow by your presence at the funeral, and that you will come to the dinner afterwards.'

'What! Is she giving a spread?'

'Well, a kind of collation. She has requested me to thank you for the help you gave us yesterday. Without you, we could not have met the various expenses.'

A sudden quivering moved the lower part of the girl's face, but she conquered her emotion, and once more looked down. During this dialogue Raskolnikoff had attentively watched her. Sonia had a thin and pale face, her small nose and chin were more or less pointed and angular, the whole face was not quite in harmony, hence she could not be called pretty. Her blue eyes, on the other hand, were so limpid that, on becoming animated, they gave to the whole face such an expression of kindliness that people felt involuntarily attracted towards her. Another characteristic peculiarity was noticeable in her face as in her person – she seemed much younger than her real age, and although only eighteen, she might almost be taken for a lassie. Some of her ways, indeed, often caused merriment.

'But is it possible that Catherine Ivanovna can have met her expenses with such a trifle? And yet she thinks of giving a dinner or something of the kind?' asked Raskolnikoff.

'The coffin will be a very simple one, everything will be done as modestly as possible so that things won't cost much. Catherine and I have just been reckoning up the expenses; and, when everything will be paid, enough will be left to give some kind of repast, for Catherine Ivanovna is very particular that there shall be one. Nobody can possibly object to that. It is a kind of consolation for her, and you know she is – '

'I know – I know – of course – I see you are looking at my room? My mother says herself that it is like a grave.'

'Yesterday you deprived yourself of everything for us!' replied Sonetchka in a low and rapid voice, once more looking down. Her lips and chin began again to quiver. From the first moment of her arrival she had been struck by the poverty which was visible in Raskolnikoff's lodging, and these words fell from her almost unawares. There was silence. Dounetchka's eyes brightened, and Pulcheria Alexandrovna herself looked at Sonia in an affable way.

'Rodia,' said the latter, on rising, 'it is, I believe, understood that we dine together. Dounetchka, let us be off. As for you, Rodia, you ought to take a short turn, then have a rest before you come to us, at your very earliest. I am afraid we have fatigued you.'

'Yes, yes, I'll come,' he made haste to reply, rising in his turn. 'Besides, I have something to attend to.'

'I suppose,' exclaimed Razoumikhin, looking at Raskolnikoff with astonishment, 'you are not going to dine alone? You can't do that!'

'No, no; I shall be sure to come. But you had better stop a minute. You won't want him just now, will you, mother? I am not taking him away from you, am I?'

'By no means! And I hope, Dmitri Prokovitch, that you will be kind enough to come and dine with us?'

'Do, pray!' added Dounia. Razoumikhin bowed, beaming. For a moment, everyone present experienced an unusual constraint.

'Adieu, Rodia, or rather *au revoir*; I hate the word, adieu. Adieu, Nastasia. Why, I positively catch myself saying it again!'

Pulcheria Alexandrovna intended to bow to Sonia, but, in spite of her kindly wish, she could not make up her mind to do so, and hurriedly left the room. It was, however, not so with Eudoxia Romanovna, who seemed to have been impatiently waiting for this moment. When, following her mother, she passed by Sonia, she made her a perfectly courteous bow. The girl became confused, and bowed, in her turn, with nervous hurry, whilst even her face betrayed an expression of sadness, as if Eudoxia Romanovna's politeness had painfully affected her.

'Farewell, Dounia!' cried Raskolnikoff in the passage. 'Give me your hand!'

'But I have just now given it to you, have you already forgotten?' answered Dounia, turning towards him with an affable air, although she felt more or less constrained.

'Then give it me again.' And he clutched his sister's slender fingers. Dounetchka smiled, blushed, hastened to free her hand, and followed her mother. She also was happy, although we are not in a position to know why.

'That is as it should be!' said the young man, on his return to Sonia, who had stayed behind. At the same time he looked at her with a serene air: 'May God give peace to the dead, and let the living live! Is that right?'

Sonia noticed with some astonishment that Raskolnikoff's face had suddenly brightened up. For some time he considered silently: everything that Marmeladoff had told him concerning her suddenly occurred to his mind. 'This is the matter I have to talk to you about,' said Raskolnikoff, drawing Razoumikhin into the recess of the window.

'Then, am I to say to Catherine Ivanovna that you are coming?' On saying which, Sonia was preparing to take leave.

'I am at your service in a moment, Sophia Semenovna; we have no secrets, don't be uncomfortable. I am anxious to say a word or two to you.' And, suddenly stopping, he said to Razoumikhin: 'You know that – what is his name? – Porphyrius Petrovitch?'

'I should think I did, he is a relation of mine! Well, what about him?' replied Razoumikhin, greatly perplexed by this question.

'Did you not tell me yesterday that he was preparing – that investigation – all about that murder, I mean?'

'Yes, I did; what about it?' asked Razoumikhin, opening his eyes wide.

'I think you told me that he was examining people who had been pledging things with the old woman. Now, I have been pledging things there also – not worth talking about, I admit. A little ring my sister gave me when I went to St Petersburg, and a silver watch which belonged to my father. The lot is not worth more than five or six roubles, but I cling to the things as so many keepsakes. What am I to do now? I do not wish these things to be lost, especially the watch. I trembled just now lest my mother should wish to see it when Dounetchka's watch was mentioned. It is the only thing left of my father's. If it were to get lost, my mother would get ill in consequence. So much for women! I want you to tell me how I am to act? I know that an affidavit must be taken before the police. But would it not be better for me to go straight to Porphyrius himself? What say you? I want to arrange about this as soon as possible. You will see that even before dinner my mother will ask about the watch.'

'You must not go to the police at all, but to Porphyrius!' cried Razoumikhin, a prey to extraordinary agitation. 'I am glad! We can go at once, it is only a stone's throw from here, we shall be sure to find him in!'

'All right – let us be off!'

'He will be delighted to make your acquaintance! I have often talked to him about you on different occasions – as late as yesterday, even. Let us go! So you knew the old woman? Everything seems to turn out admirably! Yes, Sophia Ivanovna – '

'Sophia Semenovna,' corrected Raskolnikoff. 'Sophia Semenovna, this is my friend, Razoumikhin, a good fellow.'

'If you are obliged to go out – ' commenced Sonia, whom this introduction had more and more confused, and who did not dare raise her eyes to Razoumikhin.

'Well, let us be off!' said Raskolnikoff. 'I shall call your way in the course of the day, Sophia Semenovna, if you will tell me where you live.' He said these words, not precisely in an embarrassed manner, but with a certain hurry, whilst avoiding the girl's gaze. She gave him her address, not without a blush. They all three went out.

'Don't you shut your door?' asked Razoumikhin whilst going downstairs.

'Never! Why, for the last two years I have been wanting to buy a lock!' answered Raskolnikoff carelessly. 'Not bad, is it? I mean for people who have nothing to lock up!' he added gaily, addressing Sonia. They stopped on the threshold of the large gateway. 'You turn to the right, do you not, Sophia Semenovna? By the by, how did you discover my lodging?' One could see that what he said was not what he wished to say, as he continued to watch the girl's bright and gentle eyes.

'Why, you gave Poletchka your address yesterday.'

'What Poletchka? Ah! yes, that is your little sister, is she not? So you mean to say that I gave her my address?'

'Have you forgotten having done so?'

'Oh, no! I remember.'

'I have heard my poor father speak of you. Only I did not know your name then, neither did he. I have come now – and when I discovered your name yesterday – I asked today: "Does Mr Raskolnikoff live here?" I did not know that you also lived in furnished lodgings. Goodbye. I will tell Catherine Ivanovna.'

Pleased that she was at last able to go, Sonia withdrew with rapid stride and downcast look. She was longing to reach the first corner of the street to the right, in order to escape the scrutiny of the two young men and to reflect unobserved on the various incidents of her visit. Never had she experienced anything like it. The whole of an unknown world rose confusedly to her mind. She suddenly remembered that Raskolnikoff had of his own accord given expression to his intention of visiting her today; he might therefore call in the course of the morning, or he might do so at once!

'Would to Heaven he did not call today!' she murmured sadly. 'Great heavens! In my home – in that room – he would see – heavens!'

She was too thoughtful to have noticed that since leaving the house, she had been followed by a stranger. At the moment when Raskolnikoff, Razoumikhin, and Sonia had stopped on the pavement to converse for a moment, chance would have it that this gentleman should pass closely by them. Sonia's words, 'I asked: "Does Mr Raskolnikoff live here?" ' accidently struck the stranger's ear and almost made him shiver. He stealthily looked at the three speakers, and particularly at Raskolnikoff, to whom the girl had spoken; then he examined the house to be able, if necessary, to remember it. All this was done in a moment and as unostensibly as possible; upon which, the gentleman walked on with slackened pace, as if he were waiting for someone. It was Sonia he was waiting for; he soon saw her bid the two young men good-day and take the direction of her lodging.

'Where can she live? I have seen her face somewhere,' he thought. 'I'll try and find out.'

When he had reached the street corner, he crossed to the opposite pavement, turned round, and saw the girl taking the same direction as himself; she, however, observed nothing. When she had reached the corner, she took the same side. He now followed her, continuing along the opposite pavement, without taking his eyes off her. Fifty yards farther on he crossed the roadway, and, once more catching her up, walked behind her at a few paces' distance. He was a man of about fifty, but well preserved and appearing much younger than his age. He was of more than medium height, tolerably stout, with broad and some-what stooping shoulders. His dress was as elegant as it was comfortable, his gloves new; in his hand he held a handsome cane, with which he tapped the pavement as he went on. Everything about his person bespoke the gentleman. His broad face looked pleasant; whilst his complexion and vermilion lips showed that he was not a St Petersburger. His still thick head of hair had retained its blonde colour, and was just commencing to turn grey; his long and full beard was of yet lighter colour than his hair. His blue eyes had a cold, serious, and fixed look. The stranger had had plenty of opportunity to notice that Sonia was absent in mind and thoughtful. Having reached her house, she entered it; whilst the man behind her kept on following, seeming somewhat astonished. After having entered the courtyard, Sonia took the staircase on the right – the one that ascended to her lodging. 'Bah!' said the gentleman to himself, ascending the same staircase the girl had taken. Then for the first time Sonia noticed the man's presence. Having reached the third floor, she walked down a passage and rang at number nine, where could be read on the door the two words, '*Kapernasumoff, tailor*,' written in chalk. 'Bah!' repeated the unknown man, surprised at this coincidence, whilst ringing the bell of number eight. The two doors were six paces apart.

'Are you living at Kapernasumoff's?' he asked of Sonia, with a smile. 'He mended me a waistcoat yesterday. I lodge here, close to you, in Madame Resslich's – Gertrude Karlovna's – rooms. Isn't that strange?' Sonia looked attentively at him. 'We are neighbours, then?' he went on, in a pleasant tone of voice. 'I have only been in St Petersburg since the day before yesterday. Well, till we meet again.' Sonia made no reply. The door was opened and the girl quickly entered. She felt frightened, abashed.

Razoumikhin was in excellent spirits whilst accompanying his friend to Porphyrius's.

'Capital, my dear fellow!' he repeated more than once, 'and I am delighted, I can tell you! I did not know that you yourself had been pledging things with the old woman. Was it long ago? I mean is it long since you were there?'

'Where do you mean?' answered Raskolnikoff, seeming to question his memory. 'I was there, I think, two days before she died. I am not anxious to take my things out of pawn just now,' he added somewhat hurriedly, as if this question had struck him. 'I have only got about a rouble left, thanks to the follies I committed yesterday whilst in the state of mind I was in!' He laid special stress on the words 'state of mind.'

'Yes, indeed,' Razoumikhin made haste to reply, whilst dwelling on a thought which had struck him, 'it was owing to that, then, that you – the matter did strike me – do you know that, when you were in your delirious state, you talked of nothing but rings and watch-chains? You did, indeed. It is all clear to me now, and everything is explained.'

'I see how this idea has got hold of them! I have evidence to that effect now: this man would lay down his life for mine and he is delighted to be able to account for my talking of finger-rings during my raving condition! My language must have confirmed their suspicions!' mused Raskolnikoff. 'But,' he inquired in a loud voice, 'shall we find him in?'

'Of course we shall,' replied Razoumikhin, without hesitation. 'He is a capital fellow, as you will see! A little awkward, I admit – not, let me tell you, that he is wanting in good manners. No, no; he is awkward from another point of view. He is no fool either; on the contrary, he is very sharp, only his cast of mind is a peculiar one – incredulous, sceptic, cynical. Nothing he enjoys more than to mystify people. At the same time, he sticks to the old lines – that is to say that he admits nothing but material evidence. He knows his business, I can tell you. Last year he disentangled a case of murder in which nearly every species of evidence was wanting! He is most anxious to get to know you!'

'Why should he be?'

'Oh! only because – why, latterly, during your malady, we have often had occasion to talk about you. He used to be present at our conversations. When he heard that you were reading for the law, and that you had been obliged to leave the University, he said, "What a pity!" From that I gathered – not that I attached any special importance to his remark, but rather to many other things. Yesterday, Zametoff – listen to me, Rodia. When I took you home yesterday I was intoxicated, and talked anyhow. I fear you must have taken what I said in bad part.'

'What was it you said? Did you say people took me for a lunatic? They may be right after all,' answered Raskolnikoff, with a forced smile.

They remained silent. Razoumikhin's high spirits were angrily noticed by Raskolnikoff. What his friend had just told him concerning the magistrate did not fail to cause him anxiety.

'That's the house,' said Razoumikhin.

'The main thing to know,' thought Raskolnikoff, 'is whether Porphyrius is informed of my visit yesterday to the lodging of that old hag, and as to my inquiries on the subject of blood. I must, first of all, be satisfied on that score. I must, as soon as I can, catch his eye, and make sure of that, otherwise I'll make a clean breast of it, though it cost me my life.'

'Do you know?' he went on, addressing Razoumikhin brusquely, with a sly smile, 'I fancy, old fellow, that since this morning you have been greatly agitated. Am I right?'

'In what way? Not at all!' replied Razoumikhin, vexed.

'I am right, though. Just now, for instance, you were fidgeting on the edge of your chair, a thing you never do, and people might have thought you had the cramp. You kept on starting up; your temper was continually changing; you got cross, to become a moment afterwards like honey and sugar. Why, you even blushed, and when you were asked to dinner you turned scarlet.'

'Nonsense! What makes you say that?'

'Why, you are as bashful as a schoolboy! Even now you are blushing!'

'You are unbearable.'

'But why such confusion, O Romeo? As you please, I'll mention all about it, somewhere, today. Ha, ha, ha! I shall be sure to amuse my mother and someone else.'

'Just one moment; things are getting serious – let me tell you – why after –' spluttered Razoumikhin, cold as ice. 'What will you mention to them? My dear friend, what a horrid fellow you are!'

'Just like a rose! If you only knew how it becomes you! But I hope you have taken care of your toilet today? Bless me, if I don't think you have gone in for bear's grease! Put your head down for a minute so that I may smell!'

'You horrid wretch!'

Raskolnikoff burst out laughing, and this hilarity, which he seemed unable to check, continued till the two young men reached Porphyrius Petrovitch's house. The visitors' laughter could be heard within, and Raskolnikoff trusted that it might be.

'Say another word, and I'll do for you!' muttered Razoumikhin furiously, seizing his friend's shoulder.

Chapter 5

RASKOLNIKOFF ENTERED the magistrate's house with the air of a man doing his very best to keep his countenance, but who only succeeded in doing so at great pains. Behind him came Razoumikhin, blushing like a peony, his features distorted by anger and shame. The ungainly person and discomfited aspect of this big boy were, at the moment, amusing enough to justify his comrade's hilarity. Porphyrius Petrovitch, standing up in the middle of the room, looked inquiringly at his two visitors. Raskolnikoff bowed to the master of the house, shook hands with him, and seemed to make a violent effort to stifle his laughing mood while having to answer customary questions. But no sooner had he recovered his self-possession and stammered out a few words, than, in the very act of introduction, his eyes accidentally met those of Razoumikhin. He could no longer contain himself, and his serious attitude vanished before a fit of merriment, all the more uncontrollable from its previous curb. Razoumikhin unwittingly played into his friend's hands, for this 'silly laughter' threw him into a passion, which lent to the interview an air of frank and natural gaiety.

'Wretch!' howled Razoumikhin, violently raising his arm.

The effect of this gesture was to upset a small side-table where stood a tumbler which had contained tea.

'Pray, gentlemen, why spoil the furniture? You are doing injury to the State!' exclaimed Porphyrius Petrovitch.

Raskolnikoff roared to such an extent that for some time he left his hand in that of the magistrate, and it certainly would have been unusual to have left it there too long, hence he withdrew it at the right moment in order to keep up the assumed part he was playing. As for Razoumikhin, he was more confused than ever since he had upset a side-table and broken a glass, and, after having contemplated with gloomy air the result of his bad temper, he moved to the casement, where, with back turned on the others, he looked through the windows, without, however, seeming to see anything. Porphyrius Petrovitch laughed by way of good-breeding, although he evidently expected some kind of explanation. Zametoff was seated somewhere in a corner; on the appearance of the visitors, he just rose, attempting a smile, although by no means off his guard at what had happened and considering Raskolnikoff with special curiosity. The latter had certainly not expected to meet a police official, whose presence caused him a disagreeable surprise.

'Here is another point to be taken into consideration,' he thought.

'Pray excuse me,' he commenced, with pretended embarrassment. 'Razoumikhin is – '

'That will do! You have caused me great amusement by your way of entering. I see he won't even say "How do you do?" ' added Porphyrius Petrovitch, pointing to Razoumikhin with a nod.

'I really don't know why he is so angry with me. I only told him, as we were coming along, that he was like Romeo – and I even proved it to him; that was all.'

'Wretch!' cried Razoumikhin without looking round.

'He must have had very good reason to take your little joke in such bad part,' remarked Porphyrius Petrovitch with a smile.

'There peeps out the magistrate – always sounding! I wish the deuce would take all of you!' replied Razoumikhin, who now began to laugh in his turn; he had suddenly recovered his good temper and cheerfully approached Porphyrius Petrovitch.

'No more nonsense! Let us proceed to business! Permit me to introduce to you my friend Rodion Romanovitch Raskolnikoff, who has heard a great deal about you, and is anxious to make your acquaintance; he has to discuss some little affair with you. Hallo! Zametoff, what brings you here? So you are already acquainted, and since when?'

'What can this mean now?' asked Raskolnikoff of himself with anxiety.

Razoumikhin's question seemed to annoy Zametoff somewhat; he soon, however, got over that. 'It was yesterday, at your house, that we became acquainted,' he said in his easy way.

'Then the finger of fate has been at work. Do you know, Porphyrius, that last week he expressed a very great wish to be introduced to you, but it would appear that you have been able to become acquainted without me. Have you any tobacco, by the by?'

Porphyrius Petrovitch was in morning costume – dressing-gown, slippers down at heel, speckless linen. He was a man of thirty-five, below medium height, stout, and even somewhat corpulent. He had neither beard nor moustache, and his hair was cut short. His large round head was particularly fleshy in the nape of the neck. His bloated, round, and slightly flat face was not wanting in vivacity or cheerfulness, although his complexion, of a darkish yellow, was far from indicating sound health. Had it not been for the expression of his eyes – which, hidden under almost white lashes, seemed to be continually blinking, as if to make signs of some kind or other – one might have taken his face for a good one. But it was this expression which singularly belied the rest of the countenance. At first sight, one could not help noticing the more or less rustic physique of his frame, but an attentive observer was soon undeceived as to that.

As soon as he heard that Raskolnikoff had to discuss some little affair with him, Porphyrius Petrovitch invited him to sit down on the sofa by his side, did the same at the other end, and placed himself at his disposal with the greatest eagerness. As a rule, we feel more or less constrained when a person with whom we have but slight acquaintance shows much curiosity to hear us; and our embarrassment becomes all the greater if the subject about to be discussed is, in our eyes, scarcely deserving of the extreme attention lavished on us. Nevertheless, Raskolnikoff, in a few short, and precise words, went into all the aspects of his little affair, and was even enabled, whilst doing so, to take a good look at Porphyrius Petrovitch, who on his part was not wanting in careful observation. Razoumikhin, facing them both, listened impatiently, whilst his gaze kept on wandering from his friend to the magistrate and back again, in a manner less than polite.

'The idiot!' fumed Raskolnikoff to himself.

'You must place the matter in the hands of the police,' answered Porphyrius Petrovitch in the most self-possessed manner. 'You must explain how, being cognisant of such and such a circumstance – that is, this murder – you wish to inform the magistrate entrusted with the case that certain articles are yours, and that you wish to redeem them. But you will sure to be written to.'

'Unfortunately,' replied Raskolnikoff, with feigned confusion, 'I am not in funds for the time being, and my available means do not even allow me to take these trumpery things out. To tell you the truth, I am anxious to confine myself to the statement that those things are mine, and that as soon as possible – '

'That does not matter,' answered Porphyrius Petrovitch, who hardly noticed the financial explanation; 'you can, if you like, write directly to me, and state that being cognisant and so forth, you are anxious to inform us as to those articles which are your own, and which –'

'Can I write such a letter on unstamped paper?' interrupted Raskolnikoff, pretending only to see the pecuniary side of the case.

'On any paper you like!' Porphyrius Petrovitch uttered these words in a frankly railing way, with a suggestive look at Raskolnikoff. At all events, the latter would have sworn that this look was meant for him, and was the result of Heaven only knows what secret thought. He might, after all, said he to himself, be mistaken. 'He knows!' was the momentary thought.

'Excuse my having disturbed you about such a trifle,' was the slightly disconcerted reply. 'These things are not worth more than five roubles, but association makes them particularly valuable to me, and I must own that I was greatly concerned on hearing –'

'Was that the reason you were so upset, yesterday, on hearing me tell Zosimoff that Porphyrius was examining the people who had pledged things at the old pawnbroker's?' asked Razoumikhin with evident intention.

But this was beyond a joke. Raskolnikoff could not bear it, and cast on the clumsy chatterer a look flashing anger, though knowing in a moment the imprudence he had been guilty of, and which he did his best to repair. 'You seem to me to be poking fun at me, my friend,' he said to Razoumikhin, pretending to be greatly vexed. 'I admit that I meddle perhaps too much with things which in your eyes may be insignificant, but that is no reason why you should look upon me as a selfish and greedy man; trifles like that may be of value to me. As I told you just now, the silver watch, which may not be worth more than a *groch*, is all I have from my late father. Poke fun at me, if you like, but my mother has just paid me a visit' – on saying which he turned towards Porphyrius – 'and if she knew,' he went on once more, addressing Razoumikhin, in a voice as trembling as possible, 'if she knew that I am no longer in possession of that watch, I am certain she would be in despair! Women are like that!'

'By no means! I did not mean in that way! You are quite wrong as to my thoughts!' protested Razoumikhin aggrieved.

'Have I done well? Was it natural? Did I pitch my key too high?' Raskolnikoff asked himself anxiously. 'I ought not to have said "women" in the general sense.'

'Has your mother paid you a visit?' inquired Porphyrius Petrovitch.

'Yes!'

'When did she come?'

'Last night.'

The magistrate was silent for a moment; he seemed to be thinking. 'Under any circumstances your things won't get lost,' was his calm and cold remark. 'Do you know, I have been expecting your visit for some time.' On saying which, he quickly pushed the ash-tray to Razoumikhin, who kept on dropping his cigarette-ash on the carpet. Raskolnikoff shuddered, but the magistrate did not seem to notice it, anxious as he was to preserve his carpet.

'You have been expecting his visit? But how did you know that he had pledged anything there?' cried Razoumikhin.

Porphyrius Petrovitch, without any further reply, said to Raskolnikoff: 'Your things, a ring and a watch, were at her place, wrapped up in a piece of paper, and on this paper your name was legibly written in pencil, with the date of the day she had received these things from you.'

'What a memory you must have got!' said Raskolnikoff, with a forced smile, doing his best to look the magistrate unflinchingly in the face. However he could not help adding: 'I say so, because, as the owners of the pledged articles are no doubt very numerous, you must, I should fancy, have some difficulty in remembering them all; but I see, on the contrary, that you do nothing of the kind. (Oh! fool! Why add that?)'

'But they have nearly all of them come here; you alone had not done so,' answered Porphyrius, with an almost imperceptible sneer.

'I happened to be rather unwell.'

'So I heard. I have been told that you have been in great pain. Even now you are pale.'

'Not at all. I am not pale. On the contrary, I am very well!' answered Raskolnikoff in a tone of voice which had all at once become brutal and violent. He felt rising within him uncontrollable anger. 'Anger will make me say some foolish thing,' he thought. 'But why do they exasperate me?'

'He was rather unwell! A pretty expression, to be sure!' exclaimed Razoumikhin. 'The fact is that up to yesterday he has been almost unconscious. Would you believe it, Porphyrius? Yesterday, when he could hardly stand upright, he seized the moment when Zosimoff had just left him, to dress, to be off by stealth, and to go loafing about, Heaven only knows where, till midnight, being, all the time, in a completely raving condition. Can you imagine such a thing? It is a most remarkable case!'

'Indeed! In a completely raving state?' remarked Porphyrius, with the toss of the head peculiar to Russian rustics.

'Absurd! Don't you believe a word of it! Besides, I need not urge you to that effect – of course you are convinced,' observed Raskolnikoff, beside himself with passion. But Porphyrius Petrovitch did not seem to hear these singular words.

'How could you have gone out if you had not been delirious?' asked Razoumikhin, getting angry in his turn. 'Why have gone out at all? What was the object of it? And, above all, to go in that secret manner? Come now, make a clean breast of it – you know you were out of your mind, were you not? Now that danger is gone by, I tell you so to your face.'

'I had been very much annoyed yesterday,' said Raskolnikoff, addressing the magistrate, with more or less of insolence in his smile, 'and, wishing to get rid of them, I went out to hire lodgings where I could be sure of privacy, to effect which I had taken a certain amount of money. Mr Zametoff saw what I had by me, and perhaps he can say whether I was in my right senses yesterday or whether I was delirious? Perhaps he will judge as to our quarrel.' Nothing would have pleased him better than there and then to have strangled that gentleman, whose taciturnity and equivocal facial expression irritated him.

'In my opinion, you were talking very sensibly and even with considerable shrewdness; only I thought you too irritable,' observed Zametoff off-handedly.

'Just now,' added Porphyrius Petrovitch, 'Nicodemus Thomich told me he met you late last night, in the lodgings of an official who had been run over – '

'Exactly!' put in Razoumikhin. 'This proves my own statement definitely! Did you not behave like a lunatic in that man's place? You gave all you had to pay for the funeral expenses! I admit that you wished to assist the widow, but you might have given her fifteen, or even twenty, roubles, if necessary, and have kept something for yourself; whereas you gave everything you had – you spent, in fact, your whole twenty-five roubles!'

'But how do you know that I did not find a treasure? Yesterday I was in the mood for largess. Mr Zametoff knows that I did find one! I must really apologise for having pestered you for half an hour by my useless twaddle,' he went on, with quivering lips, addressing Porphyrius. 'You are tired, I should think!'

'What do you say? Quite the contrary! If you only knew how you interest me! I am interested in seeing and hearing you – in fact, I am enchanted with your visit!'

'Do let us have some tea! We are as dry as fishes!' exclaimed Razoumikhin.

'Good idea! But perhaps you would like something more substantial before tea, would you?'

'Look alive, then!'

Porphyrius Petrovitch went out to order tea. All kinds of thoughts were at work in Raskolnikoff's brain. He was excited. 'They don't even take pains to dissemble; they certainly don't mince matters as far as I am concerned: that is something, at all events! Since Porphyrius knew next to nothing about me, why on earth should he have spoken with Nicodemus Thomich at all? They even scorn to deny that they are on my track, almost like a pack of hounds! They certainly speak out plainly enough!' he said, trembling with rage. 'Well, do so, as bluntly as you like, but don't play with me like a cat with a mouse! That's not quite civil, Porphyrius Petrovitch; I won't quite allow that yet! I'll make a stand and tell you some plain truths to your faces, and then you shall find out my real opinion about you!' He had some difficulty in breathing. 'But supposing that all this is pure fancy? – a kind of mirage? Suppose I had misunderstood? Let me try and keep up my nasty part, and not commit myself, like a fool, by blind anger! Ought I to give them credit for intentions they have not? Their words are, in themselves, not very extraordinary ones – so much must be allowed; but a double meaning may lurk beneath them. Why did Porphyrius, in speaking of the old woman, simply say "At her place"? Why did Zametoff observe that I had spoken very sensibly? Why their peculiar manner? – yes, it is this manner of theirs. How is it possible that all this cannot have struck Razoumikhin? The booby never notices anything! But I seem to be feverish again! Did Porphyrius give me a kind of wink just now, or was I deceived in some way? The idea is absurd! Why should he wink at me? Perhaps they intend to upset my nervous organisation, and, by so doing, drive me to extremes! Either the whole thing is a phantasmagoria, or – they know!

'Zametoff himself is insolent. He has thought things over since yesterday. I suspected that he would change his opinion! He behaves here as he would at home, and yet it is his first visit! Porphyrius does not consider him in the light of a stranger; he sat down even, and turned his back on him. Those two have become fast friends, and I am sure that I am the cause of their intimacy. I am sure they were talking of me when we came in! Can they know anything about my visit to the old woman's room? I am longing to know! When I stated that I had gone out to engage lodgings, Porphyrius did not notice my observation. But I did well to mention that, as it may come in handy later on! As for my condition of mind, the magistrate did not seem to want to know anything about that. He is evidently perfectly aware as to how I spent the evening. But he knew nothing about my mother's visit. And as for that hag – who made a pencil-note of the date of the pledging? No, no! Your affected assurance does not mislead me. Up to the present you are without facts; you have nothing but idle conjectures. Bring forward one single fact, assuming you can do as much as that! The visit I paid to the old woman proves nothing! It may be attributed to my condition of mind at the time. I distinctly remember what I told the journeymen and the dvornik. But do they really know that I went there at all? I do not intend leaving till I am certain on that point! Why have I come at all? But I am getting angry, a thing to be feared! What makes me so irritable? Perhaps it is better that it should be so. I shall continue my rôle of invalid. Perhaps he'll begin to worry me, so as to make me forget myself. Ah! Why have I come at all?'

All these thoughts flashed through his mind with the rapidity of lightning. Porphyrius Petrovitch came back a moment afterwards. He seemed in a very good temper. 'When I left your place yesterday, old fellow, I was really not well,' he commenced, addressing Razoumikhin with a cheeriness which was only just becoming apparent, 'but that is all gone now.'

'Did you find the evening a pleasant one? I left you in the thick of the fun; who came off best?'

'Nobody, of course. They cavilled to their heart's content over their old arguments.'

'Fancy, Rodia, the discussion last evening turned on the question: "Does crime exist? Yes or No." And the nonsense they talked on the subject!'

'What is there extraordinary in the query? It is the social question without the charm of novelty,' answered Raskolnikoff abruptly.

'The question was not put like that,' remarked Porphyrius.

'Not exactly like that, I own,' Razoumikhin immediately admitted, who had moved according to his wont. 'Listen, Rodia, and give us your opinion – I insist. Yesterday, when those fellows upset me, and I was expecting you, having told them you were coming – these Socialists then commenced by airing their theory. We all know what it is – in other words, crime is a protest against a badly-organised social state of things – that's all. When they have said that, they have said all; they admit no other cause for criminal acts; in their own opinion, man is driven to commit crime in consequence of the irresistible influence of environment, and nothing else. This is their favourite theme.'

'Talking of crime and environment' said Porphyrius Petrovitch, speaking to Raskolnikoff, 'I remember a production of yours which greatly interested me. I am speaking about your article 'On Crime' – I don't remember the exact title. I was delighted in reading it two months ago in the *Periodical Word*.'

'My article? In the *Periodical Word*?' asked Raskolnikoff astonished. 'I wrote, it is true, an article six months ago, when I left the University, in connection with some book, but I sent it to the *Hebdomadal Word*, and not to the *Periodical Word*.'

'That is the paper it came out in.'

'In the meantime, the *Hebdomadal Word* ceased to appear; that was why my article was not published at the time.'

'Quite so; but, whilst no longer appearing, the *Hebdomadal Word* became amalgamated with the *Periodical Word*, and this is how your article was published by the latter paper two months ago. Did you not know that?'

Raskolnikoff had not known it.

'Then you may go and draw the money for your copy! What a disposition is yours however! You live so hermit-like that the very things which interest you directly, do not even come under your notice! That is a fact.'

'Bravo, Rodia! I did not know anything about it either!' exclaimed Razoumikhin. 'This very day I shall ask for the number in the reading-room! Is it two months ago since the article was inserted? What was the date? Never mind – I shall find out! What a joke! And he has never said anything about it!'

'But how do you know the article was mine? I only signed it with an initial.'

'I discovered it lately, quite by chance. The chief editor is a friend of mine; it was he who let out the secret of your authorship. The article has greatly interested me.'

'I was analysing, if I remember rightly, the psychological condition of a criminal at the moment of his deed.'

'Yes, and you strove to prove that a criminal, at such a moment, is always, mentally, more or less unhinged. That point of view is a very original one, but it was not this part of your article which most interested me. I was particularly struck by an idea at the end of the article, and which, unfortunately, you have touched upon too cursorily. In a word, if you remember, you maintained that there are men in existence who can, or more accurately, who have an absolute right to commit all kinds of wicked and criminal acts – men for whom, to a certain extent, laws do not exist.'

At this false interpretation of his views, Raskolnikoff smiled.

'How? What? A right to commit crime? Did he not rather mean to say that a criminal is urged to crime by the irresistible centrifugal influence?' asked Razoumikhin with a species of anxiety.

'No, no, that is not the point in question' replied Porphyrius. 'In the article under discussion, men are divided into ordinary and extraordinary men. The former must live in a state of obedience, and have no right to break the law, inasmuch as they are nothing more than ordinary men; the latter have a right to commit every kind of crime and to break every law, from the very fact that they are extraordinary men. I think that is what you mean, unless I am mistaken?'

'But how? It is impossible that such things can be!' stammered Razoumikhin, confused.

Raskolnikoff smiled again. He had seen in a moment that they wished to get from him a statement of facts, and, remembering his article, he was ready to enter into explanations. 'That is not quite it,' he commenced in simple and modest tones. 'I must allow, however, that you have almost precisely reproduced my theory; if you like, I will go so far as to say, very precisely' (he emphasised these last words with a certain pleasure). 'I did not say, however, as you make me do, that extraordinary men are absolutely bound to be always committing all kinds of criminal acts. I even believe that the censor would not have permitted the publication of an article conceived in that sense. This is really what I maintained: An extraordinary man has a right – not officially, be it understood, but from and by his very individuality – to permit his conscience to overstep certain bounds, only so far as the realisation of one of his ideas may require it. (Such an idea may from time to time be of advantage to humanity.) You pretend that my article is not a clear one: I will do my best to make it so; perhaps I am right in surmising that such is your wish. According to my theory, if Kepler's or Newton's inventions had, in consequence of certain obstacles, not been able to get into vogue without the sacrifice of one, ten, a hundred, or even a larger number of intervening human impediments, Newton would have had the right – nay, would have been obliged – to do away with these few, these hundred men, in order that his discoveries might become known to the whole world. This does not imply, however, that Newton had a right to assassinate at his will or fancy any living thing, or to steal daily in open market.

'Further on in my article, I remember insisting on the idea that all legislators and rulers of men, commencing with the earliest down to Lycurgus, Solon, Mahomet, Napoleon, etc. etc., have one and all been criminals, for, whilst giving new laws, they have naturally broken through older ones which had been faithfully observed by society and transmitted by its progenitors. These men most certainly never hesitated to shed blood, as soon as they saw the advantage of doing so. It may even be remarked that nearly all these benefactors and teachers of humanity have been terribly bloodthirsty. Consequently, not only all great men, but all those who, by hook or by crook, have raised themselves above the common herd, men who are capable of evolving something new, must, in virtue of their innate power, be undoubtedly criminals, more or less, be it said. Otherwise they could not free themselves from trammels; and, as for being bound by them, that they cannot be – their very mission forbidding it.

'You must own that, as far as we have gone, there is nothing very new in my article. The same views have been uttered and printed a thousand times. As for my division of men into ordinary and extraordinary ones, I own to its being somewhat arbitrary, but I take no heed of the question of figures, which hampers me but slightly. But I believe that the kernel of my theory is a sound one. It confines itself to maintaining that Nature divides men into two categories: the first, an inferior one, comprising ordinary men, the kind of material whose function it is to reproduce specimens like themselves; the other, a superior one, comprising men who have the gift or power to make a new word, thought, or deed felt. Their subdivisions are naturally innumerable, but these two main categories contain distinctively marked characteristics. To the first belong, in a general way, conservatives, men for order, who live in a state of obedience and love. To my mind, such men cannot help obeying, because it is their destiny, and such an act has nothing humiliating for them.

'The next class, however, consists exclusively of men who break the law, or strive, according to their capacity or power, to do so Their crimes are naturally relative ones, and of varied gravity. Most of these insist upon destruction of what exists in the name of what ought to exist. And if, in the execution of their idea, they should be obliged to shed blood, step over corpses, they can conscientiously do both in the interest of their idea, not otherwise – pray mark this. It is in so far that my article gives them a right to commit crime. (You will remember that our starting argument was a judicial question.) There is, however, not much need for anxiety. The mass of men hardly ever concedes them such a right; it either decapitates or hangs them, and by doing so performs most virtuously its conservative mission till the day this very class erects statues in veneration of those thus executed. The first group is always predominant in the present; the second, however, is master of the future. One class keeps up the world by increasing its inhabitants, the other arouses humanity and makes it act. Both have absolutely the same right to existence – yea, even to the day of the New Jerusalem!'

'Then you believe in the New Jerusalem?'

'I do,' replied, with considerable stress, Raskolnikoff, who, during the whole of this tirade, had kept his eye obstinately fixed on some spot in the carpet.

'And – do you believe in God? Excuse my inquisitiveness.'

'I do,' repeated the young man, raising his eyes on Porphyrius.

'And in the resurrection of Lazarus?'

'Yes. But why put such questions?'

'Do you believe fully?'

'Fully.'

'Excuse my having put these questions, but I was interested. Permit me once more – I am going back to the subject we were talking about just now – they are not always executed; on the contrary, there are some who – '

'What? Who are triumphant during their lifetime? Yes, such a thing happens to some of them, and then – '

'It is they, I suppose, who give up the others for capital punishment?'

'Yes, if necessary, and, let me tell you, this is most frequently the case. From a general point of view, your observation is full of accuracy.'

'Thanks. But tell me: How is it possible to distinguish these extraordinary men from ordinary ones? Have they, at birth, any special marks? It strikes me that here we require a little more precision, and, to some extent, a more apparent definition. Excuse this fidgetiness, after all but natural to a practical and well-meaning man; but could they not, for instance, wear some special dress – an emblem of some kind or other? For, you must agree, if confusion set in; if a member of one class were to conceive that he belonged to the other, and were, according to your happy expression, to try and "overcome every obstacle," then – '

'Oh! Such a thing often happens. Your second remark is even a more clever one than the other.'

'Thanks!'

'Don't mention it; but remember that such an error is only possible with men of the first category, that is to say, in the case of those whom I have, perhaps clumsily, called "ordinary" men. Notwithstanding their inborn tendency to obey, many of them, as a result of some freak of nature, fancy themselves men that ought to be in the van, and consider themselves in the light of "regenerators" – think themselves selected to bring about a "new state of things," and this illusion is perfectly genuine in their case. At the same time, they do not, as a rule, recognise the real regenerators, they even sometimes despise them as people behind the times – lacking in genius. But in my opinion that is not a very great danger, and there is no occasion for anxiety, for they never accomplish much. They may sometimes be urged on by way of punishment for their presumption, and thus be placed once more in their right place, but that is all; even in such cases, there is no special need to harass the instrument – on the contrary, they themselves are more or less their own castigators, because their characters are sensitive ones, and this punishment they either award each other mutually or by themselves. They may be seen undergoing various open inflictions, which cannot fail to edify; in a word, anxiety on their score would be more than futile.'

'I must confess that in this particular case you have somewhat set me at rest, but here is something else which worries me: tell me, pray, are there many of these extraordinary men who have the right to destroy others? I am ready to yield them precedence, but if there are very many of them, you must own such a fact to be rather a disagreeable one, eh?'

'Pray do not let that disturb you to any great extent,' Raskolnikoff continued in the same tone. 'Generally, the number of men born with new ideas, or even capable of giving utterance to anything out of the ordinary course, is infinitesimal. It is a self-evident fact that the repartition of births in the various categories and subdivisions of humanity must be carefully regulated by some natural law. This law, unfortunately, is unknown to us as yet, but I fully believe in its existence and also that it will be discovered sooner or later. I believe that very many of us have only one duty in this world, the bringing finally into existence, after long and mysterious cross-breeding, one man out of a thousand with a trace of independence. In proportion to this increase of independence, we begin to discover one man in ten thousand, or even in a hundred thousand (my figures are approximate ones). A genius is found among several millions of men, and it is highly probable that thousands of millions pass through life before there arises one of those lofty intellects which renew the face of the globe. Unfortunately, I have had no opportunity of peeping in the retort where this process of evolution takes place. At all events there is, there must be, some immutable law at work in this process – chance has nothing whatever to do with it.'

'I really think that both of you are joking,' exclaimed, at last, Razoumikhin; 'you are mystifying one another, I fancy! You are not really talking seriously, are you, Rodia?'

Without replying, Raskolnikoff raised on him his pale and apparently suffering face. Whilst looking at its calm and woebegone expression, Razoumikhin thought the caustic, irritating, and rude manner, Porphyrius had assumed was very singular.

'Well, my dear friend, if you are really serious, of course you are perfectly right in saying that your statements are not new ones, and that they are very much like what we have read and heard a thousand times; but I am grieved to observe that the only original opinion you adduce, is a moral right to shed blood – this opinion I find you support, even defend, with fanaticism. This is, in fact, the main point of your article. Moral licence or authority to kill is, to my mind, even more terrible than official legal authority to the same effect.'

'Quite so. It is, in fact, much more terrible,' remarked Porphyrius.

'No, you said more than you really thought; you did not mean that at all! I purpose reading your article; whilst talking, people are sometimes carried away! You cannot really have such opinions. But I shall read it.'

'There is nothing of the kind in my article at all, I have hardly touched upon such a question,' said Raskolnikoff.

'Yes, yes,' went on Porphyrius, 'I now almost understand your way of looking at crime; but, excuse my persistency, if a young man fancies himself a Lycurgus or a Mahomet of the future, of course his first step will be to trample under foot every obstacle in the way of his crusade.'

'He will say to himself, "I propose undertaking a long campaign, and, in order to do so, I shall require money." And then, of course, he will get money. Can you guess how?' All at once, Zametoff sniffed in his corner. Raskolnikoff did not even look at him. 'I must admit,' he added coolly, 'that such cases occasionally occur. They are snares set by vanity for vain and foolish people; young men especially are caught in them.'

'You understand that, do you?'

'What?' replied Raskolnikoff, with a smile. 'Is that my fault? Things of that kind happen every day. Just now,' he added, pointing to Razoumikhin, 'this man reproached me for countenancing murder. What can that matter? Is society not sufficiently protected by penal servitude, prisons, magistrates, the hulks? Why, therefore, be uneasy? Find your thief first!'

'And supposing we do find him?'

'All the worse for him, of course.'

'At all events, you are logical. But what will his conscience tell you?'

'What is that to you?'

'It is a question of interest to humanity.'

'The man who has a conscience suffers whilst acknowledging his sin. That is his punishment – to say nothing of the galleys.'

'Then I suppose,' asked Razoumikhin, 'men of genius, who have a right to kill, can experience no anguish, even when doing so?'

'Why introduce here the word "can"? Suffering is neither permitted nor forbidden in their case. They may suffer, if they pity their victim. Suffering is part and parcel of extensive intelligence and a feeling heart. A man who is really great, it seems to me, must suffer considerably here below,' added Raskolnikoff, affected with a sudden melancholy which contrasted with his manner in the course of the preceding conversation. He looked up, regarded the others with dreamy eye, smiled and took his cap. His manner was much too calm, when compared with his bearing on entering the house, and he remembered it. Everyone rose. Once more Porphyrius Petrovitch touched upon the late discussion.

'One moment, if you please, taunt me or not, get angry or not, but – I want to ask one more trifling question. I am ashamed to trespass as I am doing – now that I am on the subject, and in order that I may not forget it, I should like to communicate to you a small idea which has struck me –

'All right, out with your small idea!' replied Raskolnikoff, facing the magistrate with a pale and serious countenance.

'I – really – I – hardly know how to express myself. My idea is a singular – psychological one. Whilst composing your article, it is very probable – ha! ha! – that you looked upon yourself in the light of one of those "extraordinary' men you were talking about. Am I right?'

'Very likely,' scornfully responded Raskolnikoff. Razoumikhin made a movement.

'If I am right – would you not be induced yourself – either with a view to triumph over material embarrassments, or to assist humanity in its onward course – I say would you not be induced – to step over obstacles? For instance, to kill and to rob?' At the same time, he winked his left eye, and laughed silently, as he had done just before.

'If I were induced to do so, I should certainly not tell you,' answered Raskolnikoff, with an accent of haughty disdain.

'Only a kind of literary inquisitiveness induced me to put my question; all I wanted was to get a better grip of the real meaning of your article.'

'What an obvious trap! What shallow cunning!' thought Raskolnikoff in disgust. 'Permit me to observe,' he replied curtly, 'that I neither consider myself a Mahomet nor a Napoleon, nor anyone like them; consequently I am not in a position to enlighten you as to what I should do if I were in their shoes.'

'Come, now! where is the man who at this time, in this country, does not look upon himself as a Napoleon?' retorted the magistrate, with brusque familiarity. The very intonation of his voice savoured of mental reserve.

'Is it not very likely that some coming Napoleon did for Alena Ivanovna last week?' suddenly blustered Zametoff from his corner.

Without saying a word, Raskolnikoff fixed on Porphyrius a firm and penetrating glance. Raskolnikoff was beginning to look sullen. He seemed to have been suspecting something for some time past. He looked round him with an irritable air. For a moment there was an ominous silence. Raskolnikoff was getting ready to go.

'What, are you off already?' asked Porphyrius, kindly offering the young man his hand with extreme affability. 'I am delighted to have made your acquaintance. And as for your application, don't be uneasy about it. Write in the way I suggested. Or, perhaps, you had better do this. Come and see me before long – tomorrow, if you like. I shall be here without fail at eleven o'clock. We can make everything right – we'll have a chat – and as you were one of the last that went *there*, you might be able to give some further particulars?' he added, with his friendly smile.

'Do you wish to examine me formally?' Raskolnikoff inquired, in an uncomfortable tone.

'Why should I? Such a thing is out of the question. You have misunderstood me. I ought to tell you that I manage to make the most of every opportunity. I have already had a chat with every single person that has been in the habit of pledging things with the old woman – several have given me very useful information – and as you happen to be the last one – by the by,' he exclaimed, with sudden pleasure, 'how lucky I am thinking about it, I was really going to forget it!' (Saying which he turned to Razoumikhin.) 'You were almost stunning my ears, the other day, talking about Nikola. Well, I am certain, quite certain, as to his innocence,' he went on, once more addressing himself to Raskolnikoff. 'But what was to be done? It has been necessary to disturb Dmitri. Now, what I wanted to ask was: In going upstairs – was it not between seven and eight you entered the house?'

'Yes,' replied Raskolnikoff, and he immediately regretted an answer he ought to have avoided.

'Well, in going upstairs, between seven and eight, did you not see on the second floor, in one of the rooms where the door was wide open – you remember, I dare say? – did you not see two painters, or, at all events, one of the two? They were whitewashing the room, I believe; you must have seen them! The matter is of the utmost importance to them!'

'Painters, you say? I saw none,' replied Raskolnikoff slowly, trying to sound his memory: for a moment he violently strained it to discover, as quickly as he could, the trap concealed by the magistrate's question. 'No, I did not see a single one; I did not even see any room standing open,' he went on, delighted at having discovered the trap, 'but on the fourth floor I remember noticing that the man lodging on the same landing as Alena Ivanovna was in the act of moving. I remember that very well, as I met some porters carrying a sofa and I was obliged to back against the wall; but, as for painters, I don't remember seeing a single one – I don't even remember a room that had its door open. No, I saw nothing.'

"But what are you talking about?' all at once exclaimed Razoumikhin, who, till that moment, had attentively listened; 'it was on the very day of the murder that painters were busy in that room, whilst he came there two days previously! Why are you asking that question?'

'Right! I have confused the dates!' cried Porphyrius, tapping his forehead. 'Deuce take it! This job makes me lose my head!' he added by way of excuse, and speaking to Raskolnikoff. 'It is very important that we should know if anybody saw them in that room between seven and eight. I thought I might have got that information from you without thinking any more about it. I had positively confused the days!'

'You ought to be more attentive!' grumbled Razoumikhin.

These last words were uttered in the ante-room, as Porphyrius very civilly led his visitors to the door. They were gloomy and morose on leaving the house, and had gone some distance before speaking. Raskolnikoff breathed like a man who had just been subjected to a severe trial.

Chapter 6

'I DO NOT believe it! I cannot believe it!' repeated Razoumikhin, doing his utmost to dispel Raskolnikoff's conclusions. They were already close to Bakaleieff's, where Pulcheria Alexandrovna and Dounia had been waiting some time for them. In the heat of their discussion, Razoumikhin stopped periodically in the middle of the road; he was greatly excited, for this was the first time the two young men talked about the subject which, up to the present, had only been covertly touched upon.

'Don't believe it then, if you like!' answered Raskolnikoff with a cold and indifferent smile. 'As usual, you have noticed nothing; as for me, I have weighed every word.'

'You are disposed to mistrust – that is why you discover everywhere underhanded thoughts. H'm! I admit that Porphyrius's tone was a rather strange one, and it was especially that rascal Zametoff – you are quite right, he showed an indescribable – how can that be, do you know?'

'He will have changed his mind tomorrow.'

'You are altogether mistaken. If they had had such a silly suspicion, they would have taken good care to dissimulate; they would have hidden their hand to make you confidential, and would have waited for the right moment to unmask their batteries. If your supposition is a correct one, their behaviour today would have been both clumsy and daring!'

'If they had had facts to go upon, I mean of course serious facts, or evidence with more or less of basis, then they would have done their best to hide their hand in the hope of gaining fresh advantage over me (they certainly would long since have searched my lodgings). But they have no evidence, none whatever – everything ends in idle conjectures, in suspicion without solid ground, that is why they have recourse to effrontery. Perhaps all we ought to fear in the matter is Porphyrius's disgust at having no kind of proof. He may have ulterior intentions, for the man seems intelligent; he may have wanted to frighten me – you know, old fellow, that he has some system of his own; besides, cases of that kind are always unpleasant to clear up. Let us drop the subject!'

'The thing is hateful! Hateful! I quite understand! But since we have frankly touched on this subject (and I think we have been quite right in doing so), I can no longer hesitate to confess that I had for some time given them credit for having such an idea. I know they did not dare to give utterance to it, I know that it only existed in their minds in a vague state; but it was too much of a good thing to take it up.'

'And what may have given rise to such abominable suspicions? If you only knew the temper I have been thrown in! What? Here we have a poor student struggling against poverty and hypochondria, on the eve of a serious malady, which perhaps was already germinating, a diffident young man by no means wanting in vanity, conscious of his own worth, who for the last six months has clung to his room without seeing a soul, we see him in rags, without shoes or stockings, almost face to face with some miserable police officials, whose insolence he must bear the brunt of, in respect of immediate payment of a dishonoured bill; the court swarms with people, the heat is excessive, the smell of new paint helps to make the atmosphere unbearable; the unhappy man, who has not yet broken his fast, hears talk of the assassination of a person whom he has visited the night previously! How could he help fainting under such circumstances? And it is on that fainting-fit that everything hinges. Here we have the crux of the charge! Deuce take the lot of them! I own the thing is vexatious, but if I were in your place, Rodia, I would laugh them to scorn, or, better still, I would show them my contempt as markedly as ever I could! That is what I would do with them! Cheer up! The whole thing is most despicable, most disgraceful!'

'And yet the fellow has been having his say as if he were convinced!'

thought Raskolnikoff. 'It is all very well to say that the whole thing is most despicable, but yet another examination tomorrow!' he replied with a sad strain, 'shall I have to lower myself so far as to give them even explanatory details? I am disgusted with myself at having consented to talk with Zametoff at the *traktir*.'

'Deuce take them all! I'll go myself to Porphyrius! He is a relative, and I'll use the man so as to sound him, I'll compel him to make a complete confession! And as for Zametoff –'

'The bait has taken at last!' Raskolnikoff said to himself.

'Wait!' cried Razoumikhin, suddenly seizing his friend by the shoulder. 'Wait! You are digressing just now! On careful reflection, I am convinced you are digressing! Where now do you notice a snare? You maintain that the question in connection with the journeymen painters was meant as a trap? Just reason for a moment: supposing you had done *that*, would you have been fool enough to have said that you had seen the men at work in the lodging on the second floor? On the contrary, even if you had seen them, you would not have owned to it! Who would make statements to compromise himself?'

'If I had done *that* I should not have hesitated to say that I had seen the painters,' answered Raskolnikoff, to whom this conversation seemed particularly objectionable.

'Why then make statements prejudicial to one's cause?'

'Because only moujiks and pigheaded fellows of that kind deny everything as a foregone conclusion. A prisoner with the least possible intelligence acknowledges, as far as he can, every material fact, the reality of which it would be idle for him to try and annul; only he accounts for it in another way, he modifies its purport, exhibits it in a different light. According to all probability, Porphyrius calculated that I should answer him in this strain. He believed that, in order to give a greater show of probability to my statements, I should confess to having seen the journeymen, without, however, doing so in a way unfavourable to my case.'

'But he immediately would have answered you that, two days before the occurrence of the crime, the painters could not have been there, and that, consequently, you must have been in the house on the very day of the murder, between seven and eight o'clock. He would have caught you in that way!'

'He would have reckoned that I should not have time to reflect, and that, driven to reply in the most advantageous way, I should have forgotten that circumstance, namely, the impossibility of the workmen's presence in the house two days before the committal of the crime.'

'But how forget such a thing?'

'Nothing more easy! Details like that are so many stumbling-blocks to knowing fellows; it is in answering them that they commit themselves whilst under examination. Porphyrius knows that perfectly well – he is not such a fool as he may look – '

'If that is his way, he must be a rascal!'

Raskolnikoff could not help laughing. But at the same moment he was astonished to have made his last explanation with real pleasure – he who, till then, had only carried the conversation on grudgingly, and because the object to be gained compelled him to do so. 'Should I like questions like that?' he thought. But, almost at the same time, he was seized with a sudden anxiety, which soon became intolerable. The two young men were already at Bakaleieff's door.

'Go in alone,' said Raskolnikoff quickly, 'I shall be back in a moment.'

'Where are you going to? Why, here we are!'

'I have to make another call first. I shall be back in half an hour. You had better tell them – '

'Well, then, I'll come with you!'

'I say, have you also sworn to persecute me to the end of the chapter?'

This exclamation was uttered with such an accent of passion, and in so desperate a manner, that Razoumikhin dared not insist. He stopped for some time on the outer steps, watching with gloomy look Raskolnikoff, who was taking long strides in the direction of his lodging. Finally, after having ground his teeth, clenched his fists, and promised himself that he would squeeze Porphyrius that very day like a lemon, he ascended to the ladies' room to reassure Pulcheria Alexandrovna, whom this long absence had already made uneasy. When Raskolnikoff reached his home, his temples were moist with sweat, and he felt a difficulty in breathing. He ascended his staircase in very great haste, entered his room, which had remained open, and forthwith locked himself up in it. Then, beside himself with fear, he ran to the hiding-place, thrust his hand under the wall-paper, and probed the hole in every direction. Meeting with no obstacle after having fumbled in every nook and corner, he rose again with a sigh of relief. Just now, at the very moment of his arrival at Bakaleieff's, he had been struck with the idea that one of the stolen articles had probably slipped down in a crack in the wall. Supposing, he thought, someone were to find it there at some time or other – a watch-chain, a cuff-link, or even one of the pieces of paper in which the trinkets had been wrapped up, which had on it some particulars jotted down by the old woman – what a terrible piece of evidence would not this be! He remained as if absorbed in some hazy reverie, and a strange, stupefied smile hung on his lips. He ended by taking his cap and quietly leaving the room. His ideas were getting confused. Thoughtfully he went downstairs, and reached the entrance-gate.

'Hallo! There he is!' exclaimed a loud voice. The young man looked up. The porter, standing in his box-door, pointed Raskolnikoff out to a little man of plebeian appearance. This person wore a species of khalat and a waistcoat, and might, at a distance, have been taken for a countrywoman. His head, covered with a greasy cap, was bent forwards; he seemed also very round-shouldered. Judging by his wrinkled and wan face, he must have been over fifty. His little eyes had a hard and discontented look.

'What is the matter?' asked Raskolnikoff, on getting close to the porter.

The individual looked at him out of the corners of his eyes, examined him at his leisure, then, without saying a single word, turned on his heel and moved away from the house.

'But what is the matter?' cried Raskolnikoff.

'Well, if you want to know, a man has been inquiring if a student did not live here. He mentioned you by name, and asked whom you were lodging with. At the time you were coming downstairs. I pointed you out, and he is gone; that's all.'

The porter was somewhat surprised, although not greatly. Having cogitated another moment, he retired into his box.

Raskolnikoff went in pursuit of the stranger. No sooner had he got away from the house than he perceived him keeping close to the other side of the street, where the unknown man was moving with slow and regular pace, his eyes fixed on the ground, his aspect thoughtful. The young man would soon have caught him up, but he contented himself for some time by keeping close on his heels; at last he was even with him, and looked at him askance. The stranger observed this in a moment, cast back a rapid glance, then once more continued his former contemplation. For a moment, the two kept on a level, without interchanging a word.

'You asked for me at the porter's?' commenced Raskolnikoff, without raising his voice. The man condescended no reply, and did not even look at his interlocutor. More silence. 'You have just called to ask for me, and yet you don't say a word – what is the meaning of that?' continued Raskolnikoff in jerky strain; one might have fancied that the words experienced some difficulty in leaving his mouth.

This time the man raised his eyes, and looked at the young man with a sinister glance. 'Murderer!' he hissed out suddenly in an undertone, but pointedly and distinctly.

Raskolnikoff was now walking by his side. All of a sudden he felt his legs give way, and a chill come down his back; for a moment his heart seemed to sink, then began to beat with extraordinary violence. The two men advanced in this way, side by side, for some distance, without saying a single word. The stranger took no notice of his fellow-pedestrian.

'But what do you – how? – who is a murderer?' stammered Raskolnikoff in a scarcely intelligible voice.

'It is you who are a murderer!' said the other, emphasising his reply more markedly, and more energetically than ever; seeming at the same time to have on his lips a smile of triumphant hatred, and looking hard at Raskolnikoff's pale face, whose eyes had become glassy.

The two were now approaching a public place. The stranger took a street on the left, and continued on his way without looking round. Raskolnikoff permitted him to move off, but for a long time watched his disappearance. After having advanced some fifty paces, the stranger turned round to take stock of the young man, who was still spellbound in his place. Distance did not help him much, but yet Raskolnikoff imagined that this individual kept up his cold, but triumphant, smile of hatred. Thoroughly frightened, with trembling legs, he regained as best he could his lodgings, and ascended to his room. When he had thrown his cap down, he remained several minutes stock-still. Then, worn out, he lay down on his couch, and stretched himself with a languid, feeble sigh. At the expiration of half an hour, hurried footsteps were heard, and at the same moment Raskolnikoff recognised Razoumikhin's voice; he closed his eyes, pretending to be asleep. The latter opened the door, and remained for some time in the doorway, not seeming capable of coming to any definite resolution. At last he entered the room gently, and cautiously approached the couch.

'Don't rouse him, let him sleep right out; he'll take a mouthful by and by,' said Nastasia, in a whisper.

'Quite right,' replied Razoumikhin. They moved off on tiptoe and pushed the door to. Another half-hour passed by, when Raskolnikoff opened his eyes, lay down again on his back, and clasped his hands behind his head.

'Who is that man? Who is that fellow that has risen from the bowels of the earth? Where has he been and what can he have seen? He has seen everything, that's clear. Where can he have been at the time, and from what hiding-place can he have witnessed the deed? How is it that he did not turn up sooner? And how can he have seen? Can such a thing be possible? H'm!' continued Raskolnikoff, with icy tremor, 'and as for the jewel-box which Nikola found behind the door, could anyone have expected such a thing as that?'

He felt that he was getting weaker and weaker, that his bodily strength was failing him, and he experienced in consequence great disgust at himself. 'I ought to have known that,' he thought with a bitter smile, 'how did I dare, knowing what I am, anticipating what would happen, how did I dare take an axe and shed blood? I must have known everything beforehand. Indeed, I did know it!' he muttered in despair. At moments he would reflect on a thought: 'No, people of that cast of mind are not constituted like that. The real ruler – the man who dares all – bombards Toulon, massacres in Paris, abandons an army in Egypt, gets rid of half a million of men on his Moscow campaign, and gets off scot-free at Vilna by means of a pun; when he is dead and gone, people put up statues for him; everything seems allowable in his case. No, men like that are not made of flesh, but rather of bronze!' Another idea, which suddenly struck him, nearly made him laugh: 'Napoleon, the Pyramids, Waterloo, and an old woman, the widow of a college bursar – a contemptible usurer, who hides a red morocco trunk under her bed. How would Porphyrius Petrovitch digest such an amalgam? Æstheticism could not swallow that. "Would Napoleon have crept under an old woman's bed?" he might ask. How absurd!'

Occasionally he felt that he was nearly delirious; his state was one of feverish excitement. 'As for the old woman, she is of no account!' he exclaimed by fits and starts. 'Let us grant that she has been a mistake all along! She has always been an incident. I wished to complete the thing as quickly as possible. It was not a human being, it was a principle I destroyed! The principle I have destroyed, but I could not step over it, I am no farther than before. All I could do was to kill! And in that I was not very successful, I fancy. A principle? Why on earth did that silly fellow Razoumikhin attack Socialists just now? They are hard-working business men, "they work for the common weal." No, I have but one life, I have no wish to wait for the "common weal." I wish to live myself, otherwise it would be better not to exist at all. I have no desire to neglect a starving mother, and clutch the money I have by me, on the pretext that someday or other everybody will be happy. As some of them say, I contribute my stone towards the building-up of universal happiness, and that must be enough to set my mind at ease. Ha, ha! Why then have you forgotten me? As I have but a certain time to live, I intend to have my share of happiness forthwith. After all, I am only so much atheistical vermin, nothing more!' he added all at once, laughing as if demented, and he clung to this idea. He took an acrid pleasure in turning it over and over, in surveying it from every point of view. 'Yes,

I am, *de facto*, so much vermin; first, from the fact that I am now considering whether I really am so; secondly, because during a whole month I have been pestering Divine Providence, taking it to witness that I was contemplating this attempt, not with a view to material gains, but with ulterior purposes – ha, ha! Thirdly, because in the act of doing, I was anxious to proceed with as much justice as possible; amongst various kinds of vermin I selected the most noisome, and in destroying it I determined only to take just enough to give me a suitable start in life, neither more nor less (the remainder would have gone to the convent to which she had bequeathed her fortune) – ha, ha! I am absolutely so much vermin,' he added, grinding his teeth, 'because I am probably more vile and more ignoble than the vermin that has been destroyed, and because I felt certain that after my deed I should say so! Can there be anything like my terror? Oh! platitude! platitude! I can now realise the Prophet on horseback, scimitar in hand! Allah wills it! – therefore obey, trembling creature! The Prophet was right when, in marshalling some picked troops in the open, he struck down the good and bad, without even deigning an explanation! Obey, trembling creature, and beware you have no will, because the matter at issue does not concern you! I shall never, never forgive the old woman!'

His hair was moist with sweat, his parched lips moved, his motionless gaze was fixed on the ceiling. 'How I loved my mother and sister! And why do I hate them now? For I do hate them, I detest their presence, I cannot bear them near me! I remember getting close to my mother, quite lately, and kissing her. Fancy kissing her, whilst thinking that if she but knew – how I now loathe that old woman! I believe that, if she came to life again, I should kill her as I did before! Wretched Elizabeth! Why did chance bring you there at all? Singular, however, I scarcely think of her – as if nothing had happened. Elizabeth! Sonia! Poor, gentle, dove-eyed creatures! Why are they not weeping and wailing? Resigned to their fate, they accept everything in silence. Sonia! Sonia! Gentle Sonia!'

He became unconscious, and to his great surprise, dreamed that he was in the street. It was already getting late; the darkness was increasing; the moon shone more and more brightly, and yet the atmosphere was stifling. Many persons were about the streets; busy toilers were returning home; others, again, were leisurely strolling. The air reeked with the smell of lime, mortar, dust, and stagnant water. Raskolnikoff moved on, sorrowful and in thought; he well remembered having left home with some purpose; he remembered that he had urgent duties to attend to – but what were they? He had forgotten. Suddenly he stopped, and noticed that, on the opposite pavement, somebody was beckoning to him. He crossed the street to join him, but, all of a sudden, the man turned about, and, as if nothing had happened, continued on his way, with bent head, without looking round, without seeming to call Raskolnikoff. 'Can I have made a mistake?' he thought, continuing, however, to follow the man. When he had advanced somewhat, he suddenly recognised him, and was seized with fear; it was the very man, looking on the ground as before, with the same stoop, wearing the self-same garment. Raskolnikoff, whose heart was beating fast, advanced yet a little; they both entered a pereoulok. And yet the man did not turn round. 'Can he know that I am behind him?' Raskolnikoff asked himself. The man now entered a large house. Raskolnikoff quickly advanced to the door, looking hard, thinking that this mysterious individual might now turn and call him. And when the latter was in the courtyard, he looked round all of a sudden, seeming to continue waving his hand as before.

Raskolnikoff hastened to enter the house, but once within, the man had vanished. Assuming that he had ascended the first staircase, he did the same. In truth, slow and regular steps could now be heard two floors above. How strange, he seemed to recognise these stairs! Here was the window of the first floor, through which the sad, mysterious moonlight was shining. Here was the second floor. Why! – the very room where the painters were at work! Why, then, did he not recognise the house from the very first? The footsteps of the man who was ahead of him now ceased to be heard. 'He must have stopped – have hidden somewhere. Here is the third storey – shall I go on? And the silence! – this terrible silence!' But he continued his ascent. The very echo of his own footsteps appalled him. Heavens! How dark! Surely the man is hidden in some corner? Ah! the room opening on the landing was wide open! Raskolnikoff stopped and entered. Darkness and space within. He now entered the sitting-room, keeping on tiptoe. The light of the moon shone brightly here, and cast its fullest light; the furniture had not been touched; chairs, mirror, sofa, and pictures, all had retained their former places. The moon, with its enormous round copper-coloured face, was fully visible from the window. In deadly silence he now waited. Suddenly he heard a grating noise, like that of shavings that are being torn. Silence once more. A giddy fly impinged against the window, commencing its plaintive buzz.

At the same moment, he fancied he saw, in a corner, some woman's garment hanging from the wall between the cupboard and the window. 'Why is that garment there?' he thought, 'it was not there before.' He gently approached, suspecting that someone was hidden behind it. Now cautiously removing it, he observed a chair; upon the chair sat the woman, her head bent low, her body crouching – the face he could not see. He knew it was Alena Ivanovna. 'Frightened, I suppose,' he thought. And now he gently slips the axe from off its noose and, with twice-repeated blow, strikes at her skull. But more strange still, she keeps her seat just as before, just like a statue. The youth stoops down to see his work, whilst she still crouches more and more. He stoops again – more to the ground, looks up, and, when he sees her face, grows terror-struck. The woman laughed – yet with a silent laugh, striving hard no one should hear. Suddenly it struck Raskolnikoff that the room door was open; there also was laughter, whispering. Rage overcame him. Now, with a demon's power he struck, and struck, and struck again. Yet laughter grew and whisper grew. As for the woman, she only writhed. He wished to run: – the room was filling, the door stood open, and on the landing and on the stairs – here, there, and everywhere – people, living people, they looked, looked on in silence. His heart stood still, his feet were leaden – he tried to cry out, and woke.

He breathed with an effort, but he fancied he was still dreaming, when he perceived, in the doorway of his room, a man whom he had never seen before, and who was carefully watching him. Raskolnikoff had not as yet had time to open his eyes wide before he once more closed them. Lying on his back, he scarcely moved. 'Am I still dreaming?' he thought and gently raised his eyelids to cast a timid glance at the stranger. The latter, continuing in the same place, went on with his inspection. Suddenly he entered, gently closed the door behind him, approached the table, and, after a moment's interval, sat down quietly on a chair near the couch. During the whole of this time he had not taken his eyes off Raskolnikoff. Then he deposited his hat by his side, rested both hands on the knob of his walking-stick, and allowed his chin to sink on his hands, like a man prepared to wait some time. As far as Raskolnikoff had been able to judge by a furtive glance, the stranger was no longer young; he appeared robust, and wore a thick and very fair beard.

Ten minutes went by in this way. It was yet light, although it was getting late. The profoundest silence reigned in the room. No noises were even heard on the stairs, nothing but the buzz of a big fly, which, in its course, had struck the window. This was becoming unbearable. Raskolnikoff could bear it no longer, and suddenly sat bolt upright.

'Why don't you speak? What do you wish?'

'I was perfectly aware that your sleep was only a make-believe,' replied the stranger, with a tranquil smile. 'Permit me to introduce myself: Arcadius Ivanovitch Svidrigaïloff.'

PART IV

Chapter 1

'AM I REALLY wide awake?' Raskolnikoff asked himself once more, whilst looking at his unexpected visitor with mistrustful eye. 'Svidrigaïloff? Nonsense! Impossible!' said he at last, aloud, not daring to trust his ears. This exclamation seemed to cause the stranger no kind of surprise.

'I have called on you for two reasons. The first, because I wished to make your acquaintance personally, having for some time past heard speak of you in the most flattering terms; secondly, I trust you will not refuse me your help in an enterprise directly affecting your sister Eudoxia's interests. Alone, and without introductions, I should have some difficulty in being received by her, now that she is prejudiced against me; but, introduced by you, I presume that things would be otherwise.'

'You have been wrong in relying on me,' replied Raskolnikoff.

'Permit me to ask you whether it was yesterday that these ladies arrived?' No reply from Raskolnikoff. 'It was yesterday, I know. I myself have only been here since the day before yesterday. Now, this is what I am going to tell you on the subject, Rodion Romanovitch, and I think it needless to justify myself; but let me ask you, what may there be so very vicious in this on my part, assuming one to view things healthily without prejudice?'

Raskolnikoff continued to examine him in silence.

'You are going to tell me, perhaps, that I have persecuted, under my own roof, a defenceless girl, whom I have insulted by dishonourable proposals? You see, I anticipate the charge. But remember that I am a man, *et nihil humanum* – in a word that I am susceptible of being fascinated, of falling in love, a thing doubtless independent of our will – and everything is explained as naturally as possible. The question lies in a nutshell. Am I a monster, or am I not rather a victim? When I proposed to the object of my passion to elope with me to America or to Switzerland, I harboured, with regard to herself, the most respectful sentiments, and I thought only of bringing about our mutual happiness!

Reason is only the slave of passion, and I have only injured myself.'

'That is not the point in question,' replied Raskolnikoff disdainfully. 'Whether you are right or wrong, you are odious to me; I do not wish to know you, and I show you the door. Be off!'

Svidrigaïloff burst out laughing. 'There is no way of entangling you,' said the latter with frank gaiety. 'I wanted to pretend to be sly, but that does not go down with you.'

'Why, at this very moment you are trying to entangle me.'

'After all,' repeated Svidrigaïloff, laughing heartily, 'my slyness is perfectly fair under the circumstances. But you have not permitted me to finish. To return to what I was just talking about, nothing unpleasant has happened except the incident in the garden. Marfa Petrovna – '

'Why, people say you have killed Marfa Petrovna!' interrupted Raskolnikoff brutally.

'You have been told as much? After all, that is not so astonishing! Now, as regards your question, I hardly know how to answer it, although my conscience is perfectly at ease on the subject. Do not believe that I dread the consequences of the incident. Every customary formality has been gone through most minutely; the inquest has proved that the dead woman died of an apoplectic fit brought about by a bath she had taken after a copious meal at which she had drunk nearly a bottle of wine. Nothing else has been discovered. No, this is not the matter that causes me anxiety. But several times, especially when posting towards St Petersburg, I asked myself if I had not morally contributed towards this misfortune, either by having irritated my wife or in some similar manner. I have come to the conclusion that this could not have been the case.'

Raskolnikoff began to laugh. 'What may you be thinking about now?'

'And why do you laugh? I had only given her two gentle cuts with my horsewhip which have left no marks. Don't consider me a cynic, if you please. I know that this was infamous on my part and so forth, but I also know that my fits of passion did not displease Marfa Petrovna. When the incident in connection with your sister occurred, my wife went and bruited the circumstance all over the town; she went and pestered all her acquaintances with her notorious letter. You have heard, I suppose, that she went and read it to everybody? It was then that these two whip-cuts came down like a thunderbolt.'

For a moment Raskolnikoff thought of getting up and of going out, to cut the interview short. But a kind of curiosity and a species of calculation induced him to wait a little longer. 'You are fond of using the horsewhip?' he asked absently.

'Not particularly!' replied Svidrigaïloff quietly. 'I hardly ever had a quarrel with Marfa Petrovna. We lived very harmoniously, and she was always satisfied with her husband. During our seven years of married life, I have only used the whip twice (I do not mention the third time, which was, after all an equivocal case). The first occasion was two months after our marriage, at the time of having just settled down in the country; the second and last time was on the occasion I referred to just now. You took me for a pigheaded monster, for a partisan of serfdom, did you not?'

In Raskolnikoff's opinion, this man had some preconceived plan, and was an extremely cunning fellow. 'You must have spent several consecutive days without speaking to anybody?' asked the young man.

'There is some truth in your conjecture. But you are astonished to find me such a good-natured man?'

'I am of opinion that you are extremely so!'

'Because I have taken no offence at your brutal questions? Why should I? Why should I be offended? I have answered you in the same way you have questioned me,' retorted Svidrigaïloff with a singularly good-natured look. 'In truth I hardly take an interest in anything,' he continued thoughtfully. 'At this time especially, nothing engages my attention. You may, if you like, think that I seek to enlist your good graces from interested motives, all the more as I have to do with your sister as I have just told you. Frankly, I do get very weary – especially has this been the case the last three days; so that I was really glad to see you. Do not be pained, Rodion Romanovitch, if I tell you that you yourself seem very strange to me. Say what you like, there is something very funny about you, and especially now. I do not mean at this very moment, but for some time past. All right! I shall say no more. Don't look so angry. I am not such a bear as you think.'

'Perhaps you are no bear at all,' said Raskolnikoff. 'Nay, more, you seem to me a very well-bred man, and, at all events, you know when it suits you to be so.'

'I do not care a jot for anyone's opinion,' answered Svidrigaïloff in an off-hand and slightly disdainful tone of voice. 'Why, therefore, not assume the ways of a badly bred man in a country where they are so elastic, and especially if one has a natural tendency that way?' added he with a laugh.

Raskolnikoff looked at him gloomily. 'I have heard that you know many people here. You are not what is called a man without friends. This being so, what are you doing here? – what is your purpose?'

'It is perfectly true, as you say, that I have "friends" here,' replied the visitor, without answering the principal question addressed to him; 'for the last three days that I have been looking about the metropolis, I have met several of them; I have recognised them, and I fancy that they have recognised me. I am tolerably dressed, and I am considered well off. The abolition of serfdom has not ruined us, and yet I am not anxious to renew former friendships, which used to be unbearable to me. I have been here since the day before yesterday without calling on anyone. The club society and the *habitués* of Dussaud's restaurant must try and do without me. Besides, what is the fun in cheating at cards?'

'Ah! Were you in the habit of doing so?'

'Of course I was! Eight years ago, there was quite a clique of us – very gentlemanly fellows, capitalists, men of letters – who used to spend our time in playing cards, in cheating one another to our hearts' content. Have you ever noticed that in Russia most of the nobs are more or less pickpockets? About this time a cardsharper from Nijine, whom I owed seventy thousand roubles, had me locked up for debt. It was then that Marfa Petrovna showed herself in her true colours. She made terms with my creditor, and, in consideration of thirty thousand roubles, she paid him, and secured my liberty. We were married, upon which she did her best to bury me like a treasure in her country house. She was five years older than myself, and was very fond of me. For seven whole years I never stirred from our village. Observe that during the whole course of her life she kept in her possession, by way of hold upon me, the bill I had endorsed for this card-sharper, and which she had secured by proxy. Had I tried to kick, she would have had me locked up there and then. Yes, she would; in spite of all her love for me, she would not have hesitated, I am positive. Women are so paradoxical.'

'I suppose if she had not had this hold upon you, you would have left her in the lurch?'

'I hardly know how to answer you. The document in question did not disturb me very much – I had no kind of wish to go elsewhere. Twice Marfa Petrovna, seeing that I was miserable, urged me to go abroad. But why should I? I had already been in Europe, and had never liked it in any shape or form. The grand sights of nature undoubtedly evoke your admiration; but somehow, in watching a sunrise, the sea, or even the Bay of Naples, one feels miserable – and, what is worst of all, without knowing why. No! A man is better at home. Here, at all events, you can lay the blame on others, thus justifying yourself in your own eyes. I may perhaps undertake an expedition to the North Pole, because drink, which used to be my only solace, has at last sickened me. I can't drink any more, I have tried it. But, by the by, they say there is going to be a balloon-ascent next Sunday in Youssoopoff's garden; it appears that Berg is going to attempt an aerial excursion, and that he is prepared, for a consideration, to take a few fellow-travellers. Is that so?'

'Do you want to go up in a balloon?'

'Well, yes – no,' muttered Svidrigaïloff, who seemed to have become absent-minded.

'What sort of man can this fellow really be?' thought Raskolnikoff.

'This bill,' continued Svidrigaïloff, 'did not vex me in any sort of way. I remained in the village of my own accord. Well, about a year ago, on the occasion of my birthday, Marfa Petrovna returned me this document, in addition to a large sum of money, by way of present. She had plenty of it. "See what confidence I have in you, Arcadius Ivanovitch!" said she. Those were her very words, I assure you. Do you believe me? But you must know that I played the squire's part uncommonly well: everybody knows me down the country-side. And, in order to have something to do, I sent for books. Marfa Petrovna, at bottom, approved of my taste for reading, although later on she got anxious lest I might weary from too much application.'

'It appears that Marfa Petrovna's death has left a void?'

'Perhaps it has. Such a thing is quite possible, quite possible! By the by, do you believe in apparitions?'

'What kind of apparitions?'

'Why, apparitions in the ordinary acceptation of the word.'

'Do you believe in them?'

'Yes – no, I don't if you like; and yet – '

'Have you ever seen any?'

Svidrigaïloff looked at his interlocutor with a strange look, 'Marfa Petrovna appears to me,' replied the latter, and his mouth twitched with an indefinable smile.

'Do you really mean she appears to you?'

'Yes, she has already done so three times. The first time I saw her was on the very day of her burial, an hour after my return from the churchyard. This was on the eve of my departure for St Petersburg. I saw her again on my journey, the day before yesterday she appeared to me at daybreak at the Malaia Vichera station; her last appearance occurred two hours ago, in one of the rooms of my lodgings. I was alone.'

'Were you wide awake?'

'Quite so. I was awake on every occasion. She appears, talks for a moment, and goes out by the door, always by the door. I fancy I hear her footstep.'

'I have often said that things of this kind did happen,' cried Raskolnikoff brusquely. A moment afterwards, he was astonished at his remark. He was greatly agitated.

'You have often said so?' asked Svidrigaïloff, surprised. 'Is it possible? Well, was I wrong in saying that there is a point in common between us – yes or no?'

'You have never said anything of the kind!' replied Raskolnikoff irritably.

'I have not?'

'Never!'

'I really fancy I have. Just now, on entering here and seeing you in bed with shut eyes and pretending to be asleep, I thought to myself, "That is the very man!"'

'The very man? What do you mean by such a statement? What are you alluding to?' cried Raskolnikoff.

'What am I alluding to? I hardly know, to tell you the truth,' stammered Svidrigaïloff with embarrassment. For a moment the two men looked each other hard in the face.

'All this is beside the question!' replied Raskolnikoff calmly. 'What does she say when she appears to you?'

'What does she say? She talks nonsense, talks about silly and insignificant things. It vexes me. Such is man! On her first appearance I was tired out – the funeral and service, the dinner, all this had scarcely given me breathing time. I was at last in my study, was smoking a cigar whilst giving scope to my reflections, when I saw her enter by the door. "Arcadius Ivanovitch," says she, "today, as a result of all the bother you have had, you have forgotten to wind up the dining-room clock." I had, you must know, been in the habit of winding this clock up once a week, and, if I used to forget it, my wife always reminded me of it. The following day, I started for St Petersburg. At daybreak, having stopped at a station, I got out and entered the refreshment bar. I had slept badly, my eyes were heavy; I ordered a cup of coffee – all at once, whom did I see? Marfa Petrovna seated beside me. She was holding a pack of cards. "Shall I predict what will happen during your journey, Arcadius Ivanovitch?" asked she. She used to be a capital hand at telling fortunes. I am vexed, I must own, that I did not let her tell me mine. I darted away, frightened. Luckily, the bell was going for the passengers. This very day, after a detestable dinner which I could not digest, I was in my room, and had no sooner lit a cigar when I once more saw Marfa appear. On this occasion she was carefully dressed, wore a new green silk gown with a very long train. "Good-morning, Arcadius Ivanovitch!" said she. "What do you think of my gown? Aniska can't make gowns like this one." Aniska, I must tell you, is a dressmaker in our village, an ex-serf, who has served her apprenticeship in Moscow – a fine strapping wench.

'I look at her gown, then carefully at my wife, telling her "It is useless for you to put yourself out, Marfa Petrovna, to come and talk to me about similar trifles." *"Batuchka,"* said she, "there seems no way of frightening you." "I shall marry shortly, Marfa Petrovna," I replied, wishing to tease her a little. "So you may, Arcadius Ivanovitch, you won't get thought much of for marrying so soon after your first wife's death; even if you made a happy selection, you would only gain the contempt of decent people." Upon this, she went out, and I even fancied I heard the rustling of her train. Is that not peculiar?'

'But perhaps you have been lying all along?' observed Raskolnikoff.

'It is but seldom that I do so,' replied Svidrigaïloff, absently, and without in any way seeming to heed the rudeness of the question.

'And had you never seen any apparitions before?'

'Oh, yes; but that happened only once some six years ago. I used to have a servant called Philka; he had just been buried. In a fit of absence, I called out as usual, "Philka, bring me my pipe!" He came in, went straight to the cupboard where my smoking-requisites were kept. "He is down upon me!" I thought to myself, for shortly before his death we had had a smart altercation. "How dare you," I asked, "how dare you come in my presence, out at elbow? Be off, you rascal!" He turned about face, went out, and has never appeared again. I never mentioned this circumstance to my wife – it was originally my intention to have a mass said for him, but I thought, later on, that that would be very childish.'

'Go and consult a medical man.'

'Your advice is superfluous. I know perfectly well that I am ill – although, to tell the truth, I hardly know what is the matter with me; in my opinion I am ever so much better than you are. Remember, I did not ask you, "Do you think that people see apparitions?" My question was, "Do you think that there are apparitions?"'

'Indeed, I do nothing of the kind!' replied the young man sharply, even angrily.

'What do people generally say on the subject?' muttered Svidrigaïloff, by way of soliloquy, who, with drooping head was looking askance. 'People will tell you, "You are ill: hence, what appears to you is nothing but a vision, the results of delirium." But that is not logical reasoning. I admit that apparitions only happen to the sick; but that proves that, in order to see them, one must be sick, and not that they are not in existence.'

'They are not in existence, I am positive!' replied Raskolnikoff vehemently.

Svidrigaïloff looked at him a long time. 'You are of opinion that they do not exist? But might we not say apparitions are to some extent portions, particles, from other spheres. A healthy man can have no reason for seeing them, considering that a healthy man is, above all, a material man; he must in consequence, in order to be well, live on or by his mundane life. But let him get ill, let his normal physical organisation get out of order, then forthwith becomes manifest the possibility of another world; and, in proportion to his increasing illness, his contact with the next world becomes nearer and nearer till death hurls him straight away into it. This argument I have held for a long time; and if you believe in another life, nothing can prevent you admitting this.'

'I do not believe in another life,' replied Raskolnikoff.

Svidrigaïloff remained pensive. 'Supposing we found there nothing but spiders or such-like things?' asked he, all of a sudden.

'The man is mad,' thought Raskolnikoff.

'Men always represent eternity as an incomprehensible idea, as a something immense – immense! But why should this necessarily be the case? Imagine, on the contrary, a small room – a bathroom, if you will – blackened by smoke, with spiders in every corner. Supposing that to be eternity! I often conceive it to be so.'

'What! Do you mean to say that you have not a more just, a more consoling idea of eternity?' exclaimed Raskolnikoff, ill at ease.

'More just, you ask? Who knows? This point of view is possibly true, and certainly would be so if I had my way,' answered Svidrigaïloff, with a vague smile.

This sinister reply sent a shudder through Raskolnikoff's veins. Svidrigaïloff looked up, looked the young man hard in the face, and burst out laughing. 'Is it not strange?' he exclaimed. 'Half an hour ago we had as yet not met – we looked upon each other as enemies, a something unpleasant had to be settled between us; this unpleasantness has not been touched upon, and we positively end by philosophising! Did I not say that we were birds of a feather?'

'Excuse me,' said Raskolnikoff, vexed, 'be kind enough to explain to me, without any more beating about the bush, why you have honoured me with your visit – I am in a hurry – I am obliged to go out.'

'Well and good. Is it true that your sister, Eudoxia Romanovna, is going to marry Mr Looshin?'

'I must ask you to leave my sister alone, and not to mention her name. I cannot even understand how you dare speak of her to me at all, if you really are Svidrigaïloff.'

'But as I have called to speak specially of her, it seems but natural to speak of her.'

'Very well then. Speak up, but look alive.'

'This Mr Looshin is a relative of mine by marriage. I am quite sure you must already have taken stock of him, if you have only seen him for half an hour, or if someone worthy of belief has mentioned him to you. He is not a suitable match for Eudoxia Romanovna. In my opinion, your sister would, by marrying him, sacrifice herself in an unselfish and foolish manner – in a word, she would do so for her family. From what I knew of you, I fancied that you would be delighted to see this marriage broken off, provided this could be done to your sister's advantage. Now that I know you personally, I am sure of it.'

'All this is very candid on your part – nay, even somewhat brazen-faced,' replied Raskolnikoff.

'In other words, you give me credit for nothing but selfish views? Be at ease, Rodion Romanovitch; if I only thought of myself, I should conceal my hand. I am not quite a fool – but on this subject I purpose offering you a remarkable psychological study. Just now I apologised for having loved your sister, saying that I myself had been a victim. Well, at this moment, I have no more love for her. This astonishes me beyond expression, for I had been hit hard.'

'Yours was only the caprice of an idle and vicious man,' interrupted Raskolnikoff.

'I must own to being an idle and vicious man. But your sister possesses qualities to impress even a libertine like me – after all, mine was only a temporary fascination; of that I am sure now.'

'How long have you been sure of that?'

'I have been suspecting it for some time of late; and yesterday, on arriving in St Petersburg, I became positive of it. But, whilst in Moscow, I had decided to sue for Eudoxia's hand, and to pose as Mr Looshin's rival.'

'Excuse my interrupting you, but could you not cut matters somewhat shorter, and explain to me the object of your visit? I repeat that I am in a hurry, that I have calls to make.'

'With pleasure. Having made up my mind to undertake a certain journey, I wanted before doing so to settle different matters. My children live with their aunts; they are rich and independent of me. Besides, fancy me a father! I have only brought with me the sum which Marfa Petrovna made me a present of a year ago. This is plenty for my purposes – excuse me, but I am coming to the point: – before starting, I want to have done with Mr Looshin – not that I exactly detest him, though he was the cause of my last dispute with my wife, but I was enraged when I found out that she had contrived this marriage. I now appeal to you for an introduction to Eudoxia Romanovna; you may, if you think fit, be present at our interview. To begin with: I am anxious to submit to your sister all the inconveniences which would arise from her marriage with Mr Looshin, then I would beg of her to forgive the annoyances I have caused her, begging, at the same time, her acceptance of ten thousand roubles, which would make up for a breach, which, I am persuaded, she would not regret if she saw the possibility of such a thing.'

'But you must be mad, positively mad!' cried Raskolnikoff, with more surprise than anger. 'How dare you speak in this way?'

'I expected you would protest, but I shall first show you that, although not wealthy, I can yet dispose of these ten thousand roubles, which I can very well do without. If Eudoxia Romanovna will not accept them, Heaven only knows what use I may make of them. Secondly, my conscience is perfectly at ease, my offer being in every way an unselfish one. Believe me or not, but the future will prove this to Eudoxia as well as to yourself. I own that I have behaved very badly to your respected sister; I regret it bitterly, and I am most anxious not only to make up the vexations I have caused her by some kind of pecuniary compensation, but to do her some kind of service, so that it may not be said that I have only injured her. If my proposition were not a straightforward one, I would not make it as frankly as I do, and I would draw the line today at an offer of ten thousand roubles, considering that I made a much larger offer five weeks ago. Besides, it is likely that I may marry a young girl before long, and under such conditions, I cannot be suspected of wishing to fascinate Eudoxia Romanovna. To sum up, I tell you that, if the latter does become Mr Looshin's wife, she is sure to receive this amount later, but from another man. But, pray, do not get angry, Rodion Romanovitch! Judge calmly and soberly.' Svidrigaïloff himself pronounced these words with extraordinary apathy.

'Pray cease!' said Raskolnikoff. 'This proposition is an extremely insolent one.'

'Not at all. Then you mean to imply that if in this world of ours a man can only injure his fellow-man, he has *per contra* no kind of right to do him any kind of good? You may say customary propriety is opposed to such a theory. Nonsense, say I. Supposing I were to die, and were to bequeath this sum to your sister: would she still persist in her refusal?'

'Probably she would.'

'Let us say nothing more about the matter. At all events I must beg of you to put my request to Eudoxia Romanovna.'

'I shall do nothing of the sort.'

'Then, Rodion Romanovitch, I must try to get a private interview with her, which will be impossible without causing her annoyance.'

'And supposing I were to make her your proposition, would you desist from endeavouring to see her privately?'

'I hardly know what to answer. I should like, above all things, to meet her, if only once.'

'Do not indulge in such a hope.'

'So much the worse. After all, you do not know me. Perhaps friendship may grow between us.'

'Do you think so?'

'And why not?' said Svidrigaïloff, with a smile, whilst rising and taking his hat. 'I have no wish to force myself upon you. Whilst coming here, I did not much expect – this very morning I was struck – '

'Where have you seen me this morning?' asked Raskolnikoff, uneasily.

'I saw you by the merest chance. It seems to me, somehow, that you and I are tarred with the same brush.'

'That will do! May I ask you if you intend starting before long?'

'On what journey?'

'On the journey you spoke about just now.'

'Did I speak to you about a journey? Ah! to be sure I did. If you only knew the question you have raised!' added he with an unfeeling laugh. 'Perhaps, instead of starting on this journey, I may get married. My friends are trying to arrange an alliance for me.'

'Here?'

'Yes.'

'You certainly have made the most of your time since your arrival in St Petersburg.'

'Well, I am off: by the by, I was going to forget something. Tell your sister, Rodion Romanovitch, that Marfa Petrovna has bequeathed to her three thousand roubles. Fact! Marfa Petrovna made her will in my presence a week before her death – in two or three weeks' time Eudoxia Romanovna may take possession of her legacy.'

'Is that the truth?'

'It is, indeed! Don't forget to tell her. Goodbye! I am living quite close to you.'

On going out, Svidrigaïloff passed Razoumikhin in the doorway.

Chapter 2

IT WAS CLOSE UPON eight o'clock when the two young men set out for Bakaleieff's, wishing to get the start of Looshin.

'Tell me,' asked Razoumikhin, as soon as they were in the street, 'who was the man that left your house when I entered it?'

'That was Svidrigaïloff, the landowner, with whom my sister once lived as governess, and whose house she was obliged to leave because he made love to her. Marfa Petrovna, that gentleman's wife, turned her out of doors. Later on, this very Marfa Petrovna apologised to Dounia. She has died quite lately. It was about her that my mother was talking just now. I don't know why, but I am very much afraid of the man. He is very queer, and has some firmly settled plan – one would almost fancy that he knows something. He came here shortly after his wife's burial. Dounia must be protected against him. This is what I meant to tell you.'

'Protect her! What can he do to Eudoxia Romanovna? I must thank you, Rodia, for having told me that. We will protect her, never fear! And where does the man live?'

'I know nothing about it.'

'Why did you not ask him? It is a pity! But I shall remember him.'

'Did you see him?' asked Raskolnikoff, after a certain silence.

'Yes! and have carefully, very carefully, taken stock of him.'

'Are you sure? Did you carefully notice him?' added Raskolnikoff.

'I did indeed, I remember his face and should recognise it amongst a thousand. I have a good memory for faces.'

They were once more silent. 'Do you know – it seems to – that I am perhaps the dupe of an illusion,' stammered Raskolnikoff.

'What makes you say this? I don't understand you very well.'

'Why,' pursued Raskolnikoff, with a grimace which was meant for a smile, 'all of you say that I am crazy, and, do you know, just now I was struck with the idea that you were perhaps right, and that I had seen nothing but a vision.'

'What an idea!'

'Who knows? I may be mad after all, and all the events of the last few days may only have existed in my imagination.'

'I say, Rodia, somebody has been upsetting you. But tell me, what has he been talking about? Why did he call at all?' Raskolnikoff said nothing – Razoumikhin reflected for a moment.

'Listen to my statement. Whilst calling on you, you were asleep. Afterwards, we dined; later on, I called on Porphyrius. Zametoff was still there. I wanted to begin, but was unfortunate at the outset. I could not, for the life of me, enter into details. They seemed as if they could not understand. Without, however, showing any kind of embarrassment, I took Porphyrius to the window, and began to speak with him, without, however, any greater success. He looked in one direction, I in another. At last I raised my fist, telling him that I purposed to do for him. He only looked at me in silence. I said what I had to say, and that was all. Awfully stupid, you will say. With Zametoff I did not exchange a single word. I was disgusted with my own stupidity, when a sudden reflection consoled me: for, on going down the stairs, I said to myself, "Is it worth our while to trouble ourselves in this way?" If some kind of danger threatened you, that would be quite another thing. But under present circumstances what have you to fear? You are not guilty, hence no occasion to be anxious on their account. Later on we shall laugh at their blunder, and, if I were in your place, I would delight in mystifying them. What a disgrace for them to have made such an awful mistake! Disgusting! Later on, we may be able to wake them up a bit, but, for the nonce, all we can do is to laugh at their folly.'

'Right!' answered Raskolnikoff. 'But what may you say tomorrow?' said he to himself. Strange to say, up to the present time he had not once thought of asking himself, 'What will Razoumikhin say when he shall know that I am guilty?' At this idea he looked hard at his friend. The accounts of his visit to Porphyrius had interested him but little; other things absorbed his attention at this moment.

They met Looshin in the passage; he had turned up precisely at eight, but had lost much time in looking for the number, so that they entered all three together without looking or bowing. These young men were the first on the scene. Peter Petrovitch, a stickler for propriety, stayed behind a moment to take off his overcoat. Pulcheria Alexandrovna immediately advanced towards him. Dounia and Raskolnikoff greeted each other. Peter Petrovitch, on entering, bowed to the ladies in an amiable manner, although with suitable gravity. Besides, he stood somewhat disconcerted. Pulcheria Alexandrovna, who seemed ill at ease, begged all her guests to sit round the samovar. Dounia and Looshin sat opposite to one another at the ends of the table. Razoumikhin and Raskolnikoff faced Pulcheria Alexandrovna, the former at Looshin's side, the latter by the side of his sister.

There was a moment's silence. Peter Petrovitch slowly drew a scented cambric handkerchief out of his pocket, and blew his nose. His manners were, undoubtedly, those of a kindly man, whose dignity had been somewhat wounded, and who was resolutely determined to have an explanation. As he took off his overcoat in the hall, he had already asked himself if the best punishment to inflict on the ladies would not be to retire there and then. This idea, however, he had not carried out, for he loved, above all, to see things clear before him – and here things were not quite clear to him. Since they had so openly despised his demands, there must have been some reason for it, and what could this reason have been? Perhaps it would be better to clear the matter up first, there would still be time enough for punishment – and punishment, though delayed, is none the less sure.

'I hope you have had a pleasant journey?' he asked, as in duty bound, of Pulcheria Alexandrovna.

'Thank God, I have, Peter Petrovitch.'

'I am delighted to hear it. And Eudoxia Romanovna has also, I trust, not been overtired?'

'I am young and strong, and do not get tired; but for my mother this journey has been a very trying one,' replied Dounia.

'What can you expect? Our highways are very long, Russia is a large country, and, however much I longed to do so, I was not able to meet you yesterday. I hope, however, that you have not had much inconvenience?'

'On the contrary, Peter Petrovitch, we have been in a bad plight,' Pulcheria Alexandrovna hastened to reply, with peculiar emphasis, 'and, had not God sent us Dmitri Prokovitch, I do not know what would have become of us yesterday. Permit me to introduce to you our deliverer, Dmitri Prokovitch Razoumikhin,' added she.

'Why – I have already had the pleasure – yesterday!' stammered Looshin, casting a malicious side-glance at the young man, whilst silently knitting his brows.

Peter Petrovitch was one of those men who do their best to appear amiable and lively in society, but who, under the influence of the least unpleasantness, suddenly lose all their grace, to the extent of seeming more like bags full of flour than dapper cavaliers. Silence reigned once more; Raskolnikoff became obstinately silent; Eudoxia Romanovna thought that it was wiser for her to remain silent; Razoumikhin had nothing to say. So that Pulcheria Alexandrovna saw herself in the painful necessity of renewing the conversation.

'Did you know that Marfa Petrovna was dead?' she commenced, resorting to a last resource.

'Indeed! I heard of it at once, and I can tell you that, immediately after his wife's burial, Arcadius Ivanovitch Svidrigaïloff posted in all haste to St Petersburg. I have this on the best authority.'

'To St Petersburg? And he is here?' asked Dounia, in an alarmed tone of voice, whilst interchanging looks with her mother.

'Quite so; and we may suppose that he has not come without a purpose. The hurry of his journey, and all the preceding circumstances lead one to think so.'

'Good heavens! Is it possible that he purposes pursuing Dounetchka as far as here?' exclaimed Pulcheria Alexandrovna.

'It seems to me that you need none of you be very anxious as to his presence in St Petersburg, provided, let me tell you, that you mean to avoid all kind of dealing with him. As for me, I am wide awake, and I shall soon know where he is quartered.'

'Ah! Peter Petrovitch, you have no notion how you have frightened me!' resumed Pulcheria Alexandrovna. 'I have only seen him twice, and he struck me as being terrible, terrible! I am sure that he was the cause of Marfa Petrovna's death.'

'The precise details which have come to my ears do not justify such a conclusion. I do not deny, however, that his evil doings may to a certain extent have hurried the natural course of things. But as to his general conduct, as to the real character of the man, I agree with you. I do not know what he is now, and what Marfa Petrovna may have left him. I shall shortly know it. One thing is certain, namely, that, being here in St Petersburg, he will not delay resuming his old ways, provided he has pecuniary resources. He is the most vicious, the most depraved of men. I am justified in believing that Marfa Petrovna, who was silly enough to be smitten with him, and who paid all his debts eight years ago, has been of use to him in yet another way. By dint of skill and sacrifice, she hushed up a criminal affair which would certainly have sent Mr Svidrigaïloff to Siberia. It was in connection with an assassination committed under peculiarly terrible and, I may say, odd circumstances. Now you know the man, if you are still anxious to get acquainted with him.'

'Good heavens!' exclaimed Pulcheria Alexandrovna. Raskolnikoff listened attentively.

'You speak, I presume, from certain information?' asked Dounia, in a severe tone of voice.

'I only repeat what I have heard from Marfa Petrovna herself. It must be remembered that, from a judicial point of view, this affair is a very obscure one: – at the time of the occurrence there used to live here – and it appears that she still does so – a certain woman of the name of Resslich, a foreigner, who lent money at usurious rates, and carried on other small trades. An intricate and mysterious connection had existed for a long time between this woman and Mr Svidrigaïloff. She had living with her a distant relative, a niece – a girl, I fancy of fourteen or fifteen years of age, who was deaf and dumb. Resslich hated the girl, she grudged her every mouthful of bread, and used to beat her with the utmost inhumanity. One day, this unfortunate creature was found hanging in the garret – the customary inquest ended in a verdict of suicide, and things seemed to rest there, when the police received information that the child had been violated by Svidrigaïloff. The whole matter was an obscure one, I admit; the charge came from another German female, a woman of notoriously loose morals, and whose testimony could not be of great weight. In a word, there was no trial. Marfa Petrovna started for the country, lavished her money, and succeeded in preventing pursuit. But, none the less, the most awkward reports were bruited abroad about Mr Svidrigaïloff; whilst you lived with him, Eudoxia Romanovna, you have doubtless also heard the story about his servant Philip, who died a victim of his harsh treatment. This happened six years ago, at the time when serfdom was yet in existence.'

'On the contrary, I heard that this Philip had hanged himself!'

'Quite so, but he was compelled – or, more correctly, driven – to commit suicide, in consequence of the incessant brutality and systematic vexation of his master.'

'I did not know that,' replied Dounia, dryly. 'I have only heard a somewhat strange story about this circumstance; this Philip, it appears, was hypochondriacal, a kind of philosophic servant, who, according to the statements of his fellow-servants, had gone wrong through reading; he is supposed to have hanged himself to escape his master's sneers and not his blows. I have always seen the latter treat his servants very humanely; he was beloved by them, although they attributed to him Philip's death.'

'I observe, Eudoxia Romanovna, that you have a desire to exculpate him,' replied Looshin, with a treacherous smile. 'The fact is, the man is a good hand at currying favour with the ladies; poor Marfa Petrovna, who has died under such strange circumstances, is a lamentable proof of it. I have only wished to warn your mother and yourself, by way of warning as to the attempts he will not fail to renew. As for me, I am firmly persuaded that this man will die in a debtors' prison. Marfa Petrovna thought too much about her children's interests to indulge an intention of ever securing to her husband a considerable portion of her fortune. She may probably have left him enough to live fairly comfortably, for, with his dissipated tastes, he would have squandered everything within a year.'

'Pray, Peter Petrovitch, let us talk no more about Mr Svidrigaïloff,' exclaimed Dounia. 'This subject is unpleasant to me.'

'He called upon me just now,' said, somewhat sharply, Raskolnikoff, who, up to that moment, had not said a word.

The company turned towards him with exclamations of surprise. Peter Petrovitch himself seemed curious.

'Half an hour ago, whilst I was asleep, he entered my room, roused me, and stated his name,' continued Raskolnikoff. 'He was quite at home and cheerful; he is very anxious to become friends with me. Amongst other things, he is very anxious to have an interview with you, Dounia; and he has requested me to act as go-between for this purpose. He has a proposal to make to you, and has told me the nature of it. Likewise he positively assured me that Marfa Petrovna, a week before her death, had left you, in her will, three thousand roubles, and that you could draw this sum after some little delay.'

'God be praised!' exclaimed Pulcheria Alexandrovna, whilst making the sign of the cross. 'Pray for her! Dounia, pray for her!'

'It is a positive fact,' Looshin could not help admitting.

'Well, and what more?' asked Dounetchka eagerly.

'He also told me that he himself was not rich, and that the whole of the fortune would pass to his children, who are now staying with their aunt. He has also informed me that he was living quite near me, but where I don't know – I forgot even to ask him.'

'And what is he anxious to propose to Dounia?' asked Pulcheria, anxiously. 'Did he tell you?'

'He did.'

'What was it?'

'You shall know later on.' After having made this answer, Raskolnikoff began to drink his tea.

Peter Petrovitch looked at his watch. 'An urgent matter compels me to go. I, therefore, will not disturb your party,' added he, with somewhat nettled air. Upon this, he rose.

'Stay, Peter Petrovitch,' said Dounia, 'you had intended spending the whole of your evening with us. Besides, you yourself wrote that you wanted to have an explanation of some kind with mamma.'

'You are quite right, Eudoxia Romanovna,' replied Peter Petrovitch, in an affected tone of voice, whilst pretending to sit down, holding, however, his hat in his hand. 'I certainly wanted to clear up with your respected mother and yourself some matters of the utmost gravity. But, as your brother cannot explain in my presence certain proposals of Mr Svidrigaïloff's, I am neither able nor anxious to make an explanation, before a third party, on certain points of the utmost importance. Besides I had expressed in the most formal terms a desire left unheeded.' Looshin's face had become hard and repellent.

'I admit that you asked that my brother should not be present at our interview, and, if your request has not been acceded to, it was solely at my entreaty,' replied Dounia. 'You wrote to us that my brother had insulted you; according to me, no misunderstanding ought to exist between you, and a reconciliation must take place. If Rodia has really offended you, he must apologise, and will do so.'

On hearing these words, Peter Petrovitch felt less than ever disposed to make concessions. 'With the best will in the world, Eudoxia Romanovna, it is impossible to forget certain insults. In all things there is a limit dangerous to overstep, for, once stepped over, return or retraction is impossible.'

'Put this sensitiveness on one side, Peter Petrovitch,' cried Dounia, moved; 'be the noble and intelligent man I have always known you to be, and which I always wish to see you. I have made you a sacred promise; trust me, therefore, in this matter, and believe me capable of judging impartially. The part of arbitrator, which I claim at this moment, is as great a surprise for my brother as for you. When this day, upon receipt of your letter, I urgently asked him to be present at our interview, I did not in any way communicate to him my intentions. Believe me, that if you refuse to be reconciled, I shall be obliged to declare in favour of one of you, to the exclusion of the other. It is there the question rests. I neither wish nor ought to make a wrong choice. If in your favour, I must break with my brother; if in his, I must break with you. I will, and have a right to be, enlightened as to your feelings towards me. I shall know either whether I have a brother in Rodia, or if in you a husband who loves and appreciates me.'

'Eudoxia Romanovna,' replied Looshin, vexed, 'your language suggests too many and varied interpretations – nay, more, I find it offensive, considering the position I hold with reference to yourself, to say nothing of the vexation of seeing myself placed on the same level as – a fiery young man. You seem to admit the possibility of a breaking off of our marriage. You say you must choose between your brother and me. This shows how small I am in your eyes. I cannot accept this, considering our relationship and our mutual engagement.'

'What!' cried Dounia, blushing to the roots of her hair. 'I weigh your interest with what is dearest to me in life, and you complain that you are but little in my eyes?'

Raskolnikoff smiled sarcastically; Razoumikhin pulled a face, but the girl's reply did not appease Looshin, who became more and more arrogant and intractable.

'Love for your husband, for the future companion of your life, should rise superior to a brother's love,' he cried, sententiously; 'at all events, I must not be placed on the same level. Although I stated just now that I did not wish, nay, could not explain myself in your brother's presence on the main object of my visit, there is one point, and that a very important one for me, which I am anxious to clear up, and at this very moment, with your mother. Your son,' continued he, whilst addressing himself to Pulcheria Alexandrovna, 'offended me yesterday, in presence of Mr Razoumikhin – excuse me, but I have forgotten your name,' said he to the latter, with a pleasant bow – 'by the way in which he distorted a remark made by me some time ago, as I was taking tea at your house. I stated on that occasion that, in my opinion, a poor girl, who had been familiar with poverty, offered her husband more guarantees for virtue and happiness than a girl who had always lived in affluence. Your son has deliberately attached another meaning to my words; he has attributed to me odious intentions, and, in doing so, I presume he relied on your own correspondence. It would be a great relief to me, Pulcheria Alexandrovna, if you can prove me mistaken. Tell me, therefore, I pray, in what words you reproduced my statement in your letter to Rodion Romanovitch.'

'I scarcely remember,' replied Pulcheria Alexandrovna, 'but I give it as I understood it. I do not know how Rodia has repeated the sentence to you. He may have strained the wording.'

'He can only have been able to do so under the influence of what you wrote him.'

'Peter Petrovitch,' answered Pulcheria Alexandrovna, with dignity, 'the proof that neither Dounia nor I have taken your words in bad part is the fact of our being here.'

'Well said, mamma!' exclaimed the girl.

'Then it is I who am wrong!' cried Looshin, angered.

'Let me tell you, Peter Petrovitch, you keep on accusing Rodion. Now you, in your last letter, you charge him with something untrue,' pursued Pulcheria Alexandrovna, greatly comforted by the girl's approval.

'I do not remember having written anything untrue.'

'According to your letter,' declared Raskolnikoff, without turning towards Looshin, 'I had given to a girl, whom I had only seen once, the money I was supposed to have given to the widow of a man who had been run over by a carriage. You wrote that with the intention of getting me in bad odour with my family, and, in order to succeed all the better in this, you have described in the most ignoble manner the conduct of a girl, a stranger to yourself. This is a base defamation.'

'Excuse me, sir,' answered Looshin, trembling with passion, 'if in my letter I enlarged on matters concerning you, it was solely because your mother and sister had asked me to let them know how I had found you, and what impression you made upon me. I defy you to point out a single untruthful line in the passage in question. Do you deny having squandered your money? And, as to the unhappy family in question, would you go so far as to guarantee the respectability of all its members?'

'According to my ideas, with all your respectability, you are not worth the little finger of the young woman you slander.'

'And do you mean to tell me that you would not hesitate to introduce her into the society of your mother and sister?'

'I have already done so, if you want to know. I invited her yesterday to sit down by my mother and Dounia.'

'Rodia!' exclaimed Pulcheria Alexandrovna. Dounetchka blushed, Razoumikhin knitted his brows, while on Looshin's lips played a scornful smile.

'Judge for yourself, Eudoxia Romanovna,' said he, 'if it is possible for us to be friends. I trust that this is now understood, and that there may be no more talk about it. I am off, in order to no longer embarrass your family circle; besides, you have confidences to exchange.' He rose and took his hat. 'But let me tell you, before going, that I do not wish to be exposed in future to a similar interview. Of you especially, Pulcheria Alexandrovna, do I ask this favour, all the more as my letter was addressed to you, and to no one else.'

Pulcheria Alexandrovna felt somewhat ruffled. 'You think yourself, then, wholly master here, Peter Petrovitch! Dounia has told you why your wish was not fulfilled, although her intentions were of the best. But I must tell you that your style of writing is an imperious one. Are we to look upon all your wishes as commands? Let me tell you that you ought, above all things, to treat us, under present circumstances, with consideration, for our confidence in yourself has caused us to give up everything to come here, and, consequently, you have us at your mercy.'

'You are not quite right there, Pulcheria Alexandrovna, especially as you are now aware of the legacy left by Marfa Petrovna to your daughter. These three thousand roubles come in the very nick of time, it would appear, judging from the unusual tone you assume,' added Looshin bitterly.

'Your remark seems to imply that you have been speculating on our poverty!' observed Dounia irritably.

'At the present time, however, I am not able to do anything of the kind, especially as I do not wish to prevent your hearing of the secret proposals Arcadius Ivanovitch Svidrigaïloff has wished your brother to lay before you. It would appear to me that these proposals are, for you, of considerable and perhaps pleasant significance.'

'Heavens!' exclaimed Pulcheria Alexandrovna. Razoumikhin moved impatiently in his chair.

'Tell me, sister, are you not ashamed now?' asked Raskolnikoff.

'I am, Rodion,' replied the young lady. 'Peter Petrovitch, leave the room!' said she to Looshin, pale with anger.

The latter did not expect such an end. He had been too presumptuous, had reckoned too much on his own power and on the helplessness of his victims. Even now he could hardly believe his own ears. 'Eudoxia Romanovna,' said he, pale, and with quivering lips, 'if I go now, depend upon it that I shall never return. Think well what you are about! I mean what I say!'

'Insolent man!' exclaimed Dounia, bounding from her chair. 'I have no kind of wish ever to see you here again.'

'What? Is that really so?' shouted Looshin, all the more disconcerted as, even at the eleventh hour, he had scarcely believed such a rupture possible. 'And is that the way the wind blows? But permit me to say, Eudoxia, that I am in a position to protest.'

'What right have you to speak in this way?' interrupted Pulcheria Alexandrovna vehemently. 'How can you protest? What is your right? Do you think I would entrust my Dounia to a man like you? Be off! Leave us, henceforth, in peace! We have been wrong to assent to an unmannerly thing, and I especially.'

'And yet, Pulcheria Alexandrovna,' replied Peter Petrovitch, exasperated, 'you have bound me down by making me a promise which you now decline to fulfil, and this has put me to some expense.'

This last complaint was so much in keeping with Looshin's character, that Raskolnikoff, in spite of his wrath, could hardly hear it without bursting out laughing. This was, however, not the case with Pulcheria Alexandrovna.

'Expense?' retorted she violently. 'Do you mean, perhaps, the box you sent us? But you managed to forward it carriage-free. Heavens! You pretend that we have bound you down in some kind of way! Fancy turning the tables in such a manner! Say, rather, that we were at your mercy, Peter Petrovitch, and not you at ours!'

'Enough, mamma! Enough! I must beg!' said Eudoxia Romanovna 'Peter Petrovitch, do me the favour of leaving the room!'

'I am doing so; but one word more,' he said, almost beside himself. 'Your mother seems to have completely forgotten that I asked for the honour of your hand at a time when all kinds of reports were going about concerning you. In braving public opinion for your sake, in vindicating your reputation, I had reason to hope that you would be thankful to me in consequence – indeed, I fancied I had a right to rely on your gratitude. My eyes are opened, however. I see that my conduct was indiscreet, and that I was wrong to ignore public opinion.'

'It seems that the fellow wants his head broken!' cried Razoumikhin, who had started up to chastise him for his insolence.

'You are a base, bad man!' cried Dounia.

'Not another word!' exclaimed Raskolnikoff, passionately checking Razoumikhin; and, approaching Looshin and speaking in his face, he said, in a low but distinct tone of voice: 'Be good enough to withdraw! Not another word, or – '

Peter Petrovitch, pale and trembling with anger, looked at him for a second more, turned on his heel, and went, harbouring in his heart mortal hatred for Raskolnikoff, to whom he attributed his disgrace. And, strange to say, on going downstairs, he fancied that all was not yet lost, and that there might still be a possibility of reconciliation with the two ladies.

Chapter 3

FOR THE NEXT few minutes, the whole company was very cheer-ful – its satisfaction was manifested by laughter. Dounetchka alone grew pale at intervals and knitted her brows whilst reflecting on the previous unpleasantness. But the merriest of all was Razoumikhin. His satisfac-tion, to which as yet he dared not openly give vent, was betrayed in spite of himself by the feverish tremor of his person. He was now in a position to devote himself to the two ladies. Nevertheless, he kept these hopes in his heart of hearts, fearing to give utterance to his thoughts. As for Raskolnikoff, immovable and sullen, he in no wise shared the general mirth – indeed, it might be said that his thoughts were elsewhere. After his eagerness to see a rupture with Looshin, he seemed the first man to whom this very rupture was of the smallest possible interest. Dounia could not get over the idea that he was still angry with her, and Pulcheria Alexandrovna anxiously watched him.

'Tell me what Svidrigaïloff has been saying to you?' asked the young lady, approaching her brother.

'Pray do!' exclaimed Pulcheria Alexandrovna.

Raskolnikoff looked up. 'Why, he insists absolutely on making you a present of ten thousand roubles, and is most anxious to see you once, in my presence.'

'See her! Never!' cried Pulcheria Alexandrovna. 'And how dare he offer her money?'

Upon which Raskolnikoff related somewhat curiously his interview with Svidrigaïloff. Dounia was extremely startled when she heard the nature of Svidrigaïloff's proposals. For a long time she remained thoughtful. 'He has formed some atrocious intention!' she muttered, with a shudder.

Raskolnikoff observed her fear. 'I rather fancy that I shall have further opportunity of seeing him,' he remarked to his sister.

'We shall be sure to find his whereabouts. I'll make that my business,' cried Razoumikhin energetically. 'Depend upon it, I shall not lose sight of him. I have Rodia's permission. He himself told me not very long ago, "Watch over my sister!" Do you consent to that, Eudoxia Romanovna?'

Dounia smiled whilst holding out her hand to the young man. Pulcheria Alexandrovna cast on her a timid glance; in other respects, the three thousand roubles had decidedly calmed her. A quarter of an hour later, everybody was chattering with great animation. Even Raskolnikoff, although taciturn, listened for some time attentively to what was being said. Razoumikhin engrossed all the conversation.

'And why, may I ask, why leave this place?' he exclaimed with conviction. 'What will you do in your wretched little town? The main thing to take into consideration is that you are all together here, and you know that you are indispensable to one another. Don't forget, you cannot separate. Let me urge you to remain a little longer. Look upon me as a friend, as an associate, and I am convinced that we shall start a paying business. Now listen, and I will explain to you my project in all its details. The idea came upon me this very morning, before anything had happened. Here it is: I have an uncle whom you shall know, a kindly and respectable greybeard; this uncle possesses a capital of a thousand roubles which he is scarcely in need of, for he has a pension sufficient for all his wants. For the last two years he has offered me this capital at six per cent interest. I quite understand his subterfuge: it is a kindly expedient to help me. Now, last year I was not in want of money, but this year I eagerly looked forward to my uncle's visit in order to accept his proposal. Add to his thousand roubles another thousand of your own, and behold the partnership is a settled thing! Now, what shall we start?'

Then Razoumikhin set about explaining his plan. According to him, the greater number of our publishers and booksellers did badly because they did not thoroughly understand their business; but, with good books, money could be made. For the last two years he had been connected with divers firms, understood the trade, and had a fair knowledge of three European languages. A week before, he had told Raskolnikoff that his German was poor, and had said so in order to induce his friend to help him in a translation which would bring in a few roubles. Raskolnikoff had not, however, been duped by this falsehood.

'Then why,' asked Razoumikhin, getting interested, 'why not go in for a good thing, when we have already one of the most essential means of action – money? Of course we shall have to work, we mean doing so, we shall all of us do so – you, Eudoxia, I, Rodion. Why, there are publications which pay uncommonly well! Above all, we shall have the advantage of knowing just what to translate. We shall be translators, publishers, teachers. Now I can be of immense value because of my experience. Having been close upon two years in the very thick of publishers, I know the ins and outs of the business, which is not so very difficult after all, let me tell you! When the chance does turn up of earning something, why let it go by? I could mention two or three books whose bringing-out would be something like a gold-mine. Even the fact of pointing them out to one of our publishing firms ought to be worth to me something like five hundred roubles – but catch me doing so! And, even then, the noodles might be capable of hesitating! As to the plant, the paper, printing, selling – leave that to me, I know all about it! We must commence in a small way; later on, we will do business on a bigger scale, and we shall be sure to make ends meet.'

Dounia's eyes sparkled.

'Your proposition pleases me amazingly, Dmitri Prokovitch,' said she.

'I, of course, don't understand anything about all this,' added Pulcheria Alexandrovna. 'The idea may be good. Heaven only knows. We are obviously obliged to remain a certain time here,' continued she, casting a glance on her son.

'And what do you think of the idea, brother?' asked Dounia.

'Think it an excellent idea,' replied Raskolnikoff. 'Mind, a large publishing house can't be founded in a day, but I know five or six books whose success would be certain. And one thing, you may have every confidence in Razoumikhin's capacity: he is a clever fellow – and, besides, you can talk the matter over again.'

'Hurrah!' cried Razoumikhin. 'Now stop a bit. There are, in this very house, some apartments quite separate and independent of the premises; the rent is not heavy, they are furnished, three small rooms. Hire them. You will be all right there, all the more so as you may all live together and have Rodia with you. But where are you off to, Rodia?'

'What, are you already going?' asked Pulcheria Alexandrovna anxiously.

'And at such a time as this!' exclaimed Razoumikhin. Dounia looked at her brother with surprise and distrust. He held his cap, making ready to go out.

'One would really say that this is a question of an eternal separation. Why, you are not going to bury me yet?' said he strangely. He smiled, but what a smile! 'After all, this is perhaps the last time we are in each other's company. Who knows?' added he all on a sudden. These words fell spontaneously from his lips.

'What on earth is the matter with you?' inquired his mother anxiously.

'Where are you off to, Rodia?' asked Dounia, emphasising her question.

'I must be off!' he replied. His voice hesitated, but this pale face showed a marked resolution. 'I was desirous to say, on coming here – I was desirous to tell you, mother, and you also, Dounia, that it would be better if we separated for some time – I do not feel well, I am in need of rest; I shall come later – I shall come when I can – I shall not forget you, and shall always love you. Leave me! Leave me alone! This has been my intention for some time. My resolution is an irrevocable one! Whatever may happen to me, lost or not, I must be alone – forget me, I beg. That is far better. Don't make inquiries about me – when necessary I shall come of my own accord, or – shall send for you! Perhaps everything may come right yet! But, in the meanwhile, if you really love me, give up the idea of seeing me. If not, I feel I shall hate you. Goodbye!'

'Good Lord!' groaned Pulcheria Alexandrovna. A terrible fright had seized upon both ladies as well as upon Razoumikhin. 'Rodia, Rodia! Be reconciled with us, let us be friends as in the past!' cried the poor mother.

Slowly did Raskolnikoff move towards the door, but before reaching it Dounia had joined him. 'Oh, brother! How can you behave like this to our mother?' cried the girl, with a look of passionate indignation.

He made an effort to face her. 'It is nothing. I shall come back!' he stammered in a low tone of voice, like a man not fully conscious of what he is saying. And he left the room.

'Selfish, hard, and pitiless fellow!' exclaimed Dounia.

'He is not selfish; he is mad! mad! I tell you! Can you not see that? It is you who are pitiless in this instance!' retorted Razoumikhin, whilst bending over the young lady whose hand he gripped roughly.

'I shall be back before long!' he yelled to Pulcheria Alexandrovna, now almost fainting. And he rushed out of the room.

Raskolnikoff was waiting for him at the end of the passage. 'I knew you would come after me,' he observed. 'Go back to them! Don't leave them! Stay with them tomorrow. Stay with them always! If – if I can, I will return. Farewell!'

He was moving away without holding out his hand to Razoumikhin.

'But, whither are you going?' stammered out the latter, aghast. 'What is wrong with you? How can you behave in this way?'

Raskolnikoff stopped again. 'Once for all, never question me about anything! I have nothing to say! Do not call. I may come again. Leave me; but, as for them, do not leave them! Do you understand?'

The passage was dark. They stood close to a lamp. For a moment they looked at each other in silence. At this moment Razoumikhin recalled the whole of his past life. Raskolnikoff's fixed and fiery look seemed as if anxious to probe his very soul. All at once he shivered and grew pale as a corpse; the dreadful truth had dawned upon him.

'Do you understand me, now?' suddenly asked Raskolnikoff, whose features were terribly distorted. 'Go back to them!' concluded he, and, with rapid footsteps, he left the house.

It would be needless to describe the scene which followed upon Razoumikhin's return to Pulcheria Alexandrovna. As may be guessed, the young man did his very best to pacify the two ladies. He assured them that Rodia, being ill, was in need of rest; he assured them that the latter would not fail to come again, that they would see him daily, that his temperament was more or less out of order, that he could not be disturbed, and promising to watch over his friend, whom he would entrust to the care of a competent doctor – yes, if necessary, to the care of the bigwigs of the healing art. And, from that night, Razoumikhin became to them a son and brother.

Chapter 4

RASKOLNIKOFF WENT STRAIGHT to the waterside where Sonia was living. The three-storied house was an old building painted green. The young man had some difficulty in finding the dvornik, and got from him vague information about the quarters of the tailor Kapernasumoff. After having discovered in a corner of the yard the foot of a steep and gloomy staircase, he ascended to the second floor, and followed the gallery facing the courtyard. Whilst groping in the dark, and asking himself how Kapernasumoff's lodgings could be reached, a door opened close to him; he seized it mechanically.

'Who is there?' asked a timid female voice.

'It is I. I am coming to see you,' replied Raskolnikoff entering a small anteroom. There, on a wretched table stood a candle fixed in a candlestick of twisted metal.

'Is that you? Good heavens!' feebly replied Sonia, who seemed not to have strength enough to move from the spot.

'Where do you live? Is it here?' And Raskolnikoff passed quickly into the room, trying not to look the girl in the face.

A moment afterwards, Sonia rejoined him with the candle and remained stock-still before him, a prey to an indescribable agitation. This unexpected visit had upset her – nay, even frightened her. All of a sudden, her pale face coloured up, and tears came into her eyes. She experienced extreme confusion, united with a certain gentle feeling. Raskolnikoff turned aside with a rapid movement and sat down on a chair, close to the table. In the twinkling of an eye, he took stock of everything in the room.

This room was large, with a very low ceiling, and was the only one let out by the Kapernasumoffs; in the wall, on the left-hand side, was a door giving access to theirs. On the opposite side, in the wall on the right, there was another door, which was always locked. That was another lodging, having another number. Sonia's room was more like an outhouse, of irregular rectangular shape, which gave it an uncommon character. The wall, with its three windows facing the canal, cut it obliquely, forming thus an extremely acute angle, in the back portion of which nothing could be seen, considering the feeble light of the candle. On the other hand, the other angle was an extremely obtuse one. This large room contained scarcely any furniture. In the right-hand corner was the bed; between the bed and the door, a chair; on the same side, facing the door of the next set, stood a deal table, covered with a blue cloth; close to the table were two rush-chairs. Against the opposite wall, near the acute angle, was placed a small chest of drawers, of unvarnished wood, which seemed out of place in this vacant spot. This was the whole of the furniture. The yellowish and worn paper had everywhere assumed a darkish colour, probably the effect of the damp and coal-smoke. Everything in the place denoted poverty. Even the bed had no curtains. Sonia silently considered the visitor, who examined her room so attentively and so unceremoniously. Finally, she began to tremble with fear, as if in presence of the arbitrator of her fate.

'I am here for the last time,' said Raskolnikoff, with an agitated look, seeming to forget that this was also his first visit, 'perhaps I shall never see you again.'

'What! – are you going away?'

'I don't know – tomorrow – everything.'

'You will not go then tomorrow to Catherine Ivanovna's?' asked Sonia in a trembling tone of voice.

'I don't know – tomorrow – everything. But after all that is not the present question. I am here to have a word with you.' He cast on her his dreamy look, observing that he was seated, while she was all the time standing before him. 'Why remain standing? Sit down,' said he in a tone of voice which had all of a sudden become gentle and caressing. She obeyed. For a minute he looked at her with a kindly, almost tender look. 'How thin you are! What hands! The light can almost be seen through them. Your fingers are more like those of a corpse.'

He took her hand. Sonia smiled feebly. 'I have always been like this,' she answered.

'Even whilst living with your parents?'

'Yes.'

'Of course!' cried he brusquely, a sudden change having taken place in the expression of his face, and in the sound of his voice. Once more he looked about him. 'You are lodging then with the Kapernasumoffs?'

'I am.'

'They live on the other side of this door?'

'Yes, their room is the fellow-one to this.'

'And have they but one room between them?'

'That is all.'

'If I lived in such a room as this, I should be afraid of the night,' he remarked gloomily.

'My lodgers are good kindly folk,' answered Sonia, who did not as yet seem to have recovered her presence of mind, 'and the furniture – everything is theirs. They are very kind, their children often come here.'

'They are stammerers, are they not?'

'Yes, the father stammers, and is lame. The mother also. Not that she stammers exactly, but she has an impediment in her speech. She is a very kind woman, I must say. Kapernasumoff is a former serf. They have seven children, of whom only the eldest stammers; the others are sickly, but do not stammer. But tell me, how do you know all this?' added she with some surprise.

'Your father once told me all this. He told me the whole of your story. He told me that you had gone out at six, that you had come back after eight, and that Catherine Ivanovna had knelt by your bedside.'

Sonia became agitated. 'I fancy I saw him today,' she remarked hesitatingly.

'Who?'

'My father. I was out in the street, close by here, between nine and ten; he seemed to be walking ahead of me. I could have sworn that it was he. I even wanted to mention the circumstance to Catherine Ivanovna.'

'Were you walking?'

'Yes,' muttered Sonia, lowering her eyes confusedly.

'Used Catherine Ivanovna to beat you when you were with your father?'

'Never. How can you say such a thing? No!' exclaimed the young woman, looking at Raskolnikoff half-frightened.

'So you like her?'

'Her? Of course!' replied Sonia slowly and plaintively, quickly joining her hands with an expression of pity. 'Do you? If you did but know her! I assure you she is quite child-like. Her mind is more or less deranged through misfortune! But as for her intelligence, goodness, and generosity, you know nothing – nothing. Ah!'

Sonia emphasised these words with an almost desperate emphasis. She was a prey to extreme agitation, grew sad whilst wringing her hands. Her pale cheeks had assumed a fresh colour, suffering was depicted in her eyes. A sensitive chord had been touched; she was longing to speak, to exculpate Catherine Ivanovna. Suddenly an insatiable compassion, if such an expression may be used, became visible in all her features.

'She beat me! What are you saying? Great heavens! She beat me! And even if she had? But you know nothing. She is so sad – oh, how sad! – and ill at the same time. She looks for justice. Being pure, she believes that justice reigns paramount, and she claims it as her own. Treat her badly if you will, she will not be unjust herself. She does not conceive that it is impossible for justice to exist in the world, and she becomes vexed like a child – like a little child. Yes, she is just!'

'And as for yourself – what is going to become of you?' Sonia questioned him, with a look. 'They are on your hands. I know that it always has been so. Did not the dead man worry you for money to squander on drink? And what is going to happen now?'

'I don't know,' was her sad reply.

'Will they remain?'

'I don't know. They are in debt to their landlady, and it appears that she has spoken this very day of her intention to eject them. As for Catherine Ivanovna, she maintains that she won't remain another moment.'

'Whence her confidence? She is depending on you, I suppose?'

'Don't say that! We share a common purse; our interests are identical,' answered Sonia, eagerly, whose irritation at this moment was more like the inoffensive anger of a little bird. 'Besides, what could she do?' she asked, getting more and more animated. 'And how the poor thing has wept – wept this very day! Her reason is unhinged, as you must have noticed. How she worries in a childish way, about what is to be done tomorrow, in order that everything may be decent, such as the dinner, and so on. Now, again, she wrings her hands, throws up blood, weeps, beats her head against the wall in despair, and then she grows consoled, speaks of her hope in you; says that you are going to be her mainstay; talks about borrowing money somewhere to go back with me to her native place. There, as she says, she will establish a boarding-school for young titled ladies, and will entrust to me the duties of matron to her establishment, and, hugging me, maintains "that a new life – a happy life – shall commence for us all." These thoughts console her; she has such profound faith in her vagaries! Is it, I ask, worth while to contradict her? This very day she has entirely spent in washing, in setting her place in order, and, feeble as she is, she was putting up a clothesline in her room when, unable to do more, she fainted by her bedside. This very morning we have been shopping together, anxious to buy boots and shoes for Poletchka and Lena, as theirs are worthless. Unfortunately, we were short of money; a good deal was wanted, for she had chosen such pretty little boots – she has taste, I assure you. In the shop, in presence of its owner, she burst into tears because she had not enough to complete her purchase. Oh! What a sad sight!'

'I can understand now,' retorted Raskolnikoff, with a bitter smile, 'why you live in this way.'

'And you, do you not pity her?' exclaimed Sonia. 'I know that you have deprived yourself of your last means for her sake, though you have as yet seen but little. Had you but seen all, good Heaven! And, alas! how many times have I been the cause of her tears! How many times! As late even as last week! A short week only before my father's death, I had acted with harshness. And how often has this not happened? Ah! what sorrow has the recollection of this caused me the whole of this livelong day!' Sonia wrung her hands, so sad was this reminiscence to her.

'Do you mean that you are harsh?'

'Yes, I – I. I had gone to see them,' she went on, weeping, 'when my father said to me: "Sonia, I have a headache, read me something. There is a book." It was a book belonging to Andreas Semenovitch Lebeziatnikoff, who always used to lend us very funny books. "I must really be off," I answered, as I had no desire to read, having only called on them, to show Catherine Ivanovna a purchase I had made. Elizabeth, the huckstress, had brought me cuffs and collars, pretty embroidered collars, almost new. I had them cheap. They pleased Catherine Ivanovna amazingly, and she tried them on whilst looking approvingly in the glass. "Give them me, Sonia, do," said she. Of course they were of no use to her, but she is like that. She always recalls her happy younger days! She looks at herself in the glass although for very many years she has had neither gowns nor anything else. Another thing, she never asks the least thing of anybody. So proud is she, that she would rather give away the little she has, and yet she asked me for those collars, being so pleased with them. To me it was a struggle to part with them. "What do you want with them, Catherine Ivanovna?" I asked. Yes, I did indeed. I ought not to have spoken to her like that. She looked at me so sadly in return that it was pitiful. Not that she regretted the collars – by no means; no, it was my refusal as I could clearly see. Ah, could I but recall all that now! Had those words but been left unpronounced! Yes, indeed! After all, what can all this be to you?'

'Used you to know that huckstress, this Elizabeth?'

'I did. And you, did you also know her?' asked Sonia, somewhat astonished.

'Catherine Ivanovna is in the last stage of consumption, she will die before long,' said Raskolnikoff, after a moment's silence, and without replying to her question.

'Oh no, no, no!' And Sonia, unconscious of what she was doing, seized both hands of her visitor, as if Catherine Ivanovna's fate had depended on him.

'But it would be all the better if she were to die.'

'Don't say that it would be all the better, by no means!' re-echoed the girl, frightened.

'And the children? What do you propose doing with them since you cannot have them near you?'

'I don't know!' cried she, with heart-broken accents, holding her head. It was evident that this thought must often have preoccupied her.

'Assuming Catherine Ivanovna to live somewhat longer, and that you yourself become ill, what will happen should you yourself be taken to the hospital?' continued Raskolnikoff ruthlessly.

'Don't say that! don't say that! The prospect is impossible!' Fear had distorted Sonia's face out of recognition.

'How impossible?' he answered, with a sarcastic smile. 'I suppose you are not safe from illness? What, under such circumstances, would become of the family? It would be in the street, the mother, with her cough, begging for alms, beating her head against the wall, as she did today. And the wailing children? Catherine might succumb under such circumstances, and in a dying state would be taken to the station or hospital; and, then, how about the children?'

'No, God will permit no such thing!' retorted Sonia, with choking voice. She had till now listened silently, looking fixedly at Raskolnikoff, her hands joined, as if in silent prayer, as if he called up before her the miseries he depicted. The young man rose, and commenced walking to and fro in the room. A moment passed. Sonia remained standing upright, with hanging arms and drooping head, a prey to acute anguish.

'To save! to put money by for a rainy day,' he asked, suddenly drawing up before her, 'is not possible, either?'

'No,' replied Sonia.

'Of course not! But have you ever tried?' added he somewhat ironically.

'I have tried!'

'And you have failed? So it appears! The question was needless!' And he continued his tramp about the room; then, after another moment's silence, he asked, 'You do not make money every day?'

At this question Sonia became more and more upset, her cheeks blushed crimson. 'No!' was the indistinct and sad reply.

'And as for Poletchka,' he replied, brusquely, 'I suppose it will be the same?'

'Impossible! No! Impossible!' exclaimed Sonia, cut to the quick as by a dagger. 'God will not permit such a thing!'

'But He permits much!'

'No, I tell you! No, God will protect her!' repeated Sonia beside herself.

'For all you know: besides there may be no God,' answered Raskolnikoff bitterly, and looking at the young woman with a smile.

A sudden change took place in the girl's countenance, the muscles of her face grew hard. She cast on her interlocutor a look of reproach, seemed anxious to speak, but not a word fell from her. Sobbing, she covered her face with her hands.

'You tell me that Catherine Ivanovna is troubled in her mind? So are you!' he remarked, after an interval. Several minutes went by whilst he continued his tramp, not noticing her. Suddenly he approached her. His eyes gleamed, his lips trembled, and, resting his two hands on her shoulders, he cast an angry look on this face bathed in tears. In a moment he bent downwards, kissing the girl's feet. She started back frightened, as she would have done from a madman. For Raskolnikoff's face at this moment was that of one.

'What are you doing? And to me?' stammered Sonia, growing pale with sorrow-smitten heart.

Upon this he rose. 'I did not bow down to you, personally, but to suffering humanity in your person,' said he somewhat strangely, going to lean against the window. 'Listen to me!' he pursued, on coming back to her a moment after. 'Just now, I have told some overbearing fellow that he was not a patch on you, and that this very day I have honoured my mother by inviting her to associate with you.'

'And how could you say such a thing? And that in her presence?' exclaimed Sonia, beside herself. 'An honour to associate with me? I, who am a fallen creature! How could you? How could you?'

'When I said what I did, I thought neither of your dishonour nor of your faults. I thought only of your great sufferings. Doubtless you have erred,' he continued with increasing emotion, 'but you have only done so because you have sacrificed yourself to no kind of purpose. I know you to be unhappy! To live in this mire which you detest, and to know at the same time (for you cannot delude yourself) that it is to no purpose, and that your sacrifice will avail no one! But tell me, pray,' he went on, getting more and more excited, 'how can you, with your refined soul, resign yourself to such shame? Better a thousand times be drowned, to end it in a moment!'

'And as for them, what will become of them?' asked Sonia feebly, looking at him with a martyr-like gaze; though she seemed in no wise astonished at his advice. Raskolnikoff examined her with singular curiosity.

Her look had told him all. She herself had had the same idea. Many a time and oft, in the height of despair, she had thought of the same thing, had thought of it so seriously that now she experienced no kind of surprise at this proposed solution. The cruelty of the words she had not noticed, and, as may be thought, the import of the young man's reproach had left no sting; Raskolnikoff observing at the same time that his way of looking at her sin had escaped her. He understood, however, perfectly well to what extent the thought of her wretched condition tortured her, and he asked himself more than once what it was that, up to the present, could have prevented her from committing suicide. His only answer to the question was the girl's devotion to those poor little children, and to Catherine Ivanovna, the consumptive and demented woman who beat her head against the wall. Nevertheless, it was clear to him that Sonia, with her temperament and education, could not go on indefinitely. He had already found it difficult to understand how, failing suicide, madness had not severed her from such a life. He saw, of course, that Sonia's position was an exceptional social phenomenon, but was not that all the more reason that shame had not killed her at the outset of such a life, a life against which her former state, as well as her relatively high mental culture, ought to have nauseated her? What was it then that did brace her up? Had she perhaps a taste for debauch? Surely not! – vice had not affected her character; her body alone was soiled. Raskolnikoff understood this, for he read the girl's heart like a book.

'Her lot is fixed,' thought he, 'a watery grave – the mad-house, or a brutish existence!' This latter contingency was especially repellent to him, but, sceptic as he was, he could not help believing it a possibility. 'Is it possible that such is really the case?' he asked himself. 'Is it possible that this creature, who still retains a pure mind, should end by becoming deliberately mire-like? Has she not already become familiar with it, and if up to the present she has been able to bear with such a life, has it not been so, because vice has already lost its hideousness in her eyes? Impossible again!' cried he, on his part, in the same way as Sonia had cried a moment ago. 'No, that which up to the present has prevented her from throwing herself into the canal has been the fear of sin and its punishment. May she not be mad after all? Who says she is not so? Is she in full possession of all her faculties? Is it possible to speak as she does? Do people of sound judgement reason as she reasons? Can people anticipate future destruction with such tranquillity, turning a deaf ear to warnings and forebodings? Does she expect a miracle? It must be so. And does not all this seem like signs of mental derangement?'

To this idea he clung obstinately. Sonia – mad! Such a prospect displeased him less than the other ones. Once more he examined the girl attentively. 'And you – you often pray to God, Sonia?' he asked her.

No answer. Standing by her side, he waited for a reply. 'What could I be, what should I be without God?' cried she in a low-toned but energetic voice, and, whilst casting on Raskolnikoff a rapid glance of her brilliant eyes, she gripped his hand.

'Come, I was not mistaken!' he muttered to himself. 'And what does God do for you!' asked he, anxious to clear his doubts yet more.

For a long time the girl remained silent, as if incapable of reply. Emotion made her bosom heave. 'Stay! Do not question me! You have no such right!' exclaimed she, all of a sudden, with looks of anger.

'I expected as much!' was the man's thought.

'God does everything for me!' murmured the girl rapidly, and her eyes sank.

'At last I have the explanation!' he finished, mentally, looking eagerly at her.

He experienced a new, strange, almost unhealthy feeling on watching this pale, thin, hard-featured face, these blue and soft eyes which could yet dart such lights and give utterance to such passion; in a word, this feeble frame, yet trembling with indignation and anger, struck him as weird, nay almost fantastic. 'Mad! She must be mad!' he muttered once more. A book was lying on the chest of drawers. Raskolnikoff had noticed it more than once whilst moving about the room. He took it and examined it. It was a Russian translation of the Gospels, a well-thumbed leather-bound book.

'Where does that come from?' asked he of Sonia, from the other end of the room.

The girl still held the same position, a pace or two from the table. 'It was lent me,' replied Sonia, somewhat loth, without looking at Raskolnikoff.

'Who lent it you?'

'Elizabeth – I asked her to!'

'Elizabeth. How strange!' he thought. Everything about Sonia assumed to his mind an increasingly extraordinary aspect. He took the book to the light, and turned it over. 'Where is mention made of Lazarus?' asked he, abruptly. Sonia, looking hard on the ground, preserved silence, whilst moving somewhat from the table. 'Where is mention made of the resurrection of Lazarus? Find me the passage, Sonia.'

The latter looked askance at her interlocutor. 'That is not the place – it is the fourth Gospel,' said she dryly, without moving from the spot.

'Find me the passage and read it out!' he repeated, and sitting down again, rested his elbow on the table, his head on his hand, and, looking sideways with gloomy look, prepared to listen.

Sonia at first hesitated to draw nearer to the table. The singular wish uttered by Raskolnikoff scarcely seemed sincere. Nevertheless she took the book. 'Have you ever read the passage?' she asked him, looking at him from out the corners of her eyes. Her voice was getting harder and harder.

'Once upon a time. In my childhood. Read!'

'"Have you never heard it in church?"'

'I – I never go there. Do you often go yourself?'

'No,' stammered Sonia.

Raskolnikoff smiled. 'I understand then, you won't go tomorrow to your father's funeral-service?'

'Oh, yes! I was at church last week. I was present at a requiem mass.'

'Whose was that?'

'Elizabeth's. She was assassinated by means of an axe.' Raskolnikoff's nervous system became more and more irritated. He was getting giddy. 'Were you friends with her?'

'Yes. She was straightforward. She used to come and see me – but not often. She was not able. We used to read and chat. She sees God.'

Raskolnikoff became thoughtful. 'What,' asked he himself, 'could be the meaning of the mysterious interviews of two such idiots as Sonia and Elizabeth? Why, I should go mad here myself!' thought he. 'Madness seems to be in the atmosphere of the place! Read!' he cried all of a sudden, irritably.

Sonia kept hesitating. Her heart beat loud. She seemed afraid to read. He considered 'this poor demented creature' with an almost sad expression. 'How can that interest you, since you do not believe?' she muttered in a choking voice.

'Read! I insist upon it! Used you not to read to Elizabeth?'

Sonia opened the book and looked for the passage. Her hands trembled. The words stuck in her throat. Twice did she try to read without being able to utter the first syllable.

'Now a certain man was sick, named Lazarus, of Bethany,' she read, at last, with an effort; but suddenly, at the third word, her voice grew wheezy, and gave way like an overstretched chord. Breath was deficient in her oppressed bosom. Raskolnikoff partly explained to himself Sonia's hesitation to obey him; and, in proportion as he understood her better, he insisted still more imperiously on her reading. He felt what it must cost the girl to lay bare to him, to some extent, her heart of hearts. She evidently could not, without difficulty, make up her mind to confide to a stranger the sentiments which, probably, since her teens had been her support, her *viaticum* – when, what with a sottish father and a stepmother demented by misfortune, to say nothing of starving children, she heard nothing but reproach and offensive clamour. He saw all this, but he likewise saw that, notwithstanding this repugnance, she was most anxious to read – to read to him, and that now – let the consequences be what they may! The girl's look, the agitation to which she was a prey, told him as much, and, by a violent effort over herself, Sonia conquered the spasm which parched her throat, and continued to read the eleventh chapter of the Gospel according to St John. She thus reached the nineteenth verse:

'And many of the Jews came to Martha and Mary, to comfort them concerning their brother. Then Martha, as soon as she heard that Jesus was coming, went and met him; but Mary sat still in the house. Then said Martha unto Jesus, Lord, if Thou hadst been here, my brother had not died. But I know, that even now, whatsoever Thou wilt ask of God, God will give it Thee.'

Here she paused, to overcome the emotion which once more caused her voice to tremble. 'Jesus saith unto her, Thy brother shall rise again. Martha saith unto Him, I know that he shall rise again in the resurrection at the last day. Jesus said unto her, I am the resurrection, and the life; he that believeth in Me, though he were dead, yet shall he live; and whosoever liveth and believeth in Me shall never die. Believest thou this? She saith unto Him, – ' And, although she had difficulty in breathing, Sonia raised her voice, as if in reading the words of Martha she was making her own confession of faith: 'Yea, Lord: I believe that Thou art the Christ, the Son of God, which should come into the world.'

She stopped, raised her eyes rapidly on him, but cast them down on her book, and continued to read. Raskolnikoff listened without stirring – without turning towards her – his elbows resting on the table, looking aside. Thus the reading continued till the thirty-second verse.

'Then when Mary was come where Jesus was, and saw him, she fell down at his feet, saying unto Him, Lord, if Thou hadst been here, my brother had not died. When Jesus, therefore, saw her weeping, and the Jews also weeping which came with her, he groaned in the spirit, and was troubled, and said, Where have ye laid him? They said unto Him, Lord, come and see. Jesus wept. Then said the Jews, Behold how He loved him. And some of them said, Could not this man, which opened the eyes of the blind, have caused that even this man should not have died?' Raskolnikoff turned towards her and looked at her with agitation. His suspicion was a correct one. She was trembling in all her limbs, a prey to fever. He had expected this. She was getting to the miraculous story, and a feeling of triumph was taking possession of her. Her voice, strengthened by joy, had a metallic ring. The lines became misty to her troubled eyes, but, fortunately, she knew the passage by heart. At the last line, 'Could not this man, which opened the eyes of the blind – ' she lowered her voice, emphasising passionately the doubt, the blame, the reproach of these unbelieving and blind Jews, who, a moment after, fell, as if struck by lightning, on their knees, to sob and to believe. 'Yes,' thought she, deeply affected by this joyful hope, 'yes, he – he who is blind, who dares not believe – he, also, will hear – will believe in an instant, immediately, now, this very moment!'

'Jesus therefore, again groaning in Himself, cometh to the grave. It was a cave, and a stone lay upon it. Jesus said, Take ye away the stone. Martha, the sister of him that was dead, saith unto Him, Lord, by this time he stinketh: for he hath been dead four days.' She strongly emphasised the word *four*.' Jesus saith unto her, Said I not unto thee, that, if thou wouldest believe, thou shouldest see the glory of God? Then they took away the stone from the place where the dead was laid. And Jesus lifted up his eyes, and said, Father, I thank Thee that Thou hast heard Me. And I knew that Thou hearest Me always; but, because of the people which stand by I said it, that they may believe that Thou hast sent Me. And when he thus had spoken, He cried with a loud voice, Lazarus, come forth. *And he that was dead came forth*,' – on reading these words, Sonia shuddered, as if she herself had been witness of the miracle – 'bound hand and foot with grave-clothes; and his face was bound about with a napkin. Jesus saith unto them, Loose him, and let him go. *Then many of the Jews which came to Mary, and had seen the things which Jesus did, believed on Him.*'

She read no more, – such a thing would have been impossible to her – closed the book, and, briskly rising, said, in a low-toned and choking voice, without turning towards the man she was talking to: 'So much for the resurrection of Lazarus.' She seemed afraid to raise her eyes on Raskolnikoff, whilst her feverish trembling continued. The dying piece of candle dimly lit up this low-ceilinged room, in which an assassin and a harlot had just read the Book of Books. At most, five minutes elapsed.

Suddenly Raskolnikoff rose, and, approaching Sonia, said, in a loud voice: 'I have called to speak to you about a matter.' Whilst speaking thus, he knit his brows. The young woman silently raised her eyes on him, and saw that his gaze, a peculiarly harsh one, expressed some stern resolve. 'This day,' pursued he, 'I have renounced future dealings with my mother and sister. Henceforth I shall not visit them again. The rupture between me and my family is complete.'

'And why?' asked Sonia with stupefaction. The late meeting with Pulcheria Alexandrovna and Dounia had left behind an extraordinary, although an obscure, impression. A species of terror had taken possession of her on hearing the news that the young man had broken with his family.

'At present you are all that is left me!' he said. 'Let us go together. I am here to make such a proposition. As we are both of us accursed, let us go off together!'

His eyes sparkled. 'He talks as though he were mad!' thought Sonia in her turn. 'And to go whither?' asked she, frightened, recoiling involuntarily.

'How can I tell? I only know that the way and the goal are the same for you as for me. Of that I am sure!' She looked at him without comprehending. One sole idea was clear to her from amongst

Raskolnikoff's remarks – it was that of his extreme unhappiness. 'Not one of them will understand you, should you speak to them,' he continued, 'but I – I have understood you. You are necessary to me – hence my visit.'

'I do not understand,' stammered Sonia.

'You will do so later on. Have you, also not acted – as I have done? You, also, have exceeded – You have had pluck for that – You have laid hands on yourself – have destroyed a life – your very own. (That is the same thing.) You might have lived by your talents – your understanding, and – you will die in some public place! But this you cannot bear the thought of, and, if you remain *alone*, you will reason as I do. Even now, you are more or less crazed. Therefore, we must be off together; we must follow the same road! Let us go!'

'Why? Why talk in that way?' replied Sonia, strangely troubled by this language.

'Why? you ask. Because you cannot remain here, that is why! It is necessary to reason seriously, and to see things in their true light, instead of weeping like a child, and relying on God! What will happen, I ask you, if tomorrow you be taken to the hospital? Catherine Ivanovna, consumptive and almost crazed, must shortly die; and what then will become of her children? And is not Poletchka's ruin certain?'

'What must be done – oh! what must be done?' repeated Sonia, weepingly, wringing her hands.

'You say, what must be done? The cable must be cut once for all – a forward movement must be made, happen what may. Do you understand? Well, you will later on. Liberty and power! But above all – power! To rule over all trembling creatures, over the whole ant-hill. That is the goal! Remember! – that is the heirloom I leave you. I am speaking to you perhaps for the last time. Should I not come tomorrow, you will discover all, and then remember what I have been saying. Later on, a few years hence, with life and experience, you will perhaps understand their meaning. If I come tomorrow, you will know who it was that killed Elizabeth! Farewell!'

Sonia shivered and looked at him with bewilderment. 'But do you really know who has killed her?' she asked, cold with terror.

'I know it, and I shall reveal it – but to you – to you alone! I have selected you. I shall not come to ask for forgiveness, but simply to make the revelation. It is some time since I have selected you. From the first moment your father spoke to me of you, even during Elizabeth's lifetime, the idea was upon me. Farewell! Don't shake hands. Till tomorrow!'

He went out, leaving with Sonia the impression that he was a madman; whilst she herself was like a madwoman, and felt herself to be so. Her head was giddy. 'Great heavens! How can he know who it was that killed Elizabeth? What was the meaning of his words? How strange!' And yet she had no kind of suspicion as to the truth. 'He must be sad, indeed – has left mother and sister, and why? What can have happened? And what may be his purpose? What was it all he talked about? He kissed my feet, and he said – yes, he said – that he could not live without me! Oh, heavens!'

Behind the locked door, there was a room which had long been standing empty, and which formed part of Gertrude Karlovna Resslich's set. This room was to let, judging from a board placed outside the principal entrance, and from the bills pasted against the windows overlooking the canal. Sonia knew that no one lived there. But during all the preceding scene Mr Svidrigaïloff, hidden behind the door, had not ceased to listen attentively to the conversation. When Raskolnikoff went out, Mrs Resslich's tenant reflected for one moment, returned noiselessly to the room contiguous to the empty one, took a chair out of it, and placed it against the door. What he had just heard had interested him to such an extent that he brought this chair in order that he might be able to listen more comfortably, on the next opportunity, without being obliged to stand a whole hour.

Chapter 5

WHEN, ON THE following day, precisely at eleven o'clock, Raskolnikoff called on the examining magistrate, he was astonished to have to dance attendance for a considerable time. According to his idea, he ought to have been admitted immediately; ten minutes, however, elapsed before he could see Porphyrius Petrovitch. In the outer room where he had been waiting, people came and went without heeding him in the least. In the next room, which was a kind of office, a few clerks were at work, and it was evident that not one of them had even an idea who Raskolnikoff might be. The young man cast a mistrustful look about him. Was there not, thought he, some spy, some mysterious myrmidon of the law, ordered to watch him, and, if necessary, to prevent his escape? But he noticed nothing of the kind; the clerks were all hard at work, and the other people paid him no kind of attention. The visitor began to become reassured. 'If,' thought he, 'this mysterious personage of yesterday, this spectre which had risen from the bowels of the earth, knew all, and had seen all, would they, I should like to know, let me stand about like this? Would they not rather have arrested me, instead of waiting till I should come of my own accord? Hence this man has either made no kind of revelation as yet about me, or, more probably, he knows nothing, and has seen nothing (besides, how could he have seen anything?): consequently I have misjudged, and all that happened yesterday was nothing but an illusion of my diseased imagination.' This explanation, which had offered itself the day before to his mind, at the time he felt most fearful, he considered a more likely one.

Whilst thinking about all this and getting ready for a new struggle, Raskolnikoff suddenly perceived that he was trembling; he became indignant at the very thought that it was fear of an interview with the hateful Porphyrius Petrovitch which led him to do so. The most terrible thing to him was to find himself once again in presence of this man. He hated him beyond all expression, and what he dreaded was lest he might show his hatred. His indignation was so great that it suddenly stopped this trembling; he therefore prepared himself to enter with a calm and self-possessed air, promised himself to speak as little as possible, to be very carefully on the watch in order to check, above all things, his irascible disposition. In the midst of these reflections, he was introduced to Porphyrius Petrovitch. The latter was alone in his office, a room of medium dimensions, containing a large table, facing a sofa covered with shiny leather, a bureau, a cupboard standing in a corner, and a few chairs: all this furniture, provided by the State, was of yellow wood. In the wall, or rather in the wainscoting of the other end, there was a closed door, which led one to think that there were other rooms beyond it. As soon as Porphyrius Petrovitch had seen Raskolnikoff enter his office, he went to close the door which had given him admission, and both stood facing one another. The magistrate received his visitor to all appearances in a pleasant and affable manner, and it was only at the expiration of a few moments that the latter observed the magistrate's somewhat embarrassed manner he seemed to have been disturbed in a more or less clandestine occupation.

'Good! My respectable friend! Here you are then – in our latitude!' commenced Porphyrius, holding out both hands. 'Pray, be seated, *batuchka*. But, perhaps, you don't like being called respectable? Therefore *batuchka*, for short! Pray, don't think me familiar. Sit down here on the sofa.'

Raskolnikoff did so without taking his eyes off the judge. 'These words, "in our latitude," these excuses for his familiarity, this expression, "for short," what could be the meaning of all this? He held out his hands to me without shaking mine, withdrawing them before I could do so,' thought Raskolnikoff mistrustfully. Both watched each other, but no sooner did their eyes meet than they both turned them aside with the rapidity of a flash of lightning.

'I have called with this paper – about the – If you please, is it correct, or must another form be drawn up?'

'What, what paper? Oh, yes! Do not put yourself out. It is perfectly correct,' answered Porphyrius somewhat hurriedly before he had even examined it; then, after having cast a glance on it, he said, speaking very rapidly: 'Quite right, that is all that is required,' and placed the sheet on the table. A moment later he locked it up in his bureau, chattering about other things.

'Yesterday,' observed Raskolnikoff, 'you had, I fancy, a wish to examine me formally – with reference to my dealings with the victim. At least so it seemed to me!'

'Why did I say, "So it seemed"?' reflected the young man all of a sudden. 'After all, what can be the harm of it? Why should I distress myself about that?' he added, mentally, a moment afterwards. The very fact of his proximity to Porphyrius, with whom he had scarcely as yet interchanged a word, had immeasurably increased his mistrust; he marked this in a moment, and concluded that such a mood was an exceedingly dangerous one, inasmuch as his agitation, his nervous irritation, would only increase. 'That is bad! Very bad! I shall be saying something thoughtless!'

'Quite right. But do not put yourself out of the way, there is time, plenty of time,' murmured Petrovitch, who, without apparent design, kept going to and fro, now approaching the window, now his bureau, to return a moment afterwards to the table. At times he would avoid Raskolnikoff's suspicious look, at times again he drew up sharp whilst looking his visitor straight in the face. The sight of this short chubby man, whose movements recalled those of a ball rebounding from wall to wall, was an extremely odd one. 'No hurry, no hurry, I assure you! But you smoke, do you not? Have you any tobacco? Here is a cigarette!' he went on, offering his visitor a paquitos. 'You notice that I am receiving you here, but my quarters are there behind the wainscoting. The State provides me with that. I am here as it were on the wing, because certain alterations are being made in my rooms. Everything is almost straight now. Do you know that quarters provided by the State are by no means to be despised?'

'I believe you,' answered Raskolnikoff, looking at him almost derisively.

'Not to be despised, by any means,' repeated Petrovitch, whose mind seemed to be preoccupied with something else – 'not to be despised!' he continued in a very loud tone of voice, and drawing himself up close to Raskolnikoff, whom he stared out of countenance. The incessant repetition of the statement that quarters provided by the State were by no means to be despised, contrasted singularly, by its platitude, with the serious, profound, enigmatical look he now cast on his visitor.

Raskolnikoff's anger grew in consequence; he could hardly help returning the magistrate's look with an imprudently scornful glance. 'Is it true?' the latter commenced, with a complacently insolent air, 'is it true that it is a judicial maxim, a maxim resorted to by all magistrates, to begin an interview about trifling things, or even, occasionally, about more serious matter, foreign to the main question however, with a view to embolden, to distract, or even to lull the suspicion of a person under examination, and then all of a sudden to crush him with the main question, just as you strike a man a blow straight between the eyes?'

'Such a custom, I believe, is religiously observed in your profession, is it not?'

'Then you are of opinion that when I spoke to you about quarters provided by the State, I did so – ' Saying which, Porphyrius Petrovitch blinked, his face assumed for a moment an expression of roguish gaiety, the wrinkles on his brow became smoothed, his small eyes grew smaller still, his features expanded, and, looking Raskolnikoff straight in the face, he burst out into a prolonged fit of nervous laughter, which shook him from head to foot. The young man, on his part, laughed likewise, with more or less of an effort, however, at sight of which Porphyrius's hilarity increased to such an extent that his face grew nearly crimson. At this Raskolnikoff experienced more or less aversion, which led him to forget all caution; he ceased laughing, knitted his brows, and, whilst Porphyrius gave way to his hilarity, which seemed somewhat feigned, he fixed on him a look of hatred. In truth, they were both off their guard. Porphyrius had, in fact, laughed at his visitor, who had taken this in bad part: whereas the former seemed to care but little about Raskolnikoff's displeasure. This circumstance gave the young man much matter for thought. He fancied that his visit had in no kind of way discomposed the magistrate; on the contrary, it was Raskolnikoff who had been caught in a trap, a snare, an ambush of some kind or other. The mine was, perhaps, already charged, and might burst at any moment.

Anxious to get straight to the point, he rose and took up his cap. 'Porphyrius Petrovitch,' he cried, in a resolute tone of voice, betraying more or less irritation, 'yesterday you expressed the desire to subject me to a judicial examination.' (He laid special stress on this last word.) 'I have called at your bidding: if you have questions to put, do so; if not, allow me to withdraw. I can't afford to waste my time here, as I have other things to attend to. In a word, I must go to the funeral of the official who has been run over, and of whom you have heard speak,' he added, regretting, however, the last part of his sentence. Then, with increasing anger, he went on: 'Let me tell you that all this worries me! The thing is hanging over much too long. It is that mainly that has made me ill. In one word,' he continued, his voice seeming more and more irritable, for he felt that the remark about his illness was yet more out of place than the previous one – 'in one word, either be good enough to cross-examine me, or let me go this very moment. If you do question me, do so in the usual formal way; otherwise, I shall object. In the meanwhile, adieu, since we have nothing more to do with one another.'

'Good gracious? What can you be talking about? Question you about what?' replied the magistrate, immediately ceasing to laugh. 'Don't, I beg, disturb yourself.' He requested Raskolnikoff to sit down once more, continuing, nevertheless, his tramp about the room. 'There is time, plenty of time. The matter is not of such importance after all. On the contrary, I am delighted at your visit – for as such do I take your call. As for my horrid way of laughing, *batuchka*, Rodion Romanovitch, I must apologise. I am a nervous man, and the shrewdness of your observations has tickled me. There are times when I go up and down like an elastic ball, and that for half an hour at a time. I am fond of laughter. My temperament leads me to dread apoplexy. But, pray, do sit down – why remain standing? Do, I must request you, *batuchka*, otherwise I shall fancy that you are cross.'

His brows still knit, Raskolnikoff held his tongue, listened, and watched. In the meanwhile he sat down.

'As far as I am concerned, *batuchka*, Rodion Romanovitch, I will tell you something which shall reveal to you my disposition,' answered Porphyrius Petrovitch, continuing to fidget about the room, and, as before, avoiding his visitor's gaze. 'I live alone, you must know, never go into society, and am, therefore, unknown; add to which, that I am a man on the shady side of forty, somewhat played out. You may have noticed, Rodion Romanovitch, that here – I mean in Russia, of course, and especially in St Petersburg circles – that when two intelligent men happen to meet who, as yet, are not familiar, but who, however, have mutual esteem – as, for instance, you and I have at this moment – they don't know what to talk about for half an hour at a time. They seem, both of them, as if petrified. Every one else has a subject for conversation – ladies, for instance, people in society, the upper ten – all these sets have some topic or other. It is the thing, but somehow people of the middle-class, like you and me, seem constrained and taciturn. How does that come about, *batuchka*? Have we no social interests? Or is it, rather, owing to our being too straightforward to mislead one another? I don't know. What is your opinion, pray? But do, I beg, remove your cap, one would really fancy that you wanted to be off, and that pains me. I, you must know, am so contented.'

Raskolnikoff laid his cap down. He did not, however, become more loquacious; and, with knit brows, listened to Porphyrius's idle chatter. 'I suppose,' thought he, 'he only doles out his small-talk to distract my attention.'

'I don't offer you any coffee,' went on the inexhaustible Porphyrius, 'because this is not the place for it, but can you not spend a few minutes with a friend, by way of causing him some little distraction? You must know that all these professional obligations – Don't be vexed, *batuchka*, if you see me walking about like this; I am sure you will excuse me, if I tell you how anxious I am not to do so, but movement is so indispensable to me! I am always seated – and, to me, it is quite a luxury to be able to move about for a minute or two. I purpose, in fact, to go through a course of callisthenics. The trapeze is said to stand in high favour amongst State councillors – councillors in office, even amongst privy councillors. Nowadays, in fact, gymnastics have become a positive science. As for these duties of our office, these examinations, all this formality – you yourself, you will remember, touched upon the topic just now, *batuchka* – these examinations and so forth, sometimes perplex the magistrate much more than the man under suspicion. You said as much just now with as much sense as accuracy.' (Raskolnikoff had made no statement of the kind.) 'One gets confused, one loses the thread of the investigation. Yet as far as our judicial customs go, I agree with you fully. Where, for instance, is there a man under suspicion of some kind or other, were it even the most thickheaded moujik, who does not know that the magistrate will commence by putting all sorts of out-of-the-way questions to take him off the scent (if I may be allowed to use your happy simile), and that then he suddenly gives him one between the eyes? A blow of the axe on his sinciput? (if again I may be permitted to use your ingenious metaphor). Hah, hah! And do you mean to say that, when I spoke to you about quarters provided by the State, that that – hah, hah! You are very caustic. But I won't revert to that again. By the by! – one remark produces another, one thought attracts another – but you were talking just now of the practice or form in vogue with the examining magistrate. But what is this form? You know as I do that in many cases the form means nothing at all. Occasionally a simple conversation, a friendly interview, brings about a more certain result. The practice or form will never die out – I can vouch for that;

but what, after all, is the form, I ask once more? You can't compel an examining magistrate to be hampered or bound by it everlastingly. His duty or method is, in its way, one of the liberal professions or something very much like it.'

Porphyrius Petrovitch stopped a moment to take breath. He kept on talking, now uttering pure nonsense, now again introducing, in spite of this trash, an occasional enigmatical remark after which he went on with his stupidities. His tramp about the room was more like a race – he moved his stout legs more and more quickly, without looking up; his right hand was thrust deep in the pocket of his coat, whilst with the left he unceasingly gesticulated in a way unconnected with his observa-·tions. Raskolnikoff noticed, or fancied he noticed, that, whilst running round and round the room, he had twice stopped near the door, seeming to listen. 'Does he expect something?' he asked himself.

'You're perfectly right,' resumed Porphyrius cheerily, whilst looking at the young man with a kindliness which immediately awoke the latter's distrust. 'Our judicial customs deserve your clever satire. Our proceedings, which are supposed to be inspired by a profound knowledge of psychology, are very ridiculous ones, and very often useless. Now to return to our method or form: Suppose for a moment that I am deputed to investigate something or other, and that I know the guilty person to be a certain gentleman. Are you not yourself reading for the law, Rodion Romanovitch?'

'I was some time ago.'

'Well, here is a kind of example which may be of use to you later on. Don't run away with the idea that I am setting up as your instructor – God forbid that I should presume to teach anything to a man who treats criminal questions in the public Press! Oh no! – all I am doing is to quote to you, by way of example, a trifling fact. Suppose that I fancy I am convinced of the guilt of a certain man, why, I ask you, should I frighten him prematurely, assuming me to have every evidence against him? Of course, in the case of another man of a different disposition, him I would have arrested forthwith; but, as to the former, why should I not permit him to hang about a little longer? I see you do not quite take me. I will, therefore, endeavour to explain myself more clearly! If, for instance, I should be too quick in issuing a writ, I provide him in doing so with a species of moral support or mainstay – I see you are laughing?' (Raskolnikoff, on the contrary, had no such desire, his lips were set, and his glaring look was not removed from Porphyrius's eyes.) 'I assure you that in actual practice such is really the case; men vary much, although, unfortunately, our methods are the same for all. But you will ask me: Supposing you are certain of your proofs?

Goodness me. *batuchka*! you know, perhaps as well as I do, what proofs are – half one's time, proofs may be taken either way; and I, a magistrate, am, after all, only a man liable to error.

'Now, what I want is to give to my investigation the precision of a mathematical demonstration – I want my conclusions to be as plain, as indisputable, as that twice two are four. Now supposing I have this gentleman arrested prematurely, though I may be positively certain that he is *the man*, yet I deprive myself of all future means of proving his guilt. How is that? Because, so to say, I give him, to a certain extent, a definite status; for by putting him in prison, I pacify him. I give him the chance of investigating his actual state of mind – he will escape me, for he will reflect. In a word, he knows that he is a prisoner, and nothing more. If, on the contrary, I take no kind of notice of the man I fancy guilty, if I do not have him arrested, if I in no way set him on his guard – but if the unfortunate creature is hourly, momentarily, possessed by the suspicion that I know all, that I do not lose sight of him either by night or by day, that he is the object of my indefatigable vigilance – what do you ask will take place under these circumstances? He will lose his self-possession, he will come of his own accord to me, he will provide me with ample evidence against himself, and will enable me to give to the conclusion of my inquiry the accuracy of mathematical proofs, which is not without its charm.

'If such a course succeeds with an uncultured moujik, it is equally efficacious when it concerns an enlightened, intelligent, or even distinguished man. For the main thing, my dear friend, is to determine in what sense a man is developed. The man, I mean, is intelligent, but he has nerves which are *over*-strung. And as for bile – the bile you are forgetting, that plays no small part with similar folk! Believe me, here we have a very mine of information! And what is it to me whether such a man walk about the place in perfect liberty? Let him be at ease – I know him to be my prey, and that he won't escape me! Where, I ask you, could he go to? You may say abroad. A Pole may do so – but my man, never! especially as I watch him, and have taken steps in consequence. Is he likely to escape into the very heart of our country? Not he! For there dwell coarse moujiks, and primitive Russians, without any kind of civilisation. My educated friend would prefer going to prison, rather than be in the midst of such surroundings. Besides, what I have been saying up to the present is not the main point – it is the exterior and accessory aspect of the question. He won't escape – not only because he won't know where to go to, but especially, and above all, because he is mine from the *psychological* point of view. What do you think of this explanation? In virtue of a natural law, he will not escape, even if he could do so! Have you ever seen a butterfly close to the candle? My man will hover incessantly round me in the same way as the butterfly gyrates round the candle-light. Liberty will no longer have charms for him; he will grow more and more restless, more and more amazed – let me but give him plenty of time, and he will demean himself in a way to prove his guilt as plainly as that twice two are four! Yes, he will keep hovering about me describing circles, smaller and smaller till at last – bang! He has flown into my clutches, and I have got him. That is very nice. You don't think so, perhaps?'

Raskolnikoff kept silent. Pale and immovable, he continued to watch Porphyrius's face with a laboured effort of attention. 'The lesson is a good one! ' he reflected. 'But it is not, as yesterday, a case of the cat playing with the mouse. Of course, he does not talk to me in this way for the mere pleasure of showing me his hand; he is much too intelligent for that. He must have something else in view – what can it be? Come friend, what you do say is only to frighten me. You have no kind of evidence, and the man of yesterday does not exist! All you wish is to perplex me – to enrage me, so as to enable you to make your last move, should you catch me in such a mood, but you will not; all your pains will be in vain! But why should he speak in such covert terms? I presume he must be speculating on the excitability of my nervous system. But, dear friend, that won't go down, in spite of your machinations. We will try and find out what you really have been driving at.'

And he prepared to brave boldly the terrible catastrophe he antici-pated. Occasionally the desire came upon him to rush on Porphyrius, and to strangle him there and then. From the first moment of having entered the magistrate's office, what he had dreaded most was, lest he might lose his temper. He felt his heart beating violently, his lips become parched, his spittle becoming congealed. He resolved, how-ever, to hold his tongue, knowing that, under the circumstances, such would be the best tactics. By similar means, he felt sure that he would not only not become compromised, but that he might succeed in exasperating his enemy, in order to let him drop some imprudent observation. This, at all events, was Raskolnikoff's hope.

'I see you don't believe, you think I am jesting,' continued Porphyrius, more and more at his ease, without ceasing to indulge in his little laugh, whilst continuing his perambulation about the room. 'You may be right. God has given me a face which only arouses comical thoughts in others. I'm a buffoon. But excuse an old man's cackle. You, Rodion Romanovitch, you are in your prime, and, like all young people, you appreciate, above all things, human intelligence. Intellectual smartness md abstract rational deductions entice you. But, to return to the *special case* we were talking about just now. I must tell you that we have to deal with reality, with nature. This is a very important thing, and how admirably does it often foil the highest skill! Listen to an old man! I am speaking quite seriously, Rodion' – (on saying which Porphyrius Petrovitch, who was hardly thirty-five years of age, seemed all of a sudden to have aged, a sudden metamorphosis had taken place in the whole of his person, nay, in his very voice) – 'to an old man who, however, is not wanting in candour. Am I or am I not candid? What do you think? It seems to me that a man could hardly be more so – for do I not reveal confidence, and that without the prospect of reward? But, to continue, acuteness of mind is, in my opinion, a very fine thing; it is to all intents and purposes an ornament of nature, one of the consolations of life by means of which it would appear a poor magistrate can be easily gulled, who, after all, is often misled by his own imagination, for he is only human. But nature comes to the aid of this human magistrate! There's the rub! And youth, so confident in its own intelligence, youth which tramples under foot every obstacle, forgets this!

'Now, in the *special case* under consideration, the guilty man, I will assume, lies hard and fast, but, when he fancies that all that is left him will be to reap the reward of his mendacity, behold, he will succumb in the very place where such an accident is likely to be most closely analysed. Assuming even that he may be in a position to account for his syncope by illness or the stifling atmosphere of the locality, he has none the less given rise to suspicion! He has lied incomparably, but he has counted without nature. Here is the pitfall! Again, a man off his guard, from an unwary disposition, may delight in mystifying another who suspects him, and may wantonly pretend to be the very criminal wanted by the authorities; in such a case, he will represent the person in question a little too closely, he will place his foot a little too naturally. Here we have another token. For the nonce his interlocutor may be duped; but, being no fool, he will on the morrow have seen through the subterfuge. Then will our friend become compromised more and more! He will come of his own accord when he is not even called, he will use all kinds of impudent words, remarks, allegories, the meaning of which will be clear to everybody; he will even go so far as to come and ask why he has not been arrested as yet – hah! hah! And such a line of conduct may occur to a person of keen intellect, yes, even to a man of psychologic mind! Nature, my friend, is the most transparent of mirrors. To contemplate her is sufficient. But why do you grow pale,

Rodion Romanovitch? Perhaps you are too hot; shall I open the window?'

'By no means, I beg!' cried Raskolnikoff bursting out laughing. 'Don't heed me, pray!' Porphyrius stopped short, waited a moment, and burst out laughing himself. Raskolnikoff, whose hilarity had suddenly died out, rose. 'Porphyrius Petrovitch,' he shouted in clear and loud voice, although he could scarcely stand on his trembling legs, 'I can no longer doubt that you suspect me of having assassinated this old woman as well as her sister Elizabeth. Let me tell you that for some time I have had enough of this. If you think you have the right to hunt me down, to have me arrested, hunt me down, have me arrested. But you shall not trifle with me, you shall not torture me.' Suddenly his lips quivered, his eyes gleamed, and his voice, which up to that moment had been self-possessed, reached its highest diapason. 'I will not permit it,' he yelled hoarsely, whilst striking a violent blow on the table. 'Do you hear me, Porphyrius Petrovitch, I shall not permit this!'

'But, goodness gracious! what on earth is wrong with you?' asked the magistrate, disturbed to all appearances. '*Batuchka*! Rodion Romanovitch! My good friend! What on earth is the matter with you?'

'I will not permit it!' repeated Raskolnikoff once again.

'*Batuchka*! Not so loud, I must request! Someone will hear you, someone may come; and then, what shall we say? Just reflect one moment!' murmured Porphyrius Petrovitch, whose face had approached that of his visitor.

'I will not permit it, I will not permit it!' mechanically pursued Raskolnikoff, but in a minor key, so as to be heard by Porphyrius only.

The latter moved away to open the window. 'Let us air the room! Supposing you were to drink some water, dear friend? You have had a slight fit!' He was on the point of going to the door to give his orders to a servant, when he saw a water-bottle in a corner. 'Drink, *batuchka*,' he murmured, approaching the young man with the bottle, 'it may do you good.'

Porphyrius's fright seemed so natural that Raskolnikoff remained silent whilst examining him with curiosity. He refused, however, the proffered water.

'Rodion Romanovitch! My dear friend! If you go on in this way you will go mad, I am positive! Drink, pray, if only a few drops!' He almost forced the glass of water into his hand. Raskolnikoff raised it mechanically to his lips, when suddenly he thought better of it, and replaced it on the table with disgust. 'Yes, yes, you have had a slight fit. One or two more, my friend, and you will have another attack of your malady,' observed the magistrate in the kindest tone of voice, appearing greatly agitated. 'Is it possible that people can take so little care of themselves? It was the same with Dmitri Prokovitch, who called here yesterday. I admit mine to be a caustic temperament, that mine is a horrid disposition, but that such a meaning could possibly be attributed to harmless remarks! He called here yesterday, when you had gone, and in the course of dinner he talked, talked. You had sent him, had you not? But do sit down, *batuchka*, do sit down, for Heaven's sake!'

'I did not indeed! – although, I knew that he had called, and his object in doing so!' replied Raskolnikoff drily.

'Did you really know why?'

'I did. And what did you gather from it?'

'I gathered from it, *batuchka*, Rodion Romanovitch, the knowledge of a good many of your doings – in fact, I know all! I know that you went, towards nightfall, *to hire the lodging*. I know that you pulled the bell, and that a question of yours, in connection with bloodstains, as well as your manner, frightened both journeymen and dvorniks. I know what was your mood at the time. Excitement of such a kind will drive you out of your mind, be assured! A praiseworthy indignation is at work within you, complaining now as to destiny, now on the subject of police-agents. You keep going here and there to induce people as far as possible to formulate their accusations. This stupid kind of tittle-tattle is hateful to you, and you are anxious to put a stop to it as soon as possible. Am I right? Have I laid finger on the sentiments which actuate you? But you are not satisfied by turning your own brain, you want to do, or rather do the same thing to my good Razoumikhin. Really it is a pity to upset so good a fellow! His kindness exposes him more than anyone else to infection from your own malady. But you shall know all as soon as you are calmer. Pray, therefore, once again, do sit down, *batuchka*. Try and recover your spirits – you seem quite unhinged.'

Raskolnikoff sat down once again. A feverish tremor shook his whole frame. He listened with profound surprise to the demonstrations of interest Porphyrius Petrovitch lavished on him. But he attached no faith to the magistrate's statements, although he had a singular hankering to do so. Porphyrius's account of his visit to the lodgings had greatly impressed him. 'How on earth,' thought he, 'can he know anything about that, and why should he tell me of the circumstance himself?'

'In our judicial practice there has cropped up an almost analogous psychological case, a morbid case, if you will,' continued Porphyrius. 'A man accused himself of a murder he was innocent of; naturally, he declared himself guilty, told no end of a tale, a string of hallucinations of which he had been the plaything, and his account was so lifelike, seemed so much in harmony with the facts of the act, that it defied denial. How are we to explain this? Without any kind of fault of his own, this man had, in part, been the cause of an assassination. Hearing that he had unwittingly facilitated the assassin's work, he was, as a consequence, so grieved that his reason gave way, and he fancied himself the murderer! To cut matters short, a higher tribunal examined the affair, and it was discovered that the wretched man was innocent. But, had it not been, however, for this identical tribunal, it would have been all up with the man in question. That is what you may expect, *batuchka*. Men sometimes go wrong when wandering about of a night, asking all kinds of questions about blood and bloodstains! I assure you that, in my profession, I have had great opportunities for studying psychology! It is a tendency of the same kind which sometimes induces a man to throw himself out of a window or from the top of a steeple. But you are ill, Rodion Romanovitch, you were wrong to neglect your illness at the outset. You should have consulted a medical man of experience, instead of allowing yourself to be treated by that vulgar Zosimoff! What has happened is with you the effect of delirium!'

For a moment Raskolnikoff fancied he saw everything turning about him. 'Can the fellow be lying at this very moment?' he asked himself. And he strove to dispel such a suspicion, dreading the outburst of mad passion it might cause. 'I was not delirous, I was perfectly rational!' he exclaimed, racking his mind in order to see Porphyrius's hand. 'Do you hear?'

'I do, and understand. Even yesterday you told me as much, laying particular stress on this point! I perfectly understand all you may say! Ha! Ha! But permit me, my dear Rodion Romanovitch, to submit an observation. Suppose you are really guilty or that you have had some kind of share in this cursed business – I ask you, would you insist this to have been the case whilst delirious or whilst fully conscious? In my opinion, it would be quite the contrary. If you think your case to be a doubtful one, you should doggedly maintain that you acted under the influence of delirium. Am I right?' The manner of the question permitted the suspicion of some kind of snare. Whilst putting it, Porphyrius had bent over Raskolnikoff, who sank down on the sofa silently – silently looking his interlocutor in the face. 'It's like Mr Razoumikhin's visit. If you were guilty, all you have to say is that he called here of his own accord, without admitting that he really did so at your instigation. Now, far from doing so, you admit, on the contrary, that it was you who sent him!'

Raskolnikoff had never admitted anything of the kind. Cold ran down his spinal cord. 'You persist in lying!' he said, in a slow and feeble voice, whilst attempting to smile. 'You persist in your attempts to prove to me that you can read my hand, that you know every answer of mine by way of anticipation.' He went on, feeling, however, that he no longer weighed his words as he ought to have done: 'Either you want to frighten me, or you are simply poking fun at me.' Saying this, Raskolnikoff continued looking hard at the magistrate. All of a sudden an outburst of rage once more caused his eyes to sparkle. 'You do nothing but lie!' he yelled. 'You know perfectly well that the best tactics for a guilty man are to reveal what he can no longer hide. I don't believe a word you say!'

'How you twist and turn about!' sneered Porphyrius. 'But in spite of that, you are very obstinate. That is the result of monomania. I see you don't believe me, but I am justified in saying that you do believe me to a certain extent, and I shall do my best to make you believe me fully, for I like you sincerely, and take real interest in you.' Raskolnikoff's lips began to move. 'Yes, I mean you well,' went on Porphyrius, taking the young man's arm in a friendly way, a little above the elbow, 'I tell you plainly, attend to your malady. Another thing, has not your family moved to St Petersburg? Think of it. You ought to be the cause of your relatives' happiness, and, on the contrary, cause them nothing but anxiety.'

'What does that matter to you? How do you know that? What are you prying into? You watch me, I suppose, and you mean to let me know it?'

'But it is from you, from your very self, *batuchka*, that I have heard all this! Perhaps you are not aware that, in your excitement, you speak, of your own freewill, both to me and to others, about your affairs. I admit that many interesting circumstances were communicated to me yesterday by Mr Razoumikhin. I was going to say that, in spite of your interruption and power, you had lost a healthy way of viewing things. So much for a suspicious temperament! Take, for example, the circumstance of ringing the bell: here we have an incident of the utmost value for an examining magistrate. I, as a legal functionary, tell you this plainly. Does this open your eyes? If I thought you ever so slightly guilty, do you think I should have acted as I did? Under such circumstances, my line of action would have been fully chalked out. I should, for instance, have commenced by lulling your distrust, I should have pretended to ignore this fact, I should have drawn your attention to something quite different, and then, all of a sudden – to use your expression – I should have dealt, on your sinciput, the following questions: "What, sir, were you doing at ten o'clock last night in your victim's house? Why, I beg, did you ring the bell? Why did you make inquiries about blood? Why did you astound the porters by asking them to take you to the police-office?" That was the way I should have commenced if I had had any suspicions with regard to yourself. I should have subjected you to a systematic cross-examination, I should have ordered an investigation, should have secured your person. And, if I acted quite differently, it was because I did not suspect you! But I tell you once again, you have lost the right bearing of things and understand nothing!'

Raskolnikoff trembled from head to foot, a fact Porphyrius could easily notice. 'You do nothing but lie!' the young man kept on vociferating. 'I do not know what you may be driving at, but you do nothing else. You did speak to me just now in the sense you are alluding to, and I cannot in any shape or form delude myself. I say again you are lying!'

'I am lying, say you?' replied Porphyrius, with an air of vivacity, preserving, however, a good-natured look, and seeming to attach no kind of importance to the opinion Raskolnikoff had of him. 'I am lying, you say? Now tell me how I behaved to you just now. Did I not, in my official capacity, suggest to you certain psychological arguments which you might turn to some account – such as your malady, your delirium, your offended vanity and hypochondria, lastly your affront at the police-office? Am I right? You know I am! It is true, by the way, that these means of defence do not hold good by themselves, for cutting as they may both ways, they might be turned against you. If you were to say, for instance, "I was ill and delirous, I did not know what I was doing, I can remember nothing!" – the answer might be, "Well and good, *batuchka*, but why is it that delirium always assumes the same character with you? Might it not take some other form?" Am I right?'

Raskolnikoff rose, whilst looking at him with an air full of contempt. 'Tell me once for all,' asked the latter, 'tell me one way or other, whether I am in your opinion an object for suspicion? Speak up, Porphyrius Petrovitch, and explain yourself without any more beating about the bush, and that forthwith!'

'Dear me! Why, you are just like a small child, crying for the moon!' retorted Porphyrius in his bantering way. 'But why wish to know so much, since you have up to the present been left in perfect peace? Why distress yourself then? Why come here of your own accord without being even asked to do so? Give your reasons, I beg.'

'I tell you again,' cried Raskolnikoff furiously, 'that I can no longer bear – '

'Uncertainty, I presume?' interrupted the magistrate.

'Don't drive me to extremes! I object! I tell you I object! I cannot and will not bear it! Do you hear?' replied Raskolnikoff in a voice of thunder, striking a fresh blow on the table.

'Not so loud! Not so loud! Someone will hear you! Let me give you a sound piece of advice. Take care of yourself,' murmured Porphyrius.

The magistrate had no longer the affected boobyish look which lent to his countenance its former good-natured aspect – he knitted his brows, spoke like one having authority, and seemed on the point of throwing off his mask. At first uneasy, Raskolnikoff burst all at once into a terrible passion; and yet, strange to say, although extremely exasperated, he obeyed the order to lower his voice. He felt, besides, that he could not do otherwise, and this thought contributed to additional irritation.

'I will not permit myself to be tortured!' he went on. 'Arrest me, search me, order your investigations, but act legally and don't trifle with me! Do not dare to have the audacity – !'

'Do not, I must request, disturb yourself on the subject of the law,' replied Porphyrius, in his cunning tone of voice, whilst considering Raskolnikoff with a show of exultation, 'it was only in a familiar friendly kind of way that I invited you to come and see me.'

'I don't want to have anything to do with your despicable friendship! Do you hear? But I am off. Have you any kind of intention to arrest me?'

As he neared the door, Porphyrius once more seized his arm a little above the elbow. 'Would you not like to see a little surprise?' chuckled the magistrate, who seemed more and more lively, more and more bantering, a mood which drove Raskolnikoff absolutely beside himself.

'What little surprise? What do you mean?' asked the young man, stopping suddenly, whilst watching Porphyrius with anxiety.

'A little surprise I have behind there! hah! hah!' – pointing to the closed door which gave admittance to his quarters on the other side of the wainscoting. 'I have even taken care to place it under lock and key so that it may not escape.'

'What is the nature of it? What?' Raskolnikoff went towards the door, wishing to open it, but he could not succeed in doing so.

'It is locked, here is the key.' Saying which, the magistrate drew the key from his pocket and showed it to his visitor.

'You keep on lying!' shouted the latter beside himself, 'you keep on lying, you miserable mountebank!' At the same time he wished to throw himself on Porphyrius, who, however, without testifying to any kind of fear, backed towards the door. 'I understand all, all!' vociferay Raskolnikoff. 'You keep on lying and putting me out so commit myself.'

'But there is nothing for you to commit yourself about, *batuchka*, Rodion Romanovitch. Look at the state you are in! Don't shout, or I shall call for help!'

'You liar! you will do nothing of the kind! You knew I was ill, and all you wanted was to exasperate me, to drive me to extremes so that you might get some kind of confession out of me! That was your object! Produce your proofs! I see through it now! You have no proofs, you have nothing but miserable suppositions, or perhaps only Zametoff's conjectures! You know my disposition, you wanted to do nothing but put me out, and then to send all at once for popes and deputies. You expect them, don't you? What is it you do expect? Where are they? Out with them!'

'What on earth do you mean by talking about deputies or delegates, *batuchka*? What ideas! Why, the law, to use your own word, does not permit anything of the kind! My dear friend, you are not very well acquainted with our means of procedure! But formalities shall be observed, as you shall see!' murmured Porphyrius, who had moved to listen at the door. A certain noise was, in fact heard in the next room.

'Are they coming?' cried Raskolnikoff. 'You have sent for them, have you? I see, you were waiting for them! You had reckoned, I presume – Well, introduce the lot of them, officials, witnesses, anybody you fancy! I am quite ready!'

And then occurred a singular incident out of the usual way of things, and one which neither Raskolnikoff nor Porphyrius Petrovitch could have anticipated.

Chapter 6

THIS IS THE RECOLLECTION this scene left on Raskolnikoff's mind. The noise which was being made in the next room increased all of a sudden and the door was opened. 'What is the matter?' cried Porphyrius Petrovitch, in a passion. 'I gave instructions – '

No reply, but the cause of the noise was easily to be guessed at. Someone wanted to enter the magistrate's study, and was being prevented from doing so.

'What on earth is the matter there?' once more cried Porphyrius anxiously.

'It is the prisoner Nikola who is being brought up,' was the reply.

'I do not want him! I have no wish to see him! Take him away! But, one moment! How has the man been brought here? How very irregular!' growled Porphyrius, darting towards the door.

'But it is he who – ' answered the same voice, suddenly stopping.

For a moment or two, there could be heard the noise of two men struggling; then one of them overpowered the other one, and rushed noisily into the study. This new-comer was a strange-looking person. He looked straight ahead, without seeming to see anyone. Resolution was visible in his glittering eye, whilst at the same time, his face was livid, like that of a condemned man who was being led to the scaffold. His blanched lips were slightly trembling. He was still a very young man; thin, of medium height, and dressed like a journeyman; his hair was cut all round, his features drawn and harsh. The man whom he had overpowered rushed after him into the room, and seized him by the shoulder. The latter was a police official, whose hold Nikola succeeded once more in shaking off. Many idlers collected in the doorway. Some of these even seemed anxious to come in. All this had occurred in very much less time than we have required in relating.

'Be off! You are before your time! Wait till you are called! Why has the man been brought here so soon?' growled Porphyrius Petrovitch, with as much irritation as surprise. But in a moment, Nikola fell on his knees.

'What are you doing, man?' cried the magistrate, with increasing astonishment.

'Pardon! I am guilty! I am the murderer!' said Nikola, abruptly, in a loud voice, in spite of the emotion which was suffocating him.

For a few moments there was a silence so profound that one would have imagined all the bystanders to have been struck by catalepsy; the police official did not even attempt to recapture his prisoner, and mechanically moved towards the door, where he remained immovable.

'What's that you say?' exclaimed Porphyrius Petrovitch, when his stupefaction permitted him to speak.

'I am the murderer!' repeated Nikola, after a moment's silence.

'What? You? What? Whom have you murdered?' The magistrate was visibly disconcerted. Nikola waited another moment before answering.

'I killed – Alena Ivanovna – with a hatchet – as well as her sister, Elizabeth Ivanovna! I was mad!' added he, all at once, and then he was silent, though still on his knees.

After hearing this reply, Porphyrius Petrovitch seemed to reflect profoundly; whereupon, with an imperious gesture, he requested the witnesses to withdraw. The latter immediately obeyed, and the door was closed. Raskolnikoff, standing in a corner, contemplated Nikola with a singular air. For some moments the magistrate's gaze wandered from the visitor to the prisoner, and vice versa. Finally, he addressed Nikola with more or less of passion.

'Wait till you are asked, before you tell me that you are mad!' he observed, in an irritable tone of voice. 'Up to the present, such a question has not been put to you! Now then, speak up! You say you are guilty of murder?'

'I confess I am the murderer!' replied Nikola.

'Very well! What did you commit the murder with?'

'With a hatchet I bought for that purpose.'

'Don't be in such a hurry! Did you do this alone?' Nikola did not understand the question.

'Had you any accomplices?'

'None. Dmitri is innocent; he had no kind of share in the crime.'

'Don't be in such a hurry, man, to whitewash Dmitri; I asked no such question! But how is it that the porters saw both of you bolt down the stairs?'

'I ran after Dmitri on purpose. It was only a feint to turn away suspicion,' answered Nikola.

'Good! That will do,' cried Porphyrius angrily. 'The man is not speaking the truth!' he growled to himself. All of a sudden his eyes met those of Raskolnikoff, whose presence he had evidently forgotten during his examination of Nikola. On perceiving his visitor, the magistrate seemed to get uneasy. He immediately went towards him. 'Rodion Romanovitch, *batuchka*! Excuse me, pray, for there is nothing more here for you to do. I myself – You see the surprise! Pray therefore –' He had taken the young man by the arm, and was showing him the door.

'You don't seem to have expected this!' remarked Raskolnikoff. Naturally, what had just taken place was an enigma for him as yet. He had, however, to a considerable extent, regained his self-possession.

'Neither did you, *batuchka*! But see how your hand is trembling!'

'You are trembling too, Porphyrius Petrovitch.'

'You are right; I certainly did not expect this.' They were already in the doorway. The magistrate was eager to get rid of his visitor.

'And won't you show me your little surprise?' asked the latter somewhat offendedly.

'Why, you have scarcely found your voice again, and you are already getting satirical! Hah! hah! you are a caustic fellow! Well, *au revoir*!'

'No, no, you should say adieu!'

'That shall be as God wills,' stammered Porphyrius, with a forced smile.

Whilst going through the outer office, Raskolnikoff noticed that several of the clerks looked hard at him. In the anteroom he observed, in the midst of the crowd, the two porters of *the house*, those whom he had requested the other day to take him to the police-superintendent. They seemed to be expecting something. But no sooner was he on the landing, when he once more heard Porphyrius's voice behind him. He turned round, and perceived the magistrate running after him, out of breath.

'Just one word, Rodion Romanovitch. This affair will end as God knows best; but still, by way of form, I may have to ask you a few more questions. Hence we are certain to meet again!' And with a smile Porphyrius stopped before the young man. 'Certain!' he repeated. One might have fancied that he wished to say something more. But he did not do so.

'Forgive my strange manner just now, Porphyrius Petrovitch, I was hasty,' began Raskolnikoff, who had regained all his self-possession, and who even experienced an irresistible wish to chaff the magistrate.

"Don't say any more, it was nothing,' replied Porphyrius in almost joyful tone. 'I myself am – my disposition, I must confess, is a very disagreeable one. But we shall meet again. Please God, we shall meet again often!'

'And we are likely to become intimate?' asked Raskolnikoff.

'We are likely to become intimate,' repeated Porphyrius Petrovitch like an echo, and, with a wink, he looked at his interlocutor very seriously. 'You are off to a dinner-party, are you not?'

'To a funeral, you mean!'

'Ah! yes. Well, look after your health – '

'As for me, I hardly know what good things to wish you!' answered Raskolnikoff. He had already commenced going downstairs when, turning suddenly towards Porphyrius, he added: 'I think I ought to wish you more success than you have had – today, that is. Your functions are certainly comical ones!'

At these words the magistrate, who was on the point of going back to his room, pricked up his ears. 'What is there comical about them?' he asked.

'Why, look at this poor Nikola: how you must have tormented and pestered him to get a confession out of him! No doubt you have been telling him night and day, in every key, "You are the murderer – you are the murderer!" According to your psychological method you must have persecuted him relentlessly. Now that he admits his guilt, you continue aggravating him by singing to him in another scale: "You lie, you are not the murderer – you can't be – you don't speak the truth!" Well, after all this, am I not entitled to consider your functions comical ones?'

'Hah! hah! then you noticed just now that I pointed out to Nikola that he was not speaking the truth?'

'How could I avoid doing so?'

'Yours is a subtle mind – nothing escapes you. Besides, you like a joke, and yours is a humorous vein! ha! ha! That, I am told, used to be the distinct attribute of our writer Gogol?'

'So it was.'

'So it was! Till we meet again!'

'Till we meet again!'

The young man forthwith went home. Having got there, he threw himself on his couch, and for a quarter of an hour he tried to arrange his ideas somewhat, inasmuch as they were very confused. He did not even try to account for Nikola's conduct, feeling that there was beneath it a mystery, the key to which he would seek in vain. Besides, he did not delude himself as to the probable consequences of the incident. The man's statements would not be long in being found false; and then, once more suspicion would again fall on him, Raskolnikoff. But in the meanwhile he was free, and had to take precautions in anticipation of the danger he considered imminent. How far, however, was he threatened? The situation commenced to clear up – the young man shuddered on recalling his late interview with the magistrate – doubtless it would be difficult for him to probe all Porphyrius's intentions, but what he guessed of them was more than enough to make him understand the terrible danger he had just escaped. A little more, and he would have been irretrievably done for. Knowing his visitor's nervous irritability, the magistrate had gone thoroughly into the subject, and had shown his hand a little too boldly, although his game was a certain one. Raskolnikoff, it is true, had nearly become too much compromised; however, the imprudence he reproached himself for was as yet no proof-positive against himself – it was only relative. Was he right in thinking so? What was the object Porphyrius had in view? The latter had undoubtedly planned something today, and if there were a got-up affair, what was the nature of it? Without the unexpected appearance of Nikola, how would this interview have ended?

Raskolnikoff was seated on his couch, his elbows resting on his knees, and his head on his hands. A nervous trembling continued to agitate the whole of his body. At last he rose took his cap, and, after having reflected for one moment, moved towards the door. For this day, thought he, there would at all events be nothing to fear. All at once, he experienced a kind of pleasure – the idea struck him to go as soon as possible to Catherine Ivanovna. Of course it was too late to go to the funeral, but he would at all events be in time for the dinner, and there he would see Sonia. He stopped, reflected, and a sickly smile appeared on his lips. 'Today – today!' he repeated. 'Yes, this very day. It must be so.' At the moment of opening the door, it did so of its own accord. He recoiled frightened, on seeing appear the enigmatical person of yesterday; the man, in short, who had risen from the bowels of the earth. The visitor stopped on the threshold, and, after having looked at Raskolnikoff in silence, advanced into the room. He was dressed as yesterday, but his face was no longer the same. He seemed afflicted, and sighed painfully.

'What do you want?' asked Raskolnikoff, pale as death. The man did not reply, and bowed suddenly, almost down to the ground. At least he touched the carpet with the ring he wore on his right hand. 'Who are you?' cried Raskolnikoff.

'I ask your pardon!' said the man in a low tone of voice.

'For what?'

'For my evil thought!' They looked at one another. 'I was angry when you came the other day, having perhaps your mind disturbed by drink. You put questions about bloodstains, and asked the porters to take you to the police-office. I was pained to see that your words were unheeded, and that you were taken to be a drunken man. That vexed me to such an extent that I was unable to sleep. But I remembered your address, and yesterday I called here.'

'It was you who called?' interrupted Raskolnikoff. Light was beginning to dawn in his mind.

'Yes, I insulted you!'

'You were in that house then?'

'Yes, I was standing under the principal entrance at the moment of your visit. Have you forgotten that? I have lived there for a long time. I am a furrier.'

Raskolnikoff hereupon suddenly remembered the whole of the scene in question: independently of the dvorniks, there were several persons, men as well as women, under the gateway. Someone proposed to take him there, and then to the superintendent of police. He could not remember the name of the man who had given this advice, and even now he did not recognise him, but he remembered having answered him something, and having turned towards him in order to do so. Thus was cleared up, in the simplest way in the world, the terrible mystery of yesterday. And, under the impression of the anxiety which so insignificant a circumstance caused him, he had nearly been done for! This man could have revealed nothing, unless it was that Raskolnikoff had called in order to see the old woman's room, and had put questions on the subject of bloodstains. Hence, save this proceeding of a *person suffering from delirium*, save this *double-edged psychology*, Porphyrius knew nothing, he was without data – had, in fact, nothing positive. 'Consequently,' thought the young man, 'if no new charges crop up (and none will crop up, I am certain), what harm can be done to me? Even assuming I were arrested, how bring my guilt definitely home to me?' Another conclusion resulted for Raskolnikoff from his visitor's words, for was it not quite lately, only just now in fact, that Porphyrius had got scent of his visit to the victim's home?

'You told Porphyrius today, did you not, that I had gone there?' he asked, struck with a sudden idea.

'What Porphyrius?'

'The examining magistrate.'

'I did tell him as much. As the porters would not go to him, I went myself.'

'Today?'

'I got there a moment before you did. In fact, I heard everything that passed between you and him; you must have spent an uncomfortable time there.'

'Where? How? What?'

'Why, I was in his house, in the very room next to his study. I was there all along.'

'What? Do you mean to say that you were the surprise? But how could this have come about? Speak, I beg!'

'When I saw,' began the man, 'that the porters objected to go to the police under pretext that it was too late and that they might find the office closed, I experienced great dissatisfaction, and determined to do so myself: the following day, that is, of course, yesterday, I made inquiries, and today I called upon the magistrate. The first time I called, he was absent. I called again an hour later without being admitted; the third time, I was introduced. I went through the whole story in detail, just as it had happened, and whilst listening to me he jumped about the room, and, beating his breast, kept on shouting: "That is the way you do your duty, you ruffians; if I had known anything about this sooner, I would have had him sent for by the police." Upon this, he rushed out of the room all in a hurry, called someone and talked with him for a moment aside, then came back to me, and began questioning me, swearing all the time. I didn't hide anything from him – told him that you had been afraid to answer me yesterday, and that you had not even recognised me. He went on beating his chest, vociferating, and dancing about his room. In the midst of all this you were announced. "Get behind that partition," he called out, bringing me a chair, "and don't budge whilst you are there, whatever you may hear. I may yet have to put a few more questions to you." Then he locked me in. As soon as Nikola was brought up, he dismissed you, and then let me out, saying once again: "I may have to examine you further." '

'And did he examine Nikola in your presence?'

'I went out immediately after you, and then only he began to examine the latter.' His story at an end, the man bowed again to the ground. 'Forgive me my denunciation, and the wrong I have done you!'

'May God forgive you!' was Raskolnikoff's reply. At these words the man bowed once again, but only half-way, then withdrew with slow step.

'No precise charges, only proofs that may be explained away!' thought Raskolnikoff, with renewed hope; and he left the room. 'Now we can continue the fight,' he said to himself with an angry smile on going down the stairs. He was disgusted with himself on thinking of his faint-heartedness.

PART V

Chapter 1

ON THE MORROW OF the fatal day when Peter Petrovitch had had his explanation with the Raskolnikoff ladies, his ideas cleared; and, to his extreme regret, he was obliged to own that the rupture, in which even the day before he would not believe, was in good earnest an accomplished fact. The serpent of wounded vanity had gnawed his heart all night long. On rising, Peter Petrovitch's first thought was to go and look at himself in the glass – fearful, lest in the course of the night an overflow of bile might have occurred. This apprehension was, however, luckily, a groundless one. Whilst examining his pale and distinguished countenance, he was consoled for a moment by the thought that he would not find it so difficult to replace Dounia, and – who knows? – perhaps advantageously! Soon, however, he banished such a chimercial hope, and, vigorously clearing his throat, he provoked a sneering smile on the part of his young friend and bedroom-companion, Andreas Semenovitch Lebeziatnikoff. Peter Petrovitch, noticed the silent sneer, and entered it to the account of his young friend – an account which had already been considerably overdrawn for some time past. His anger increased on reflecting that he ought not to speak of this mischance with Andreas Semenovitch. This was the second folly which anger had led him to commit last night, he had succumbed to a need of extravasating his excessive irritability.

During the whole of the morning, bad luck contrived to persecute Looshin. In the very courthouse, the case in which he was engaged reserved for him another disappointment. What vexed him more than all, however, was that he could not bring to reason the owner of the lodging he had secured with a view to his pending marriage. This individual, a German by birth, was a quondam working-man on whom fortune had smiled. He would hear of no kind of compromise, and insisted on the uttermost farthing of the forfeit stipulated in the contract, although Peter Petrovitch gave up his apartments almost entirely renovated. Neither did the upholsterer show himself less harsh. He insisted on retaining the very last rouble of the deposit he had received for the sale of the movables, of which Peter Petrovitch had not as yet taken possession. 'Am I absolutely to marry for the sake of so much furniture?' asked himself the unfortunate man of business, grinding his teeth. At thought of this, a last ray of hope flashed through his mind: 'Is it possible that things are so desperate? Can nothing more be tried?' The thought of Dounetchka's charms had pierced his heart like a thorn. This was a trying ordeal for him to pass through and, if desire alone could have done it, Peter Petrovitch would have killed Raskolnikoff there and then.

'Another folly of mine was not to have given them any money,' thought he, on going slowly and sadly to Lebeziatnikoff's room. 'Why the deuce was I so Jew-like? That was a foolish calculation! By leaving them temporarily in difficulties, I fancied I should prepare them later on to look upon me as a kind of Providence. Whereas now they have entirely slipped through my fingers! If, for instance, I had given them fifteen hundred roubles, say just enough to get an outfit with – if, perhaps, I had bought them a few presents at the English stores, such an act would have been at one and the same time generous and – clever! They would not have dropped me as easily as they have! With their notions, they would certainly have believed themselves obliged, in case of rupture, to return me both presents and money, a restitution they would have found unpleasant and difficult! Besides, the thing would have been with them a matter of conscience: "How," they would have asked, "turn a man out who has proved himself so generous and so sensitive?" Hem! I have made a mistake!'

Once more Peter Petrovitch ground his teeth and considered himself in the light of a fool – in his heart of hearts only, be it understood. Having come to this conclusion about himself, he went to the lodging-house in a much more ill-humoured and discontented mood than ever previously. His curiosity, however, was excited to a certain point by the confusion to which the preparations for Catherine Ivanovna's dinner had given rise. The day before even he had heard talk of this repast; he remembered even that he had been invited to it, but his personal preoccupations had prevented his paying any attention to that. In the absence of Catherine Ivanovna (who was then at the cemetery), Madame Lippevechzel bustled about the table on which the things were laid. Whilst talking with the landlady, Peter Petrovitch learned that it was a regular dinner-party, that almost all the lodgers of the house had been invited, amongst them several who had not even known the defunct. Andreas Semenovitch Lebeziatnikoff himself had received an invitation, notwithstanding his rupture with Catherine Ivanovna. Indeed, they would think themselves highly favoured if Peter

Petrovitch were to consent to honour the repast with his presence, considering that he of all the tenants was the most noteworthy personage.

Catherine Ivanovna, forgetting all her grievances in connection with her landlady, thought it her duty to address to the latter a formal invitation; hence was it that at this moment Amalia Ivanovna occupied herself with a kind of joy about the dinner. Madame Lippevechzel was, besides, in full dress, and, although in mourning, she experienced extreme pleasure in showing off a beautiful new silk gown. Informed of all these details, Peter Petrovitch was struck with an idea, and returned pensively to his room, or rather to that of Andreas Semenovitch Lebeziatnikoff, for he had just heard that Raskolnikoff would be amongst the guests. That day, for some reason or other, Andreas Semenovitch spent the whole of the morning at home. Between this gentleman and Peter Petrovitch there existed a strange connection, which after all is easily explained: Peter Petrovitch hated and despised him beyond all measure, almost from the first day he had come to ask his hospitality; he seemed, at the same time, to be somewhat in fear of him.

On arriving at St Petersburg, Looshin had at first put up at Lebeziatnikoff's, not only for the sake of economy, but also for another reason. In his part of the country, he had heard speak of his former pupil, Andreas Semenovitch, as one of the most advanced young Liberals of the metropolis, and even as a man likely to hold an eventual position in certain circles which had passed into a legendary condition. This circumstance struck Peter Petrovitch. For a long time he had experienced a vague dread with regard to these powerful confraternities which knew all, respected no one, and waged war with everybody. It is needless to add that his absence from the capital did not give him the opportunity of having distinct notions on the subject. Like other people, he had heard that there existed in St Petersburg Liberals, Nihilists, restorers of wrong, and so forth – names which in his mind, as in the minds of the majority, had assumed a meaning of absurd exaggeration. What he particularly dreaded were the *inquiries* made concerning this or that individual by revolutionary parties. Certain reminiscences going back to the outset of his career contributed not a little to magnify within him this fear, which had greatly increased since the time he hugged the wish to settle in St Petersburg. Two persons, more or less of high rank, who had started him in life, had been exposed to the ill-will of the Radicals, and the result was for them an extremely nasty one. This was why, from the very first moment of his arrival in the metropolis, Peter Petrovitch had been so anxious to find out how the land lay, in order to gain, if possible, the good graces of 'our younger folk.' He reckoned on Andreas Semenovitch to assist him in the matter. Looshin's conversation on the occasion of his visit to Raskolnikoff has shown us that he had already succeeded in catching to a certain extent the language of the advanced party.

Andreas Semenovitch was a clerk in a Government office. He was short, puny, scrofulous, had almost white hair and mutton-chop whiskers, of which he was very proud. In addition, he was nearly always afflicted with sore eyes. Although a decent enough fellow at bottom, he showed in his language a presumption which frequently savoured of overwhelming conceit, which contrasted ridiculously with his insignificant exterior. He was, however, considered one of the most gentlemanlike lodgers of the place, because he did not drink, and paid his rent regularly. With exception of these good points, Andreas Semenovitch was, after all, rather a fool. An inconsiderate fascination had induced him to side with the party of progress. He was one of those innumerable simpletons who become infatuated with new fleeting ideas – who, by their silliness, throw discredit on the cause they may be greatly infatuated with. In other respects, notwithstanding his kindly disposition, Lebeziatnikoff had got so far as to find his former fellow-lodger and tutor, Peter Petrovitch, unbearable. This antipathy was a mutual one. In spite of his simplicity, Andreas Semenovitch began to have an inkling that Peter Petrovitch detested him at heart, and that nothing could be done with such a man. He had done his best to expound to him Fourier's system and Darwin's theory; but Peter Petrovitch, who at first had seemed to listen with sneering looks, now no longer restrained himself in making cutting remarks to his young instructor. The fact is that Looshin had come to the conclusion that Lebeziatnikoff was not only a fool, but a braggart, without any kind of importance in his own set. His special craze was the *Propaganda*, with reference to which he was by no means an authority, for he frequently floundered in his explanations. So what could be feared from such a man?

Let it be observed, by the way, that, since his visit to Andreas Semenovitch (especially in its early days), Peter Petrovitch had cheerfully, or at all events without protest, accepted his friend's singular compliments, when – for example, the latter gave him great credit because of his zeal for the founding of a new Commune in the Meschtschanskaya Street, when he used to tell him: 'You are much too intelligent to become enraged if your wife, one month after marriage, were to take a lover; or, a man of your capacity would never have his children christened,' and so on. Peter Petrovitch, on hearing this fulsomeness, would wince in no kind of way, so agreeable was flattery to him. In the course of the morning, he had negotiated some shares, and now, seated at his table, he was counting the money he had received. Andreas Semenovitch, who had hardly ever any money, was strutting about the room, affecting to regard these bundles of banknotes with contemptuous indifference. Of course, Peter Petrovitch did not believe by any manner of means that this contempt was sincere. On his part, Lebeziatnikoff guessed, not without pain, Looshin's scepticism, thinking that the latter was, doubtless, greatly delighted to show his money off in his presence, with a view to humiliate him and to remind him of the distance fortune had placed between them. On this occasion, Peter Petrovitch was more ill-disposed and more inattentive than ever, although Lebeziatnikoff was developing his favourite sub- ject – the establishment of a new species of Commune of peculiar nature. The man of business only interrupted his calculations, to give vent from time to time to some sneering and rude remark. But of this, Andreas Semenovitch took no kind of heed. In his eyes, Looshin's bad temper was owing to the disgust of a discarded lover. He, therefore, lost no time in broaching this subject, wishing to express, concerning it, a few advanced opinions which might console his worthy friend, and which, he trusted, might, at any rate, be of use in bringing about his prospective regeneration.

'It appears that a funeral-repast is being prepared at that widow's?' asked Looshin point-blank, interrupting Andreas Semenovitch in the most interesting part of his statement.

'Do you mean to say you knew nothing about it? I spoke to you yesterday on the subject, giving you my opinion about the whole ceremonial. From what I heard, she has also invited you. Didn't you yourself have a word with her yesterday?'

'I certainly never would have believed, considering the poverty she is in, that the silly woman would go and spend on a dinner all the money she had received from that other ass – Raskolnikoff. Just now, on getting home, I was aghast on seeing the wine and all the preparations! She has invited no end of people – the deuce only knows why!' continued Peter Petrovitch, who seemed intentionally to have turned the conversation on this topic. 'Do you mean to say that she has invited me, too?' he added all at once, looking up. 'And when did she? I don't remember anything about it. At all events, I shan't go. What on earth should I be doing there? All I know of the woman is having chatted with her yesterday for a minute or so, when I told her that, as the widow of a Government official, she might perhaps get temporary help. Can she have invited me because of that?'

'I don't intend going either!' replied Lebeziatnikoff.

'Well, that would crown all! Having thrashed her once, I can quite understand your scruples about going to dine with her.'

'Whom have I thrashed? Whom are you talking about?' retorted Lebeziatnikoff, angry and blushing.

'I am talking to you about Catherine Ivanovna, whom you thrashed about a month ago! I found that out yesterday. How now about your convictions? Is that the way to solve the question of female suffrage? Hah! hah! hah!' After this sally, which seemed to have eased his mind somewhat, Peter Petrovitch resumed counting his money.

'That's nonsense, to say nothing of calumny!' replied Lebeziatnikoff, excitedly, who did not like being reminded of this incident. 'Things did not happen in this way at all! What you have been told is false. With reference to the particular circumstance you allude to, all I did was to defend myself. It was Catherine Ivanovna herself who, at the first going off, rushed on me to scratch my face. She pulled one of my whiskers. I rather fancy that every man has a right to defend his own person. Besides, I am opposed to violence, wherever it may be, and that on principle, because it is a form of despotism. What was I to do? Was I to let her abuse me just as she pleased? All I did was to push her off.'

'Hah! hah! hah!' Looshin continued to chuckle.

'You want to pick a quarrel with me because you are in a bad temper, but that does not matter, and has nothing whatever to do with the question of women. This has been my argument. Assuming a woman to be in every respect man's equal, even in the matter of bodily strength (and people are beginning to hold this theory), then equality must exist here also. Of course, I have reflected that there really was no occasion to put such a question, for in future society, in which occasions for quarrelling will be impossible, there will also be no open violence. Hence the consideration of equality may be left out in the contention. I am not such a fool – although, of course, quarrels may arise – I should say, although they still exist for the time being, that later on none will be left. But hang it! a fellow is likely to fall out with you! It is not that matter which prevents my acceptance of Catherine Ivanovna's invitation. If I don't go to dinner there, it is simply on principle, in order to discourage by my absence the idiotic custom of funeral feasts! That's why! I might go, to be sure, to make fun of them; but unfortunately there will be no clergy, otherwise I would go without a moment's hesitation.'

'Then you mean to tell me that you would partake of her hospitality and insult both her and it?'

'Not insult, only protest, and that with a useful purpose. I can indirectly aid the civilising propaganda which is every man's duty. Perhaps such a task is all the more readily performed with the fewest formalities. I can start the idea, sow the seed, and this seed will generate – a fact. Would you call behaviour of such a kind offensive? People may, at first, get ruffled more or less, but they will soon understand that a service has been done them.'

'Have it your own way,' interrupted Peter Petrovitch. 'But, by the by, do you know the dead man's daughter, that skinny little thing – is it true what people say of her?'

'Well, what of it? According to my way of thinking, her condition is woman's normal state. Why not? Let us analyse for a moment. In society as it is, such a kind of life is not quite a normal one, because it is unnatural; but in future society it will be normal, because it will be free. Even now she has a perfect right to give way to it; she was wretched, why not dispose of her own free will of what is after all her capital? In future society, I may as well tell you, capital will be of no earthly kind of use, but the position of the gay woman will be of quite a different character, and will be rationally regulated. As for Sophia Semenovna, I consider that, under present circumstances, her doings are an energetic protest against society as now organised. I esteem her in consequence – nay more, I regard her with delight.'

'And yet I have been told that you had her turned out of this very house!'

Lebeziatnikoff grew angry. 'Another lie!' he went on energetically. 'The circumstances did not happen at all like that! Catherine Ivanovna has told the story in the most blundering manner, because she has not understood it! I have never run after Sophia Semenovna's favours. All I did was to try and develop without any other kind of intention, whilst striving to awaken in her a spirit of protest. I wanted nothing else; she herself felt that she could no longer remain here!'

'Did you not invite her to join the Commune?'

'Yes, I am at this very moment doing my best to absorb her into it. But she will be part of it under quite different conditions than here! Why laugh? We are anxious to found our Commune on a broader basis than any former one. We go much further than our predecessors – we annul more! If Dobroliouboff and Bielinsky were to rise from the tomb, they would have me as an opponent! In the meanwhile I shall continue to develop Sophia Semenovna. Hers is a beautiful, a very beautiful disposition!'

'You make the most of this beautiful disposition, don't you?'

'By no means; quite the contrary!'

' "Quite the contrary!" he says. Hah! hah!'

'You may believe me or not; why should I have secrets from you? There is, on the contrary, something which astonishes me. With me, she seems ill at ease – shows a kind of nervous reserve!'

'Granted for a moment that you are engaged in developing her. Hah! hah! You prove to her than that this nervous reserve is silly?'

'By no means! By no manner of means! What a coarse, nay, foolish, meaning you apply to the word "development"! Good heavens, how very much you are behind! You understand nothing! We seek liberty for woman, and you only think – Whilst leaving untouched the question of female modesty, a useless and even absurd thing, I can fully understand the girl's reserve with reference to myself, considering that she only uses her liberty, only exercises her right. If she, of her own free will, were to say to me: "Be mine," I should be delighted, for the girl pleases me. But, under existing circumstances, no one has ever been more polite, more considerate towards her than I, no one has ever done more justice to her worth. I wait and I hope! And that is all!'

'I would recommend you to make her a little present instead. I wager you have not as yet thought of that?'

'You do not understand anything, as I have already told you. Her condition, doubtless, authorises your sarcasms, but the question is quite another one! You only despise her. Going by a fact which to you seems falsely dishonourable, you refuse to regard humanely a human creature. You do not know what her nature is!'

'Tell me,' resumed Looshin, 'can you – or, to speak more plainly, are you friends enough with the girl in question, to ask her to step in here for a moment or so? They must, all of them, have returned from the cemetery. I fancy I heard them coming up the stairs. I should just like to see her for a moment.'

'Why?' asked Andreas Semenovitch with astonishment.

'I must speak to her. I must be off from here either today or tomorrow, and I have something to tell her. Besides, you may be present at our interview, which, after all, would be preferable. Otherwise, Heaven only knows what you might think.'

'I should think nothing at all. I put the question to you without attaching any importance to it. If you have any business with her, nothing will be easier than to have her here. I'll go for her at once, and, you may depend on it, I shall not disturb you.'

Five minutes afterwards, Lebeziatnikoff led Sonetchka into the room. She stepped forward, extremely surprised and anxious. Under such circumstances she was always frightened; fresh faces disconcerted her. This was, in her case, one of the impressions of childhood, and age had only increased this shyness. Peter Petrovitch showed himself polite and kind. Receiving, as a serious and respectable man, so young, and, in a sense, so interesting a creature, he thought himself entitled to greet her with some show of cheery familiarity. He did his best to set her at ease, whilst asking her to take a chair facing him. Sonia sat down, looked in turns at Lebeziatnikoff and at the money on the table, when, all of a sudden, her eyes turned on Peter Petrovitch, from whom she could not withdraw them. A species of fascination had seized on her. Lebeziatnikoff moved towards the door. Looshin rose, made a sign to Sonia to sit down again, and stopped Andreas Semenovitch at the moment the latter was going out.

'Is Raskolnikoff there? Has he arrived?' he asked of him, in a whisper.

'Raskolnikoff? Yes. Well! Yes, he is there; he has just arrived; I saw him! What then?'

'In that case. I ask you, urgently, to remain here, and not to leave me alone with this – lady. The matter under consideration is an insignificant one, but Heaven only knows what kind of conjectures might be made. I don't want Raskolnikoff to go and tell *there* you understand why I say this to you?'

'I understand – I understand!' replied Lebeziatnikoff. 'Yes, you are perfectly right. In my personal conviction, your fears are greatly exaggerated, but that does not matter – you are justified. As you wish it, therefore, I will remain. I will go and stand by the window, and shall not disturb you. To my mind, it is your right.'

Peter Petrovitch once more came and sat down opposite Sonia and watched her attentively. Suddenly his face assumed a grave, almost severe, expression, seeming to say: 'Nor must you, madam, either, imagine things which are not.' Sonia entirely lost countenance.

'To begin with, Sophia Semenovna, be kind enough to make my apologies to your greatly-respected mother. I am right, I believe, in using the word? Catherine Ivanovna is a mother to you, is she not?' began Peter Petrovitch, in a serious, though, on the whole, friendly tone.

'Yes, you are right; she is a mother to me!' poor Sonia hastened to reply.

'Well, then, be kind enough to tell her how much I regret that circumstances, independent of my will, do not permit me to accept her graceful invitation.'

'I will do so forthwith.' And Sonetchka rose.

'But that is not *yet* all,' continued Peter Petrovitch, who smiled on seeing the simplicity of the girl, and her ignorance of worldly ways. 'You scarcely know me, my dear Sophia Semenovna, if you think that, with so futile and unimportant a motive, I would have presumed to disturb a person like yourself. I have another object in view.'

At a gesture from her interlocutor, Sonia hastened to sit down again. The many-coloured banknotes lying on the table struck her once more, but she quickly turned her eyes away, and raised them on Peter Petrovitch; to look at another person's money seemed to her extremely out of place, especially for a person in her position. By turns she examined the gold-rimmed eyeglass which Peter Petrovitch held in his left hand; then the heavy ring, set with a yellow stone, which was twinkling on the middle finger of this hand. Finally, no longer knowing what to do with her eyes, she fixed them straight on Looshin. The latter, after having preserved for some moments a majestic silence, went on:

'I happened yesterday to interchange, by the way, a word or two with poor Catherine Ivanovna. This was enough to prove to me that she is in a state – anti-natural – if I may use such a word – '

'Yes – anti-natural,' repeated Sonia gently.

'Or – to speak more simply and more intelligently – ailing.'

'Yes, more simply and more intel— Yes, she is ailing.'

'Quite so. Now, from a feeling of humanity and – and – if I may say so, and of compassion, I should like, on my part, to be useful to her – anticipating, as I do, that she is likely to find herself in a sorry plight. It would appear that at this moment this unfortunate family has only you as mainstay.'

Sonia rose brusquely. 'May I ask you, sir, whether you did not tell her that she might get an annuity? Only yesterday she told me that you had taken upon yourself to get it for her. Is that correct?'

'By no means, and even in a certain sense that is absurd. I confined myself to making her understand that, as the widow of an official who had died at his post, she might get some kind of temporary help, provided she had patronage. But it appears that, instead of having served long enough to claim superannuation, your late father was not even in the service at the time of his death. In a word, we may yet hope, but hope is a quicksand; for in this case there is no claim for help – on the contrary. And was she really dreaming about a pension? Ha! ha! The good lady makes sure of everything!'

'Yes, she was dreaming about a pension. She is credulous and kind, her good nature makes her believe anything. As for her mind – you must excuse her!' said Sonia, who rose once more to depart.

'One word! – you have not yet heard all!'

'I have not yet heard all?' stammered the girl.

'Precisely. Pray be seated once more!' Sonia, in great confusion, sat down for the third time. 'Knowing her to be, as I do, with children of tender age, in such a plight, I was anxious, as I have already said, to be of some use to her as far as my means would permit – nothing more. For instance, a subscription, a raffle, or something of the kind might be got up for her; just as, under similar circumstances, people who want to benefit relatives or even strangers, often do. Such a thing is possible.'

'That is kind indeed! God will – ' stammered Sonia, looking hard at Peter Petrovitch.

'Such a thing is possible – but we will talk of this later on, At all events, some kind of steps might be taken this very day. We shall meet again tonight, when we shall talk about the matter, and lay the foundations, if I may use such an expression. Call in about seven. I am sure that Andreas Semenovitch will kindly be present at our conference. But there is one point which must first of all be thoroughly gone into. It is for that very reason that I took the liberty of disturbing you when I asked you to come here. In my opinion, no money should be entrusted in Catherine's own hands. Indeed, it would be inadvisable to do so; witness, for instance, today's banquet. She is without shoes and stockings, and yet goes and buys Jamaica rum and Madeira coffee. I noticed that, by the way, quite incidentally. Tomorrow you are likely to have the whole family on your hands again, even to the extent of providing it with a loaf. Why, such a thing is monstrous! I am, therefore, of opinion that a subscription be got up – unknown, however, to the poor widow – and that you alone have the management of the money. What do you think of my idea?'

'I hardly know how to answer you. It is only to say that she is like this – such a thing only occurs once in a lifetime. She was very anxious to do honour to her late husband's memory, but she is, for all that, very intelligent. But, as you wish, I shall be very, very – they will all be – and God – and the orphans.' Sonia could say no more, and burst into tears.

'Then it is a settled thing. Let me ask you to accept for your relative this sum, which must represent my own subscription. I am most anxious that my name should not be connected with this matter. Being myself, to some extent, in pecuniary straits, I regret not being able to do more.'

Upon which Peter Petrovitch handed to Sonia a ten-rouble note, after having carefully unfolded it. The girl received it with a blush, stammered a few indistinct words, and made haste to withdraw. Peter Petrovitch escorted her as far as the door. Finally she left the room, and returned to Catherine Ivanovna, a prey to extraordinary agitation. During this scene Andreas Semenovitch, unwilling to disturb the interview, had remained near the window, or had moved about the room. No sooner had Sonia left, however, when, approaching Peter Petrovitch, he held out his hand to him with solemn gesture.

'I have heard and *seen* all,' said he, with peculiar emphasis. 'Your conduct was noble – nay, rather, humane, for I do not admit such a word as noble. I saw your desire to escape being thanked. And, although I am, to tell you the truth, opposed, on principle, to private charity – which, far from rooting out misery, encourages its increase – I must still own that I have watched your act with pleasure – yes, with real pleasure.'

'It is a matter of no consequence,' murmured Looshin, somewhat embarrassed, looking at Lebeziatnikoff with particular attention.

'No, no! it is not. A man who, like yourself, grieved by a late humiliation, is still capable of being interested in the misfortunes of others, may act contrary to sound social economy: yet such a man is none the less worthy of esteem. I did not expect such a thing from you, Peter Petrovitch, considering your ways of viewing things. But, how fettered your ideas are, to be sure! How can you be so distressed by yesterday's mishap?' cried good-natured Andreas Semenovitch, experiencing a return of sincere sympathy for Peter Petrovitch. 'And why, after all, stand in need of being *legally* married, my generous and very dear Peter Petrovitch? What can you care about *legal* unions? Strike me if you will, but your disappointment delights me. I am happy at the thought that you are free, that you are not yet wholly lost to humanity. I am candid, you must admit.'

'I am a supporter of legal marriage because – I don't want to wear horns, because I don't want to bring up another man's children, as is the case with your free marriages,' answered Peter Petrovitch, for the sake of saying something. He was thoughtful, and only listened casually to his friend's talk.

'Children? You talk about children?' resumed Andreas Semenovitch, rousing himself all at once, like a war-steed that has heard the sound of the trumpet: 'Children! Here we have a social difficulty which will be solved in its own good time. Many people go so far as to ignore them *in toto*, as they do every family obligation. We will talk about children a little later on; for the present, let us discuss "the wearing of the horns." I must own that that is my fancy topic. This vulgar and coarse expression, circulated by Pooshkin, will have no place in the dictionaries of the future! What in fact is meant by "wearing the horns"? Vain bogy! On the contrary, dear friend, in free marriages such a contingency will not exist. The condition of cuckoldom is the natural consequence and, we may say, the antidote to legal wedlock, a protest against an indissoluble bond. From this point of view there is nothing humiliating about it, and if I ever – avaunt the thought! – were to contract a legal union, I should be delighted to wear the very horns you dread so greatly; I would say to my other half: "Formerly I had but love for you, but now I esteem you because you have known how to protest." But you are laughing, and that because you have not strength enough to break with prejudice! Deuce take me! I can readily understand that, in the case of a legal union, to be hoodwinked, must be very disagreeable – but that is the result of a condition debasing to both contracting parties. Let this wearing of horns be a recognised and open thing, as it would be in free unions – the fact would no longer exist, its very meaning would die out. Your partner would, on the contrary, prove to you that she esteems you, since she would think you incapable of interfering with her happiness, and much too enlightened to be likely to take vengeance on a rival. In truth, I sometimes think if I were wedded (freely or legally, that matters not), and my spouse were to be backward in finding a particular friend, that I would procure her one myself. "My dear," I would say, "I love you, but I wish above all things that you should esteem me!" Am I right?'

These words scarcely brought a smile to Peter Petrovitch's lips: his thoughts were elsewhere; he rubbed his hands with an anxious air. Andreas Semenovitch remembered later on his friend's absence of mind.

Chapter 2

IT WOULD BE DIFFICULT to explain accurately how the idea of this insane banquet had taken root in Catherine Ivanovna's distracted brain. At all events, she spent, on the dinner-question, the greater half of the sum she had received from Raskolnikoff for Marmeladoff's funeral. Perhaps Catherine Ivanovna believed that she was, with a view of pleasing Mrs Grundy, obliged thus to do honour to her late husband's memory, in order to prove to all the lodgers, and especially to Amalia Ivanovna, that the dead man 'was as good as they were, if not a great deal better.' Or perhaps she was a slave to this pride of the poor – who, under certain circumstances of life, such as a christening, wedding, or burial, are induced to sacrifice their last penny with a view 'of doing things quite as decently as others.' We are even permitted to suppose that, at the very moment she saw herself reduced to the greatest misery, Catherine Ivanovna wished to show to all these 'paupers,' not only that she 'knew how to live, and how to receive,' but that, as the daughter of a colonel, 'brought up in a noble or, more accurately still, an aristocratic family,' people might see that she had not been cut out to scrub the floor with her own hands and to wash every night her brats' underlinen.

The bottles of wine were neither very numerous nor of very varied brands, and the Madeira was conspicuous by its absence. Peter Petrovitch had much exaggerated things. At all events, wine and brandy, rum and liqueurs, all of very inferior quality, but plentiful in quantity, had been procured. The fare, which had been prepared in Amalia Ivanovna's own kitchen, comprised, in addition to the *koutia*, three or four varied dishes, and so forth. Two samovars were, in addition, kept ready for those of the guests who were anxious to take tea and punch after dinner. Catherine Ivanovna herself purchased what was wanted with the assistance of one of the lodgers, a starving Pole who lived – Heaven only knows how! – with Madame Lippevechzel. This poor wretch had from the very first moment placed himself at the widow's disposal, and for six-and-thirty hours ran here and there on errands, and quickly, with a zeal which he took care to make the most of on every possible occasion. At every moment, for the least trifle he would hurry up, with the utmost fussiness, to ask for instructions from '*panna* Marmeladoff.' After having declared that, without the civility of 'this serviceable and magnanimous man,' she really did not know what would have become of her, Catherine Ivanovna finished by discovering that her factotum was absolutely useless. It was one of her ways to get straight-way infatuated with the first best-comer; she would view such a person under the most favourable light, and would give him credit for a thousand qualities, which only existed in her own imagination, but in which, however, she placed implicit faith. But, all of a sudden, disillusion would follow upon enthusiasm, and she would, with many an uncalled-for remark, drop the very person she had overwhelmed a few hours previously with excessive praise.

Amalia Ivanovna, likewise, assumed sudden importance in Catherine's eyes, and grew considerably in her esteem, perhaps from the sole reason that the landlady had used every care in catering for the feast, for it was she who took upon herself to lay the table, to provide the plates and dishes, linen and so on, and to cook the provisions. On starting for the cemetery, Catherine Ivanovna entrusted her authority to the latter – and Madame Lippevechzel showed herself worthy of such confidence. The dinner-things were even laid in somewhat superior fashion. The plates and dishes, glassware, cups, forks, and knives, borrowed from different lodgers, did certainly, by strange disparities, betray their varied sources, but, in spite of all this, everything was in its right place. When the mourners returned to the deceased's house, an expression of triumph could be read on Amalia Ivanovna's face. Proud of having so well executed her functions, the landlady strutted about in her new mourning-gown, having, at the same time, retrimmed her cap. This pride, although a perfectly legitimate one, did not seem to please Catherine Ivanovna. 'As if it would have been impossible to lay the dinner-things without Amalia Ivanovna!' The cap, with its new ribbon, also seemed to displease her. 'Lo and behold that silly German woman with all her fuss! She (the landlady) has been high-minded enough to come and help her poor lodgers. High-minded, to be sure! Just fancy that! At Catherine Ivanovna's home – her father was a colonel, you must know – there used to be sometimes as many as forty people at dinner, and such a person as Amalia Ivanovna, or, rather, Ludwigovna, would not even have been admitted to the servants' hall.' Catherine did not want to give way to her feelings there and then, but she promised herself that she would put this bold creature back in her right place that very day.

Another circumstance likewise contributed to irritate the widow. With the exception of the Pole, who followed the coffin to the cemetery, scarcely a single one of the lodgers invited had done so. But to make up for all this, when it was time to sit down at table, the scrubbiest and least desirable of them bustled in. Some of them even appeared in guise more than unstudied. The better ones seemed to have given each other the cue to stay away, beginning with Peter Petrovitch Looshin, the most gentlemanlike amongst them. Catherine Ivanovna, however, had said no end of flattering things of him to everybody the evening before – that is, to Madame Lippevechzel, to Poletchka, to Sonia, as well as to the Pole. He was, she assured them, a most noble and magnanimous man, who was, at the same time, immensely rich, with grand relatives, and, according to what she said, he had been her first husband's particular friend, had formerly visited at her father's; indeed, he had promised to use all his influence to procure her a snug pension. It may be observed by the way, that, when Catherine Ivanovna extolled the wealth and connections of any one of her acquaintances, she always did so without any personal kind of reason, and that only in order to augment the prestige of the person in question.

Next to Looshin, and probably 'to ape him,' that 'fellow' Lebeziatnikoff also failed to put in an appearance. What did the man really think of himself? Catherine Ivanovna had been very considerate, to say the least of it, to invite him, and this she had only done because Peter Petrovitch and he lived together; if civility was shown to one of the two, it was of course, necessary to do the same to the other. The absence likewise of a lady of fashion and of her daughter, who was 'withering on the stalk,' was commented on. These two persons had only lived about a fortnight at Madame Lippevechzel's; they had, however, more than once complained of the noises made in the Marmeladoffs' room, especially when the deceased used to come home intoxicated. As may readily be thought, the landlady had not been slow in bringing these complaints to Catherine Ivanovna's ears, and, in the course of one of her incessant disputes with her lodger, Amalia Ivanovna threatened to turn all the Marmeladoffs out of doors, considering, she shouted, 'that they disturbed the repose of distin-guished persons in whose boots they were not fit to stand.' Under present circumstances, Catherine Ivanovna had been very particular to invite these two ladies 'in whose boots she was not fit to stand,' all the more so as, whenever they met on the stairs, the distinguished lady turned her back on her disdainfully. This was a way of showing the minx how superior Catherine Ivanovna was to her in feeling – she, who could forget unhandsome behaviour; besides, the lady and her daugh-ter would have had an opportunity of convincing themselves, during the course of the meal, that she had not been born to the position in which circumstances had placed her. She was fully resolved to make this clear to them at table, to let them know that her papa had performed the functions of a governor, and that, consequently, there was no occasion to turn their heads away on meeting her. A corpulent lieutenant-colonel (he was in reality only a half-pay staff-captain) also failed to put in appearance. He, however, had an excuse, the gout having pinned him to his easy-chair since the previous day.

To make amends, however, for all this, there first appeared – leaving the Pole out, of course – an ugly, pimply Government clerk, got up in a greasy dress coat, unsavoury as to his person, and as silent as a fish. Then an ex-post office official, a little deaf and nearly blind old man, whose rent somebody paid at Amalia Ivanovna's since time immemo-rial. These two individuals were followed by a lieutenant on half-pay, or, to speak more correctly, a retired sutler, who, being the worse for drink, made his entry laughing most indecently at the top of his voice, and, 'just fancy!' without his waistcoat! One of the guests sat down abruptly without even bowing to his hostess. Another one, for the want of suitable clothing, appeared in his dressing-gown. This was, however, too much of a good thing, and this free-and-easy gentleman was turned out by Amalia Ivanovna, aided by the Pole. The latter had introduced two of his fellow-countrymen who had never lodged at Madame Lippevechzel's, and whom no one in the place knew. All this caused

Catherine Ivanovna keen dissatisfaction. It certainly was worth while to make so many preparations for such a gang. Fearing lest the table, which took up the whole breadth of the room, might be too small, care had been taken to provide the children's dinner on a travelling-trunk standing in a corner: Poletchka, as being the eldest, had to attend to the two young ones, to see that they ate properly and made right use of their handkerchiefs. Under these conditions, Catherine Ivanovna could not help receiving her guests with almost insolent haughtiness. Holding, goodness only knows why, Amalia Ivanovna responsible for the absence of the principal guests, she all at once assumed so rude a tone towards her landlady that the latter remarked it in a moment, and was greatly ruffled in consequence. Thus the feast commenced under unfavourable auspices. At last, everyone sat down.

Raskolnikoff appeared almost immediately after his return from the cemetery. Catherine Ivanovna was enchanted to see him – firstly, because, of all the persons present, he was the only cultured man (she introduced him to the company as being likely, within a year or two, to occupy a chair at the University of St Petersburg); next, because he apologised respectfully for not having been able, in spite of his utmost desire, to be present at the obsequies. She did her best to induce him to sit on her left, Amalia Ivanovna having taken a seat on her right, and then in an undertone she commenced with the young man such a conversation as her duties of hostess admitted of. On the other hand, the malady she was subjected to had assumed for the last few days a more alarming character than ever, and the cough which racked her breast often prevented her from finishing a sentence; nevertheless, she was delighted to have someone to whom she could confide the indignation she experienced face to face with this heterogeneous gathering. At first her anger was manifested by jeering remarks made at the expense of the guests, and especially of the landlady herself.

'It is all the fault of that idiotic woman! You know very well whom I am talking about.' And Catherine, with a movement of the head, pointed to the landlady. 'Look at her!' she exclaimed, 'she is opening her eyes as wide as she can, she guesses that we are talking about her, but can't make out what we are saying, that's why she is making such goggle-eyes. Oh! the laughing-stock! Ha! ha! ha! Hi! hi! hi! And what does she pretend to prove with her bonnet? Hi! hi! hi! She wants to make everybody believe that she is honouring me awfully by sitting down at my table! I had requested her to invite a few good people, and, in preference, those who had known my husband. Just look at the collection of vulgar fellows and scrubs she has scraped together for me! Look at that animal! – he has not even washed himself, disgusting beast! And as for those unhappy Poles – Ha! ha! Nobody about here seems to know them. This is the first that I see of them. Why, I would wish to know, have they come at all? They are like so many strings of onions, one neck to the other. I say, you – !' she called out to one of them. 'Help yourself! Don't forget the beer! Or would you prefer brandy? Look, he has got up, he is making his bow! I suppose they are some poor devils, people hard-up! All is one to them, provided they can eat! One thing in their favour is that they don't make any noise, only – only I am so afraid for my landlady's plate! Amalia Ivanovna!' – she went on almost aloud, addressing Madame Lippevechzel – 'if your spoons should by chance get stolen, I must warn you that I am not answerable for them!'

After having thus satisfied her resentment, she once more turned towards Raskolnikoff and chuckled on, drawing his attention to the landlady. 'Hah! hah! hah! She has not even understood! She never does! There she is, with her mouth wide open. Just look, do; she is a screech-owl – a regular screech-owl, with fresh ribbons, hah! hah! hah!' This laugh was followed by a fit of coughing, which lasted five minutes. She raised her handkerchief to her lips, and silently showed it to Raskolnikoff: it was stained with blood. Beads of sweat glistened on her brow, her cheek-bones grew red, and her breathing more and more difficult. Nevertheless, she continued her chatter in a low tone of voice, with extraordinary animation. 'I had entrusted her with the mission, a very delicate one, I may say, of inviting that lady and her daughter – you know, I presume, whom I mean? It was, of course, necessary to set about it with a good deal of tact. Well! She did it in such a way that that foolish creature, that countrified pea-hen who has come here to solicit a pension, as being the widow of a major, and who haunts from morning till night every Government office in the place, with an inch of paint on her face, though she is more than fifty-five – the affected thing! – has refused my invitation without even an apology, which the commonest civility after all requires in such a case! Another thing I can't make out is, why Peter Petrovitch has not come either. But where can Sonia be? What can have become of her? Ah! Here she comes! Where have you been, my dear? It is very singular that, on such a day as this, you should be so unpunctual! Rodion Romanovitch, let her sit down next to you. That's your place, Sonia – and help yourself. Try the caviar, it's very good. I hope the children have been helped? They are not forgetting you down there, Poletchka. are they? Come, I am glad of that. Mind your manners, Lena; and you, Kolia, don't fidget about with your legs like that, hold yourself as becomes a child of good family. What did you say, Sonetchka?'

Sonia hastened to deliver Peter Petrovitch's excuses to her step-mother, making a point of speaking rather loudly so that everybody should hear her. Not satisfied with repeating the well-bred formula Looshin had made use of, she did her best to amplify them. Peter Petrovitch, she added, had begged of her to tell Catherine Ivanovna that he would call, as soon as possible, to talk over business, and to come to some kind of understanding with her as to further steps, and so forth. Sonia knew that this would quiet Catherine Ivanovna, and that her vanity, especially, would be satisfied. The girl sat down beside Raskolnikoff, to whom she hastily bowed, casting on him, at the same time, a rapid and inquisitive look. But, during the remainder of the dinner, she appeared to avoid looking at him or addressing him. She seemed even absent in mind, although she kept her eyes fixed on Catherine's face, with a view to divine her stepmother's wishes.

For want of clothes, neither of the two ladies was in mourning. Sonia wore a dark cinnamon costume; the widow had put on a print-gown of sombre colour – the only one she possessed. Peter Petrovitch's excuses were well received. After having listened with an affected air to Sonia's account, Catherine Ivanovna assumed an important tone of voice whilst inquiring after Peter Petrovitch's health. Then, without con-cerning herself very greatly about the remaining guests who might hear her, she remarked to Raskolnikoff that so respectable and esteemed a man as Peter Petrovitch would have been very much out of his element in the midst of so singular a society; she therefore understood why he had not come, in spite of the former ties which united him to her family.

'That is why, Rodion Romanovitch, I am so particularly obliged to you for not having despised my hospitality, although offered under such conditions,' she added, almost aloud; 'besides, I am convinced that it was only your friendship for my poor husband which induced you to keep faith with me.' Then once more, Catherine Ivanovna began to make fun of her guests. Suddenly, addressing herself with particular solicitude to the deaf old gentleman, she called out to him, to the other end of the table: 'Would you like some more roast meat? Have you been helped to port wine?' The guest thus addressed made no reply, and it was long before he understood what they asked him, although his neighbours did their utmost to explain it to him. He, however, looked all round, with his mouth wide open, which added to the general merriment. 'What a clod! Just look at him! And why has he been invited?' inquired Catherine Ivanovna of Raskolnikoff. 'As for Peter Petrovitch, I always counted on him, I did,' she went on, addressing herself to Amalia Ivanovna, with a look of such severity as to cow the person in question; 'he certainly is not like some got-up finical creatures; why, my papa would not have looked at such persons for kitchenmaids, and, if my late husband had honoured them with an invitation, it would only have been from pure kindliness!'

'Yes, he was fond of drink, he had quite a weakness for the bottle!' shouted out all at once the retired sutler, emptying his twelfth glass of brandy.

Catherine Ivanovna sharply took up this ill-timed remark. 'I own that my late husband had this failing, everybody knows that, but he was a good and noble fellow, who loved and respected his family. All one could reproach him with was his excess of kindliness. He took much too easily for friends all kinds of debauchees, and God only knows with whom he has not drunk! The persons he fraternised with were not worth the soles of his feet! Just fancy, Rodion Romanovitch, we even found in one of his pockets a little gingerbread-cock. In spite of his drinking he never forgot his children.'

'A little cock, did you say? A little cock?' cried the sutler.

Catherine Ivanovna did not deign to reply. Having become thoughtful, she heaved a sigh. 'You doubtless believe, like everybody else, that I was too hard upon him,' she resumed, speaking to Raskolnikoff. 'But that is a mistake! He held me in esteem – he entertained the greatest respect for me! His heart was so good! – and, at times, he would inspire me with so much pity! When seated apart, he used to raise his eyes to mine. I would be so affected that I had some difficulty to hide my emotion, but I used to say, "Flinch, and he will again take to drinking!" The only way to check him was by a gentle kind of severity.'

'Yes, he used to get his hair pulled – that happened more than once,' bawled the sutler, and he tossed off another glass of brandy.

'There are certain idiots who ought not only to have their hair pulled, but to be sent about their business with the broomstick. I am not now, however, alluding to the deceased,' retorted Catherine Ivanovna vehemently. Her cheeks grew purple, her chest heaved more and more. Another moment and there was likely to be a scene. Many laughed, finding this droll. Some incited the sutler; they spoke to him in a whisper – in a word, they all vied with one another as to who should add fuel to the flame.

'Permit me to ask whom you are talking about? Whom do you mean?' inquired the ex-sutler with a threatening voice. 'But no, it's useless! It's of no importance after all! A widow! Only a poor widow! I forgive her! Never mind!' And he tossed off another glass of brandy.

Raskolnikoff listened in silence. He experienced a feeling of disgust. Out of consideration only, and in order not to displease Catherine

Ivanovna, he tasted the viands with which she filled his plate at every moment. The young man kept his eyes fixed on Sonia, who, more and more anxious, followed with anxiety the progress of Catherine's exasperation. She anticipated that the dinner would come to an unpleasant end. Amongst other things, the latter knew that she was the principal cause which had prevented the two country ladies from being present on the occasion. She had heard from Amalia Ivanovna's own lips that, on being invited, the insulted mother had asked 'how she could let her daughter sit down by the side of *that young lady.*' Sonia fancied that her stepmother was already informed of the insult. Now, an insult to Sonia was, in Catherine Ivanovna's eyes, worse than an insult offered to herself, her children, or her father's memory. It was a mortal outrage. Sonia concluded that Catherine Ivanovna had, at present, but one thing at heart – namely, to prove to these artificial women that they were both of them, etc., etc. Just at this moment a guest, seated at the other end of the table, sent down to Sonia a plate on which were deposited two hearts, pierced by a dart and made of bread crumbs. Catherine Ivanovna, glowing with anger, forthwith declared, in a loud tone of voice, that the author of this joke was assuredly 'some drunken fool.'

Upon this she announced her intention of retiring, as soon as she obtained her pension, to T—, her native town, where she would start an educational establishment for the use of young ladies of rank. All at once she produced the 'honorary certificate' of which the late Marmeladoff had spoken to Raskolnikoff at their meeting in the tavern. Under existing circumstances this document proved Catherine's right to open a boarding-school; she had, however, above all provided herself with it with the object of confusing the two 'finicals,' supposing them to have accepted her invitation; she would have demonstrated to them, by means of conclusive evidence, that 'the daughter of a colonel, the descendant of a noble, if not aristocratic family, was rather above adventuresses, whose number had become so large nowadays.' The document had soon made the round of the table, the drunken guests passing it from hand to hand without opposition on Catherine's part, for this certificate designated her in full the daughter of a Court councillor, which authorised her in part, if not wholly, to call herself a colonel's daughter.

Then the widow enlarged on the charms of the happy and quiet life she promised herself to lead at T—; she would, she maintained, appeal for aid to the masters of the town college, amongst whom there was a respectable old man, Mr Mangot, who had once upon a time taught her French; he would not hesitate to come and give instruction at her house, and would show himself considerate as to his fees. Lastly, she announced her intention of taking Sonia with her to T——, and entrusting her with the general management of her establishment. At these words, somebody burst out laughing at the other end of the table. Catherine Ivanovna pretended to have heard nothing; but, raising her voice, declared that Sonia Semenovna possessed every necessary quality to assist her in her enterprise. After having extolled the girl's gentleness, patience, unselfishness, mental capacity, and nobility of character, she gently tapped her cheek and twice kissed her effusively. Sonia blushed, and suddenly Catherine Ivanovna burst into tears.

'My nerves are greatly agitated,' said she, by way of apology, 'and I am so tired that I can do no more; therefore, as you have all done, we will take tea.'

Amalia Ivanovna, greatly vexed because she had not been able to squeeze a single word in during the preceding conversation, chose this opportunity to make another attempt, and, with much tact observed to the future schoolmistress that she should pay the utmost attention to her pupils' linen, and that, above all, she should prevent their reading novels in bed. Fatigue and irritation had rendered Catherine Ivanovna not over-patient; hence she took this wise counsel in very bad part, and, to believe her, the landlady knew nothing of what she was talking about. In a seminary for young ladies of rank, the care of the linen belonged to the housekeeper and not to the manageress; as for her remark in connection with the reading of novels, it was simply uncalled for. In a word, Amalia Ivanovna was requested to hold her tongue. Instead of complying, however, with this request, the latter retorted sharply that she had only spoken 'with reason' – that her intentions were always of the best, and that for a long time Catherine Ivanovna had not paid her a single penny. 'You are not telling the truth when talking of your good intentions,' retorted the visitor; 'as late as yesterday, when the deceased was laid out on the table, you came and abused me about the rent.' Thereupon the landlady observed with some show of logic, that 'she had invited those ladies, but that they had failed to come, because they were people of rank, and could not think of visiting any lady who was not so.' Upon which, her opponent replied that a kitchenmaid had not the capacities requisite for sitting in judgement on real nobility.

Amalia Ivanovna, stung to the quick, retorted that 'her *vater* was a most important man in Berlin, and was in the habit of walking about with his hands in his pockets, and always going "Puff, puff!" ' And, in order to give a more precise notion of her *vater*, Madame Lippevechzel rose, thrust her hands in her pockets, and, puffing out her cheeks, began to imitate the noise of a blacksmith's bellows. At this there was general merriment amongst the various lodgers, who, in the hope of a battle – royal between the two women, did their utmost to excite Amalia Ivanovna. Catherine Ivanovna, losing all control over herself, declared in a loud voice that Amalia Ivanovna had never had a *vater*, that she was nothing more nor less than a Finn from St Petersburg, and must have been, once upon a time, a cook, or perhaps even something worse. Then came a furious repartee from Amalia Ivanovna. It was Catherine Ivanovna herself, more likely, who had never had a *vater*. As for her, her own *vater* was a Berliner, who was in the habit of wearing long frock-coats, and was always going 'Puff, puff!' Catherine Ivanovna answered contemptuously that her birth was known to everyone, and that some honorary certificate, in printed characters, stated her to be a colonel's daughter, whilst Amalia Ivanovna (even assuming her ever to have had a father at all) could, probably, only trace her origin to some Finnish milkman; but, more likely, she had never had a father at all, considering that no one knew for certain what her real patronymic was, whether her name was Amalia Ivanovna or Amalia Ludwigovna. The landlady, beside herself, exclaimed, striking the table with her fist, that she was an Ivanovna, and not a Ludwigovna; that her *vater's* name was Johann, and that he was a bailiff, which Catherine Ivanovna's father had never been. Upon this the widow rose, and in a calm tone of voice, which the pallor of her face and the agitation of her bosom belied, shouted:

'If you again dare to place your miserable *vater* on a level with my papa, I will pull your cap off, and trample it under foot.'

Amalia Ivanovna now began to run about the room exclaiming at the top of her voice that she was the landlady, and that Catherine Ivanovna should clear out there and then; then she hastened to take the plate from the dinner-table. There now ensued an indescribable confusion and hubbub, the children commenced to weep, Sonia rushed to her stepmother to prevent her giving way to violence, but Amalia Ivanovna having suddenly made an allusion to the yellow ticket, Catherine Ivanovna pushed the girl on one side and marched straight up to her landlady prepared to execute her threat. At this moment the door was opened. Peter Petrovitch suddenly appeared on the threshold. He cast a severe look on the united company. Catherine Ivanovna ran towards him.

Chapter 3

'PETER PETROVITCH!' she exclaimed, 'come and protect me! Make this foolish woman understand that she has no right to speak as she does to a high-born and unhappy lady! It's shameful! I shall complain to the Governor-General himself. She will be held responsible. Come, in memory of the hospitality you have received at my father's house, to the help of these poor orphans!'

'Permit me, madam, permit me, I beg,' answered Peter Petrovitch, making a movement to put her aside, 'I never had the honour, as you know very well yourself, of your papa's acquaintance. Excuse me, madam!' – (here someone began to laugh aloud) – 'and I do not intend to take part in your continual squabbles with Amalia Ivanovna. I am here for a matter which is personal to myself. I am anxious to have an immediate explanation with your stepdaughter, Sophia Ivanovna. That is her name, I believe? Allow me, therefore, to come in.' And, leaving Catherine Ivanovna to herself, Peter Petrovitch went to Sonia's part of the room.

Catherine Ivanovna remained as if glued to her place, she could not understand Peter Petrovitch's denial as to ever having been her father's guest. This hospitality, which only existed in her imagination, had been to her a species of dogma. What struck her, likewise, was Looshin's haughty, and even threatening, tone of voice. Silence was, however, somewhat restored at his appearance. The careful dress of the man of law jarred extremely with the untidiness of Madame Lippevechzel's lodgers, each of whom felt sure that a motive of exceptional gravity could alone account for the latter's presence in such a gathering; hence all expected some unusual result. Raskolnikoff, who happened to be by Sonia's side, made way to allow Peter Petrovitch to pass; the latter did not seem to observe the young man. Lebeziatnikoff appeared a moment after in his turn, but, instead of entering the room, he remained in the doorway, listening inquisitively, without succeeding in understanding what was the matter.

'Excuse my troubling your company, but I am compelled to do so for a sufficiently weighty reason,' commenced Peter Petrovitch, without addressing anyone in particular. 'Indeed, I am delighted at having the opportunity of coming to an explanation in such a large assembly. Amalia Ivanovna, I must ask you most humbly in your capacity as landlady, to listen to the conversation I purpose holding with Sophia Ivanovna.' Then, turning towards the surprised and already frightened girl, he added: 'Sophia Ivanovna, I discovered, immediately after your visit, the loss of a hundred-rouble note on the National Bank, which had been lying on a table in my friend Andreas Semenovitch Lebeziatnikoff's room. If you should happen to know what has become of this note, and will tell me so, I give you, in the presence of everybody here, my word of honour that the matter shall go no further. Otherwise, I shall be compelled to have recourse to very serious measures, and then – you will only have yourself to blame.'

A profound silence, followed upon these words. Even the children left off crying. Sonia, pale as death, looked at Looshin without being able to answer. As yet she did not seem to have understood. A few seconds elapsed. 'Well, what is your reply?' asked Peter Petrovitch, attentively watching the girl.

'I do not know – I know nothing,' was the answer in a feeble tone of voice.

'No? You don't know?' continued Looshin, who, after a few more seconds, resumed in a severe tone: 'Think about it, miss, and reflect, I will give you time to do so. Let me tell you that, if I were less certain of my case, I would take care not to charge you with so formal an accusation. I am too experienced a man of business to lay myself open to an action for libel. This morning I went out to negotiate several bonds, representing a nominal value of three thousand roubles. On my return home, I recounted my money – Andreas Semenovitch was witness to that. After having counted two thousand three hundred roubles, I placed them in a book, which I secured in the breast-pocket of my overcoat. Thus there were left on the table about five hundred roubles in banknotes, and especially three notes of one hundred roubles each. It was then that, on my invitation, you came to me, and were, during the whole of your visit, a prey to extraordinary agitation. Three different times you attempted to go out, although our interview was not yet at an end. Andreas Semenovitch can prove all this.

'You will not deny, I believe, that I got Andreas Semenovitch to call you with the sole intention of talking to you about the sad condition of your relative, Catherine Ivanovna (with whom I could not dine), and as to some kind of a way of helping her, either by means of subscriptions, a lottery, or some other plan. You thanked me with tears in your eyes (I am going into all these details in order to prove to you that not a single circumstance has escaped my memory). I then took a ten-rouble note from my table, and handed it to you, as a temporary assistance for your relative. Andreas Semenovitch was a witness to all this. Then I escorted you to the door, and you went away, showing the same agitation as previously.

'After you had gone, I conversed for about ten minutes with Andreas Semenovitch. At length he left me, and I went to the table to take the remainder of my money, when, lo and behold, I discovered the absence of a hundred-rouble note. Now, judge, how can I suspect Andreas Semenovitch? The mere thought of such a thing is impossible to me. Neither have I made any mistake in my reckoning, for a moment before your entrance I had gone through it carefully. You must own yourself that, remembering your agitation, your hurry to be gone, and the fact that you had for some time your hands on the table; finally, whilst considering your social status and the habits it implies, I have been obliged, in spite of myself, in spite of my own free will, to give way to a suspicion, cruel I admit, but nevertheless legitimate. However convinced I may be of your guilt, I admit that I am well aware to what I expose myself in making such a charge against you. I do not, however, hesitate in doing so, and I will tell you why: it is solely in consequence of your base ingratitude! I ask you to come to me, because I am interested in your unfortunate relative; I make you a present of ten roubles for her benefit, and it is thus you reward me! See! That is not right! You must learn a lesson. Reflect, think; I urge you to do so as your best friend, for that is your only course at this moment! If not, I shall be inflexible! Well, do you confess?'

'I have taken nothing from you!' murmured the frightened Sonia. 'You gave me ten roubles, here they are, take them back!' The young girl pulled her handkerchief out of her pocket, undid a knot she had made in it, and produced a ten-rouble note, which she handed to Looshin.

'You persist, then, in denying having stolen the hundred roubles?' he asked, in a reproachful tone, without taking the note back.

Sonia looked round the room, and on the different faces saw nothing but a severe, angry, or jeering look. She looked at Raskolnikoff, who, standing upright against the wall with folded arms, had his ardent gaze fixed on her. 'Good heavens!' she groaned.

'Amalia Ivanovna, it will be necessary to communicate with the police; consequently, I must most humbly ask you to get the porter to come upstairs,' said Looshin in a gentle and even affectionate voice.

'*Gott der barmherzig*! I knew the creature was a thief!' exclaimed Madame Lippevechzel, beating her hands together.

'Did you?' resumed Peter Petrovitch; 'previous circumstances, I suppose, must have authorised you to come to such a conclusion. I must ask you, respected Amalia Ivanovna, to remember what you have just said. Moreover, there are witnesses.'

Everybody in the room was talking noisily. All the guests had become excited.

'What!' cried Catherine Ivanovna, recovering all at once from her stupor, whilst darting with a rapid movement towards Looshin. 'What! accuse her of theft? She? Sonia? You coward! You coward!' And then she went quickly up to the girl, whom she strained closely in her bony arms. 'Sonia! How could you have accepted ten roubles from him? Foolish child! Give them up! Give the money up immediately! Here!'

Catherine Ivanovna took the note from Sonia's hand, crumpled it between her fingers, and threw it in Looshin's face. The rolled-up paper hit Peter Petrovitch, and rebounded on the floor. Amalia Ivanovna hastened to pick it up. The lawyer grew angry.

'Hold that madwoman!' he exclaimed.

At this moment many persons came and stood in the doorway beside Lebeziatnikoff; amongst them were the two ladies from the country.

'Madwoman, say you? Is it me you treat as a madwoman, you idiot?' shouted Catherine Ivanovna. 'You yourself are an idiot, a vile agent of some kind or other, a base man! And to say that Sonia has taken his money! Sonia a thief! Why, you idiot, she is more likely to give it you!' And Catherine Ivanovna burst out in a nervous laughter. 'Do you see that idiot?' she added, going from one lodger to another, and pointing Looshin out to them; all of a sudden she saw Amalia Ivanovna, and her anger knew no longer any bounds. 'What! you also, you cat, you also, you miserable German woman! You pretend to say that Sonia is a thief? Is it possible? Why, she has not left the room; on leaving you, you rascal, she came straight here to sit down to table with us, everybody has seen that! She went and sat down by the side of Rodion Romanovitch! Turn her pockets inside out! As she has been nowhere else, she must have got the money about her! Search! search away! Only, if you don't find anything, my man, you will be held answerable for your behaviour! I shall complain to the Emperor, to the merciful Czar; I shall go and throw myself at his feet this very day. I am an orphan, and I shall gain admittance. You think it will be refused? But you are wrong, I shall gain an audience. Because she is gentle you thought you would have nothing to fear, you counted on her timidity, did you not? But, if she is timid I, my man, am not afraid, and your calculation will be upset! Search, therefore! Go on and search, but be quick about it!' And Catherine Ivanovna seized Looshin by the arm, and dragged him towards Sonia.

'I am ready, I ask no better – but be calm, madam, be calm!' he stammered. 'I see clearly that you are not afraid! But it must be done at the police-office; although, it is true, there are more than sufficient witnesses here. I am ready! Yet it is somewhat difficult for a man – considering her sex – if Amalia Ivanovna would kindly assist. It is not like this, though, that such matters are settled.'

'Have her searched by whom you please!' cried Catherine Ivanovna. 'Sonia, show them your pockets! There! there! Look, monster, you see it is empty; there was a handkerchief in it, nothing more, as you can prove to yourself! Now for the other pocket, now! There! there! Do you see?'

Not satisfied with emptying Sonia's pockets, Catherine Ivanovna turned them inside out, one after the other. But, at the very moment of her thus showing the lining of the right-hand pocket, there dropped out of it a small paper which fell at Looshin's feet. Everyone saw it, several even uttered a cry. Peter Petrovitch stooped to the ground, picked up the paper with his two fingers, and unfolded it *coram populo*. It was a hundred-rouble note, folded eight times. Peter Petrovitch held it up within sight of all, in order to leave no doubt as to Sonia's guilt.

'Thief! begone! Police! Where are the police?' shouted Madame Lippevechzel. 'She ought to be sent to Siberia! Away with her!'

Exclamations were heard on all sides. Raskolnikoff, silent, only left off looking at Sonia to cast from time to time a rapid glance at Looshin. The girl, immovable in her place, seemed more stupefied than surprised. All of a sudden she blushed, and covered her face with her hands.

'No, it is not I! I have taken nothing! I know nothing about it!' she cried in heartrending tones, whilst rushing towards Catherine Ivanovna, who opened her arms as a kind of inviolable refuge for the young girl.

'Sonia, Sonia, I do not believe it! You see that I do not believe it!' repeated Catherine Ivanovna, blind to the evidence. These words were accompanied by a thousand caresses, whilst showering kisses on the girl, seizing her hands and straining her in her arms like a child. 'You to have stolen something? But how stupid these people are! Good Heaven! You are idiots, idiots every one of you!' she cried out to those present. 'You do not as yet know this loving young heart! She rob? She? Why, I tell you, she would sell her last garment, she would go barefooted rather than leave you without help if you were in need – that is what she is! She even accepted the yellow ticket because my children were dying with hunger – she has sold herself for us! Oh! my poor husband, my poor dear husband! Great God! But, why don't you defend her, you, all of you, instead of remaining impassive? Rodion Romanovitch, why don't you take up the cudgels for her? Do you think her guilty? You, every one of you here, are not fit to be compared to her! Great God! come to her help!'

The tears, the supplications, and the despair of poor Catherine seemed to make a profound impression on the bystanders. Her consumptive face, parched lips, her almost inaudible voice, expressed so deep-seated a suffering, that it was almost impossible to remain unaffected by them. Peter Petrovitch at once awakened to gentler feelings. 'Madam! madam!' he exclaimed earnestly, 'this unpleasantness concerns you in no kind of way! Nobody thinks of accusing you of complicity; it was you yourself who, in turning the girl's pockets inside out, discovered the stolen note; that only suffices to establish your own complete innocence. I am disposed in every shape and form to show myself indulgent for an act to which misfortune may have impelled Sophia Semenovna, but why should she object to confess? She fears dishonour, I can well understand! It was her first fault, I believe! Perhaps she had lost her presence of mind! The thing is clear, perfectly clear! But look to what she exposes herself! Gentlemen,' said he to the bystanders, 'moved by pity, I am ready to forgive even now, in spite of the personal insults levelled at me.' Then, turning once more to Sonia, he added: 'Young girl, may this day's humiliation serve you as a lesson for the future! I shall not proceed further in this matter, bygones shall be bygones. Enough!'

Peter Petrovitch cast a hypocritical look at Raskolnikoff. Their eyes met; those of the young man flashed fire. As for Catherine Ivanovna, she seemed to have heard nothing, and continued to hug Sonia with a species of frenzy. In imitation of their mother, the children likewise pressed the girl in their little arms. Poletchka, without understanding what it was all about, sobbed as if she would break her very heart; her pretty face, bathed in tears, was resting on Sonia's shoulder.

But, all of a sudden, a sonorous voice was heard in the doorway: 'What a base thing to do!' Peter Petrovitch turned quickly round. 'What a base thing to do!' repeated Lebeziatnikoff, looking hard at Looshin. The latter felt a kind of shudder pass through him. Everyone saw, and remembered it afterwards. Lebeziatnikoff entered the room. 'And you dared to call upon me as a witness?' continued he, approaching the lawyer.

'What do you mean, Andreas Semenovitch? What are you talking about?' stammered Looshin.

'I mean that you are a calumniator, that is what I mean!' answered Lebeziatnikoff passionately. He was a prey to violent passion, and whilst looking hard at Peter Petrovitch, his small sickly eyes had an expression of unaccustomed harshness. Raskolnikoff listened intently, his gaze fixed on the young Socialist's countenance. There was a moment of silence. At first Peter Petrovitch was almost disconcerted.

'If it is I you mean – ' he stammered. 'But what is the matter with you? Are you in your sound senses?'

'Yes, I am in my sound senses, and you – you are a knave! How base! I have heard all, and have not spoken before because I wished to understand all; although I own there are yet some things I cannot account for – I am trying to find out what your motive can be for doing all this.'

'But what have I done? Have you nearly finished talking in riddles? You have been drinking, I fancy!'

'Base wretch I if one of us has been drinking, it is you rather than I! I never touch spirits, because such a thing is contrary to my principles! Just conceive that it is he, he himself, who, with his own hand, gave that hundred-rouble note to Sophia Semenovna! I saw it, I was a witness to it, and I can swear to it! It was he, he!' went on Lebeziatnikoff, addressing everyone by turns.

'Are you mad or not, you simpleton?' retorted Looshin passionately. 'She herself acknowledged here, but a moment ago, in presence of everybody, that she only received ten roubles from me. How then is it possible that I could have given her more?'

'I saw it, saw it with my own eyes!' repeated Andreas Semenovitch energetically, 'and, although it is in opposition to my principles, I am ready to swear to it in open court; I myself saw you stealthily slip the money in her pocket! Only, in my folly, I believed you were acting from generosity! At the moment you wished her goodbye at the door, whilst offering her your right hand, you slyly slipped in her pocket a piece of paper you were holding in your other hand. I saw it, I say, – saw it with my own eyes!'

Looshin grew pale. 'What yarn are you spinning us here?' retorted he insolently. 'How could you, when standing near the window, see the paper at all? Your wretched eyes have been the dupe of some illusion. You saw wrong, let me tell you!'

'By no means, there was no illusion! In spite of the distance I was at, I saw clearly and saw everything! I admit that it was difficult to see the paper from the position I was in – in so far your observation is a just one; but, in consequence of a particular circumstance, I knew for a positive fact that it was a hundred-rouble note. After you gave Sophia Semenovna ten roubles, I was then quite close to the table, I saw you at the same time take up a hundred-rouble note. This did not escape me, because at the very moment I was struck with an idea. When you had folded the paper, you held it tightly in the palm of your hand. I then thought no more about it, but, on rising, you passed it from your right hand to the left one, and nearly dropped it. I remember that distinctly, for I was struck again with the same idea – namely, that you were anxious to assist Sophia Semenovna without my knowing. You may imagine with what attention I was now following your doings. Yes, I saw you thrust the paper in her pocket. I saw it, I tell you once again, and I will swear to it!'

Lebeziatnikoff was almost suffocated with indignation. On all sides were heard various exclamations; most of them expressed astonishment, but some were proffered in a tone of menace. Everybody crowded round Peter Petrovitch. Catherine Ivanovna rushed to Lebeziatnikoff.

'Andreas Semenovitch! I have misjudged you! You – defend her! You alone – side with her! It is God, yes, God Himself, who has sent you to aid the orphan! Andreas Semenovitch, my dear friend, *batuchka*!' And Catherine Ivanovna, without seeming conscious of what she was doing, fell at the young man's feet.

'This is nonsense, sheer nonsense!' vociferated Looshin, beside himself with rage. 'You are talking folly, sir! – "I forgot, I remember, I remember, I forgot" – what is the meaning of such contradictions? To judge, then, from what you say, you wish to imply that I slipped a hundred roubles in her pocket? And pray, why? Pray, again with what object? What on earth can I have in common with that – '

'You wish to know why? That is what I cannot comprehend either – I merely confine myself to relating things as they occurred, without pretending to explain them, and, in so far, I can vouch for their entire precision! I am so very certain of my statement, you vile criminal, that I remember having asked myself a similar question at the very moment I was complimenting you by shaking hands. I asked myself why you should have made your present in so clandestine a fashion. Perhaps, said I to myself, he is so particular to hide his good act, knowing me to be on principle opposed to private charity, which, as he knows perfectly well, I look upon as a useless palliative. Then, again, I thought you wished to surprise Sophia Semenovna, for there are plenty of people who love to give to their favours the zest of surprise. But another idea came upon me. I fancied you wanted to try the girl – you wanted to know whether, on finding these hundred roubles in her pocket, she would come and thank you. Or, again, I thought perhaps you wished to evade her gratitude on the principle that the right hand ought not to know – In a word, God alone knows all the conjectures which occurred to my mind!

'Your conduct puzzled me to such an extent that I determined to think it over later on at my leisure; in the meanwhile, I thought that I should be wanting in delicacy if I were to let you know that I was a party to your secret. In the midst of all this, one fear came upon me: – I thought that Sophia Semenovna, not knowing your generosity, might perchance lose the note. That was why I made up my mind to come here: I wanted to take her aside to tell her how you had conjured the money into her pocket. But, previous to doing so, I called for a moment at Madame Kobyliatnikoff's to hand them the *General View of the Positive Method*, and to recommend specially Piderit's article (Wagner's is also worth something). A moment afterwards I came here, and was a witness to this scene! Now, answer me, could I have had all these ideas, could I have indulged in all that reasoning, if I had not seen you introduce the hundred roubles into Sophia Semenovna's pocket?'

When Andreas Semenovitch had had his say, he was overpowered with fatigue, and his face was bathed in perspiration. Alas! Even in Russian, he had some trouble to express himself suitably, although he knew no other language. His oratorical effort had exhausted him. His words, nevertheless, produced an extraordinary effect. The tone of sincerity with which he uttered them left conviction on the minds of his hearers. Peter Petrovitch felt that things were beginning to look bad for him.

'What do I care about the insane questions which suggest themselves to your mind!' he exclaimed. 'They are not proofs! You have probably dreamed all this idle talk! I tell you, you are lying, sir! You are lying, and are slandering me, to gratify a spite. The fact is, you dislike me, because I am opposed to the impious radicalism of your anti-social doctrines!'

But this attack, far from turning to Peter Petrovitch's account, only roused violent murmurs round about him.

'And that is all you have to say in reply! It is not much, after all!' replied Lebeziatnikoff. 'Send for the police! I will take my oath! One thing, however, remains a puzzle to me: what can have been the motive which induced him to commit so base an act? The miserable coward!'

Raskolnikoff stepped forward from the crowd. 'I can account for his conduct; and, if necessary, can also take my oath!' he said in a firm tone of voice. At first sight, the young man's tranquil assurance proved to everyone concerned that he knew the ins and outs of the mystery, and that the imbroglio was about to be cleared up.

'I understand all now, I understand all!' pursued Raskolnikoff, speaking pointedly to Lebeziatnikoff. 'From the very commencement of this incident, I suspected some contemptible intrigue. My suspicions were based on certain circumstances known to myself alone, and which I purpose going into, for they will show the matter in its true light. It is you, Andreas Semenovitch, who, by your invaluable statements, have definitely shed light in my mind. I must request everyone to pay attention. This gentleman,' he went on, pointing to Peter Petrovitch, 'has of late solicited the hand of my sister, Eudoxia Romanovna Raskolnikoff. Having only of late come to St Petersburg, he called to see me the day before yesterday. But at our very first interview we commenced quarrelling, and I ejected him, as two witnesses can prove. This man is a very malicious individual. The day before yesterday, I was not as yet aware that he was lodging with you, Andreas Semenovitch – thanks to this circumstance, which I was unacquainted with, he was present the day before yesterday, that is, on the very day of our quarrel, at the moment when, as a friend of the late Mr Marmeladoff, I offered his wife, Catherine Ivanovna, a little money to meet the funeral expenses. He immediately wrote to my mother, informing her that I had given this money, not to Catherine Ivanovna, but to Sophia Semenovna, speaking at the same time, of this girl in the most outrageous manner, and leading my mother to suppose that I was on too intimate terms with her. His object, you will understand, was to get me in bad odour with my relatives by insinuating that I spent in debauch the money they deprive themselves of to supply my wants.

'Last night, in an interview with my mother and sister, an interview at which he was present, I established the truth of facts misrepresented by himself. The money in question, I explained had been given to Catherine Ivanovna to pay for her husband's funeral, and not, as alleged, to Sophia Semenovna, whose very face had been unknown to me till that day. Enraged to see that his slander did not obtain the wished-for result, he grossly insulted my mother and sister. An irreparable rupture was the result: he was shown the door. All this occurred last night. Now, reflect, and you will understand what interest he had in establishing Sophia Semenovna's guilt. If he had succeeded in proving her guilty of theft, it was I who would be guilty in the opinion of my mother and sister, since I had not feared to introduce the latter to a thief; he, on the contrary, whilst injuring me, had protected my sister's, his future wife's, respectability. In a word, his plan was to set me at variance with my family, so that he might be restored to their favour. At the same time he would be avenged on me, having reason to believe that I was greatly interested in the honour and comfort of Sophia Semenovna. This was his scheme! You see how well I understand it. Such is the explanation of his conduct, and there can be no other!'

With these words Raskolnikoff finished his remarks, which were frequently interrupted by the exclamations of an audience who were, on the whole, extremely attentive. But, in spite of interruptions, his observations preserved to the very end an imperturbable calmness, assurance, and clearness. His vibrating voice, his convinced accent, and his severe face profoundly affected his hearers.

'Yes, yes, it is so!' Lebeziatnikoff made haste to admit. 'You must be right, for, at the very moment that Sophia Semenovna entered my room, he asked me with great interest if you were there, if I had seen you among Catherine Ivanovna's guests. He drew me into the recess of a window to whisper this question to me. He must have desired your presence! Yes, yes, you are quite right!'

Looshin, who was very pale, remained silent, and smiled scornfully. He seemed to be looking for some way of getting out of his difficulty. Perhaps he would gladly have made off there and then; but, at that moment, retreat seemed almost impossible – to have left would have been an implicit acknowledgement of the justice of the accusations made against him, and to own his culpability in having slandered Sophia Semenovna. On the other hand, the attitude of the various guests after their carouse was anything but an assuring one. The sutler, though without a very accurate idea of the matter under discussion, shouted louder than anybody else, and proposed certain measures by no means pleasant for Looshin. Nearly everybody was more or less intoxicated; moreover, the scene had gathered together in the room a number of other lodgers who had not feasted with Catherine Ivanovna The three Poles, who were greatly excited, kept uttering in their own language all sorts of threats against Peter Petrovitch's person.

Sonia listened with sustained attention, but did not as yet seem to have recovered her presence of mind; one might also fancy that she was just recovering from a fainting-fit. She did not take her eyes off Raskolnikoff, feeling that her sole hope was in him. Catherine Ivanovna seemed in great suffering, for, at every breath she took, a husky sound escaped from her lungs. The silliest face was that of Amalia Ivanovna. She seemed as if she could understand nothing – with gaping mouth, looked on amazed. All she could make out was that Peter Petrovitch was in a bad way. Raskolnikoff wished again to speak, but was obliged to give up his intention through inability to make himself heard. On all sides fell insults and threats against Looshin, around whom a compact and hostile group had collected. But the lawyer did not lose countenance. Knowing that his game was up, he had recourse to effrontery.

'Permit me, gentlemen, permit me, but do not crowd round me like that – once more permit me to pass,' he said endeavouring to make his way. 'It is quite useless, I assure you, to seek to intimidate me by menace, such trifles don't frighten me. It is you on the contrary, gentlemen, who will have to answer in a court of law for your connivance in a criminal act. The theft has been more than proved, and I shall lay my charge. We have an enlightened – fortunately not besotted magistracy, it will challenge the testimony of two sceptics, of two confirmed revolutionary persons, who accuse me with a view to personal vengeance, as they themselves have most foolishly admitted – permit me!"

'I will no longer breathe the same air as yourself, and I must ask you to leave my room – all is up between us! When I reflect that I have for the last fortnight done my utmost to –'

'Only just now, Andreas Semenovitch, I announced to you my departure at the time you were imploring me to stay; I will now, however, say no more than that you are an idiot! wish you every kind of enlightenment – mental as well as ocular. Permit me, gentlemen!'

He succeeded in making his way out, but the ex-sutler, finding that insult was not a very effective punishment, took a glass from the table, and threw it with all his might in the direction of Peter Petrovitch. Unfortunately, the projectile, meant for the latter, caught Amalia Ivanovna, who began to utter piercing screams. Whilst brandishing the glass, the sutler lost his balance, and rolled heavily under the table. Looshin returned to Lebeziatnikoff's rooms, and an hour afterwards left the house. Being naturally timid, Sonia had known, long before this incident, that her position exposed her to many a charge, and that the first best-comer might insult her with impunity. Up to the present, she had always hoped to be able to disarm ill-will, by dint of circumspection, gentleness, and humility, towards one and all. This illusion had now vanished. She had, doubtless, patience enough to bear her late accusation with resignation and without a murmur, but for a moment the deception was too cruel a one. Although her innocence had gained a victory over calumny, her heart sank, as soon as her first dread had passed away and she was in a position to explain things to herself, at the thought of her abandonment and isolation in the world. A nervous crisis set in, and, beside herself, she rushed from the room and returned to her own abode in all haste. Her exit took place only a few moments after Looshin's.

The accident that had happened to Amalia Ivanovna had caused general hilarity, but the lady in question took it so badly to heart that, in a burst of passion at the expense of Catherine Ivanovna, who, overcome by pain and anguish, had been obliged to take to her bed, she exclaimed: 'Begone from here! At once! Begone!' Whilst yelling these words in an infuriated tone of voice, Madame Lippevechzel seized every article belonging to her lodger, and threw it in a heap on the floor. Exhausted and faint, poor Catherine Ivanovna nevertheless jumped from her bed and rushed on Amalia Ivanovna. But the contest was too unequal a one – the landlady had no difficulty in repelling the assault.

'What! It is not enough to have slandered Sonia, but this creature must now attack me! What! Am I to be ejected on the very day my poor husband has been taken to his grave? And, after having partaken of my hospitality, am I to be turned adrift, with my children? Where shall I go? Where shall I go?' sobbed the poor woman. 'Great God!' she exclaimed all at once, rolling her glittering eyes, 'is it possible that there is no justice? Whom wilt thou defend, unless it be us, we who are fatherless? But wait! There are yet magistrates and law courts left in the world. I shall appeal to them! Wait but a while, infamous woman! Poletchka, stay with the children, I shall be back in a moment. In case you are turned away, wait in the street. We shall see if there is any justice left here below!'

Catherine Ivanovna placed, bandanna-fashion, on her head the identical green handkerchief mentioned in Marmeladoff's story, and, battling her way through the tipsy and chattering crowd of lodgers who persisted in haunting the room, she went, with woebegone face, down into the street, to search at all costs where justice could be found. Poletchka, frightened out of her life, clung to her little brother and sister; and the three little children, huddled together in a corner next to the travelling-trunk, awaited with fear and trembling their mother's return. Amalia Ivanovna, more like one of the Furies, moved to and fro in the room, howling with rage and throwing about her whatever came in her way. Some of the lodgers commented on the preceding scene, while others quarrelled; and others, again, struck up refrains.

'It is time I should be off!' thought Raskolnikoff. 'And now, Sophia Semenovna, we shall see what you are likely to say after this!' And he started in the direction of the girl's home.

Chapter 4

RASHKOLNIKOFF HAD VALIANTLY pleaded the cause of Sonia against that of Looshin, although he himself had his own heavy share of cares and sorrows. Independently of the interest he felt in the girl, he had joyfully, after the morning's torture, seized the opportunity of shaking off impressions which had become unbearable. On the other hand, his pending interview with Sonia preoccupied, nay even frightened, him at times: he was *bound* to reveal to her who it was that had killed Elizabeth, and, anticipating the pain of such a confession, he strove to dispel the very thought of it.

When, on leaving Catherine Ivanovna's he had said: 'And now, Sophia Semenovna, what will you say after this?' He was, like the gladiator excited by the contest, still warm from his victory over Looshin, who had thrown down the glove of challenge. But, strange to say, when he reached Kapernasumoff's place, his self-possession forsook him all at once, to make way for fear. Undecided, he stopped at the door, saying: 'Must I confess who has killed Elizabeth?' The question was a strange one, for, at the moment of putting it, he felt not only the impossibility of his making the confession, but his wish to put it off a moment longer. As yet, he did not know why it was impossible – he only *felt* it to be so; and he was almost weighed down by the painful consciousness of his weakness face to face with necessity. To spare himself further torture, he hastened to open the door, and, before entering, looked at Sonia. She was seated, her elbows resting on her small table, her face hidden in her hands. On perceiving Raskolnikoff, she forthwith rose to meet him, as if she had been in expectation of him.

'What would have become of me without you?' she asked passionately, whilst accompanying him to the middle of the room. According to appearances, she only thought of the service the young man had done her, and she was anxious to thank him in consequence. Then she stood waiting. Raskolnikoff approached the table and sat down on the chair the girl had just vacated. She remained standing close to him, just precisely as she had done the night before.

'Well, Sonia,' said he, perceiving all at once that his voice trembled, 'the whole charge was based on your social position, and the habits it implies. Did you understand that fully?'

Sonia's face assumed an expression of sorrow. 'Don't speak again as you did yesterday!' she replied. 'Pray, pray don't begin like that again! I have suffered more than enough.' She hastened to smile, fearing lest her reproach might pain her visitor. 'Just now, I left there, more like a madwoman. What is going on now? I was anxious to return, but I fancied all along that you would come.'

He informed her that Amalia Ivanovna had turned the Marmeladoffs out of doors, and that Catherine Ivanovna had gone in search of justice!

'Heavens!' cried Sonia. 'Let us go!' Upon this she seized her cape.

'Always the same thing!' replied Raskolnikoff vexed. 'You think only of them! Stay a moment with me.'

'But Catherine Ivanovna?'

'Well! As for Catherine Ivanovna, she will not fail to call, you may be sure,' he replied in a disappointed tone of voice. 'If she does not find you, it will be your own fault.' Sonia sat down, a prey to cruel perplexity. Raskolnikoff reflected with drooping eyes. 'I admit that all Looshin wanted to do today was to injure your reputation,' he began, without looking at Sonia. 'But if it had suited him to have had you arrested, and if neither Lebeziatnikoff nor I had been there as we were, you would now be in prison, would you not?'

'Yes!' said the girl in a feeble voice. 'Yes,' she repeated mechanically, indifferent to the conversation, in consequence of the anxiety she experienced.

'I might indeed not have been there at all; and it was quite a chance that Lebeziatnikoff came in as he did.' Sonia remained silent. 'If, now, you had been imprisoned, what would have happened? Do you remember what I told you yesterday?' She continued silent, whilst he awaited for a moment her reply. 'I thought you were again going to exclaim: "Pray, do not talk of that case!" ' resumed Raskolnikoff with somewhat far-fetched laughter. 'Are you still silent?' he asked, after a moment. 'Then I suppose I must keep the conversation going. I am anxious to know how you would solve a question, to quote Lebeziatnikoff.' (His embarrassment was becoming apparent.) 'No, I am speaking seriously. Suppose, Sonia, that you had been previously aware of Looshin's intentions, and that you had known his projects meant to bring about the ruin of Catherine Ivanovna and of her children, to say nothing of your own (for that you count for nothing); suppose that, as a consequence, Poletchka should be condemned to a life like your own; suppose such to be the case, and it were to depend on you either to annihilate Looshin, thereby saving Catherine Ivanovna and her family, or let Looshin continue his infamous machinations – what would you decide upon, I am anxious to know?'

Sonia looked at him with anxiety. Under such words, pronounced in a faltering voice, she feared some far-fetched mental reserve. 'I expected some such question,' she said, looking at him.

'That is possible; but once again, tell me, what would you decide upon?'

'What interest can you have in knowing what I would do in a contingency which may not even come about?' answered Sonia with repugnance.

'Then you would rather let Looshin live and commit villainies? And yet you have not courage to say that you would do so?'

'Let me tell you that I am not in the secrets of Divine Providence. And what can be the good of asking me what I would do in an improbable case? Why such idle questions? How is it possible that the existence of some other person should depend on my will? And who has selected me to act as arbitrator of the life and death of others?'

'Introduce Divine Providence, and there is nothing more to be said!' retorted Raskolnikoff in a bitter tone of voice.

'Tell me, candidly, what have you to say?' cried Sonia. 'As yet, you are only using subterfuges. Have you only come to torture me?'

She could no longer bear it, and burst into tears. For five minutes he watched her with a gloomy air. 'You are right, Sonia,' he said, at last, in a low tone. A sudden change had taken place in him; his forced self-possession, the off-hand manner which he had previously affected, had suddenly disappeared – he could hardly be heard now. 'I told you, yesterday, that I would not come to beg pardon, and yet I have almost commenced this interview by doing so. When speaking of Looshin, I was seeking to excuse myself, Sonia!'

He wished to smile, but, do what he would, his countenance retained its sorrow-stricken look. He lowered his head, covering his face with his hands. All at once, he fancied that he was beginning to hate Sonia. Surprised, frightened even, at so strange a discovery, he suddenly raised his head and attentively considered the girl, who, in her turn, fixed on him a look of anxious love. Hatred fled from Raskolnikoff's heart. It was not that; he had only mistaken the nature of the sentiment he experienced. It signified that the fatal moment had come. Once more he hid his face in his hands and bowed his head. Suddenly he grew pale, rose, and, after looking at Sonia, he mechanically went and sat on her bed, without uttering a single word. Raskolnikoff's impression was the very same he had experienced when standing behind the old woman – he had loosened the hatchet from the loop, and said to himself: 'There is not a moment to be lost!'

'What is the matter?' asked Sonia, in bewilderment.

No reply. Raskolnikoff had relied on making explanations under quite different conditions, and did not himself understand what was now at work within him. She gently approached him, sat on the bed by his side, and waited, without taking her eyes from his face. Her heart beat as if it would break. The situation was becoming unbearable; he turned towards the girl his lividly pale face, his lips twitched with an effort to speak. Fear had seized upon Sonia.

'What is the matter with you?' she repeated, moving slightly away from him.

'Nothing, Sonia; don't be afraid. It is not worth while, it is all nonsense!' he murmured, like a man absent in mind. 'Only, why can I have come to torment you?' added he all at once, looking at his interlocutress. 'Yes, why? I keep on asking myself this question, Sonia.'

Perhaps he had done so a quarter of an hour before, but at this moment his weakness was such that he scarcely retained consciousness; a continued trembling shook his whole frame.

'Oh! How you suffer!' said she, in a voice full of emotion, whilst looking at him.

'It is nothing! But this is the matter in question, Sonia.' (For a moment or so, a pale smile hovered on his lips.) 'You remember what I wished to tell you yesterday?' Sonia waited anxiously. 'I told you, on parting, that I was, perhaps, bidding you farewell for ever, but that if I should come today, I would tell you who it was that killed Elizabeth.' She began to tremble in every limb. 'Well, then, that is why I have come.'

'I know you told me that yesterday,' she went on in a shaky voice. 'How do you know that?' she added vivaciously. Sonia breathed with an effort. Her face grew more and more pale.

'I know it.'

'Has *he* been discovered?' she asked, timidly, after a moment's silence.

'No, *he* has not been discovered.'

For another moment she remained silent. 'Then how do you know it?' she at length asked, in an almost unintelligible voice.

He turned towards the girl, and looked at her with a singular rigidity, whilst a feeble smile fluttered on his lips. 'Guess!' he said.

Sonia felt on the point of being seized with convulsions. 'But you – why frighten me like this?' she asked, with a childlike smile.

'I know it, because I am very intimate with *him*!' went on Raskolnikoff, whose look remained fixed on her, as if he had not strength to turn his eyes aside. 'Elizabeth – he had no wish to murder her – he killed her without premeditation. He only intended to kill the old woman, when he should find her alone. He went to her house – but at the very moment Elizabeth came in – he was there – and he killed her.'

A painful silence followed upon those words. For a moment both continued to look at one another. 'And so you can't guess?' he asked abruptly, feeling like a man on the point of throwing himself from the top of a steeple.

'No,' stammered Sonia, in a scarcely audible voice.

'Try again.'

At the moment he pronounced these words, Raskolnikoff experienced afresh, in his heart of hearts, that feeling of chilliness he knew so well. He looked at Sonia, and suddenly read on her face the same expression as on that of Elizabeth, when the wretched woman recoiled from the murderer advancing towards her, hatchet in hand. In that supreme moment Elizabeth had raised her arm, as children do when they begin to be afraid, and ready to weep, fix a glaring immovable glance on the object which frightens them. In the same way Sonia's face expressed indescribable fear. She also raised her arm, and gently pushed Raskolnikoff aside, whilst touching his breast with her hand, and then gradually drew back without ceasing to look hard at him. Her fear affected the young man, who, for his part, began to gaze on her with a scared expression.

'Have you guessed?' he murmured at last.

'My God!' exclaimed Sonia.

Then she sank exhausted on the bed, and buried her face in the pillows; a moment after, however, she rose with a rapid movement, approached him, and, seizing him by both hands, which her slender fingers clutched like nippers, she fixed on him a long look. Had she made a mistake? She hoped so, but she had no sooner cast a look on Raskolnikoff's face than the suspicion which had flashed on her mind became certainty.

'Enough, Sonia! Enough! Spare me!' he implored in a plaintive voice. The event upset all his calculations, for it certainly was not *thus* that he had intended to confess his crime.

Sonia seemed beside herself, she jumped from her bed, went to the middle of the room wringing her hands, she then quickly returned in the same way, sat once more by the young man's side, almost touching him with her shoulder. Suddenly she shivered, uttered a cry, and, without knowing why, fell on her knees before Raskolnikoff. 'You are lost!' she exclaimed, with an accent of despair. And, rising suddenly, she threw herself on his neck and kissed him, whilst lavishing on him tokens of tenderness.

Raskolnikoff broke away, and, with a sad smile, looked at the girl: 'I do not understand you, Sonia. You kiss me after I told you *that* – You cannot be conscious of what you are doing.'

She did not hear the remark. 'No, at this moment there cannot be a more wretched man on earth than you are!' she exclaimed with a transport of passion, whilst bursting into sobs.

Raskolnikoff felt his heart grow soft under the influence of a sentiment which for some time past he had not felt. He did not try to fight against the feeling; two tears spurted from his eyes and remained on the lashes. 'Then you will not forsake me, Sonia?' said he with an almost suppliant look.

'No, no; never, nowhere!' she cried. 'I shall follow you, shall follow you everywhere! Heaven! Wretch that I am! And why have I not known you sooner? Why did you not come before? Heaven!'

'You see I have come.'

'Now? What is to be done now? Together, together!' she went on, with a kind of exaltation, and once more she kissed the young man. 'Yes, I will go with you to the galleys!'

These words caused Raskolnikoff a painful feeling; a bitter and almost haughty smile appeared on his lips. 'Perhaps I may not yet wish to go to the galleys, Sonia,' said he.

The girl rapidly turned her eyes on him. She had up to the present experienced no more than immense pity for an unhappy man. This statement, and the tone of voice in which it was pronounced, suddenly recalled to the girl that the wretched man was an assassin. She cast on him an astonished look. As yet, she did not know how nor why he had become a criminal. At this moment, these questions suggested themselves to her, and, once more doubting, she asked herself: 'He, he a murderer? Is such a thing possible? But no, it cannot be true! Where am I?' she asked herself, as if she could have believed herself the sport of a dream. 'How is it possible that you, being what you are, can have thought of such a thing? Oh! why?'

'To thieve, if you wish to know. Cease, Sonia!' he replied in wearied and rather vexed accents.

Sonia remained stupefied; suddenly a cry escaped her; 'Were you hungry? Did you do so to help your mother? Speak!'

'No, Sonia! no!' he stammered, drooping his head. 'I was not so poor as all that. It is true I wanted to help my mother, but that was not the real reason – Do not torment me, Sonia!'

The girl beat her hands together. 'Is it possible that such a thing can be real? Heaven! is it possible? How can I believe such a thing? You say you killed to rob; you, who deprive yourself of all in favour of others! Ah!' she cried suddenly. 'That money you gave to Catherine Ivanovna! – that money! Heavens! can it be that?'

'No, Sonia!' he interrupted somewhat sharply. 'This money comes from another source, I assure you. It was my mother who sent it to me during my sickness, through the intervention of a merchant, and I had just received it when I gave it. Razoumikhin saw it himself, he even went so far as to receive it for me. The money was really my own property.' Sonia listened in perplexity, and strove to understand. 'As for the old woman's money, to tell the truth, I really do not know whether there was any money at all,' he went on hesitatingly. 'I took from her neck a well-filled chamois-leather purse. But I never examined the contents, probably because I had no time to do so. I took different things, sleeve-links, watch-chains. These things I hid, in the same way as the purse, on the following day, under a large stone in a yard which looks out on the V— Prospect. Everything is still there.'

Sonia listened with avidity. 'But why did you take nothing, since, as you tell me, you committed murder to steal?' she went on, clinging to a last and very vague hope.

'I don't know – as yet I am undecided whether to take this money or not,' replied Raskolnikoff in the same hesitating voice; then he smiled. 'What silly tale have I been telling you?'

'Can he be mad?' Sonia asked herself, but she soon dispelled such an idea; no, it was something else, which she most certainly did not understand.

'Do you know what I am going to tell you, Sonia?' he went on in a convinced tone: 'If nothing but need had urged me to commit a murder,' laying stress on every word, and his look, although frank, was more or less puzzling, 'I should now be *happy*! Let me tell you that! And what can the motive be to you, since I told you just now that I had acted badly?' he cried despairingly, a moment afterwards. 'What was the good of this foolish triumph over myself? Ah! Sonia, was it for that I came to you?' She once more wished to speak, but remained silent. 'Yesterday, I made a proposal to you that we should both of us depart together, because you are all that is left to me.'

'Why did you wish me to accompany you?' asked the girl timidly.

'Not to rob or to kill, I assure you,' answered Raskolnikoff, with a caustic smile. 'We are not of the same way of thinking. And – do you know, Sonia? – it is only of late that I have known why I asked you yesterday to accompany me. When I asked you to do so, I did not as yet know what it would lead to. I see it now. I have but one wish – it is that you should not leave me. You will not do so, will you, Sonia?' She clasped his hand. 'And why have I told her this? Why make such a confession?' he exclaimed, a moment afterwards. He looked at her with infinite compassion, whilst his voice expressed the most profound despair. 'I see, Sonia, that you are waiting for some kind of explanation, but what am I to say? You understand nothing about the matter, and I should only be causing you additional pain. I see you are once more commencing to weep and to embrace me. Why do so at all? Because, failing in courage to bear my own burden, I have imposed it on another – because I seek in the anguish of others some mitigation for my own. And you can love a coward like that?'

'But you are likewise suffering!' exclaimed Sonia.

For a moment he experienced a new feeling of tenderness. 'Sonia, my disposition is a bad one, and that can explain much. I have come because I am bad. Some would not have done so. But I am an infamous coward. Why, once more, have I come? I shall never forgive myself for that!'

'No, no! – on the contrary, you have done well to come,' cried Sonia; 'it is better, much better, I should know all!'

Raskolnikoff looked at her with sorrowful eye. 'I was ambitious to become another Napoleon; that was why I committed a murder. Can you understand it now?'

'No,' answered Sonia, naïvely and in a timid voice. 'But speak! speak! – I shall understand all!'

'You will, say you? Good! We shall see!' For some time Raskolnikoff collected his ideas. 'The fact is, that one day, I asked myself the following question: "Supposing Napoleon to have been in my place, supposing that to commence his career he had neither had Toulon, nor Egypt, nor the crossing of Mont Blanc, but, in lieu of all these brilliant exploits, he was on the point of committing a murder with a view to secure his future, would he have recoiled at the idea of killing an old woman, and of robbing her of three thousand roubles? Would he have agreed that such a deed was too much wanting in prestige and much too – criminal a one? For a long time I have split my head on that question, and could not help experiencing a feeling of shame when I finally came to the conclusion that he not only would not have hesitated, but that he would not have understood the possibility of such a thing. Every other expedient being out of his reach, he would not have flinched, he would have done so without the smallest scruple. Hence, I ought not to hesitate – being justified on the authority of Napoleon! You think that laughable? You are quite right.'

The girl had no kind of desire to laugh. 'Tell me frankly – without precedents,' she said in a more timid and almost indistinct voice.

He turned towards her, looked at her sadly, and took her hands. 'You are indeed right, Sonia. What I have been saying is absurd – is nothing but gibberish! As you know already, my mother is almost penniless.

Circumstances have given my sister the opportunity of a good education, and in consequence she is condemned to the drudgery of teaching. I was their sole hope. I entered the University, but, for want of means, was obliged to put a stop to my studies. Supposing even I had continued them: – I might, looking at everything in a most favourable light, at the expiration of ten or fifteen years, have been appointed to a mastership at a public school, or have obtained some kind of Government position with a salary of a thousand roubles.' (He gave the impression of repeating a lesson.) 'But, in the meanwhile, care and sorrow would have ruined my mother's health, and as for my sister – something worse might have happened to her. To deprive oneself of everything, to leave one's mother in want, to submit to a sister's dishonour – is that life? And to undergo all that to obtain – what? After having buried my kith and kin, I might have reared a fresh family, with the probability of leaving, at my death, wife and children without a mouthful of bread! Well – well, I argued with myself that with the old woman's money, I should cease to be on my mother's hands, that I could again return to the University, and thus secure an introduction to life – that was all. Of course I was wrong to kill the woman – but enough!' Raskolnikoff seemed exhausted, and sank his head with dejection.

'That was not it! that was not it!' cried Sonia plaintively. 'Is it possible? – no, there was something else!'

'You are of opinion that there was something else! And yet I have told you the whole truth!'

'The whole truth! Oh! heavens!'

'After all, Sonia, all I did was to kill some ignoble malevolent vermin.'

'But yet the vermin was a human being.'

'I am well aware that it was not vermin in the literal meaning of the word,' continued Raskolnikoff, looking at her with strange look. 'Besides, I am not talking common-sense,' he added. 'You are right, Sonia, that is not it. Totally different motives impelled me! For some time past I have avoided human intercourse, Sonia – and this conversation has given me a violent headache.'

His eyes glistened with a feverish gleam. Delirium had almost affected him again; a restless smile hovered on his lips. Beneath his forced animation could be read extreme lassitude. Sonia knew that he was suffering. She also was beginning to lose her self-control. 'What singular language! To offer similar explanations as plausible ones!' She was thoroughly amazed and wrung her hands in an excess of despair.

'No, Sonia, it is not that!' he went on, suddenly raising his head; his thoughts had all at once taken a new turn, and he seemed to have acquired, in consequence, another lease of vivacity. 'It is not that! Conceive rather that I am excessively vain, envious, ill-disposed, vindictive, and, what is more, inclined to folly. I told you just now that I had been obliged to leave the University. I might perhaps have been able to remain. My mother would have paid my fees, and I could have gained enough by work of some kind for food and clothing, I could have accomplished that! My lessons were bringing me in fifty kopecks each. Razoumikhin works hard, I can tell you! But I was exasperated and would not. Yes, exasperated is the word! Then I took to my rooms as the spider does to its corner. You knew my den – you visited me once, I think. Do you know, Sonia, that a man's mind becomes paralysed in small poky rooms? How I used to detest the place! And yet I could not leave them. I stopped there whole days, always in bed, unwilling to read, indifferent even to food. I used to say to myself, "If Nastasia brings me up anything, I will take it; if not, I will go without." I was too angry to ask for anything! I had given up reading and sold my books; my notebooks are covered with an inch of dust. In the evening I was without light, for want of means to buy candles; I ought to have studied, but would not – no, I preferred musing on my couch. I need not tell you what my vagaries were all about. Then it was that I commenced to think – But I am wrong! I am not telling things correctly! I used to keep on asking myself: As you know that the majority are fools, why not try and be more enlightened than they? Then I admitted, Sonia, that, if a man were to wait for the moment when everybody else should be enlightened, very considerable patience would be required. Later on, I got so far as to acknowledge that that moment would never come about, that men would never change, and that one would lose one's time in striving to improve them! I am quite correct! Such is the rule. I now know, Sonia, that the foremost amongst them is he who possesses marked intelligence. The man who dares much is the right man in his fellow's opinion. The one who defies and scorns them acquires their respect! That has always been and always will be! Not to be able to observe that, is a sign of blindness!'

Whilst speaking thus, Raskolnikoff looked at Sonia, but he was no longer troubled to know if she understood. He was a prey to a gloomy fanaticism. For a very long time he had had no kind of dealing with other men. The girl understood that this austere code was his belief as well as his law.

'Then I became certain, Sonia,' he went on; growing more and more excited, 'that power is only given to the man who dare stoop to pick it up. Nothing more is needed, except courage. From the moment this truth had dawned upon me – a truth as clear as the light of the sun – I longed to dare, and I committed murder. All I wanted was to do some daring thing, Sonia; that was my sole motive!'

'Cease, cease, I pray!' cried the girl, beside herself. 'You turned away from God, and God has punished you, by giving you up to Satan!'

'Then, by the way, Sonia, do you mean to infer that when those ideas came upon me in my room, it was Satan who was tempting me?'

'Cease! Jest not, unbelieving man; you understand nothing! O Lord! will he ever understand?'

'I am not jesting, Sonia; I am not, indeed. I know that it was Satan who was tempting me. But, Sonia, say no more, I ask of you!' he repeated, with gloomy persistency. 'I know all. Whatever you may say to me, I have said to myself, over and over again, whilst dreaming in the dark. Oh! the inner struggles I have had! How unbearable my reflections were, and how I longed to throw them off for ever! Do you think that I went thither like a hare-brained madman! Far from it. I acted on ripe reflection, and that was my loss! Do you think I indulged in illusions? When I examined myself as to how far I really had a right to power, I knew full well that my right was naught, from the fact of doubting such a thing. When I asked myself if a human creature was so much vermin, I comprehended that it was not so for me, but for some audacious individual who would not have questioned such an idea, and would have gone on his way without vexing himself about such a thing. Why, the very fact of asking myself: "Would Napoleon have murdered this woman?" was sufficient proof that I was no Napoleon. At last I gave up looking for subtle justifications. I wished to commit murder without casuistic argument – to do so only for myself, and nothing else! Even in so terrible a thing, I scorned beguiling my conscience. When I committed murder, it was not to relieve my mother's misfortunes, nor to devote to the wellbeing of humanity the power and wealth which, in my opinion, such a deed ought to help me to acquire. No, no, such thoughts were not mine. At that moment, I did not in any way care to know if I should ever benefit anyone, or if I should continue, for the remainder of my life, a social parasite! Neither was money the main factor in the deed – no, another reason induced me to commit it. I see that now. Understand me: if the past could be recalled, I should most probably not do so again. But, at the time being, I longed to know if I was vermin, like the majority – or a Man, in the full acceptance of the word – whether, in fact, I had the power to break through obstacles; if I was a timorous creature, or if I had the right –'

'What! the right to kill?' cried Sonia, stupefied.

'Yes, Sonia!' was the irritable reply; a longer reply was on his lips, but he scornfully abstained from putting it into shape. 'Do not interrupt me, Sonia! I only wished to prove one thing to you: Satan led me to the house of the old woman, making me understand that I had no kind of right to go there, considering that I am vermin as much as others! He mocked me – hence I am now here with you! If I were no vermin, should I have paid you this visit? Listen! Upon going to the house of the old woman, I only wished to make an *experiment* – Don't forget that! – '

'And you committed murder, murder?'

'But let us see how I did so! Do men kill as I did? Do they set about the matter in the way I set about it, when starting with such an intention? You shall know all the details some day – Did I really kill the old woman? No, it was myself I killed! – it was myself I have irrevocably ruined! As for the old woman, it was Satan, and not I, who killed her. But enough, enough Sonia, enough! leave me!' he cried all at once in a heartrending voice, 'leave me!' Raskolnikoff rested his elbow on his knees, and convulsively gripped his head between his hands.

'How he is suffering!' groaned Sonia.

'And what must be done now? Tell me!' he asked, suddenly raising his head. His features were terribly distorted.

'What must be done?' exclaimed the girl, rushing up to him, whilst her eyes, which had hitherto been filled with tears, brightened up all of a sudden. 'Rise!' (Saying which, she seized Raskolnikoff by the shoulder; he rose slightly, looking at Sonia with astonishment.) 'Go forthwith, go this very moment to the nearest public place, prostrate yourself, kiss the earth you have stained, bow down in every direction, and proclaim at the top of your voice to the passers-by, "I am a murderer!" and God will give you peace again! Will you go? Will you go?' she asked trembling, whilst seizing his hands with ten-fold strength, and fixing on him a burning glance.

The girl's sudden exaltation plunged Raskolnikoff in a profound stupor. 'You wish me to go to the galleys, then, Sonia? You wish me to accuse myself, is it not so?' he asked in his depressed way.

'You must make atonement, so that you may be redeemed thereby!'

'I shall not accuse myself, Sonia!'

'And yet live? And how will you live?' she replied forcibly. 'Is such a thing possible under existing circumstances? How look your mother in the face? (What, oh! what will become of them now?) But what am I talking about? Have you not already left mother and sister? I now see why you have broken with friends and family. Heavens!' she continued, 'he himself understands it all now! How keep from human intercourse? What will become of you?'

'Be reasonable, Sonia,' continued Raskolnikoff, gently. 'Why give myself up to the authorities? What should I say to them? What has occurred is of no importance – they themselves make away with thousands of people, and even take a pride in doing so. They are cowardly scamps, Sonia! I will not go. What should I say to them? That I have been guilty of murder, and that, not daring to benefit by the stolen money, I went and hid it under a stone?' he added with a splenetic smile. 'Why, they would laugh at me, they would call me a fool, for not having made use of it. Fancy! – a cowardly fool! They could not understand such a thing, Sonia, they are incapable of understanding. Why, then, give myself up? No, I shall do no such thing. Therefore, Sonia, be reasonable, I beg – '

'And to carry a burden like that – a lifetime!'

'I shall get used to it,' he replied in a fierce tone. 'Listen!' he went on a moment later, more or less moved, 'it is time to speak seriously; I am here to tell you that the police are in search of me, that they are going to arrest me – '

'Ah!' exclaimed Sonia, alarmed.

'Well, what is the matter with you? Since you are anxious that I should go to the galleys, why be afraid? But one thing, however – they have not got me yet. I will give them some trouble, and everything will end in smoke. Positive clue they have none whatever. I certainly did run great danger yesterday, and I really believed that it was all up with me. Today, the danger is over. All their proofs go either way – I mean, the charges against me I am able to explain away to my advantage, do you hear? and I should have no difficulty in doing so, for I have gained experience. And yet, I am positive that I shall be imprisoned. It would have happened today, but for a lucky circumstance; and I still run the risk of finding myself under lock and key before night. But that is nothing, Sonia. They will arrest me, but they will also be compelled to let me go, because they are without actual proof, and, you may depend, will get none out of me. With suppositions only, such as they have got, a man is not condemned. But, enough! I only wished to warn you. As for my mother and sister, I shall manage in such a way that they shall not be upset. My sister is now out of reach of want; all I have to do is to make sure as far as my mother is concerned. That is all. Whatever you do, be prudent; and as soon as I am in prison you will come and see me?'

'Yes, yes!'

They were seated side by side, sad and dejected, like two ship-wrecked persons whom the tempest had cast on some desert-shore. In looking at Sonia, Raskolnikoff was convinced of her love; and, strange to say, the tender love, of which he was the object, suddenly caused him a pang of grief. He had visited Sonia, saying that his sole refuge, his sole hope, was in her; he had yielded to an irresistible desire to air his grief, and now that she had given him her whole heart, he acknowledged that he was infinitely more unhappy than before.

'Sonia,' said he, 'it would be better that you should not come and see me in prison!'

The girl made no reply, but wept. A few moments went by. 'Are you wearing a cross?' she asked unexpectedly, as if struck with a sudden idea. He did not at first understand the question. 'You have none, I see? Well, take this one, it is made of cypress-wood. I have another of brass, which was left me by Elizabeth. We made an exchange – she gave me her cross, and I gave her an image. I shall now wear hers, and you – you may wear this one. Take it, it is mine!' she insisted. 'As we shall mutually go and make atonement, so shall we mutually wear the cross.'

'Give it to me!' said Raskolnikoff to save her pain; and he held out his hand, which, however, he immediately withdrew. 'Not now, Sonia. Later on – that will be better,' added he, by way of concession.

'Yes, yes, later on,' she replied with animation. 'You shall have it at the moment of your expiation. You shall come to me, I will put it round your neck, we will say one short prayer, and then we will go.'

At that moment, three knocks were struck on the door. 'Sophia Semenovna, may I come in?' asked a pleasant and well-known voice.

Sonia, uneasy, ran to the door. The visitor was no other than Mr Lebeziatnikoff.

PART VI

Chapter 1

ANDREAS SEMENOVITCH looked upset. 'I am in search of you, Sophia Semenovna. Excuse me, I rather expected to find you here,' he said brusquely to Raskolnikoff. 'Of course, I need hardly say that I did not give you credit for anything wrong – but I was just thinking – by the by, Catherine Ivanovna has – gone back home mad!' he concluded, once more addressing Sonia. The girl uttered a shriek.

'At all events, she gives that impression. None of us know what to do! She has been driven from the place she had moved to, and, for all we can make out, she may have been turned out of doors with blows. She went to Simon Zakharitch's chief without finding him – he was dining at the time with one of his colleagues. And, would you believe me? she immediately went to the house of that other General, where she insisted upon seeing Simon Zakharitch's chief, whilst he was yet at table. Of course, they turned her out there. She says that she insulted him right and left, and had even thrown something at him. I can't conceive why she has not been locked up. She now explains her future plans to everybody, even to Amalia Ivanovna! Unfortunately, her excitement is so great that people can't glean very much from her flow of words. Why, she even maintains that, as no other resource is left her, she means to turn organ-grinder, that her children shall sing and dance for charity, and that she intends to go every day outside the General's house. People, she says, shall see the children of noble family beg in the public streets! And yet she beats them so as to make them weep. Lena is being taught the "Little Farm," whilst her little boy and Polya Mikhaïlovna are being instructed in dancing. She even cuts their clothes up to convert them into acrobats' costumes; and, being in want of musical instruments, she purposes using a wash-hand-basin as a species of drum. But advice and counsel she objects to. Can you conceive such a state of things?'

Lebeziatnikoff would have gone on much longer in this strain, had not Sonia, who had listened to him with bated breath, suddenly seized her bonnet and cloak previous to rushing out of the room. Her toilet was completed as she went along. The two young men followed her.

'She is positively mad!' said Andreas Semenovitch to Raskolnikoff. 'I told Sophia Semenovna that she only seemed so, as I did not want to frighten the girl; but doubt is out of the question. It would appear that tubercles form in the brain with people in consumption. I wish to goodness I knew something of doctoring. Of course, I did my best to influence Catherine Ivanovna, but she won't hear anything.'

'Did you talk to her, then, about tubercles?'

'Not exactly about tubercles. Why, she would have understood nothing about that sort of thing. What I want to say is this: – If you logically try to persuade a person that there is no absolute reason for shedding tears, the person in question will cease weeping. That's self-evident. Why, I should like to know, should such a person continue doing so?'

'If such were the usual course of things, life would be a very easy matter,' replied Raskolnikoff.

Having got to his door, the latter nodded to Lebeziatnikoff and went in. Once inside his room, Raskolnikoff asked himself why he had returned at all. His eyes surveyed the yellowish ragged carpet, the dust, the sofa he used as bedstead, whilst from the yard there came an uninterrupted sound of tapping, like that of a hammer; was somebody driving in nails? He approached the window, raised himself on tiptoe, and looked hard with extraordinary attention in the direction of the yard. But he could see nobody. A few windows were open on the left, pots of geraniums were standing on their sills, linen was hanging out to dry. All this he had seen over and over again. He, therefore, quitted his post, and sat down on the couch. Never, as yet, had he experienced such a terrible feeling of isolation! But one thing was certain – that he once more felt as if he really hated Sonia, and that, too, after having added to her sorrow. Why had he called to make her weep? What need had he to embitter her existence? How cowardly!' I shall remain alone,' he exclaimed resolutely, 'she shall not visit me in prison!' Five minutes afterwards he once more looked up, smiling at a strange idea, which had suddenly struck him: 'Perhaps, after all, it would be better if I were to go to the hulks,' he thought. How long had this reverie lasted? He could not remember. Suddenly the door opened, giving admittance to Eudoxia Romanovna. At first, the girl stopped in the doorway, looking at him in the same way he had lately looked at Sonia. Then she drew nearer, and sat down on a chair facing him, in the same spot as the day before. He silently watched her, without, however, betraying anything in his stare.

'Do not be vexed, brother dear. I have only called for a moment,' said

Dounia. Her face had a serious, but not severe, expression; her gaze, a sweet limpidity. The young man felt that his sister's proceeding was dictated by affection. 'Brother, dearest, I know all – all! Dmitri Prokovitch has told me everything. You are being persecuted and tormented, you are under the onus of suspicions as false as they are hateful. But Dmitri Prokovitch is positive that you have nothing to fear, and that you are wrong in getting affected in the way you do. I am not precisely of his way of thinking, for I can quite understand the indignation you must feel, and I should not at all be surprised if your whole life suffered from its effects. And I do fear that. You have left us, have you not? Well, I do not presume to sit in judgement on your resolution, I dare not do so, and I implore you to forgive me for the reproaches I have levelled at you. I feel that, if I were in your place, I, like yourself, should withdraw from the world. But I shall not let mother know anything about that. On the contrary, I shall always talk to her about you, and shall tell her, on your behalf, that you will be sure to come and see her. Do not be anxious about her in any way. I shall make it a point to reassure her, and you, on your part, cause her no pain; but come, if only once. Remember always that she is your mother! And my only object in paying you this visit was to tell you,' said Dounia, rising, 'that, if, by chance, you needed me – whatever might be the purpose – that I would be yours in life, as in death. Call, and I will come. Farewell!' She turned on her heel, and moved towards the door.

'Dounia!' exclaimed Raskolnikoff, getting up and advancing, 'this Razoumikhin Dmitri Prokovitch is a most excellent man.'

Dounia slightly blushed. 'What of that?' she asked, after a moment's interval.

'He is an active, hard-working, honest fellow, capable of sincere attachment. Farewell, Dounia!'

The girl had become perfectly crimson, but a sudden fear took possession of her. 'But surely, brother dearest, we are not parting for ever? You are not telling me your last wishes?'

'Never mind – Farewell!' He moved away towards the win-dow. She waited another moment, looking at him anxiously, and withdrew sadly troubled.

No, it was not indifference he experienced concerning his sister. There had been one moment, and that the last one, when he felt a violent desire to clasp her in his arms, to bid goodbye, and tell her all; and yet he could not even make up his mind to hold his hand out to her. 'Perhaps, later on, she might shudder at such a recollection – she might even say I had stolen a kiss! Besides, would she be able to bear such a confession?' he added mentally a moment or two afterwards. 'No, she could not; women like her can do no such thing – ' And once more his thoughts turned on Sonia.

A cool breeze was blowing in at the window. It was getting dusk. Suddenly, Raskolnikoff took up his cap and went out. Of course he was neither able nor anxious to worry himself about his health. But this continual fear and anguish could not fail to have their consequences, and, if fever had not as yet laid him low, it was perhaps owing to the artificial strength which this moral awakening was temporarily giving him. He now wandered about without aim or purpose. The sun had set. For some time Raskolnikoff experienced a form of suffering which, without being specially acute, was remarkable for a character of continuity. He thought of the years he would have to pass in mortal anxiety, 'a species of eternity within the space of a square foot.' And it was usually of a night that this thought haunted him most. Under the influence of this stupid physical discomfort which sunset favours, how could he help doing foolish things? 'I had better go to Sonia, and to Dounia as well!' he muttered, irritated. Hearing himself called, he turned round. Lebeziatnikoff was running after him.

'Why – do you know? – I have been to your place wanting you! What do you think? She has positively done as she said she would, and has started off with her children! Sophia Semenovna and I have had all the trouble in the world to find them. She is beating a frying-pan, and her children are dancing to the tune! Poor things, they are all in tears. They hang about public places and shops, and a lot of gabies are following them about! Look sharp!'

'And how about Sonia?' asked Raskolnikoff anxiously, whilst doing his best to keep up with Andreas Semenovitch.

'She is quite off her head. I should say, rather, that it is Catherine Ivanovna, and not Sophia Semenovna, who is like that; but it's six of one and half a dozen of the other. As for Catherine Ivanovna, it's a clear case of insanity. I assure you that she is positively deranged. They are all of them about to be taken to the station-house, and you can imagine the effect that will have on her. They are now by the waterside, near the bridge – not far from Sophia Semenovna's. We are close there.'

By the canal, not far from the bridge, there was a crowd, mainly composed of little boys and girls. Catherine Ivanovna's harsh and husky voice could already be heard on the bridge itself. Of a truth, the sight was singular enough to attract the attention of the passers-by. Wearing a wretched straw-hat – dressed in her old gown, over which she had thrown a shawl bandanna-fashion – Catherine Ivanovna justified but too well Lebeziatnikoff's statements. She was exhausted and panting. Her consumptive face more than ever testified to her sufferings (for people afflicted with this malady look worse out in the open than in their own homes), and yet, notwithstanding her weakness, she was a prey to an excitement which kept on momentarily increasing. She rushed towards her children, scolded them severely, and there, in presence of everyone, busied herself with their choregraphic and musical education – reminded them why they had to dance and sing, and then, grieved to find them so wanting in intelligence, set about beating them. These proceedings she interrupted by addressing the public. If amongst the crowd she happened to see a fairly well-dressed man, she would hasten to explain to him to what extremities the children 'of a noble, nay, even aristocratic, family' were reduced. Did she hear laughter or jeering remarks, she would forthwith turn on the propagators thereof, and begin to bandy words with them.

Many lookers-on certainly tittered – others shook their heads – all inquisitively watched this crazed woman surrounded by frightened children. As for the frying-pan, Lebeziatnikoff had made a mistake – at all events, Raskolnikoff saw none. By way of accompaniment, Catherine Ivanovna would beat her hands in time, whilst Poletchka sang and Lena and Kolia danced. Sometimes she would even try and sing, but as a regular thing she would, after a note or two, be interrupted by a fit of coughing; this would throw her in despair – lead her to curse her malady, whilst rendering her incapable of checking her tears. But what more especially put her out of temper were the tears and fear of Kolia and Lena. As Lebeziatnikoff had said, she had done her best to dress her children after the fashion of street-singers. Her little boy wore a sort of red-and-white turban to represent a Turk. Not having stuff enough to make Lena a dress, she had confined her adornments to a red head-dress, or to speak more accurately, to the nightcap of the late Simon Zakharitch. This article was decorated with a white ostrich feather which once upon a time had belonged to Catherine Ivanovna's grandmother, and which she had preserved up to the present in her trunk as a precious heirloom. Poletchka wore her everyday dress. She never left her mother's side, guessing her mental derangement, and, looking at her timidly, strove to spare her the sight of her tears. The child was abashed to find herself thus in the streets, in the midst of crowds. Sonia kept close to Catherine Ivanovna, and unceasingly implored her to come home with her. But Catherine remained inflexible.

'Don't talk to me, Sonia!' she would exclaim, coughing. 'You don't know what you ask, you are more like a child. Have I not told you that I would on no account go back to that drunken German woman? Everybody, the whole of the town, shall see reduced to beggary the children of a high-born father, who loyally served his country during his lifetime, and who may be said to have died in her service.' (Catherine Ivanovna had already succeeded in worming this idea into her head, and it would now have been impossible to make her relinquish it.) 'Let that good-for-nothing General be witness of our distress! But you must be silly, Sonia! And you wish us to live on you? No! We have sponged quite enough as it is! Is that you, Rodion Romanovitch?' she exclaimed on seeing the latter; and, darting towards him, she cried: 'Do make that silly goose understand that this is our best move! People give alms to organ-grinders, don't they? And they will be sure to distinguish us from them; people will know that we are high-born folk in distress, and mark my words, that vile General will yet have to go about his business! We intend hanging about his place every day, and when the Emperor passes there, I will throw myself at his feet and draw his attention to my children, and implore his protection in their behalf. He is the father of the friendless, and what's more, he is merciful – you'll see how he will protect us. And as for that atrocious General – Lena, keep straight! Now, Kolia, just you go through that step once more! And what may you be whining and sniggering about? Will there never be any end to that? What are you afraid of, you silly? Lord! What am I to do with them, Rodion Romanovitch? If you only knew how dense they are! There is nothing to be done with them!'

Catherine herself was almost in tears (this did not, however, prevent her incessant chatter) whilst drawing Raskolnikoff's attention to her woebegone charges. The young man did his best to persuade her to go home again; thinking to appeal to her vanity, he even reminded her that it was not seemly to ramble about public thoroughfares like so many organ-grinders, especially in the case of persons purposing to open a boarding-school for young ladies of rank.

'A boarding-school – ha, ha, ha! What a joke!' exclaimed Catherine Ivanovna, who was immediately taken with a violent coughing fit. 'No, Rodion Romanovitch, that vision has collapsed! Everybody has forsaken us! And as for that General – you must know, Rodion Romanovitch, that I threw at his head the inkstand which I found on the hall-table side by side with the sheet on which visitors registered their names. And when I had inscribed mine, I threw the ink-well and ran away. Oh! the contemptible cowards! But I snap my fingers at the lot of them, for I shall support my own children, and nobody shall catch me bowing and scraping! She has had more than enough to put up with!' she added, drawing his attention to Sonia. 'Poletchka, how much money have we got together? Show your takings! What! Only two kopecks? Scurvy lot! They give nothing, but persist, for all that, in following us about, whilst making game of us all the time! Now, what can that idiot be laughing at?' (She pointed to someone in the crowd.) 'But it's all Kolia's fault, her pig-headedness is the cause of everyone's merriment! What do you want, Poletchka? Speak in French. I have given you some lessons, and you ought to know a sentence or two! If you don't do that, how can you expect people to know that you are of good stock, that you are well brought up and not common wandering minstrels? We don't mean to have anything to do with trumpery songs, I can tell you, we intend to go in for nothing but troubadour-ballads.

'But what are we going to sing, now, for you keep on interrupting me, and we – I ought to tell you, Rodion Romanovitch, that we have stopped here to choose our programme, for, as you may suppose, we have been taken quite unawares, having nothing prepared, so we really want some kind of rehearsal; and then we mean to go to the Nevsky Prospect, where there are no end of nobility. Of course, they will know us in a moment. Lena knows the "Little Farm' very well, the only thing is, that it's getting rather stale, for you hear it all over the place. We ought to go in for something more elaborate. Now then, Polya, give me some kind of idea; do come to your mother's help! My poor memory is quite gone! By the by, why shouldn't we sing, "As on his sword the hussar leans"? No, I have got something better than that; let us sing in French, the song of "Five sous"! I have taught it you, don't you remember? And, as it happens to be a French song, people will see in a moment that you belong to the upper ten, and that will make it all the more touching. We might even add, "Now to the wars our Marlborough goes"! That would be all the more desirable, especially as this happens to be a children's ditty which is in use in every good house as a lullaby:

> Now to the wars our Marlborough goes;When he'll come
> back deuce only knows.

She commenced to sing. 'But no! – "Five sous!" that's the song. Now then, Kolia, strike your attitude, a little more smartly; and as for you, Lena, face me; and Poletchka and I will play the accompaniment:

> Five sous, five sous,To start housekeeping with –

Ha, ha, ha! Poletchka, child, pull your dress up, it's slipping all down your shoulders,' the mother remarked, coughing. 'You know under present circumstances, you can't mind your p's and q's too much. If I were you, I'd just let them have a peep at my instep to show them that you are the children of gentlefolks. Here's another soldier! What might you be wanting, my man!'

A constable was pushing his way through the crowd. At the same time there stepped forward a gentleman, about fifty years of age, of imposing mien, showing, under his cloak, an official uniform. This new-comer, whose face expressed sincere compassion, wore a decoration on his breast, a circumstance which caused Catherine Ivanovna exquisite pleasure and did not fail to produce its effect on the police-constable. He silently handed to Catherine a three-rouble note. On receiving this donation, she bowed with the ceremonious politeness of a well-bred woman.

'Many thanks, sir!' she commenced in a tone full of dignity. – 'The causes which have reduced us to – Take care of the money, Poletchka. You see there are still generous and high-minded men left, ready to help a high-born dame reduced to misery. The orphans you see here, sir, belong to a great family, I might go so far as to say that they are connected with the highest in the land. And that horrid General was eating spring chicken and stamping about in his tantrums because I had dared to disturb him. "Your Excellency," I said to him, "you no doubt remember Simon Zakharitch; take upon yourself the care of the orphans he has left behind; on his burial-day one of his daughters was slandered by the basest of men." Here's this soldier again! Do protect me!' she exclaimed, addressing the official in the cloak. 'Why should this soldier fasten on me like that? We have already been driven out of Meschtschanskaya Street. What may you want, you fool?'

'People are not allowed to cause scandal in the streets. Mind your behaviour, if you please!'

'Mind your own behaviour! I am in the same position as organ-grinders; please leave me alone!'

'Organ-grinders must have a licence; you have got none, and you cause a crowd to gather. What is your address?'

'What, a licence?' shouted Catherine Ivanovna. 'I buried my husband today, and that's sufficient licence, I should hope!'

'Madam, madam, pray be calm!' interposed the gentleman in the cloak; 'permit me to accompany you home; you are not in your place in this crowd – you are ill.'

'Sir, you know nothing; allow me to inform you!' cried Catherine Ivanovna. 'We are going to the Nevsky Prospect. Sonia, Sonia! Where is she gone to? What is she crying about? What ever is the matter with you all? Kolia, Lena, where are you?' she inquired, with sudden anxiety. 'Foolish, foolish children! Kolia! Lena! What has become of them?'

On seeing a soldier who was about to take them into custody, Kolia and Lena, who were already much frightened at the presence of the crowd and the strange behaviour of their mother, had been seized with a species of panic, and taken to their heels. Poor Catherine Ivanovna, weeping and wailing, rushed in pursuit. Sonia and Poletchka followed her.

'Sonia, make them come back; call them! Oh, the stupid, ungrateful children! Polya! Catch them up. It is for you I – ' But as she ran her foot caught in some kind of obstacle, and she fell.

'She is hurt; she is all over blood. Lord!' cried Sonia, stooping over her.

A crowd was not slow in gathering round both women. Raskolnikoff and Lebeziatnikoff were the first to hurry up, in addition to the official and the constable. 'Move on, move on!' the latter continued to exclaim, whilst doing his best to drive away the lookers-on. But, on careful examination, it transpired that Catherine Ivanovna had not been hurt in the way Sonia had fancied, and that the blood which stained the pavement had spurted from her lungs.

'I know what that means,' whispered the gentleman in the cloak to the two young men, 'that is consumption; blood spurts out in that manner, and then the patient gets choked. Not so very long ago, I saw an instance of it at the house of a lady-relative. She lost close upon a pint of blood quite unexpectedly. Nothing can be done for her. She will die.'

'This way, this way, to my lodgings!' implored Sonia. 'That is where I am living. The second house, my lodging. Quick, quick! Send for a medical man. Good Lord!' she went on, going from one to another.

Thanks to the active intervention of the cloaked officer, matters were soon arranged; even the constable helped to move Catherine Ivanovna. She was, however, nearly dead when placed on Sonia's bed. The hæmorrhage continued for some little time, but the patient soon came to herself again. In addition to Sonia and Raskolnikoff, Lebeziatnikoff and the official entered the room. They were soon joined by the constable, after having first dispersed the idlers, several of whom had accompanied the dreary procession as far as the doorway. Poletchka came back, leading the two trembling and weeping fugitives. Kapernasumoff's people likewise hurried in; the tailor, a lame and one-eyed man, was a singular type, with hair and beard like pig's bristles; his wife seemed scared, which was, however, her normal look; the children's faces expressed a condition of stupefied surprise. Suddenly Svidrigaïloff appeared amongst those present. Not knowing that he inhabited this house, and not remembering having even seen him in the crowd, Raskolnikoff was greatly surprised at their meeting. There was a talk as to the advisability of sending for a doctor and a priest. The gentleman in the cloak, however, considered the resources of art of no avail under the circumstances, and said as much to Raskolnikoff; nevertheless, he did what was necessary to obtain for the patient both spiritual and medical assistance. It was Kapernasumoff who took upon himself to go in search of a medical man. Catherine Ivanovna was now, fortunately, somewhat more at ease, and the hæmorrhage had ceased for the time being. The wretched woman cast a sickly, but sharp and penetrating look on Sonia, who pale and trembling, was sponging her brow with a handkerchief. At last she begged to be propped up. In this position they raised her on the bed, holding her on both sides.

'Where are the children?' she asked in a feeble voice. 'Have you brought them home, Polya? Oh, the silly creatures! And what could have induced you to run away?' Once more blood covered her parched lips. She looked round the room. 'And this is how you live, is it, Sonia? I had not even paid you a single visit, and to come under such circumstances!' She cast a pitying glance on the girl. 'We have lived on you, Sonia. Polya, Lena, Kolia, come here. Here they are, Sonia, take them all. I entrust them to your hands. I am wearied! The game is up! Let me go, let me die in peace.' She was obeyed; and sank back on her pillow.

'What say you? – a priest? I am not in need of one. Do any of you happen to have a rouble to spare? My conscience is free from sin! And, even were it not, God must forgive me. He knows how I have suffered! If He does not forgive me, so much the worse for me.' Her ideas were getting more and more confused. Sometimes she would start, would look round and recognise for a moment those who were near to her, but delirium soon overpowered her once more. She breathed with difficulty, a kind of gurgling was heard in her throat. 'I said to him: "Your Excellency!" ' she exclaimed, stopping at every word. 'That Amalia Ludvignovna – Ah! Lena, Kolia! your hand on your hip – smarter, smarter than that, glide, slide! Stamp with your feet – gracefully!

Diamonds and pearls are thine –

What comes next? That's the song for us –

> And eyes that ever brightly shine,
> Maiden, what wilt thou more?

Ah, yes, indeed! What more can the silly creature want? Here is something more:

> In a Daghestanian valley,
> Beneath a torrid sun –

How I used to like it! Poletchka, dear, your mother loved that ballad to distraction! Your father used to sing it before we were married. Happy days! That shall be our song! But how? – what? Why, I have forgotten, can't you remind me of the rest?'

And, a prey to terrible excitement, she strove to sit up on the bed. At last, in a harsh, broken, and unmusical voice, she commenced, drawing breath at every word, whilst her face expressed increasing terror:

> In a Daghestanian valley,
> Beneath a torrid sun
> Sore wounded in the breast –

Suddenly Catherine Ivanovna burst into tears, and with poignant grief she cried, 'Your Excellency, protect the orphans! In memory of former hospitality received at the hands of Simon Zakharitch! It might even be called princely? Ah!' she shuddered forth all of a sudden and as if trying to recall where she was; then she looked with a sort of anguish at all the bystanders, but only recognised Sonia, and seemed surprised to see her there. 'Sonia, Sonia!' she exclaimed in gentle and tender accents; 'Sonia, dearest, are you here?' She was once more propped up. 'Enough! All is over! I am done for!' cried the sick woman with an accent of bitter despair, and she allowed her head to sink again on the pillow.

Once more she became drowsy, but it was not for long. Her ghastly and fleshless face fell back, her mouth opened, her legs stretched convulsively, she heaved a heavy sigh, and died. Sonia, more dead than alive herself, threw herself on the corpse, clutched it in her arms, and leaned her head on the dead woman's lean bosom. Poletchka, in her turn, kissed her mother's feet, in the midst of sobs. Too young as yet to understand what had happened, Kolia and Lena had none the less a suspicion of a terrible catastrophe. They twined their arms round each other's necks, and, after having looked hard at one another, burst into tears. The dresses they wore were their acrobatic suits; the one in a turban, the other wearing a nightcap trimmed with an ostrich-feather. How did the 'honorary certificate' get all at once on the bed, side by side with Catherine Ivanovna? For there it was, on the pillow. Raskolnikoff saw it with his own eyes. He went towards the window. Lebeziatnikoff hastened to do the same.

'Dead!' said Andreas Semenovitch.

And now Svidrigaïloff drew near to them. 'Rodion Romanovitch, I want a word with you.'

Lebeziatnikoff immediately made room, and discreetly moved away. Nevertheless, Svidrigaïloff thought it advisable to take Raskolnikoff aside, who, on his part, was much puzzled by such proceedings.

'As for the whole of this business – I mean the burial, and so on – I purpose being responsible. You know that it will cost something, and I have told you before that I have more than I want. Poletchka and the two younger ones I purpose getting into an orphanage, where they will be taken good care of. I shall also invest a sum of fifteen hundred roubles in favour of them all, till the time of their majority, so that Sophia Semenovna may have no anxiety on the score of their mainte-nance. As for her, I purpose drawing her out of the mire, for she is a good creature, is she not? Very well, tell Eudoxia Romanovna the use I have made of her money.'

'Why so generous?' asked Raskolnikoff.

'Sceptical as ever!' replied Svidrigaïloff, with a laugh. 'Have I not told you that this money was of no use to me? Very well, then, give me credit for acting from humanity. But perhaps you do not admit anything of the kind? After all,' he added, pointing to the corner where the corpse was resting, 'that woman, at all events, was not "vermin," like a certain old money-lender. Do you grant that it was "better for her to die," and that Looshin continued living to do infamous things? Without my help, for instance, Poletchka would be condemned to the same existence as her sister.'

His somewhat spiteful tone of voice was full of suggestive meaning, and whilst speaking he did not take his eyes off Raskolnikoff's face. The latter grew pale, and felt a chill on hearing almost the identical words he had made use of in his conversation with Sonia. He started back and eyed Svidrigaïloff with a singular look. 'How do you know that?' he stammered forth.

'Why, I live there, on the other side of that wall, in Madame Resslich's rooms. She is a dear old friend of mine. I am Sophia Semenovna's next-door neighbour.'

'You are?'

'I am,' continued Svidrigaïloff, writhing with laughter, 'and I give you my word of honour, my dearest Rodion Romanovitch, that you have greatly interested me. I told you we should meet again – in fact, I had a foreboding to that effect. Well, we have met, as you see. And you shall see how well-favoured I am, and that people can yet manage to live with me.'

PART VII

Chapter 1

THIS WAS A STRANGE TIME for Raskolnikoff: it seemed as if a haze had fallen upon him, and wrapped him in an impenetrable and gloomy solitude. In recalling the time, long afterwards, he recollected that his powers of perception were dim and inelastic, and that this hazy condition lasted, with the exception of rare intervals, right up to the final catastrophe. He was fully convinced that his errors had been numerous in many cases – for example, as regards the date, time, and order of many events. At last, when trying to bring back reminiscences of past times, and explaining them to himself, he was often obliged to admit outside evidence to assist him. One incident he would confound with another, or regard another as the consequence of an act which, perhaps, existed in his imagination only. At times he experienced a sickly disturbing fear which gradually worked itself up into a state of panic-stricken terror. Then he recollected that there were moments, hours, and even days when complete apathy held him, a complete contrast to the terror spoken of, and like to death itself.

In such days as these, far from wishing clearly to survey his position, he strove to avoid all contemplation of his state. Such circumstances of daily life as required prompt solution, he was, of course, obliged to be interested in, but he was only too glad to bury in oblivion and avoid just those questions which were for him of most vital moment. Principally the question of Svidrigaïloff disturbed him – his mind stopped at him. With Svidrigaïloff's fearful and too plainly expressed words in Sonia's chamber, at the time of Catherine Ivanovna's death, the thoughts of Raskolnikoff took a new departure. But, notwithstanding this new fact greatly upset him, he resolutely refrained from bestowing any thought upon the matter. Sometimes, when his feet led him to some distant and solitary part of the town, and he found himself seated in a miserable drinkshop without knowing how he got there, it would suddenly strike him that he must see this man at once, as soon as possible, and claim a prompt and full explanation.

Once, in passing some place, he recollected that it was here on one occasion he had given a rendezvous to Svidrigaïloff. One morning he rose before dawn and was astonished to find his bed had been under a bush, upon the bare earth; why he was there he knew not. Casually, he came across Svidrigaïloff twice during the few days following the death of Catherine Ivanovna – on both occasions near Sonia's quarters, where Raskolnikoff aimlessly loitered. They simply exchanged a few ordinary words, never approached the great point; it would seem that was avoided by common consent. The body of Catherine Ivanovna still lay in the room. Svidrigaïloff informed Raskolnikoff that the children of Catherine Ivanovna were provided for; that, thanks to some influential friends of his and the means of the orphans, they were placed in very good hands. He also touched upon Sonia, and promised himself to visit Raskolnikoff, and confer with him upon certain affairs. This conversation took place on the staircase. Svidrigaïloff was looking straight in Raskolnikoff's eyes when, breaking the silence in a low voice, the former asked:

'What has come over you, Rodion Romanovitch? You listen, but seem to be in a daze; pluck up your spirits, man. We must have a talk together – pity 'tis I'm so busy. Ah! Rodion Romanovitch,' added he suddenly, 'how necessary it is to a man to have air – air alone, all air.'

He stepped aside to make room for a priest and his clerk, who came to perform the service of the dead. Svidrigaïloff was particular that this duty should be performed twice a day. They parted, and after a moment of indecision, Raskolnikoff followed the priest into Sonia's room. He stood upon the threshold. The service commenced softly and sadly. The idea of death always evoked in Raskolnikoff a sort of mystical awe, which had always kept him away from such celebrations. Besides, now there was something still more awful to him. He looked on the children; all were on their knees round the body. Poletchka cried. Near them, and silently weeping, Sonia prayed. 'All these days she has never looked at me, or spoken a word,' Raskolnikoff suddenly thought. The sun shone clearly into the room, the fumes of the incense rolled along the ceiling, and the priest read from his book: 'Give unto her, O Lord, thy eternal peace.'

Raskolnikoff remained during the whole service, and, upon its conclusion, went up to Sonia. She took him by both hands and inclined her head upon his shoulders. This marked demonstration took Raskolnikoff completely by surprise. 'How! Sonia?' Betraying not the slightest aversion towards him, her hand as firm as possible. It was the height of personal abnegation. At least, this was the construction he placed upon the action. Sonia did not speak, and Raskolnikoff, pressing her hand, left the room. He felt fearfully oppressed. If it were possible to go at once into perfect solitude even for life, he would have felt happy; however, that was impossible, for, although he was almost always alone, in reality he could never feel so. Strange to say, the more solitary the place, the more Raskolnikoff felt haunted by an invisible presence, which, however, did not so much terrify as irritate him. Then he hastened back to life again, mixing with the crowd, and frequenting the cafés and dramshops.

One evening he passed a whole hour in an eating-house listening to some singing he pronounced agreeable. But towards the end he became uneasy again, the remorse of conscience awoke in him. 'Have I nothing to do but listen to songs?' And he recollected the fearful question that was awaiting solution. 'Better the strife! Better Porphyrius! Better Svidrigaïloff! Hurrah for the battle and attack, come whence it may! Yes, yes!' thought he.

He jumped up and rushed out of the tavern. Thoughts of his mother and sister threw him into extreme agitation. On this night he woke up before the dawn, found himself under a tree on Krestovsky Island, and, trembling with fever, made the best of his way home. After some hours of sleep the fever left him, but he did not rise until late – at two o'clock in the afternoon. He called to mind that this was the day of the funeral of Catherine Ivanovna, and he felt glad that he was not present. Nastasia brought him his dinner, and he ate with a very good appetite, almost with avidity. His head felt much clearer, and his spirits were brighter than they had been for many a day. As usual, he was astonished at the excessive depression that had been upon him. The door now opened, and Razoumikhin entered.

'Ah! Eating? Then there's not much the matter,' said the visitor, taking a chair and seating himself at the table opposite Raskolnikoff. Razoumikhin was annoyed and did not trouble himself to conceal the fact. He spoke with evident temper – without, however, raising his voice. It was easy to discern that his mission was a serious one. 'Listen!' he commenced in a firm tone. 'There's no making head or tail of you and your ways; now, don't think I am come to cross-examine you. That's not my wish; on the contrary, it is very probable, if you offered to tell me your secrets, I should not listen to you. I am simply come to satisfy myself on one point. Are you out of your mind or are you not? There certainly exists the idea that you are on the road to it. I am quite inclined to endorse that opinion – firstly, judging from your incredible and almost swinish behaviour; and, secondly, your conduct of late towards your mother and sister – only a fool or a cad would have acted like you, unless you are a lunatic – '

'Have you seen them lately?'

'Just now. Have you not seen them all this time? Tell me now, where do you hide yourself all day? I myself have been here three times today. Your mother was taken very ill last evening, but she would see you. Eudoxia Romanovna did all she could to dissuade. Nothing would prevent her. "If he is ill and his mind is deranged, who is there to nurse him if not his own mother?" She was dreadfully agitated, and as we could not leave her alone, we all came over here and tried to soothe her all the way. Behold, you were out! She sat down and waited ten minutes in silence. At last she stood up and said, "If he can go out, he is not ill, his mother is forgotten, it does not become me to sue for his affection – let us go away!" When at home again, she began crying bitterly. "I see," she said, "his time is not for us." Her idea is that Sophia Semenovna is either your fiancée or your mistress. I called on her to see how things stood. I went and saw a coffin and a host of wailing children. Sophia was busy putting them into mourning, but you were not there! I returned and reported the result to Eudoxia Romanovna. Evidently, love was not the explanation – more probably the other reason, and, now, I behold you coolly sitting here, devouring boiled beef, as if you had not tasted food for days. Your mental condition does not interfere with your appetite – but you are not mad. No, no, I'll swear. Nevertheless, I've done with you, and am not going to crack my head over your mysteries. I only came here to have a row and relieve my feelings. I now know what to do!'

'What are you going to do?'

'That is nothing to you!'

'You will start drinking.'

'How do you know?' Razoumikhin was silent. 'You always were a pretty intelligent man and never were mad,' he observed suddenly with warmth. 'You are right, and I am off for a drink. Goodbye!' and he prepared to go.

'I was speaking to my sister about you, the day before yesterday,' said Raskolnikoff.

Razoumikhin paused. 'About me? But where did you see her, then?' asked Razoumikhin, changing colour. He was agitated.

'She came here alone, and we talked together.'

'She?'

'Yes, she – '

'What did you say – I mean about me?'

'I told her that you were very good-hearted, honest, and persevering. I did not tell her that you love her, because she knows it.'

'She knows it?'

'Well, now, wherever I go or whatever may become of me, you must be their good providence. I give them into your hands, Razoumikhin. I tell you this because I am certain that you love her, and am convinced of the purity of your heart. I know, also, that she is well disposed towards you, if she does not love you already. Now, decide for yourself whether to go drinking or not.'

'Rodia – you see – devil take it! What are you going to do? If it is a secret – well, let it be; but I know this much, and am certain your notions are all moonshine, and have nothing serious about them. Well, well, you are a good fellow – the best of good fellows.'

'I was about to add, only you interrupted me, that you were quite right to leave my secrets alone; don't worry about them, all will come out in time, and when they should. Yesterday a man told me that air was necessary to every man. Air! air! I am thinking about going to him to ask him what he meant.'

Razoumikhin stood in doubt, an idea came into his head. 'He is a political conspirator, no doubt, on the eve of some desperate venture. Can it really be that Dounia is privy to it all?' Then he added aloud, weighing each word: 'Eudoxia Romanovna comes here to see you, and you yourself wish to see a man who says you want air. Perhaps that letter came from some such person?' he said, apart.

'What letter?'

'A letter she received yesterday which upset her – in fact, very much. I was about to speak of you when she bade me be silent. Then she said that perhaps we might be separated very soon, and began to pour out her thanks; and finally withdrew hastily in agitation.'

'She received a letter?' Raskolnikoff repeated.

'Yes, a letter – and you did not know?'

They were both silent a minute.

'Adieu, Rodion! There once was a time, my friend – but now, goodbye, goodbye. You will not find me drinking now, there is no need.' He went out quickly, but had hardly closed the door upon himself, when he reopened it and said: 'By the by, you recollect that murder – Porphyrius's affair – the old woman? Well, they've discovered the murderer, who has confessed all. Fancy, it is one of those very two workmen I used to defend so hotly! Can you believe, all that scene of fighting and laughter on the stairs was simply concocted to divert suspicion. What depth, what cunning, it is almost incredible; but he has confessed it all. How I was taken in! He is the very incarnation of dissimulation.'

'Tell me, I beg, where have you gleaned this, and why you take so much interest in the affair?' asked Raskolnikoff with evident emotion.

'What a question! Porphyrius told me among other persons. He knows all about it.'

'Porphyrius?'

'Porphyrius.'

'What – what did he say?' asked Raskolnikoff anxiously.

'He explained it to me very lucidly, psychologically – you know his way.'

'He explained – he himself?'

'Himself, yes, goodbye, I have no time for more. There was a time when I thought – Ah! Well – Some other time. What need is there to drink? You intoxicate me without wine. I am drunk, Rodia, without wine, I am drunk. Ah! Goodbye. I will come again very soon.' He departed.

'He is a conspirator, undoubtedly,' Razoumikhin decided as he made his way downstairs. 'And he has drawn his sister in, very likely, and congenial to her character. They have had interviews; now I can understand many of her words and allusions. All chimes in. Besides, what other solution is there? I used to think – oh, Lord, what did I not think? Such horrible thoughts! How well it is that Nikola has confessed. His illness, his strange behaviour, even long ago at the University how sombre his thoughts were! But what does the letter signify? From whom is it? I suspect – But, no, I will make sure first.' He thought of Dounia, and his heart beat.

Raskolnikoff, as soon as Razoumikhin had departed, rose, approached the window, then marched up and down the room, quite unmindful of the small space there was, and finally sat down again on the sofa – he felt as if renovated once more. It was necessary to come to an issue. Yes, yes, this entombment must end. The thought of Nikola with Porphyrius took his breath away, whilst the scene with Sonia exercised a sense of dissatisfaction. He had agreed with her that his burden was too heavy to be borne. And Svidrigaïloff, he was an enigma. Svidrigaïloff disgusted him, but still he was not such a formidable person as Porphyrius. Ah! Porphyrius was a bird of another feather.

'So Porphyrius explains to Razoumikhin Nikola's guilt psychologically, once more his damnable theories! But, how can Porphyrius believe for a single moment in Nikola's guilt? And that scene, eye-to-eye, which admitted of only *one* interpretation? All Nikola's assertions could never efface the effect of that interview from Porphyrius's mind. But what?' continued Raskolnikoff dubiously. 'After the scene in the corridor, no doubt he ran straight away to Porphyrius. But how could he be duped? He has some aim, what is it? There has been plenty of time since the morning – too much. And I have seen nothing of Porphyrius. The more evil the portent.'

Raskolnikoff took up his cap and made for the door, deep in thought. For the first time he felt in the best of health, really well. 'I must finish with Svidrigaïloff, the sooner the better, and besides, he expects me to visit him.' At this moment such a hatred arose in his heart that he could have murdered either of the two detestable persons, Svidrigaïloff or Porphyrius. 'We shall see – we shall see!' said he to himself. He opened the door, and encountered Porphyrius face to face. The latter entered. Raskolnikoff staggered for a moment, but quickly recovered. The visit did not dismay him. 'Perhaps this is the finale, but why does he come upon me like a cat, with muffled tread? Can he have been listening?'

'You did not expect visitors, Rodion Romanovitch?' said Porphyrius, smiling graciously. 'I have been thinking for a long time of calling on you, and, as I was passing, I thought I might drop in for a few minutes. Where are you off to? I won't detain you long, only the time to smoke a cigarette, if you will allow me?'

'Be seated, Porphyrius Petrovitch, be seated,' said Raskolnikoff to his guest, assuming such an air of friendship that he himself could have been astonished at his own affability. Thus the victim, in fear and trembling for his life, at last does not feel the knife at his throat. He seated himself in front of Porphyrius, and gazed upon him without flinching. Porphyrius blinked a little, and commenced rolling his cigarette.

'Speak! Speak!' Raskolnikoff mutely cried in his heart. 'What are you going to say?'

Chapter 2

'OH, THESE CIGARETTES!' Porphyrius Petrovitch commenced at last, 'they'll be the death of me, and yet I can't give them up! I am always coughing – a tickling in the throat is setting in, and I am asthmatical. I have been to consult Botkine of late; he examines every one of his patients at least half an hour at a time. After having thumped and bumped me about for ever so long, he told me, amongst other things: "Tobacco is a bad thing for you – your lungs are affected." That's all very well, but how am I to go without my tobacco? What am I to use as a substitute? Unfortunately I can't drink, ha, ha! Everything is relative, I suppose, Rodion Romanovitch?'

'There he is beginning with some more of his legal palaver!' Raskolnikoff growled to himself. His late interview with the magistrate suddenly occurred to him, at which anger affected his mind.

'Did you know, by the by, that I called on you the night before last?' continued Porphyrius, looking about. 'I was in this very room. I happened to be coming this way, just as I am going today, and the idea struck me to drop in. Your door was open – I entered, hoping to see you in the course of a few minutes, but went away again without leaving my name with your servant. Do you never shut your place?'

Raskolnikoff's face grew gloomier and gloomier. Porphyrius Petrovitch evidently guessed what the latter was thinking about.

'I have called, my dear Rodion Romanovitch, just to clear things up a bit. I owe you an explanation,' he went on, smiling and gently slapping the young man on the knee; but almost at the selfsame moment his face assumed a serious and even sad expression, to Raskolnikoff's great astonishment, to whom the magistrate appeared in quite a different light. 'At our last interview, an unusual scene took place between us, Rodion. I somehow feel that I did not behave very well to you. You remember, I dare say, how we parted; we were both more or less excited. I fear we were wanting in the most common courtesy, and yet we are both of us gentlemen.'

'What can he be driving at now?' Raskolnikoff asked himself, continuing his inquisitive scrutiny of Porphyrius.

'I have come to the conclusion that it would be much better for us to be more candid to one another,' went on the magistrate, turning his head gently aside and looking on the ground, as if he feared to annoy his former victim by his survey. 'We must not have scenes of that kind again. If Nikola had not turned up on that occasion, I really do not know how things would have ended. You are naturally, my dear Rodion, very irritable, and I must own that I had taken that into consideration, for, when driven in a corner, many a man lets out his secrets. "If," I said to myself, "I could only squeeze some kind of evidence out of him, however trivial, provided it were real, tangible, and palpable, different from all my psychological inferences!" That was my idea. Sometimes we succeed by some such proceeding, but unfortunately that does not happen every day, as I conclusively discovered on the occasion in question. I had relied too much on your character.'

'But why tell me all this now?' stammered Raskolnikoff, without in any way understanding the object of his interlocutor's question. 'Does he, perhaps, think me really innocent?'

'You wish to know why I tell you this? Because I look upon it as a sacred duty to explain my line of action. Because I subjected you, as I now fully acknowledge, to cruel torture, I do not wish, my dear Rodion, that you should take me for an ogre. Hence, by way of justification, I purpose explaining to you what led up to it. I think it needless to account for the nature and origin of the reports which circulated originally, as also why you were connected with them. There was, however, one circumstance, a purely fortuitous one, and which need not now be mentioned, which aroused my suspicions. From these reports and accidental circumstances, the same conclusion became evolved for me. I make this statement in all sincerity, for it was I who first implicated you with the matter. I do not in any way notice the particulars notified on the articles found at the old woman's. That, and several others of a similar nature, are of no kind of importance. At the same time, I was aware of the incident which had happened at the police-office. What occurred there has been told me with the utmost accuracy by someone who has been closely connected with it, and who, most unwittingly, had brought things to a head. Very well, then, how, under such circumstances, could a man help becoming biased? "One swallow does not make a summer," as the English proverb says: a hundred suppositions do not constitute one single proof. Reason speaks in that way, I admit, but let a man try to subject prejudice to reason. An examining magistrate, after all, is only a man – hence given to prejudice.

'I also remembered, on the occasion in question, the article you had published in some review. That virgin effort of yours, I assure you, I greatly enjoyed – as an amateur, however, be it understood. It was redolent of sincere conviction, of genuine enthusiasm. The article was evidently written some sleepless night under feverish conditions. That author, I said to myself whilst reading it, will do better things than that. How, now, I ask you, could I avoid connecting that with what followed upon it? Such a tendency was but a natural one. Am I saying anything I should not? Am I at this moment committing myself to any definite statement? I do no more than give utterance to a thought which struck me at the time. What may I be thinking about now? Nothing – or, at all events, what is tantamount to it. For the time being, I have to deal with Nikola; there are facts which implicate him – what are facts, after all? If I tell you all this now, as I am doing, I do so, I assure you, most emphatically, so that your mind and conscience may absolve me from my behaviour on the day of our interview. "Why," you will ask, "did you not come on that occasion and have my place searched?" I did so, ha, ha! I went when you were ill in bed – but, let me tell you, not officially, not in my magisterial capacity; but go I did. We had your rooms turned topsy-turvy at our very first suspicions, but *umsonst*! Then I said to myself: "That man will make me a call, he will come of his own accord, and that before very long! If he is guilty, he will be bound to come. Other kinds of men would not do so, but this one will."

'And you remember, of course, Mr Razoumikhin's chattering? We had purposely informed him of some of our suspicions, hoping that he might make you uneasy, for we know perfectly well that Razoumikhin would not be able to contain his indignation. Zametoff, in particular, had been struck by your boldness, and it certainly was a bold thing for a person to exclaim all of a sudden in an open *traktir*: "I am an assassin!" That was really too much of a good thing. Well, I waited for you with trusting patience, and, lo and behold, Providence sends you! How my heart did beat when I saw you coming! Now, I ask you, where was the need of your coming at that time at all? If you remember, you came in laughing immoderately. That laughter gave me food for thought, but, had I not been very prejudiced at the time, I should have taken no notice of it. And as for Mr Razoumikhin on that occasion – ah! the stone, the stone, you will remember, under which the stolen things are hidden? I fancied I can see it from here; it is somewhere in a kitchen-garden – it was a kitchen-garden you mentioned to Zametoff, was it not? And then, when your article was broached, we fancied we discovered a latent thought beneath every word you uttered. That was the way, Rodion Romanovitch, that my conviction grew little by little. "And yet," said I to myself, "all that may be explained in quite a different way, and perhaps more rationally. After all, a real proof, however slight, would be far more valuable." But, when I heard all about the bell-ringing, my doubts vanished; I fancied I had the indispensable proof, and did not seem to care for further investigation.

'At that moment, I would willingly have paid a thousand roubles out of my own pocket to have seen you, with my own eyes, walking close to that man who had called you an assassin, and to whom you did not dare to give the lie! I admit that the ravings and sayings of a person suffering from delirium should not be taken too seriously. Then, Rodion Romanovitch, how could you be surprised at my conduct towards you? And why, pray, call on me then? Some demon, I fancy, must assuredly have impelled you to do so, and, of a truth, if Nikola had not separated us – You remember his coming in, do you not? It was more like a clap of thunder! And how did I receive him? You remember that I did not attach the least faith to his statements, don't you? When you had gone, I continued cross-questioning him. His replies on certain points were of so topical a character that I was astonished myself; his utterances, however, left me quite incredulous, and I continued like a rock in my previous convictions.'

'Razoumikhin told me, however, just now, that at present you are convinced of Nikola's guilt – you yourself having assured him so!' He could not continue, his breath failed him.

'Mr Razoumikhin!' exclaimed Porphyrius Petrovitch, who seemed quite happy to have at last heard an observation come from Raskolnikoff. 'Ha, ha! What I had to do was to get rid of Mr Razoumikhin, who used to come to me with a long face, and who has nothing to do with this matter. I would rather leave him out, with your permission. As for Nikola, would you like to know what he is like, or at least my notion of him? First of all, he is more like a child – he has not yet forgotten baby-ways. Without being exactly of craven disposition, he is as sensitive as an artist. Don't laugh if I give him that character. He is unaffected, lively, whimsical. When he is in his village he sings, dances, tells stories, which the country lads round and about come and hear. He will drink till he loses his senses – not, I must tell you, that he is a sot, but because he cannot throw off the force of example when he is with his fellows. He cannot realise having committed a theft by taking possession of the jewel-case he came across. "As I found it lying on the ground," he says, "I had a perfect right to take it."

'If one is to believe what his friends from Zaraïsk say, he must have been exceedingly religious, for he used to spend his nights in prayer, and was continually reading good books. What is told must be true. St Petersburg has done him no good; for no sooner did he come here than he took up with women and drank, and has quite forgotten about religion. I know for a fact that one of our artists took a great interest in him, and had commenced to give him instruction, and then that unfortunate affair came about. The poor fellow gets frightened, and manages to get within the clutches of the law. What was to be done? People here cannot get it out of their minds that a man wanted by the police must be done for. Whilst in prison, Nikola remembered his earlier religious mood. What he wants now is to make atonement of some kind or other, and that has been his idea in making a confession of guilt. My conviction in connection with this matter is based on certain facts he himself is unacquainted with. But he is bound to make a clean breast of everything. You think, perhaps, that he will persist in his statement to the very end? Wait a bit, and you shall see that he will deny everything. Besides, if in certain respects he has succeeded in giving an air of probability to his confession, there are points totally at variance with actual facts, which he does not expect himself.

'No, *batuchka*, Rodion Romanovitch, Nikola is not the real culprit. We are face to face with a weird and gloomy case – a case of a contemporary character, if I may say so – a case possessing, in the fullest sense of the word, the hall-mark of time, and circumstances pointing to a person and life of different surroundings. The real culprit is a theorist, a bookworm, who, in a tentative kind of way, has done a more than bold thing; but this boldness of his is of quite a peculiar and one-sided stamp; it is, after a fashion, like that of a man who hurls himself from the top of a mountain or church-steeple. The man in question has forgotten to cut off evidence, and in order to work out a theory, has killed two persons. He has committed a murder, and yet has not known how to take possession of the pelf; what he has taken he has hidden under a stone. The anguish he experienced whilst hearing knocking at the door and the continued ringing of the bell, was not enough for him; no, yielding to an irresistible desire of experiencing the same horror, he has positively revisited the empty place and once more pulled the bell. Let us, if you like, attribute the whole of this to disease – to a semi-delirious condition – by all means; but there is yet another point to be considered: he has committed a murder, and yet continues to look upon himself as a righteous man! No, no, my dear Rodion Romanovitch, there is no question here of Nikola; he is not the culprit!'

This home-thrust was all the more unexpected, as it followed upon the apology made by the magistrate. Raskolnikoff trembled in every limb. 'Then, who – who is it – that has committed the murder?' he stammered forth, in jerky accents.

The examining magistrate sank back in his chair as though astonished at such a question. 'Who committed the murder?' he retorted, as if he could not believe his own ears. 'Why, you – you did, Rodion Romanovitch! You – ' he added, almost in a whisper, and in a tone of profound conviction.

Raskolnikoff suddenly rose, waited for a few moments, and sat down again, without uttering a single word. All the muscles of his face were slightly convulsed.

'Why, I see your lips tremble just as they did the other day,' observed Porphyrius Petrovitch, with an air of interest. 'You have not, I think, thoroughly realised the object of my visit, Rodion Romanovitch,' he pursued, after a moment's silence, 'hence your great astonishment. I have called with the express intention of plain-speaking, and to reveal the truth.'

'It was not I who committed the murder,' stammered the young man, defending himself very much like a child caught in the act of doing wrong.

'Yes, yes, it was you, Rodion Romanovitch, it was you, and you alone,' replied the magistrate with severity.

Both were silent, and, strange to say, this silence lasted some ten minutes. Leaning on the table, Raskolnikoff passed his fingers through his hair. Porphyrius Petrovitch waited without showing signs of impatience. Suddenly the young man looked at the magistrate with scorn. 'I see you are returning to your old tricks, Porphyrius Petrovitch! You stick to your beaten tracks. I should have thought that would have wearied you in the long run?'

'Never mind my tricks! Things would be very different if we were in presence of witnesses; here, however, we are talking confidentially. You must own yourself that I have not called to hunt you down like so much game. Confess or not, as you think best; for the time being, that is nothing to me. In either case, my conviction is arrived at.'

'If that is so, why have you called?' asked Raskolnikoff angrily. 'I once more repeat the question I have put you: If you think me guilty, why not issue a warrant against me?'

'What a question! But I will answer you categorically. To begin with, your arrest would not benefit me!'

'It would not benefit you? How can that be? From the moment of being convinced, you ought to – '

'What is the use of my conviction, after all? For the time being, it is only built on sand. And why should I have you placed *at rest*? You yourself know why, since you yourself ask to be so placed. Supposing you were brought face to face with that man, and you were to say to him: "Had you been drinking, yes or no? Who was it that saw me with you? I only took you for what you were, a drunken man!" What could I probable one than his statement – after all, a purely psychological one – and that, in addition, you would come off victorious in this case, the man being known for a drunkard? Have I not more than once told you in all candour that psychology has a double way of viewing things, and that, were it not for that, I have absolutely nothing whatever against you for the time being? Of course, I purpose having you arrested – I have called to give you a hint to that effect – and yet I do not hesitate to tell you that I shall gain nothing by it. The second object of my visit – '

'Well, and what may that be?' asked Raskolnikoff, panting. 'I have already told you. I was anxious to account for my behaviour, not wishing to appear in your eyes as an ogre, especially – you may believe me or not – as I am all in your favour. Considering, therefore, the interest I feel for you, I earnestly urge you to go and acknowledge your crime. I called before to give the same advice. It is by far the wisest thing you can do – for you as well as for myself, who will then wash my hands of the affair. Now am I candid enough?'

Raskolnikoff considered a moment. 'Listen to me, Porphyrius Petrovitch! To use your own statement, you have against me nothing but psychological sentiments, and yet you aspire to mathematical evidence. Who has told you that you are absolutely right?'

'Yes, Rodion Romanovitch, I am absolutely right. I hold a proof! And this proof I came in possession of the other day: God has sent it me!'

'What is it?'

'I shall not tell you, Rodion Romanovitch. But I have no right to procrastinate. I am going to have you arrested! Judge, therefore: whatever you purpose doing is not of much importance to me just now; all I say and have said has been solely done for your interest. The best alternative is the one I suggest, you may depend on it, Rodion Romanovitch!'

Raskolnikoff scowled. 'Your language is more than absurd – it is impudent. Assuming me to be guilty (which I in no wise acknowledge), why should I denounce myself, since, as you tell me yourself, I shall be *at rest* when in prison!'

'You should not, Rodion, take these words too literally; you may or you may not find *rest* there. I am undoubtedly of opinion that prison pacifies a culprit, but, after all, that is only a theory – and a theory peculiar to myself. Now, can I be an authority for you? Who knows but that I may at this very moment be hiding something from you? You cannot expect me to give you an insight into all my secrets, ha, ha! As to the gain you will get from following my advice, it is simply incontestable. You will be sure to have your punishment shortened. Think for a moment, at what an auspicious time you will make your confession: at a time when another man is lying under suspicion and has thrown confusion into magisterial investigations! As far as I am personally concerned, I solemnly pledge myself, in the presence of God, to give you legally the full benefits of your initiative. The judges, I promise you, shall know nothing of the psychological aspect of the case) nor of any suspicion bearing on yourself; so that your step shall have, in their eyes, the character of absolute spontaneity. They will see in your crime nothing more than the result of a fatal impulse – and, in truth, it is nothing else. I am an honest man, Rodion Romanovitch, and I shall keep my word.'

Raskolnikoff dropped his head and thought long; at last, he smiled once more, but with a gentle and melancholy smile. 'I do not care for it!' he said, without seeming to observe that his words were almost tantamount to a confession. 'What do I care about the shortened punishment you talk of? I don't want it!'

'That is just what I feared!' Porphyrius exclaimed, as if beside himself. 'Alas! I suspected that you would scorn our kindliness!' Raskolnikoff looked up with a grave and sorrowing look. 'Do not despise life!' continued the magistrate. 'You have yet much of it ahead of you. And you refuse shortened punishment! You must be very hard to please!'

'What should I have to look forward to?'

'Life! Are you a prophet that you can say what it may have in store for you? Seek, and you will find. God may perhaps have been expecting you there. Besides, yours will not be a life-punishment.'

'I shall obtain the benefit of extenuating circumstances,' remarked Raskolnikoff, with a smile.

'It is an undignified form of shame (though, perhaps, you may not be aware of it) which prevents you from making a confession. I would be above that!'

'By no means!' muttered the young man scornfully. He once more pretended to rise, but sat down again, a prey to visible dejection.

'You are mistrustful, and you think I am endeavouring in a coarse kind of way to decoy you, but answer me – have you lived really as yet? What do you know of existence? You have conceived a theory, which, when put to the test, has ended in consequences whose want of originality you are now ashamed of! You have committed a crime, it is true, but you are far from being a hopeless criminal. What is my opinion about you? I look upon you as one of those men who, with a smile, would permit their executioners to tear their bowels out, provided they had found their fetish! Find it, and you will live! Besides, you have been wanting a change of air for a long time! Again, suffering is a very good thing. Suffer, therefore! Nikola may have his reasons for wishing to suffer. I know you are sceptical, but simply from want of having reasoned; join in with the ordinary current of life, and it will take you somewhere. Whither, you ask? Have no care on the subject, you will land and take root somewhere yet! Where? I cannot say, I only believe you have yet long to live. Perhaps you may be saying, now, that I am playing my part of magistrate; later on, perhaps you will remember my words and benefit by them; that is why I speak now as I do. It was a lucky thing, after all, that you only killed a wicked old woman. Had you had a different theory, you might have committed an act a hundred mil-lion times worse. You have occasion to thank God. Who knows? – He may have plans with regard to you. Therefore, be plucky, and do not from faint-heartedness recoil from what justice claims at your hands. I know you do not believe me, but, with time, your love of life will return. What you require at present is air, air, air!'

Raskolnikoff shuddered. 'But,' exclaimed he, 'who may you be thus to prophesy? What lofty wisdom permits you thus to divine my future?'

'Who am I? I am a man who has had his day, that is all. A sensible and kindly man, to whom experience may have taught something, but a man who has had his day. With you, now, it is quite another thing; you are on the threshold of life, and – who knows? – this adventure may leave no traces in your life. Why dread so much the change that may come about in your condition? Is it comfort a mind like yours should regret? Do you fret at the prospect of being confined for a long time in darkness? The duration of that darkness will depend upon yourself. Become like the sun, and men will notice you. Why still smile? You may say that this is the idle talk of a magistrate? Possibly! You need not believe me, Rodion Romanovitch, on my word of – I do my duty, be assured of that. I only add this: time will show whether I am a knave or an honest man!'

'When do you propose arresting me?'

'I can yet give you one or two days' liberty. Think! Ask God to inspire you, friend! Believe me, the advice I am giving you is the very best for you to follow!'

'And supposing I escaped now?' asked Raskolnikoff, with his singular smile.

'You will do no such thing. A moujik may do so – one of our present revolutionists – who apes some other man's individuality, simply because he has some article of faith, which he blindly accepts for the remainder of his life. But as for you, you no longer believe in your theory. What then can you be depriving others of in your flight? Besides, how ignoble and hard is the life of a fugitive! If you do escape, you will return of your own accord. *You cannot do without us.* When I shall have had you arrested – at the expiration of a month or two, or even three, if you like – you will remember my words, and you will confess. You will be led to do so insensibly, almost without being conscious of it. I am even of opinion that, after careful consideration, you will make up your mind to make atonement. You do not believe me at this moment, but wait and see. In truth, Rodion Romanovitch, suffering is a grand thing. In the mouth of a coarse man, who deprives himself of nothing, such a statement might afford food for laughter. Never mind, however, but there lies a theory in suffering. Nikola is right. You won't escape, Rodion Romanovitch.'

Raskolnikoff rose and took his cap. Porphyrius Petrovitch did the same. 'Are you going for a walk? The night will be a fine one, as long as we get no storm. That would be all the better though, as it would clear the air.'

'Porphyrius Petrovitch,' said the young man, in curt and hurried accents, 'do not run away with the idea that I have been making a confession today. You are a strange man, and I have listened to you from pure curiosity. But remember, I have confessed to nothing. Pray do not forget that.'

'I shall not forget it, you may depend – How he is trembling! Don't be uneasy, my friend – I shall not forget your advice. Take a little stroll, only do not go beyond certain limits. I must, however, at all costs,' he added with lowered voice, 'ask a small favour of you; it is a delicate one, but has an importance of its own; assuming, although I would view such a contingency as an improbable one – assuming, during the next forty-eight hours, the fancy were to come upon you to put an end to your life (excuse me my foolish supposition), would you mind leaving behind you something in the shape of a note – a line or so – pointing to the spot where the stone is? – that would be very considerate. Well, *au revoir*! May God send you good thoughts!'

Porphyrius withdrew, avoiding Raskolnikoff's eye. The latter approached the window, and impatiently waited till, according to his calculation, the magistrate should be some distance from the house. He then passed out himself in great haste.

Chapter 3

HE WAS IN A GREAT HURRY to see Svidrigaïloff. As to what there was to hope for from that man – he did not know himself. The man in question, however, had a mysterious kind of power over him. Since Raskolnikoff had become convinced of its necessity, anxiety was consuming him; there was now no longer any occasion to put off the moment of explanation. One question, however, engaged his attention very fully on his way: had Svidrigaïloff gone to Porphyrius? 'No,' was his reply, as far as he could judge. No, Svidrigaïloff had not gone there! This he could have sworn to. On recalling mentally every circumstance in connection with Porphyrius's visit, he repeatedly came to the same negative conclusion. But even assuming Svidrigaïloff not to have gone to the magistrate as yet, might he, however, not do so sooner or later?

Even on this point, the young man was disposed to answer himself in the negative. But why? He could not have explained the reasons of his conclusion, and, even had he been able to do so, he certainly would not have gone far out of his way to find the answer. All this worried, and yet at the same time left him indifferent. What was stranger and yet more incredible still, was that, in spite of the critical nature of his present position, Raskolnikoff had not much anxiety about it; what did, however, torture him, was a much more important question, a question, too, which interested him personally; but this was not the one. He experienced in addition a species of mental torpor, although he was at this time in a much better mood for reasoning than he had been for days previously. After all the skirmishing he had gone through, was it absolutely necessary to commence another to enable him to get the mastery of all these distressing difficulties? Was it, for instance, worth while (if the expression be permissible) to lay siege to Svidrigaïloff, to endeavour to circumvent him, fearing lest the latter might pay a visit to the magistrate? All this enervated him!

He hastened, however, to go in search of Svidrigaïloff. Did he really expect from him something new, advice of some kind, the means, perhaps, of getting out of his difficulty? Drowning men, it is said, cling to wisps of straw! Was it destiny or instinct which drew these two men together? Raskolnikoff may have taken this step simply because he no longer knew which way to turn. Perhaps he felt the need of someone else than Svidrigaïloff, and merely clung to the latter as a kind of makeshift? Would Sonia have been the better of the two? But, why go now to Sonia? To see her tears once more? Besides, Sonia frightened him; Sonia represented in his eyes a form of irrevocable sentence, a sentence beyond appeal. But, at this moment, he felt himself unfit to face the girl. It would perhaps be better to feel his way with Svidrigaïloff; for, in spite of himself, he had long since come to the conclusion that Arcadius Ivanovitch was, to a certain extent, indispensable to himself. And yet what could there possibly be in common between these two men? Their very profligacy was not of a nature to bring them together. The man was in reality objectionable to him; he was evidently a thorough rake, decidedly crafty and knavish, probably utterly depraved. Evil reports were in circulation about him. It is true that he seemed interested in Catherine Ivanovna's children; but did people know the real reason? With men of his stamp one could hardly avoid the suspicion of underhanded intentions of some kind or other.

Another thought had for many days disturbed Raskolnikoff, and, although he did his best to drive it away, it was none the less painful to him. 'Svidrigaïloff persists in hovering about me,' he often said to himself, 'Svidrigaïloff has evidently discovered my secret. Svidrigaïloff has had, and may yet have, intentions towards my sister; the latter idea is the most probable. Supposing he knows my secret, might he not try and wield it as a kind of hold on Dounia?' This thought, which occasionally even worried him in his sleep, had never struck him so forcibly as at this very moment of his visit to Svidrigaïloff. At first it occurred to him to tell his sister everything – a step which would make a striking difference in the situation. Then he thought it best to give himself up, to prevent any kind of outward proceeding on Dounetchka's part. As for the letter – for Dounia had received one that very morning – who could have written to her in St Petersburg? (Might it not have been Looshin?) Razoumikhin certainly kept most excellent watch, but he knew nothing. 'Ought I not to take him fully into my confidence?' Raskolnikoff asked himself, with a pang. 'One thing is certain – I must see Svidrigaïloff as soon as possible. Thank God, in this case, details are of less importance than the thing itself; but, should he have the audacity to do anything to Dounia's detriment, I shall simply kill him,' he determined.

A feeling of pain was oppressing him; he stopped in the middle of the road, looking about him. Which way had he taken? Where could he be? He was in the Prospect, from thirty to forty paces from the Haymarket, which he had just crossed. The second floor of the house on the left was wholly used as a *traktir*. All the windows were wide open. Judging from the faces looking out of them, the place must have been full In the large hall they were singing songs, playing the clarionet, the violin, and the drum. Women's voices were likewise heard. Surprised to find himself in this neighbourhood, the youth was on the point of recovering his footsteps, when, all of a sudden, he discovered at one of the windows of the *traktir*, Svidrigaïloff seated, pipe in mouth, at one of the tea-tables. This caused him astonishment, mixed with fear. Svidrigaïloff looked at him in silence, and what astonished Raskolnikoff still more was that the former was making preparation to rise, as if anxious to steal gently away before anyone should have seen him. Raskolnikoff, on his part, pretended not to see him, and looked sideways, whilst, nevertheless, continuing his watch. Anxiety caused his heart to beat. Svidrigaïloff was evidently desirous not to be noticed. He took his pipe out of his mouth and wished to escape Raskolnikoff's gaze, but on rising and moving his chair he probably found that it was already too late. There was between them nearly the same game as on the occasion of their interview in Raskolnikoff's room. Each knew himself observed by the other. A malignant smile appeared on Svidrigaïloff's face. At last he burst out laughing.

'Come in if you like, I am here!' he shouted from the window.

The young man went upstairs. He found Svidrigaïloff in a very small room opening into a large one, where were seated a large number of guests: tradesmen, Government officials, and others were drinking tea, whilst listening to a few singers who were making a terrible hubbub. In another room some people were playing billiards. Svidrigaïloff had before him an uncorked bottle of champagne, and a half-empty glass;

he was hob-nobbing with a couple of nomad musicians, a little organ-grinder, and a singer. This one, a girl eighteen years of age, of fresh complexion and good-looking, was dressed in a gown of striped material, and wore a Tyrolese head-dress trimmed with ribbons. Accompanied by the organ, she was singing in a rather powerful contralto some trivial ditty, in the midst of the noise which came from the other room.

'That will do,' interrupted Svidrigaïloff, upon Raskolnikoff's entrance. The girl forthwith ceased, and waited in a respectful attitude. Just now, whilst singing her melodious nonsense, she showed a glimmer of respect in her seriously expressive face. 'Here, Philip, a glass!' cried Svidrigaïloff.

'I'll take no wine,' said Raskolnikoff.

'As you please. Drink, Katia! I shall want you no more now, so you may go.'

He poured out a large glass of wine for the girl, and gave her a small note of yellow colour. Katia drank her glass gingerly, just as ladies take their wine; and, after having taken the note, she kissed Svidrigaïloff's hand, who accepted in the most serious manner this testimony of servile respect. Upon this, the singer withdrew, followed by the little organ-grinder. Although Svidrigaïloff had not yet been a week in St Petersburg, anyone would have taken him for an old *habitué* of the house. Philip, the waiter, knew him, and showed him particular attention. The door opening into the larger room was locked. Svidrigaïloff was quite at home in this small apartment, where he probably spent whole days. The *traktir*, dirty and third-rate as it was, did not even belong to the ordinary run of houses of this kind.

'I was about to call on you,' began Raskolnikoff, 'but somehow, on leaving the Haymarket, I took the Prospect. I never come in this direction at all. I always go to the right as soon as I get across the Haymarket. That does not happen to be the best way, either, to find you. No sooner had I turned than I saw you. Very strange, is it not?'

'Why don't you say, straight off, it is a miracle?'

'Because it may, after all, only be chance.'

'That is a way everybody has here,' answered Svidrigaïloff with a smile. 'Even those who in their hearts believe in miracles would not dare say so. You say yourself that it only may be a chance. You have no idea, Rodion Romanovitch, how few people here have the courage of their opinions. Present company excepted, of course. You have opinions of your own, and are not afraid to give vent to them. You very much excite my curiosity from that fact alone!'

'From that alone?'

'It is sufficient.' Svidrigaïloff was visibly excited, although he had only drunk half a glass of wine.

'When you called upon me you were not aware, I believe, if I could have what you call opinions of my own,' remarked Raskolnikoff.

'That was quite a different thing. Every man has his own special business. But as for the miracle, I must tell you that you have evidently been asleep for the last few days. I myself gave you the address of this very house. It is, therefore, not so astonishing that you should have come to it straight away. I told you the way to come, and at what time I could be found here. Don't you remember?'

'I don't,' replied Raskolnikoff with surprise.

'I believe you. I have, however, given you those particulars on two occasions. The address has become mechanically fixed on your memory, which has brought you here in spite of yourself. Why, whilst I was talking to you just now, I could see that you were absent in mind. You do not take care enough of yourself, Rodion Romanovitch. But here is something else: I am convinced that there are in St Petersburg no end of people who talk to themselves as they walk about. The town is half-full of lunatics. If we had any savants, then doctors, lawyers, and philosophers would be able to make very interesting studies here, each one in his own special branch. There does not exist another place where the human mind can be subjected to such gloomy and singular influences. The effect of the climate itself is unfavourable. Unfortunately, St Petersburg happens to be the administrative centre of the country, and its character affects the whole of Rusisa. But I am not talking about that now, all I wanted to tell you was that I had seen you more than once passing through the street. When you leave your rooms, you walk erect. When you have gone about twenty paces your head hangs, and you cross your hands behind your back. You look up, but it is evident that you see nothing, either ahead of you or by your side. At last your lips begin to move, you talk to yourself, sometimes even you gesticulate, you recite, you stop in the very middle of the causeway for a longer or a shorter time. What can be the use of such goings-on? Others, besides myself, may notice you, and that may have dangers of its own. Of course, these things in no way concern me, I don't pretend to be able to influence you; but you nevertheless understand me, I hope.'

'Do you mean that I am being followed?' asked Raskolnikoff, fixing an inquiring look on Svidrigaïloff.

'I know nothing of the kind,' answered the latter astonished.

'Then pray don't talk of me again,' growled Raskolnikoff with an angry look.

'Very well, you shall not be spoken of again.'

'Just answer me this question – If it is true that on two occasions you drew my attention to this *traktir* as a place where I could see you, why then did you just now, when I looked up at the window, hide and try to move away? I distinctly saw that.'

'Ah! ah! but why, when I entered your room the other day did you pretend to be asleep, though you were wide awake all the time? I distinctly saw that.'

'I may have had my reasons, as you know.'

'And I too may have had my reasons, though you did not know them.'

For a moment Raskolnikoff had carefully watched his interlocutor's face, a face which continually caused him new astonishment. Although beautiful it had points that were exceedingly unattractive. It might almost have been taken for a mask; the complexion was too bright, the lips too ruddy, the beard too fair, the hair too thick, the eyes too blue, the gaze too rigid. Svidrigaïloff wore an elegant summer-suit, his linen was irreproachable as regards colour and quality, a massive ring set with a valuable stone shone on one of his fingers.

'Subterfuge must be out of the question between us,' brusquely observed the young man, 'and, although you may be in a position to do me much harm supposing you had such desire, I purpose speaking to you candidly and plainly. Know, therefore, that, if you still have the same views with reference to my sister, and if, in order to gain your object, you intend to make use of the secret you discovered the other day, I purpose killing you before you get me put in prison. I give you my word of honour to that effect. Secondly, I fancy having noticed of late that you are anxious to have a conversation with me; if such is the case, have your say, for time is precious, and soon it may be too late.'

'Why be in such a hurry?' asked Svidrigaïloff, looking at him inquisitively.

'Every man has his own special business,' replied Raskolnikoff gloomily.

'You have just asked me to be candid, and the very first question I put to you, you refuse to answer,' remarked Svidrigaïloff with a smile. 'You give me credit for certain plans, yet you look upon me with mistrustful eye. I can quite account for that in the case of a man in your position. But, however anxious I may be to live on friendly footing with you, I shall not take the trouble to undeceive you. I assure you the game is not worth the candle, and I have nothing in particular to communicate to you.'

'Then what do you want with me? Why are you continually turning round and about me?'

'Simply because you are an object of interest. You have interested me, because there is about you a fantastic side, that is all! You are also the brother of a lady who has greatly struck me; she has often mentioned you to me, and her language had induced me to think that you have great influence over her. Do such reasons not suffice? Hah! hah! In other respects, I must own that your question strikes me as a very complex one, and I therefore find it difficult to answer. You, for instance, in calling, do so not only on business, but in the hope that I might tell you something new. Am I right? Yes or no?' repeated Svidrigaïloff with a sly smile. 'Well, I likewise, do you know, when coming to St Petersburg – I likewise reckoned that you would tell me something *new*, I hoped to be able to get something from you! Now you know what we rich men are like?'

'Get something from me? What?'

'How do I know? You see the miserable den I spend my days in,' went on Svidrigaïloff, 'not that I am amused here, but a man must spend his days somewhere. I am amused by this poor Katia, who has just gone out. If I had the luck to be a glutton, some club gourmand – but I have not. You see that is all I can eat!' (He pointed to a tin platter standing on a little table in a corner, containing the remnants of a wretched steak and potatoes.) 'By the by, have you dined? As for wine, I seldom touch it, and then only champagne – even of that, a glass lasts me the whole evening. Although I ordered a bottle of it today, it was because I have to go somewhere presently, and I wanted, by way of a start, to get some Dutch courage. You find me in quite a peculiar mood. Just now I played the truant, after a fashion, because I expected that your visit might upset me a bit, but I think I shall be able to get through an hour with you – it is now half-past four,' he added, after having looked at his watch. 'Would you believe me? – there are times when I regret being a nonentity, neither country gentleman, nor paterfamilias, nor uhlan, nor photographer, nor journalist! It sometimes is hard on a man when he finds that he is nothing in particular. I really thought you would tell me something new.'

'Who are you, and why have you come here at all?'

'You ask me who I am! You know: a nobleman, who has served a year or two in the cavalry; after which I have been dawdling about St Petersburg; then I married Marfa Petrovna and went and lived in the country. That's my biography!'

'You gamble, I think?'

'I gamble? No; call me a cardsharper, if you like.'

'Used you to cheat at cards?'

'Of course I did.'

'You have had your face slapped, have you not?'

'I have. Why do you want to know?'

'Well now, you might fight a duel; there's a sensation for you.'

'I can't raise any objections on that score. But I am really not up in philosophic discussions. I must tell you that I specially came here on account of the fair sex.'

'As soon as you had buried Marfa Petrovna?'

Svidrigaïloff smiled. 'Well, yes,' he replied, with extraordinary candour. 'You seem shocked at what I am telling you?'

'Are you astonished that debauchery should shock me?'

'Why should I fight shy, please? Why give up dealings with the fair sex, considering that I like it? It is, at all events, occupation.' Raskolnikoff rose. He felt ill at ease, and regretted having gone there. Svidrigaïloff struck him as the most depraved scoundrel in existence. 'You had better stop a little longer. Have some tea. Sit down, do. I am going to tell you something. Shall I tell you how a low woman has tried to convert me? That would be a kind of reply to your first question, considering that your sister is involved in this. May I begin? We shall, at all events, kill time.'

'You may, but I trust you –'

'Don't be alarmed! Even in the case of a man as vicious as I am, Eudoxia Romanovna can only inspire the profoundest esteem. I believe I understand her, and I take credit to myself in consequence. But you know, when one does not know people very well, one is liable to be mistaken, and that is just what has happened to me in connection with your sister. Deuce take me! But why should she be so handsome? Is that my fault? In a word, a most irrepressible caprice was originally at the bottom of it. I ought to tell you that Marfa Petrovna did not mind so much about the country-wenches. Well, somebody got us a lady's maid, a girl from a neighbouring village. Her name was Paracha. She was very pretty, but a perfect fool; her tears, her shrieks, brought about a regular to-do. One day, after dinner, Eudoxia Romanovna took me aside, and, looking at me with gleaming eyes, insisted that I should leave Paracha alone. That was, I believe, the first time we ever had a private chat. Naturally I was eager to comply with her request, I did my best to appear affected, vexed; in a word, I was thoroughly conscientious in what I did.

'From that time we often used to have private interviews, when she used to read me a lecture, would implore me with tearful eyes to change my mode of life. Yes, with tearful eyes! That will tell to what extent a passion for proselytism can go with young women. Of course I attributed all my shortcomings to my unlucky star. I posed as a man longing for light, and finally I used an instrument which never fails in its effect on the feminine heart: in other words – flattery. I hope you will not be angry if I add that Eudoxia Romanovna did not turn a deaf ear to the eulogy I lavished on her. Unfortunately, I spoiled the whole thing by my impatience and want of discretion. Whilst talking with your sister, I ought to have put some kind of damper on my eyes. My way of looking frightened her to the extent of becoming odious. Without going into details, let it suffice to say that a rupture took place between us. As a result, I committed still further indiscretions. I indulged in offensive criticism at the expense of proselytisers. Paracha was more than once the cause of unpleasantness and so on; in a word, my existence was becoming quite a ridiculous one.

'My dear Rodion Romanovitch, if you had only seen your sister's eyes on those occasions, you would know how they can flash from time to time. I assure you that her looks haunted me even in my sleep; things had got so bad that I could no longer bear to hear the rustling of her dress. I really thought I should have had an epileptic fit. I never would have believed that infatuation could have got such a hold upon me. It was absolutely necessary I should become reconciled with Eudoxia Romanovna, and reconciliation was impossible! Fancy what I did then! You have no idea to what degree of imbecility anger can lead a man! Never do anything when you are in that state, Rodion Romanovitch. Knowing that Eudoxia was to all intents and purposes, a pauper (forgive me! I really do not mean that – but, after all what is a word?), that she depended on her exertions, that both her mother and yourself were on her hands (hang it! you are still scowling!), I made up my mind to offer her the whole of my fortune (I could have realised thirty thousand roubles at the time), and to propose that we should elope to St Petersburg. Once there, I need scarcely add, I would have sworn eternal love, and so on, and so on.

'Would you believe it? I was so smitten with her at this time that, if she had said "Kill or poison Marfa Petrovna and marry me," I would have done so there and then! But the catastrophe you are acquainted with put a stop to all that, and you can imagine how furious I was on hearing that my wife had arranged a marriage between Eudoxia Romanovna and that miserable pettifogger, Looshin; for, on the whole, your sister would have done better to have accepted my offers than throw herself away on such a fellow. Am I right? I see you have been listening very attentively – most interesting young man –'

Svidrigaïloff struck a heavy blow on the table. He was very red, and, although he had hardly drunk two glasses of champagne, intoxication was beginning to show its effects on him. Raskolnikoff noticed it, and determined to make the most of this circumstance to find out the secret intentions of the man he looked upon as his most dangerous enemy. 'Well, after all that, I no longer doubt that you have come here after my sister,' he declared all the more boldly as he wished to throw Svidrigaïloff off his guard.

The latter did his best to destroy the effect produced by his statements: 'Nonsense! did I not tell you. Besides, your sister can't bear the sight of me.'

'Of that I am persuaded, but that is not the point, however.'

'Are you really persuaded that she cannot bear the sight of me?' resumed Svidrigaïloff with a leer and a mocking smile. 'You are right, she does not love me; but never make sure of what passes between husband and wife, or between a lover and his mistress. There is always some little nook hidden from the world at large, and only known to the interested parties. Would you dare to affirm that Eudoxia Romanovna used to view me with disfavour?'

'Certain words in your own statement prove to me that, even at this moment, you have dishonourable intentions with reference to Dounia, and that you purpose putting them into effect as soon as ever you can.'

'What? I have dropped statements of that character?' replied Svidrigaïloff, who had suddenly become very anxious, without, however, taking exception to the epithet with which his intentions were qualified.

'Why, at this very moment your ulterior intentions are apparent. Why are you so afraid? Whence this sudden fear you manifest at this moment?'

'I afraid? Afraid of you? What fable are you favouring me with? It is you rather, my dear friend, who ought to fear me. Besides, I am intoxicated, I feel it; a little more, and I should have let slip more nonsense. Deuce take the wine! You there, some water!' He seized the bottle, and without any kind of ceremony, threw it out of the window. Philip brought some water. 'All that is so much absurdity,' went on Svidrigaïloff, wetting a towel, which he afterwards passed over his face; 'indeed, I am able to dispel every one of your suspicions. Do you know that I am going to get married?'

'You have already told me as much.'

'I have? I must have forgotten it then. But, when I spoke to you about my pending marriage, I could only do so with more or less uncertainty, for at that time nothing was as yet certain. The thing is settled now, and, if I were free at this moment, I would take you to the house of my intended. I should like to know if you approve of my selection. The dickens! I have only ten minutes left. I should like, however, to tell you the story of my marriage, which is an interesting one. Well, do you persist in going?'

'No; now I intend to stick to you.'

'To stick to me? We shall see, dear friend! Of course you shall know my future wife, but not now, for we must be thinking of separating. You to the right, I to the left. You may have heard talk of Madame Resslich, at whose house I am lodging for the present? She has hatched it all for me. "Time hangs heavy on your hands," she used to say, "and that will be a temporary distraction." I am, it is quite true, a sulky and soured man. You think, perhaps, I am cheerful? Do not run away with that idea, my temper is a morose one. I injure no one, however, although I sometimes spend three consecutive days alone, without speaking to anybody. That hussy, Resslich, has some ideas of her own; she reckons that I shall soon be sick of my wife, that I shall leave her in her charge, for her to do as she likes. I heard from her that the father, a former Government official, is infirm; that for the last three years he has lost the use of his legs, and does not get out of his easy chair; that the mother is a very intelligent woman that the son serves somewhere in the provinces, and does not help his parents; that the eldest daughter is married and never writes home. These good people have two young nephews on their hands, and their youngest daughter has been taken away from the High School before she had finished her education; she will be sixteen in a month – that is the one meant for me.

'Provided with these particulars, I call on the family in the capacity of country gentleman, widower, in possession of friends and means. My fifty years do not seem to raise the least objection. You should have seen me talking with papa and mamma! It was really too good! The young lady enters, wearing a short dress, and bows, blushing like a peony (I dare say she had some little preliminary drill). I don't know what your taste is in the matter of female faces; but, in my opinion, these sixteen years, these yet childlike eyes, this timidity, these modest tears, all have more charm than beauty; besides, the little thing is very pretty, with her fair hair, her wayward curls, her ruddy and slightly pouting lips, her tiny feet. In a word, we have become acquainted, I mentioned that family affairs made it necessary to hasten my marriage, and the following day, that was the day before yesterday, we were betrothed. When I call there now, she remains seated on my knee the whole of my visit, and I kiss her momentarily. She blushes, without however, objecting; her mother has no doubt given her to understand that a future husband may indulge in such little familiarities. Taken in that light, the privileges of betrothal are scarcely less agreeable than those of matrimony.

'I may truthfully say that the natural and the true are equally balanced in this little maid! I have talked twice with her, she is by no means wanting in understanding; she has a sly way of looking at me which fires me wholly. Her face is somewhat like that of the Sistine Madonna. You may have noticed the fanciful expression which Raphael has given to that virginal face? She is something like it. The day following the betrothal I bought for my future wife presents to the value of fifteen hundred roubles: diamonds, pearls, and a silver-mounted dressing-case; you should have seen her slight Madonna-like countenance beam! Even yesterday, I was not backward in taking her upon my lap; she blushed, and I saw in her eyes little tears she strove to hide. We were left together, then she threw her arms round my neck, and, in hugging me, swore that she would be to me a good, obedient, and faithful spouse, that she would make me happy, that she would devote to me every moment of her life, and that, in return, she would ask of me but one thing – *my esteem*! "I want no presents!" she said. To hear a little angel of sixteen, with cheeks burning with virginal modesty, make you a similar declaration, with tears of enthusiasm in her eyes, acknowledge yourself, is not that delicious? Listen, I purpose introducing you to my betrothed, only I cannot do so immediately.'

'In a word, this unnatural difference in your ages whets your sensuality? Is it possible you can seriously think of contracting such a marriage?'

'You are an austere moralist!' sneered Svidrigaïloff. 'Where will virtue build its nest? Hah! hah! Do you know that your exclamations of indignation amuse me very much?' Then he called Philip, and, after having paid for his refreshments, arose. 'I very much regret,' he continued, 'not to be able to enjoy your company any longer, but we shall meet again – only wait a little longer.'

He left the *traktir*. Raskolnikoff followed him. Svidrigaïloff's intoxication disappeared visibly; his brows contracted, he appeared lost in thought, like a man on the point of undertaking an extremely important thing. For some moments a kind of impatience was observable in his movements, whilst his language was getting caustic and aggressive. All this seemed to justify Raskolnikoff's apprehensions more and more; he, therefore, resolved to follow this troublesome individual. They reached the street together.

'We part here. You go to the right and I to the left, or vice versa. Goodbye, my friend, till we meet again!' And he went in the direction of the Haymarket.

Chapter 4

RASKOLNIKOFF FOLLOWED close behind Svidrigaïloff.

'What are you doing?' the latter exclaimed, turning round. 'I thought I had told you – '

'It means that I have made up my mind to go with you.'

'What?'

Both stopped, and, for a moment, took each other's measure.

'You have told me enough in your half-tipsy condition,' retorted Raskolnikoff, 'to convince me that, far from having renounced your odious intentions on the subject of my sister, you are now more than ever infatuated. I am aware that my sister received a letter this morning. So you, evidently, have not allowed the grass to grow under your feet since your arrival in St Petersburg. I can quite understand your having secured a wife in your wanderings. That, of course, is nothing. But I am anxious to make sure – ' It is doubtful whether Raskolnikoff could have stated what he wanted to make sure of.

'Indeed! Now, do you wish me to call for the police?'

'Call, by all means!'

They stopped once more, continuing their scrutiny. Svidrigaïloff's face at last changed expression. Seeing that his threat did not in any way intimidate Raskolnikoff, he suddenly exclaimed in the merriest and friendliest tone: 'You are a funny fellow! I did not speak to you about your affairs on purpose, notwithstanding the natural curiosity it has aroused in me. I wanted to postpone doing so till some later period; but, to tell you the truth, you would make a saint swear. Come along with me, but I must tell you that I am only going indoors to get some money; I shall then take a vehicle to go and spend the evening in the Islands. Why should you follow me, therefore?'

'I have something to do at your house, but it is not to your rooms, but to Sophia Semenovna's, that I am going. I must go and apologise for not having turned up at her stepmother's funeral.'

'Just as you please, but Sophia Semenovna is away from home. She has taken the three children with her to an old lady's whom I have known for some time, and who is at the head of several orphanages. I have caused this dame the greatest pleasure in handing to her some little money for Catherine Ivanovna's babies, in addition to some pecuniary aid for the use of her homes; lastly, I have told her the whole of Sophia Semenovna's story, without omitting a single detail. It produced an indescribable effect. That is why Sophia Semenovna has been invited to call today at the — Mansion, where the lady in question has been temporarily staying since her return from the country.'

'That does not matter, I shall call on her all the same.'

'Do as you please, only I won't accompany you; what would be the good? But do you know I am positive that you mistrust me, because up to the present I have been considerate enough not to bother you with ticklish questions? You know what I am alluding to, of course? I venture to say that you look upon my discretion as something extraordinary! So you had better be considerate by way of gratitude!'

'Do you think it considerate to listen at keyholes?'

'Hah! hah! I should have been surprised if you had not said that!' replied Svidrigaïloff with a smile. 'If you think it is not allowable for people to listen at keyholes, but that they may assassinate old women when so disposed, and as a magistrate might not be of that way of thinking, you had better be off to America as soon as possible! Be off at once, young man! There may yet be time. I am speaking in all sincerity. Is it money you want? If so, I can supply your travelling expenses.'

'I am not thinking about that,' replied Raskolnikoff disdainfully

'I understand: you are asking yourself if you have acted ethically, as it behoves a man and a citizen. You ought to have asked yourself that question before; at the present time it is somewhat of an anachronism, hah! hah! If you think you have been guilty of a crime, you should blow your brains out, that's what you want to do, is it not?'

'It seems to me that you are doing your very best to irritate me in the hope I may free you of my presence.'

'Oh! You eccentric man! But here we are, be kind enough to ascend. Look, here is Sophia Semenovna's door, there is nobody within! Don't you believe me? Ask the Kapernasumoffs, she leaves her key with them. Why, here comes Madame Kapernasumoff herself. Well? What? (She is slightly deaf.) Has Sophia Semenovna gone out? Where is she gone to? Are you satisfied now? She is not at home, and she won't probably come back till late in the evening. Now then, come into my rooms. Did you not intend calling on me at the same time? This is my set. Madame Resslich is gone out. That woman has always a thousand and one things to attend to, but she is an excellent woman, I assure you; she might, perhaps, be of use to you if you were a little more reasonable. You see what I am doing. I take from my desk a five-per-cent bond (look at the lot left), which I shall convert this very day into cash. Have you had a good look? I have done here, I lock my desk, I lock my rooms, and here we are once more on the staircase. If you like, we will take a cab, as I am going to the Islands. Would not a short drive tempt you? You hear me tell the coachman to take me to the Pointe d'Elaguine. You still refuse? Come, let me tempt you. The rain threatens, but never mind, we can have the hood up – '

By this time Svidrigaïloff was in the vehicle. In spite of his excessive distrust, Raskolnikoff thought that there could be no danger in delay. Without, therefore, saying anything, he turned round and once more went in the direction of the Haymarket. Had he looked round, he might have seen that Svidrigaïloff, after having gone a short distance in the cab, got out and paid the driver. But the young man advanced without doing so. He had soon got round the corner, and, as was his habit when alone, sank into a profound reverie. Having reached the bridge, he stopped at the railing, and kept his eyes fixed on the canal. Not far off stood his sister Eudoxia, carefully watching him. After having made his way over the bridge, he passed close, without, however, seeing her. Dounetchka, on the contrary, at sight of her brother, experienced a feeling of surprise and of anxiety. For a moment she stopped, asking herself whether she should address him, but suddenly perceived Svidrigaïloff rapidly approaching her from the direction of the Haymarket. He was advancing prudently and mysteri- ously, stopped on the pavement, avoiding the bridge, thus doing his best to escape Raskolnikoff's gaze. He had already noticed Dounia, and now beckoned her. The girl thought he was calling her to him, and telling her to avoid attracting Rodion Romanovitch's attention. Obedi- ent to Svidrigaïloff's signals, Dounia quickly withdrew from her brother and joined the former.

'Come a little quicker,' whispered Svidrigaïloff. 'I am very particular that Rodion Romanovitch should know nothing of our interview. I ought to tell you that he hunted me up some short time ago in a *traktir* close by, and that I had all the trouble in the world to get rid of him. He knows that I have written to you, and suspects something. Surely you can't have told him, and yet, if not you, who can?'

'Now that we have turned the corner,' interrupted Dounia, 'my brother will no longer be able to see us. I must tell you that I cannot come any farther with you. Tell me everything here; whatever you may have to say can very well be said in the street.'

'Excuse me, but private matters cannot be very well mentioned in an open thoroughfare; secondly, you ought to see Sophia Semenovna; thirdly, I must show you certain papers; lastly, if you should refuse to come to my rooms, I shall refuse every explanation, and move off in a trice. But, pray, don't forget that I am the depository of a very singular secret affecting your dearly-beloved brother.'

Dounia remained undecided, and cast a searching look on Svidrigaïloff. 'What are you afraid of?' observed the latter tranquilly. 'We are not in the country here. And even in the country you did me more harm than I you.'

'Does Sophia Semenovna know?'

'I have not told her a single word – in fact, I very much doubt whether she is at home just now. And yet she must be. She has been burying her stepmother today, and on such an occasion people don't go out calling. I shall for the present say nothing about the matter to anybody; and I regret, to a certain extent, having mentioned anything about it to you. In cases of this kind, the slightest word heedlessly dropped is almost tantamount to an accusation. I live close by here, in the house you see there. Here is our porter, he knows me very well: do you see? he gives the salute. He sees I am with a lady, and I dare say he has already caught your face. That ought to set you at ease, supposing you to mistrust me. Excuse my blunt way of speaking. This is my place, and I am only separated from Sophia Semenovna's lodging by a thin partition. The whole flat is inhabited by different lodgers. Why, then, be so childishly frightened? Is there anything so very terrible about me?'

Svidrigaïloff essayed an easy smile, but his face refused to obey him. His heart beat loud, his breast was oppressed. He did his best to speak up to hide his increasing agitation, a heedless precaution, for Dounetchka did not observe anything special about him; his last words had irritated the high-minded girl to such an extent that she could think of nothing beyond the insult to her self-respect.

'Although I know you to be a man without honour, I am not in the least afraid of you. Show the way!' she said in a tone of voice, the calm of which was belied by the excessive pallor of her countenance.

Svidrigaïloff stopped at Sonia's door. 'Allow me to make sure whether she is in. No, she is not. That's awkward! But I know that she will shortly be home again. She is only gone out to see a lady on the subject of the orphans she is so interested in. I have also had to do with the same case. If Sophia Semenovna does not come back within ten minutes, and you insist on speaking with her, I will send her to you this very day. There is my set: two rooms. Madame Resslich, my landlady, lives on the other side of that door. Now, just look here, I purpose showing you my principal papers: close to my bedroom – which is this – there are unoccupied rooms. Pay attention – for you must get the right bearings of the place.' The two furnished rooms forming Svidrigaïloff's lodging were fairly spacious. Dounetchka inspected them with considerable mistrust, but she discovered nothing of a dubious character either in the furniture or the arrangement of the place. She might, however, have noticed Svidrigaïloff was quartered between two other partly-occupied sets of rooms. To get to his own, he was obliged to go through two nearly empty ones, which formed part of his landlady's occupancy. Opening the door of his bedroom he showed Dounetchka the empty set. The girl hesitated on the threshold, not understanding why she was requested to make an inspection, but Svidrigaïloff soon set her at rest on that score.

'Just look at that second big room. Look at that locked door. You see that chair, the only one in the place? I moved it there from my own room, to be able to listen under comfortable conditions. Sophia Semenovna's table stands just on the other side of that door. The girl sat there, and was talking confidentially with Rodion Romanovitch, whilst I was sitting in this chair listening to their conversation. I spent here two successive evenings, and, on each evening, two successive hours. So you can imagine I have been able to find out a thing or two. What do you think about it?'

'Were you eavesdropping?'

'I was. Now let us return to my own room. There is not even sitting accommodation here.'

He once more conducted Eudoxia Romanovna to his parlour, and offered the girl a seat near the table. As for himself, he sat at a respectable distance from her, but his eyes had the selfsame look which had so greatly frightened Dounetchka some time previously. The latter shuddered, in spite of the self-possession she was doing her best to make a show of, and once more cast a mistrusting look around. The isolated position of Svidrigaïloff's room particularly struck her. She was most anxious to inquire whether the landlady was within, but her pride would not permit her to formulate such a question. Besides, her anxiety on the subject of her personal safety was as nothing in comparison to that other anxiety which was gnawing at her heart.

'Here is your letter,' she commenced, laying it on the table. 'Can the thing you have written about, be possible? You insinuate that my brother has committed a crime. Your insinuations are but too clear, therefore do not endeavour to have recourse to subterfuge. I may as well tell you that I had already heard talk of this absurd tale of which, by the by, I do not believe one word – long before I was favoured with your pretended revelations. They are as ridiculous as they are monstrous. I know all about these suspicions, and I also know how they have been generated. You have no kind of proof, although you have promised to do so – therefore speak up! But I warn you that I shall not believe you.' Dounetchka pronounced these words with extreme rapidity, and for a time, the emotion she experienced brought blushes to her face.

'If you did not believe me, how could you have resolved upon coming here alone? Why have you come at all? From sheer curiosity? Surely not?'

'Pray do not torture me – speak out!'

'One thing I must admit, and that is that you are a plucky girl. I really thought at first that you might have asked Mr Razoumikhin to have accompanied you. One thing I was certain of – namely, that, if he did not come with you, he would not have followed you. That was very sensible on your part – doubtless you did not wish to offend Rodion Romanovitch. In other respects everything about you is divine. But as for your brother, what shall I say? You saw him just now yourself. What did you think of him?'

'Surely you are not basing your accusations on such a slight foundation?'

'By no means – but on Rodion Romanovitch's own words. He came two successive days to spend his evening here with Sophia Semenovna. I showed you where they were seated. He made a complete revelation to the girl. In other words, he is a murderer. He murdered an old usurious money-lender, with whom he had pledged various articles. A few moments after the murder, the victim's sister, a huckstress, by name of Elizabeth, came in by accident, and she was likewise murdered. To effect his purpose, he made use of a hatchet he had brought with him. Theft was his intention, and theft was his act – he took money and various other things. This is what he told Sophia Semenovna, word for word. She alone knows the secret, but she has had no share in the deed. On the contrary, on hearing the account, she was every bit as much frightened as you are now yourself. Be easy, she will not denounce your brother.'

'Impossible!' stammered the panting girl with pallid lips, 'impossible! he had no kind of reason, not the slightest motive to commit such a crime. The thing is false!'

'The theft, however, gives the key to the murder. He stole money and jewels. It is true that he owns himself having touched neither the one nor the other, and that he had hidden them under a stone, where they still remain. But he did that because he was afraid to use them.'

'Is it at all likely that he has stolen? Can he even have had such thoughts?' cried Dounia, quickly rising. 'You know him, you have seen him; do you think he can be a thief?'

'That class, Eudoxia Romanovna, contains many varieties. In a general way of speaking, thieves are conscious of their fault: and yet I have heard speak of a man of noble character who had robbed his own lackey. How can we judge? Your brother may have thought that he was committing a praiseworthy act. I, like you, would most assuredly have turned a deaf ear to this story, had I heard it indirectly, but I could not doubt the evidence of my own ears. Where may you be going to, Eudoxia Romanovna?'

'I must see Sophia Semenovna,' Dounetchka replied in a feeble voice. 'Whereabouts is her door? She may be back by this time, and I must see her at all costs. She must – ' Eudoxia Romanovna could say no more. She was literally stifling.

'According to all appearances, Sophia Semenovna will not be back before night. Her absence was not to have been a long one. But, as she has not yet returned, she is likely to be very late.'

'Ah, is that the way you tell falsehoods? You have been lying, I see you have said nothing but untruths! I do not believe you! No, I do not believe you!' exclaimed Dounetchka, in an outburst of passion, depriving her of self-control. Almost fainting, she sank on a chair which Svidrigaïloff had hastened to offer her.

'Eudoxia Romanovna, what is the matter with you? Pluck up your spirits! Here's some water; take a mouthful.' He sprinkled her face with water. The girl trembled, and once more came to herself. 'It produced some effect,' Svidrigaïloff murmured to himself, with knitted brows. 'Eudoxia Romanovna, be calm! Remember that Rodion Romanovitch has friends. We will save him; we will extricate him. Would you wish me to leave the country with him? I have means, and, in three days hence, I can realise my capital. As for the act itself, your brother will do all kinds of good deeds which shall wipe it out; don't be uneasy about that. He may yet become a great man. What is the matter with you? How do you feel now?'

'Wretch! To mock at such a time! Leave me.'

'And where do you intend to go?'

'To him. Where is he? You know, do you not? Why is that door shut? We came in that way, and now it is locked. When did you lock it?'

'I did not think it advisable for the house to hear what we were talking about. Why go in search of your brother, in your present condition? Do you want to bring about his destruction? Such a step would drive him beside himself, and he would denounce himself. Besides, remember, if you please, that he is being watched, and that the slightest imprudence on your part would be fatal to him. Wait a little longer. I saw him and spoke to him just now; there is yet time to save him. Sit down, and we will examine together what has to be done. It was to go into this matter privately with you that I asked you to come here. But pray sit down!'

'How can you succeed in saving him? Is such a thing possible?' Dounia sat down. Svidrigaïloff took a chair beside her.

'That all depends on you, and on you alone,' he commenced in a low tone. His eyes sparkled, his agitation was such that he could hardly speak. Dounia, frightened, moved some distance away from him. 'You – one word from you, and he is saved!' he continued, trembling in every limb. 'I – I will save him. I have both money and friends. He shall go abroad forthwith, and I myself will procure him a passport. I will get two: one for him and one for me. I have friends on whose devotion and intelligence I can rely. What say you? I can also get a passport for you, and for your mother. Why think of Razoumikhin at all? My love is surely worth his. I love you devotedly. Let me but kiss the hem of your garment! Pray, do! The rustling of your dress affects me beyond control! Speak, and I will execute your behests, whatever they may be! I will do wonders! Your wishes shall be mine. But do not look like that; for, let me tell you, you are killing me!'

He was beginning to rave. It seemed as though aberration of mind was setting in. Dounia, with a bound, reached the door, which she commenced shaking with all her might. 'Open! open!' she exclaimed, hoping she might be heard from without. 'Open, I say! Is there nobody about the place?'

Svidrigaïloff rose. He had now in part recovered his self-possession. A bitter, mocking smile hovered on his yet-quivering lips. 'Nobody is near,' he said slowly; 'my landlady has gone out, and you are wrong to shout thus; you are giving yourself needless trouble.'

'Where is the key? Open the door at once – at once, you base man!'

'I have lost the key, I cannot find it.'

'Then this is a snare?' cried Dounia, pale as a spectre, and, rushing to a distant part of the room, she barricaded herself behind a small table accident had placed within her reach. Then she became still, without ceasing to fix her look on her enemy, whose slightest movements she surveyed. Standing bolt – upright on the other side of the room, Svidrigaïloff did not budge from his position. To all outward appearance, he had once more regained complete self-control. Nevertheless, his face remained pale, and his smile continued to defy the girl.

'Just now you made use of the word, "snare," Eudoxia Romanovna. If there really be such a thing, you must be aware that all my precautions are taken. Sophia Semenovna is away from home. Five other rooms separate us from Kapernasumoff's set. Also, I am at least twice as strong as you are, independently of which I have nothing to fear, for, should you lodge a complaint against me, your brother would be lost. Besides, nobody would believe you, every appearance is dead against a young woman who goes alone to a man's house. And, even supposing you were to forget your brother, you could prove nothing. To prove a criminal assault, Eudoxia Romanovna, is a very difficult matter.'

'Wretch!' exclaimed Dounia in a low voice vibrating with indignation.

'Be it so! But remember that up to the present moment I have simply argued from your own standpoint. Personally, I hold the same opinion as you do, and consider such an assault an abominable crime. What I have said on the subject, was done to reassure your conscience in case you – in case you might of your own free will consent to save your brother in the way I propose. You may justify yourself on the score of circumstances, or even main force, if it were absolutely necessary to use the word. Reflect: your brother's and mother's fates are in your hands. I will be your slave the remainder of my days. I will wait here.'

He now sat down on the sofa some eight steps from Dounia. The girl felt certain that the man's resolution was an unalterable one. Besides, she knew what he was. Suddenly she drew a revolver from her pocket, cocked it, and placed it on the table within easy reach. At sight of this, Svidrigaïloff uttered a cry of surprise, and made a sudden forward movement. Ah, so that's your answer!' he said with a malicious smile. 'Well, that changes the situation completely! You singularly lighten my bark, Eudoxia Romanovna! But pray where did you get that revolver? Has Mr Razoumikhin perhaps lent it to you? Why, it's mine – I recognise it! I had hunted for it without being able to find it. The shooting-lessons I gave you in the country were not quite wasted.'

'This revolver was not yours, but Marfa Petrovna's, whom you killed, you vile man! Nothing was yours in her house. I took possession of it as soon as I commenced to suspect what you were capable of. Move but a single step nearer, and I swear that I will shoot you!' Dounia, now beside herself, was getting ready, in case of necessity, to put her threat into execution.

'Well, and how about your brother? It is only out of curiosity I put that question,' said Svidrigaïloff, continuing in the same position.

'Denounce him if you like! But do not stir, or I'll fire! You have poisoned your own wife, as I know full well, you are yourself a murderer!'

'Are you quite sure that I poisoned Marfa Petrovna?'

'Yes! You yourself led me to believe as much; you spoke to me about poison. I know you procured some. It was you – most certainly you – infamous man!'

'Even supposing such a thing were true, I must have done it for you – you were the cause.'

'You lie! I have always – always detested you.'

'You seem to have forgotten, Eudoxia Romanovna, how in your zeal for my conversion, you bent over me with languishing looks. I read it in your eyes – it was evening-time – do you remember? The moon was shining – the nightingale was singing.'

'You lie!' (Anger caused Dounia's eyes to flash.) 'You lie! Slanderer.'

'I lie, say you? Very well then, I lie! I have lied all along. Women do not like being reminded of such trifles,' he went on with a smile. 'I know that you will fire, you pretty little monster. Fire away!'

Dounia aimed, waiting for his slightest movement to fire. A deathly pallor covered the girl's face; her lower lip was quivering with the quiver of passion, and her large black eyes flashed fire. Never had she seemed so beautiful to Svidrigaïloff before. He advanced a step. A report followed. The ball had grazed his head and gone and imbedded itself in the wall behind. She stopped.

'Only a wasp's sting!' he observed with a slight laugh. 'It was my head she aimed at – What's this? Blood!' He drew out his handkerchief to wipe away a trickling streak running down his right temple; the ball had grazed the skin of the cranium. Dounia lowered her weapon, and regarded Svidrigaïloff with a kind of stupor. She seemed incapable of realising what she had just done. 'I see you have missed me – fire again – I am waiting,' went on Svidrigaïloff, whose indifference seemed of a sinister character. 'If you delay, I shall have time to seize you before you can defend yourself.'

With a shudder, Dounetchka rapidly cocked her revolver, and once more threatened her persecutor. 'Leave me!' she exclaimed in despair, 'I swear I shall fire again – I shall kill you!'

'It is indeed impossible you should miss me four paces off. But if you don't kill me, then – ' The remainder of his thought could easily be read in Svidrigaïloff's glittering eye. He advanced another two steps. Dounetchka pulled the trigger, the revolver missed fire. 'Your weapon has not been properly loaded. Never mind, better luck next time; you have got another cap, so I'll wait!'

Standing at two paces from the girl, he fixed on her an amorous look, suggestive of his indomitable resolution. Dounia concluded that he would rather die than yield up his resolve. 'Yes, she would surely kill him, now that he was only two paces from her!' Suddenly she threw the revolver away.

'You refuse to fire!' exclaimed Svidrigaïloff amazed, breathing slowly The fear of death was perhaps not the heaviest burden of which he felt his mind freed; yet he would have had difficulty to explain the nature of the relief he experienced. He approached Dounia, and gently encircled her waist. She offered no resistance, but, trembling, looked at him with suppliant eyes. He wished to speak, his mouth could produce no sound.

'Let me go!' implored Dounia.

On hearing himself addressed in a key different from her former one, Svidrigaïloff trembled. 'And you do not then love me?' he asked in hushed accents. Dounia shook her head. 'And could you not do so? What – never?' he continued with despairing accent.

'Never!' was the murmured reply.

For a moment a terrible struggle was at work in Svidrigaïloff's mind. His eyes were fixed on the girl with an unutterable expression. All at once he removed the arm with which he had encircled her waist, and, withdrawing rapidly, went and stood at the window. 'There is the key!' he said after a moment's silence (he took it out of the left pocket of his coat, and laid it on the table behind him without turning towards Eudoxia Romanovna). 'Take it, and be gone quickly!' he went on, intently looking out of the window. Dounia approached the table to take the key. 'Quick! quick!' repeated Svidrigaïloff. He had not changed his position, nor looked at her he was addressing, but the word 'quick' was pronounced in a tone of voice, the meaning of which was not to be mistaken.

Dounia seized the key, darted to the door, opened it in all haste, and quickly left the room. A moment after, she rushed as if demented, along the canal bank, in the direction of the bridge. Svidrigaïloff remained another three minutes near the window. At last he slowly turned round, looked about him, and passed his hand across his brow. His features, which a strange smile had distorted, revealed the most heart-rending despair. Perceiving that there was blood upon his hand, he angrily looked at it, wetted a cloth, and washed the wound. The revolver which Dounia had thrown away had rolled as far as the door. He picked it up, and began to examine it. It was a small old-fashioned three-chambered weapon, and there were still two charges and one cap. After a moment's reflection, he thrust the revolver in his pocket, took his hat, and went out.

Chapter 5

TILL TEN THAT NIGHT, Arcadius Ivanovitch Svidrigaïloff haunted every pot-house and *traktir*. Having again met Katia in one of these localities, he treated her, as well as the organ-grinder, waiters, and two little clerks, for whom he had contracted a strange liking. With reference to these last two, he discovered that their noses had not grown straight, that the nose of one of them had grown to the right, whereas the nose of the other had grown to the left. Finally, he permitted himself to be enticed by them into a tea-garden, to which he paid their admissions. This establishment, dubbed Vauxhall, was in reality a low music-hall. The clerks met there a few 'chums,' with whom they commenced to have words. Blows very nearly followed upon the latter. Svidrigaïloff was chosen as umpire. After having listened for about a quarter of an hour to the confusing recriminations of the contending individuals, he fancied that he gathered one of the clerks to have stolen something, which he had sold to a Jew, without having, however, permitted his companions to have their share of the result of this commercial operation. At last it turned out that the stolen article was one of the teaspoons belonging to Vauxhall. It was recognised by some of the attendants of the place, and the circumstance threatened to take a nasty turn, had not Svidrigaïloff compensated the losers. He forthwith rose and left the garden. It was then close upon ten.

The whole of that evening he had not taken a single drop of wine; at the Vauxhall he had confined himself to nothing but tea, and that only because custom compelled him to order some kind of refreshment. The temperature was stifling, and black clouds began to pile up in the sky. A violent thunderstorm broke about ten. Svidrigaïloff got home drenched to the skin. He locked himself up in his rooms, opened his writing-desk, from which he took all his money and tore two or three papers. After having put his cash in his pocket, he thought of changing his clothes, but, as the rain continued to fall, he thought it hardly worth while, took his hat and went out, without shutting the outer door. He thereupon went straight to Sonia's place, whom he found within. The girl was not alone; on the contrary, she was surrounded by four young children belonging to the Kapernasumoffs. Sophia Semenovna was helping them to tea. She respectfully received her visitor, looked with surprise at his drenched garments – without, however, any comment.

At sight of the stranger, all the children scampered off, seized with indescribable fear. Svidrigaïloff sat down close to the table, and invited Sonia to do the same. The latter timidly prepared to listen to what he had to say.

'Sophia Semenovna,' he commenced, 'I shall perhaps be going to America, and, as in all probability this will be our last interview, I have called to settle a few things. And did you go to that lady's house? I know what she told you, you need not tell me anything about it.' (Sophia made a movement and blushed.) 'People like that have prejudices. As far as your sisters and brother are concerned, they are provided for, the money I destined for each of them has been entrusted by me to safe hands. Here are the receipts – take them. Here are, in addition, for yourself, three five-per-cent bonds, representing a sum of three thousand roubles. I am anxious that the knowledge of this transaction should remain between us. The money is indispensable to you, Sophia Semenovna, for your continuing to live as you are doing is out of the question.'

'You have been so kind to the orphans, to the dead woman, and to myself!' stammered Sonia, 'and, if I have scarcely thanked you up to the present, do not believe that – '

'That will do!'

'As to this money, Arcadius Ivanovitch, I am very grateful to you, but I am not in want of it now. Having only myself to look after, I shall always be able to help myself. Do not accuse me of ingratitude if I refuse your offer. And, since you are so generously disposed, this money – '

'Take it, Sophia Semenovna, and do not, I beg, raise any further objections, as I have no time to listen to them. Rodion Romanovitch has but a choice of two alternatives: either to blow his brains out or to go to Siberia.' At these words, Sonia began to tremble, and looked at her interlocutor in bewilderment.

'Don't be uneasy,' pursued Svidrigaïloff, 'I know everything from his own lips, and I am no chatterbox, I shall say nothing to anyone. You were gloriously inspired when you advised him to accuse himself. It is by far the wisest thing he could do. And when he goes to Siberia, you are going with him, are you not? In that case you will require money – you will require money for him, do you understand? The sum I offer you is meant for him, through you as an intermediary. You have, besides, promised Amalia Ivanovna to pay off what is owing to her. Why, then, Sophia Ivanovna, burden yourself always so lightly with similar responsibilities? The debtor of this German woman was Catherine Ivanovna, and not you; you should have sent the German woman to the very deuce! People want some kind of calculation in this life. Now, if tomorrow or the day after tomorrow, someone begins by asking you questions about me, don't say one word about my visit, nor tell anyone that I have given you money. And now farewell.' (He rose.) 'Remember me to Rodion Romanovitch. And, by the by, you would do well to entrust your money to Mr Razoumikhin. You know him, do you not? He is a good fellow. Take it to him tomorrow, or when you have the opportunity. But, between now and then, mind someone does not rob you of it.'

Sonia had risen and fixed an anxious look on her visitor. She was very anxious to say something, to put some kind of question, but she was frightened, and did not know how to commence. 'And do you, then, purpose starting in such weather as this?'

'When people are going to America, do they bother about the rain? Farewell, my dear Sophia Semenovna! May you live long and happily, for you are useful to others. By the by, give my regards to Mr Razoumikhin. Tell him that Arcadius Ivanovitch Svidrigaïloff wishes him well. Don't forget.'

When he had left her, Sonia remained weighed down by a vague feeling of fear. That same evening, Svidrigaïloff made another singular and very unexpected call. The rain kept on. At twenty minutes past eleven, he presented himself, dripping wet, at the house of his future wife, whose parents occupied a small flat in Vasili-Ostroff. He had considerable difficulty in gaining admittance, and his appearance at so unreasonable an hour caused at first excessive astonishment. At first it was set down as the freak of a drunken man, but this impression was of short duration, for when he was so disposed, Arcadius Ivanovitch had the most taking manners. The thoughtful mother brought forward the easy chair of the invalid father, and forthwith opened the conversation with a few ambiguous questions. The good lady could never go straight to the point; if, for example, she wished to find out when it would suit Arcadius Ivanovitch to have the ceremony solemnised, she would commence by putting some pointed question about Paris, or Parisian high-life, in order to bring him, little by little, back to Vasili-Ostroff. On previous occasions this little manœuvre had succeeded very well; but this time Svidrigaïloff showed himself more impatient than usual, and insisted on immediately seeing his affianced, although he was told that she had retired for the night. His request was, however, granted. He informed the young lady that an important piece of business required his absence for some time from St Petersburg, that he had brought her fifteen thousand roubles, and that he begged of her to accept this trifle, of which for some time previously he had intended to make her a present before their marriage. As there was no kind of cohesion between this present and his announced departure, it did not seem that such a nocturnal visit, in the midst of a pouring rain, was an absolute necessity.

Nevertheless, in spite of their suspicious nature, these explanations were well received; indeed, the young lady's parents did not show any special surprise as a result of his peculiar behaviour; chary in respect of questions and exclamations of astonishment, they lavished, by way of gratitude, the most effusive thanks – to which the shrewd mother added her quota of tears. Svidrigaïloff rose, kissed his intended, gently patted her cheek, assuring her that he would soon be back again. The girl regarded him uneasily, her look betrayed simple childish inquisitiveness. Arcadius Ivanovitch noticed the look, once more kissed her, and withdrew, thinking, with genuine disgust, that his present would surely be kept under lock and key by that most considerate of mothers. At midnight he returned to town by the — Bridge. The rain had ceased, but the wind continued to howl. For nearly half an hour, Svidrigaïloff rambled about the endless – Prospect, apparently in search of something. Some time previously he had observed on the right-hand side of this street, an hotel, which as far as he could remember, was called the Adrianople Hotel. At last he found it. It was a long wooden edifice, where, in spite of the lateness of the hour, a light could yet be seen He entered it, and asked a slipshod attendant, whom he met in the passage, to show him a room. After having cast a glance on Svidrigaïloff, the man led him to a small apartment situated at the extreme end of the corridor, below the staircase. It was the only one at their disposal.

'Have you any tea?' asked Svidrigaïloff.

'I can get some made for you.'

'What have you got besides?'

'Veal, brandy, and some *hors d'œuvre*.'

'Let me have some tea and veal.'

'Do you require anything else?' asked the attendant hesitatingly.

'Nothing else.'

The seedy waiter moved away disappointed.

'This is a queer house, I suppose,' thought Svidrigaïloff. 'I fancy that I am taken for some fellow who has been to a place of amusement, and who has had some fun by the way. I should like to know what sort of people put up here.'

He lit his candle, and carefully inspected his bedroom. It was very small, and so low in the ceiling that a man of Svidrigaïloff's build could scarcely stand upright in it. The furniture consisted of a very dirty bed, a table of polished wood, and one chair. The rotten carpet was so dusty that it was difficult to tell its original colour. The staircase cut slanting through the ceiling, which made the place look like a garret. Svidrigaïloff placed his candle on the table, sat down on the edge of the bed, and became thoughtful. But a continued chattering in the next apartment at last attracted his attention. He rose, took his candle, and peeped through an opening in the partition. In a room, somewhat larger than his own, he saw two persons, one of them standing up, the other seated on a chair. The former, who was in his shirt-sleeves, had woolly hair, and looked angry. He reproached his companion with sobbing voice: 'You had no status. You were down on your luck; it was I who pulled you out of the mire, and it is I who can plunge you in it again.' The man thus addressed seemed as if desirous to sneeze, a wish he could not execute. From time to time he cast a drowsy look on his opponent, but evidently did not understand a single word of what was being said; indeed, he may not even have heard it. On the table was a nearly empty brandy-bottle, glasses of various dimensions, a loaf, some cucumbers, and a tea-service. After having attentively contemplated this scene, Svidrigaïloff quitted his coign of vantage, and resumed his place on the bed.

On bringing the tea-things, the waiter was once more induced to ask whether something else was not required. Being assured in the negative, he finally withdrew. Svidrigaïloff made haste to pour himself out a tumblerful of tea, in order to get some warmth, but eat he could not. The fever which had commenced to get a hold on him had destroyed his appetite. He took off his overcoat and jacket, wrapped himself up in the blankets, and went to bed. He was cross. 'I ought to be pretty well on an occasion like this,' he said, with a smile. The atmosphere was stifling, the candle gave but an indifferent light, the wind roared without, a mouse made itself heard in some nook or corner; in fact, the whole room was impregnated with an odour of mice and leather. Stretched on his bed, Svidrigaïloff mused, rather than thought, his ideas crowded confusedly, he longed to fix his mind on something tangible. 'That must be a garden beneath the window, the trees seem stirred by the wind. How I do hate the rustling of trees of a night, especially in rough and dark weather!' He remembered how, just before, as he was passing by the Petrovsky Park, he had been struck with the same lugubrious idea. He then thought about the Lower Neva, and experienced the selfsame shiver as when he had stood on the bridge looking at the river. 'I never could bear water, even in a landscape,' he thought, and a strange idea begot a smile. 'Why, at such a time as this, I ought to snap my fingers at æstheticism and all the rest of it; and yet, I am all at once as particular as a dog looking for a corner? Why didn't I go just now to Petrovsky Ostroff? I suppose the cold and the dark must have frightened me! Not bad that! I like to feel nice! But why not blow the candle out?' (He did so.) 'Those two fellows have gone to bed, I suppose,' he went on, seeing no longer any light through the chink of the partition. 'It is now, Marfa Petrovna, that your visit would have some sense. It is pitch dark, the place is propitious, the situation an exceptional one. And, somehow you don't come.'

Sleep continued to shun him. Gradually Dounetchka's image rose before him, and a sudden trembling affected his frame at the recollection of the interview he had had with her a few hours previously. 'That's all over. Strange to say, I have never particularly detested anybody; I have never had any special longing to take vengeance on any living thing – bad sign, that! Neither have I ever been quarrelsome, or violent – another bad sign. But, the promises I made the girl this morning! She could have done anything with me.' He became silent and set his teeth. His fancy once more evoked Dounetchka, just as she appeared at the moment when, having dropped the revolver, incapable of further resistance, she fixed on him her terror-stricken look. He remembered how he pitied her that moment, how heavy at heart he was. 'The devil take such thoughts! No more of them!' He was now getting drowsy, when suddenly it occurred to him that something was moving beneath the bedclothes and running down his arm and leg. He trembled: 'Hang it all! a mouse I suppose,' he thought. 'There's that meat on the table.' Objecting to take cold, he neither rose nor uncovered, but all at once a similar feeling affected his foot. He thrust aside the blankets, lit his candle, and with a shiver bent over his bed which he unsuccessfully examined. He shook the bedclothes and suddenly a mouse leaped forward. He did his best to catch it, but, remaining in bed, the mouse indulged in many a gyration, and slipped through his groping fingers; all at once it disappeared beneath his pillow. Svidrigaïloff threw the pillow down, but at the same moment he felt that something else had leaped upon him, and was crawling over his body beneath his shirt. A nervous quiver seized on him, and he awoke. The room was perfectly dark; he was lying on his bed, wrapped in the blankets as before. The wind continued its moan in the open: 'This fidgets me!' he exclaimed, angrily.

He now got up and seated himself on the bedside, with his back to the window. 'I think I had better keep awake,' he remarked. A cold and damp chill came through the lattice and, without quitting his place, Svidrigaïloff drew the bedclothes together and wrapped them round him. As for the candle, he left it untouched. He thought of nothing, he did not want to think; but fancies, incoherent ideas rushed through his mind. He was dozing. Was it the effects of the cold, the darkness, the damp, or of the wind which was stirring in the trees – at all events his fancies had taken a fanciful, fantastic turn – his mind now dwelt on flowers. He thought it was Trinity Sunday, and that, in glorious weather, he saw before him a smiling landscape. In the midst of some blossoming flower-beds, there stood out an elegant English cottage; honeysuckle was climbing about the doorway; on either side of a richly-carpeted staircase there rose Chinese vases containing exquisite exotics. In the windows, in bowls half-filled with water, he saw bouquets of white hyacinths weighing down their green supports, whilst shedding overpowering perfumes. These flowers particularly attracted Svidrigaïloff's attention – he longed to be quite near them: he now ascended the stairs and entered a large and lofty dining-room. There also, as well as everywhere else – at the windows, near the door opening on the terrace, nay, on the terrace itself – flowers, flowers everywhere. The floors were strewn with freshly cut grass, which exhaled a sweet perfume. A delicious breeze made itself felt through the open lattice; birds were warbling beneath the windows. But in the very middle of the room, on a table covered with a silken cloth, there stood – a coffin. Wreaths of flowers surrounded it everywhere; the inside was padded with *gros-de-Naples* and white frilling.

On this bier there rested, in the midst of flowers, a dainty maiden, clad in a spotless gossamer shroud. Her arms were crossed on her breast; they might have been taken for those of a marble statue. Her bright, fair hair was dishevelled and dank; a crown of roses encircled her brow. The well-defined and already hardened outline of her face seemed as if hewn out of marble, but it was the smile on her pale lips which expressed heart-rending anguish – the anguish known only to childhood. Svidrigaïloff knew this maiden, near whose corpse was neither holy picture nor blazing taper, nor anyone praying. It was the body of a suicide – one who had drowned herself. In her fourteenth year her heart had been broken by an outrage which had appalled her virgin soul, had filled her mind with unmerited shame, and wrung from her despairing wails – wails hushed by soughing winds one lowering gloomy night. Svidrigaïloff awoke, left his bed, and approached the casement. After having groped for the window-fastening, he opened it, exposing thereby his face and nearly naked body to the nipping of the icy air which came rushing into the small room. There must have been a garden under the window, probably a tea-garden, where, most likely, in the daytime comic songs were sung, and tea was served on little tables. But now darkness reigned supreme, and indistinct blackish patches took the place of solid things. For five minutes Svidrigaïloff, resting on the windowsill, looked down into the darkness. In the middle of the night two cannon-shots were heard.

'That's a signal! The Neva is rising,' he thought, 'the lower portions of the town will be inundated by morning, rats will be drowned in their cellars; the cursing and swearing occupants of ground floors will be saving their goods and chattels, in spite of wind and rain; they'll have to shift to higher rooms. But what time can it be?' At the very moment he asked himself this question, a clock near at hand struck three. 'Another hour, and it'll be day. Why wait any longer? I'll off in a trice to the Petrovsky Island.' Hereupon he closed the window blew the light out, and dressed, when, candlestick in hand, he left his room to rouse the waiter, pay his bill, and leave the inn. 'This is my best time, I could not have a better.' For a long period he rambled about the long and narrow corridor, and, meeting no one, he was on the point of shouting out, when, lo and behold! in a dark corner between an old cupboard and a door he discovered a strange object, something which seemed to live. On stooping down, light in hand, he saw that it was a little trembling and weeping girl of about five years of age. Her little dress was drenched, like a dish-clout. Svidrigaïloff's presence did not seem to frighten her, for she fixed on him her large dark eyes with an expression of pained surprise. At times she sobbed, as happens in the case of children who, after a bout of weeping, recover cheerfulness. Her face was pale and ghastly, she was bitterly cold. But – 'what could have brought her there? No doubt she had lain hidden all night long in that corner, without a wink of sleep.'

He began to question her. Recovering all at once, the little maid commenced, in childlike and yet affected voice, some endless story about 'mamma' and a 'broken cup.' From this, Svidrigaïloff gathered that this was some unhappy waif, her mother, perhaps, one of the attendants in the kitchen, with a taste for drink, and careless as to her offspring. The child had, it appeared, broken a cup, and, fearing punishment, had, in the course of the evening, made away from the house in the midst of the pelting rain. After having been long enough outside, she had at last returned, and hidden behind the cupboard, where she had spent the whole night trembling, weeping frightened at the dark, yet more frightened still at the thought of being, perhaps, cruelly beaten, not only for the broken cup, but for the prank she had indulged in. Svidrigaïloff raised the child up in his arms, took her to his room, and, having laid her on his bed, proceeded to undress her. She was stockingless, and her wretched boots were as damp as if they had stood the whole night long in a puddle. When he had undressed her, he laid her down, and carefully wrapped her in the blankets. In a moment the child was asleep. Having now seen to all this, Svidrigaïloff once more gave way to his morose thoughts. 'What on earth am I meddling with?' he asked himself angrily 'What absurdity!' In his vexation he took up the candle to go in search of the waiter previous to leaving the place. 'After all, only a little girl!' he exclaimed, uttering an oath at the moment of quitting the room. He turned round, however, to cast one more glance at the little thing, to make sure that she was sleeping, and sleeping comfortably.

He carefully raised the coverings which hid her head. The child was sound asleep. She had become warm in bed, and her pale cheeks had already regained their colour, and yet, how strange! the colour of that complexion was much redder than is usual with children in a normal state. 'It is the flush of fever,' thought Svidrigaïloff. 'Can she have been drinking? These purple lips seem burning.' Suddenly he fancies he sees the long black lashes of the little sleeper gently move; beneath the half-closed eyelids there seemed a tendency to some cunning, sly, in no wise childish twinkle. Can the child be awake and only pretend to sleep? Yes, her lips smile – they quiver as with a desire to check a laugh. But now she throws aside constraint – she merrily laughs – there is, in that small face, a bold, brazen, luring look, without one trait of youth, for it is the face of a French harlot. Suddenly she opens both eyes wide – they gaze on Svidrigaïloff with a lewd and amorous look – they ask, they smile. Nothing so repugnant as this childish face, whose youthful traits betoken lust. 'What! at such an age?' he cries, a prey to horror. 'Can such things be?' And now she turns on him her painted face with outstretched arms. 'Accursed thing!' exclaims Svidrigaïloff with a cry of horror; he raises his hand to strike her, and at the same moment wakes.

He was lying on his bed – wrapped in his blankets – the candle had not been lit – day was dawning. 'I have had the nightmare all night!' He sat bolt-upright, and noticed with disgust that he was cramped and jaded. A thick fog was hanging without, through which nothing was visible. It was nearly five o'clock; Svidrigaïloff had slept too long! He rose once more, put on his damp garments, and, feeling for the revolver in his pocket, took it out to make quite sure that the cap was correctly fixed. He then sat down, and on the first page of his notebook wrote a few words in large letters. Having re-read them, he once more rested his elbows on the table, lost in thought. The flies were feasting on the untouched meat. He watched them for some time, then chased them away. At last, astonished at the occupation he was now engaged in, and regaining all at once consciousness of the situation, he quickly left the room. Another moment and he was in the street. A dense fog hung over the city. Svidrigaïloff now moved in the direction of the Lower Neva. Whilst walking along the slippery wooden pavement, he saw in his mind's eye the Petrovsky Island, with its pleasant paths, lawns, trees and copses. Not a pedestrian – not a single cab could be seen along the Prospect. The little yellow houses, with their closed shutters, looked dirty and miserable. Cold and damp were beginning to affect the early wanderer. The occasional signboards on his way he read mechanically.

Having reached the end of the wooden pavement, on a level with the large stone-mansion, he saw a very ugly dog crossing the road, its tail between its legs. A drunkard was lying right across the pavement, his face downwards. Svidrigaïloff for one moment contemplated the drunkard, and then passed on. On his left he observed a belfry. 'Hah!' he thought, 'that place will do – why go to the Petrovsky Island at all? Under these circumstances the thing can be officially spoken to by an eye-witness – ' Smiling at this new idea, he turned down — Street. There was the building surmounted by the belfry. A little man wrapped in a military cloak and wearing a helmet, was resting against the door. On seeing Svidrigaïloff approach, he cast on him a sullen look. His face had that sulky, sour expression which has been from time immemorial the characteristic sign of the Hebrew countenance. For some time both looked at one another in silence. At last it seemed strange to the sentinel that a sober man should stop so close, and should look at him without a word.

'What do you want?' asked the man, without changing his position.

'Why, nothing, my friend – good-day!' replied Svidrigaïloff.

'Go along, then.'

'I am going abroad, my friend.'

'Abroad, you say?'

'To America.'

'To America? oh!'

Svidrigaïloff now took the revolver from his pocket and cocked it. The soldier looked up. 'I say, none of that nonsense here!'

'Why not?'

'Because this is not the right place.'

'Never mind, my friend, the place will do very well; if anyone should ask you, say I've gone to America!' He pressed the barrel of his revolver against his right temple.

'I say, you can't do that here, this isn't the place!' again said the soldier, opening his eyes more and more.

Svidrigaïloff pulled the trigger.

Chapter 6

THAT SAME DAY, between six and seven in the evening, Raskolnikoff called on his mother and sister. The two ladies occupied at this time, in the Bakaleieff mansion, a floor which Razoumikhin had recommended them. On ascending the staircase, Raskolnikoff seemed to hesitate once more. Nothing in the world, however, would have induced him to swerve from his purpose; he had, therefore, made up his mind to pay his visit. 'To begin with, they do not as yet know anything,' he thought, 'and by this time they have got into the way of taking me for an eccentricity.' His clothes were mudstained and torn; and the bodily fatigue, to say nothing of the mental struggle he had undergone for nearly twenty-four hours, had affected his face almost beyond recognition. Heaven only knows where the youth had spent the whole night. One thing was certain, he was resolved. He tapped at the door, which his mother opened. Dounetchka had gone out; the housemaid likewise was absent at the present moment. Pulcheria Alexandrovna remained at first dumb with joyful surprise; then seized her son's hand and pulled him into the room.

'Here you are then at last!' she exclaimed in a voice trembling with emotion 'Do not be vexed, Rodia, if I receive you with tears, put them down to happiness. Perhaps you think I am depressed? On the contrary I am merry, full of laughter, only I have got into this absurd way of shedding tears. Since your father's death, I weep in this way for the least thing. Sit down, darling, I see you are tired. And, by the by, what makes you so dirty?'

'I was caught in the rain yesterday, mother!' began Raskolnikoff.

'Nonsense!' interrupted quickly Pulcheria Alexandrovna. 'I suppose you fancied I was going to cross-question you in my grandmotherly way? Don't be afraid, I know and can understand, I am to some extent initiated in St Petersburg ways; and, really, it strikes me that people are cleverer about here than with us. I have said to myself, once for all, that I had no right to meddle with your concerns, and to haul you over the coals. When you may have your head full of goodness knows what sort of things, I would on no account dream of worrying you with troublesome questions! On no account! – Do you know, Rodia, I am positively reading for the third time the article you contributed to a review and which Dmitri Prokovitch has lent me. It has been quite a revelation for me and I have ever since been able to account for everything, and to see what a silly creature I have been. "That is the sort of thing which takes up all his time," I have said to myself; "he keeps turning over in his head new ideas, and does not like being taken out of them, savants are all like that." Well, in spite of all my pains to read your article, there are many things in it quite beyond me; but, knowing how ignorant I am, I have no occasion to be puzzled if I can't quite make it all out.'

'Just let me look at it, mother!' Raskolnikoff took the review, and cast a rapid glance over his article. An author always experiences great satisfaction on seeing himself in print for the first time, especially when he is not more than twenty-three. Although full of grave cares, our hero could not escape this satisfaction, which was, after all, only a momentary one. Having read a few lines, he became thoughtful, and a terrible pang gnawed at his heart. This perusal had suddenly aroused the mental anguish of the last few months, and it was with a feeling of violent antipathy that he threw the pamphlet on the table.

'Silly as I am, Rodia, I am quite positive that in a short time hence you will hold one of the first, if not the foremost, places in the scientific world. And yet some of them have dared to think you were insane! Hah! hah! hah! You, perhaps, have never heard that opinion? Oh! the silly people! How, I should like to know, could they judge intellect? And yet to think that Dounetchka, yes, Dounetchka herself, had her doubts! Is it possible? A few days ago, Rodia, I was quite grieving as to the way you lodged, dressed and lived. But now I can quite understand how foolish I was. I am certain that, if you only choose, you will before long succeed, with your powers and talent. I suppose you are not very ambitious for the time being, engaged as you evidently are with more important –'

'Where is Dounia, mother?'

'She is out, Rodia. She is often out, and leaves me quite alone. Dmitri Prokovitch is kind enough to come and see me, and he is always talking about you. He likes and respects you, dear. As for your sister, of course I do not complain about the little attention she pays me. She has her disposition just as I have mine. She is not disposed to let me know any of her concerns – as she pleases, of course! I have never had secrets from my children. I know, of course, that Dounia is very clever, and that she loves both you and me. But I cannot quite see things in their real light, and I very much regret that she cannot share the pleasant visit you are paying me. When she gets home, I will tell her: "Your brother called during your absence; where were you all the time?" Mind you don't spoil me overmuch, Rodia; call here whenever you can do so without disturbing yourself – I can wait, as long as I only know you love me. I shall read your productions, and I shall hear everybody talk about you, and, of course, I shall get an occasional visit. What more can I want? I see that you called here today to comfort your old mother.' All at once, Pulcheria Alexandrovna burst into tears. 'Here I am again! Don't mind me dear; I know I am foolish! But, bless me, I am forgetting everything!' she exclaimed, rising all at once. 'There is some coffee, and I forgot to offer it you. Now you know what is meant by the selfishness of elderly people. Wait a moment.'

'It's really not worth while, mother, I am off directly. I did not come here for that. Listen to me, I pray.' Pulcheria Alexandrovna timidly approached her son. 'Mother dear, tell me, will you, in spite of anything that may happen, in spite of anything you may hear, will you always love me as much as you do now?' he asked all at once.

These words rushed spontaneously from his very heart of hearts long before he had time to weigh their import. 'Rodia, Rodia, what is the matter with you? How can you ask me such a question? Who will ever presume to say one word against you? Should anyone dare to do so, I would refuse to listen, and would drive him from my presence.'

'The object of my visit was to assure you that I have always loved you, and I am delighted that we should happen to be alone just now; yes, even without Dounetchka,' he went on with the same ardour; 'and, even should you be unhappy, remember that your son loves you now more than himself, and that you have been wrong to doubt his affection. I shall never cease to love you. But enough! I thought that I was bound above all things to give you this assurance.'

Pulcheria Alexandrovna silently embraced her son, pressed him to her bosom and wept. 'I cannot really conceive what is wrong with you, Rodia,' she said once more. 'Up to the present I have honestly thought that our society wearied you; now I dread that some great misfortune is threatening, and that you are living in fear. I have been suspecting something of the kind, Rodia. Excuse my mentioning the subject at all, but I am always thinking about the matter, and cannot sleep in consequence. Last night your sister was delirious, and in her ravings your name was foremost. I picked up stray words here and there, but I do not know what the subject was about. Since this morning, up to the very moment of your visit, I have been more like a culprit awaiting execution. I anticipated something! Where are you going to, Rodia? – for you are on the point of going away, are you not?'

'I am.'

'I thought as much! But, if you must go, let me go with you. Dounia shall also come, for she loves you dearly. And, if necessary, Sophia Semenovna might come, for I may tell you I am ready to look upon her as a daughter. Dmitri Prokovitch will help us in our preparations for departure, but where are you going to?'

'Goodbye, mother!'

'What, this very day!' she exclaimed, as if there had been question of an eternal separation.

'I can remain no longer, I am obliged to leave you.'

'And may I not go with you?'

'No; but you may kneel down and pray to God for me. Perhaps He will hear your prayer.'

'I hope He may! Take my blessing – Oh! Lord!'

He was, indeed, glad that his sister was absent from this interview. To unbosom himself, it was necessary there should be no witness – the presence of his sister would have constrained him. He fell at his mother's feet and kissed them. Pulcheria Alexandrovna and her son embraced with tears. The mother asked no more. She felt her son to be passing through a crisis, and that his fate would be decided in a moment.

'Rodia, beloved, my firstborn!' she said in the midst of sobs, 'you are now as you were in early boyhood, when you came to me with your love and kisses. When your father was yet alive, we had no joy but you in our troubles, and, since his death, how often have not you and I wept on his tomb, embracing as we do just now! My sorrowing days, attribute them to the fact that my mother's heart had gloomy forebodings. The very night we reached St Petersburg, at our very first interview, your face told me all, and this day, on opening the door to you, I thought, on seeing you, that the fatal hour had come. Rodia, you surely cannot be going at once?'

'No.'

'You'll come again?'

'I will, indeed.'

'Rodia, do not be vexed, I do not like to ask – but tell me only a word or two: are you going far off?'

'Very far.'

'Will you have some occupation, a position, there?'

'I shall have what God may think best – only pray for me.' Raskolnikoff wished to go out, but his mother clung to him, and looked him full in the face with an expression of despair. 'Enough, mother!' said the youth, who, at the sight of her terrible anguish, deeply regretted that he had called at all.

'But you are not going for good? You surely do not purpose starting forthwith? You intend coming once more?'

'I do, I do – farewell!' and he succeeded in making his escape.

The evening was warm without being stifling, however. Since morning, the weather had cleared up. Raskolnikoff quickly reached home. He longed that everything should be finished before night. Meetings with others would, under the circumstances, have been objectionable to him. On going upstairs, he noticed that Nastasia, who was engaged at the time in getting his tea, had stopped her preparations and was wistfully looking at him. 'Can there be anybody waiting for me?' he asked himself, thinking of the odious Porphyrius. But when he opened his outer door he discovered Dounetchka. The girl, lost in thought, was seated on the couch; she had evidently been waiting a long time for her brother. He stopped before entering. For a moment she was unnerved, started up and closely scrutinised him. Profound dejection was visible in her look, and proved to Raskolnikoff that his sister knew all.

'Am I to approach or to withdraw?' he asked hesitatingly.

'I have been waiting all day long for you at Sophia Semenovna's – we expected to see you.'

Raskolnikoff entered the room, and sank on a chair, visibly overcome. 'I feel done, Dounia, I am very tired, and at this time above all, I need all my strength.' He looked suspiciously at his sister.

'Where did you spend the whole of last night?'

'I hardly know, dear. I have been wanting to come to some definite conclusion, and more than once I went to the Neva; that's all I can remember. I wanted to settle things in that way, but somehow I could not make up my mind,' he concluded in indistinct accents, whilst trying to gather from the girl's face the impression his words had made.

'Thanks be to God! That was the very thing we were all so afraid of – I mean, Sophia Semenovna and I! You still cling to life then? Praise be to God!'

Raskolnikoff smiled bitterly. 'I used not to do, but just now I called on our mother, and we embraced with tears; I am incredulous, and yet I asked her to pray for me. God only knows, Dounetchka; as for myself, I can no longer account for my thoughts and feelings!'

'You have seen our mother, you say? And you have spoken to her?' exclaimed Dounia, alarmed. 'But, tell me, you surely cannot have told her *that*?'

'I have not, indeed! – that is, in so many words; but I think she suspects something. She heard you in your delirious state last night. I am sure she already half – guesses the secret. I ought, perhaps, not to have seen her; and I really do not know what could have induced me. I am a miserable man, after all, Dounia!'

'Yes, but a man ready to make atonement. You mean to do that, do you not?'

'Without delay. To shun dishonour, I purposed drowning myself, Dounia; but at the moment of doing so I thought to myself that a courageous man ought not to fear disgrace. Is that pride, Dounia?'

'It is, Rodia!'

A sudden gleam appeared in his wearied eyes; he seemed happy at the thought of having preserved his pride. 'I hope you don't think, Dounia, that I was merely afraid of the water?' he asked with a strange smile.

'Enough, Rodia! Enough!' replied the girl, grieved at such a supposition.

Both remained silent for some time. Raskolnikoff was looking down, whilst Dounetchka was contemplating him with anxious gaze. Suddenly he started up. 'Time is slipping by, it is meet I should be gone. I purpose giving myself up, although I do not know why I do so.' Tears were streaming down his sister's face. 'I see you weep, Dounia; but can you clasp my hand?'

'Have you ever doubted it?' And she pressed it convulsively to her heart. 'You surely know that in offering to expiate your offence you are washing out half your crime?' she exclaimed, whilst clasping her brother in her arms.

'My crime? What crime, say you?' he retorted in a sudden fit of frenzy. 'Is it a crime to have killed some vile and noisome vermin, an old usurer that was obnoxious to all, a vampire living on the life of the poor? Why, murders of that kind ought to make up for many a crime! I do not even give it a thought! As to atonement – bah! Why should everyone hiss out to me the word, "Crime, crime!" Now that I am determined of my own free will to face dishonour, the absurdity of such a resolution strikes me more than ever! It is only weakness and puerility that is leading me to take that step, unless it may be self-interest, as Porphyrius counselled.'

'Brother, brother! How can you talk like that? Are you not guilty of shedding blood?' answered Dounia aghast.

'Suppose I am. And does not everybody do so?' he pursued, with growing fury. 'Has it not always flowed in streams down here below? Do not men, who have spilt it like water, immediately ascend the Capitol, where they are hailed as saviours of their kind? Look into things before you judge. I, also, wished to benefit my kind, for hundreds, thousands of sensible deeds would amply have made up for this mad freak or rather blunder, for my original purpose was not so mad as one may think; though often, for want of skill, the brightest schemes look hollow. I only wanted to make myself an independent position, to assure my entrance into life, to find the means, for then success would have been certain. But I have failed, and am a villain! Had I but carried my point, the victor's wreath would have been mine; whilst now I'm only good for the dogs!'

'But, brother dear, that is not the point at issue!'

'I own I have broken through the laws of æstheticism! But I cannot conceive in how far it is more glorious to shell some besieged town, than to destroy by the blows of an axe! The fears of æstheticism are the surest signs of impotence! Never have I felt that truth more strongly than now, and never have I so slightly realised the nature of my crime! Never have I felt more capable, more convinced than now!'

His pale and fagged face had certainly recovered colour. But, on giving utterance to his last words, his eyes accidentally met those of Dounia. She looked at him with such sorrow that his mood once more became normal. He was obliged, he admitted, to acknowledge that, on the whole, he had brought about the misfortune of these two poor women.

'If, Dounia darling, you think me guilty, forgive me, although pardon cannot be in case of proven crime. Farewell! do not let us haggle. It is time, high time, I should be gone. But I ask you on no account to follow me. I have one other call to make. Go, go without delay to our mother, and stay with her! I ask this as a favour – the last I shall ever ask! Do not forsake her, she is now in bitter anxiety, and I dread her incapacity for contending with grief; she will die or go out of her mind. Watch, therefore! Razoumikhin will not forsake you; I can depend on him. And, above all, do not bewail me; for, though a murderer, I'll strive to the end of life for courage and what's good. Someday, perhaps, you may hear of me. And I shall cause you no shame; for, be assured, I will yet prove – But now farewell!' he hastened to add, on remarking an unusual expression in Dounia's eyes whilst making her these promises. 'Why weep like that? Don't weep! it is not for ever. One moment more. I was forgetting – ' He took from the table a thick, dust-covered book, opened it, and took from it a small ivory miniature. It was the likeness of his landlady's daughter, the girl he had loved. For a moment he contemplated this expressive and sorrowing face, kissed it, and handed it to Dounetchka. 'I more than once talked with her about – *that*, but with her alone,' he went on absently. 'I trusted her with that project which was destined to have so lamentable an ending. Be at ease,' he continued whilst addressing Dounia, 'she was as horror-stricken as yourself, and I'm glad to think that she's dead and gone.'

Then, returning to the main point at issue, he went on: 'The principal thing for me to know at this moment is, whether I have carefully considered what I am going to do, and whether I am ready to take all its consequences. Can it be true? What moral power shall I have left on leaving the hulks, crushed, perhaps, by twenty years of suffering? Will life be worth living then? And so I really purpose bearing the weight of such an existence! I was a coward indeed this morning, when I was on the point of throwing myself in the Neva!'

And then they both left the house. During the whole of this distressing interview Dounia had only been kept up by her love for her brother. They parted in the street. After having gone some distance, the girl turned round to have one last look at him. On reaching the corner of the street, he himself did the very same thing. Their eyes met, but, observing that his sister's gaze was fixed on his, he made a gesture of impatience, and even of anger, in order to induce her to continue on her way; then he disappeared.

Chapter 7

IT WAS GETTING DARK when he reached Sonia's lodging. The whole of that day the girl had been impatiently waiting for him. In the earlier part, she had been favoured by a visit from Dounia, who, having heard the day before from Svidrigaïloff that Sonia knew every detail, had determined on calling. We do not purpose to give in detail the conversation of the two women: suffice it to say that they wept together, and became fast friends. At this interview Dounia acquired some consolation from the thought that her brother would not be alone. It was Sonia who had received his first confession; it was her he had addressed on feeling the need of human confidence; she it was who would accompany him to wherever destiny might send him. Without having put any more definite questions on that subject, Dounia was, nevertheless, convinced of it; she watched Sonia with a kind of reverence which quite confused the poor girl, for she believed herself quite unworthy to lift her eyes on Dounia. Since Sonia's visit to Raskolnikoff, the image of the charming lady who so graciously bowed to her on that occasion had remained imprinted on her memory as one of the most beautiful and striking episodes of her life.

Dounetchka had resolved, as her last chance, to wait for her brother at his lodging, saying to herself that he would be certain to come sooner or later. No sooner had Sonia been left to herself than the thought of Raskolnikoff's probable suicide deprived her of all rest. This had also been Dounia's fear. But, after some conversation, both girls had adduced various reasons in the way of tranquillisation, and had to some extent succeeded. As soon as they had parted, however, they again became tortured by anxiety. Sonia remembered how Svidrigaïloff had told her the day before: 'Raskolnikoff has but two alternatives, either Siberia or – ' She knew, besides, the young man's pride and want of religious conviction. 'Is it possible he can care to live solely from faintheartedness, from fear of death?' she thought in despair. She already dreaded lest the unhappy man had taken his life, when he unexpectedly entered the room. A cry of joy escaped the girl's bosom. But when she had examined her visitor's face, she suddenly grew pale.

'Yes,' said Raskolnikoff, with a smile, 'I am come to bear the cross, Sonia. It was you advised me to go and make a public confession, and, now that I am on the point of doing so, why should you be alarmed?' Sonia looked at him with astonishment. The young man's tone struck her as being strange; a shudder passed through her frame; but in another minute she concluded that his promise was not a genuine one. Raskolnikoff, whilst speaking, looked aside, evidently fearful of looking the girl in the face. 'I think, Sonia, that it is the best thing to do after all. There is one circumstance – it would take me too long to go into; besides, my time is precious. Do you know what is vexing me? I am savage at the thought that, before long, all those rough men will surround me, will be glaring at me, will put to me all sorts of questions I shall have to answer, will hold me up to public execration. You know, of course, that I do not purpose going to Porphyrius. I can't bear the man. I would much rather go to my friend Powder. Won't he be surprised! If there is one thing I can make sure of – it will be people's amazement! I wish I had more self-possession though. I have grown terribly fidgety of late. Would you believe me? I was very nearly raising my fist to my sister just now, and simply because she turned round in the street to have one more look at me. I have, indeed, degenerated! Now, then, where are the crosses?'

The young man no longer appeared in his usual state of mind. He could not remain a moment in one and the same spot, nor fix his attention on any special object; his ideas came without sequence – or, to speak more accurately, his mind wandered, his hands were slightly trembling. Sonia preserved silence. From a little box she produced two crosses – one in cypress, the other in copper; she then crossed herself, and, after having done the same for Raskolnikoff, hung the cypress cross round his neck.

'This is a symbolic way of showing that I am taking a cross upon myself, hah! hah! As if this were my first day of suffering! The cypress cross is one used by humble folk; the copper one belonged to

Elizabeth; keep it for yourself, but let me have a peep at it! So, you mean to tell me that she was wearing it at that moment? I am acquainted with two other religious objects: a silver cross and an image. I – *on that occasion* – threw them at the old woman. I ought to put them round my neck now. But I am talking rubbish, and forget what is before me; I am unhinged. I think I ought to let you know, Sonia, that I called here on purpose to tell you, so that you might make quite sure. I think that is all. That is why I called (and yet I fancy I had something more to say to you). Yes, by the by, you yourself have induced me to take this step, I am going to be imprisoned, your wish will be satisfied. Why weep, then – you also? Enough, no more of it! If you but knew how painful this is to me!' At sight of Sonia in tears his heart became oppressed. 'What, after all, am I to her?' he asked himself. 'Why should she be interested in me, in the same way that my mother and Dounia are?'

'Do make the sign of the cross, say just one short prayer!' implored the girl in a trembling voice.

'I will pray as much as you like! And that earnestly, Sonia, earnestly.'

He was longing to say much more. He now made several signs of the cross. Sonia tied round his head a green handkerchief, the same one probably that Marmeladoff had spoken about in the tavern, and which at that time was used by the whole family. The recollection of this circumstance flashed through his mind, but he abstained from broaching the subject. He was beginning to notice how he was becoming more and more distracted, and that he was very much agitated. This made him uneasy. Suddenly he observed that Sonia was making preparations to go out with him.

'What are you doing? Where are you going to? Stop here, do! I want to be alone!' he cried in an irritable voice, whilst moving to the door. 'Why go there accompanied by a crowd!' he grumbled as he went out. Sonia did not persist. He did not even take leave of her, he had forgotten her. Only one thought was supreme at this moment: 'Is the game really up?' he asked himself on going downstairs. 'Is there no possibility of retracting, of making everything right, and of keeping away from there?'

Nevertheless he went on, understanding suddenly that the hour for hesitating was past. Once in the street, he remembered that he had forgotten to bid Sonia goodbye, how she had stood stock-still in the middle of the room, how a word of his had almost glued her to the spot. He then asked himself another question which had been haunting his mind for some moments without assuming full shape: 'Why did I make that call at all? I told her I came on business. What business? I have absolutely none whatever. Did I call to let her know that I was going there? That was hardly necessary! Did I call to tell her I loved her? Nonsense! Why, I have just pushed her aside like a veritable cur! And as to her cross, what do I want with it? Oh, how I have degenerated! No, what I wanted were her tears; what I wanted was to see her anguish of heart! Perhaps by calling I only wanted to gain time, to delay the fatal moment a little longer! And I have positively dared to think of a lofty destiny, I have fancied myself called to bring about great things – I, who am so vile, wretched, and cowardly!'

He was advancing along the canal-bank, and had not much farther to go; but on reaching the bridge, he stopped his progress for a moment, then quickly moved to the Haymarket. His looks wandered eagerly from right to left; he strove to examine every object within view, without being able to concentrate his attention on anything. 'In a week, in a month,' he thought, 'I shall again be crossing this bridge – a prison-van will be taking me somewhere; how shall I then contemplate this canal? Shall I notice that signboard? The word "company" is written on it; shall I read it in the same way I do today? What will my feelings and my thoughts be like? How trumpery my anticipations are! The matter is interesting in a way – what am I going to distress myself about? I am behaving like a child. I am posing, as it were, to myself; and yet, why should I blush at my thoughts? Look at that crowd! That fat fellow – a German, I should think – who has just knocked up against me; does he know what kind of man he has come into contact with? That woman who is leading a child and asking alms thinks me, perhaps, happier than herself. Strange! I ought to give her something, if only for the curiosity of the thing. Bah! I happen to have five kopecks by me, for a wonder. Here, *matouchka*.'

'Heaven save you!' said the beggar, in a whimpering voice.

The market-place was now full of people. This fact displeased Raskolnikoff greatly; nevertheless he went to that part of it where the crowd was thickest. He would have bought solitude at any price, but he felt that he could not enjoy it for a single moment. Having got to the centre of the place, the young man suddenly recalled Sonia's words: 'Go to some public place, bow to the crowd, kiss the earth you have soiled by your sin, and say in a loud voice, in the presence of everyone: "I am a murderer."' At the recollection of this he trembled in every limb. The anguish of the last few days had hardened his heart to such an extent, that he felt satisfied to find himself yet open to feelings of another kind, and gave himself entirely up to this one. Sincere sorrow overpowered him, his eyes filled with tears. He knelt in the very middle of the place, bowed earthwards, and joyfully kissed the miry ground.

After having risen, he knelt down once more.

'There's a fellow who has got a tile loose!' observed a lad standing by.

This observation was received with shouts of laughter.

'He is a pilgrim bound for Jerusalem, lads; he is taking leave of his children and his native land; he is wishing everybody goodbye, even St Petersburg and the ground of the capital,' added a respectable man, slightly the worse for drink.

'He is still very young,' said a third.

'He is of noble birth,' observed another, seriously.

'Nowadays you can't distinguish those of noble birth from those who are not.'

On seeing himself the object of general attention, Raskolnikoff lost his self-possession somewhat, and the words: 'I have killed,' which he had on the tip of his tongue, died away. The exclamations and jokes of the crowd did not particularly affect him, and it was in a calm state of mind that he went in the direction of the police-office. On his road, only one apparition struck him: he had, it must be owned, expected to see it – and therefore it did not surprise him. At the very moment when he had prostrated himself for the second time in the public market-place, he had perceived Sonia at a short distance from him. The girl had done her best to escape his observation, whilst hiding behind one of the wooden stalls which stand about the place. She was, therefore, accompanying him whilst he was ascending his Calvary! From that moment Raskolnikoff acquired the certainty that Sonia was his for ever, would follow him anywhere, even if destiny were to lead him to the end of the world. This is the fatal spot. He entered the courtyard with a tolerably firm footstep. The police-office was on the third floor. 'Before I get there I shall still have time to turn back,' the youth thought. All the while he had not confessed – he liked to tell himself that he might change his mind.

As on the occasion of his first visit, he found the staircase covered with filth – made fouler still by the smells coming from the various kitchens opening on every lobby. His legs were giving way as he mounted the stairs. For a moment he stopped to take breath – to collect himself – to make ready for his interview. 'But for what purpose? Why?' he suddenly asked himself. 'As the cup must be emptied, it cannot matter how it is taken. The bitterer the better.' Then all at once he remembered Elia Petrovitch, Lieutenant Powder. 'Is that the man I have to see? Might I not see somebody else – Nicodemus Thomich for instance? Supposing I were to go instead to the home of the superintendent of police and tell him everything in a private conversation? No, no! I will tell it to Powder; it will be over all the sooner.' With a shudder, with scarcely any self-control left, Raskolnikoff opened the door of the superintendent's office. On this occasion, he only saw in the outer room a porter and a labouring man. The constable did not even heed him. Raskolnikoff now entered into the inner room, where two clerks were busy. Zametoff and Nicodemus Thomich were both absent.

'Are they all out?' asked the visitor, addressing one of the clerks.

'Whom do you want?'

'A-a-ah! Without hearing his words – without seeing his face, I guessed the presence of a Russian – as somebody relates in some story or other – At your service!' suddenly exclaimed a well-known voice. Raskolnikoff started. He was face to face with Powder, who had just left an inner room. 'Fate wills it – how can he have got here?' thought the youth. 'You visiting us? What's up?' exclaimed Elia Petrovitch, who seemed in a very good temper, and even somewhat merry. 'If you have called on business, you are too early. It is quite by accident I am here. But, pray, in what can I – I must really say that I – What? What do you –? Excuse me – '

'Raskolnikoff.'

'Of course! Raskolnikoff! You surely do not run away with the idea I can have forgotten you? Pray do not, on any account, think me so – Rodion – Ro – R – Rodionitch, I think?'

'Rodion Romanovitch.'

'Yes, yes, yes! Rodion Romanovitch – Romanovitch! I had it on the tip of my tongue. I must confess that I sincerely regret the way in which we treated you when But I had things explained later on: I discovered you were a young writer – a real savant, I was told. I knew, of course, that you intended to go in for literature. Bless me! where is the man of letters – the pundit, who in his early days has not lived more or less loosely? Both my wife and I adore books, but as for my wife, it is quite a passion! She dotes on literature and art! With the exception of birth, everything else can be got by talent, knowledge, intellect, and genius! What, for instance, is a hat? A hat is like a cake – I can always buy one at Zimmermann's; but, as to what there is under the hat, that is a thing which can't be bought! I ought to say that I even intended to call on you with a view to apology and explanation; but I thought perhaps you – Still, I am forgetting to ask you why I am favoured with this visit. It appears that your family is now in St Petersburg?'

'Yes, my mother and sister.'

'I have even had the honour and pleasure of meeting your sister – she is as charming as she is well-bred. Now, really, I sincerely deplore that altercation of ours on that special occasion. As to the various conjectures that were started with reference to your sudden disappearance, their apparent falsehood has long been recognised. I can fully understand your indignation on the subject. And, now that your family is living in St Petersburg, you are perhaps going to change your quarters?'

'No, not for the present. I called to – in fact, I thought I should see Zametoff.'

'Yes, I remember. You were rather intimate with him; at all events, so I have heard. Well, Zametoff is no longer engaged here. Yes, we have lost Alexander Gregorievitch! He left yesterday, and I am sorry that, previous to leaving, there was an interchange of hard words between him and some of us. He is a little inconsistent monkey, that's what he is. At first he was rather a promising kind of fellow, but he has been foolish enough to take up with some of our gay dogs, and he has got the idea that he is to pass this and that examination, just for the show of the thing, and to be considered a man knowing a thing or two. Mind, I don't compare Zametoff with you, you understand, nor with your friend Mr Razoumikhin; for one of your stamp have gone in for scientific studies seriously, and reverses do not affect you particularly. The pleasures of life have no kind of hold on men like you; yours is the austere, ascetic, monkish life of the book-man. As long as you have a book, a pen behind your ear, and some scientific inquiry to make, you have all you want. Even I, you must know, up to a certain point – By the by, have you read Livingston's *Travels*?'

'No.'

'Well, I have. I notice, by the way, that the number of Nihilists has greatly increased – which is not to be wondered at in such times as these. Between ourselves, you are no Nihilist, I suppose? Answer me frankly, quite frankly!'

'N – o.'

'You may be quite as frank with me as you would be with yourself! As for the service, that is quite another thing. I suppose you thought I was going to say *friendship*, but you are mistaken there. Not friendship, but the feelings of a man and citizen, feelings of humanity and of love for the Almighty. I may be an official personage, a red-tapist: I am none the less, however, a man and a citizen. You were talking just now of Zametoff. Well, Zametoff, I must tell you, is a young man who goes in for French style, who does the big in shady localities when he has been drinking an extra glass of wine. Now you know what he is. I may have been rather hard on him; but, if my indignation did carry me a little too far, I acted from high motives – zeal for the good of the service. Besides, I hold a high position, and have a social importance! I am, in addition, a married man with children. I do my duty as a man and as a citizen, whereas he – what is he? allow me to ask you. I am speaking to you as a man blessed with education. Why, do you know, midwives have increased almost beyond calculation?

Raskolnikoff looked at the lieutenant with some confusion. Elia Petrovitch's remarks (he had evidently just been dining) struck the young man's ears as so many empty sounds. And yet he understood a word here and there. He once more looked inquiringly at his interlocutor, not knowing how all this would finish.

'I am talking about those young women who have their hair cut Titus-fashion,' continued the inexhaustible Elia Petrovitch. 'I call them midwives, and I rather consider the name a good one. Hah! hah! Why, they attend lectures on medicine, and study anatomy! Now, do you think, if I were taken ill, that I should allow myself to be treated by a young lady? Hah! hah!' Elia Petrovitch began to laugh, well satisfied with his own wit. 'I can understand the love of learning, but surely people can learn without going to extremes? What occasion is there for insolence? Why insult persons of rank, as that good-for-nothing Zametoff does? Why should he insult me, I should like to know? Another mania which is making terrible headway is suicide. A man squanders every penny he possesses, and kills himself there and then! Even quite young girls, striplings, and greybeards put an end to their lives! Why, just now we have heard of a gentleman, who has settled here quite lately, having done so. I say, Nil Paulitch! Nil Paulitch! What was the name of that gentleman who blew his brains out this morning in the Peterburgskaia?'

'Svidrigaïloff,' answered someone, in a husky voice, from the next room.

Raskolnikoff shuddered. 'Svidrigaïloff! Svidrigaïloff has blown his brains out?' he exclaimed.

'What! did you know him?'

'I did. He arrived here some short time ago.'

'He did, you are quite right; he had lost his wife. The fact is, the fellow was a rake. He killed himself with a revolver, under peculiarly offensive circumstances. They found on his body a pocketbook, in which he had written: "I die in possession of all my mental faculties; let no one therefore, be accused of my death." They say the man was wealthy. But how is it you know him?'

'I – my sister had been a governess in his family.'

'Bah! bah! Then, perhaps you may be able to let us know something about him. Had you any idea of his intention?'

'I saw him yesterday – he was drinking – but I never suspected anything.' Raskolnikoff felt a load on his chest.

'You seem to me to be getting pale again. The atmosphere of this room is very stifling – '

'Yes, it is time I should be gone,' stammered the visitor. 'Excuse me for having disturbed you.'

'Nonsense! I am always at your orders. You have caused me real pleasure, and I am delighted to have the opportunity of declaring – ' Saying which, Elia Petrovitch held out his hand to the young man.

'I only wished – I wanted to tell Zametoff – '

'I quite understand – quite – charmed to have seen you!'

'Enchanted, I am sure! *Au revoir!*' said Raskolnikoff with a smile.

He staggered out. His head was giddy. He could hardly stand upright, and, going downstairs, he was obliged to clutch the wall to save himself from falling. It struck him that a porter who was going to the police-office, touched him whilst passing; that a dog was barking somewhere on the first floor and that a woman was shouting out to silence the animal. Braving got down the stairs, he entered the yard. Standing, not far from the door, he saw Sonia, pale as death, watching him with a singular look. He stopped opposite her. The girl was beating her hands together; her countenance expressed the utmost despair. At the sight, Raskolnikoff smiled – but such a smile! A moment afterwards he had gone back to the police-office. Elia Petrovitch was in the act of ransacking some papers. Before him stood the same moujik who just now, on ascending the stairs, had come into contact with Raskolnikoff.

'Ah! There you are again! Have you forgotten something? But what is the matter with you?'

With pale lips and fixed gaze, Raskolnikoff slowly advanced towards Elia Petrovitch. Resting his head upon the table behind which the lieutenant was seated, he wished to speak, but could only give vent to a few unintelligible sounds.

'You are in pain, a chair! Pray sit down! Some water!'

Raskolnikoff allowed himself to sink on the chair that was offered him, but he could not take his eyes off Elia Petrovitch, whose face expressed a very unpleasant surprise. For a moment both men looked at one another in silence. Water was brought.

'It was I – ' commenced Raskolnikoff.

'Drink.'

With a movement of his hand the young man pushed aside the glass which was offered him; then, in a low-toned but distinct voice he made, with several interruptions, the following statement:

'It was I who killed, with a hatchet, the old money-lender and her sister,

Elizabeth, and robbery was my motive.'

Elia Petrovitch called for assistance. People rushed in from various directions. Raskolnikoff repeated his confession.

Chapter 1

SIBERIA! On the banks of a broad waste-river stands a town, one of the administrative centres of Russia; in the town is a fortress, in the fortress a prison. In the prison Rodion Raskolnikoff had lain for nine months, a transported convict of the second class. A year and a half had passed since the commission of the crime.

Justice took its course with him without much difficulty. The criminal fairly and clearly maintained his confession, without in any way confusing himself as to details or extenuating any circumstance. Neither did he mutilate any fact, nor spare the most minute detail. He recounted every incident of the crime, and cleared up the mystery of the pledge (the little package of wood and iron) which he showed to the woman; explained his taking of the old woman's keys, described their shape, and the trunk with its contents, and even enumerated some of the particular articles, and, finally, explained the murder of Elizabeth – up to that moment a profound enigma; further, Koch's coming and knocking at the door, his being followed by the student, their conversation; then how he, the criminal, went downstairs, and, hearing the noise made by Nikola and Dmitri, crept into the empty room. Finally, in full confirmation of all he said, Raskolnikoff described the exact court and gate where, underneath a stone, he had hidden the jewellery and purse. These were duly found. In one word, the thing became clear. The examining magistrate and judges were greatly astonished that he should have concealed the things, instead of profiting by them; but, above all, that he gave no particulars of the articles taken, and could not even furnish the number. It was quite incomprehensible to them that he had never opened the purse, and that he did not know how much it contained seemed very improbable; its contents consisted of three hundred and seventy roubles in notes, and a few copper pieces; the notes were very much damaged, as may be imagined.

They expended a long time in trying to discover the prisoner's motive in concealing this knowledge from them, whilst, in all other facts of the case, he openly and readily avowed the truth. It was inexplicable that in this particular instance the accused should lie. In the end a few (especially among the psychologists) admitted the feasibility of his assertion that he knew nothing of the contents of the purse by admitting the conclusion that the crime had been committed under the influence of monomania, impelling the accused, without any primary or ulterior motive, to murder and theft. This fitted in very well with the latest theory of temporary insanity, as the explanation of most crimes, which was much in vogue. Besides, there were many witnesses to testify to Raskolnikoff's hypochondriacal condition – among others the doctor (Zosimoff), some old acquaintances, his landlady, and Nastasia, whose evidence strongly supported the idea that Raskolnikoff's case was not that of ordinary murder and theft. Unfortunately for the theorists, the culprit refused to take up this line of defence – in fact, made hardly any defence whatever. Upon being called upon to declare the motives of his crime, he replied bluntly and curtly that the cause of all was his wretched condition, his misery and helplessness, and his desire to secure, at least, the means of starting on his career. For this purpose he had calculated upon 3,000 roubles, as proceeds of the robbery. Asked why he denounced himself, he replied that he had repented.

However, even taking these facts into consideration, the sentence was more favourable than could have been expected, and the leniency of the judges seemed to be influenced by the absence of defence on the culprit's part, and his evident desire to make no extenuation of his crimes. Furthermore, every strange circumstance of the deed was taken into account. The illness and poverty of the murderer were not subject to any doubt. As he did not profit by his act, the court supposed either that he was immediately stricken with remorse, or that his mind was unhinged at the time of the crime. The murder of Elizabeth even contributed in his favour, to a certain degree. A man commit two murders, and at the same time to forget that the door is wide open! Finally, his denunciation of himself at the very time when Nikola's confession so complicated matters that suspicion was entirely diverted from the real culprit. (Porphyrius Petrovitch kept his word.) All this helped to mitigate the punishment.

Furthermore, several circumstances, strongly favourable to the accused, were brought to light during the course of the trial. His co-student, Razoumikhin, deposed, and proved, that during Raskolnikoff's stay at the University he considerably assisted, out of his own poor and inadequate means, a sick and consumptive comrade, indeed almost keeping him entirely for six months. When the latter died, Raskolnikoff went to the old and infirm father (whom his son had supported since he was thirteen years of age), and finally succeeded in placing him in an asylum; and, upon his death, also decently buried him. His former landlady, the mother of Raskolnikoff's deceased sweetheart – the widow Zarnitzin – testified to his extreme bravery upon the occasion of a fire near the dwelling, when Raskolnikoff, at the peril of his life, succeeded in extricating two children from the flames. These facts were duly corroborated by other and independent witnesses. Briefly the court, influenced by these facts, his confession, and previous good character, sentenced him to eight years' hard labour, with transportation to Siberia.

During the course of the trial, Raskolnikoff's mother became very ill. Dounia and Razoumikhin found it advisable to remove their residence from St Petersburg, and the latter chose a town upon the railway, a little distance from the city only, so that he was able to follow closely all the details of the case, and at the same time to enjoy the company of Eudoxia Romanovna. This illness of Pulcheria Romanovna was rather peculiar, and of a nervous character, accompanied by hallucinations. Dounia, upon returning from her last interview with her brother, found her mother excited and delirious. The same evening, conferring with Razoumikhin, they agreed how to meet the inquiries of the mother, and invented tales to explain the absence of Raskolnikoff – how he had gone upon a mission to a distant land upon the borders of Russia, a mission which would procure him both money and repute. But Pulcheria never asked after her son – on the contrary, she herself met them with a complete history of Raskolnikoff's sudden departure. She related to them, with tears, how he had taken his farewell; at the same time she hinted that she knew of very serious and secret circumstances, which it was necessary to keep unmentioned, as Raskolnikoff had many powerful enemies. She assured them that he would ultimately become a man of mark in the State, and mentioned the article as a proof of his great talents.

This article she read unceasingly, at times aloud, and almost slept with it. Dounia and Razoumikhin became at last very much alarmed at her peculiarities, and especially at her omissions. For instance, now she did not even complain of her son's silence, whilst formerly, living in her quiet village, her one hope and one joy was to receive a letter from her beloved child. This last circumstance, so inexplicable, was very alarming to Dounia, and led her to believe that her mother knew of some evil which had befallen him, and dreaded the question for fear of learning something even worse. In any case, Dounia saw that her mother's condition was very critical.

Twice it happened that the mother directed the conversation in such a manner that it was impossible to reply without mentioning the whereabouts of her son, and on Dounia's answers, which were necessarily equivocal and unsatisfactory, she fell into a deep melancholy. Dounia saw at last how difficult it was to invent, and decided to keep silent upon the matter entirely – it became, however, more and more apparent that Pulcheria suspected the worst. Dounia remembered, from the words of Raskolnikoff, that her mother had heard her speak in her sleep during the night which followed the interview with Svidrigaïloff. After days of obstinate silence, she would become hysterical and talk loudly and incessantly of her son, his hopes, and his future. Her fancies were at times very strange. They tried to divert her, but she saw their object clearly, and only talked on.

The sentence was pronounced about five months after the confession to Elia Petrovitch. Razoumikhin visited him in gaol as soon as possible; Sonia also. At last came the transportation. Dounia declared her conviction, along with Razoumikhin, that the adieu was not for ever. The latter's head was full of projects for the future, involving their emigration to Siberia in three or four years, where the soil was rich, and wanting only labour and a little capital to yield a livelihood; and, in fact, to settle in the very town where Raskolnikoff would be, and commence a new career. All wept on taking leave. Raskolnikoff during the last few days was very much preoccupied, spoke of his mother, and was much concerned about her. When he was informed of her critical condition, he became very gloomy. With Sonia he was specially uncommunicative and distant. Sonia, with the aid of the money given by Svidrigaïloff, had already arranged to accompany the batch of prisoners with whom he was to be dispatched. She had never mentioned a word of her intention to Raskolnikoff, but both knew it would be so. At the last moment he wore a strange smile when listening to the ardent assurances of his sister and Razoumikhin with regard to the bright future which would open before them when he returned from hard labour. He foresaw the certainty of his mother's death. He and Sonia at last set off.

Two months after, Razoumikhin married Dounia. The nuptials were sad and quiet. Among the invited guests were Porphyrius Petrovitch and Zosimoff. For a long time Razoumikhin's character had been growing firmer and more decided. Dounia believed blindly that this improvement was permanent, and that he would carry out all his resolutions. He commenced by re-entering the University to finish his course. The two elaborated incessantly the plans they had formed to emigrate to Siberia within four or five years. Until then, they relied upon Sonia.

Pulcheria Alexandrovna joyfully blessed her daughter's union with Razoumikhin, but after the marriage she relapsed still more into her gloomy condition. Razoumikhin tried to rouse her by telling her the story of Raskolnikoff's gallant conduct at the fire. The recital enraptured her. She could do nothing but talk of it and enter into conversation about it to perfect strangers, in the streets, shops, and carriages (although Dounia was always with her). Dounia hardly knew how to restrain her, and went in fear of coming across somebody who might know of his crime and fate, and mention it to her mother. Pulcheria managed to learn the address of the two children, and wanted to set out at once to visit them.

At last her condition reached its utmost limits. She then gave way to floods of tears, and became delirious. One morning, she announced positively that Rodion's return was at hand and declared that he had promised to be back again after nine months. She at once set about arranging her rooms, polished the furniture, scoured the floors, and hung up new curtains, etc. Dounia was disquieted, but said nothing, and humoured her mother by assisting her. After an alarming day, passed in foolish imaginings and stupid freaks, Pulcheria Alexandrovna broke down entirely, and next morning was in a high state of fever; in a fortnight she died. During the delirium, she spoke words which left no doubt that she knew more of the fearful fate of her son than Dounia and her husband were aware of.

Raskolnikoff did not learn for a long time the death of his mother, although the mode of a regular correspondence had been arranged through Sonia. Every month a letter came to Razoumikhin, and equally regular ones went to Siberia. The letters of Sonia at first appeared to Dounia and Razoumikhin, dry and unsatisfactory, but afterwards they came to understand that the letters could not be better, as they always contained the most complete statement of the condition of their unhappy brother. Sonia described very simply and clearly the everyday realities and surroundings of Raskolnikoff's life. She did not speak of her own self, her own hopes, her feelings, her future, and instead of giving her own impressions of the prisoner, she contented herself with chronicling his own words. She related what questions he had asked, the desires expressed, and finally reported the state of his health.

But little consolation could Dounia or her husband draw from these communications, especially at first. Sonia reported his state as always sombre and taciturn; when she told him the latest news from St Petersburg, he gave no attention, and even upon her announcing the death of his mother, which, no doubt he anticipated, he showed no signs of emotion. He seemed to comprehend his situation thoroughly, and manifested no astonishment at anything in a life so different from his former one. His health was satisfactory. He performed his duties without repugnance. To his food he was indifferent, but, excepting on feast-days and holidays, this was so bad that he accepted some money from Sonia to procure him some tea. Any further attention he refused to accept, and told Sonia that they only vexed him. In prison, she further wrote, he lived in common with the rest, and slept upon a felt rug. He could obtain advantages and privileges, but made no effort to do so, simply through apathy and indifference to his fate. Sonia confessed that at first, far from viewing her with pleasure, Raskolnikoff showed a decided aversion and even rudeness towards her. Later on, these interviews were treated by him as a simple matter of course. On feast-days they saw each other at the porter's gate or in the guard-house, when a prisoner was brought out to anyone wishing for an interview, but on ordinary days she saw him at his work in the brick-fields or sheds near the river.

As regarded herself, Sonia informed them that she employed herself in sewing, and, as there was hardly a dressmaker in the place, she was almost indispensable. What she did not tell, was that, thanks to her, he had obtained the good graces of the authorities, who had lightened his work, etc. At last, there arrived the news (Dounia had detected some alarm in Sonia's latter letters) that he had hardly spoken for many days, and looked very ill. The next letter quickly reported that he had fallen dangerously ill, and was lying in the prison hospital.

Chapter 2

HE WAS ILL a very long time, but it was not the prison life, the labour, rags, food, or shaven head that brought him low. Oh, what did any of these signify? One thing, he was glad of his work. Tired out, physically, he could at least hope for some hours of restful sleep. The thin cabbage-soup, with the cockroaches floating in it, what did it matter? Had he not been glad to have even that when he was a student? His clothes were warm and suited to his life. As for his fetters, he never felt them. And before whom was he to blush for his cropped head? Before Sonia? Sonia feared him.

But what? He was ashamed before Sonia; he felt he had acted contemptibly towards her. Thus his shame arose not from his hair and chains: his pride was bitterly wounded – in fact, he was ill from wounded pride. How happy he would have been to reproach himself; then he could have endured everything – even the shame and dishonour. But, although he severely examined himself, he failed to find any specially dreadful cause in his past life, except a silly *error*, which might have happened to any man. What principally humiliated him was that he, Raskolnikoff, should be so utterly lost through an error, the consequences of which he must submit to if he wished for a moment of calmness.

An aimless anxiety in the present – a continual sacrifice – by which nothing could be acquired in the future. This was what was left him on earth. And after eight years he would be only thirty-two! Vain idea, to think he could commence life anew. For what object? What aim in life? Live to exist? But, in old times, he was ready a thousand times to give up his existence for an idea, for a hope – a phantom, even. He was always insatiable. Perhaps the influence of his desires made him believe that he was a man to whom more was revealed than to any other, and, therefore, more was permitted. Still, had destiny only given him the faculty of repentance – the burning regret which crushes the heart and drives away sleep – repentance, whose torments drive to the noose or river – oh, he would have rejoiced. Sorrow, tears, that would be life. But he did not repent of his deeds. One thing, he might have lashed himself with his foolishness – and that most stupid action of his which had led him to prison – as he had always done. But now in the quiet of his prison, he again reflected upon his past conduct, and did not find it so foolish and ugly as it appeared to him in that fatal time – the past.

'How,' thought he, 'were my thoughts more stupid than other thoughts or ideas which have existed since the world was made? It is only necessary to look upon the deed from a broad view, without prejudice, and free from all influences of the day. My idea will then not appear so strange. Oh, you twopenny-halfpenny philosophers and wise men! Why do you stop half-way? And why does my behaviour appear so guilty?' he continued to himself. 'Because it is a crime? What does the word crime mean? My conscience is easy. My act was, decidedly, unlawful. I certainly broke the letter of the law, and shed blood. Well, let the letter of the law take my head, that's all. Undoubtedly, many benefactors of humanity, who have not inherited power, but have attained to it, should have been punished for the very first of their steps; but these people prevailed, and are justified, whilst I have not known how to shape my steps; consequently, I was wrong in making the attempt.'

He owned to one fault only – his feebleness in confessing; he suffered from the thought. Why did he not kill himself? Why, when choosing between the river and confession, had he preferred the latter? Was the desire to live so difficult to conquer? Did Svidrigaïloff, who feared death, surmount it? He tormented himself with this question, and could not understand that his decision against suicide arose from a presentiment of future resurrection and a new life. He attributed it, rather, to a weakness in his character. He looked upon his convict companions, and marvelled to see how they all loved life – how they prized life. It appeared to him it was prized more in prison than in liberty. What pains and tortures would not these miserable creatures endure! Looking farther, he discovered much more inexplicable.

In the prison many things escaped him. He lived, as it were, with lowered eyes; he recognised nothing. But, after a time, he commenced, involuntarily, to receive impressions. One thing he remarked was the impassable abyss which existed between him and the other convicts. They were as different nations, and they looked upon one another with distrust, and evident hostility. Independent of the ordinary criminals, there were to be found within the prison a number of Polish political offenders. These looked upon the others as brutes, and despised them from head to foot. But Raskolnikoff could not so regard them. He clearly saw that some of these insignificant creatures were far more intelligent than the Poles themselves. Among the Russians were an officer and two seminarists, who loathed the *canaille* of the prison. Raskolnikoff saw this error, too. As for himself, he was not liked, and was avoided by all. He even came to be hated. Why? He knew not. Many, far guiltier than he, despised him, laughed at him, and derided his crime.

'You are a gentleman,' they would say to him. 'It was not a very gentlemanly act to kill with a hatchet.'

On one occasion he went with the others to church. How it happened he knew not, but suddenly his companions fell upon him, and assailed him with fury. 'Impious man! You do not believe in God!' they cried. 'We must kill you.'

He had never spoken to them of belief in God, but they wished to kill him as an atheist. He did not reply. One prisoner was about to rush upon him, Raskolnikoff awaited him calmly and silently, not a line of his face trembled. The escort had just time to throw himself between them, and bloodshed was avoided.

Another thing struck him: why did they all adore Sonia? She never seemed to ingratiate herself with them, indeed, they rarely met her – sometimes when she came to see him for a moment while at work. However, they all knew her, and her history, how she had followed him; they knew how she lived, where she lived. She never gave them money nor showed special favours to anyone. Once only, at Christmas, she distributed amongst them white rolls and cakes. But, little by little, between them and Sonia, an intimacy became established. She wrote letters for them to their friends and relations, and took them to the post. When friends arrived, it was upon the recommendations of the prisoners that the former placed in Sonia's hands little parcels, and even money. The wives and sweethearts knew her and went to her. When she appeared where they were at work, all took off their hats and made a bow. 'Little mother, Sophia Semenovna, thou art our mother, tender and compassionate,' these churlish and branded felons said to her. She smiled in return; they loved even to see her walk, and turned to look upon her as she passed by. They praised her for being so little, and knew not what not to praise her for. They even went to her with their ailments.

Raskolnikoff lay ill in the hospital during all the latter part of Lent and Eastertide. Whilst returning to health, he called to mind the dreams which he had during the period of delirium. The whole world was desolated by an unknown and terrible plague, which, coming from the interior of Asia, spread over all countries; all perished except a few elect. Parasites of a new character, microscopical beings fixed their home in the human body. But these animalculæ were breathing creatures, endued with intellect and will. Persons affected became immediately mad. But, strange to say, the stricken were, at the same time, imbued with a strong sense of their own good judgement, never did they believe themselves so strongly endowed with wisdom and intellectual vigour or scientific conclusions and moral perception so correct as now. Whole villages and towns, the entire population became tainted, and lost their reason. They were incapable of understanding one another, because each believed himself the sole possessor of truth, and looking upon his unenlightened neighbours, beat his breast, threw up his arms and wept. They could not agree upon any point, knew not what to consider evil, what good, and they fell upon one another in anger and killed, they formed great armies, but, once in motion, they tore each other to pieces.

In the towns the alarm was great, meetings were called, but for what and by whom, none knew. The commonest trade was abandoned, because everybody had his own idea as to the mode of pursuing it, but no two agreed. Agriculture was also abandoned. People gathered together in crowds, agreed upon a common action, swearing never to abandon one another, then immediately rushed to something else, forgot their agreement, and ended in rushing upon and murdering each other. Incendiarism was rife everywhere and famine set in.

Everything perished. The pestilence raged more and more. Of the whole world only a few remained; these were the pure and elect, predestined to found a new race, to inaugurate the new life and purify the earth; but the chosen were not recognised. None knew their voices or heard their words.

This nonsensical dream, so weird and horrifying, lingered so strongly in his recollection, that he could hardly realise it was only a dream. It was now the second week after Easter, the days were clear and bright, and they opened the iron-barred windows of the prison for the first time. During his long illness, Sonia was able to see him but twice. The prison rules were stringent, and it was difficult to obtain a permit. But she often came to the prison doors, principally towards evening, and stood under the hospital windows for a short time. One evening, when almost convalescent, he rose after sleep, and suddenly went to the window, and there, at the prison gate, beheld Sonia. Something pierced him to the heart, he trembled and quickly withdrew from the window. The following day, Sonia did not appear, nor next evening either. He noticed that he awaited her appearance with impatience. At last came his discharge from the hospital. Returning to prison, he learned that Sonia was ill, and confined to the house.

He was much distressed, and sent to inquire after her. He quickly discovered that her illness was not dangerous. On learning, on her part, that he was concerned about her, Sonia scribbled a note in pencil to him, that she was only suffering from a chill, and that she would soon, very soon come to see him at his work. When he read this letter his heart beat. The day was again bright and genial. In the early morning, about six, he was sent to work by the side of the river, where were arranged sheds for the preparation of alabaster. Only three workmen were sent there. One of the prisoners, with the guard, returned to the prison for some tools; the other entered the shed to prepare the fires. Raskolnikoff went down to the water-side, and, sitting down upon a log, sat gazing upon the wide and shallow river. From his position he could view the immense steppes, and far off, almost imperceptible, he could detect the black points of the tents of nomads. There was liberty, and other people not resembling those here; there time itself had stood still, and had not moved since the days of Abraham and his flocks! Raskolnikoff sat looking, immovable; he fell into a reverie, and thought of nothing, but he felt agitated.

Suddenly he found himself with Sonia; she had come up to him silently, and sat by his side. It was still very early, and the morning air was not yet softened by the sun. Her face still bore traces of illness, and was very pale and wan. She glanced up at him affably, and timidly extended her hand, as of old. She always proffered her hand in a timid fashion, as if doubtful whether it would be taken. But now he seized it with rapture, and rapidly looked up in her face. Not a word was spoken, and her eyes sought the ground. They were alone. How it happened he knew not, but a strong impulse came upon him, and he threw himself at her knees. He wept and clutched her. At first she became dreadfully frightened, and her face was pale as death. She rose, and, in agitation, looked upon him. But one glance showed her all, and in her eyes shone ineffable happiness. She clearly saw, and did not doubt, that he loved her – loved her – at last!

They tried to speak, but could not, and tears stood in their eyes. They were both pale and ill, but in those white and worn faces already beamed the dawn of a restored future, and full resurrection to a new life. Love and affection rose upon them; the heart of one held within it an eternal store of light and love for the heart of the other. They resolved to wait, and have patience. For him there still remained seven years of much pain and suffering, but so much happiness! He was saved! He knew it, and was conscious fully of his renewed being. And she – she was part of his life!

The evening of that day came, and Raskolnikoff lay and thought of her. His fellow-convicts seemed to have looked kindly upon him during the day. He spoke to them, and they replied cheerfully. He thought of this change, and said, 'Perhaps all will now change!' He recollected how he had treated her, but these memories hardly troubled him. He knew the unending affection which had ended all her sufferings. Yes; and what were now all these torments of the past! All – even his sin, and sentence, and exile – appeared to him, in the first transports, as if they had not occurred, or were swept away. He could not, that evening, bring his thoughts to bear long upon anything; he only felt! Life – full, real, earnest life, was coming, and had driven away his cogitations. Under his pillow lay the New Testament. He took it up mechanically. The book belonged to Sonia; it was that same from which she had read to him of the raising of Lazarus. At the commencement of his confinement he thought that she would pester him with religious teaching, and force the book upon him; but, to his astonishment, she never spoke of religion, nor ever mentioned the Scriptures. He himself asked for it during his illness, and she silently laid the book by his side. It had remained unopened.

He did not open it now, but one thought burned within him: Her faith, her feelings, may not mine become like them? Sonia was very agitated during all the day, and at night was ill again. But she was so happy that nothing could mar her joy. Seven years – only seven years!

At the commencement of their happiness they were ready to look upon these seven years as seven days. They did not know that a new life is not given for nothing; that it has to be paid dearly for, and only acquired by much patience and suffering, and great future efforts.

But now a new history commences: a story of the gradual renewing of a man, of his slow progressive regeneration, and change from one world to another – an introduction to the hitherto unknown realities of life. This may well form the theme of a new tale; the one we wished to offer the reader is ended.

WORDSWORTH CLASSICS

General Editors: Marcus Clapham & Clive Reynard

JANE AUSTEN
Emma
Mansfield Park
Northanger Abbey
Persuasion
Pride and Prejudice
Sense and Sensibility

ARNOLD BENNETT
Anna of the Five Towns

R. D. BLACKMORE
Lorna Doone

ANNE BRONTË
Agnes Grey
*The Tenant of
Wildfell Hall*

CHARLOTTE BRONTË
Jane Eyre
The Professor
Shirley
Villette

EMILY BRONTË
Wuthering Heights

JOHN BUCHAN
Greenmantle
Mr Standfast
The Thirty-Nine Steps

SAMUEL BUTLER
The Way of All Flesh

LEWIS CARROLL
Alice in Wonderland

CERVANTES
Don Quixote

G. K. CHESTERTON
*Father Brown:
Selected Stories*
*The Man who was
Thursday*

ERSKINE CHILDERS
The Riddle of the Sands

JOHN CLELAND
*Memoirs of a Woman of
Pleasure: Fanny Hill*

WILKIE COLLINS
The Moonstone
The Woman in White

JOSEPH CONRAD
Heart of Darkness
Lord Jim
The Secret Agent

J. FENIMORE COOPER
*The Last of the
Mohicans*

STEPHEN CRANE
*The Red Badge of
Courage*

THOMAS DE QUINCEY
*Confessions of an English
Opium Eater*

DANIEL DEFOE
Moll Flanders
Robinson Crusoe

CHARLES DICKENS
Bleak House
David Copperfield
Great Expectations
Hard Times
Little Dorrit
Martin Chuzzlewit
Oliver Twist
Pickwick Papers
A Tale of Two Cities

BENJAMIN DISRAELI
Sybil

THEODOR DOSTOEVSKY
Crime and Punishment

**SIR ARTHUR CONAN
DOYLE**
*The Adventures of
Sherlock Holmes*
*The Case-Book of
Sherlock Holmes*
*The Lost World &
Other Stories*
*The Return of
Sherlock Holmes*
Sir Nigel

GEORGE DU MAURIER
Trilby

ALEXANDRE DUMAS
The Three Musketeers

MARIA EDGEWORTH
Castle Rackrent

GEORGE ELIOT
The Mill on the Floss
Middlemarch
Silas Marner

HENRY FIELDING
Tom Jones

F. SCOTT FITZGERALD
*A Diamond as Big as the
Ritz & Other Stories*
The Great Gatsby
Tender is the Night

GUSTAVE FLAUBERT
Madame Bovary

JOHN GALSWORTHY
In Chancery
The Man of Property
To Let

ELIZABETH GASKELL
Cranford
North and South

KENNETH GRAHAME
*The Wind in the
Willows*

**GEORGE & WEEDON
GROSSMITH**
Diary of a Nobody

RIDER HAGGARD
She

THOMAS HARDY
*Far from the
Madding Crowd*
The Mayor of Casterbridge
*The Return of the
Native*
Tess of the d'Urbervilles
The Trumpet Major
*Under the Greenwood
Tree*

DISTRIBUTION

AUSTRALIA
& PAPUA NEW GUINEA
Peribo Pty Ltd
58 Beaumont Road, Mount Kuring-Gai
NSW 2080, Australia
Tel: (02) 457 0011 Fax: (02) 457 0022

CYPRUS
Huckleberry Trading
3 Othos Avvey, Tala Paphos
Tel: 06 653585

CZECH REPUBLIC
Bohemian Ventures spol s r o
Delnicka 13, 170 00 Prague 7
Tel: 02 877837 Fax: 02 801498

FRANCE
Copernicus Diffusion
23 Rue Saint Dominique, Paris 75007
Tel: 1 44 11 33 20 Fax: 1 44 11 33 21

GERMANY
**GLBmbH (Bargain, Promotional
& Remainder Shops)**
Schönhauser Strasse 25
D-50968 Köln
Tel: 0221 34 20 92 Fax: 0221 38 40 40

**Tradis Verlag und Vertrieb GmbH
(Bookshops)**
Postfach 90 03 69
D-51113 Köln
Tel: 022 03 31059
Fax: 022 03 3 93 40

GREAT BRITAIN & IRELAND
Wordsworth Editions Ltd
Cumberland House, Crib Street
Ware, Hertfordshire SG12 9ET

INDIA
OM Book Service
1690 First Floor
Nai Sarak, Delhi – 110006
Tel: 3279823-3265303 Fax: 3278091

ISRAEL
Timmy Marketing Limited
Israel Ben Zeev 12
Ramont Gimmel, Jerusalem
Tel: 02-865266 Fax: 02-880035

ITALY
Magis Books SRL
Via Raffaello 31/C
Zona Ind Mancasale
42100 Reggio Emilia
Tel: 1522 920999 Fax: 0522 920666

NEW ZEALAND & FIJI
Allphy Book Distributors Ltd
4-6 Charles Street, Eden Terrace
Auckland,
Tel: (09) 3773096 Fax: (09) 3022770

NORTH AMERICA
Universal Sales & Marketing
230 Fifth Avenue, Suite 1212
New York, NY 10001, USA
Tel: 212 481 3500 Fax: 212 481 3534

PHILIPPINES
I J Sagun Enterprises
P O Box 4322 CPO Manila
2 Topaz Road, Greenheights Village
Taytay, Rizal
Tel: 631 80 61 TO 66

PORTUGAL
International Publishing Services Ltd
Rua da Cruz da Carreira, 4B,
1100 Lisbon
Tel: 01 570051 Fax: 01 3522066

**SOUTHERN, CENTRAL
& EAST AFRICA**
**P.M.C.International Importers &
Exporters CC**
Unit 6, Ben-Sarah Place, 52-56 Columbine
Place, Glen Anil, Kwa-Zulu Natal 4051
 P.O.Box 201520
 Durban North, Kwa-Zulu Natal 4016
 Tel: (031) 844441 Fax: (031) 844466

SCOTLAND
Lomond Books
36 West Shore Road, Granton
Edinburgh EH5 1QD

**SINGAPORE,
MALASIA & BRUNEI**
Paul & Elizabeth Book Services Pte Ltd
163 Tanglin Road No 03-15/16
Tanglin Mall, Singapore 1024
Tel: (65) 735 7308 Fax: (65) 735 9747

SLOVAK REPUBLIC
Slovak Ventures spol s r o
Stefanikova 128, 94901 Nitra
Tel/Fax: 087 25105

SPAIN
Ribera Libros, S.L.
Poligono Martiartu, Calle 1 - no 6
48480 Arrigorriaga, Vizcaya
Tel: 34 4 6713607 (Almacen)
      34 4 4418787 (Libreria)
Fax: 34 4 6713608 (Almacen)
      34 4 4418029 (Libreria)